YANNIS

This is the story of Greek sufferers from Hansen's Disease (leprosy). All the events that took place in the Athenian hospital and on Spinalonga are true.

There was never any suspicion of embezzlement of Hospital Funds in Heraklion, and all the characters in this novel are entirely fictitious. Any resemblance to actual persons, living or dead, is entirely coincidental.

My thanks to Anita Darby who found a sufferer who had been sent to Spinalonga as a young man. His information and reminiscences were invaluable to me.

Titles available in this series

Yannis
Anna
Giovanni
Joseph
Christabelle
Saffron
Manolis
Cathy
Nicola
Vasi
Alecos

YANNIS

Beryl Darby

JACH

Copyright © Beryl Darby 2006

Beryl Darby has asserted her right under the Copyright,
Designs and Patents Act, 1988, to be identified
as the author of this work.

All rights reserved.
No part of this publication may be reproduced, stored in a
retrieval system, or transmitted in any form or by any means,
electronic, mechanical, photocopying, recording or otherwise,
without prior written permission of the publisher.

ISBN 978-0-9554278-0-0

Printed in the UK by
MPG Books Group, Bodmin and King's Lynn

Reprinted 2011
2nd Reprint 2012

First published in the UK in 2006 by

JACH Publishing
92 Upper North Street, Brighton, East Sussex, England BN1 3FJ

website: www.beryldarbybooks.com

For Fayne, for his fortieth birthday

Family Tree

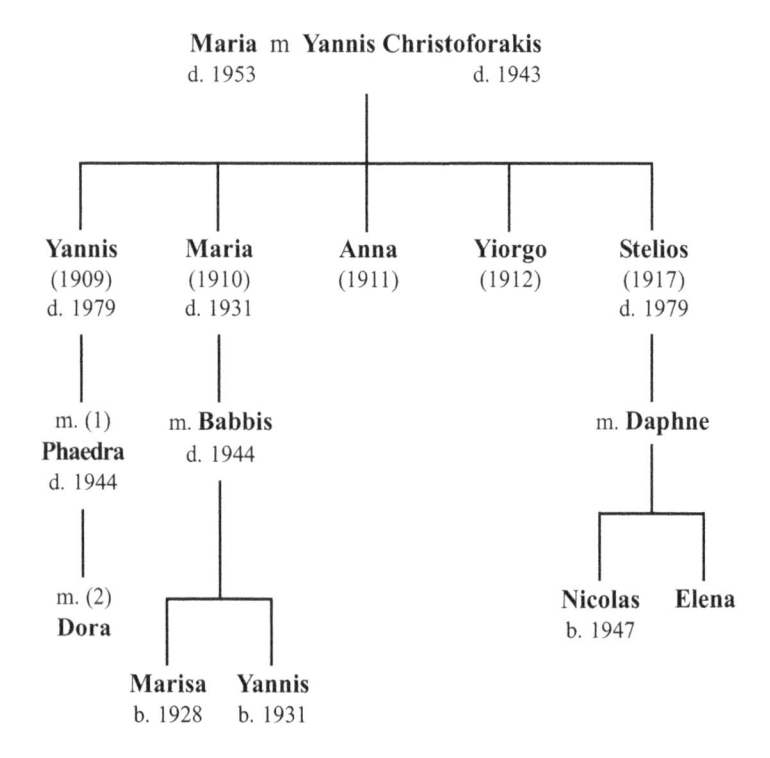

Maria m **Yannis Christoforakis**
d. 1953   d. 1943

- **Yannis** (1909) d. 1979
  - m. (1) **Phaedra** d. 1944
  - m. (2) **Dora**
- **Maria** (1910) d. 1931
  - m. **Babbis** d. 1944
    - **Marisa** b. 1928
    - **Yannis** b. 1931
- **Anna** (1911)
- **Yiorgo** (1912)
- **Stelios** (1917) d. 1979
  - m. **Daphne**
    - **Nicolas** b. 1947
    - **Elena**

1918 - 1926

Yannis pulled his roll-neck jumper a little higher to hide the slight swelling on the side of his neck. His throat hurt, but he did not want to worry his mother. The next baby was due at any time and the last few weeks had not been easy for her.

It was hot in the fields, but Yannis refused to remove his jumper, although his father had removed his jacket and rolled his sleeves above the elbow. He felt cold and shivery and wanted to lie down and sleep, but his father urged him to hurry. Rain was threatening and he wanted to get the grass stored whilst it was still dry. Patiently the donkey allowed Yannis to pile the grass higher and higher on her back until he could no longer reach.

Yannis eased the neck of his jumper with fingers stained by the grass and earth. The first finger of his left hand oozed a small amount of blood where he had cut it on a small glass bottle he had found. He had never seen a bottle like it before, coloured deep blue with swirls of yellow decorating it from the base to the lip. He sucked his finger a couple of times, then forgot it as he collected together the pieces of broken pottery he had found.

'I've finished, Pappa.'

'Off you go, then.'

Yannis took the rope, which was both leading rein and tether for the donkey and urged her towards the track that led to the village. Slowly they plodded homeward. Only a few yards from the main street the rain began to fall, large drops, wetting their clothes and trickling down their necks. Yannis's father took the donkey's rope from him, under the impression that the animal would move faster under his controlling hand. With the heavy, unwieldy load of grass the donkey continued at the same sedate pace, only quickening almost imperceptibly as the farm buildings came into view.

His mother straightened up from the oven as they entered the kitchen. Yannis saw the wince of pain on her face and her hand went involuntarily to her bulging stomach.

'Best go for the Widow,' Yannis's father spoke softly. None of the fear that he felt for the safe delivery of his wife and child was communicated to the boy. Yannis nodded and without a word left the house to run the length of the village street. The rain was harder now and he was glad he had not yet changed into dry clothes.

Yannis knocked and opened the door of the old lady's cottage at the same time. Widow Segouri looked up. Her nose had a slight Semitic hook, dressed all in black; she looked more like a witch than a competent, but untrained midwife.

'What's the hurry, Yannis?' Her voice was soft and composed.

'Pappa said to come – Mamma – the baby,' he panted.

Widow Segouri rose reluctantly from her chair. She thrust her feet into a pair of stout wooden clogs and placed her shawl around her shoulders. From inside a dark cupboard she took a reel of thread and a pair of scissors and slipped them inside a pocket in her voluminous skirt. She looked outside and shrugged; the rain showed no sign of abating. A fifth child and Maria did not take her time like some women.

Slowly they walked back along the street. Yannis could feel the eyes of the villagers watching their progress. By evening there would be callers to ask after the mother and child. If the news were bad, Widow Segouri would spread the word on her return journey. Then the villagers would come in black, to weep and wail to express their sorrow. Yannis had seen that happen once before. He remembered shivering at the shrill keening of the women as they had sat by a neighbour's bed when she had lost her child.

Yannis pushed open the front door to the house. In the main room sat his two younger sisters, their eyes round and wondering. The older girl, called Maria after her mother, had five-year-old Yiorgo on her lap and was rocking him gently.

'Upstairs, all of you,' ordered the Widow and silently the children obeyed. Yannis stood in the communal bedroom, cold, tired and hungry. It would be hours before his mother could attend to them and his father had forgotten their existence.

'I'll get some soup,' he said to Maria and crept back down the stairs. He cast a surreptitious glance towards the high bed that stood in the corner of the living room, hurriedly averting his eyes from his mother's naked legs.

Yannis lifted the pot of warm soup from the embers of the fire and tucked a loaf of bread beneath his arm. Yannis senior looked at his son and was about to order him out of the room when he realised the errand he was carrying out.

'Good boy, Yannis.'

The children dipped the bread into the soup as they sat on the floor eating hungrily. Yannis shivered. He must change his clothes. He stripped off the sodden pullover and trousers. As he pulled the dry jumper over his head he was conscious once again of the small lump just below his ear. His finger was bleeding slightly again, so he stuck it in his mouth whilst he watched Anna tickling Yiorgo. Vaguely he wondered if he would have a brother or sister. It did not matter very much. Babies were all the same.

It seemed an eternity before their father called to them, relief and pride in his voice. 'Children, come and see your brother.'

Silently the children returned to the living room and gazed at the small, crumpled face in their mother's arms. The tiny forehead puckered and the eyes screwed tighter, sensing the presence of more people.

Anna smiled. 'He's beautiful.'

YANNIS

Yannis looked at his mother. Her hair hung limply and she exuded exhaustion. 'What will you call him?' he asked. He had been named after his father and paternal grandfather; Yiorgo had been called after his maternal grandfather, long since dead. This baby had to have a new name.

'Stelios,' his father said firmly and his mother smiled in agreement. Yiorgo stretched out his arms to his mother and Yannis placed him on the high bed beside her where he grabbed at the baby, anxious to investigate this new source of interest.

Widow Segouri stepped forward, her presence having been forgotten. 'I'm going home now. You'll be all right. I'll call in again tomorrow.'

Maria nodded. 'All I want to do is sleep.' It was a signal for their dismissal. Yannis picked Yiorgo up from the bed and set him on his feet.

'Yannis!' His mother's voice was sharp. 'You haven't washed.'

Yannis looked sheepishly at her. 'I'm sorry. I forgot.'

He walked out into the yard and worked the pump, ducking his face quickly beneath the gushing water before rubbing his hands to remove the grime from the fields. He returned to the kitchen and rubbed himself dry on a rough towel. 'I'm going to bed,' he announced.

'Ask Maria to see to Yiorgo,' his mother spoke sleepily and Yannis nodded.

Yannis senior looked at his oldest son. 'Look after them, Yannis. I'm going out for a while.' Yannis senior looked very different from the man who had returned from the fields a few hours earlier. In place of the old trousers and check shirt with a torn sleeve he had donned a white shirt and his Sunday suit of black. It was a little tight, he had put on some weight since he had first bought it, some eleven years ago for his wedding, but it was still his best and only suit. He had a family to be proud of, and now he planned to visit the taverna and spread the news of his latest addition.

Once upstairs Yannis looked at the tiny room. Soon there would have to be another bed. Maybe he and Yiorgo would share a mattress, as did the girls. Anna wriggled down beneath her blanket, leaving room for Maria. Yannis placed Yiorgo on his small pallet in the corner and covered him before pulling across the curtain, which divided the room and gave him a modicum of privacy.

Yannis lay beneath his blanket. His throat felt raw, his head throbbed and his ears began to ache. He fell into a restless sleep full of dreams. He was cutting grass, picking carob, loading the donkey, all the time hot and sweaty and his father would not let him rest or take a drink. He wanted a drink so much. He turned to run to where the water was stored away from the heat of the sun, only to find a beggar standing there, staring at him with pain-filled eyes. Yannis screamed.

Maria was awake in a moment. 'Yannis? What is it?'

'I had a dream.' He realised his voice was almost a sob. His throat felt as though it had closed. 'I need a drink,' he whispered hoarsely. He groped his way downstairs, helped by the dim light of the oil-lamp in the living room.

'Yannis,' called his mother, 'What's wrong?'

'A drink,' mumbled Yannis, and continued on his way to the kitchen.

'Come here afterwards.'

Yannis swallowed the water, which did little to ease the burning sensation in his throat, and went obediently to her bed. His mother ruffled his hair affectionately.

'Your hair's all wet! I thought you went for a drink, not a bath.'

Yannis tried to smile. He shivered and his mother touched his forehead. 'You're like a fire. Here, let me look at you.' She noted the flushed skin and over-bright eyes. 'You've got a temperature. Not changing those wet clothes quickly enough. Back to bed now.'

Yannis escaped thankfully. His legs felt weak. He crawled back onto his mattress and resorted to the childish habit of sucking his fingers for comfort.

YANNIS

Sunlight filtered through the bedroom window, the rays falling on Maria's face. She stirred slightly, refusing to accept that morning had arrived. The rays extended their fingers to touch Anna who rubbed her eyes and sat up.

'Maria,' she whispered. 'Time to get up.'

Maria grunted and opened a sleepy eye. Yiorgo was still asleep. She could dress and wash herself and perhaps see her mother for a moment before he started demanding attention. She slid off the mattress, followed by a bouncing Anna. Anna did not stop to dress, but clambered down the stairs to her mother. She peered at the wizened face of the baby, regarding him quizzically, her head on one side. She was still watching him as her mother woke.

'Anna, come here, my little one.'

Anna scrambled up to her mother's outstretched arms, nestling down in their security. 'Can I hold Stelios today, please, Mamma?'

Maria smiled. 'I'm sure you can. After the Widow has been.'

Anna was content. She slipped off the bed and returned to her room.

Maria was dressed and preparing to go downstairs, Yiorgo and Yannis still slept. It was unusual for Yannis to sleep late; maybe everyone else was early. She pulled on her clothes and returned to the lower floor.

'Is Yannis awake?' asked her father as she entered.

'Not yet.'

Yannis senior rose to his feet and climbed the stairs. His wife had told him Yannis had been up in the night and not appeared at all well. He was tired. The villagers had drunk his health and that of his baby son until four in the morning and he had slept in the hard chair with his head resting on the table rather than disturb his wife. He looked down at the flushed face of the sleeping boy. He was obviously ill.

'Yannis.'

Yannis opened his eyes, tried to move his head on the pillow and emitted a low groan. 'A drink,' he croaked.

Yannis senior returned to his wife. 'He has a fever. Will the Widow look at him when she comes to see you?'

'Of course she will. I'll have a look at him myself.' Cautiously Maria swung her legs over the side of the bed and slowly mounted the stairs. She knelt beside the mattress and took Yannis's hand. 'Do you hurt anywhere?'

'My throat and ears.' Tears welled up in Yannis's eyes. He felt so ill.

She smiled at him to allay his fears. 'I expect you have a chill. A day in bed and you'll be better. I'll ask the Widow to have a look at you when she comes.' She kissed his forehead and returned to her own bed.

The day passed in a haze of faces for Yannis. The Widow diagnosed mumps, probably caught from Nicolas and Louisa and warned Maria to keep him away from the baby. Stelios cried intermittently for attention and whilst their mother was occupied Maria and Anna took turns to take their brother a drink, often interrupting his feverish dreams.

It was a week before he was well enough to leave his bed. His attack of mumps had been quite severe and a chill had hampered his recovery. It was a pale, thin little boy who joined the family for a meal on Sunday evening. As he recuperated he helped his mother around the house, and although his brother and sisters caught mumps they were hardly ill and needed no looking after. Baby Stelios thrived and Maria regained her strength and energy.

The winter was particularly wet, they frequently returned to the house soaked to the skin. Maria had clothes drying continually before the fire and soup became the regular evening meal to warm them through. Yannis began to think of the summer and would look eagerly each morning for blue sky. Almost overnight winter disappeared and spring was with them. He was able to remove his pullover when he worked in the fields with his father at the weekends and the work seemed less arduous as the weather improved.

YANNIS

Yannis pulled off the tight fitting jumper that he had worn most of the winter. Soon it would have to go to Maria as he had grown considerably during the last few months.

'Here, let me look. What's that? Can't be mumps again.' His father touched the small swelling gently. 'Does it hurt?'

Yannis shook his head. The lump had been there since the onset of mumps and now he accepted it as he did his crooked tooth. Yannis senior frowned. He would mention it to Maria.

Maria made Yannis remove his shirt and she examined him carefully. The lump showed white against the brown of his skin. Maria shrugged. It was probably nothing. She would ask the Widow after church tomorrow.

The Widow was comforting. It was probably a blocked gland. She eyed Maria suspiciously. Was this concern over Yannis the prelude to asking for another attendance in a few months time? Maria's body, thickened by childbearing, showed no visible signs of pregnancy.

'How are you keeping, Maria?'

'I'm feeling fine. Now the children are growing up they're able to help me. I've even started to embroider again.'

The Widow calculated rapidly. Maria's embroidery was good.

'I know a woman who has a small shop, no promises, but she might be willing to take some from you, for a small commission, of course.'

'Of course.' Maria smiled. She knew the commission would be shared between the woman and the Widow, but it would be a start. She took her leave, contented with life. She would light two candles next Sunday; one for her healthy family, and the other for her good fortune in being offered an outlet for her embroidery.

Yannis was happy. He had easily caught up with the work he had missed at school whilst he was ill and his father spoke of him with pride to his friends. He wished he could go to a proper school, not one that was taught by the village priest. He did not dislike being up in the fields working with his father, but he would prefer to sit at the kitchen table and read a book the priest had lent to him or complete an exercise.

The days he did not have to attend school his sisters and Yiorgo went to the fields with him, leaving just Stelios at home with his mother. Maria was enjoying her newfound leisure and spent long hours sitting at her embroidery. She was saving hard. A second donkey was needed as Aga was getting old, and she wanted to surprise her husband with the purchase money. Easter was only three days away and she must make the bread and cakes, that was more important than earning an extra lepta.

An hour later, to Maria's surprise, she heard her family returning from the fields. Yannis was dragging his feet and had given the honour of leading the donkey to Maria so he could lean on his father's arm. Maria left her baking.

'What's wrong?'

'Yannis isn't well. His breath won't come.'

'Into bed,' commanded Maria.

Yannis did not argue. The attack of breathlessness had not only frightened him, but also left him feeling weak and exhausted. His legs were a little unsteady as he climbed the stairs. He did not undress, but lay on his mattress fully clothed, he was so tired. He must have slept, as the next thing he knew was his mother shaking him.

'Yannis, wake up. The Widow is here to see you.'

Yannis brushed the sleep from his eyes. 'The Widow? Why?' He struggled into a sitting position and his mother pulled his jumper off over his head.

'He looks fit enough,' declared the Widow. 'What's this lump?' She ran her fingers over the slight swelling.

'The blocked gland,' explained Maria.

The Widow frowned. 'Maybe it sticks out inside and is hindering his breathing,' she suggested. 'Maybe a doctor could say.'

Maria smiled. As usual the Widow had reassured her. They had talked of a trip to Aghios Nikolaos and a visit to a doctor would be an added excuse for the journey.

As they entered the small town Yannis's eyes widened. He had never seen so many people bustling around, intent upon their business. So many fishing boats in the harbour, men mending their nets, vendors crying their wares of oranges, apples, bread, olives and other goods. The main road was lined with small shops, gaily-coloured clothes, weaving and embroidery hanging outside to attract the passer-by. Interspersed were the usual tavernas where the old men spent all day, sitting with their cups of black coffee, clicking their beads and discussing politics.

They filed into a taverna, ostensibly for food, but also to ask for directions. Coffee was ordered for Maria, and Yannis was treated to a glass of fresh lemon juice whilst they waited for their moussaka to arrive. Yannis senior began to converse with two men at the next table and Maria and her son waited until he turned back to them.

'Our luck is in. Yiorgo hasn't gone out today. When we've eaten we'll go and find him.'

Maria smiled happily. Her cousin had visited them occasionally and she was excited at the prospect of meeting his wife and family and showing off her own son.

The moussaka was not as good as his mother served, but Yannis was hungry. He cleared his plate, then wiped it round with bread, wishing there could have been more. Having eaten well and drunk two glasses of wine Yannis senior was in no hurry to move. Yannis began to fidget. Although he was tired after the long walk across the hills he wanted to see more of this new town. Maria coughed to attract her husband's attention and reluctantly he rose to his feet. The bill paid, the little group made their way down to the quay until Maria gave a shout.

'There he is.'

A tall, bronzed man looked up from his nets. His face was weathered by the open-air life he led, his hands gnarled and misshapen from his work.

'Maria! I don't believe it.'

Yiorgo packed up his nets, checked the moorings were secure, then led the way to his cottage. Coffee, lemon juice and raki were produced. Elena and Maria, wary of each other at first, were soon chatting amicably about their children. Yannis had been tongue-tied with Annita and Andreas initially, but when Andreas suggested they showed him the town he accepted with alacrity.

'Be back in an hour,' insisted Elena. 'I will need Annita to help me then.'

'I could stay now, Mamma.' Annita had no particular desire to wander around her hometown with her cousin.

'Off you go, all of you,' her father ordered. 'We have business to discuss.'

The children left the house obediently and Yiorgo smiled happily at his relatives. 'It's good to see you, but what has brought you all this way? If you just wanted to visit I could have brought you down in my boat next time I called at Plaka.'

'Maria wishes to sell more embroidery and we need to see a doctor.'

Yiorgo raised his eyebrows. 'Who is ill?' Both Maria and Yannis looked the picture of middle-aged health.

Yannis explained. It was nothing much, just a small lump on Yannis's neck that gave him a little trouble breathing sometimes.

Yiorgo nodded. 'The doctor will know what it is. Maybe he should have his tonsils out. I'm pleased you've come, though. There are a couple of things I need to talk over with you, and the first concerns Yannis. Have you any plans for the boy?'

'Plans?' Yannis looked puzzled.

Yiorgo leant forward across the table. 'You say he's an intelligent boy. Maybe if he went to a proper school he could become a shopkeeper. There's money in that – and you're not out in all weather every day of the week.'

'He's used to being up in the fields with me.'

'Does he want to be a farmer? The last time I visited you he was working away at an exercise the priest had set him and was reluctant to leave it unfinished. Also, I've looked around. Annita's a good girl. She's been brought up properly, knows how to cook and run a house. What's more she goes to school with Andreas and can read and write. She'll make a good wife, but there's no one in Aghios Nikolaos that I would consider suitable for her. They're mostly young ruffians and not likely to improve as they get older.'

Maria sucked in her breath. 'Are you suggesting that Yannis and Annita are betrothed?'

'Unofficially. Just an understanding between us for a few years time.'

Yannis was calculating rapidly. He had one farm and three sons. It was unlikely to provide a living for all of them. 'I've no objection to a betrothal, but the schooling, that's another matter.'

'Yannis could stay with us and go to school with Andreas. See how he gets on. If he's unhappy he could always return to the farm.'

Yannis shook his head doubtfully. 'I'd need to think about this carefully. Go into the finance. I haven't got a great deal of savings.'

Yiorgo rubbed the side of his nose and winked. 'We'll leave the ladies here to chat whilst we walk down to the taverna.'

Yannis followed Yiorgo obediently from the house and they strolled down to the quay. 'Just thought we could do with a bit of privacy,' smiled Yiorgo as he helped Yannis aboard his fishing boat. 'Come and look in the hold.' He ducked inside the small doorway and lit the oil-lamp that hung from a hook to give a feeble light. 'This is my living,' grinned Yiorgo.

Yannis looked around the empty hold. 'There's nothing here.'

'When the Turks were here they ran a very profitable business. Often I would lend my boat for a few hours and be well paid. The Turks have gone, but the business is still here.'

'How do you mean?'

'Sometimes goods have to be stored until they can be collected. Storage places can be difficult to find. You have two outhouses. Maybe they need enlarging?'

Yannis looked down at his clasped hands. He guessed Yiorgo was offering him a small part in a smuggling operation. If he was careful there should be little risk involved.

'What would you want me to do?'

'You have a contract from the Government to send produce to Spinalonga for the lepers. No one will notice an extra crate occasionally. You'll make more money that way. The Government will pay you and you'll be paid for storage.'

To Yannis it seemed too easy for words. Yiorgo winked at him. 'I don't need to tell you to keep it to yourself, you know what women are like, a little gossip with the neighbours and before you know it half a dozen people are offering storage space and wanting a share in the profits.'

Yannis had no intention of telling Maria. He had an idea that she would disapprove. He deliberately ignored the fact that if he and Yiorgo were caught moving contraband they would both face a spell of imprisonment. The immediate benefits were more important to him.

'Now, we'll visit that taverna.' Yiorgo jumped off his boat and held out his hand to steady Yannis.

The two men finally returned to the fisherman's cottage an hour after the children. Yannis's eyes were aglow and he was recounting to his mother all the wonders he had seen. The school where not only Andreas attended every day, but Annita also, was enormous when compared with the tiny back room that belonged to the village priest. The shops sold all manner of exciting items. There was even a bookshop where you could by newspapers, which had been sent over from Athens. If you wanted information you could visit the library and spend hours sitting in there reading to your heart's content. Aghios Nikolaos, when compared with Plaka, was the most wonderful place on earth.

Yiorgo led them to a taverna by the side of a deep pool where they ate a delicious mixture of fish and rice. Yiorgo and Yannis entered into a very quiet conversation over their raki, whilst Maria and Elena discussed bringing up their families and running their homes. Yannis put his head down on his arms and was almost asleep before they noticed him. Shaking him gently, Maria made ready to leave with Elena and her children, leaving the men to talk and drink.

Yannis hardly remembered the walk home. He stumbled along, clutching at his mother's hand, until he finally tumbled onto the mattress he was to share with Andreas. No sooner had his eyes closed than it was morning. He screwed his eyes up tighter and tried to ignore the light, but it was useless. He squirmed his way out of his bed. Today he had to see a doctor. He had never seen a doctor before in his life. The Widow with her scanty knowledge and common sense was the person he trusted if he were ill. He dressed in clean underclothes as his mother had instructed and went down to the kitchen to wash. Yannis was fascinated by the tap he could turn to get water into a bowl and turned it on and off three times.

'Haven't you seen a tap before?' Annita was gazing at him curiously.

Yannis felt his face redden. 'No,' he answered honestly. 'We have to use the pump in the yard at home.'

Annita raised her eyebrows. 'Tell me about your farm.'

Yannis sat down at the kitchen table and told her how he helped his father in the fields.

'Isn't it boring?'

'Sometimes,' admitted Yannis, 'And it can be cold and wet.'

'Tell me about your school.'

Without waiting for him to answer she began to tell him how fortunate she was to be able to go to school with Andreas. There were only four other girls in the school and she was the cleverest.

The adults appeared and joined the boys at the table whilst Annita made coffee for them and cut slices of Madeira cake at her mother's request. Yiorgo consulted his pocket watch and declared the doctor would be open in an hour and he would show them the way. He insisted, winking broadly at Yannis as he did so, that the wind was too strong for him to venture out fishing that day.

Apart from the Red Cross above the doorway there was nothing to distinguish the building from all the other offices and homes along the road. Inside it was cool and bare. A few chairs were placed along a wall for waiting patients to sit and most were already occupied. The waiting people looked at them curiously as they entered and a woman spoke to Maria.

'Why are you here?'

'My son,' explained Maria. 'He has trouble with his breath sometimes.'

The woman nodded, satisfied. 'I've had a bad throat. The doctor says my tonsils should come out, but at my age ….'

She broke off as an inner door opened and a voice called 'Next.'

She scuttled into the surgery and was lost to their view. Yannis shifted uncomfortably on his seat. He did not want to go to a hospital and have his tonsils out. The other patients began to discuss their various ailments until Yannis began to believe he would catch something very nasty if he stayed much longer. The time dragged as people went in and came out until finally it was Yannis's turn.

He sat in an upright metal chair whilst the doctor peered down his throat.

'Nothing there,' he declared. He looked into Yannis's eyes and ears, sounded his chest and felt his throat around the lump. 'Does it hurt when I do this?'

'No,' whispered Yannis.

'Good.' The Doctor turned to Yannis's parents. 'I can find nothing. How long do you say the lump has been there?'

'Five years, about.'

'Then forget about it. If it troubles you in the future come and see me again.'

Yannis's father dug into his pocket for the necessary drachmas. The doctor had said there was nothing wrong. It had been a waste of time and money. The Widow had told them it was a blocked gland. He felt a reluctance to part with the money, which could have been better spent. He handed the coins over and thanked the doctor politely for his time, waiting until he was outside in the street before commenting to his wife on the futility of their visit. Maria did not agree with him.

'I'm glad we know it's nothing to worry about. Suppose Yannis had been ill and we hadn't bothered to take him to a doctor until it was too late? We would never forgive ourselves.'

Grudgingly her husband had to admit she was right.

'Come,' she said, slipping her hand through his arm, 'Let's go to the church and light a candle to say thank you that Yannis is fit and well.'

Solemnly they entered the church, which was magnificent when compared with the tiny, whitewashed building in their home village. The candle was duly lit and a picture of the Virgin kissed reverently.

'Now,' smiled Maria, brightly, 'Let us go and tell Yiorgo and Elena the news from the doctor, then we should think about leaving.'

Maria shifted herself restlessly. Her husband seemed enthusiastic about her cousin's proposal that Yannis should live with them and attend the Gymnasium in Aghios Nikolaos, but where would they find the money? Schooling was expensive and the meagre amount she earned from her embroidery would not cover the additional cost to the family. There was also Yannis to think of, would he want to leave his home and live with strangers? What would he do when he finished at the Gymnasium? Would he want to become a shopkeeper as Yiorgo had suggested and marry Annita? Then there were the other two boys to consider. If Yannis went to Aghios Nikolaos to be better educated they should also have the opportunity. She sighed deeply and turned over again, disturbing Yannis as she did so.

'What's wrong?'

'I'm worried about Yannis.'

'Why? The doctor said he was fit enough.'

Maria sat up and hugged her knees. 'It's this idea Yiorgo has about him going to school in Aghios Nikolaos. I'm not sure about it.'

Yannis sighed. He knew from experience that if Maria had something troubling her there would be no sleep for him until he had put her mind at rest. He sat up beside her and placed his arm around her shoulders.

'We don't have to make any decision tonight. We need to speak to Father Theodorakis and see what he has to say. There's no point in sending the boy if he hasn't got the ability. If Father Theodorakis thinks it's a good idea, then we'll speak to Yannis and see how he feels.'

Maria nodded in the darkness. 'But the money? How are we going to pay?'

'You don't need to worry about that. Yiorgo and I have come to an understanding on a business matter. There will be more than enough money from that to cover Yannis's schooling.'

'What kind of business?'

'A contract to send food to the island. Leave it to Yiorgo and myself. We'll speak to Father Theodorakis tomorrow evening. Now that you've thoroughly woken me up, I can think of something that will take your mind off Yannis.' Her husband reached out an exploratory hand and Maria gave a girlish giggle.

Maria busied herself in the kitchen and by the time her husband entered the house his supper was ready for him. He muttered to himself as he washed and changed into his best suit, then to Maria's consternation insisted on sitting and smoking a cigarette before strolling leisurely down the road to the church.

Father Theodorakis greeted them with a glass of wine and a considerable amount of curiosity. Maria had asked if they could visit that evening, but had not disclosed the nature of their errand.

'This is a pleasure,' he beamed. 'How can I help you?'

'It's about Yannis.'

'Yannis? I thought you were coming to ask if I had room for Stelios in the school room!'

Maria smiled. 'Stelios is too young. In another year, maybe.'

'Is he intelligent? If we sent him to the Gymnasium would he be able to keep up with the work there?'

Father Theodorakis smiled at the anxious father. 'Yannis is the most intelligent boy I have taught in a long time. With the proper education he could become a school teacher, go into politics, almost anything he had a mind to do.'

Maria settled herself more comfortably in the chair and took a sip from her wine. Yannis shifted uneasily. 'Are you sure? If he went to the Gymnasium and had his head stuffed full of fancy ideas what happens when he leaves?'

'If he is successful at the Gymnasium there are scholarships offered for the University in Heraklion, even in Athens. He would have to work hard, but the opportunity would be there.' Father Theodorakis could not help but think how his estimation would go up in the eyes of the villagers if a pupil of his went on to University.

'And if he didn't get a scholarship? If he's not as clever as you think? He would hardly want to come back here and be a farmer.'

'Have you asked Yannis what he wants? He might not want to go to the Gymnasium, he might want to be a farmer.' Father Theodorakis avoided the question.

Yannis shook his head. 'We wanted to speak to you first.'

Father Theodorakis drained his glass. 'You speak to Yannis and let me know what decisions you make. I will happily write a recommendation for him.'

Yannis took the empty glass as a signal for them to take their leave. He rose and shook the schoolteacher's hand. 'We'll think about it and let you know within a day or two. There's just one other thing.'

Father Theodorakis frowned. What else could there be?

'If Yannis did go to Aghios Nikolaos, there would be a space in your class. I'd like my Maria to get a bit of schooling, just to read a bit and do her numbers.'

Taken unawares Father Theodorakis could think of no good excuse to refuse the request. 'I suppose I could have her, for a couple of mornings maybe.'

Yannis was sitting at the kitchen table reading when his parents returned. His father looked over his shoulder. 'What are you reading?'

'Aristophanes, "The Birds".'

Yannis nodded. It meant nothing to him. 'You enjoy reading?' He could struggle through a newspaper, but he had never attempted to read a book.

'I love reading. Aristophanes is so clever with words.'

'What did you think of Aghios Nikolaos when we visited?'

Yannis noted the number of the page and closed the book. It was evident that his father was not going to let him read in peace. 'I enjoyed it. Everything was so much bigger than here, even the fishing boats were bigger, and the shops, they were marvellous.'

'Did you like your cousins?'

'Yes. Andreas was a bit quiet, but I liked him.'

'And Yiorgo and Elena, did you like them?'

Yannis nodded.

His father seemed at a loss for words, finally he continued, 'Yannis, what would you like to do when you leave school?'

'I don't want to be a fisherman with Uncle Yiorgo,' his lip trembled. He was going to be sent away to work on his uncle's boat. 'Please, Pappa, don't send me away. I'll work harder on the farm for you, I promise.'

'Do you like working on the farm?'

'Yes, I love it.'

'Better than reading?'

'Much better than....' Yannis voice trailed off and he reddened. 'No, I love reading best, but I don't mind working in the fields.'

'Suppose I said you could leave the village school, what would you say to that?'

Yannis's face fell. 'And work in the fields all the time?' He felt his eyes begin to fill with tears. 'I don't want to be a farmer, Pappa, or a fisherman.'

'What would you like to do?'

'I don't know.'

'Would you like to go to the Gymnasium in Aghios Nikolaos? See how you get on, then make up your mind.'

Yannis opened his mouth to reply and no words came.

'Think about it, let me know tomorrow.' His father patted him on the shoulder. 'I'll let you get back to your reading.'

'Pappa! There's nothing I would like more.' The unshed tears began to spill from Yannis's eyes. 'Pappa, do you really mean it?'

Yannis drew out the chair and sat down next to his son. 'Father Theodorakis says that you are a clever boy, but you'd have to work hard. You could stay with Yiorgo and Elena, you'd have to help Yiorgo on his boat at the weekends, the same as Andreas, but that won't hurt you. Maybe you could get a job in Aghios Nikolaos when you've finished your schooling, in a shop or something.'

Yannis nodded, still hardly daring to believe his father. 'Would I go to the proper school, with Annita and Andreas? They learn about different countries and things that happened in the past, like the way that Aristophanes lived when he was alive and the great battles that Alexander fought. Annita can add up faster than I can, and she doesn't use her fingers.'

'That's settled then. I'll ask Father Theodorakis to write you a recommendation. I'll send a message to Yiorgo at the same time and he can make the arrangements.'

It was June before a reply was received from Aghios Nikolaos. Maria straightened up from her vegetable garden as her cousin shouted to announce his arrival and Stelios was sent running to fetch his father from the fields. Maria fussed around her cousin, longing to know the news he brought with him, but dutifully waiting for her husband to arrive.

The children were sent out into the yard to play and Yannis produced a bottle of raki. 'Is your visit business or pleasure?'

'Both,' smiled Yiorgo and lifted his glass. 'I have the letter from the Gymnasium offering a place for Yannis. I decided to deliver it myself. Your letter took five weeks to reach me. Takis made three trips to Aghios Nikolaos before he remembered.'

Maria crossed herself. 'What does it say, Yannis?'

'I'll call Yannis. He'll be able to read it.'

Yannis took the flimsy piece of paper in trembling fingers. His throat felt so dry he could hardly utter the words.

"On the recommendation of Father Theodorakis we will be pleased to offer Yannis Christoforakis, a place at the Gymnasium of Aghios Nikolaos for one year.

At the end of this time, if his results are of a satisfactory standard, he will be eligible to apply to a High School if this is your wish.

If you accept the place offered to him we should point out that suitable accommodation should be found for him in Aghios Nikolaos, as we are a day school only.

All fees are payable termly in advance.

Please advise us of your decision."

Maria clasped her hands together. 'That's wonderful.' She

held out her arms to Yannis and hugged the trembling boy to her, trying hard to hold back her tears.

The two men raised their glasses. 'To Yannis,' said Yiorgo, and drained his glass, holding it out to be refilled.

'Now,' Yannis leaned forward, 'We must talk about expenses.'

Yiorgo grinned. 'That should be no problem, but that kind of business is better man to man.'

Maria kissed her cousin. 'Thank you, Yiorgo, and thank Elena for me. I know you'll look after Yannis. I must go back to the garden. Yannis, go and look after the children.' Covered with both elation and confusion she shepherded her son before her as she left the room, making sure the door was firmly closed behind her. If the men wanted to talk business they needed privacy.

The rest of the summer passed like a dream for Yannis. His mother mended shirts and darned socks, packing them away in a clean sack as she finished them, alternately telling him to behave whilst he was away from home and how much she would miss him.

The day Yannis was due to leave he examined his neck carefully. The small white lump was still there, as big as his thumbnail, he decided. He pressed it, but it did not hurt, he tried to squeeze it, but no pus came. The doctor was right. It was nothing.

He felt both excited and apprehensive as he kissed his family goodbye. His mother was fighting hard to suppress her tears and the other children seemed tongue-tied. Yannis senior was fidgeting to leave. He would walk to Elounda with Yannis and Yiorgo would meet them there and take Yannis on to Aghios Nikolaos. As Yannis turned back and waved to the little group he felt a lump rise in his throat and tears pricked at the back of his eyelids. He was determined not to cry.

His family disappeared as he and his father rounded the corner. The sun warmed their backs and they walked briskly, quickly covering the few kilometres between the two villages. A boat could be seen slowly tacking towards the quay and they went into the waterfront taverna to await Yiorgo's arrival. They drank coffee, Yannis being allowed a cup of the hot, sweet, sticky liquid as a sign that he was being treated as an adult. In due course Yiorgo appeared and more coffee was ordered. Yannis began to feel slightly sick and sipped at his glass of water to cleanse his mouth of the cloying effect of the coffee.

At last the men made a move. Yannis kissed his son affectionately on both cheeks and held him tightly for a moment.

'Do as your mother has told you. Help Yiorgo all you can and look after your cousins. Mind you work hard at school; it's not many boys who have your opportunity. We're proud of you, Yannis.'

Yannis was relieved when they reached the port of Aghios Nikolaos. He was not sure if the strange feeling in the pit of his stomach was due to the motion of the boat, nervousness or the two cups of coffee. As they walked along the waterfront men called out a greeting to Yiorgo and stared curiously at Yannis.

'Makkis called,' Elena said to Yiorgo after greeting Yannis. 'Asked if you were planning a fishing trip tonight.'

Yiorgo nodded. 'It will make up for lost time today.'

Yannis felt guilty. Because of him his uncle had lost a day's work and had to go out at night. 'I'm sorry,' he mumbled.

Yiorgo laughed. 'What are you sorry for? I often go out at night. The fishing can be better then. When you've got your sea-legs I'll take you with me, it's very different from the day.'

Annita and Andreas came tumbling through the door and stopped when they saw Yannis.

'Oh!' exclaimed Annita. 'I didn't think you'd be here yet.'

They sat down beside Yannis at the table and helped themselves to the bread, cheese and olives. Yannis ate steadily, racking his brains for something to say. At last he had an idea.

'After we've eaten would you show me the school again, please, Annita?'

'If you like,' she replied. 'You'll soon see more than enough of it.'

'I'd like you to show me round the town again as well. I don't want to get lost.'

Having helped her mother clear the table she called to Yannis. 'Come on, then, if you want me to show you round.'

Yannis rose quickly and opened the door for her. Annita looked surprised and went through without a word. She led the way down to the harbour, then up a steep hill and veered to the left. 'Here we are,' she announced.

Yannis gazed at the building. 'It's so big.' He was admiring, but his heart was fluttering. On Monday he would have to walk through the doors amongst children he did not know. Would he find the work too difficult and be laughed at, called the village dunce and mocked until his life was a misery?

'Come on,' said Annita. She saw no point in looking at the closed door. 'We have four classes,' she informed him and added with pride, 'I'm in the top class because I'm clever.'

Yannis did not comment and Annita led him to the centre of the town, waiting impatiently as Yannis looked into every shop. Never had he seen such an array of goods.

'Who buys all these things?' he asked.

'We're beginning to have tourists here in the summer. They buy things to take home. Mamma does embroidery for that shop.'

'My Mamma does embroidery also, but I don't know which shop it goes to.'

'They're all much the same.' Annita dismissed the subject and waved frantically to a girl standing in a shop doorway. 'Come and meet my friend Thalia.'

Yannis was duly introduced to the girl and spent a self-conscious ten minutes whilst Thalia was told his history, which obviously did not impress her.

Leaving Thalia with a promise to see her the following day, Annita led Yannis round the corner to the lake. They scrambled up a steep hill until the panorama of Aghios Nikolaos was spread before them.

'It's a wonderful view. I didn't realise there were two harbours.'

'That one is where the ferries dock, the ones that bring the tourists,' explained Annita.

Yannis looked at the ships. 'I shall go on those when I'm older,' he said, confidently.

'Where to?'

Yannis shrugged. 'I don't know. Athens, maybe.'

'I'd like to go to Athens. Maybe we could go together. Come on, race you.'

Annita took to her heels and went flying down the hill, Yannis following more carefully. He did not want to fall and ruin his new trousers. By the time they returned to the cottage Yiorgo had left to make ready for the night's fishing. A salad, bread and brawn were sitting in the kitchen and Annita helped herself and Yannis, leaving plenty for Andreas who returned home just as they were finishing their meal.

Whilst Elena chatted to Yannis, Annita spent the evening sitting in a corner, her head bent over her embroidery. Surreptitiously she studied her cousin. He was not as good looking as Dimitrakis, and he did not spend his time making silly jokes like Nicolas who made her laugh, but she liked him, she decided. She hoped he would not be a dunce at school. He was, after all, her cousin and if he were stupid people might thinks she was stupid also. She sighed heavily.

'Time for bed all of you. You must be tired, Yannis, you've had a long day.' Elena was fussing over him, as she never did her own children.

Obediently Annita folded her embroidery and led the way up the stairs. The room she shared with her brother had been partitioned by a flimsy piece of wood a few years earlier to give her a certain amount of privacy now she was older. Yannis fell asleep immediately, but Annita lay awake, listening to the regular breathing of her cousin and brother. She wanted Yannis to like her, but she also wanted to impress him and have him admire and respect her. When she woke the sun was up and she could hear her mother in the kitchen. The boys were probably already up she realised and dragged on her clothes hurriedly. As she entered the kitchen Yannis stood up and offered her his chair. She looked at him, nodded and sat down without a word.

'Your father is going to take me out fishing today. Are you coming?'

Annita hesitated, she was a good sailor and she doubted if the same was true of her cousin. 'May I go, Mamma?'

'I didn't think you were very fond of the sea.'

Annita wrinkled her nose. 'I like the sea, it's the smell of fish.'

Elena wagged a finger at her daughter. 'You should be used to it by now.'

Yiorgo was already on his boat and he held out his hand to help them jump aboard. Yannis carried out Yiorgo's instructions with the ropes to cast off and stood with his face held up to the breeze. Annita smiled to herself. Wait until they turned the headland, then her landlubber cousin would know what sailing was all about. Annita went and stood by his side. He smiled at her shyly.

'Do you often come out with your father?'

'I'm not very interested in fishing.'

As they rounded the headland the boat pitched and tossed violently for a few moments. Yannis slid into a sitting position, his face white. Annita laughed at his discomfort. She was still standing, moving with the motion of the boat.

'This is nothing,' she said. 'Today it's calm, you should be out here in a storm.'

The colour returned to Yannis's face as the boat ceased its erratic movement and continued to glide smoothly through the water. 'I'll get used to it,' he said, confidently. 'I'm going to help your father at the weekends.'

Yiorgo showed Yannis how to drop and secure the net, and they trawled gently for an hour. Yannis was enjoying himself. If this was fishing it was not as bad as he had thought. True, there was nothing to do whilst waiting to haul in the net, but the sun was pleasant and he could always bring a book with him and read.

At a signal from Yiorgo the children began to heave the net up. The boat rocked violently as the catch came aboard. Once again Yannis turned white and clutched at a rope to steady himself. His fear was overcome by his fascination with the gleaming, silver fish, wriggling and gasping as they struggled in the mesh. The children turned their attention to sorting them into boxes, keeping two large lobsters to one side as Yiorgo directed.

They rounded the headland again, but this time Yannis was prepared for the motion.

'Move with it,' Annita advised him. 'Don't try to sit still.'

He tried to carry out her instructions and found it helped. His stomach did not jump up to the back of his throat each time the boat pitched.

'Haul in the sail, Yannis,' directed Yiorgo.

Yannis loosened the ropes and before he realised what was happening he was completely covered in the coarse cloth. Annita and Andreas were helpless with laughter as he fought his way out and their father was grinning.

'You'll have to do better than that. Suppose we hit a squall one day and you ended up in a heap on the deck? That wouldn't be much help to me. Let me show you the right way to do it.' Deftly Yiorgo raised the sail again, and then showed the boy which ropes to slacken off first.

Yannis tried again and was more successful on his second attempt.

'I'm better at harnessing a donkey,' he declared ruefully.

Yiorgo ruffled his hair. 'You'll soon learn. Help me pull on this rope; then I'll pass the boxes out to you. Come on; get those lobsters to your mother, Annita. We'll come back later and see to the nets.'

Elena had spent the morning sitting at her embroidery which she packed away carefully as they arrived, then took the lobsters into the kitchen. The children soon heard them squealing as their shells shrunk and they sniffed the air hungrily.

'They won't be ready until supper,' announced Elena. 'Have your lunch now and think of the treat in store for you later.'

Yannis yawned hugely. 'It must be the sea air,' he apologised.

'You could sleep for a while this afternoon, Yannis.'

'No he can't.' Yiorgo contradicted his wife. 'The nets have to be hung out to dry and I expect they'll need mending. He can sleep tonight.' Yiorgo sounded quite grim as he spoke. 'Fishermen don't rest until everything is in readiness for the next trip. If you leave it you'll forget it, and that can be dangerous if you get caught out at sea in bad weather.'

Yannis could see the sense of Yiorgo's argument and forced thoughts of sleep from his mind. The afternoon passed in the sunshine, Yannis holding the net up a few feet from the hole Yiorgo was mending. 'Try your hand now.' Yiorgo handed the shuttle to Yannis. Under Yiorgo's direction he threaded the slim piece of wood in and out, knotting the thread as Yiorgo had done.

'Not bad,' Yiorgo eyed his handiwork critically. To Yannis it looked very clumsy and had taken him twice as long as any of the larger holes that Yiorgo had mended. 'Have another try.' This time Yiorgo gave no instructions and Yannis struggled and fumbled until Yiorgo finally took the shuttle from him and untangled the mass of knotted thread. Yannis flushed with embarrassment.

'It takes a lot of practice to mend a net. You'll learn.'

Patiently Yiorgo directed the boy's efforts a second time. Yannis continued to mend nets until late in the afternoon and he was able to repair a hole without tangling the thread, although he was still slow and clumsy.

Yiorgo clapped him on the back. 'You've certainly got tenacity. Many others would have given up long ago and sneaked away with some excuse. Leave it now. We'll go and have supper. Next weekend will be the test – to see if you can remember the knack.'

Yannis smiled. He felt so tired. He would be quite happy to have his supper and go to bed. On their way home they met Makkis slouching along by the harbour.

'Fishing tonight?' he asked.

'No,' said Yiorgo decisively. 'I was out last night, besides it's Elena's birthday.'

Makkis shrugged. 'Another time.'

'Does he sail with you?' Yannis was curious; the man had not accompanied them that morning.

'Sometimes. He works for anyone who will hire him. He wants the money, he's saving for a boat of his own.'

The smell of lobster and newly baked bread met them as they opened the door. Annita wrinkled her nose as they entered and she smelled their clothes. She took her place at the table, not even the odour of stale fish could detract from the succulent smell of the lobsters and ruin her appetite. Yannis found the lobster unexpectedly delicious.

'Do you often eat lobster?' he asked hopefully.

Yiorgo shook his head. 'I often catch them, but they sell for a good price. This was a treat for Elena's birthday.'

Elena smiled happily. Yiorgo never forgot either her name day or birthday.

When Yannis awoke the next morning he had mixed feelings as he washed and dressed ready for school. He walked between Annita and Andreas feeling conspicuous. Every child who greeted them looked at him curiously and once in the playground Annita began to introduce him to her classmates. There was a note of pride in her voice as she told them Yannis was her cousin, but the children seemed unimpressed.

YANNIS

'Where have you come from?' asked a plump, rather foolish looking boy.

'Plaka,' answered Yannis, and was about to explain where the village was when the boy stuck out his tongue and waggled his fingers above his head.

'Village boy! Village boy! Looks like a donkey!'

'Take no notice of him,' said Annita, taking Yannis's arm. 'He's not as clever as a donkey.'

A bell rang from inside the building and the children began to enter. Yannis followed Annita to a room where a young man was busily writing on a blackboard.

'Good morning, sir. I've brought my cousin, Yannis.'

The man turned and flicked back the lock of dark hair that hung down over his eyes. He wiped his hand down his black trousers, leaving white streaks, then extended his hand to Yannis.

'How do you do?' he asked politely and not waiting for Yannis to answer he continued. 'I've had a letter from your teacher at Plaka. He seems to think you have some promise. We'll see. I'll put you next to your cousin for a few days until you find your feet. I shall expect you to work hard. I won't waste my time on lazy boys. Ask me if you don't understand, now, take your seat and don't talk.'

'Yes, sir.' Yannis followed Annita to a spare desk and chair.

'Here you are,' she said, pushing pen, pencil and ruler towards him. 'Mr Pavlakis will give you any paper or book that you need.'

'Shh,' said Yannis.

Annita laughed. Mr Pavlakis had already turned back to the blackboard ignoring the children who were noisily entering the room. 'He always tells us not to talk.'

Gradually the children settled and Mr Pavlakis turned to face them. 'Now don't talk,' he said, flicking back the offending lock of hair. 'We have a new boy with us, Yannis Christoforakis, Annita's cousin. Make him feel welcome, please. Now, turn to page fifty six of your Homer,' he passed a book to Yannis, 'And Yannis will read for us.'

Yannis was pleased. He had borrowed a copy of the book from Father Theodorakis and thoroughly enjoyed reading about the siege of Troy. Yannis read fluently and with expression.

'You've read this before, I think?'

'Yes, sir.'

'Then you can answer some questions for me.'

To Yannis the questions were simple, the answers to all of them being found in the text he had just read.

Mr Pavlakis pushed back his hair and looked at Yannis speculatively. 'Now, no talking. Mental arithmetic.' As he spoke he was passing out sheets of paper. 'Name on the top. No cheating.' For the next fifteen minutes he reeled off subtraction, addition, multiplication and division. Yannis found it difficult to keep up and was relieved when the teacher stopped and asked for the papers.

'Now, no talking. Whilst I mark them you can draw a map of Africa.' Mr Pavlakis marked Yannis's arithmetic paper first and was pleasantly surprised. The boy had done well. Nearly all right. At the sight of the blank sheet of paper Yannis handed to him later he raised his eyebrows.

Yannis flushed and wriggled uncomfortably. 'I didn't know the shape, sir.'

The class tittered and Mr Pavlakis frowned. 'Everyone else seems to know all about the country. Let's make sure.' He fired questions at the children, which they struggled to answer. 'Not quite as clever as you all thought,' observed the teacher. He made a quick note on his pad. 'Come to me after school, Yannis. You have some catching up to do in that area.'

Yannis felt most embarrassed and hoped he would not be asked to do other things he had never heard about. When the children were given a short break he found himself surrounded and being bombarded with questions.

'Did you really not know what Africa looked like?'

'Did you know it was a continent?'

'Did you know the people there are black, really black?'

Yannis shook his head miserably. 'We didn't learn things like that in the village school.'

'Donkey! Village donkey!' The mocking voice of the fat boy drifted over to him.

'Take no notice of him. I'm Costas.' A swarthy, stocky boy pushed himself to Yannis's side. 'I come from a farm just outside Aghios Nikolaos. Tell me about yours. Do you have animals or just crops?'

The morning passed quickly for Yannis and by the end of the day he felt quite at home in the class. When the bell rang to signify the end of school Yannis went up to his teacher.

'You asked me to see you.'

Mr Pavlakis handed him an atlas. 'Have a look at that and familiarise yourself with the shape of the countries, which ones they border and their main towns. Give yourself a couple of weeks. I don't expect you to learn it all overnight. When you've caught up on your Geography I'll make you a book list. You can join the library and read them as you want. Reading is the best way to education. Reading, observation and travel.'

Yannis was delighted. 'I love reading. I've read every book in Plaka.'

'It might take you a little longer to read all the books in Aghios Nikolaos,' remarked Mr Pavlakis dryly. 'Off you go now.'

Annita was waiting for Yannis by the gate. 'What have you got there?'

'Homework.' Yannis held the atlas up for her inspection. 'Mr Pavlakis is going to give me a book list.'

'Pappa won't be very pleased if you have your head stuck in a book all the time. He expects you to help him.'

'I'll help him all he wants,' replied Yannis. 'I can read in the evenings.'

Annita sniffed. She enjoyed school, but saw no need for any homework.

'Where's Andreas?' Yannis looked around for the younger boy.

'He's already gone,' Annita called as she ran down the hill.

Yannis caught her up. 'What's the rush?'

'I just felt like running,' she panted and came to a stop. 'Look, there's Pappa just arriving. Let's go and meet him.'

'How did it go, Yannis?' called Yiorgo.

'Fine. Mr Pavlakis is going to give me a book list and I'm going to join the library.'

When Yannis handed the atlas back to Mr Pavlakis at the end of a week the teacher looked at him in disbelief. 'Have you done all I asked?'

'Yes, sir. Annita helped by asking me questions and I've drawn all the maps from memory.'

Mr Pavlakis pursed his lips. 'The proof will be in the work you do for me. Here's the book list I promised you.'

Yannis studied the list. 'I've never heard of some of these,' he admitted.

'Don't worry. They'll have them in the library. When you've had enough of those you can start on the classics, and, Yannis, don't forget the Bible.'

'I won't, sir, and thank you.'

The days passed swiftly for Yannis. He found he could easily keep up with the class and was accepted by them. After school he would either sit and read or help Yiorgo with the nets, at the weekends he went with him to the fishing grounds and he began to enjoy the sea. Whenever he finished a book he would wait after school and talk to Mr Pavlakis. Yannis found the teacher fascinating. He seemed able to talk on any subject that was mentioned with knowledge and insight, often giving new ideas to Yannis.

'How do you know so much, sir?'

Mr Pavlakis smiled at the eager boy. 'I've read widely and I've been to University in Athens.'

'University.' Yannis said the word with awe.

'All teachers have to go to University,' explained Mr Pavlakis.

'I should like to go so I could become a teacher,' sighed Yannis wistfully.

'There's no reason why you shouldn't if you continue to work hard.'

Yannis shook his head. 'I have brothers and sisters. My parents couldn't afford to send me to University.'

'They do give scholarships, you know.'

Again Yannis shook his head. 'You'd have to be very clever to gain a scholarship.'

'We shall see.' Mr Pavlakis did not want to raise the boy's hopes. At present he had all the makings of scholarship material. 'Now, I must go or I shall be late.'

'Late?' Yannis looked surprised. School was over for the day.

'I work in a taverna in the evening,' explained Mr Pavlakis. 'I'm saving up to visit Italy this year.' His eyes glowed with enthusiasm. 'I want to see Rome, Florence, Venice, two weeks will not be long enough for me.'

'Have you been to other countries?' asked Yannis as they walked together.

'I've been to Egypt twice, to Turkey and also to Cyprus.'

Yannis gazed at him in wonder. 'Please, sir, when you have time, will you tell me all about them?'

They parted company at the school gate and Yannis ran down to the harbour where he could see Yiorgo examining his nets.

'More books, Yannis? Can you put them down long enough to come out with me tonight?'

'Oh, yes.' His eyes shone, his uncle had been promising him a night trip for some time now.

'What time do we leave?'

'After supper, about nine.' Yiorgo turned back to his nets.

Yannis waved his hand and rushed off down the street. Excitedly he told his aunt he was going fishing that night.

She frowned. 'You should be in bed, not out fishing.'

The interval before supper dragged for Yannis. He could not lose himself in his book and continually fidgeted until Annita asked him what was wrong.

'Nothing,' replied Yannis. 'I'm just excited. I'm going fishing tonight.'

Once away from the shore the excitement drained from Yannis. It was difficult carrying out his uncle's instructions with only the light of the moon to help him. He fumbled with the ropes, his fingers becoming numbed with the cold far more quickly than they did during the day, and he was relieved when his uncle told him to take the tiller and keep the boat on course. They had rounded the headland, but in the darkness Yannis had no idea of their direction.

The slap of the waves against the hull seemed far louder than usual and the pitching and rolling of the small craft more pronounced. He was thankful when Yiorgo lowered the sail and told him to take the oars.

'Aren't we going to drop the nets?'

'Not tonight. I've a delivery to make.'

They strained at the oars rounding the end of the long finger-shaped piece of land until they were running into the channel between the island of Spinalonga and Yannis's hometown. Skilfully Yiorgo manoeuvred the boat alongside the quay and made fast the rope.

'Don't make a sound,' ordered Yiorgo.

Yiorgo swung himself over the side of the boat and within a few moments was swallowed up in the darkness. Yannis sat on the gently rocking boat for an age before he saw Yiorgo a short distance away. Two large, unwieldy bundles were passed up to Yannis and Yiorgo disappeared into the night again. Yiorgo returned twice more with bundles that he handed up to Yannis before climbing aboard, casting off quickly and exhorting Yannis to row as fast as he could. Yannis obeyed and they were soon through the channel and back out to the sea.

Yiorgo raised the sails and then took the oars from Yannis. On the horizon there was a wink of light and Yiorgo steered straight towards it. The light became larger as they drew closer, until Yannis could make out the hull of a trawler. Yiorgo dropped the anchor before taking the lantern from the cabin. He lit it carefully, shading it with his hand he began to swing it back and forth until an answering flicker came from the trawler.

Satisfied Yiorgo blew out the lamp and passed it to Yannis to return to the cabin. They sat and waited until the splash of oars could be heard, Yannis straining his eyes in the darkness. Finally a rowing boat came into view and Yiorgo sent Yannis to the hold to pass up the bundles. 'Stay down there until I call you,' he ordered.

Yannis was not sure whether he was excited or frightened, but he was certainly not going to disobey. It seemed an eternity before his uncle called to him.

'Yannis, come and get this lot below.'

Boxes of fish were pushed towards him and he placed them carefully, the weight evenly dispersed on each side, as Yiorgo had shown him. Cautiously he made his way back on deck and looked around. There was no sign of the trawler.

'Take the tiller, Yannis. We may as well return; we've made a good catch.'

'Yiorgo,' Yannis spoke tentatively, 'I don't really understand.'

'It's quite simple. I store a few things for some friends of mine. When they collect them they give me a share of their catch for my trouble.'

'Why don't they come to Aghios Nikolaos for them?'

'They have their reasons. Nothing you need to worry about, and you don't tell anyone. The other fishermen might not like the idea of a trawler catching fish for me.'

'Do you do this every time you go out at night?'

Yiorgo shook his head. 'Only occasionally. Now, any more questions, or can we make for home?'

'Where did we go when we moored and went along the beach?'

'Spinalonga.'

'Spinalonga!' Yannis gasped in horror. 'But the lepers...'

'Did you see any? I didn't. That was why I told you to be quiet, didn't want to wake them up.'

Yannis swallowed and shuddered. 'I hate that place. You can see them sometimes when the boats deliver their supplies and they come down to the quay to collect them.'

Yiorgo shrugged. 'There's no harm in going onto the quay. Now, let me get those sails up and we'll get going.'

It soon became routine to Yannis to go with Yiorgo on some of his night fishing trips. Gradually he became accustomed to the night sounds and was able to perform his duties on the boat by touch. Yannis yawned surreptitiously. He had been out the previous night with his uncle and felt decidedly sleepy in the hot classroom. Mr Pavlakis was explaining an exercise to them and he was finding it very hard to keep his eyes open and concentrate.

When he left the classroom, Yannis was surprised to find a strong wind blowing and clutched his books tightly. As the children left the shelter of the buildings the full force hit them and they bent their heads as sand and dust swirled around, stinging their faces and making their eyes water.

'I hope Pappa isn't out in this,' observed Annita.

The wind, coming across from Africa, was the dread of both fishermen and farmers. Boats would be overturned in the harbour, nets torn to shreds, or crops of olives and grapes shaken from their precarious hold on the branches and complete harvests ruined. When they reached the quay they could see that Yiorgo's boat, along with the others was moored, the fishermen talking disconsolately in groups, looking at the horizon, trying to calculate the severity of the storm.

YANNIS

'It will blow itself out by morning,' declared Yiorgo. 'I might as well come home with you children. There's nothing I can do here.'

The wind howled around the little house, rattling the shutters and sending debris along the street. Tired as he was, Yannis found it difficult to ignore the sound of the waves crashing against the rocky shore and he shivered involuntarily at the thought of being at sea. He fell into a deep sleep shortly before dawn and the next thing he knew Andreas was shaking him vigorously.

'Come on, lazy. Pappa wants us to help him with the nets.'

Yannis rubbed his eyes. Was it really morning? He pulled on a shirt and trousers and hurried downstairs after Andreas. The sea was unbelievably calm and it was strangely quiet now the wind was no longer blowing. The little harbour was almost empty as the fishermen tried to make up for the lost fishing hours.

Yannis and Andreas worked hard all morning, taking it in turns to hold the nets whilst the other mended. Yiorgo washed the deck, greased the rowlocks and checked the ropes to the sails, finally declaring himself satisfied. Annita arrived, waving to her father and sitting down on a coil of rope.

'I've been talking to Mr Pavlakis,' she announced to Yannis.

'Where did you see him?'

'In the square. He said he was on his way to work, but there's no school today.'

Yannis smiled. 'He works in a taverna in his spare time, then saves the money so he can travel abroad during the school holidays.'

Annita sniffed. 'Fancy working in a taverna when you're a teacher.'

'What does it matter where you work if you make enough money to do something you want? He probably enjoys it anyway.'

Annita began to giggle. 'I wonder if he tells his customers not to talk?'

Andreas and Yannis laughed with her, and Andreas began to walk between them, pretending to carry a tray.

'Yes, sir,' he mimicked. 'What can I get for you? A coffee? Thank you, sir. Anything to eat, sir? Baklava? Certainly, sir. Now don't talk and I'll go and fetch it.' Andreas flicked back an imaginary piece of hair from his forehead and wiped his hand down his trousers. The two children watching him laughed uproariously and Yiorgo turned round.

'What's so funny?'

Yannis wiped his eyes. 'It was Andreas, pretending to be Mr Pavlakis.'

Yiorgo smiled. He doubted if he would understand. It was probably some school joke. He had met Mr Pavlakis once and thought him an annoying young man with his habit of pushing back his hair.

Yannis turned to Annita. 'He told me he was going to Italy in the summer holidays.'

'Italy?' Her eyes widened. 'What for?'

'To see the buildings and art they have there. He's been to Athens and Egypt. I'm going too.'

'Oh? When?'

'When I'm older and have saved some money,' said Yannis confidently.

Yiorgo stepped ashore. 'Until you two boys have finished mending that net you haven't even earned your lunch.' He started to stroll back up the road with Annita dancing along beside him.

'What are you going to do this afternoon?' asked Andreas.

'Read, I expect.'

'You're always reading.'

'I enjoy reading. I want to know all about the different places ready for when I visit them.'

Andreas looked at his cousin in concern. 'Don't you like Crete?'

Yannis smiled. 'I love it, but I want to see other countries. I want to see where the Venetians came from before they came here and built forts. The Romans came here, the Arabs, the Turks.

I want to see why Crete was so much better than their own country.'

Andreas did not understand. If you loved Crete why bother to go elsewhere? It must be all the reading that made Yannis odd.

The walk to Elounda, where he would meet Yiorgo, was cold. Maria had accompanied him part of the way, but now he bent his head against the wind as he trudged along the country road alone. It had been good to spend a week with his family. He had been surprised and delighted when Yiorgo had given him a whole drachma to spend before leaving Aghios Nikolaos. He had spent a long time looking in the shops deciding what he should buy as presents. Finally, with Annita's help, he had chosen hair ribbons for his sisters, coloured marbles for his brothers; a skein of embroidery silk for his mother and a small packet of tobacco for his father. He had been quite unprepared for their joy over the insignificant little gifts and glowed with pleasure at their thanks.

He was almost as excited to be returning to Aghios Nikolaos as he had been on his first visit and once he was aboard the boat he felt as if he had never been away. Throughout January and February the weather continued to be wet and windy, Yiorgo continually coming home soaked to the skin, began to cough and sneeze. One by one the children caught his cold, staying home from school until the worst was over.

The term passed uneventfully for Yannis. He had sought out Mr Pavlakis and asked if there was a certain date when applications had to be made to a High School, but Mr Pavlakis had seemed vague and disinterested. Yannis was miserable and when he went to church he prayed long and fervently for a solution to his problem. He could hardly believe his eyes the day he returned from school and saw his father sitting at the table with Yiorgo.

'Pappa! What are you doing here? Is Mamma all right?'

Yannis senior hugged his son closely to him. 'Everyone is fine. How you've grown since Christmas!'

Yannis sat down beside his father. 'Why are you here, Pappa?'

'I was sent for. I had a letter from your teacher asking me to come to Aghios Nikolaos as soon as I could, so here I am.'

'From Mr Pavlakis? What have I done?'

'That I hope to find out when I meet him. I hear you know where to find him in the evening so you'd better lead the way.' Yannis rose from the table and placed an arm around his son's shoulders. 'I don't think you need to worry too much, though.'

Yannis led his father through the maze of side streets until he found the shabby taverna. As they entered Mr Pavlakis was in the act of pouring himself a glass of wine.

'Good evening – why, Yannis. What brings you here?'

'This is my father, Mr Pavlakis.' Yannis felt very nervous.

Mr Pavlakis held out his hand. 'I'm pleased to meet you. Won't you sit down and have a glass of wine with me?'

'Thank you.' Mr Christoforakis was also feeling nervous. 'You sent a message to me asking me to come to Aghios Nikolaos to see you about Yannis. Something to do with the High School in Heraklion.'

Mr Pavlakis nodded. 'I've found out details for you about a scholarship, if you're willing for Yannis to continue with his education. You may have other plans for him.'

Yannis's father drew on his cigarette. 'How do you feel, Yannis? Do you want to go to High School?'

'Oh, yes, Pappa. I want that more than anything.'

Yannis senior shrugged. 'You'll have to explain to me. I'm a farmer. What does he have to do to go to a High School, and more important, what does he do when he's finished there?'

Mr Pavlakis smiled. 'It's quite simple. He has to complete some examination papers. If he reaches a high enough standard he will be given a scholarship. That means you will only have to pay for his lodgings and books. What he does afterwards,' he spread his hands eloquently, 'that will be up to him. He has a brain, Mr Christoforakis, a good brain, that should be trained and used.'

'If he completes the papers, but doesn't get a scholarship, what happens then?'

'If he doesn't gain a scholarship he could still be offered a place, but then you would be asked to pay his fees. You don't have to accept a place. It would cost a good deal of money. Would you like me to find out the cost involved before you commit yourself to anything?'

Yannis was sitting on the edge of his chair, willing his father to agree to him taking the examination. His father appeared to be considering as he sipped his glass of wine.

'If he went to Heraklion where would he live?'

'That would be up to you to arrange. Do you have any relatives there?'

Yannis senior shook his head.

'I could make some enquiries when I next visit the town,' offered Mr Pavlakis. 'Let's see how he gets on before you worry about where he is to live.'

'You're quite sure, Yannis, that this is what you want?'

'I'm quite sure, Pappa. I want to go on to University as well.'

Mr Pavlakis smiled. 'One step at a time, young man.' He refilled their glasses and handed one to Yannis. 'To your success with the examination.'

The glasses clinked and each took a long draught. Yannis felt his head swimming, not from the wine, he was used to drinking wine with his meals, but the thought that he was going to High School. He was convinced that he would pass the examination. He could hardly wait to tell Annita. He excused himself from the men as the taverna began to fill up with its regular customers and ran back across the town to his uncle's house.

'Annita, Annita,' he called. 'I'm going, I'm really going.'

'Where?' Annita raised her head from her embroidery.

'I'm going to the High School in Heraklion. 'I have to take an examination first, then I might get a scholarship.'

'Suppose you don't get one?'

'Pappa can pay for me to go.'

'I thought your Pappa was a poor farmer. Where's he going to find enough money to send you to High School?'

Yannis sat down. His world had suddenly begun to crumble around him. 'Pappa seemed to think he would be able to.'

Annita snorted. 'He probably doesn't know how much it will cost yet.'

'I thought you'd be pleased, Annita. Why are you being horrid?'

She folded her embroidery together. 'I'm not being horrid. I just face facts.' She flounced from the room, leaving Yannis feeling hurt and puzzled.

Annita walked down to the harbour, hoping Yannis would follow her. She sat on the wall gazing out to sea and tried to think rationally. She had overheard her parents discussing her future with Yannis and since that day she had looked at him in a different light, no longer as her cousin, but as her prospective husband. She had thought Yannis would stay and work in Aghios Nikolaos and in a couple of years they would be married, now he was planning to leave and would probably not want to return and settle down. She sighed deeply. A voice in her ear nearly made her fall off the wall.

A bearded man was eyeing her. 'I don't like to see a beautiful young lady by herself and looking sad. Won't you join me for a drink?'

Annita jumped to her feet and ran. Her mother had warned her about such strangers. Her heart was pounding as she reached her home and tumbled inside, slamming the door shut and leaning against it to regain her breath.

'Annita – what's wrong?'

'A man!' gasped Annita. 'He wanted to take me for a drink.'

'What!' Yannis was horrified. 'Where is he?' The boy clenched his fists menacingly.

'I don't think he followed me. He only asked me to go for a drink. I was only frightened because I didn't know him. There's no need to go looking for him.'

Yannis scrutinized his cousin gravely. 'He didn't touch you? He only spoke to you?'

Annita nodded, she was feeling distinctly braver now she was safely indoors with Yannis. 'Let's forget it.' She smiled shakily.

To her surprise Yannis put his arms round her and held her tightly to him. 'I couldn't bear anything to happen to you, Annita.'

Annita felt a thrill go through her. 'Do you mean that, Yannis?'

'Of course. You're as precious to me as one of my sisters. You mustn't go anywhere on your own in the evening again.'

'I'm sorry you thought I was being nasty to you earlier,' she apologised humbly.

'You were being nasty,' retorted Yannis.

'I was just surprised. We've talked about it for so long, and now it seems to be happening.'

'I have to get the scholarship first. You're right, Pappa probably has no idea how much the fees would be. I expect he'll want me to go back to Plaka to help on the farm during the summer. Maybe I'll change my mind and become a farmer after all.' Yannis smiled, knowing that nothing would make him change his mind.

'I wouldn't mind being a farmer's wife.' Annita could have bitten her tongue for the indiscreet remark.

Yannis appeared not to notice. 'You've never been on a farm. You don't know how hard the work is, much harder than fishing. You don't ever have a day off because the weather's bad. Maybe you and Andreas could come and visit us during the holidays.'

Annita smiled. 'I'd like that.'

'Let's go and find Pappa now and ask him about the holidays.' Yannis took Annita by the hand.

Annita agreed readily and they toiled up the hill and down the far side, Yannis avoiding the back streets, which were a short cut. Annita had not been to the taverna before and wrinkled her nose in disgust as they entered, the smell of wine, smoke and stale food assaulting her nostrils. Yannis was sitting where his son had left him and Mr Pavlakis was working behind the bar where a young girl sat at the end looking thoroughly bored. Every so often she would be handed some coins, which she placed in a pot and gave the correct change.

Yannis approached his father. 'Are you ready to go home, Pappa? I thought you might not know your way, so Annita and I came to meet you.'

'That was thoughtful of you, but this is no place for Annita. Go and wait for me outside, both of you. I'll just say goodbye to Mr Pavlakis.'

The cousins retreated from the smoky interior; glad to be back in the fresh air and after a short time Yannis's father joined them.

'We wanted to ask you a favour, Pappa. When school finishes here will you want me to come back to the farm to work before I go to High School, if I get a place, that is?'

'It would certainly help. What had you in mind?'

'I wondered if Annita and Andreas could come also.'

'I see no reason why they shouldn't, if Yiorgo and Elena don't need them.'

Annita clapped her hands. 'Thank you, uncle Yannis, that would be lovely.'

Yannis's father smiled at her exuberance. 'I don't think you'll find it very exciting. We haven't all the shops that you have here.'

'I don't mind. It will be different.'

Elena was in the kitchen preparing fresh coffee. 'Is Andreas with you?' she asked of Annita as they entered.

Annita shook her head. 'I've been with Yannis to meet his father.'

'Where has he got to?'

YANNIS

'I expect he's at a friend's house.' Annita dismissed her brother. 'Mamma, please say yes, uncle Yannis says that Andreas and I can go and stay on the farm during the holidays.'

Andreas entered quietly, but his mother noticed him. 'Where have you been?'

'I'm sorry, Mamma. I was with some friends and we were talking. It was later than I realised.'

'Andreas, would you like to go to Plaka and stay on the farm with Yannis during the holidays?' asked Annita.

'I'm sure I should enjoy it very much. I've never been on a farm.'

'To bed, young man, or you won't be going anywhere,' Elena said firmly and Andreas disappeared obediently. 'You two should also be in bed,' she continued, turning to Annita and Yannis. 'Yannis you will have to share Andreas's mattress tonight as your Pappa is having yours.'

Yannis nodded. 'I don't mind. I'll go up now, and then I won't disturb Andreas. Goodnight, Pappa, and thank you. I'll see you in the morning.'

'Would you mind having them in the holidays?' asked Elena when she was finally alone with her cousin.

'Not a bit, they'll be able to help around the farm. You've been so good to Yannis that it won't hurt us to show a bit of hospitality to your children. He's a lucky boy. Mr Pavlakis thinks he shows great promise and has every hope of him gaining a scholarship. Tell me, do you have any relatives in Heraklion? If Yannis does go there he'll have to stay somewhere and I know no one.'

Elena shook her head. 'I can't think of anyone. I'll ask Yiorgo tomorrow. We may as well go to bed. There's no telling what time he'll be back.'

She began to clear the table of coffee cups and stack them in the kitchen. 'What time do you plan to leave tomorrow?'

'Don't worry about me. I'll be up with the sun. I'll see Yannis before I leave, but if Yiorgo is sleeping late I shan't disturb him. We had a chat today. I'd like to be back in Plaka by mid-day, so I'll have to make an early start.' Yannis held out his hand to Elena. 'I'd like to thank you, Elena. You've been like a mother to Yannis. We do appreciate it.'

'Go on with you,' Elena was embarrassed. 'He's a nice boy; besides it's given him and Annita time to get to know each other. They've become as thick as thieves. I think that match will work out well.'

Yannis held his breath and crossed his fingers behind his back.

'I've had a letter from the High School. I'm pleased to say that you have been accepted and gained a full scholarship.'

Yannis sat back on the desk behind him, his legs no longer able to support him. 'Thank you, sir,' he managed to whisper, then realisation dawned and a broad grin spread over his face. 'It's wonderful!'

'You've worked hard for it. Don't think it's the end of the road, you'll have to continue to work hard for the next few years if you want to get anywhere in life. Have you any ideas for a career?'

Yannis shook his head. 'I don't know. Something to do with history I think.'

Mr Pavlakis nodded. 'A wise choice, but don't force yourself into a career. You are one of the few who will be able to choose their occupation. Now, something else before you go; I've been giving serious thought to you going to Heraklion. Your father said you have no relatives there that you could stay with.'

'That's true. We're quite a small family really. I suppose I'll have to find a room somewhere.'

'I've lived on my own in a strange town and it's a very lonely experience. This is confidential at the moment, Yannis, but I am also leaving at the end of this term and taking up a position in Heraklion. I wondered how you and your parents would feel if I tried to find rooms for us in the same house? We could be a certain amount of company for each other until we found our feet and made our own friends.'

'I would really appreciate that and I'm sure my parents would, too.' At this moment Yannis did not care where he would live.

Mr Pavlakis picked up his books from his desk and held out his hand. 'Congratulations on your success, and let's hope I manage to find somewhere suitable to stay together. I shall go to Heraklion during the holidays and look around. When I've found something I'll pay you a visit in Plaka and talk to your parents.'

'I'm sure they'll be very grateful.'

'Come along then, I must go or I shall be late for work.'

Mr Pavlakis walked rapidly away from his pupil who watched him out of sight before walking slowly back to his uncle's cottage. His dreams had come true. He was going to High School. His imagination began leaping ahead of him, finishing High School and going to University in Athens, finishing University and becoming famous. How proud of him his parents would be!

Annita was helping with the washing when he arrived. She looked at him a little fearfully. 'Why did Mr Pavlakis want you?'

'Why do you think?'

'You've a scholarship to High School?'

Yannis clasped his cousin around her waist, the wet washing between them. 'I've passed and I'm really going! Isn't it the most marvellous thing that has ever happened?'

Annita hugged him back. 'I'm so pleased for you. Wait 'til we tell Mamma and Pappa!'

'That's not all, Mr Pavlakis is going to Heraklion,' he flushed in mortification. 'That's supposed to be confidential, so don't tell anyone, please. He's going to find us rooms together.'

'Do you want to live with him?' Annita was surprised at Yannis's pleasure.

'It will be better than being on my own in a strange town, and I do enjoy talking to him.'

Annita disentangled herself from Yannis's embrace and the wet sheet. 'What will your parents say?'

'I expect they'll be pleased that there will be someone with me. It seems strange to think that I won't be coming back here.' He gazed around the kitchen as if he were seeing it for the first time.

'I must put the washing out.' Annita went out to the yard so that Yannis did not see her eyes were full of tears. She would miss him so much.

Yiorgo had agreed to take the children to Plaka by boat, using the canal at Olous as a short cut. It would be more work for him, as the sail would have to be lowered so they could pass beneath the concrete bridge, but it would save the children a long walk in the blazing sun.

'A special treat for Yannis,' he grinned. 'He'll be able to see the houses.'

Yannis smiled contentedly. He had tried in vain to see the remains of the village that had been lost beneath the sea whenever his uncle had sailed in that direction, but never managed to catch more than a glimpse. Yiorgo and Yannis rowed strongly over the smooth water, whilst Andreas sat at the tiller. At Yiorgo's instruction they shipped their oars and allowed the boat to glide gently over the clear, blue-green water.

'Look, Yannis,' he called and pointed into the sea. The three children hung over the side.

'They're just blocks of stone,' said Andreas in disgust.

'Could be anything,' added Annita.

Yannis shook his head. 'No, look. There's the outline of a wall. See that large stone over there? That's where the door would have been. You can see another wall going that way. Please, Yiorgo, move on a bit.'

Yiorgo did as he was asked, Yannis pointing out where the

YANNIS

walls were until even Annita and Andreas became interested. Finally the water deepened until it was impossible to see the weed-encrusted blocks and Yannis sat up

They began to negotiate the tiny canal. There was just enough room for a boat to pass beneath the low concrete bridge with the mast down. The water looked so shallow that Yannis held his breath; sure they would be grounded. They passed through safely into the bay and Yannis's heart skipped a beat as Spinalonga came into sight. He hoped Yiorgo would not sail too close.

Annita and Andreas began to look for lepers, but saw no one until they rounded the island and were nearing Plaka. At the quay was a boat and a quantity of barrels had been off-loaded. As the boat began to row away lepers appeared through the archway and began to manhandle the barrels away from the quay. Yannis watched, horrified and fascinated. The men who were collecting the barrels looked like any other villager.

'I feel so sorry for them,' said Annita quietly. 'They've done no harm, and yet they're treated like criminals.'

'No harm! They infect people with their terrible disease. An island is a good place for them.' Yannis shivered despite the warmth of the sun.

'They don't infect people deliberately, and they couldn't help getting the disease. It's like having measles,' reasoned Annita.

'Don't they frighten you?' asked Yannis

Annita shook her head. 'No, I just feel sorry for them and sort of helpless.'

Yannis looked at her with disbelief written all over his face. 'We're here,' he said, announcing the obvious to change the subject.

His family were waiting at the tiny jetty to welcome him. The children jumped ashore and Yannis found himself in his mother's arms. To his surprise he found he was considerably taller than she was. He knew he had grown by the way his arms had been poking out from his shirts and the gap there was between his trouser legs and his shoes, but he had not realised by how much.

His brothers and sisters hung back; shy of their cousins and also of their older brother whom they had not seen since Christmas. Yannis threw his arms round all of them in turn, and then introduced them to Annita and Andreas.

As soon as they arrived at the farmhouse Yannis wanted to see the new donkey his father had purchased. Aga seemed to know him and looked at him with sad, old eyes that wrenched at Yannis's heart. The younger donkey eyed him uneasily and shifted away. Yannis ignored her; there would be time to get to know her later. He talked softly to old Aga and she responded to his voice by twitching her ears and nuzzling close to him. Eventually Maria came to find him.

'Are you coming? Mamma has lunch ready.'

Yannis nodded. 'Poor old Aga.'

Maria took his arm. 'She has a good life. Pappa still takes her with him and lets her graze. She never works now, the young one does it all.'

'It will be nice to be in the fields again, to smell the earth instead of fish.'

They laughed together. 'It's good to have you back, Yannis. I wish you were going to stay.'

'I couldn't do that.'

'Do you prefer to live in a town – and smell of fish?'

'No,' Yannis smiled. 'Do I still smell?' He sniffed at his shirt.

'Will you ever come back?'

'I don't think I will ever live here again, but I'll always come back to visit.'

The fields fascinated Annita and Andreas. The vines, planted in such straight rows and the earth around them turned regularly to keep the weeds at bay, the olive trees which were planted irregularly with the grass for the donkeys being allowed to grow as it wished between them.

YANNIS

Annita lay on her back in the shade of a carob tree. 'This is lovely. So peaceful. It can be peaceful at sea, but you always have to be ready for trouble there. Here you can just lay and relax.'

Yannis poked her with his toe. 'I thought you were supposed to be working. You might marry a farmer and you'd look silly not knowing what to do.'

'He could teach me,' answered Annita nonchalantly, 'besides, your mother doesn't work in the fields.'

'She used to,' Yannis assured her. 'Now she plants herbs and vegetables and looks after the chickens.'

Annita sighed. She would have to get up. Yannis showed her how to dig around the roots of the vines to aerate them, but not to damage the young shoots. He also explained how to look for parasites that could blight a crop overnight, or moulds that would make the plant whither and die.

'I don't think I want to marry a farmer,' she groaned as she straightened up. 'Yannis, what are you doing?'

'I found this.'

'It's only a broken pot. I expect someone threw it away.'

Yannis ignored her and stuffed the pieces into his pocket. He began to look for more shards until Annita lost interest and walked away. Yannis searched around the area, but no more pieces came to light. He straightened up and decided to search systematically along each row, bending to examine more closely the small stones, which were mixed with the red-brown earth. He was on the verge of giving up when he saw another piece sticking out of the ground, far larger than anything he had found earlier. He tried to pull it out, but met with resistance. With eager fingers he scraped away at the soil and tugged again. He wriggled it in the earth and dug a little deeper. The shard gave, and to his surprise the piece he had been pulling at was the base of a pot, with at least half of one side still attached. The boy fingered it curiously, brushing away the earth and rubbing it against his trousers. He looked into the hole it had left and found another small slither.

'Have you lost your bone?' Maria's voice sounded behind him.
He looked up and smiled. 'I've found some pottery.'

'I should think Pappa would be quite pleased to have his fields cleared. You could take the stones as well.'

'Don't you find it interesting?'

Maria shook her head. 'It's just useless pieces of a broken pot. No good to anyone, so they've been thrown away.'

'You're probably right,' admitted her brother. 'What have you been doing?'

Maria produced a pad of paper. 'Drawing.'

Yannis took the proffered pad. 'Maria, these are good.' There was surprise and respect in his voice as he looked at the sketches of the family working or resting and finally one of him, walking, his head bent as he examined the ground. 'When did you do that?'

'I was sitting higher up the hill and could see you. It isn't very good.'

Yannis examined the drawings with their bold lines again. 'I think they're marvellous, so life-like. How do you do it?'

'They're easy. You just copy people. Come on, we ought to go. Pappa has packed up and the others are going with him.' Maria retrieved her pad from Yannis and they began to walk down the hill, Yannis cradling his precious pieces of pottery.

'Do you like Annita and Andreas?' Yannis asked his elder sister.

'I like Annita. I'm not sure about Andreas. Is he always so quiet, or is he just a bit shy at the moment?'

Yannis grinned. 'He's the same in Aghios Nikolaos. Annita and I talk and argue, but Andreas just sits and doesn't say a word. He doesn't even seem to be listening.'

'What does Mr Pavlakis say about him? Is he clever?'

'He's never mentioned him to me. We only talk about people in history. What about you? Does Father Theodorakis think you're clever?'

Maria shrugged. 'I can read and write now, but I don't think he likes me.'

'Why not?'

'I drew a picture of him and he saw it. He said I should be doing my lessons, not wasting my time drawing pictures.'

'Was it rude?'

Maria shook her head indignantly. 'No, it just showed what a little, fat man he is, with his glasses perched on the end of his nose and the wart on his chin.'

Yannis laughed uproariously. 'No wonder he doesn't like you!'

The days passed happily for the children. Having helped with the work in the fields, Maria would sit and draw, whilst Annita chattered to her and Yannis wandered off to search for pieces of pottery. His collection was growing, and he found himself fascinated by their different textures and thickness. Babbis from the neighbouring farm was a frequent visitor, but his attention appeared to be on Maria. The younger children would play together, although Andreas was often missing or would be seen sitting under a tree deep in thought.

Annita was puzzled by her brother's behaviour. He had always been quiet, but now he seemed to have withdrawn into himself. It crossed her mind that he might be missing their mother and decided to ask him.

He smiled gently at her. 'Of course I miss Mamma, but I'm not unhappy. I'll see her again very soon. I just enjoy sitting quietly and thinking.'

'You're not ill?' Annita asked anxiously.

'Not a bit,' he replied cheerfully. 'I'm happier sitting here than I would be if I were chasing around. I wish these holidays could go on for ever.'

Annita studied him. He certainly looked well and did not appear to be miserable. She decided he always behaved like this and it was only noticeable because of the energy of his cousins. It occurred to her that although she sat and worked at her embroidery most evenings, Andreas was nearly always out.

'What do you think about?'

'Many things,' Andreas evaded the question.

Annita realised her brother was going to tell her nothing. She shrugged and wandered away to find Yannis and Maria, finally running them to earth in the stable with Aga. She was lying in the straw, her breathing laboured and her eyes glazed.

'Go and fetch Pappa,' ordered Yannis.

Annita fled back to the house, bursting into the living room. 'Aga's sick, maybe dying.'

Yannis senior jumped to his feet and followed the girl back to the stable. Maria was sobbing, burying her face into the donkey's soft neck. Yannis was talking softly to Aga, the twitching of her ears showing she was conscious. The farmer took one look and turned to Annita. 'Go back to the house and ask Maria for my shot-gun.'

'No, Pappa.' Both Maria and Yannis looked up at him in horror.

'It's kinder to shoot her. She's old and won't recover. Her time's come and I'd rather shoot her than see her suffer.'

Yannis could feel hot tears pricking behind his eyelids. He loved Aga, he had ridden her to and from the fields since before he could walk and to him she was part of the family.

Annita returned with the gun and handed it to her uncle. 'I'll hold her,' she said calmly and pushed Maria gently out of the way.

'There's no need. Say goodbye to her, then all of you outside.'

Annita put her arm around Maria and pulled Yannis by the sleeve. Once outside the stable Yannis buried his face in his hands, waiting for the shot. For what seemed like an age they stood and no sound came. Yannis came out from the stable.

'She's dead,' he announced. 'As I lifted the gun she died,' he said simply.

'I'm glad you didn't shoot her, Pappa.' Maria slipped her hand into his and gave it a squeeze.

'I'm glad too. Now, Annita, take the gun back in. We'll have to dig a grave for her.' Solemnly the children followed Yannis to the olive grove.

'Where are you going to bury her?' asked Annita.

'By the wall. The soil won't wash off her down here.'

The three children helped Yannis dig. It was a long and arduous task and before the hole was deep enough it had become dark.

'That's enough,' said Yannis, leaning on his spade. 'We'll finish it tomorrow.'

'Why do we have to dig it so deep?' asked Maria.

'For a number of reasons,' explained her father. 'As the carcass rots it will smell if it's near the surface. The smell would be most unpleasant to us when we worked here and also attract animals that would dig it up for food. Bits of her would then be left exposed to the sun and soon there would be a swarm of flies followed by maggots and in no time we should all be suffering from a disease.'

'Is that how people become ill, really ill?' asked Annita.

'Sometimes, but there can be many causes of illness. Only a doctor can say what kind of illness you're suffering from and how to cure it.'

'The Widow Segouri knows,' said Yannis.

'The Widow knows some things,' admitted his father. 'She trained as a nurse for a while before she married and the rest of her knowledge comes from experience.'

'Where does she live?' asked Annita curiously.

'At the end house,' replied Yannis, heaving his shovel onto his shoulder. He was feeling deathly tired now, but proud that he had managed to keep up with his father, not needing to stop for frequent rests as the girls had. The sad procession made their way back to the house, Yannis pointing out where the Widow Segouri lived on the way. The rest of the family were waiting for them, Anna had obviously been crying.

'I'll clean the spades,' Yannis muttered and slipped back out to the yard.

He rubbed off the cloying earth with a piece of rag and took them to the outhouse; then he returned to the stable. Aga was lying where he had last seen her. He stroked her nose gently. There was no response, no flick of the ears, no nuzzling in his hand. Yannis thought his heart would break; sobs racked his body as he expressed his grief over the dead animal. He did not hear his father enter the stable and walk over to him.

'Yannis, do you feel better now?'

The boy nodded dumbly.

'It was sad, but she didn't have a bad life. I looked after her, made sure she had enough to eat, never beat her, and she hadn't earned her keep for a long time.'

'I know, Pappa. It's just that I loved Aga and I think she loved me. I know you kept her when you could have sold her for the price of her skin.'

Yannis senior's voice was gruff. 'I don't regret keeping her. You mustn't grieve. Come inside and have a glass of wine. It will help you sleep.'

Yannis took a last look at Aga and followed his father from the stable, automatically latching the door behind him.

Yannis senior finally declared the pit they had dug was deep enough and the cart bearing the animal was manoeuvred into position. Together they tilted it and the dead donkey slid slowly into the deep hole, landing in an ungainly heap.

'Fill it in,' ordered Yannis. He did not want the children to stand and look for too long.

Filling in the hole was much quicker and easier than digging it and they had nearly finished before the girls asked for a rest. Yannis took the opportunity to pull out some pottery he had spotted and place it to one side.

'Come on, let's finish the job.' Yannis senior was not prepared to lose a day's work over a donkey. When the last of the earth had been shovelled in he stamped it down hard whilst Yannis continued his search for pottery in the remaining clods.

Anna looked at her father. 'Shouldn't we say prayers for her, like they do in church?' she asked solemnly.

Her father smiled at her. 'You can say a prayer if you wish.'

'I'll say one,' said Andreas suddenly. 'Come and stand by the grave, all of you.'

Surprised, the children did as he bade them. Andreas drew himself up to his full height, clasped his hands together and spoke in a clear, quiet voice.

'Dear God, in your mercy, please look after this donkey who has entered your Heavenly Kingdom. She carried heavy burdens in her lifetime on earth; please lighten her load now that she is in your care. Amen.'

Yannis senior looked at the boy in amazement. He had said the words so confidently, yet they were unrehearsed and came from the heart. They turned from the grave and Anna picked a few flowers that she scattered onto the stamped earth. The action brought a lump to her father's throat and he spoke gruffly.

'To work, now, all of you, to make up for the time we've spent.'

Yannis spent the evening out in the yard washing the mud from his pottery. By the morning it would be dry and he would be able to look at it properly. He could already see there were a number of pieces that looked the same.

Annita came out to him. 'What are you doing?'

'Washing the pottery I found.'

'Why?'

'You can see the differences between the pieces more easily,' explained Yannis.

'Can I see?'

'It would be better in the morning when they're dry.'

Annita looked at Yannis speculatively. Was he trying to avoid showing her?

Yannis guessed her thoughts. 'It's quite simple, really.' He held up a thick, buff coloured shard and a thin, dark red piece. 'Those two could hardly come from the same pot.' Annita was forced to agree with him. 'It's more difficult when they're all the same colour.'

Annita fingered a few. 'I don't see how you can tell if they're old or not.'

'It's something to do with the way they're made. I'm going to ask Mr Pavlakis if there is a book I can read that will tell me.'

Annita shook her head – Yannis and his books! She changed the subject. 'Wasn't Andreas odd today?'

'Odd? When?'

'When he said a prayer for Aga. He made me feel, well, all goose-pimply and embarrassed, like the priest does when you know you've done something wrong and then he talks about the same thing in his sermon.'

Yannis smiled. 'I thought it was rather nice. He sounded so grown up. I couldn't have done it. Can you put those pieces on the wall for me, please?'

Annita placed the pieces haphazardly along the low wall.

'Can't you put them straight and in some sort of order,' admonished her cousin, pushing buff ones away from the red.

Annita sighed. Her brother was acting strangely and Yannis had become obsessed with pieces of broken pottery. Thank goodness for Maria. Having finished laying out the pieces to his satisfaction, she sat on the wall and watched as he rubbed the mud off the remaining shards he had found. There was a tiny "ping" in the bucket.

'What was that?'

'A stone I expect.'

'It didn't sound like a stone.'

Yannis began to grope amongst the mud at the bottom of the bucket, letting it run slowly through his fingers. He felt something hard settle in his hand and closed his fingers around it. When he withdrew his arm and opened his clenched fist there was a small, flat, circular piece of metal resting in his palm.

'Annita!' His voice was a hushed whisper. 'It's a coin.'

'Let me see.' Annita was suddenly excited.

Yannis sat down beside her; his heart was racing. Annita scratched at the coin with her fingernail.

'It's so black you can't see it properly.' She turned the coin this way and that. 'I think I can see a figure.'

Yannis held out his hand and she returned it to him. He gazed at the round, black object with reverence and awe. 'I know what I want to do,' he said, somewhat shakily. 'I want to go to University and then work with someone like Mr Evans and discover pottery and coins. That way I can find out about the past properly, not just by reading.'

'What do you think your parents will say?'

Yannis gave a grin. 'Goodness knows, but it will stop Mamma keep trying to persuade me to be a doctor.'

'A doctor?' Annita's eyes opened wide. 'Why does she want you to be a doctor?'

'So she can boast to all the villagers. Come on, it's getting late. I'm going to ask Maria if I can put my coin in her needlework box to keep it safe.'

Mr Pavlakis arrived in Heraklion after his fortnight in Italy. He had been greatly impressed by the sights he had seen in Rome, vowing to return as soon as he had saved enough money. He decided to find some cheap lodgings for a few nights whilst he looked around for suitable rooms for Yannis and himself.

He walked past the school where he was to teach. It looked small and dark, situated between high buildings at the back of the Venetian palace. He began to wonder if he had made the right decision. On reaching Eleftherias Square he entered a taverna and ordered an omelette, eating it slowly as he watched the people bustling by. He ordered a carafe of wine and invited the owner to join him, as he was their only customer.

'You're a stranger here?'

'I'm coming to live here in September. I'm a teacher. Can you recommend anywhere I might find some lodgings?' He flicked the offending lock of hair from his eyes.

The taverna owner eyed him speculatively. 'I might.'

'I'd be very grateful.' Mr Pavlakis watched as the man took a bill from his pad, licked the end of his stumpy pencil and wrote laboriously. 'How do I get there?'

The man waved his hand. 'Follow the main road until you reach Vassileos Konstantinou and on to Kalokerinou. About half way down Kalokerinou there's a turning, which takes you to the church of Ayios Minas. Go past the church until you reach Ferou Square. It's a couple of streets down from there.'

'Thank you very much.' Mr Pavlakis offered him a cigarette for his trouble and paid his bill.

As Mr Pavlakis crossed the road he spotted the museum. It was still early. He had time to visit the building before finding any lodgings. He gazed at the large glass cases, pottery on every shelf. Half assembled vessels had pride of place in the forefront, whilst behind them odd shards of pottery lay in untidy heaps. Each case was labelled in faded Greek characters, the information utterly useless. After the displays he had seen in Rome he was bitterly disappointed.

He seemed to walk for a long while before the church of Ayios Minas came into view. From there it was only a short walk to Ferou Square, but then he became hopelessly lost in a maze of side streets and alleys. He looked around him in dismay.

'Looking for company, dear?' A woman emerged from a doorway and Mr Pavlakis recoiled from the touch of her hand on his arm.

'No, no,' he stuttered. 'I'm looking for lodgings.'

The woman's eyes gleamed. 'I could help you.'

Mr Pavlakis shrank back from her in disgust. He turned and

retraced his steps towards the church, her shrill abuse following him up the narrow road.

He rounded the corner and almost bumped into a priest. 'Excuse me, Father. Can you direct me, please? I'm looking for lodgings.'

The priest looked perplexed. The man was decently dressed and well spoken. He would have to be desperate for a roof over his head and have very little money to be looking in such an area.

"I could not recommend anything around here. I suggest you return to the main road and ask at the tavernas. One of them may have a room for the night.'

'Thank you for your help.' Mr Pavlakis retraced his steps up the cobbled road.

On reaching the main road he looked right and left. If he went right he would return to Eleftherias Square, if he went left he would gradually reach the outskirts of the town. He crossed the main road and took the first right turn that presented itself. Within a few minutes he found he was alone, away from the crowds of the main road and looking at the blank, impersonal facades of buildings he gauged to be offices. Each street and alley Mr Pavlakis came to appeared to be residential now, and he came to the conclusion that he would have to return to the Square. He had no clear idea of where he was at all as he twisted and turned through side streets and it was with a feeling of relief that he saw a dim light in the distance.

Mr Pavlakis pushed open the door of the small taverna and took a seat. He looked at the menu written on a blackboard above the counter and decided he would have peppers, stuffed with a mixture of goat meat and herbs.

'Yes?' Before him stood a young girl, her dark, limpid gaze fixed on him.

The words stuck in his throat and he swallowed hard as his hand went to his forehead to smooth back the lock of hair. 'Stuffed peppers, please, and wine.'

Whilst he sipped his wine he watched her covertly. The brown hands, with long, slim fingers, worked deftly and she soon approached with a loaded tray, which she balanced expertly whilst transferring the dishes to the table. Mr Pavlakis smiled at her and she smiled back, showing a set of perfect white teeth. As she walked back to the counter he watched the sway of her hips and felt the blood quickening in his veins. He dragged his eyes from her and began to eat slowly. In between each mouthful he shot a glance in her direction. He hoped her father or mother would not come in and send her away. He tried to calculate her age, but found it useless. He gave himself a little shake and tried to concentrate on his meal. She passed close to him to clear away his dirty plates and her perfume lingered after her.

'May I have some coffee, please?' Any excuse for her to be close to him again.

'Certainly.' She deposited the tray on the counter and quickly returned with a cup of coffee and a glass of water.

'Please, may I speak to you for a moment.' He remembered the object of his visit.

A flicker of amusement showed in her dark eyes. 'For a moment. I am busy.'

He nodded. 'Quite. I understand. I have worked in a taverna myself.' She looked surprised and he continued. 'I'm a school teacher by profession, but I have worked in a taverna in the evenings.'

Suspicion took the place of surprise. 'We have no work here.'

'No, please, don't misunderstand me. I'm not looking for work. I'm coming to Heraklion in September to teach at the school behind the Venetian palace. I wondered if you knew of any rooms to let?'

She relaxed visibly. 'I could ask for you.'

'Would you?' Mr Pavlakis was genuinely surprised and grateful. 'I would prefer two rooms. I'm bringing a young student with me. He's going to the High School.'

The girl nodded. 'I'll ask.'

'Would you know of a room I could rent for tonight?"

'We have one."

Mr Pavlakis's heart leapt, but before he had a chance to speak the door opened and a slight young man entered. The girl smiled a greeting to him and indicated with her head that she wanted him. He crossed to the counter and placed an arm about her waist. Their heads were close together and he guessed she was talking about him. The young man turned and inspected Mr Pavlakis, then they both approached his table. This time she pulled out a chair and sat down opposite him. Mr Pavlakis caught his breath. She was incredibly beautiful.

'This is my brother, Pavlos.'

'Brother, brother, brother' the word seemed to hammer into his brain as Pavlos shook the man's hand.

'My sister says you are looking for rooms. We have some to rent.'

Yiorgo Pavlakis could hardly believe it. 'You are too kind. What can I say?'

'When would you want the rooms?'

'One for tonight, maybe longer, and two in September. I shall be working in Heraklion and I'm bringing a young student with me. He's going to the High School and I promised his parents I would find him some lodgings and keep an eye on him. I can pay a retaining fee, if the rooms are suitable, of course.'

'Louisa, show our guest the rooms we have available.'

Louisa led the way up the stairs. She pointed to the first two doors. 'My brother's room and mine.' She opened the two opposite doors. 'These would be yours.'

Mr Pavlakis looked at the clean rooms. In an alcove stood a washstand with a mirror above and on the opposite wall was the bed. A rag rug covered most of the floor and beneath the window was a table and chair, there was also a chest for clothes and some open shelves.

'It's perfect,' he declared. 'How much do you charge?'

Pavlos calculated rapidly. 'Shall we say sixteen drachmas a week each? That would include your meals and laundry.'

Mr Pavlakis was elated. 'I'll pay.' He had a desire to shout for joy. He would be under the same roof as the girl he thought was the most beautiful he had ever seen and the rooms were ideal.

On returning to the taverna Louisa brought wine for the men, but not a glass for herself. 'I must go to bed,' she explained. 'I have to be up early tomorrow. Goodnight, sir.'

Mr Pavlakis held her hand. 'Please, call me Yiorgo.'

Louisa inclined her head slightly. 'Very well; goodnight, Yiorgo.'

Yiorgo Pavlakis realised how very tired he was. 'I must go to bed also. I've had a very tiring day, and I was travelling most of last night. I am most grateful to you. I had thought Heraklion a most unfriendly place until I met you and your sister.'

Pavlos grinned. 'When you come to stay here you'll meet many more people and they'll all be friendly.'

'Thank you, my friend.' Mr Pavlakis clasped Pavlos's hand. 'I shall never forget your kindness to me.'

'It was nothing. Goodnight, Yiorgo.' Pavlos watched as the man climbed the stairs, then bolted the door firmly, a pleased smile on his face. He ran up the stairs and knocked on Louisa's door before entering.

'That was a good evening's work.' He said quietly. 'You might have to be a bit careful when you use your room, but they'll be out most of the day.' He took his sister's chin between his hard fingers, turning her face towards him. 'And you don't approach him. He's our bread and butter. We don't want to lose him.'

Louisa knocked his hand away. 'I know how to be discreet.'

When Mr Pavlakis rose he found only Pavlos down in the taverna. Mr Pavlakis looked around. He must not appear too eager. 'Where is Louisa? I hoped I might get some coffee.'

'She needed to go shopping. I'll get it for you.' Pavlos returned with alacrity and sat down opposite Mr Pavlakis. 'Louisa has a hard life. My parents would be sad if they knew how hard she has to work.'

'Forgive me,' Mr Pavlakis sipped his coffee. 'I assume your parents to be dead?'

Pavlos pointed to a photograph of a large, smiling man and a small, delicate looking woman. 'That was taken only a few months before my father had a stroke. Five years ago he was fit and well, we were a happy family. I'd just left High School and I was to go to Athens to train as a hotel manager. Two weeks before I was due to leave my father had a stroke, his right side was useless. I didn't go to Athens; I had to stay here, helping my mother to lift Pappa and also working in the taverna. When Louisa came home from school she would do the cleaning and the washing – and there was a lot of washing from Pappa. We tried to give our mother as much rest and time to spend with Pappa as possible. Then he had another stroke. Mamma had to do everything for him, wash him, and feed him, just like a baby. Louisa left school and took over the running of the house and the taverna and I found some work. Slowly Pappa became worse, he died just over a year ago.' His forehead puckered. 'It was as though our mother died with him and just her body stayed with us. She had no interest in anything and would sit by his bed, doing nothing. I think she was just exhausted.'

'I am sorry.'

Pavlos shrugged. 'We're getting back on our feet. Somehow we have managed to pay our bills, the doctor and the funeral were the largest. We persuaded them to wait a little while and they gave us three months. The bank agreed to lend us a little money and now that you'll be staying here we'll be able to repay that also. That is enough about us. Tell me about this student you are bringing with you.'

Mr Pavlakis told Pavlos all he knew about Yannis. It occurred to him that he really knew very little about the boy's background. Whilst they talked Louisa returned and soon the savoury smell from the kitchen reminded him that he had not eaten since the previous night. She placed a plate in front of him and he smiled appreciatively.

'Could I ask a favour of you?' he asked the beautiful vision before him.

'You may ask. I may not grant it.'

'I'm a stranger in this town. Would you be able to spare the time to show me around? If I leave the main street I become hopelessly lost.'

Louisa giggled. 'It seems strange that anyone can get lost in Heraklion. May I, Pavlos?'

Pavlos nodded. 'I'll wash the dishes and prepare a meal for this evening. You can have an afternoon off.' He winked and his meaning was not lost on her.

It seemed to Mr Pavlakis that whichever road they took there was always someone who knew Louisa and called out a greeting to her. She took him to the library and introduced him to a young man who worked there, arranging for him to borrow books immediately. She sat and talked to the young librarian whilst Mr Pavlakis browsed amongst the shelves. He settled for two large volumes of the history of Rome, explaining that he had recently returned and wished to read more about the wonders he had seen there.

From Eleftherias Square she pointed out the direction of the bus station and two of the largest churches. 'That road leads to Knossos and ....'

'Of course,' interrupted Mr Pavlakis. 'I'd almost forgotten that I'd planned to visit Knossos. I went there last year and I want to see how they've progressed. Would you care to come with me?'

'Maybe. I've never been there.'

Mr Pavlakis stopped and swung her round to face him. 'You've never been! Then you must certainly come with me. Your education has been neglected.'

Louisa laughed. 'I'm not greatly interested.'

'I'll make you interested.' He continued to hold her elbow, relishing the softness of her skin beneath his hand, and began to extol the virtues of Knossos. She allowed him to continue for a while, then held up her hand.'

'That's enough. My head's whirling and I don't understand a quarter of what you're telling me. Let's go for some wine.' To Mr Pavlakis's indescribable joy she slipped her hand into his and led the way into a taverna.

'Hello, Louisa, who's your friend?'

'This is Mr Pavlakis. He's taken a room in our taverna. I'm showing him the town as he's a stranger here.'

'Only the town?' The waiter raised his eyebrows quizzically.

Louisa scowled at him as he sniggered and disappeared behind the bar to fulfil their order.

Finishing their wine Louisa led the way to the school where Mr Pavlakis would teach. This time it did not seem so dark and forbidding and Louisa assured him it was a good school.

'Pavlos and I went there,' she said.

'What would you have liked to do, Louisa, if your parents had not died?'

A far away look came into her eyes, and for a moment she seemed about to confide in him, then she shrugged. 'I don't know. I was worried about Pappa and I had to help Mamma and Pavlos so I didn't give it very much thought.'

Yiorgo Pavlakis squeezed her hand gently. 'So sad,' he murmured, and continued to walk along holding her hand, which she made no effort to withdraw.

Arriving back at the taverna they found Pavlos with a companion. He eyed Mr Pavlakis with suspicion and left without waiting to be introduced. Pavlos brought some wine to the table and Louisa told her brother where she had taken Yiorgo during the afternoon.

'He wants to take me to Knossos, now. I thought he had enjoyed his afternoon, now it looks as if I am to be punished for giving him a conducted tour.'

Pavlos looked surprised. 'Why do you want to go there?'

'I'm interested in antiquities and the sites where they have been found. I visited Knossos last year and there should be more to see now. Louisa's never been there and she should. Everyone should see Knossos.'

Pavlos laughed at the enthusiasm shown by Mr Pavlakis. 'I'm working there and I can tell you it's not very exciting. Mr Evans is trying to rebuild it. He's quite crazy about the place. People come and look at the walls and floors he's uncovered and think it's wonderful. Why? It's just an old building.'

Yiorgo leaned forward in his chair. 'You have no imagination. Think how it would have looked when the king lived there. The ceremony, the colour, the magnificence.'

'You should meet Mr Evans. He talks about Knossos like that. I'm sick of it, the dust, it gets down my throat and my back feels as if it will break by the end of the day. All the time I'm told to go slowly, be careful, examine everything - what is there to examine? Pieces of old broken pottery and rubble from the walls!' Pavlos drained his glass and set it down hard on the table.

'Why do you stay if you dislike it so much?'

'We need the money.'

Louisa put her arm across her brother's shoulders. 'It may not be for much longer. We've paid off all the outstanding bills, we'll soon pay back the bank loan, and then we'll be able to start saving a little. Maybe in a year or two you could go to Athens.'

'Don't be silly,' Pavlos was scornful. 'How could I go off to Athens and leave you here alone?'

Mr Pavlakis cleared his throat. 'Maybe your sister will be married by then. You would surely have no qualms about going to Athens if she had a husband to look after her?'

'I don't think Louisa is ready to get married yet, besides, she has no dowry.'

'A dowry is of no importance to a genuine suitor,' insisted Mr Pavlakis. He must find an opportunity to speak to Pavlos alone and see if the young man would consider him a suitable brother in law.

The day before Mr Pavlakis was due to leave Heraklion he made his way to a jewellers and asked to examine a finely wrought gold bracelet which fastened with a snake's head, the two tiny emeralds shining wickedly as eyes. There would be no new suit for the beginning of the new term now!

He hurried back to the taverna and was surprised to find the door locked. He knocked and rattled, but there was no response. With a sigh he turned to leave, Louisa must be out shopping. He crossed the narrow road and looked up at the façade of the building. Was it his imagination of had he seen a figure at the window of Louisa's room? He screwed his eyes up against the bright sunshine and stared. It must have been an illusion. Disconsolately he wandered towards the market, hoping he might meet Louisa on the way. After half an hour he realised he would be unlikely to spot her amongst the crowd of women who were pushing around him. With a heavy heart he left the market and strolled back to the taverna to await her return. As he rounded the corner he saw the door open and a young man leave, waving a hand to someone inside. Mr Pavlakis quickened his pace. He was sure it was the young librarian. He opened the door and Louisa looked up from behind the counter.

'Why was the door locked when I came earlier?'

She shrugged. 'I always lock the door when I go out.'

'Where have you been?'

Louisa raised her eyebrows. 'What business is it of yours?'

Mr Pavlakis swept back his hair. 'I have bought you a present.'

Louisa looked at him, her dark eyes wary. 'Why?'

Yiorgo Pavlakis moved closer to her and took her hand. 'Louisa, to me you are the most beautiful girl I've ever seen. I wish I didn't have to go away for a week. I'd like to stay with you for ever.'

Gently Louisa withdrew her hand. 'I doubt you will always think that way. First impressions can be misleading.'

'Not with you, Louisa. You are perfection in my eyes.'

'Don't be silly, Yiorgo. You're embarrassing me.'

'Louisa, I mean it.' He tried to take her in his arms but she stiffened and drew away.

'Stop, please stop this.'

Reluctantly he released her. 'I'm sorry, Louisa. I didn't mean to rush you. I've spoken to Pavlos and he has no objection to me courting you. I'd planned to wait until you were more used to me, but how can I?'

Louisa looked at the schoolteacher, her mind working rapidly. He was shouting "security" to her and it was very tempting. She decided evasion was her best plan; to dangle hope in front of him, yet give no definite answer. 'I hardly know you.'

Yiorgo Pavlakis regained control of himself. 'I've spoken too soon. Please forgive me. I bought you a small present today. Will you accept it? As a token of our friendship.' He took the small packet from his pocket and handed it to her.

Louisa gasped as she opened the box. 'I can't, Yiorgo. This is far too expensive. Please return it and ask for your money back.'

'I want you to have it Louisa. I want you to think of me when you're wearing it.'

Louisa gazed up at him from under her long, dark lashes. She would be a fool to refuse the gift and also the man as a suitor. He so obviously adored her that it should not be difficult for her to call the tune and him to dance to it.

'Thank you, Yiorgo. It's the most beautiful bracelet I've ever seen.' She turned her cheek towards him and allowed him to kiss her briefly. 'Let me go now. There's work to be done.'

YANNIS

When Pavlos returned that evening she showed him the bracelet. He raised his eyebrows and whistled. 'Are you promised to him? He asked my permission to approach you, but I didn't think he would do so yet.'

Louisa shook her head. 'I've told him I hardly know him. I'll keep him waiting; after all, he's planning to stay for at least a year. Who knows, the student he's bringing could be a more suitable match.'

Pavlos grasped her arm hard. 'Be careful, Louisa. You've got your regulars. Keep Yiorgo Pavlakis dangling on a string for as long as you want, but don't do him any favours or he may not be so keen.'

Louisa pulled her arm free and rubbed it. 'I know how to keep him interested.'

'I'm sure you do.' Pavlos eyed his sister speculatively. 'Just be discreet.'

Yannis greeted his teacher shyly, introducing him to his mother, brothers and sisters. He listened politely whilst Mr Pavlakis explained the arrangements he had made for their lodgings in Heraklion

'Will he travel down with you?' asked Yannis senior. 'It's a long journey for him to make alone.'

Mr Pavlakis leant his elbows on the table and pushed back his hair. 'I will return today with Yiorgo and his children. I have to meet my replacement teacher on Wednesday and I plan to take the bus to Heraklion on Friday. If Yannis is in Aghios Nikolaos by then we can travel down together and he will have the weekend to get to know his way around the town.'

'I can pick him up from Elounda,' offered Yiorgo, 'and I can take some of his belongings with me today.'

'I'll pack my clean clothes and books now.' Yannis rose from the table. 'I can easily carry the others with me.'

'I'll walk with you to Elounda,' his father promised. He looked very deliberately at Yiorgo. 'I'll have a word with him on the way.'

The Thursday morning dawned bright and clear. Yannis rose early and went down to the yard. To his surprise his father was out there talking quietly to a man whom Yannis did not know. The conversation stopped abruptly.

'You're up early.'

Yannis nodded. 'I suppose I'm excited. Would you like some coffee when I go in?'

The man shook his head. 'I must go. I'll be in touch.' He handed Yannis senior a small parcel.

Maria put her arms around her oldest son and held him tightly. 'I shall miss you, Yannis. Heraklion is so far away.'

Yannis felt a lump coming into his throat. 'I'll miss you, too, Mamma, but I'll be back at Christmas.'

His brothers and sisters were quiet and gazed at him with something akin to awe. They had become used to their big brother being at the Gymnasium in Aghios Nikolaos, but to be able to gain a scholarship to the High School was beyond their comprehension. As he kissed them goodbye Anna was crying openly.

'This is no way to say goodbye,' he exclaimed. 'You'll be surprised how quickly the time will go; then I'll be back home again. I'll write to Mamma and Pappa and Maria will be able to read the letters to you. I'll tell you everything I'm doing and all about Heraklion.'

The children pressed small gifts into his hands, Maria and Anna had each embroidered his initials on a handkerchief, Yiorgo had carved him a model of a donkey, which Yannis insisted was the image of Aga, and Stelios gave him a pencil. His mother wiped her eyes surreptitiously on her apron and pressed a screw of paper into his hand.

'Open it later,' she whispered as he kissed her goodbye for the last time.

YANNIS

Together Yannis and his father walked along the main street. From every doorway a person wished him luck and pushed a gift into his hands. Sometimes it was a coin, other times an apple, a screw of paper with a few olives or a small loaf of bread. Yannis stopped and thanked each person, promising to visit them on his return. By the time they came to the last of the straggle of buildings the boy was close to tears. He turned and waved to his family, then strode forward, his father at his side.

When they reached Elounda Yannis senior led the way into a taverna and they dropped their bundles at their feet. After they had been served with coffee Yannis spoke seriously to his son. 'You're a man, now, Yannis, and you'll soon find you have a young man's appetites. It wouldn't be natural to suppress them, but be careful whom you choose. Don't take any casual woman from the streets.' Yannis flushed to the roots of his hair, suddenly realising what his father was talking about. 'There again, I don't expect you to form a serious relationship with anyone. Years ago Yiorgo and I came to an agreement. You and Annita will marry in a few years time, provided you don't find each other objectionable.' He waited to let his words sink in.

'You mean – Annita and I – we're to get married?'

'Not yet. You're both young, but we think you'll be suitable for each other. Finish your education and begin to make your way in life. I'm just saying that no one expects you to live like a monk until that time comes. And there's another thing,' Yannis withdrew a wad of notes from his pocket and handed them to his son. 'I've paid Mr Pavlakis for your lodgings for the year. He'll pay the taverna owner so you have nothing to worry about there. This money is for you. I want you to buy any clothes you may need. The people in Heraklion won't dress like farmers and I don't want you to be embarrassed before your friends.'

'Pappa!' Yannis gazed at the notes and his father alternately. 'So much money! I've never seen so much. I shan't need all that.'

'You look after it. It's yours, but I don't expect you to waste it. Buy what you need, go out with your friends, buy books, travel around. You never know when you'll get another chance.'

Yannis looked at his father doubtfully. 'Pappa, this must be all of your savings. I can't take this. You might need it for Mamma or the others.' He tried to press the bundle back into his father's hands.

'I've more savings. This is your share. Put it away. I can see Yiorgo.' Yannis pushed it back to him. Yannis stowed the notes deep into his trouser pocket and held out his hand to his father. Yannis senior ignored the hand and embraced his son. 'Take care, boy. Do your best.' His voice was gruff.

'Goodbye, Pappa. Thank you for everything.' He swallowed rapidly. 'I'll write to you as soon as I can.'

He gave his father a last hug before scrambling aboard his uncle's boat, checking his pocket involuntarily before pushing his bundles into the hold, hoping they would not smell too fishy when he retrieved them later. He waved until his father could no longer be seen, before turning to his cousins, a grin spreading over his face.

'I really believe it's true, now. Tomorrow I'll be in Heraklion.'

'I'm going to be busy, too.' Annita spoke softly, looking at Yannis from the corner of her eyes. 'I'm going to train as a nurse at the hospital.'

'Really!' Yannis shook his head. 'How long have you been thinking about this?'

'I decided when I talked to the Widow Segouri. I really enjoyed talking with her, but she couldn't answer all my questions. She couldn't tell me why you took certain medicines, or what they did; she just knew they were right for that complaint. I suppose I'm a bit like you with your pieces of pottery, wanting to know how old they are and who made them. I feel like that about people. I want to know why they're ill and what I can do to help them get better. Do you understand, Yannis?' She turned to him, her eyes glowing with enthusiasm.

'No, I don't. How anybody can want to spend their time with people who are sick and ill amazes me. I know there has to be someone to look after them, but how they can want to,' his voice tailed off and he shuddered.

Annita looked at him, her eyes dancing with amusement. 'I can't understand why anyone should want to spend all day grubbing around in the earth hoping to find a bit of pottery.'

'Pottery can tell you so much about how people lived and…' Yannis broke off as Annita gave him a push that nearly sent him overboard.

'Idiot! I was teasing. I was just trying to explain that I feel the same as you do, but about something totally different.'

Yannis held up his hands for peace. 'What about you, Andreas? Do you have any great revelation for me?'

Andreas smiled. 'One is surely enough.'

'We're nearly there.' Annita jumped to her feet. 'I feel so excited about everything.' She hugged Yannis in her exuberance, and then drew away from him, blushing.

During their meal Annita chattered about her desire to become a nurse until Yannis finally pushed his plate away. 'I can't eat any more with you talking like that. It makes me feel ill.'

Annita giggled. 'You're silly. Wouldn't you like me to look after you if you were ill?'

'I'm not at all sure that I would. I've a feeling that if I said I had a bad arm you would treat my leg!'

The humour left Annita and she rose to her feet. 'You may be very clever, Yannis, but you are also a very stupid little boy at times.' She pushed her chair away and ran up to her tiny bedroom.

Yannis looked at her mother and father helplessly. 'I was only joking. I didn't mean to hurt her feelings.'

Elena patted his hand sympathetically. 'We know that, and I think Annita does really. Her decision came upon us rather suddenly and we've all teased her. She probably thought you wouldn't.'

'Excuse me. I'll go an apologise to her.' When Yannis reached the top of the stairs he could hear muffled sobbing from behind Anita's closed door. He stopped aghast. He had never known Annita to cry, not even when she had fallen and cut her knees quite badly. Cautiously he tapped on the door. 'Annita. May I come in?'

The sobbing stopped. He tapped again. 'I'm coming in.'

'Go away. Leave me alone.'

Yannis opened the door and walked over to where she had thrown herself on her mattress, her face buried in the pillow. He stroked her hair gently. 'I didn't mean it, Annita, when I said you wouldn't know the difference between an arm and a leg. I was only teasing.'

Annita began to sob again. Yannis stroked her shoulders gently. 'Come on, now. I've always thought you such a brave little girl, you never cried when you were hurt. Now you're crying because I teased you.'

'I'm not a little girl.' Annita spoke through clenched teeth. She turned her tear-stained face towards him. 'I'll prove to you I'm not a little girl.' She pulled his head downwards until their lips met, kissing him long and passionately, toppling him off balance and pressing her body tightly against his.

'I'm not a little girl, Yannis.' This time she spoke the words quietly, looking into his eyes. 'I overheard Mamma and Pappa say that we are going to be married eventually. I wanted to make you proud to have me as a wife - and I'm going to miss you, Yannis.' Her lips trembled and her eyes brimmed with tears.

Yannis pulled himself back into a sitting position and took her hand in his, noticing for the first time how strong and capable it was. 'I'm going to miss you, too. Pappa told me before I left Elounda about our parents' plans, but I was still thinking of you as the little girl I'd played with, not as the girl I'm going to marry.'

'Do you want to marry me, Yannis?'

'I think so.'

YANNIS

'Suppose you meet someone else in Heraklion?'

Yannis remembered his conversation with his father. 'You might meet someone. One of your sick people that you want to look after.'

'Yannis don't joke.'

'I'm not joking. I've heard that people can become very fond of others who are dependent upon them. Maybe when you've done some training here you could come to Heraklion?'

Annita shook her head. 'Don't be silly, Yannis. If we said we wanted to be in Heraklion together they would certainly say no. All the time they think we are just friends with no ideas for the future we can do as we please. The moment they think we have other ideas someone will always be with us, watching what we do. Look at Maria and Babbis. The village watches them as they walk down the street. You or I were supposed to be with them if they went anywhere. I don't want it to be like that.'

Yannis took her hands. 'I wish now that I was staying here longer.' He pulled his cousin towards him and kissed her very gently, revelling in the novelty of the sensations she aroused in him. 'We should go down. Your Mamma will be wondering what's happened to us. Come with me to find Mr Pavlakis. You can say you want to tell him your news.'

'Don't be long, Yannis. I want you to help me with some fishing for a couple of hours,' called Yiorgo.

Yannis sighed. He had not expected to have to go fishing on his last evening in Aghios Nikolaos.

Once outside Yannis hesitated. 'I expect he's at the taverna, saying goodbye to his friends.'

Yannis was right. At the taverna Mr Pavlakis was surrounded by his acquaintances, empty bottles and glasses stood around and toasts to his future success were being drunk. Mr Pavlakis waved them in to join him.

'You can't go in there,' Yannis decided. 'Wait here. I won't be long.'

He pushed his way forward to where his teacher was standing unsteadily with his glass raised. 'What time does the bus go tomorrow, please?'

'The bus?' Mr Pavlakis looked puzzled.

'Tomorrow we're catching the bus to Heraklion. What time does it leave, please?'

'Oh, tomorrow! Tomorrow I shall see Louisa again. Drink, my friends, drink to Louisa. The most beautiful girl in the world.'

A glass was thrust into Yannis's hand and he had no choice but to drink the rough wine. 'What time does the bus go?' he tried again.

'It doesn't matter. Come and enjoy yourself.' Mr Pavlakis splashed more wine into Yannis's glass. 'Drink. Drink to Louisa.'

Yannis raised his glass in salutation, then placed it on the table and slipped back through the little gathering to the door where Annita was waiting. She raised her eyebrows questioningly.

'He's drunk. I couldn't get any sense out of him. Let's go to the bus station.' Yannis took her hand and they strolled along the almost deserted streets together. Once they reached the main part of the town they released hands and walked side by side until they arrived at an area of rough ground where the bus, which ran from Aghios Nikolaos to Heraklion, was parked when not in use. From the wooden shack, which sold sweets, cigarettes, lottery tickets and a weekly newspaper, information about the time of the bus was given and tickets could be bought.

'Excuse me.'

The man dragged his eyes from a three-day-old newspaper. 'Yes?'

'Can you tell me what time the bus for Heraklion leaves tomorrow morning, please?'

'Ten.' He dropped his eyes again to the newspaper.

'Thank you.' Yannis turned to Annita. 'I hope he's told me correctly. Come on, we'd best get back. Your Pappa will be waiting for me.'

'There is Pappa,' said Annita in surprise and pointed across the road to where her father was speaking to a small boy who shook his head and shrugged his shoulders.

'He must be looking for us.' Together they strolled across the street. 'I'm not late, am I?' asked Yannis.

Yiorgo shook his head. 'No, I was looking for Andreas. I've seen most of his friends and they don't know where he is. I wondered if he'd wandered over this side of town. He seems to disappear without anyone knowing where he goes. Have you seen him?'

Both Yannis and Annita shook their heads. 'He used to do the same when we were at Plaka, he always turned up again, though.' Yannis felt guilty that he had never enquired into his cousin's whereabouts.

'Shall we help you look?' asked Annita.

'No,' Yiorgo sighed. 'He'll doubtless turn up when he's hungry. You two go on. I'm going for a glass of wine.'

Yiorgo sat in morose silence as he toyed with his glass. He realised for the first time that he hardly knew his son. A vague feeling of concern assailed him, which his common sense told him was stupid. Andreas was a naturally quiet, self-disciplined boy, who kept his own council. He could be relied upon not to have done anything foolish. Yiorgo sighed deeply, placed a few coins on the table and left. He walked down the hill until he reached the church and there he saw Andreas standing on the steps talking to the priest. Yiorgo stopped in surprise and waited until Andreas saw him and walked over.

'Hello, Pappa.'

'Have you been naughty, Andreas?'

'No, Pappa.'

'Why did you need to see the priest?'

'I wanted to tell him I was staying home this evening as Yannis is here, so I couldn't come for instruction.'

Yiorgo looked at his son. 'What instruction?'

'The instruction Father Dhakanalis gives me.' Andreas was being evasive.

'Don't you understand the services?'

'Of course I understand, Pappa.'

'Then why do you go for instruction?'

Andreas took a deep breath. 'I want to be a priest.'

'You want to…..?' Yiorgo could not believe his ears.

'I want to be a priest,' Andreas repeated.

Yiorgo walked a few steps in silence. Pride and sadness fought inside him. 'You're sure? It means a life spent bound by rigid laws, no wife, no children, continually putting the welfare of others before your own.'

'I know, Pappa, but that's what I want.'

'Have you told your mother?'

'I've told no one. People might laugh at me.'

'Why should they laugh? It's a good, honourable profession.'

Andreas shrugged. 'Some people wouldn't understand how I feel. To me it's the only thing worth doing.'

Yiorgo looked at his son in disbelief. 'You won't make any money as a priest.'

'That doesn't matter. I just want to help people.'

'If that's how you really feel.' Yiorgo shrugged. Who was he to insist that his son became a fisherman if he had been called to the church? As they entered the house Yiorgo shouted to his wife. 'Elena, Andreas has some news for you.'

'What is it?'

Andreas grinned sheepishly. 'I want to be a priest, Mamma.'

'A priest!' She was incredulous. 'My son a priest!'

'If I'm clever enough; I'll have to pass exams.'

'You'll pass them,' said Elena with confidence. 'You're a clever boy. A good boy. I'm so proud, so pleased.' She sank into a chair and fanned herself with her apron

Andreas winced. He hated to be called good. 'Please don't tell anyone, not even Annita and Yannis.'

'Why ever not? They'll be pleased for you.' Elena was surprised by his request.

'They might tell people who would whisper and laugh at me.'

'They wouldn't dare!' Elena was indignant.

'They wouldn't understand. Please, Mamma, promise me.'

'We must do as he asks, Elena. Suppose he changes his mind? If we've told everyone he has a vocation for the priesthood he would certainly be laughed at then.'

Elena was disappointed. She had immediately planned to tell her neighbours, but Andreas was still young to make such a decision.

'I have to go,' Yiorgo reached for his jacket. 'Where's Yannis? Have he and Annita come back yet?'

'They're upstairs. Go and call them, Andreas. Tell them Pappa's waiting.'

Andreas mounted the stairs quietly and pushed open the bedroom door. 'Oh!' He stopped, blushing with embarrassment as the two sprung apart. He closed the door behind him. 'I'm sorry. I had no idea.'

Yannis squeezed Annita gently to him. 'We had no idea either, until today.'

'Are Mamma and Pappa pleased?'

'We haven't told them yet. You won't say anything; will you, Andreas? You know how it is once parents think a couple are courting. They never have a minute alone.' Annita turned beseeching eyes upon her brother.

'I shan't tell them. Yannis goes away tomorrow, so they couldn't chaperone you anyway.'

'Mamma would want to tell everyone,' persisted Annita.

'I know!' Andreas's comment was heartfelt. 'Actually I came up to tell Yannis that Pappa is ready to leave. I'll tell him you're just getting a pullover.' He slipped out of the room, leaving them for a last few moments alone.

The tide was exactly as Yiorgo had known it would be when

he slipped the mooring rope and headed towards the open sea.

'Which way?' asked Yannis.

'Lobster pots,' Yiorgo answered briefly. 'I laid them on my way to meet you.'

Yannis nodded. At least this work would be pleasant. He hated hauling in the net, full of wet, slippery fish, which had to be sorted and made you smell like a fish yourself. Pulling in pots, removing lobsters or crabs and tying their claws was clean, easy work by comparison. Yiorgo steered near to a rocky headland and the two boys leant over the side, attaching a rope to the loop on each pot.

'How many?' called Andreas.

'Fifteen,' answered Yiorgo, intent on avoiding a sharp reef that he knew lay just beneath the surface.

The roping of the pots completed Yiorgo relinquished the oars to the boys, who made a half circle turn out towards the open sea, then rowed back slowly, giving Yiorgo time to hoist each pot aboard.

Once back on the quay they removed the lobsters from the pots, tying their claws and placing them in a galvanised bath with some old netting at the bottom. It made Yannis feel unaccountably sad to see them, their antennae searching for a way of escape, whilst their legs became more deeply entangled in the net.

'I would hate to be a lobster,' he remarked as he began to check the pots for damage. 'One minute you're crawling along the sand looking for lunch and the next you're whisked up through the water, trussed up and sent off to be cooked for lunch. It's a good job they don't know what's in store for them.'

'Do we?' asked Andreas.

Yannis stared at him thoughtfully. 'I suppose not, but at least we know we're not going to be captured and cooked. Hurry up. There are only a couple of pots to mend. I'm hungry.'

The pots repaired they hurried back up the hill and were

greeted by the savoury smell of lobster. 'I don't believe it. It isn't a name day.'

Andreas said nothing. He knew his father had captured two lobsters the day before and set them aside for Yannis's last meal with them. Taking Yannis out fishing had been an excuse to get him from the house whilst they were being finally prepared.

'I am honoured,' mumbled Yannis with embarrassment. 'You always said you only had them on special occasions like Elena's birthday.'

'This is a special occasion.' Yiorgo raised his glass. 'This is to wish you success and good fortune, Yannis. We will miss you. Just remember you always have a home here.'

Beneath the table Yannis squeezed Annita's hand. He rose with his glass held aloft. 'I should just like to say thank you. Without you giving me a home none of this would have been possible. I promise I'll work very hard and hope you'll never regret having had me for this last year.'

Throughout the evening neighbours and school friends would knock the door, staying for a glass of wine to toast Yannis on his way. Yannis's head was beginning to spin and the buzzing in his ears was disconcerting. He sidled over to his uncle.

'Can I go to bed? I know everyone means well, but I've had more than enough to drink, and I'm tired.'

Yiorgo grinned. 'Wait until you come back from Heraklion. You'll be used to drinking half the night by then and think nothing of it. Off you go. I'll tell people you have to rise early.'

Thankfully Yannis slipped away up the stairs. Once in his bed he knew no more until the room lightened. He tried to raise his head from the pillow and groaned.

'What is it?' Andreas paused in the act of buttoning his shirt.'
'My head. It feels as though it will burst.'

Andreas grinned at him. 'You probably had too much to drink. I'll go down and get some coffee on. You'll soon be all right.'

Yannis tried again to struggle up into a sitting position. The room seemed to sway slightly. Cautiously he placed his feet on the floor and an overwhelming desire to be sick overtook him, all weaknesses forgotten, he rushed down the stairs and out to the yard. Feeling a little better he staggered into the kitchen where Andreas regarded him with amusement.

'I've made your coffee. I suggest you drink two or three cups. I'll get your trousers.'

Yannis looked down at his bare legs. 'Please, and a pullover, I'm freezing.' He sipped at the scalding coffee. His head began to clear a little and he remembered he had a bus to catch. He emitted a groan and sipped again at the coffee.

Annita entered, 'You're early,' she commented; then giggled at the sight of Yannis's bare legs. 'No wonder you're early, you've forgotten to dress.'

'Stop it, Annita. I feel terrible.'

Immediately Annita became all concern. 'What is it? Are you ill?'

'No.' Yannis tried to shake his head and emitted another loud groan.

'Have you got a pain somewhere?'

'I drank too much last night.' Yannis sipped again at the coffee.

'You'll soon feel better. Drink more coffee. I'll get your trousers.' Annita had often seen her father in far worse condition after a night of merry making.

'Andreas is getting them. I do feel terrible. I think I might be sick again.'

'Serves you right.' Annita helped herself to a cup of coffee. Now that she knew Yannis was suffering from nothing more serious than a hangover she had no sympathy for him.

Yannis made another dash for the yard as Andreas returned with his clothes. He dumped them on the chair and shrugged his shoulders at his sister. 'It's probably a good thing he's feeling ill. He'll be far less inclined to drink too much in Heraklion.'

On shaky legs Yannis returned to the kitchen, sitting down to put his feet into his trousers and holding onto the table to keep his balance whilst he pulled them up. 'I'll never drink again,' he vowed.

'Yes you will. You'll forget after a while. I've heard Pappa say that so many times, and I expect your Pappa has said the same. Everyone does when they feel ill.'

Yannis groaned again and held his head in his hands.

'You'd better eat.' Annita pushed a roll across the table to him. 'When you've had that you can go back up and sleep for a while. I'll wake you in plenty of time for the bus.'

Miserably Yannis did as he was bid and clawed his way back up the stairs and lay on his bed. It seemed only a matter of moments before Annita was shaking him awake. To his relief he felt better and was able to stand without his head spinning. He appeared downstairs and grinned sheepishly at his aunt and uncle.

'I'm sorry. Your farewell party was a little too much for me.'

Yiorgo nodded sympathetically. 'Elena's made you some lunch to take with you. Collect your bags. We should be off.'

Yannis splashed his face under the tap, checked that his precious bundle of money was safely packed away and followed his relatives from the house. The bus was standing on the waste ground and Yannis purchased the necessary ticket. He embraced Elena, shook hands with Yiorgo and Andreas and kissed them formally on both cheeks. Lastly he turned to Annita, her eyes moist with unshed tears. Taking her in his arms he kissed her cheeks.

'Don't cry,' he whispered. 'I'll be back soon. Write to me and tell me all about your sick people. You've got my address, haven't you?'

Annita attempted a watery smile. 'If you don't write back to me I'll come looking for you.'

He gave Annita a last quick kiss. 'I have to go.' He jumped up the steps onto the bus, pushed his bundles under the seat and waved from the window to the little group as the bus revved its engine and moved forward slowly.

Bumping and rocking the bus made its way ponderously over the waste ground until it reached the dirt road and began to climb the hill towards the square, hooting to warn pedestrians that it was on its way. They coasted down the other side towards the pool and Yannis clapped his hand to his head.

'Oh, no! I've forgotten Mr Pavlakis.' Yannis rose from his seat and walked down the bus.

'Sit down,' called the driver. 'You're not allowed to walk around.'

'I want you to stop,' called back Yannis. The other passengers craned their necks to see what the interruption was.

'Why? Are you ill?'

'No. A friend of mine should be on this bus. Can you wait whilst I go and fetch him?'

'Sit down! I can let you off, but I'm not waiting.'

Yannis sat down miserably in his seat. It was hot and stuffy on the bus and Yannis pressed his head against the glass to try to cool his forehead. The journey to Heraklion seemed endless. For a while the bus travelled through countryside, dipping down to Neapolis, before returning to the coast where the sea threatened to lap at the tyres at any moment. After a run on level ground they began to climb and Yannis looked at the drop below the dirt road with some trepidation. The driver seemed totally unconcerned, chatting to his companion, or bringing the bus to a screeching halt to pick up a stray traveller. Yannis continued to look out of the window until a larger town than he had ever imagined loomed into view and the bus began to thread its way through narrow streets, hooting loudly at each corner. Slowly it crawled up one hill and down the next, finally halting beside a small wooden hut. The engine was cut and the driver climbed out.

'We're here.'

Yannis gathered his bundles again and left the bus. He looked around, feeling very nervous and approached the driver. 'Can you help me, please? I have to go to this address.' He dug the piece of paper from his pocket and showed it to the man.

The driver read it and called to his friend. 'Look where he's going!'

His friend looked at the scrawled address and sniggered. 'Why don't we all go?'

'My wife would kill me! Walk up the hill there, boy, until you come to Eleftherias Square. You want the main road, Konstantinou, follow it down until it becomes Kalokerinou. Ask again round there. Anyone will be able to direct you. I just hope you can afford it.'

'Thank you. My father has already paid.' The two men doubled up with laughter that bewildered Yannis.

The sun struck Yannis with full force as he made his way up the deserted road towards the Square. To his relief when he reached the top of the hill there were a number of small tavernas and he was able to enter a gloomy interior and sit in the welcome coolness with a cup of coffee. He opened the package Elena had prepared for him, but re-wrapped it when he saw the taverna owner watching him. He ordered another coffee and lingered as long as he dared before returning to the hot sunshine.

The main road was easy to find and he gazed entranced at the shops, one after another they stretched as far as he could see. He wished his mother could see all the craft and embroidery shops; she would have a ready market for her work. He almost made a detour into the market, which was bright, noisy and enticing on the other side of the road, but his cumbersome bundles deterred him. He decided to squat in a welcome patch of shade and eat whatever the cloth held in the way of food. No one took the slightest notice of him and he realised how very alone he was for the first time in his life.

The realisation destroyed his appetite. Pushing the remains of the roll and cheese back into the cloth he rose and dusted the crumbs from his trousers. He must find the taverna. They were expecting him and they would be company, albeit they were strangers.

He had no difficulty in finding where the road became Kalokerinou and Yannis asked at the first shop for directions. The man in the gift shop regarded him curiously, but told him the simplest way to find his destination. Yannis turned into a maze of side streets and walked far further than necessary before reaching the correct street. He was walking on the opposite side of the road and regarded the taverna with interest. It looked clean, despite being in need of a coat of paint, also, to his dismay, it looked deserted. He crossed the road and tried the door, but it did not yield. He knocked, then again more loudly. He dumped his bundles on the step and leaned against the wall. He would just have to wait. He returned to the shaded side of the road and sat down on a doorstep feeling thoroughly miserable. He had expected to arrive in Heraklion with Mr Pavlakis and be welcomed, not be alone and locked out from the only address he had.

It seemed an age before he saw a young woman open the door of the taverna and disappear inside. He waited a few moments, gathered his possessions, crossed the road and knocked hard on the door, opening it as he did so. The woman had her back to him and she turned with a smile as she heard the door.

'Hello,' he said. 'I'm Yannis. Are you Louisa?'

She nodded, a small frown playing between her eyes. 'Yannis?'

'I'm with Mr Pavlakis, but he's been delayed. He'll catch a later bus.'

'I see. Why was Yiorgo delayed?'

'I'm not sure. Would it be alright to go to my room? I'm sick of carrying these bundles.'

'Of course.'

Yannis followed the girl up the wooden stairs to the two rooms he and Mr Pavlakis were to occupy and placed his belongings thankfully on the floor.

YANNIS

'Is there somewhere I can wash? I feel filthy after that long bus ride.'

Louisa nodded and led him back down the stairs to the kitchen where she showed him the tap let into the wall, underneath stood an earthenware pot.

'If you want hot water it has to be heated on the stove.'

'I'm used to cold. May I take some to my room?'

'As you please. Come back down when you've unpacked. My brother will be back shortly.'

Yannis carried a heavy jug of water back to his room. He removed all his belongings from his bags and placed them carefully inside the chest. His books and precious pieces of pottery, along with his coin, he placed on a shelf, then he removed his shirt and washed the dust and sweat from his body. He was beginning to feel distinctly better, but very tired. He loosened his boots and lay back on the bed, hoping he would not roll off when he was asleep. He had only ever slept on a mattress on the floor before.

An insistent tapping awaked him. He rose and flung the door open, expecting to see Mr Pavlakis. A stranger stood there, who held out his hand and smiled. 'Welcome to Heraklion. I'm Pavlos. Louisa told me you'd arrived.'

Yannis shook Pavlos's hand and smiled back. 'I'm pleased to meet you.'

'I hear Yiorgo has been delayed, but never mind. Come down and see what Louisa has prepared for our supper.'

Yannis followed Pavlos into the taverna. There were a few young men seated at a table who stared at the boy curiously. Pavlos motioned him to a seat and called to his sister to bring them some wine and their meal. Yannis looked at the men, then at Pavlos. They all wore black trousers that buttoned at the front and white shirts, beneath the table their boots shone.

'Does everyone wear clothes like this in town?'

Pavlos looked at Yannis's traditional baggy trousers, then at the men and shrugged. 'Usually.'

'I'll have to get some. Pappa was right when he told me to buy my new clothes when I arrived and saw the fashions.'

'You don't have clothes like this at home?'

'Oh, yes, but they're not very practical when you're working on a farm or a boat. I gave my best clothes to my younger brother, as they were getting too small for me. He'll wear them on Sundays as I used to do.'

Pavlos nodded understandingly, wishing Yiorgo Pavlakis were there. What did one talk about to a country boy?

Yiorgo Pavlakis awoke, his head felt as if it were stuffed with cotton wool. He tried to rise and fell back, closing his eyes against the bright sunlight. He opened them again as his memory jolted him back to reality.

'The bus!' he exclaimed.

He rose from the narrow bed as quickly as he was able, swaying slightly and feeling nauseous as he stood and splashed his face with cold water. A glance at his pocket watch told him he had missed the bus and he sank back onto the bed with a groan. Why had his landlady not woken him as he had asked? He groped his way down the dark stairway to where he could hear the woman at work in her kitchen. She looked at him in disgust as he entered.

'Awake at last, are you? Have you got a civil tongue in your head now?'

'Why didn't you call me? I've overslept and missed the bus, you stupid old woman.'

'Stupid, am I? Not as stupid as those who drink themselves senseless. Have to be brought home by their friends and put to bed!'

'You didn't call me,' shouted Mr Pavlakis.

'I called you three times. I even shook you to wake you up. What was I supposed to do? Carry you to the bus? After the way you shouted at me and told me to leave you alone!' She snorted and turned away to continue her cleaning.

Mr Pavlakis sank into a chair. 'You didn't call me,' he insisted. 'I've missed the bus. How am I supposed to get to Heraklion now?'

'Catch the next one.'

'The next one is Monday and I have to be there by Monday morning.'

'You could walk.'

'I could, but my trunk cannot.'

'Why don't you ask Costas? He may be willing to take your trunk next time he goes.'

'Of course.' Mr Pavlakis sprang to his feet. 'Maybe he's going up today.'

He rushed from the house and through the streets to the home of the van driver. He was a drinking acquaintance, but could hardly be called a friend. On reaching the house Mr Pavlakis pounded on the door until it was finally opened a crack.

'What do you want? Oh, it's you.'

'Costas, are you going to Heraklion today? I've missed the bus and I have to be in Heraklion by Monday.'

Costas opened the door wider. 'You'd better come in.' Mr Pavlakis followed him to the kitchen where he was invited to sit and a cup of coffee was placed before him. 'Now what's all this about Heraklion? I've only just woken up.'

'I overslept this morning and missed the bus. I've got to be in Heraklion by Monday.'

Costas chuckled. 'I'm not surprised you overslept the state you were in last night.' He yawned widely. 'I'm not going up today. No need.'

'What can I do?' asked Mr Pavlakis desperately. 'Do you know if anyone else is going?'

Costas shrugged. 'I'm going tomorrow. Early, mind, I can't wait if you oversleep.'

Mr Pavlakis grabbed the man's hands and pumped them up

and down. 'I'll be here at whatever time you say. You're my saviour.'

'Be here at six.'

'Thank you, thank you, my friend. It will be worth your while.'

Costas nodded. 'Yes.'

Mr Pavlakis took his leave and made his way back to his lodgings. The old woman regarded him balefully. 'Recovered from your temper?'

'I'm very sorry. Please forgive me. I must have been disgustingly drunk. I've seen Costas and he's willing to take me to Heraklion tomorrow morning. May I stay an extra night?'

'You can stay, but you'll get yourself up. I'm not waking you.'

'Thank you. I shan't go out this evening.'

He spent the rest of the day wandering disconsolately around the town. His head still felt like cotton wool and his first glass of wine nauseated him. By the evening, having eaten, he felt considerably better. Not daring to meet his friends and spend the evening drinking in a taverna he returned to the small room he had considered his home for a number of years and tried to write. He could remember his friends acclaiming his theories as brilliant the night before. If only he could remember how he had thought the economy could be improved and the standard of living raised. He tried to put pen to paper, finally giving up the unequal struggle and forcing himself to go to bed.

For the first few hours he tossed restlessly, then fell into a heavy slumber, waking with a start and checking his pocket watch. Five in the morning! He must get up or he might be late meeting Costas. With a sigh he rose and dressed. He checked the cupboard and the chest to make doubly sure he had forgotten nothing, and crept down the stairs. To his surprise his landlady was already in the kitchen and the coffee pot was on the stove.

'You're early,' he remarked.

'I'm always up early. I like to work before it gets hot; besides, I wanted to see you before you left. You owe me an extra day's rent.'

YANNIS

Grudgingly Yiorgo had to admit she was right and dug into his pocket. 'Thank you for looking after me,' he said sincerely. As he looked at her he saw for the first time the soiled black dress and grubby apron, the lined face and gnarled work-worn hands. He would make sure Louisa did not look like her in a few years.

He bade her farewell in good time to reach the house that Costas shared with his mother. The heavy trunk, which he pulled behind him, hindered his progress and he arrived panting. He knocked vigorously on the door and waited. The driver took his time in answering and Yiorgo was anxiously checking his pocket watch when the door opened a crack.

'What do you want?'

'You told me to be here at six. You're taking me to Heraklion.'

'I'm not ready yet. You'll have to wait.'

The door closed and Yiorgo leant against the wall, trying to remain patient. It seemed an age before Costas reappeared and signalled to him to follow as he led the way through the outskirts of the town until they reached a piece of waste ground where an inelegant vehicle was parked.

Costas unlocked the doors and the engine, taking the starting handle from beneath his driving seat and inserting it in the hole beneath the radiator. Costas turned the handle vigorously and the engine spluttered and died. Costas turned, again the engine died, and at a third attempt, after a cough, the engine sprang into life. The handle was removed and stowed beneath the seat. Yiorgo was left to heave his trunk into the back whilst Costas waited for him impatiently.

Once Yiorgo was also inside Costas removed the hand brake, pressed the accelerator and they began to jolt over the stony, uneven ground. The teacher gripped his seat, his knuckles showing white; convinced he would shoot through the windscreen at any moment. The journey did not become any smoother when they reached the road, as Costas appeared to have only a rudimentary knowledge of driving procedure. His foot would press the accelerator almost to the floor until a flock of sheep came into view when it would switch quickly to the brake, bringing the van to a screeching halt, panicking both sheep and shepherd.

Costas did not speak to his companion and Yiorgo gave up any attempt at conversation. At the larger towns they stopped and Costas sat with his hand on the horn. Someone always appeared to hand over a letter or parcel and pass a few coins to Costas. He kept the engine running continually, rather than have to start it again and Yiorgo began to feel quite sick. By mid-morning they had reached Malia and he begged to be allowed to stop long enough to purchase a cup of coffee.

Grudgingly Costas agreed and whilst his passenger was gone he checked his petrol tank, topping it up from a can he carried in the back. He left the engine ticking over and strolled into the taverna. He ordered wine and drank the glass swiftly, staring at Yiorgo as he did so. As soon as the wine was finished Costas made for the door and Yiorgo had no choice but to hurry after him. His hasty coffee had only served to increase his nausea and he wished heartily he had not missed the bus.

The journey seemed to go on forever, the road no more than a cart track in places, as Costas made detours to collect or deliver items. The van rattled, bumped, shook and jolted. Costas appeared to delight in hitting each pothole at speed until Yiorgo was convinced he could have driven equally as well, if not better. He sat in agonised silence until Costas spoke.

'We're here.'

Yiorgo sighed with relief as they sped down the hill towards the harbour. Costas drew to a screeching halt and held out his hand. Yiorgo pulled out a selection of coins from his pocket, counted out the same as the bus fare, added a little to it and offered it to Costas.

The driver shook his head. 'I charge three times the bus fare.'

'Three times!'

Costas nodded. 'Or I can take you back for nothing.'

Yiorgo vowed silently that he would never travel with Costas again. He added to the amount of coins, heaved his trunk from the back and bade the man a polite farewell. Costas did not bother to reply, but shot rapidly into a turn and back up the hill. Yiorgo cursed himself for not asking to be dropped at the taverna, and then considered how much more that might have cost him.

Alternately pulling and pushing his trunk Yiorgo trudged towards the taverna. By the time he reached the door he felt exhausted, despite having stopped frequently to rest. As he pushed open the door he could hear a clattering of dishes in the kitchen.

'Louisa.'

Pavlos's head appeared round the doorway. He grinned widely. 'Welcome back. Louisa's gone shopping and your young friend is upstairs.'

Yiorgo Pavlakis sank into a chair and Pavlos brought a bottle of wine. 'You look like a man in need.' He poured a glass for each of them and raised his in salutation.

Yiorgo drank deeply. 'I've had a terrible journey.'

'You haven't walked! Why didn't you come by bus?'

Yiorgo shook his head. 'I was driven up by a friend. I'd better tell Yannis I'm here. Can you help me up with my trunk at the same time?'

Together they manhandled the cumbersome trunk up the stairs and into the room that was to be the teacher's. 'Yannis,' he called.

'I'm here.'

Yannis was writing a letter to Annita, telling her about the journey and the little he had seen of Heraklion. Opening the door he almost fell into the arms of Mr Pavlakis.

'Come down, Yannis, and I'll tell you my troubles.'

Yannis followed the two men obediently and joined them at the table, a glass of wine being passed to him, which he sipped at slowly, whilst Mr Pavlakis recounted his journey with Costas. Before he had finished Louisa returned and he had to start again.

She had no sympathy for him and laughingly told him it was his own fault. A customer entered and was invited to join the group for Yiorgo to tell his story yet again and Yannis excused himself, he had no wish to hear it for a third time.

Yannis returned to his letter writing. He finished the one to Annita and placed it on top of the one to his parents. As he did so he remembered the screw of paper his mother had pressed into his hand as he left. The excitement of the past few days had driven it from his mind, and even when he had unpacked he had hidden it away with the money his father had given him.

He rummaged amongst his socks until he found it and opened it carefully. Inside was a small, blue stone, set in silver, which his mother had always worn on a ribbon around her neck to ward off evil. He sat down on the bed and turned it between his fingers. He would have to buy a chain so he could wear it also. He took some notes from the pile and pushed them deep into his pocket before returning the charm to its hiding place. He picked up his letters and returned downstairs to see if there was any lunch available.

Yiorgo seemed to have recovered his spirits now he was finally in Heraklion and whilst they were eating Yannis asked if he would show him the town that afternoon.

'I've wandered down to the harbour, but I don't know the way to the High School.'

'Certainly I will. Maybe Louisa could come with us. She knows her way far better than I. I'll ask her.' Yiorgo went into the kitchen, returning a few moments later looking downcast. 'She says she will be busy this afternoon.'

They walked first down to the port, the teacher pointing out the impressive Venetian fort that guarded the harbour entrance. From a kiosk on the corner Yannis purchased stamps for his letters and when they reached the Square he was able to post them. Together they strolled down the main street, which Yannis recognised from his arrival. They walked through the market at Yannis's request and he was fascinated by the variety of goods on sale. He resisted the temptation to spend money on novelties he had never seen before, but when they reached the street of the cobblers he insisted on trying a pair of high, shiny boots and purchasing them.

'What I want now,' said Yannis, 'Is a silver chain for my neck.'

Yiorgo looked somewhat surprised, but agreed to take him to a reputable jeweller on their way back to the taverna. The façade of the school left him unimpressed, and he turned away from it after a few minutes, looking around to fix the location in his mind.

'Look!'

'What at?'

'Over there.' Yannis pointed. 'The museum. Can we go in?'

'If you want. I told you I was disappointed, just a jumble of old pottery and faded labels.'

They made their way inside the building and Yannis gazed in bewilderment at the dark glass cases with pottery arranged haphazardly inside and an occasional complete vessel.

'It's such a mess,' said Yannis sadly. 'Most of it you can't see properly, and if you can see it there's no label saying what it is. That piece there is the same as in the previous case. It all needs sorting out.'

'I've seen much better museums in Rome and Turin,' agreed Yiorgo. 'The one in Athens is remarkable, but this ...' he shrugged eloquently. 'Shall we go?'

'Do we have to? I wanted to look more closely at some of it.'

Yiorgo sighed; he was bored. Taking his pocket watch out he studied it carefully. 'I think it would be better if you returned another time, if you want to buy that chain tonight.'

Regretfully Yannis agreed and followed his companion out through a dimly lit hall, noticing for the first time the old man sitting on a chair in the corner.

'Who's that? Are we supposed to pay him?'

'I've no idea. I'll give him a coin.' Yiorgo dropped a lepta into the earthenware pot that stood at the man's feet. He touched his forehead and looked after them as if wondering where they had come from.

Once outside Yannis stopped abruptly. 'Where's the library?'

'A street away; I'll show you as we pass.'

'Can you arrange for me to borrow some books?'

'I'm sure the High School will arrange that for you.'

'I want one now,' Yannis spoke urgently. 'I want to read about the finds they have in the museum, then when I return I might know what I'm looking at.'

Yiorgo resigned himself to spending at least an hour in the library and was pleasantly surprised when Yannis quickly selected two books and expressed his wish to return to the taverna as soon as he had purchased a chain.

On reaching the taverna Yannis retired to his room. First he fixed the silver charm to the chain and hung it round his neck, he then eased his feet into his new boots. Sitting on his bed, his legs elevated so he could admire his new footwear frequently, he opened the first of his books from the library. He had chosen well, each book contained illustrations of the pottery, which was in the museum, the original location, and the approximate date of manufacture. On more than one occasion he went to the shelf and picked up a piece of his own pottery to compare with a line drawing. His excitement knew no bounds when he finally decided his coin was a tetradrachm and would have been minted around 490 B.C.

During their meal he could not stop talking about the pottery and Louisa and Pavlos were amazed at the change in him. He appeared to have come to life before their eyes, questioning Pavlos about the finds that had been made at Knossos and asking to be taken the following weekend to see the site for himself.

The ringing of the church bells woke Yannis early the following morning and he remembered his promise to his mother to attend services. His hand hesitated on the silver charm. Should he take it off? He decided to leave it and buttoned his shirt so that it would not show. Unlocking the taverna door he crept out quietly and made his way to the main road.

The church was not difficult to find, but after the tiny church in Plaka where he had worshipped and the larger one in Aghios Nikolaos this one was enormous. Over-awed Yannis took a seat at the very back. He concentrated little on the service and spent the time gazing around. He had never seen such magnificence in his life. He bought two candles from the blind man who was sitting on the steps and lit them both to the Virgin Mary before placing his lips reverently on her picture and kneeling to pray. Finally he rose and once outside took deep breaths of the fresh air to clear his head after the smell of incense.

He walked past the museum, and, as he had expected, it was closed. He sat on the harbour wall and watched the fishermen unloading their catch, before he strolled out to the Venetian fort, walking as far as he could around each landward side and wished he could go inside the massive, barred entrance to look at the interior. He wondered idly if the one on Spinalonga was as large and if that was where the lepers made their home.

That evening the taverna seemed to be quite busy when Yannis finally dragged himself away from his books and went down for a meal. Louisa smiled briefly at him as he entered.

'The hermit has come to honour us with his presence,' she announced.

Yannis flushed and slid into an empty chair between Pavlos and Yiorgo. He tried to follow the conversation, finally asking Mr Pavlakis what he was talking about. The teacher explained he was discussing the foreign policy of Greece, but Yannis was none the wiser. He wondered if he could introduce himself to the young men who were laughing and joking together and if they would accept his company. One of them looked his way and he smiled tentatively, risking a rebuff he walked over to their table.

'Hello. May I join you?'

'Certainly. I'm Costas. This is Dimitris and this is Nicolas.' The young man waved his hands.

Yannis shook hands with each of them. 'I'm Yannis. I've only just come to Heraklion.'

'Are you looking for work?'

'No, I've come to study at the High School.'

Nicolas rolled his eyes. 'You are looking for work, then! What are you studying?'

'Classical Greek and History.'

Nicolas whistled. 'Rather you than me.'

'There's nothing wrong with that.' The boy who had been introduced as Dimitris came to Yannis's defence.

Nicolas shrugged. 'Just because you enjoy studying.'

Yannis turned to him with interest. 'Are you at the High School?'

Dimitris nodded. 'I'm studying mathematics. I want to go into banking.'

'Will you have to go to University?'

'Oh, no, once I've finished at High School I can start work.'

'His Pappa happens to be the manager of the local bank,' put in Costas with a grin. 'What does your Pappa do?'

'He's a farmer.'

There was an imperceptible silence. 'I thought he would be a teacher,' Costas tried to cover their lapse of etiquette.

'Whatever gave you that idea?'

Costas shrugged. 'I don't know. The subjects you're taking, I suppose. Didn't you want to be a farmer?'

'No. I waste too much time looking for things in the fields. I'd never get any work done.'

'What things?' Three pairs of eyes looked at Yannis curiously.

'Pottery, mostly, but I've also found a bottle and a coin.'

'What kind of pottery?' Dimitris was genuinely interested.

Yannis began an enthusiastic description of the different types of pottery he had found in his father's fields. They listened for a while; then he sensed they were bored. 'Tell me about yourselves,' he said, by way of changing the subject. 'I seem to have been monopolising the conversation.'

'You know about me. I'm studying mathematics, my Pappa is a banker and I also plan to be a banker.' Dimitris signalled to Louisa to bring some more wine.

Costas took up the conversation. 'Nicos is going to be a doctor. He's the clever one, and I'm nothing.'

'You can't be nothing.'

Costas yawned and stretched his hands above his head. 'I can. I'm not very good at anything. I don't know what to do with myself, so my Pappa said I'd have to go to High School for a couple of years to make up my mind.'

'What does your Pappa do?'

Costas grinned. 'Nothing.'

'Nothing!' Yannis could hardly believe his ears. 'He must do something.'

'No, he has no need. He won a lot of money on the lottery.'

'You're joking!'

'I'm telling the truth, aren't I?'

Dimitris and Nicolas nodded. 'Incredible though it might seem, this layabout will always have more money than the three of us put together, however hard we work,' remarked Dimitris. 'He's trying terribly hard to spend it.'

Yannis looked at the three young men. He found them interesting and amusing. 'Could I meet you on Monday before school? So we could go in together? I'm terribly nervous.'

'There's no point in going in on Monday. I'm not bothering.' Costas refilled their glasses.

'You have to go in on Monday. That's when the term starts.'

'That's when they say it starts. That's to get everyone there to take their names and addresses, give them some books and tell them to be good and work hard. They have my name and address, I can collect the books on Tuesday, and I have no intention of being good and working hard.' Costas looked at the others, daring them to challenge his decision.

'What will you do instead?' Yannis found his attitude hard to comprehend.

Costas rolled his eyes. 'What shall I be doing? I shall spend the day with the most beautiful girl you have ever seen.'

Nicolas and Dimitris exchanged glances. 'Take no notice of him, Yannis. Every week he has a beautiful girl who he's in love with, by the end of the week he's met someone more beautiful.'

'This time it's different,' insisted Costas. 'This is the only girl in the world for me.'

'Last week Elena was.'

'And before that it was Maria.'

'They were nothing,' Costas waved his hands airily. 'Now I've met Penelope I'll never love anyone else.'

Dimitris winked at Yannis. 'Ignore him. Have you got a girl?'

Yannis nodded. 'I'm betrothed to my cousin. She's going to be a nurse.'

'Is she beautiful?' asked Costas.

'Probably not by your standards,' smiled Yannis.

The boys continued to talk, continually refilling their glasses, until Yannis realised he had drunk far more than usual and hoped he would not regret it in the morning. Twice he tried to leave them, only to be drawn back into the conversation, until at last he spoke firmly.

'I've really enjoyed this evening, but for me it has to end now. I'll meet you at school, on the steps at seven thirty.' He placed some coins on the table. 'For my share of the wine.'

Costas shook his head. 'I'm paying tonight. Save it for next time. We take it in turns to foot the bill.'

Yannis turned to Dimitris and Nicolas, both of them nodded in confirmation.

The morning came too soon and it was with great reluctance that

YANNIS

Yannis dragged himself from his bed when Louisa knocked with hot water for him. He groaned. He had been foolish to drink so much. By the time he had drunk three cups of sweet black coffee he felt a little better, managing to finish the roll he had been toying with. Mr Pavlakis appeared none the worse, although Yannis knew he had stayed in the taverna drinking long after him. Together they walked to the main road where Yiorgo stopped.

'You know your way from here, don't you? Have a good day. I'll see you this evening.' With a wave of his hand he was gone and Yannis suddenly felt very much alone. He hoped his friends of the night before would be on the steps to meet him as they had promised.

As he drew closer to the school he could see more young men hurrying in the same direction. Outside the building were little groups, chatting animatedly, all appearing to know each other. Yannis hesitated uncertainly at the foot of the steps whilst others jostled past him. He jumped with surprise when a hand clapped him on the back.

'You've arrived first. We'll give Dimitris a few minutes; then go in.' The friendly grin on Nicolas's face restored Yannis's confidence.

'I'm glad you're here. There seem to be an awful lot of us.'

'Three hundred, I expect. That's the usual number. There's Dimitris.' Nicolas began to wave wildly above Yannis's head and Dimitris pushed his way to their side.

Once inside the building the scene that met Yannis's eyes was one of total confusion. There were three men seated at desks taking down details from each student. The first took their names and addresses, confirming they were on the list for that term, the second checked the details of their course and handed out a book list, the third gave them a ticket for the library, the name of their tutor and the room number where they would find him.

'What do I do now?'

'Follow us.'

Dimitris and Nicolas began to elbow their way through the throng of students until they reached a wide staircase. Once there they compared lists and looked on each door for their room numbers. Dimitris and Nicolas quickly found theirs and decided Yannis must be on the floor above. The upper floor was a replica of the one below and Yannis found his room at the far end. The top floor housed the library and it was there that the three boys found a long queue.

'Maybe Costas was right not to come today,' murmured Nicolas. 'I'll give it an hour, then I'm off to the nearest taverna.'

Despite the queue their wait was well under an hour, by which time they were bowed down by the weight of books, all of which had to be signed for and they were told the penalty for loss or damage was the cost of a replacement and a fine for carelessness.

'Let's dump these and go to a taverna,' suggested Nicolas. 'Meet you down on the steps.'

They clattered their way down the stone staircase, leaving Yannis to go to his room. Timidly he pushed the door open with his foot and then stood hesitantly in the doorway. He cleared his throat.

'Excuse me, may I sit anywhere?'

The grey haired man who had been reading scrutinized the youth. 'What's your name?'

'Yannis Christoforakis.'

A well-manicured finger ran its way down a list of names. The man looked at Yannis with renewed interest. 'Scholarship, I see. Well done. Sit where you please. You're first, so the choice can be yours.'

Yannis walked to the centre desk in the middle row. 'Will my books be safe if I leave them for a short while?'

'I should think so. Write your name on this paper and leave it on the top. Where are you off to?'

'I've arranged to meet my friends for coffee. That is allowed, isn't it?'

YANNIS

'I shall start the class in three quarters of an hour.'
'I'll be back,' promised Yannis.

Arm in arm the trio made their way to the nearest taverna and ordered coffee and baklava. Nicolas rolled a cigarette and offered it to Yannis. For a moment Yannis hesitated, then accepted. He did not want to lose face in front of these new friends by admitting that he did not smoke. He drew on it slowly and exhaled a cloud of smoke, which stung his eyes.

'I didn't know you smoked, Nicos.'

Dimitris laughed. 'He's been practising. He started this morning.'

Nicolas looked at his cigarette. 'I quite like it, provided I don't swallow too much smoke and start to choke.'

Yannis drew on his again, this time allowing the smoke to trickle down his throat, enjoying the acrid taste. He began to cough. He tried to draw breath, but his cough increased, his eyes began to stream with tears. He gulped a mouthful of water and to his relief the coughing subsided. 'I see what you mean.' He drew again tentatively, this time exhaling some of the smoke and managing not to cough.

The day passed uneventfully for Yannis, reading passages from the Iliad and discussing them, each being encouraged to give their own interpretation of the text. At four o'clock a bell was heard and the tutor looked up in surprise.

'Is it lunch time?'

'No, sir, it's the end of lessons for today.'

The tutor frowned and took a timepiece from his pocket, holding it to his ear and checking it was still working. Finally convinced he turned to the class.

'Very well, homework. You are to read the first book of the 'Iliad' and make a character study of Telemachus. I only want the information you gather from the first book, don't go on further. You will then read it tomorrow in the first lesson and we shall discuss the points each of you have found out and see if we are all in agreement. If we are not that will lead to further discussion and it will be up to the pupil to convince the class that he has discovered something the others have missed, or change their opinion. There could be some interesting results.' The beady brown eyes flickered over the class, resting momentarily on each pupil. 'You may go now.'

Yannis gathered his books under his arm and made for the door.

'What's your rush?' asked Vassilis who sat next to Yannis.

'I want to get to the museum and see if they're still open.'

'I didn't think much of it when I visited. Have you been to Knossos?'

'Not yet; I'm hoping to go next weekend.'

'Hope you enjoy it. 'Bye. See you tomorrow.' With a wave of his hand Vassilis shot down a side road whilst Yannis hurried towards the museum.

On reaching the museum he found the elderly man was sitting in a chair by the door, a newspaper in his hand. He completely ignored Yannis as he entered.

'Excuse me.'

The old man raised his eyes reluctantly. 'Yes?'

'Who is in charge here?'

'Mr Kouvakis.'

'May I see him, please?'

'Why?'

'I have something to show him.'

The attendant rose stiffly from his seat and shuffled across the hall. 'Follow me.'

A narrow passage marked "private" led off the hall to a number of rooms. The third door along bore the name "P. Kouvakis" and the old man knocked gently.

'Come in.' The voice sounded weary. A bald headed man with gold-rimmed spectacles looked up. 'Can I help you?' He waved his hand and the door closed quietly, leaving Yannis alone with the curator. He placed his fingertips together and looked at the boy. 'Yes?'

'I am Yannis Christoforakis. May I sit down?'

Mr Kouvakis indicated the chair. 'What can I do for you?'

Yannis cleared his throat. 'I come from the village of Plaka. My father is a farmer. We were digging in one of the fields and I found some pottery and a coin. I've looked them up in a book I borrowed from the library and I believe the coin is a tetradrachm, which would date the pottery I found to the Classical era.'

Mr Kouvakis raised his eyebrows. 'Really. Illustrations in books can be very misleading, you know.'

'Would you look at the coin for me, please.'

With a sigh Mr Kouvakis stretched out his hand for the coin. 'I know very little about coins.'

'You are the curator.'

For the first time Mr Kouvakis smiled. 'I am an administrator. My interest is in sculpture.'

'I see. That explains why the cases are in such a bad state.'

'What do you mean?' A red flush spread up from the man's neck until it reached his bald head.

'The pottery is all jumbled up together and you can't read the notices on the cases. It all needs sorting out.'

Mr Kouvakis glared at Yannis. 'What do you know about Minoan pottery?'

Yannis flushed. 'Not very much. I've read a number of books on the subject. It would be much easier and more interesting for visitors if the pottery were grouped into different types, although originating from one site and of the same period. Also, if the labels were re-written, so many of them are dusty or faded that it's impossible to read them.'

'I have no one who could undertake that kind of work.'

The germ of an idea was forming in Yannis's head. He was amazed at his own audacity. 'I'd be willing to work on it. To sort it out and make new displays and labels.'

'Why should you want to do that?'

'I've collected bits and pieces from my father's fields since I was a small boy. I've gained a scholarship to the High School and I want to go to University. I hope one day I might be an archaeologist.'

Mr Kouvakis looked at the boy before him with renewed interest. 'Let me see your coin.'

The curator examined the coin carefully under a magnifying glass. He reached for a book from the shelf, flipping through the pages. Finally he looked at Yannis.

'You seem to be correct in your dating, young man.'

A broad grin spread across Yannis's face. 'That's wonderful. I wish I'd brought my pottery with me. Maybe I could bring it tomorrow?'

Mr Kouvakis nodded. 'I'd be interested to see it. Where did you say you found it?'

'In my father's field at Plaka.'

Mr Kouvakis looked at the map on the wall. 'It's quite possible there was a small settlement there. Probably working the salt mines at Olous.'

Yannis shook his head. 'I disagree. I think the mineworkers would have lived in and around the city that fell into the sea. Anyone living at Plaka would have been a farmer or fisherman.'

Mr Kouvakis raised his eyebrows and looked again at the map. 'You could be right,' he admitted grudgingly. The boy was obviously intelligent. 'Maybe you could try your hand at sorting out the pottery, on a trial basis.'

Yannis held out his hand. 'You don't understand how much this means to me.'

'I can't offer you much in the way of wages.'

'Wages!' Yannis gasped. 'I had no idea I'd get any money for doing it. I can only work at weekends and after school.'

'Hmm. Well, we'll see.' Mr Kouvakis was annoyed with himself for mentioning money. He had not expected the young man to offer his services for nothing.

'May I stay until you close today? I'd like to have another look at the cases and decide where I should start tomorrow.'

Mr Kouvakis smiled at Yannis's enthusiasm. 'By all means, I have work of my own I should attend to.'

Yannis became engrossed in the pottery displayed in the cases. The more he looked the more errors he noticed. He was disturbed by an apologetic cough and turned to see Mr Kouvakis.

'I have to close now and I'm sure you must have some homework. I must not be blamed for interfering with your studies.'

Yannis almost ran back to the taverna, longing to tell Mr Pavlakis his news. He found him sitting with Louisa, talking to her earnestly. They both jumped as he burst through the door, his eyes shining with delight.

'What's wrong?' Yiorgo was half out of his chair.

'Nothing's wrong. I've got a job.'

'You've what?'

Yannis sat down at the table with them. 'I have a job at the museum. I'm going to sort out the pottery and I'm going to get paid for doing so.'

'I don't believe it,' murmured Yiorgo Pavlakis. 'What about your studies?'

'Oh, it's only after school and at weekends,' Yannis assured him. 'I shan't let it interfere with my school work.'

Each day after his classes Yannis hurried to the museum. He never seemed to have enough time there and was frustrated each night when Mr Kouvakis told him it was time to leave. Yiorgo showed an interest each evening, but Yannis had an idea that he was more concerned that he was not neglecting his studies. When he entered the taverna that evening it looked deserted, but the smell from the kitchen told him Louisa had been busy.

She greeted him with a smile. 'Good day at school and the museum?' she asked.

'Fine. I've got a lot of homework tonight, though.'

'That's a pity. Pavlos and Yiorgo are out and I was hoping for some company.'

'Oh? Where've they gone?'

Louisa shrugged. 'To a political meeting at the Town Hall.' Louisa sat on the edge of the table, exposing her legs almost to the knee. 'I thought maybe we could get to know each other better,' she suggested.

Yannis was embarrassed by the amount of Louisa's leg he could see, but maybe the behaviour of women in Heraklion was different from the countrywomen. 'We could sit and talk whilst I eat,' he suggested.

Louisa flashed her smile at him again. 'I have stuffed tomatoes ready. I haven't eaten yet myself, so I'll join you.' She disappeared into the kitchen, returning almost immediately with a bottle of wine. 'They won't hurt for another five minutes. We'll have a drink first.' She poured the wine and held her glass up in salutation. 'To your long and happy stay in Heraklion.' Louisa leaned across the table towards him. 'Tell me what you've been doing at the museum.'

'Can we eat whilst I tell you? I'm terribly hungry.'

'Of course.' Louisa went to the kitchen and returned with two steaming plates. 'I hope you like them. It's my own recipe.'

Yannis ate hungrily and agreed the tomatoes were delicious. In between mouthfuls he told her about the pottery he had listed. Louisa poured more wine into Yannis's glass and he held up his hand in protest. 'Please, Louisa, I have to do my homework. I'd love to stay and talk to you, but I can't. Maybe a customer will come in and you can chat to them.'

'I'm not expecting any customers tonight. They'll have gone to the meeting.' Louisa looked morosely into her glass. 'I suppose you wouldn't look after the taverna for me, Yannis?'

'Me?' Yannis was most surprised.

'I really should go to visit an old friend of my father's. This would be an ideal opportunity. You could bring your homework down here and I should be back before you've finished.'

'Suppose a customer comes?'

'Just give them whatever drink they ask for. If they want any food tell them the cook isn't here tonight. I doubt that anyone will come, though.'

Yannis agreed doubtfully and to his embarrassment Louisa squeezed his hand.

'You are a kind boy, Yannis.' She whisked away from the table and Yannis heard her hurrying upstairs, in a few moments she had returned, a shawl about her shoulders and her hair freshly brushed. 'I shan't be very long.' She smiled and blew a kiss to Yannis from the doorway. 'Be good.'

Yannis grinned. He was relieved she had decided to go out. He had a suspicion that she planned to chat to him all evening. Thankfully he carried the plates to the kitchen, washed them in the bowl of murky water and returned to the table with his books. His homework took him a good deal longer than he had anticipated, although he was able to work without interruption. Finally, with a sigh, he closed the book and shuffled the papers together. He withdrew his notebook from his pocket and began to look at the notes he had made in the museum, making additional comments to some of them.

His thoughts were interrupted as the door of the taverna opened. A tall blond man stood there, his eyes roving round the room. 'Louisa?'

Yannis shook his head. 'Louisa has gone out. Can I help you?'

The man frowned. 'Louisa?' he repeated.

Yannis realised the man did not speak Greek. He pointed to the door. 'Louisa out.'

Without another word the man left, slamming the door behind him. Yannis dismissed him from his mind and bent his head back over his notes. It was another hour before Louisa returned.

'I'm so pleased I went. He said a visit from me had made all the difference to him. Did we have any customers?'

Yannis shook his head. 'I've finished all my work.'

'Good.' Louisa produced the bottle of wine and glasses again. 'You have time to sit and chat now.'

Yannis hesitated. 'I'd planned to go to bed as soon as you returned.'

'Five minutes won't make any difference.' She poured a glass of wine and handed it to him. She sat opposite and gazed at him over her glass. 'Tell me about Yiorgo Pavlakis.'

Yannis looked at her in surprise. 'I don't know anything about him.'

'Don't be silly. You're his friend. You must know him.'

Yannis smiled at her. 'Yiorgo and I are friends now, until July he was my schoolteacher. He's been very good to me. I doubt I would have passed my exams without his help, but I don't know anything about him.'

Louisa shook her head. 'You're just not thinking along the right lines. What is he like as a person?'

Taking a sip from his glass Yannis considered his answer carefully. 'Well, I know he's always worked hard. He used to work in a taverna in the evenings so he could save enough money to visit Europe. He's been to a number of countries, to visit the historical sites and museums.'

Louisa nodded and refilled their glasses. 'Go on.'

'He's very interested in politics, not just in Crete, but in the whole of Greece, in fact he has a worldwide interest. Comparing the system of government in other countries with our own. He loves to talk about his ideas for a better society. I don't understand all he talks about, but the men in Aghios Nikolaos used to listen to him when he spoke and seemed to agree with him. What else do you want to know?'

Louisa finished her glass of wine. 'Has he any family?'

Yannis shook his head. 'I don't think so. He told me his parents were dead and I've never heard him mention any other relatives. Why?'

YANNIS

Louisa smiled. 'Yiorgo has asked me to marry him. I would look very foolish if I agreed and he was already married.'

Yannis threw back his head and laughed. 'I can assure you that Yiorgo has no wife in Aghios Nikolaos. I've never seen him with a woman. I don't think he knew they existed before he met you. Are you going to marry him?'

Louisa ignored his question. She rose and took the glasses over to the counter. 'I thought you wanted to go to bed?'

Yannis felt he had been dismissed. He gathered his books and bade the beautiful girl goodnight. He was half way up the stairs when he remembered the man who had called for her. Returning he opened the door of the taverna in time to see Louisa pushing a bundle of notes into the box which served as a till.

'Have you forgotten something?'

'A young man came looking for you. I told him you were out.'

'Did he say what he wanted?' asked Louisa sharply.

'No. He didn't appear to speak Greek. Good night again.'

Yannis withdrew from the door and made his way to his room. He felt uncomfortable. There was something very disconcerting about Louisa. He heard the sound of voices below and guessed Pavlos and Yiorgo had returned from their meeting. His first instinct was to go down and join them; then he changed his mind, undressed quickly, extinguished the oil lamp and climbed into bed. Sleep evaded him; the noise that floated up from the taverna announced more arrivals. Yannis buried his head under the blanket, trying to muffle the sound of talk and laughter. Gradually exhaustion took over and he fell into a deep sleep.

Through long habit Yannis woke as dawn broke. For a short while he lay in his bed until doubts about the quality of his homework assailed him and he decided to read it through and check that he had assembled his facts correctly. By the light of day it did not seem as lucid as it had the night before. With a sigh Yannis put it to one side. It must have been the wine he had been drinking, but it would have to do. There was no time to re-write it.

Louisa set his breakfast before him. She looked tired and strained and Yannis guessed she had been kept busy after he had retired to bed. Yiorgo was full of enthusiasm for the meeting he had attended and began to relate the context to Yannis.

'Tonight some of the speakers are coming here again, we want to continue our discussion. I hope we didn't disturb you last night. Louisa said you were tired and had gone to bed. Your lamp was out or I would have asked you to join us.'

Yannis shook his head. 'You didn't disturb me. I heard you arrive, but I soon slept. I must go. I want to compare notes with some of my class.'

Yannis hurried to the High School, hoping he would have a chance to visit the library before his tutor arrived. The point he had wished to check had not been covered in the books he had at the taverna. He ran up the stone steps two at a time until he reached the top floor where the library was situated. The door was shut and locked. He waited patiently, hoping the librarian would arrive before the bell for the commencement of lessons rang.

He was unlucky. Mr Angelakis, his tutor turned the corner towards the classroom at the same moment as the bell rang. Yannis raced for the stairs. Somehow his feet went from under him and he bounced and rolled down the full flight, banging his head and cutting his face against the iron railing. He lay in a crumpled heap causing alarm and consternation amongst both his classmates and Mr Angelakis.

Vassilis knelt by his side, his face white. 'Yannis, Yannis! Can you speak?'

Yannis groaned, and Mr Angelakis let out a sigh of relief. The boy was alive.

'Can you hear me? Yannis, try to sit up.'

His head throbbing Yannis raised himself on one elbow and with the help of Vassilis struggled into a sitting position. The cut on the side of his head was pouring blood and Vassilis pulled his own shirt from over his head and tried to staunch the flow.

'I'm all right,' he muttered.

'No, you're not. You sit still. Don't try to get up until we've stopped this bleeding. Do your legs hurt? What about your arms? Can you move them or have you broken something?'

Cautiously Yannis flexed his arms and legs. 'It's just my head. Can I get up now?'

Vassilis removed his stained shirt from the side of Yannis head and was relieved to see the blood was reduced to a trickle. 'Sit up on the stairs and I'll make you a bandage. You'll have to go to the doctor and have a stitch.'

Obediently Yannis sat whilst Vassilis proceeded to rip the arms out of his shirt. Folding one to make a pad he pressed it firmly against the wound and wound the other around Yannis's head, tying it in a knot above his ear.

Mr Angelakis looked on uncomfortably. 'I suggest you escort Yannis to the nearest doctor, Vassilis; then go home for a new shirt. You are excused lessons this morning. The rest of you into the classroom.' He picked up the books and papers that were scattered around Yannis and strode after his pupils.

'I'm sorry, Vassilis.'

'There's nothing to be sorry about. Thank goodness you've no more than a few cuts and bruises. Do you think you can walk?'

Yannis nodded and decided not to do that again in a hurry. His head felt as if it would split in two and stars flashed before his eyes making him feel sick. He took a deep breath and steadied himself. With one hand on the banister rail and the other on Vassilis's shoulder he stood, trying not to sway, and became aware of the pains in his legs.

'I'll have to take it slowly.'

'There's no rush. I have the morning off, remember.' Vassilis looked at the makeshift bandage. Already the blood was beginning to seep through and he longed to get Yannis to a doctor as quickly as possible.

Their progress was slow, Yannis was badly bruised and he could tell by the pain that his ankle and knee were damaged. Every step made his head hurt more and Vassilis refused to let him rest. It seemed an age to him before they stopped before a shabby door with a red cross painted above to denote a doctor's residence. Vassilis pushed Yannis into an empty seat and called loudly, making Yannis wince with pain.

Annoyed, the doctor emerged from his inner room. 'What's all the noise about? I have patients who are sick.'

'This is an emergency. My friend has had a bad fall down a flight of stone steps. He hit his head and it needs stitching.'

The doctor looked from the young man who wore only his trousers to the other who was fully dressed but covered in blood. 'You'd better bring him in.'

The doctor removed the makeshift bandage and peered at the gash on Yannis's head. 'A few stitches needed there.' He swabbed at the wound and the blood began to flow again. Deftly he threaded a needle and rubbed Yannis's face with alcohol before inserting six large stitches from the hairline to just above the ear. He surveyed his handiwork and nodded.

'Now, young man, having dealt with that, where else are you hurt?'

'I'm not sure. My head feels terrible and my knee and ankle hurt.'

With experienced hands the doctor felt Yannis's knees and ankles, his spine and his ribs. Sometimes Yannis gave a gasp of pain and the doctor would feel again. Finally he straightened up, satisfied.

'You're very badly bruised. As far as I can tell there's nothing broken. Where were you going when you had your fall?'

'I was at school. I fell down the steps from the library.'

'I'm sure they'll understand if you don't return for a day or two. I want you to go home and take it very quietly. Keep moving around or you'll stiffen up. An hours rest for every ten minutes of exercise is the prescription, then a good night's sleep. You'll probably feel worse tomorrow, the bruising will come out fully. If you have any acute pain come back to me. I'll check you over again next week when you come back to have those stitches out.'

'Thank you.' Yannis rose to his feet unsteadily and the doctor cleared his throat.

'My bill,' he reminded them.

'I'll see to that,' Vassilis said swiftly. 'You can sort it out with me later, Yannis.'

Half carrying his friend along the road they made slow progress to the taverna. As they entered Louisa looked up with a smile, which turned to a frown of annoyance. 'What's happened to you?'

'Yannis fell down the stairs at school. He's cut his head,' explained Vassilis. 'I went to the doctor with him and he's had some stitches put in. The doctor says he must rest for a couple of days.'

'I'm not a nurse,' she declared.

'He doesn't need nursing,' Vassilis assured her. 'I'll help him up to his room and come back for some water for him to have a wash. I could do with one myself.' He looked down at his blood stained hands and trousers.

Once upstairs Yannis began to cry. 'I'm sorry Vassilis, so sorry. Your shirt and trousers are ruined.'

Vassilis sat beside him on the bed and placed an arm around his shoulders. 'Come on, now. You're in shock. Have a good cry, then I'll go and get that water and we'll both have a wash. You'll feel better then. You don't need to worry about my clothes, they were old ones.'

'My head hurts so much.'

'I'm sure it does. Let's get that dirty shirt off you and I'll go and get some water.'

There was no sign of Louisa when Vassilis returned to the kitchen. He drew a jug of water and helped himself to a glass from the shelf. As he returned to Yannis he heard movement from behind one of the doors.

'I'm just going to help Yannis have a wash, then I'll be going,' he called. There was no reply from behind the closed door and Vassilis shrugged. Louisa could have answered him, she must have heard.

Vassilis cleaned Yannis's hands and face; then removed his boots, swinging his legs up onto the bed. 'I've left you a glass of water, and there's some more in the jug. If you decide to go downstairs, make sure you don't fall. You don't want to add to your bruises! Do as the doctor told you and I'll call in after school to see how you're feeling.'

'Thanks for everything, Vassilis.' Yannis was already half asleep as his friend left the room.

Yannis awoke some two hours later, his mouth dry and his body racked with pain. He sat up and waited for the room to stop spinning before he dared place his feet on the ground. He sipped at the water, and then decided he would experiment with walking. He winced with pain each time he placed any weight on his left foot and he could feel that his knee was swollen through his trousers. He looked at his torso as best he could in the small square of mirror he used for shaving and was horrified at the purple wheals on his back. He remembered the doctor's advice and walked across the room twice more before lying back on his bed.

He heard Louisa laughing, a deep, throaty laugh and someone laughed back before a door closed quietly. Idly he wondered who it was; then drifted back to sleep. The next time he woke his head felt a little better and he decided a trip to the yard was necessary. He bent to pull on his boots, but changed his mind as the pain in his head increased. Very carefully he made his way down the stairs and out to the yard, shielding his eyes against the glare of the sun. Despite the doctor's advice of ten minutes exercise every hour he stood by the wall, letting the sun fall on his back, warming his damaged muscles, for a full five minutes before attempting to return to his room.

He took the stairs slowly, and half way up the door of Louisa's room opened and a young man emerged. He looked surprised to see Yannis, and nodded briefly to him as he passed him on his way down to the taverna. Louisa slammed her door furiously as Yannis came into view, the noise making him groan in pain.

By late afternoon Yannis decided he was well enough to go down to the taverna. It was true; his body was beginning to stiffen up. He would go for a walk along the road and back and see how he felt then. Louisa sat in the taverna stitching a blouse. She scowled as Yannis entered.

'I'm just going for a walk, Louisa. The doctor said I should exercise to stop myself stiffening. I won't be long.'

Louisa nodded and bent her head back to her embroidery. She hoped Yannis was not going to become a problem.

When Yiorgo arrived back at the taverna he was shocked by Yannis's appearance and insisted on being reassured time and again that the boy was not badly hurt. 'You could have broken your neck!' he exclaimed.

'I could have done, but I haven't. The worst thing was the blood from the cut on my head. I'm just bruised. It will soon wear off. Vassilis was so capable. He said he would call in tonight to see how I am.'

Vassilis was not the only caller. To his surprise Mr Angelakis accompanied his friend and was as relieved as Yiorgo to find that Yannis was not seriously hurt. He placed Yannis's books on the table and handed his essay to him.

'I'd completely forgotten about my books,' admitted Yannis. 'Thank you for retrieving them. I hope they're not damaged.'

'I've had a word with the librarian and in this instance he's prepared to overlook any minor damage. There's only one you'll need to pay for. The spine is broken and some of the pages are blood-stained.'

'Thank you, sir. I'll see the librarian tomorrow.'

'You will not!' Mr Angelakis spoke vehemently. 'You must stay away from school until the doctor says you're fit enough to return.'

Yannis was about to protest, but both Yiorgo and Vassilis agreed with Mr Angelakis, insisting Yannis stayed home for at least another day. Yiorgo called for a bottle of wine and was soon deep in conversation with Mr Angelakis. Vassilis winked at Yannis.

'I suggest we leave them to it. I'll have a quick drink with you, and then I shall be off. I'm sure you shouldn't be over-tired.'

'I'm not an invalid,' grumbled Yannis. 'I'd like to ask you another favour, though. I usually meet friends from some other classes at lunchtime and they'll wonder what has happened to me. Could you give them a message, please?'

'If they were in school today they know what's happened to you. The whole school does! The library was put out of bounds whilst the stairs were cleaned and the Principal went round to every class reminding us that we shouldn't run up and down them.'

Yannis smiled sheepishly. 'I do feel stupid. Fancy falling down the stairs!'

He spent a further half an hour down in the taverna; then decided to return to his room and write to Annita. He found it hard to concentrate on the letter and it was with relief that he heard a tap at his door and Costas walked in, a bottle and glass in his hand.

'Do you mind?' He settled himself on the end of Yannis's bed. 'We missed you at lunchtime.'

'My scintillating wit and brilliant conversation I dare say.'

'Not exactly, more your serious thoughts and studious attitude. When are you coming back?'

'Mr Angelakis has told me to take tomorrow off. I'm sure I'll be fine by then, so I thought I might go into the museum for a while. To make up for missing today.'

Costas threw back his head and laughed. 'Are you sure you didn't fake your fall just so you could have some time off?'

Yannis smiled ruefully. 'I can assure you that after the way my head hurt I certainly wouldn't throw myself down a flight of stairs.'

'There was an awful lot of blood. You caused a terrible panic.'

'Did I? I was too concerned with trying to walk to notice. It was lucky for me that Vassilis was there. He knew just what to do. He took me to the doctor and then brought me back here.'

'He certainly deserves a drink.'

'He's already had one. He called tonight to see how I was and brought Mr Angelakis with him.'

'I wondered how he came to be here. He's downstairs talking to Yiorgo.' Costas poured another glass of wine, but Yannis shook his head.

'I've had two already. I don't want to wake up with a worse headache.'

'Now tell me,' Costas leaned towards Yannis and lowered his voice. 'How much does Louisa charge you? Do you have an inclusive rate?'

Yannis shrugged. 'I've no idea. Yiorgo sorted all that out with my father.'

Costas slapped his leg. 'What a father! Have you got unlimited credit?'

'I shouldn't think so. My food's included, but if I want a bottle of wine I pay for it.'

Costas choked on his wine. 'I don't believe you!'

'I'm telling the truth,' protested Yannis.

'You don't understand what I'm asking. The girl I have is nowhere near as good looking and she charges three drachmas an hour. I thought if Louisa charged the same I'd ask her when she's free.'

Yannis's face flamed. 'What are you suggesting, Costas?'

Costas looked at him, his turn now to be embarrassed. 'I'm sorry. I shouldn't have asked. I didn't realise you didn't know.'

'You're going to have to tell me now.'

Costas dropped his voice lower. 'I thought as you lived here you would have been told what else she did besides run the taverna and probably taken advantage, having her to hand, so to speak.'

'That can't be true. Yiorgo wants to marry her.'

Costas whistled. 'More fool him.'

Yannis shook his head. 'I've not noticed anything amiss.' As he said the words he recalled the blond stranger, the bundle of notes Louisa had pushed into the till, the laughter he had heard that morning and the man he had met on the stairs.

'I expect she does her business whilst you're at school.'

'You must be wrong, Costas.' Yannis spoke without conviction.

Costas drained his glass. 'I'll ask her on the way out. If you see me with a black eye tomorrow you'll know I was wrong. You'll be well enough for lunch, won't you?'

Yannis grinned at him. 'Sure to be – and I'll expect to see you with two black eyes.'

Costas grinned back. 'Don't bank on it, my friend.'

Yannis did not sleep well and laid the blame on the amount of sleep he'd had during the day. He lay in his bed long after he would normally have risen, luxuriating in the unaccustomed novelty. He heard Yiorgo and Pavlos leave, and Louisa moving around down in the taverna. He recalled his conversation with Costas the previous evening and thought about Louisa. His thoughts produced a most disconcerting effect and he realised the wisdom of his father's words. Maybe Costas would give him the name of the girl he visited.

He was about to rise from his bed when the twinges in his muscles reminded him of his fall. He was not as stiff as he thought he would be and his headache had completely disappeared. He looked at the dark growth on his chin, but decided against shaving as he might wet the bandage. The last thing he wanted was to make his head bleed again. Maybe he could grow a beard.

Yannis dressed slowly. There was no immediate rush to get to the museum. He went down to the taverna and made himself a cup of coffee, lingering over it whilst he smoked a cigarette. Louisa ignored him as she washed spilt wine from the tables and emptied the ashtrays.

'I'm going to the museum, Louisa, and then I'll meet my friends for lunch. I don't know what time I'll be back.'

'As you please.' She retired into the kitchen and Yannis gazed after her speculatively until he realized that once again she was having an embarrassing effect on him.

'I must do something about this,' he thought. 'I really will have to speak to Costas.'

Mr Kouvakis expressed horror at the bandage on Yannis's head. 'I fell down the stairs at school,' he explained.

'Are you sure you're fit enough to be here?'

'I'm fine. I have to go back to the doctor next week to have the stitches out. I would have gone into school, but my tutor insisted I had the day off.'

Mr Kouvakis nodded. 'As you wish, but don't do too much. As soon as you feel tired you must go home and rest.'

Yannis agreed, wishing to get away from him and continue with his listing. He walked into the first room and felt in his pocket for his notebook. With an exclamation of annoyance he realised he had left it in his room.

He hurried as fast as his aching limbs would let him back to the taverna. There was no sign of Louisa, but when he reached his room he could hear a man's voice from behind her closed door. He had an idea that Costas would not be sporting a black eye when he met him at lunchtime.

Yannis found his work in the museum soothing, taking his mind off Louisa completely. He was surprised when Mr Kouvakis came in and asked if he would care to join him for lunch, but hastily made his apologies and set off for the taverna to meet his friends. Dimitris and Nicolas were waiting for him, wanting to know all the details of his fall the previous day and how he was feeling now. Yannis answered their questions and looked around for Costas.

'He came to see me last night and we arranged to meet for lunch. Where do you think he is?'

'I didn't see him this morning at break,' frowned Nicolas. 'Maybe he decided to take the day off. You know what he's like.'

'He's coming now,' said Dimitris, and Costas could be seen hurrying towards them. Yannis studied his face with interest. He had no black eye.

Costas swung a chair out from the table and sat leaning across the back of it. He winked at Yannis and offered his cigarettes. 'So, what have all of you been up to this morning? Working your poor brains to death I don't doubt.'

'More to the point, what have you been up to? I didn't see you at break.'

'Because I wasn't there. I have had the most incredible morning with the most beautiful girl you have ever seen.' Costas winked again at Yannis.

Nicolas groaned. 'Not another one. I thought Penelope was the love of your life?'

'She is,' Costas assured them, 'but unfortunately she is always chaperoned. A little light relief is needed now and again.'

'Why don't you get married?' asked Dimitris.

'Married!' A look of horror crossed Costas's face. 'Why should I get married? Besides, I might marry someone and then find a girl more beautiful. What would I do then?'

The boys laughed at him, but Yannis was longing to speak to Costas alone. Finally Dimitris and Nicolas rose from the table.

'Are you coming, Costas?'

'Not much point coming in just for the afternoon. I'll see you tomorrow.'

YANNIS

Yannis offered his friend a cigarette. 'So?'

'So what?'

'Did you ask Louisa? You haven't got a black eye.'

'She charges three drachma an hour, the same as the other girls, but she's way above their class. She is pure heaven.'

'You don't mean it? You're just stringing me along.'

Costas crossed himself. 'I swear I am telling you the truth, Yannis. That girl is out of this world. I spent three hours with her this morning and the time flew by. I told her I'd be back next week, but I'm not sure if I can wait until tomorrow.'

'I still think you're kidding me,' said Yannis, although he was quite sure Costas was telling the truth.

'You can prove it for yourself. Just beneath her right shoulder blade she has three tiny moles, they form a triangle. Now how would I know that if I hadn't tried to kiss them off her back?'

'I'll think about it,' promised Yannis. 'I'm going back to the museum for a while – are you coming my way?'

Costas shook his head. 'No, I promised my mother I would call in at her dressmaker's. It's in the opposite direction. I'll see you tomorrow.'

Despite Yannis's intention of staying at the museum until closing time, by mid-way through the afternoon he was feeling incredibly tired and bade Mr Kouvakis goodbye. 'I'll be back tomorrow at my usual time.'

'Very wise; you mustn't overdo things, Yannis.

On his return to the taverna Yannis slept for two hours and awoke thinking it was morning and wondering why he was already fully dressed. Feeling foolish he splashed his face with cold water and went downstairs. Louisa, as always at that time of day, was sitting at her embroidery. She looked at him guardedly as he entered.

'I've had a lovely day,' he announced. 'I spent most of it at the museum. How about you?'

'The same as usual,' she answered. 'Are you feeling better?'

Yannis nodded. 'Considerably. I've slept for a couple of hours. I shall go into school tomorrow. Can I help myself?' She nodded and Yannis reached across her for a bottle of wine and a glass.

'No doubt you needed the rest.'

Once again Yannis felt she had dismissed him. He drank slowly, and was on the point of returning to his room when Yiorgo entered. Louisa folded her embroidery and stood leaning against the bar. A customer would often call in on their way home from work and it was as well to look prepared. Despite talking to Yannis and enquiring after his health, Yiorgo could not take his eyes from the girl. If only she would give him an answer.

Yannis returned to the doctor the following week to have the stitches from his head removed, a process he found far more painful than when they had been inserted.

'How are you feeling? You complained about your knee and ankle. Are they still giving you any trouble?'

'None at all,' Yannis assured him. 'I really was very lucky.'

'I'll just check you over quickly. Take off your shirt.'

Yannis did as he was asked and the doctor's hard fingers probed his back and ribs for any sign of damage. 'All seems well. Take a deep breath for me. Does that hurt?'

Yannis shook his head.

'Good. I was a bit concerned that you might have broken a rib. What's that?'

'A blocked gland. I had mumps,' explained Yannis.

The doctor pushed the boy's head to one side. 'Does it hurt?'

'Oh, no, not at all.'

The doctor picked up a needle from his desk and began to prick the lump and surrounding area.

'Ouch!' Yannis started involuntarily as the doctor pricked the skin at a point below his chin.

'Hmm.' The doctor stood back. 'How long ago did you have mumps?'

Yannis shrugged. 'It was when my brother was born,' he wrinkled his forehead. 'I must have been about nine.'

'And you've had it ever since?'

'I think so.'

'Has it grown any larger?'

'Just a little – as I've grown.'

'I'd like to take a little scrape of skin from it?'

'Why?'

'Just as a precaution, to make sure there's no infection there.' He picked up a scalpel and without waiting for Yannis's consent took a sliver of skin from the lump.

'What kind of infection?' Yannis's hand went involuntarily to the charm he wore.

'Any kind. You can put your shirt back on now.' He placed the sample safely inside an envelope and wrote Yannis's name in the left hand corner before putting it in his desk.

'When will I know the result of the test?'

'If there's any problem the hospital will write to you. My fee is five drachma, please.'

Yannis left the doctor and began to walk towards his school. Half way there he remembered what Costas had said about Louisa having three little moles. Did he dare go and ask her? He hesitated, standing in a doorway having a cigarette whilst he made up his mind. He rehearsed what he would say to her, and finally decided he would return to the taverna and see if she was alone.

As he walked in Louisa looked round the kitchen door. 'Oh, it's you.'

'Who were you expecting?'

Louisa shrugged. 'I thought you were a customer.'

'What kind of customer?'

Louisa frowned. 'What do you mean?'

'Some one has told me that you have three moles in the shape of a triangle just below your right shoulder blade.'

'Really?'

'I'd like to see them.'

'I'm sure you would. Shouldn't you be in school?'

'I've been to the doctor.'

Louisa looked at him speculatively, then without a word she led the way up the stairs. Yannis followed her to her room and closed the door behind them. Once inside Louisa untied the ribbon at the neck and slipped her blouse over her head before sitting down on her bed. Yannis gasped as her small, perfectly shaped breasts were exposed. She turned her back to him and he could clearly see the three small moles. He could understand why Costas had tried to kiss them from her back as he had an overwhelming desire to do the same. He ran his hand across them, as if to brush them away, then slipped it beneath her arm and cupped her breast in his hand. He felt quite dizzy with longing and turned her to face him, bending and kissing her breasts gently.

He felt Louisa's fingers undoing the buckle of his belt and the buttons on his trousers as he lifted her skirt to explore beneath. It seemed he had only tasted the delights her body had to offer for a few moments before the world exploded around him. He rolled his body off hers, damp with sweat from his efforts. She lay with her legs apart, looking up at him mockingly.

'Better now?'

Yannis nodded dumbly.

'It doesn't take much to satisfy some people,' she observed sarcastically as she picked up her blouse.

'No, let me look at you. You're so beautiful, Louisa.' Again he reached out his hand and began to fondle her breasts.

'You look ridiculous.'

Yannis looked down at himself and was forced to agree. His trousers were around his thighs; his shirt was damp and sticky around the tail. He stood up, removed his boots and allowed his trousers to fall to the floor, stepping out of them whilst he unbuttoned and discarded his shirt. Louisa gazed unashamedly at his nakedness.

'That's an improvement.'

He lay beside her, stroking her body, revelling in the soft silkiness of her skin. His hand slipped between her thighs and he kissed her again. 'Take your skirt right off. It gets in the way.'

Louisa did as he bade her. 'Satisfied?'

Yannis pressed his body against hers. 'No, but I intend to be.' He kissed and stroked her until he could contain himself no longer. Desperately he tried to delay the final exquisite joy.

'I must go,' she said finally, 'and you should be in school.'

Yannis watched as she replaced her clothes. 'How much do I owe you?'

'Ten drachmas.'

Yannis shook his head. 'I've heard that you charge three drachmas an hour.'

'You have to pay for experience.'

Yannis flushed. 'I'll pay this time, but in future I expect the going rate.'

Louisa raised her eyebrows, but all she said was 'Get dressed.'

'Why do you do it, Louisa?'

'To make money, of course.'

'You have the taverna.'

'The takings from the taverna would never have paid our debts after Mamma and Pappa died.'

'Don't you mind?'

Louisa shrugged. 'Mind? What is there to mind about?'

'What about Yiorgo? If you married him you wouldn't have to worry about money any more. He has a good job and you could keep the taverna running.'

'Yiorgo,' Louisa spoke his name scornfully. 'Why should I want to marry him?'

'He loves you, Louisa.'

'But I don't love him. Are you dressed?'

Yannis nodded. 'I'll just go and have a wash. I'll bring your money down with me.'

By the time Yannis reached school the bell had rung for lunch and he made his way to the taverna where he regularly met his friends. They examined his head, which clearly showed the marks of the stitches, but assured him they would soon fade.

'I suggest we have a little celebration tonight,' said Costas. 'Let's meet up and have a night on the town.'

'Could I ask Vassilis to join us?' asked Yannis. 'He was so good to me when I fell. I've replaced his shirt, but I'd like to buy him a drink.'

'Ask whoever you like. We'll meet at your taverna and go from there. Now, what time shall we say?'

On returning to his class Yannis asked Vassilis and Stavros to meet him that evening. Stavros was quite overcome to be asked and blushed and stammered his thanks.

'Why did you ask him?' asked Vassilis. 'I find him so difficult to talk to. He never seems able to get his words out.'

'I feel so sorry for him. I know he's terrible to listen to in class, it takes him half an hour to say yes or no to a question, but if you talk to him on your own he's fine. He just gets so embarrassed if he's the centre of attention.' Yannis defended the young man.

'Are you off to the museum after school?'

Yannis nodded. 'Why?'

'I thought you would probably need to stay behind and catch up on the work you missed this morning.'

Yannis flushed, feeling guilty that he had not returned directly to school from the doctor. 'I'll ask Mr Angelakis what he wants me to do. Hopefully he'll want to leave promptly.'

Mr Angelakis smiled at the eager boy. 'We spent most of the morning drawing a map. You'll need four copies of it by tomorrow morning; each one needs to be in a different colour to represent the different periods of history. I'd like you to be able to draw it from memory by the end of the week as we shall be using it most of the time this term.'

'Yes, sir.' Yannis's hope of spending an hour in the museum faded. It would take all his time before his friends arrived to make four satisfactory copies of the map. He had also planned to write to Annita and tell her his stitches had been removed that day. He sighed, wishing he had not asked his tutor.

The taverna was deserted when he arrived and he was deliberately noisy as he climbed the stairs to his room. Louisa's door was closed, but he had an idea she was not alone behind it and he wished it were he who was with her. Mentally shaking himself, he set about the task of reproducing the map, determined to put all thoughts of Louisa from his mind. He was surprised to find that after drawing three maps the fourth one was considerably easier and he attempted a copy from memory. He compared each one and re-drew the first one to his satisfaction before starting a letter to Annita.

Usually he found writing to Annita a pleasurable task, the words flowing smoothly onto the paper, but having told her he had been to the doctor and had his stitches removed he could think of nothing else to say. He wanted to tell her he loved her and missed her, but the words seemed false when they were written down. The vision of a slim, supple body, perfect in its proportions, three little moles and a cloud of black hair that smelt faintly of almonds, continually invaded his mind. He decided he would put the letter aside until the following day. Maybe he would have something more to tell her after his evening out.

Yiorgo was engrossed in his newspaper when Yannis went down to the taverna for a meal before his friends arrived, continuing to read whilst he ate the liver and tomatoes that Louisa put before them. Pavlos flung open the door and marched into the kitchen where a low, but obviously heated exchange, took place between brother and sister. He emerged, a pleased smile on his face and raised his hand to Yannis.

'Had a good day?'

Yannis, his mouth full, could only nod.

'Ah, Pavlos, I've just read something so interesting. Have a seat ....'

'Can't stop at the moment, Yiorgo. Tell me tomorrow.'

Yiorgo looked bemusedly at the closed door and shook his head. He folded his newspaper and placed it on his chair before taking his empty plate into the kitchen.

'Louisa, I want to talk to you. Have you come to a decision yet?'

'A decision?' Louisa was deliberately evasive.

'I asked you a question before I returned to Heraklion. I'm waiting for your answer,' replied Yiorgo patiently.

'Look at that!' Louisa slammed a tomato down on the table. 'How can I possibly put tomatoes like that in a salad? I'm taking them back.'

Yiorgo Pavlakis put out a restraining hand. 'Louisa.'

'Not now, Yiorgo,' she brushed him aside. 'I must take these back and get some fresh ones. I haven't time to stop and talk now.'

The restraining hand dropped to his side and he moved to let her pass through the doorway. Disconsolately he made his way up to his room.

Stavros and Vassilis arrived within minutes of each other and Yannis asked Louisa for a bottle of wine. 'We may as well make a start whilst we wait for the others.'

'Who else is coming?'

'Dimitris, Nicolas and Costas. You've probably seen me around with them.'

'Isn't Costas the rich boy?' asked Stavros.

Yannis nodded. 'His father had a big win on the lottery apparently.'

'A useful friend to have,' remarked Vassilis.

'I think his father gives him an allowance, so he's really no better off than us.'

'Maybe not, but no doubt he can always ask for a little more if he overspends.'

'Here he comes. You can ask him.' Yannis grinned at Vassilis and called for another bottle of wine to be brought to the table as Costas slid into the seat next to him.

Louisa frowned when she saw who was with Yannis. She hoped he would say nothing out of place to her. 'I thought you were going out,' she said to Yannis.

'We are, but we thought it only right to start here. Where's Yiorgo? You must meet him. I'll give him a shout.'

From the bottom of the stairs Yannis called to Yiorgo to join them. When he arrived he was obviously preoccupied, gazing around as though someone or something was missing.

'What have you lost, Yiorgo?'

'My newspaper; I thought I'd taken it up with me, but I must have left it down here, but I can't see it.'

Yannis raised himself from his chair and pulled the newspaper out from beneath him. 'I'm sorry. I just sat down. Is there something important in there?'

Yiorgo nodded. 'There's an article on Bulgaria that I wanted to read more thoroughly. When I've finished with it I'll pass it on to you. You'll find it interesting also.'

Yannis raised his eyebrows at his friends. He doubted very much if he would find the politics of Bulgaria interesting. 'Here's Dimitris,' he announced, distracting Yiorgo from the subject. 'I wonder what kept him.'

'Sorry. Am I late? I just had to finish my homework and then my father arrived and was asking me how I was getting on. I thought I'd never get away.'

'Well you're here now. Where shall we go? You all know the town far better than I do.'

'You only know your way to school and the museum,' laughed Dimitris. 'How did you find your way to the doctor?'

'I asked Louisa.'

'Let's do the rounds,' suggested Nicolas.

'Be careful where you go boys,' warned Yiorgo Pavlakis.

'There are some unsavoury areas here, worse than Aghios Nikolaos, Yannis.'

'Would you like to come with us?'

Yiorgo Pavlakis pushed back his hair and appeared quite startled at the idea. 'No, I couldn't. I'm expecting some acquaintances here later. That's why I needed the paper.'

The boys called out goodbye to Louisa and left the taverna. Once outside Dimitris turned to Yannis. 'Is he always like that?'

'Like what?'

'Well, concerned for your safety.'

'Not usually; I think it's just where I fell down the stairs. He promised my parents he'd look after me whilst I was here and I don't know Heraklion very well, particularly at night.'

'You're safe enough with us. The waterfront is the place to steer clear of. You get so many different nationalities at the harbour and they get drunk and brawls start. If you're not careful you can get involved.' Vassilis was leading the way to the centre of the town.

'Another place is behind the market,' added Nicolas. 'It's the prostitutes' area,' he explained to Yannis. 'If you want to take a short cut it becomes embarrassing with them all calling out to you, and sometimes their pimps will push you into a doorway and take your money. If you complain to the police they say you shouldn't have been in the area in the first place.'

Dimitris dived down a side street and opened the door of a taverna. 'Let's start here.' Two elderly men who were playing dominoes looked at the boys and sighed. Their peaceful game was about to be interrupted.

It was past midnight when they finally bade each other farewell and Yannis stumbled back to the taverna. He was surprised to find the oil lamps still lit and a number of men sitting at a table with Mr Pavlakis. He hardly glanced at Yannis as he entered, so intent was he on the speech he was making. Louisa was leaning on the counter, obviously tired; yet knowing she would be called upon for further bottles of wine.

'What's going on?' asked Yannis.

'Yiorgo is talking to them about the article he read on Bulgaria. I don't understand what he's on about, but they appear to think he's right. I just wish they'd all go to bed,' she yawned openly.

'I'll call out goodnight to you and say how late it is. It might encourage them to move.' He went to the bottom of the stairs and called loudly. 'Goodnight, Louisa. It's after midnight so I'm off to bed.'

'Goodnight,' called back Louisa. 'I had no idea it was so late.'

Yannis stood and watched. The group of men did not appear to have heard, but continued listening to Yiorgo as intently as before. He glanced at Louisa who shrugged her shoulders in resignation.

Before going to sleep Yannis looked at the map he had to learn. He hoped he would remember it the following day, although at the moment he really felt too tired to care. He remembered his last evening in Heraklion and hoped he would not feel ill in the morning.

The day dragged for Yannis. He disliked having to draw the map again and again, each time inserting different information at Mr Angelakis's direction. The list of places that had sent ships to aid in the Trojan War was more interesting, but when Mr Angelakis explained they were now to make graphs from the information they had compiled that day Yannis groaned. He hated graphs. However hard he tried they never seemed to end up accurate. Making a tentative start he was pleased when the bell rang and he could hurry off to the museum.

If he worked really hard he should finish listing the pottery in the room within a few more days. When he had done that he planned to ask Mr Kouvakis if he could move it so the pieces could be grouped together. As he peered through the grubby glass he could hardly believe his eyes. Lying, half hidden between the broken pieces of pottery and the black edges of the display case was a tiny gold axe. Excitement surged through him. Did anyone else know it was there? He doubted it. Closing his notebook he went in search of Mr Kouvakis and met him as he was coming down the passage.

'Perfect timing, Yannis. I was just coming to tell you we were closing.'

'Can you spare me a moment? There's something I want to show you.'

'Yes, of course.' Inwardly Mr Kouvakis felt impatient. He was hungry and his room had been chilly, as he had forgotten to light the stove until mid-day.

'Look at that.' Yannis indicated the tiny axe.

'Yes?' Mr Kouvakis looked at the pottery. 'What is so remarkable about that?'

'Not the pottery; look, in the corner. A tiny gold axe.' Yannis's voice was trembling with excitement.

Mr Kouvakis leaned forward. 'You're right.' The incredulity sounded in his voice. He drew a large bunch of keys from his pocket and began to try them in the lock, finally having success as the mechanism creaked and the key turned. He lifted the heavy glass lid. 'Take it out, then.'

With baited breath Yannis stretched his hand into the case and picked up the tiny, precious object between his finger and thumb. He laid it on the palm of his hand and gazed at it in delight. 'It's beautiful.'

'I'd better put it in the strong room with the others.'

'The others?'

'We have a number of them, all weights and sizes. I'll show you.' Mr Kouvakis led the way back along the passage and unlocked a door at the far end. The door swung open to reveal another behind it, made of very stout wood with cross braces. Two more keys were produced and the inner door was opened to reveal a long, narrow room. One side was shelved, on each shelf a collection of boxes sat in confusion. Mr Kouvakis selected one and lifted the lid.

YANNIS

'Look.' Inside was a glittering array of small, gold axes, identical to the one Yannis had discovered inside the display case. Mr Kouvakis ran his hand through them. 'Put it in, Yannis.'

Yannis looked at the tiny object once more, then placed it gently in the box. He looked curiously around the room. On the far side were large, flat, packing cases, stacked almost from floor to ceiling.

'What are they?' he asked.

'The frescoes Mr Evans has examined. When they build the new museum they'll be put on show.'

'Will the axes go on show also?'

'I expect so.' Mr Kouvakis turned to go and Yannis followed him.

'Thank you for showing me. They're far too beautiful to be locked away. I hope they build the new museum quickly so everyone can see them.'

Mr Kouvakis shrugged. 'Who knows? They may have found better specimens by then and have no use for these.'

'I'm sure they won't. I wonder, excuse me; I must go to the library before it closes. There's something I want to look up.'

Suddenly Yannis could not wait to be out of the museum. He was sure he had seen pictures of a funeral ritual where a person was shown holding a large axe. Maybe the gold axe he had he had seen and held was a talisman, carried around as a charm against death. By the time he reached the library he was convinced his idea was correct and it took him only a few minutes to find the book with the illustration he wanted. With a sigh of satisfaction he closed the book and began to walk back to the taverna.

To his surprise he found Stavros and Vassilis waiting for him. 'We felt a bit guilty running out of here last night, so we decided we would come for a meal with you,' explained Vassilis.

Yannis nodded, hardly hearing him. 'I must tell you my news. I found a little gold axe at the museum today.' Stavros and Vassilis looked at him with interest. 'I could hardly believe it. It was just lying there. Mr Kouvakis unlocked the case and let me take it out.'

'Where is it now? Have you brought it with you?'

'Of course not. Mr Kouvakis took me into the strong room and we put it in the box with the others. They have hundreds there.'

'Why aren't they put on display?'

'They will be when the new museum is built. Yiorgo, come and hear this.'

Yiorgo came obediently to their table and Yannis told his story again, he then went on to tell them his theory of the axe being a lucky charm.

'You could well be right, Yannis. If you look in the jewellers you will see replicas made up as earrings or on a chain. People probably regard them just as decorative jewellery now, but they may have been very precious to them in the past.'

Although Yiorgo was speaking to Yannis he was watching the man who was talking to Louisa at the counter. He appeared to be getting impatient. Louisa glanced at the four at the table and shook her head again.

'Do you have a problem, Louisa?' Yiorgo was at her side.

She smiled sweetly at both men. 'Mr Manyakis has some goods for Pavlos and was hoping he would be here.' She nodded her head imperceptibly. 'I'm sure he'll be available tomorrow if you'd care to come back.'

'I shall certainly be here.' He nodded determinedly and strode out of the taverna, slamming the door behind him.

Louisa returned to the kitchen and Yiorgo followed her. 'Louisa, I don't like to see you having to deal with people like that. Have you thought any more about my proposal?'

'What proposal?'

'I asked if you would marry me.'

'Oh, that,' she answered nonchalantly, not taking her eyes from the lettuce she was chopping.

Yiorgo slipped an arm round her slim waist. 'Please, Louisa, you're driving me crazy.'

She wriggled away from him. 'Be careful, or I'll cut my finger.'

'Louisa, please give me an answer.'

'I'm too busy to think of things like that.'

'Louisa!' Yiorgo's patience snapped. He grabbed the knife from her hand, flinging it to one side, pushed her against the wall and kissed her passionately. He felt the rigidity of her body but refused to release her as his body pressed urgently against her. 'Louisa, Louisa,' he murmured, beginning to kiss her neck. For a few minutes she permitted his kisses and caresses, then pushed him roughly away.

'Don't be so silly, Yiorgo. I have a meal to prepare.'

'Louisa,' his voice was hoarse with emotion.

'Stop saying 'Louisa' in that silly way and move. I don't want to get married yet, not to you or anyone else.'

Yiorgo dropped his arms to his sides and stepped back. 'I'm sorry. I shouldn't have behaved like that. You drive me crazy. I see you talking and laughing with the customers and I feel so jealous.'

'I have to be pleasant to them. Besides, most of the people who come here in the evening come to see you. I'm just the person who cooks and serves.'

Yiorgo pushed back his lock of hair. 'I love you Louisa. I'd do anything for you.'

A mocking eyebrow was raised at him by way of reply. 'Then move out of my way and let me get this meal ready.' She pushed a bottle of wine into his hands. 'Go and join the boys.'

Yiorgo resumed his seat and listened to the conversation of the young men, which he very quickly found boring. He brushed back his hair, wiped his hand down his trousers and cleared his throat. 'Have you heard the latest news from Greece?'

The three looked at him in surprise. 'What's happened?'

Yiorgo leaned forward on the table. 'I will tell you.' He began to talk knowledgably about the political unrest that was taking place on the mainland. He talked whilst they ate their food, and continued whilst they finished a second bottle of wine. At first they had listened with interest, whilst they were eating they had allowed Yiorgo to talk, but now their attention was wandering. Vassilis even gave a surreptitious yawn, hoping the political tirade would soon end.

'Yiorgo, with your knowledge of politics, why don't you stand for election as Governor of one of the provinces?'

'Are you serious?'

Vassilis nodded. 'Perfectly serious.'

Yiorgo sat back in his chair and laughed. 'I couldn't possibly. I have my work. I would never be able to fit in all the duties of a Governor; besides, I'm trying to write a book on the political history of Greece. It's fascinating. When I've finished I'll let you read it. I have one great problem with it.'

'What's that?' grinned Yannis. 'When to stop?'

'Exactly.' Yiorgo was quite serious. 'When do I stop? Do I say that at the end of a certain page it is finished, or after a particular event, or do I continue until the day I die and others say it is finished?'

'If you plan to write it continually, won't you get bored?'

'Bored!' Yiorgo was shocked at the idea. 'How can one get bored with politics? They are forever changing. One day's policy is the next day's history. Politics are the basis of Greek history, even the mythological stories are based on the politics of the time, a power struggle between ruling factions, put into story form to explain the situation to the uneducated peasants. Think of your Homer, basic politics.'

Stavros had suddenly become interested. 'Tell me more.'

Yiorgo was only too willing to talk, and the boys found his discussion and explanation of ancient political manoeuvrings far more interesting than their modern counterparts. During the evening Pavlos returned and after listening to the conversation for a few minutes suggested they had a game of cards. Yiorgo agreed, and Yannis was surprised to find the teacher was an astute gambler.

'You have a lot to learn, Yannis,' he smiled as he scooped the money from the table for the third time.

'I'll win it back next time,' he smiled. 'Don't break up the game on my account, but I really must go and do my homework.'

'I must go as well,' Stavros was relieved to find an opportunity to excuse himself. 'I also have my homework to do, and I can't afford to play any more tonight.'

'Come again tomorrow,' suggested Pavlos.

'Maybe.' Stavros was not going to commit himself to regular gambling. 'Are you coming, Vassilis?'

They left the taverna together and Pavlos smiled. Now he would see just how good the schoolteacher was at cards when pitting his wits against a professional.

The days passed swiftly for Yannis. He found his schoolwork easy to cope with and enjoyed the hours he was able to spend in the museum. He met up with his friends at the weekends and they would spend their time walking around the town or drinking in a taverna. He avoided playing cards with either Yiorgo or Pavlos as he found he always lost and the thought that Pavlos cheated had crossed his mind more than once. Three times, when he was supposed to be working in the library, he had sneaked back to the taverna to spend the morning with Louisa, feeling both guilty and elated afterwards.

The weather became colder and he suddenly realised that the end of term exams and Christmas were not far away. He must begin to think about presents for his family but could not think of a single item that would be suitable. There would be no point in asking Yiorgo for help, but maybe Costas or Dimitris would have some ideas. He approached Costas as they walked back from the taverna at lunchtime.

'Have you thought about Christmas presents for your family yet?'

'I shall probably buy my mother some perfume and a new pipe each year for my father keeps him happy.'

Yannis nodded. He could not imagine his mother wearing perfume. 'Where do you usually go to buy them?'

Costas shrugged. 'Depends how much money I want to spend. I buy most of them from the market, after I've looked in the shops. The goods are just the same.'

Yannis wondered if he dared ask Yiorgo how much Louisa's bracelet had cost and whether he could afford something similar for Annita. He sighed deeply. He must not compare Annita with Louisa, but he was no longer sure he wanted to marry his cousin.

He approached Yiorgo that evening whilst they were eating their meal, but Yiorgo was evasive. 'You cannot put a price on a gift that you give for love. The bracelet was expensive, but there are other smaller items you could give. After all, that was my betrothal gift to Louisa, so it had to be worthy of her.'

'You're sure she will marry you?'

'She's young yet. She needs time to get used to the idea of marriage. She has no mother to advise her about these things. I have to persuade her gently that there is nothing to fear.'

'I don't think Louisa would be frightened about getting married,' remarked Yannis.

Yiorgo wagged his finger at the boy. 'You don't know her like I do. She needs to be looked after, to be protected from the world. What does she know of life? She left school to look after her ailing parents and has looked after the taverna and her brother since their death. She has had no experience of the world. When we're married I plan to take her to Athens, Rome, Venice, all the most beautiful cities in the world for the most beautiful girl in the world.'

'Have you told her this?'

'Not yet.' Yiorgo bent his head confidentially towards Yannis.

'She has asked me to give her time. I'm intending to run for office in the elections, if I'm successful I shall ask her again. Being the wife of a government official is far superior to being the wife of a schoolteacher.'

'Do you mean it?' Yannis had heard Yiorgo speak to men in the taverna, starting quietly and rationally, but becoming noisier as he received encouragement from his audience, until they would end by saluting him as capable of solving all their problems.

Yiorgo nodded. 'Don't tell Louisa, I want it to be a surprise for her.'

'How will you have time to write your political history?'

'I shall make time,' Yiorgo smiled confidently. 'This time next year I expect to be a schoolteacher, a government official and a married man. What more could I ask for?'

Yannis walked around the centre of the town. He gazed in jeweller's windows and was appalled at the prices that were displayed on the plainest ornament. From the main street he entered the market, the busy thoroughfare was full of people and he elbowed his way through until he came to a collection of small shops, which sold souvenirs. A boy behind the first stall gave him a cheeky grin.

'What would you like? Ribbon for your sister, a scarf for your mother?'

Yannis smiled. 'I'm just looking today.'

The boy nodded and picked up a penknife, flicking it open to show the number of blades. 'Very good, very strong.'

Yannis shook his head. Penknives for his brothers were an excellent idea but they could be bought at any time. He stood on the corner debating whether to go along the street where the leather workers would be making boots and shoes or to continue along the main thoroughfare. He was still hesitating when he saw Costas sauntering along, a package in his hand. He fell into step beside him. 'What have you bought?'

'A little present for my mother. Her old ones have worn thin.'
'Her old what?'
'Slippers.'
'Slippers?' Yannis had no idea what his friend was referring to.
'Yes, you know, to wear in the evenings, when she's sitting by the stove.'

As he had hoped, Costas undid the package and withdrew one. It was grey coloured with orange and blue embroidered knots at the front for decoration. Yannis was disappointed. His mother had made similar shoes for them to wear in bed during the winter.

'Very nice,' he said and turned it over. To his surprise the sole was leather.

Costas held out his hand. 'I'd better wrap it with the other one or she'll see it when I walk in. Are you going home or coming with me to buy something special for the most wonderful girl in the world, who just happens to have three little moles on her back?'

Yannis laughed. 'You were right about those moles.'

'She is delicious. I'd like to eat her.'

'Yiorgo Pavlakis wants to marry her!'

'Why? He can have everything he wants without marrying the girl.'

'He says he loves her. He has no idea what she really does for a living.'

Costas whistled. 'Do you think we should tell him?'

Yannis shook his head. 'I doubt if he'd believe us, besides she's told me she has no intention of getting married.'

Costas shrugged. 'Oh, well, not our problem. I'm going down that way.' He pointed back towards the centre of the town.

'I've just come from there. I'm just looking for ideas today.'

Yannis wandered past the boot makers until he saw rows of slippers hanging up in a doorway. They were all made from goat hair, but each pair had a different colour combination of knots. Finally Yannis chose a pair with red and blue decoration, checked he had enough money with him, and went inside to make his purchase. Now his mother would be able to take off her working shoes in the evening and be more comfortable. Night shoes were impractical to wear anywhere but in bed as the soles would be worn through within a matter of days if used for walking, even inside the house.

For a further half an hour Yannis wandered through the market. He placed his letter in the sack for delivery to Aghios Nikolaos and was told there was one for him to collect. His heart missed a beat, would it be from the hospital? To his delight it was from Maria and he tore it open eagerly. She wrote in a stilted, hesitant hand, her information often disjointed, making it necessary to read the letter through a second time before the meaning became clear.

She started by hoping Yannis was keeping well and asking if he intended to return home for Christmas. She then went on to say that they had managed a good crop of carob, and were hoping to have the last of it harvested that week. The letter was not dated so Yannis had no idea to which week she was referring. She then returned to the subject of Christmas and said that she and Anna had started to make presents for everyone and their mother had received a special order from the shop where she sold her embroidery.

At the end of the letter Yannis was most intrigued. *"I will have something very exciting to tell you when I see you,"* she wrote. *"I went to Aghios Nikolaos with Mamma last week."*

Yannis could not imagine what she was talking about. The rest of the letter had pleased him. It was always good to know the crops had been successful and he could imagine the pleasure his mother had from completing a special order. On his return to the taverna he found Yiorgo eating moussaka.

'That does smell good. I hope Louisa has enough for me.'

Yannis waited until she had placed the plate in front of him and returned to the kitchen, then he leaned across the table towards Yiorgo. 'Which shop did you go to for Louisa's bracelet? I want to make sure that whatever I buy is gold, not gilt.'

'The little shop round the corner from Eleftherias Square. They showed me the gold mark and wrote "gold" on the bill. Enjoy your meal. I'm going out for a while.'

Yannis was surprised, but he made no comment. Usually Yiorgo was happy to spend the evening in the taverna, waiting for his friends to arrive and watching Louisa. The newspaper was lying where he had left it earlier and Yannis picked it up and glanced through the pages. His attention was caught by a small announcement at the foot of a column. "The closing date for all application forms for Local Government is the end of this week."

A wide smile spread over Yannis's face. That was where Yiorgo had gone. Carefully Yannis refolded the paper and replaced it, he had little interest in politics and he did not feel he could face Yiorgo later that evening and listen for any length of time to him expounding his theories.

'I shall be upstairs, Louisa, if any of my friends call.'

Louisa nodded. It had been a disappointing day. No one had called except her brother, who had demanded money from her to pay a pressing gambling debt. She hoped Costas might call in asking for Yannis and she could charge him for a few stolen moments in the kitchen.

The examinations were easier than Yannis had dared to hope and he asked Mr Angelakis if he would care to join him for a drink at lunchtime. He was relieved when the tutor declined and determined to take the teacher's advice to take some books home with him to read in the holiday.

Mr Kouvakis accepted his offer and they spent a pleasant couple of hours whilst the curator related to Yannis how he had excavated at Tylissos. He stretched his arms to show the size of the cauldrons that had been carefully preserved until Yannis was convinced the man was exaggerating.

On his way back to the taverna he visited the market, having finally decided that a new belt for his father in tooled leather and with a bronze buckle would make him the envy of the village men, and for his sisters fine silk scarves to wear to church on Sundays and feast days. Annita was still a problem to him and he was torn between buying a pair of very tiny gold stud earrings or a pair that had a minute seed pearl inset for decoration. In the jewellers he lingered, hesitating until the shopkeeper announced he would be closing shortly and began to hang up his shutters.

'The pearls, please.'

'Very wise, sir, a very wise choice.' Rapidly the gift was wrapped and handed to him before he could change his mind.

Flowers for Louisa presented no problem to him. He had spoken to the flower seller earlier and agreed to call back to collect the bouquet. He smiled to himself as he walked along. He must look a comic figure. One hand was clasped against his pocket to ensure that the precious earrings did not fall out; whilst in his other hand he clutched two packages and an enormous bunch of flowers. He pressed the blossoms into her arms and for a moment a spark of warmth showed in her eyes as she thanked him for thinking of her.

'I'll put them in my room.'

She disappeared up the stairs, carrying the flowers and a large water jug. Yannis followed and went into his own room where he laid out the presents for his family and checked them carefully to make sure he had forgotten no one. Later he would pack them ready to catch the bus to Aghios Nikolaos the following morning.

'Yannis,' he heard Louisa call. 'Come and see. They're beautiful.'

Yannis crossed the hall and Louisa closed the door behind him. 'I have a present for you, Yannis.' Very deliberately she undid the buckle of Yannis's belt and slipped her hand inside his trousers.

Yannis needed no further encouragement; he was kissing her hungrily and pulling at her clothes to feel the smooth flesh beneath, striving desperately for a relief to his passion.

'Did you enjoy your present?' her voice was mocking.

'Wonderful. Thank you Louisa.' He twisted his hand in her hair, holding her head back, kissing her throat, breast and navel until he reached her hips.

'No, Yannis; there's no more time,' she struggled to rise. 'Let me go or Yiorgo will be back.'

Yannis groaned. 'What is it you do to me, Louisa?'

'I make you feel good.'

The taverna door was heard to open and close. Yannis looked at her in horror. In a trice she had replaced her blouse and skirt and was brushing her hair. By the time the footsteps had reached the top of the stairs she was emerging breathless from her room.

'Louisa, how beautiful you look.' Yannis heard Yiorgo's voice and cringed with shame.

'Come and have some wine with me. It isn't often we have time to sit together.'

There was a wheedling note in her voice and Yannis realised she was trying to persuade Yiorgo to return to the taverna to enable him to escape to his own room. Yiorgo needed no second invitation and followed her innocently, opening the bottle she indicated and pouring for them both. He took her hand and kissed her fingers.

'Louisa, I am a man tormented. Please, give me your answer.'

'I'm not ready to answer you yet, Yiorgo.' She withdrew her hand. 'Shall we invite Yannis to have a drink with us as he leaves tomorrow?'

'Is he in?'

'He arrived shortly before you. I'll go and ask him.' Before Yiorgo could answer she had whisked away up the stairs and was knocking on Yannis's door. 'You must come down,' she insisted in a low voice. 'Yiorgo will wonder what's wrong if you refuse to drink with us.'

After they had eaten the taverna seemed to get far busier than usual. Everyone who entered seemed to want to speak to Yiorgo, whilst Pavlos was listening, his eyes aglow with enthusiasm. Yannis made his excuses to slip away and joined Louisa at the counter.

'What's happening?' she asked.

'I've no idea,' replied Yannis honestly. 'I'm going to get packed and then have an early night.'

'Lucky you! I have a feeling I shall be late.'

The bus jolted, shuddered and rattled along the badly made road, the few passengers holding their breath and clutching at the hard, wooden seats as they careered along the narrow road within a hair's breadth of the cliff edge. Yannis gazed at the countryside in delight. He had walked to the outskirts of Heraklion, but the scenery could not compare with Mirabello, being much more barren. He leaned forward eagerly to catch his first glimpse of Aghios Nikolaos as it nestled in the hollow of the hills. The bus hooted to announce its arrival and people appeared from nowhere. Yannis craned his neck to see if his aunt or uncle was waiting to meet him, but he could see neither of them. He gathered his possessions and slowly dismounted.

'Yannis! Yannis!'

Delighted he spun round to greet Annita. 'You were the last person I expected to see here. Why aren't you at the hospital?'

'I changed my day off. Your letter came just in time for me to do so.'

'Let me look at you. You've no idea how good it is to see you.'

They walked along the quay until they could see Yiorgo spreading his nets to dry.

'We'll tell him you've arrived, then go up to Mamma.'

Yiorgo clasped Yannis to him and slapped him on the back. 'Welcome back. Elena's waiting for you. Annita can carry your supper.' Two large lobsters, claws already tied, were thrust into Annita's hands. 'Special treat,' grinned Yiorgo. 'Come on, no need to hang around.'

Happily Yannis followed Yiorgo to his house where Elena greeted him rapturously. 'Where's Andreas?' he asked, once he could regain his breath.

Yiorgo and Elena exchanged glances. 'He'll be in soon, I expect. He knows you're expected today. Come and sit down. We want to hear all your news.'

Yannis sat by the open fire and described his room in the taverna, his school, his friends and the museum. Elena continually exclaimed "Fancy that!" or "Wait until your mother hears that!" whilst Annita sat silently. Finally Yannis turned to her.

'Your turn now. I want to hear all about the hospital.'

'It's not very exciting. I spend all day rolling bandages or washing people. They say after Christmas I can begin to change dressings myself. That might be a bit more interesting.'

'Why do you stay if you don't like it?'

'I'm not saying I don't like it,' Annita groped for her words. 'It's just not how I thought it would be. I want to be able to help people get better, like Widow Segouri does.'

'I'm sure you will, dear. Just give it time.' Elena had heard the complaint before. 'Go and find Andreas, Yiorgo. He must have forgotten the time.'

'How long are you staying, Yannis?' asked Annita.

'Until tomorrow morning, if you'll have me,' he looked at Elena.

'Foolish boy! Of course we'll have you. You can stay as long as you want.'

Andreas followed his father inside. 'Yannis - I'm sorry I wasn't here to meet you.'

Yannis looked at his cousin in surprise. 'You've grown so tall. I swear you're taller than I am.'

Andreas grinned with delight and rubbed his hand across his chin where a dark shadow was beginning to appear. He drew up a chair, trying to fold his long legs underneath. 'Tell me your news,' he demanded, and once again Yannis repeated his description of his life in Heraklion.

'And how's school this year?' asked Yannis eventually. 'What's the new teacher like?'

Andreas pulled a face. 'He's so boring. Not a bit like Mr Pavlakis.'

'Yiorgo is planning to run for a place on the local government.'

Andreas and Annita laughed. 'What on earth does he want to do that for?'

'It started with a chance remark by a friend of mine when we were sick of him talking politics to us. He took him seriously.'

'Has he married the girl in the taverna?' asked Annita.

Yannis felt himself redden. 'No, she says she's not ready to settle down yet. He's hoping that if he wins the election she'll change her mind. Shall we go out for a walk?' Yannis was suddenly desperate to turn the conversation away from Louisa.

Despite the cold Yannis and Annita spent most of the afternoon wandering around the town, which to Yannis seemed to have diminished considerably. Everywhere they went friends and acquaintances wanted to know about Heraklion as though he had been away years rather than a few weeks. Finally they climbed the hill where they could look down on the natural lake, which lay at the foot. To Yannis's surprise they found a house under construction on the summit.

'I'm surprised anyone should want to climb up here each day,' he remarked, 'But what a wonderful view of the bay they will have.'

Annita did not seem to be listening. She had sat herself down on the rough grass, her head bowed.

'What is it?' asked Yannis. 'You don't seem very happy.' He sat down beside her. 'Aren't you pleased to see me?'

'Of course I am.' Tears began to course their way down her cheeks.

Yannis pulled her towards him. 'Tell me, Annita.'

'You don't care about me any more. You've found new friends and I'm just your country cousin.'

'Annita!' Yannis was genuinely shocked.

'You haven't kissed me since you arrived. You didn't even hold my hand until we started climbing the hill. I thought when you suggested going for a walk it was so we could be alone for a while.'

'It was,' Yannis assured her. 'I just wanted to make sure we were well away from any prying eyes.' He pulled Annita to him and kissed her gently. She responded passionately and Yannis's head began to spin due to her proximity and encouragement. He pushed his hand up her jumper and caressed her breast. She made no effort to resist him, simply strained her body closer to his. Unbidden a picture of Louisa entered Yannis's head. He froze. This was Annita he was holding in his arms. He pulled himself away from her.

'Get up,' he ordered.

For a moment Annita looked at him in stunned surprise, then took his hand and pulled herself to her feet, brushing down her skirt.

'I'm sorry,' he apologised gruffly. 'We ought to get back.'

Silently Annita walked with him down the hill. Neither could think of anything to break down the barrier that had been created between them. Yannis opened the door and she passed through and up the stairs to her room without a word. Elena looked up in surprise as Yannis joined her in the kitchen.

'Where's Annita?'

'She went upstairs. That smells delicious. How long do I have before supper's ready?'

'About an hour.'

'Good. I've an errand to run before then.'

Flower sellers seemed more difficult to find in Aghios Nikolaos and it took Yannis some time before he finally discovered an old lady in a back street. He was able to slip upstairs unnoticed when he returned and quickly found the presents he had bought for the family. He was unsure when he should give them, but as the flowers could not be hidden, he decided to do so immediately.

Elena was delighted with her bouquet, although Yannis wished he had bought her a silk scarf as he had his sisters, somehow flowers seemed an inadequate way of thanking her for looking after him during his time in Aghios Nikolaos. Yiorgo and Andreas were surprised when Yannis produced a sheath knife for each of them. Yiorgo assured him he needed a new one, and showed a blade worn thin by continual sharpening over the years. Andreas seemed more impressed by the tooling on the sheath than the knife, but agreed that it would be very useful to him when he accompanied his father.

Annita sat quietly, wondering what Yannis had chosen for her. When he drew the tiny packet from his pocket she knew it had to be jewellery of some kind. 'They're a special present for a special girl,' Yannis whispered in her ear.

She gasped with pleasure when she gazed upon the earrings, placed them in her ears and kissed him. 'They're beautiful, Yannis. Thank you.'

'You really like them? I spent ages choosing them. The jeweller threatened to close his shop if I didn't decide.'

Annita laughed. 'What would you have done if I hadn't liked them?'

'Gone back to the shop and asked the man to change them,' replied Yannis, relieved to see that Annita seemed happy again.

Yiorgo cleared his throat. 'Is there a meaning behind Annita's present? You don't usually give young ladies gifts of jewellery unless you're betrothed.'

Yannis flushed deeply. 'It's a promise for the future, for when I've finished University.'

Yiorgo nodded, satisfied, and raised his glass in approval.

The party became gayer as neighbours called to greet Yannis, more wine was poured and finally Yiorgo produced a bottle of brandy.

'For a toast,' he announced. 'Yannis and Annita are betrothed with our blessing.'

Embarrassed they smiled at each other, feeling very self conscious and foolish as glasses were raised to them. Yannis felt a sudden sinking in the pit of his stomach. He was not at all sure that he wanted to marry Annita, but an official declaration of their betrothal had been made before witnesses and he knew that everyone present would remember and hold him to his agreement.

A neighbour began to strum on his bouzouki. Annita clapped her hands. 'Let's dance.'

'You can't dance in here,' her mother remonstrated.

'We could dance outside,' she suggested. 'It's not very cold, anyway, dancing will keep us warm.'

In twos and threes they left the living room, making a line on the cobbled path. Keeping in time with the music they began to dance, slowly at first, then faster and faster as the tempo increased. More neighbours, hearing the revelry, joined them until most of the immediate area was congregated in the street. The word went round that Yannis and Annita were betrothed, coins were thrown to them and one or two of the wealthier pushed a note into Yannis's pocket.

Annita had drunk little, but there was a pleasurable flush to her cheeks and she was enjoying being the centre of attention. Andreas had joined them and was standing on the fringe of the crowd, clapping in time to the music.

The dancing and carousing continued until the early hours of the morning. The bouzouki player seemed tireless and willing to play forever. The women slipped away first, gathering in little knots in the doorways, watching as the men continued to dance, jumping and slapping their boots. Yannis felt exhilarated, this time he was the central figure, before he had only been one of the neighbours joining in when there had been a party like this one. He wished his friends from Heraklion could be there to watch and join in also. Parties like this only took place in small towns and villages and he doubted that they had ever experienced the like in Heraklion. The dancers continued, their numbers dwindling, as they made their way back to their homes, exhausted and the worse for drink in most cases. The bouzouki player continued, even when the street was clear.

Annita giggled. 'Shall I tell him the party's over?'

'I think he's realised.' A last wailing note was heard; then the shuffling, unsteady footsteps grew fainter.

The family looked at one another uncertainly. Andreas was the first to come to a decision. 'I'm off to bed. Don't anyone wake me tomorrow.'

Elena smiled wearily. 'I agree. We may as well get what little sleep we can. You particularly, Annita, you have to be off early.'

Annita pouted. During the last exciting hours she had forgotten she would have to leave for the hospital again in the early morning. With a sigh she mounted the stairs.

'I'll wake you before I leave, Yannis.'

'Wake me in good time. I'll walk to the hospital with you.'

On impulse she took his face between her hands and kissed him. 'I'm sorry I was so horrid to you earlier. I do love you, Yannis.'

Yiorgo cleared his throat. 'Come on. I want to get to bed myself now.'

Annita and Yannis walked to the hospital in silence, their heads heavy and their eyes dull from lack of sleep. Yannis squeezed her hand.

'I'll try to get a message to you before I return to Heraklion to say what day I'm travelling. You might be able to get the day off again.'

'I will, somehow I will.' She clung to him, her eyes wet with tears. 'I wish I could come to Heraklion with you.'

Gently Yannis disentangled her hands. 'You concentrate on your nursing and I'll concentrate on my studies. It will make the time go quicker.' He bent and kissed her, wishing he could feel the same passion rising in him as he did when he kissed Louisa.

From inside the hospital a bell could be heard. 'I must go.' She jerked herself away. 'I'll be late.' She ran through the iron gates and opened the massive door, raising her hand fleetingly to Yannis as she entered. For a while Yannis stood and looked at the door as though he expected Annita to reappear, then he turned and walked slowly away, trying to sort out the turmoil of his emotions.

Yannis disturbed Andreas as he scrabbled in his bundle to find a pullover that would be thick enough to protect him from the chill of the wind whilst he was on the boat.

'What are you up to?'

'I'm getting a pullover. Your Pappa is taking me to the canal.'

Andreas grunted and turned over, then rolled back again. 'I'm sorry you're not staying longer. I'd have liked to talk to you more about Heraklion.'

'I'll be back after Christmas. We can talk then.'

Yannis shouldered his bundle and began to trudge along the dusty path to Plaka. The cluster of cottages drew nearer and his steps quickened until he was almost running. As he rounded the curve of the track he saw his father.

'Pappa!'

Yannis senior looked up. 'Yannis! Hey, Yannis is here.'

Figures appeared from inside the house and rushed to greet him. Yannis found himself surrounded by his brothers and sisters. He gazed at them incredulously. 'You've all grown so much. It's only a few weeks since I saw you last – and look at you now.'

They plied him with questions and he answered as best he could, promising to tell them more later. 'I want to see Mamma. Where is she? When we're all together I'll tell you about Heraklion and Aghios Nikolaos.'

Stelios led the way inside calling excitedly for his mother, who left her baking to fling her arms round her eldest son, then she released him and held him at arm's length.

'You look pale, Yannis. You need some country air – and what's this?' She indicated the scar from Yannis's hairline to his ear.

'It's nothing. I'm very tired, Mamma. I'll tell you all about it in a moment. I'd love some coffee first.'

Seated at the table in the living room Yannis described the party that had taken place in Aghios Nikolaos the previous night. 'That's why I'm tired. I wish you could have been there, but it just happened. I didn't expect Yiorgo to ask me if Annita's earrings were a betrothal gift, and then for him to tell the neighbours.'

'There's no harm done, but you'll finish your schooling before you think of marriage, won't you, Yannis?'

'Of course, Mamma. If I get married I shall need a job. The pay I get for working in the museum wouldn't keep me.'

He told them about listing the pottery and his excitement at finding a golden axe, how well he had done in his exams and how he had fallen down the stairs and cut his head.

'Is your head quite healed?' His mother was all concern.

'It's fine. It's just a bit pale where I had to wear a bandage for a week.'

'Maybe we could ask the Widow to have a look at you,' suggested Maria.

'Mamma, I'm fine, really. I've seen a doctor.'

His mother still looked dubious and Yannis decided it was time to change the subject. He turned to his sister. 'What was your exciting news from Aghios Nikolaos, Maria?'

'Oh, yes, I'd almost forgotten. I sold a picture to some tourists.'

'Really!' Yannis was impressed. 'What was it of?'

Maria giggled. 'Pappa and Uncle Yiorgo.'

Yannis raised his eyebrows. 'What were they doing?'

'Drinking and talking. I just happened to be sitting on the wall and I sketched them for something to do. Some people passing by liked it and bought it from me.'

'That's wonderful. Have you done some more? I'd like to see them.'

'I'll show you later,' promised Maria. 'They're not really very good.'

The day wore on, Yannis felt refreshed when he had eaten the meal his mother had prepared, but still very tired. By the early evening he was yawning surreptitiously, but his mother noticed.

'You must go to bed. We shall none of us be late.'

Yannis was grateful. He longed for nothing more than to lie down and sleep. The revelries of the previous night had caught up with him. He had no idea how much later the rest of the family went to their beds; once his head touched the pillow he knew no more until Stelios shook him awake.

'I want to show you where I found some pottery.'

Yannis groaned. 'Not yet, Stelios; I'm not awake.' Stelios sat back on his haunches and Yannis could feel his brother's eyes on his face. He tried to ignore him, but found it impossible. 'All right, I'll get up. Give me a little while to dress and have some coffee.'

Stelios waited until he saw Yannis draw on his trousers; then he scampered away. His father would be wondering why he had taken so long to fetch his cigarettes.

By the time Yannis joined his family in the fields it was nearly mid-day. He had been more tired and slept longer than he had realised. No wonder Stelios had been impatient and woken him. He stood and watched the scene before him. The girls chattered and giggled as they worked, piling up discarded vegetation well away from the vines and carob trees. Yiorgo plodded slowly, attending to the vines, which they tried hard to grow on the poor soil, pulling up weeds that threatened to choke the roots, cutting off a dead piece, trailing a tendril that was trying to go its own independent way. Stelios was supposed to be helping him and Yannis was forced to smile at the similarity between his brother and himself. For a short while Stelios would pull weeds assiduously, then sit on his haunches and examine something he would either discard or put in his pocket. Yannis made his way up the hillside to where his father was planting, each vine the same distance apart, the line as straight and true as if he had used a rule to measure.

'Pappa, Stelios wants to show me where he's found some pottery. Is that all right? I'll help later.'

Yannis senior sighed. 'If I can find a place where there isn't any pottery I'll put Stelios to work there. He's becoming as bad as you were.'

Yannis grinned and ambled over to his youngest brother. Stelios led the way to the other end of the vineyard. It was land his father had only recently begun to cultivate.

'It was here,' announced Stelios.

Yannis went down on his knees. 'Scrape over the top layer with your trowel, then look to see if you have found anything,' directed Yannis. They pored over the ground together, removing small shards of pottery and placing them in a pile. Yannis watched as Stelios scraped diligently and the pile grew, occasionally he would stretch out his hand and examine a piece more closely, pointing out details to Stelios. It appeared to be mostly Roman, hard, red and shiny. Stelios listened open-mouthed as his brother told him how the Romans had banded together to become a nation with a most formidable army.

Yannis senior caught scraps of the conversation as he worked. He was impressed by Yannis's knowledge and also by his patience with the younger boy, answering all his questions, however obvious the answers. Yannis and Stelios were too engrossed in their conversation to notice that the others had taken a break until Anna ran over.

'Come along, it's lunch time.'

Yannis looked up in surprise. 'I didn't realise. Come on, Stelios, we'll finish later.'

Babbis appeared, as he had in the summer months, and greeted

Yannis with pleasure. His attention seemed focused mainly on Maria as before and Yannis envied him. His mother was a widow and there would be plenty of room for Maria to move into the cottage if they married. Babbis was content to stay and work on the land as his father had done before him, seeming to have no other ambition than producing a healthy harvest.

Yannis could sit still no longer. 'Come on, Stelios. Let's see what else we can find.'

The brothers wandered off together and their father shook his head. It was a good job he had Yiorgo who asked for nothing more than to be out in the fields tending the vines and olives. His other two sons would make useless farmers. A few more years and he would have to ask Yiorgo and Elena to take Stelios under their wing so he could attend the Gymnasium.

The temperature dropped rapidly during the afternoon and Yannis senior scanned the sky anxiously. He hoped the rain would hold off just a few more days and that his oldest son would be more useful on the morrow. An extra hand could make all the difference.

Maria had their meal waiting for them when they returned, Yannis and Stelios surreptitiously emptying their pockets before they entered the house. Yannis ate with relish, much to his mother's delight. The day out in the open air had given him an appetite. They settled round the table comfortably for the evening, asking Yannis to tell them once again about Heraklion and all he did whilst he was there.

Yannis sighed and was most relieved when his old school master knocked the door, having heard that Yannis was home and wanting to ask how he found the High School. Once again Yannis related the events of the past few months and Father Theodorakis's eyes became misty as he began to recollect his own youth spent in the town.

'Do you meet by the fountain, Yannis?'

'Yes, every day, we eat at the taverna just across from it.'

YANNIS

Father Theodorakis smiled. 'Do they still do the best kebabs?'

'We think so.'

The talk continued, but Yannis was interested once again. It was no longer him that was relied upon for information; the attention had turned to the schoolmaster. The younger children were sent to bed when their mother noticed Stelios was falling asleep and Maria was sent out to tell the Widow that Yannis was there and invite her to join them.

The little house gradually filled with people and Yannis senior refilled glasses continually. Yannis remained the centre of attention for the villagers, many of whom had never been further than Elounda, and although he tried to describe Heraklion he felt they did not believe his stories of water coming from a tap in the kitchen and a toilet that could be flushed clean. The shed behind the house, with an earth floor that the chickens could pick clean, was their excuse for a toilet, although some families, like Yannis's, had their own water pump in the back yard.

Yiorgo sidled out of the room and slipped off to bed and Yannis wished he could join him. He had been allowed to oversleep that morning, but he had no doubt that his father would expect him to do his share of work whilst he was staying. By the time the last neighbour left the house Yannis was yawning widely. His mother was most concerned for him.

'I am tired,' Yannis admitted. 'I usually go to bed at a reasonable hour, but these last few days it's been the early hours of the morning.'

'Poor boy. Off you go. We won't disturb you tomorrow.'

His father looked at him scathingly. 'It just shows how unhealthy it is to live in a town. No stamina. I'll be up as usual tomorrow.'

'You're used to it,' Maria tried to placate her husband.

'There's a lot to be done before the weather breaks. I was counting on Yannis as an extra hand,' Yannis senior continued to grumble.

'I will help, Pappa. I'll have recovered by tomorrow, then I'll be able to work as hard as you.'

Yannis senior doubted his son's boast, but he too was tired and not averse to going to bed. 'Go on up,' he said. 'I forget you use your brain for work and not your back.'

The slight hurt Yannis, but he made no reply. 'Goodnight,' he called from the foot of the stairs. 'Wake me when you get up.'

It was Yiorgo who woke Yannis just after dawn. 'Come on, sleepy head. Pappa has work for us.'

Yannis groaned and rolled over. Yiorgo and Stelios were already dressed. 'Can we look for pottery again today, Yannis?' asked Stelios eagerly.

Yannis shook his head. 'I don't think so. Maybe if we work hard for Pappa we can look when we've finished.'

'If I work hard for Pappa I'll be too tired to look for pottery,' grumbled Stelios, as he fought to get his head and arms through a pullover that was almost too small for him.

'You need a bigger pullover,' remarked Yannis, then a horrifying thought struck him and he rushed down to the kitchen. 'Mamma, is Stelios going without new clothes so that I can go to High School?'

'What a question! Of course not.'

'Stelios's jumper is far too small for him. He can hardly get into it.' Yannis felt rather foolish.

'He insists on wearing that one. I bought him two new ones when I went to Aghios Nikolaos last, but he says they're too good to wear in the fields.'

'Why didn't you make them? You always used to make our jumpers.' Yannis was surprised to hear that his mother had bought clothing.

'I was too busy with my embroidery.'

'I do wish you didn't have to work so hard,' sighed Yannis. 'I feel guilty. I'm at school enjoying myself and you're working hard to keep me.'

YANNIS

'You've no need to feel guilty. I love embroidery, besides, what would I do with myself if I didn't embroider in my spare time?'

Yannis had no answer, but the feeling of guilt remained. 'Suppose Yiorgo wants to go to High School?'

'He can go if he wants.' Maria smiled at the concern her son was showing. 'We've plenty of money now. Pappa sells to the island under government contract.'

'To Spinalonga? To the lepers?' Yannis was aghast.

'They have to eat, and it's cheaper for the government to buy from Plaka or Elounda and send it out to them than bring it from elsewhere.'

'Pappa's sending some food out to them this week,' chimed in Stelios. He gave his mother a quick kiss on the cheek. 'We'll see you later, Mamma.'

Together the brothers hurried up the hill towards the field where they could see their father was already loading boxes onto a low cart. He beckoned urgently as he sighted them.

'Come on,' urged Yannis. 'Pappa looks pretty impatient.'

'About time,' observed their father as they reached him. 'Help the girls whilst Yiorgo and I finish loading. Get a move on, they're nearly here.'

Shading his eyes Yannis looked towards the sea. A small boat was making good headway, the wind filling the sail as it neared the land. Yannis began to place the beans carefully into one of the boxes.

'Not like that, just throw them in,' said Anna setting him an example.

'You won't get so many in like that.'

'It doesn't matter. They're for the lepers.' Skilfully she tacked a piece of cardboard over the top and Yiorgo hoisted it onto the cart with the others. Ten more minutes saw the load complete. Yiorgo ran to the donkey and backed her into the shafts and coaxed her down the path to the track leading to the village.

Yannis hurried behind until he was able to walk beside his brother.

'Shall I take her?'

With a grin Yiorgo handed Yannis the leading rein. The donkey stopped in her tracks. Yannis pulled at her. 'Come on, walk.' He pulled again. 'Come on, I said, walk, you cussed beast.'

Yiorgo held out his hand and took the rein from Yannis and the donkey immediately continued on her way.

'I don't believe it!' exclaimed Yannis. 'Why wouldn't she walk for me?'

'She only ever walks for Pappa or myself. The girls and Mamma can't budge her.'

The brothers arrived at the quay as the boat moored and the boys had to wait whilst the boatmen off-loaded a quantity of large, wooden barrels.

'What are those for?' asked Yannis.

'Water,' explained Yiorgo. 'They fill them from the pump and take them across when there's a space in the hold. There's no water on the island.'

Two men returned to the boat and the boys began to hand the boxes up to them. The hold was only half full by the time they had finished.

'Come on,' said Yiorgo, as he turned the donkey and cart round. 'Back for the next load.'

Yannis looked behind him as he plodded back up the hill and saw the men rolling some of the barrels back to the boat where they heaved them aboard. There were still a considerable number left beside the pump.

The family worked feverishly to fill boxes and load the cart and Yannis was surprised when his father called to him.

'That's enough on the cart, Yannis. You and I will go down this time. Yiorgo, you can take charge here.' Yannis senior took the leading rein and father and son began to trek back down the hill. The boat could be seen still unloading at the island and Yannis was puzzled why his father should be leaving with only half a load when there was plenty of time. Instead of continuing down towards the quay they turned into their own yard. Yannis senior tethered the donkey to the gate.

'Come and help me,' he directed.

They crossed to the outhouses where, half hidden behind a pile of grass was a large crate. Straining their muscles they lifted a side each and staggered to the cart.

'Gently. Gently with it,' warned Yannis to his son.

'What's in there, Pappa?'

Yannis senior averted his eyes. 'You don't need to know.'

Yannis hung his head, feeling ashamed of his curiosity. He watched whilst his father turned the donkey and cart and followed them down the hill. As they arrived at the quay the small boat was nosing its way carefully amongst the other craft that were moored there. Yannis senior raised a hand to Spiriton who nodded and instructed three men to go ashore to help manhandle the crate aboard and into the hold.

'How many more trips, Pappa?' asked Yannis as they climbed back up the hill.

'Eight, I should think.'

'Eight! How many people are there on the island?'

Yannis senior shrugged. 'I don't know.'

Yannis shuddered. 'I wish we were nowhere near the island.'

Yannis senior clapped his son on the shoulder. 'You should be grateful that we are. The government contract has made a great deal of difference to me. Your sisters will have good dowries when they marry.'

'What about Yiorgo and Stelios?'

'Yiorgo will have the farm eventually. Stelios seems to be taking after you, so I'll send him to Aghios Nikolaos in a couple of years.'

Yannis thought it could be a good time to ask his father if he and Stelios might search for pottery later and he asked the question tentatively.

'When the packing and loading's finished you can do as you please.'

Three more trips were made to the quay before Yannis senior called a halt, and they sat down with the cart behind them for shelter from the stiff breeze whilst they ate their lunch.

'No point in lingering. We may as well finish as soon as we can.' Yannis senior seemed more relaxed than he had earlier in the day. 'You boys load the cart and get down to the quay ready for Spiriton. He should have some empty boxes for you to bring back this time.'

They did as their father bade them, Yiorgo whistling tunelessly. Yannis felt mildly irritated by his brother's obvious pleasure in the manual labour. By the time they had completed the last trip to the boat, returning the donkey to her stable and the cart to the yard on their way back to the field, he was thoroughly bored. The girls were sent home to help their mother with the evening meal, whilst Yiorgo and his father collected tools and stacked the remaining boxes. Yannis took the opportunity of going to the other end of the field with Stelios. Together they scraped and scrabbled, oblivious to the rest of the world.

'Enough,' announced Yannis finally, and rose to his feet, flexing his knees. 'We'll do some more tomorrow.'

'I'm hungry,' announced Stelios.

'I shouldn't have let you stay so late. It was thoughtless of me.'

'I'm only hungry now we've stopped,' insisted Stelios.

They sauntered down the road as the darkness began to close around them. The island becoming a dark, crouched shape out on the navy blue sea, faintly menacing to Yannis in his imagination. The smell of cooking wafted out to them making them quicken their steps. Their mother clucked at them impatiently as they entered.

'Your supper will be ruined. Go and wash, both of you. Your hands are filthy.'

They looked at their begrimed hands and went outside

obediently. The pump clattered and splashed in the silent yard.

'Hurry up,' Stelios urged his brother.

Having eaten Yannis yawned hugely and his mother looked at him in surprise. 'Why so tired, Yannis?'

'I'm not used to walking up and down the hill. Come and play backgammon, Maria. Beating you will keep me awake.' To his surprise Maria beat him easily time and again. At last he threw up his hands in despair. 'You're far too good for me.'

'I play with Pappa.'

'That explains it!' Yannis senior was the acknowledged backgammon master of the village. 'I'll read for a while,' said Yannis, realising he had not picked up a book for a number of days. 'Shall I read aloud to you?'

'What is it?'

'Plato.'

'No thank you. I wouldn't understand a word. No, Yannis,' she stopped her brother as he was about to speak. 'I don't want you to explain it to me, I still wouldn't understand.'

Yannis grinned and settled himself nearer the oil lamp. Despite his intention to read he began to yawn again and his eyelids continually dropped, making the words swim before his eyes. He tried drinking another cup of coffee, but it was no use. He had to admit defeat and go to bed.

It was about an hour later that his mother shook him. 'Yannis, come down. Your Pappa's had an accident.'

'What do you mean?' Yannis sat up, blinking rapidly in the light of the candle his mother held. 'Let me put my trousers on.'

Maria led the way downstairs, Yiorgo following them. The back door stood open, making the candle flame flicker in the draught.

'Light the lamp, Mamma, and tell me what's happened.'

'Pappa went out to the yard and slipped. He can't get up.'

Yannis took the candle from his mother and walked to where his father lay, his leg bent beneath him. 'Pappa.'

A groan answered him.

'Mamma, bring the lamp. Yiorgo, you light some more. I'll go for the Widow.'

'It's the middle of the night, Yannis.'

'No matter; I'll go and wake her. Pappa's hurt.'

Yannis walked carefully down the village street. It was rutted from the carts and in some places there were loose stones. It would not help anyone if he fell. He reached the Widow's house and hammered on her door. Before he had gained her attention he had woken most of the neighbours. Clothes were hurriedly donned, oil lamps lit, and the villagers made their way up to the yard where Yannis's father lay. The Widow, leaning heavily on Yannis's arm, was one of the last to arrive. The small group opened a way for her and held their lamps so she could see her patient. Yannis senior opened his eyes. He tried to speak, but only a groan of pain passed his lips. The Widow forgot her age and knelt down beside him. Experienced hands ran over his legs.

'It's broken. I have to straighten it. Hold him tight.'

Firm hands pinioned his shoulders to the ground, then the world spun before him in a burning, searing flash of pain that ended in darkness and oblivion. When Yannis senior regained consciousness he was lying on his bed, his leg hurting intolerably. Maria was beside him, sponging his face to remove sweat and mud.

'What happened?'

'You fell over in the yard.'

Yannis senior struggled to sit up, the movement bringing a return of the excruciating pain.

'Lie still.' Maria placed a restraining hand on his shoulder. 'Your leg's broken. The Widow has splinted and bandaged it, but you must lay still.'

Her husband sank back. 'I have to work.'

'Don't be silly. You can't work with a broken leg! Try to sleep now. We'll talk about it in the morning.' Maria settled herself beside him. She felt drained and exhausted, but sleep would not come. Thank goodness Yannis was home. He would have to stay until his father recovered, despite his schooling.

The morning saw them all heavy eyed and lethargic. Yannis senior lay in bed, his leg throbbing, whilst Maria hovered over him, trying to make him comfortable. Yannis waited for his father's instructions.

'You must take the rest of the boxes up to the fields. Spiriton will bring more back from the island when he returns from the first trip. Yiorgo can handle the donkey and the unloading. The rest of you stay in the fields and do the packing. Try to do ten trips or I'll be losing money and so will Spiriton.' He shifted uncomfortably. 'I'll try and get up tomorrow and help.'

'Pappa, you have to be sensible. A broken leg takes weeks before you can stand on it again. You have to lay still. Yiorgo is sensible and knows how to run the farm. You tell us what you want done and we'll manage.'

Yannis senior nodded wearily. 'You're good boys. Off you go. Yiorgo will need as much help as possible.'

Yiorgo was already on his way down the hill with the first load when Yannis arrived. Spiriton's small boat was moored in the harbour, the men filling the water barrels whilst they waited. Yiorgo had to walk up and down with the donkey on every trip as she would walk with no one else. Whilst he was gone the others worked as hard and fast as they could to fill the boxes and be ready for his return. By mid-day they were exhausted by their efforts and glad of a break in the shelter of the trees. By the time the sun began its descent behind the hill Yannis realised they could do no more. Maria and Anna were stumbling, whilst Stelios was yawning and rubbing his eyes.

'Home you go. See if you can help Mamma. Yiorgo and I will finish here.'

Gratefully they made their way down the hill towards their home. Yannis wished he could go with them and wondered how Yiorgo could continue for so long without a rest. It was completely dark by the time the two boys took the loaded cart down the hill for the last time that day. Maria was waiting for them.

'Spiriton's gone. He said it was too late to do any more. He'll be back tomorrow.'

Yannis sighed with relief. 'We can leave the cart loaded. Was Spiriton annoyed because we were late?'

Maria shook her head. 'He understood. He thought you'd done well. Come as soon as you can, supper's ready.'

As they washed the day's grime from their hands and arms Yannis felt closer to his brother than ever before. 'You love the farm, don't you?'

Yiorgo nodded as he scrubbed at his hands.

'You've worked harder than any of us,' said Yannis, admiringly, 'Yet you don't seem tired.'

'I'm used to it,' Yiorgo answered simply.

'You know Pappa wants you to have the farm when he's old?'

Yiorgo looked up, delight written all over his face. 'Did Pappa tell you that?'

Yannis nodded in confirmation.

'I hoped he might, but there's you and the others.'

'Don't worry about me. I couldn't be a farmer. The girls will probably marry and Pappa's talking of sending Stelios to school in Aghios Nikolaos. I know Pappa wants you to have it.'

Yiorgo beamed contentedly at his brother's words.

Yannis senior was propped up in his bed listening to Anna's account of the day in the fields. He beckoned Yannis to join them.

'Yiorgo knows better than I how we managed,' said Yannis, shaking his head. 'He's the boss.'

Yiorgo and his father discussed the number of boxes that had been dispatched to the island and the number they still had to fill the following day. 'Don't forget the potatoes have to be lifted, then the beans and peas need to be cleared away and the soil turned ready for replanting. I had hoped to clear some of that marginal land so I could plant there.'

YANNIS

Yiorgo smiled at his father. 'Don't worry, Pappa. We'll try and finish the island tomorrow. The girls can strip the beans and peas whilst Yannis and Stelios help me with the potatoes. When we've done that we'll start on the marginal land. We'll have to turn it, once we've cleared rubbish. If we do a strip at a time it will be easy.' Yiorgo spoke more confidently than he felt. He knew what heavy work it was lifting and gathering potatoes. He shot a glance at his older brother. Weariness showed in his every movement as he sat, elbows on the table, slowly eating his supper.

As soon as he had finished eating Yannis excused himself. 'I'm going to bed. Wake me when you get up, Yiorgo.'

Yiorgo nodded. He had every intention of waking his brother at first light, and began to plan the day in his head whilst he ate.

It seemed to Yannis that he had no sooner laid on his mattress than Yiorgo, already dressed, was shaking him into wakefulness. 'Not yet,' he groaned.

'Come on,' urged Yiorgo. 'There's more to do than you realise.'

Obediently Yannis put his feet on the rag rug and groped for his clothes. He knew his brother was right and being tired was no excuse. It was barely light, but everyone was up. Maria busy packing their lunch to take up to the fields, whilst her mother poured coffee and tended to her husband.

Christmas Day came and time was taken from the fields to go to church to offer prayers for their father's speedy recovery and thanks that his injury had been no worse. Yannis prayed particularly fervently for a speedy recovery, as he knew he would be expected to stay and help on the farm until his father was able to move around again. He was too tired most of the time to be bored, but a feeling of frustration was building up inside him.

Maria had baked a magnificent meal for their return and Yannis had instructed her to produce his special brandy from the cupboard for a toast to his family who were working so hard. Yannis decided this was the time to give the presents he had kept carefully hidden and watched with delight as they were examined and exclaimed over. The girls tied their scarves around their heads and danced sedately in the small amount of floor space available to them. Stelios was pleased Yannis regarded him as old enough to possess a penknife the same as his brother's, but secretly he wished it had been a book. Yannis senior tried his belt for size as best he could from a sitting position, but Yannis's greatest pleasure came from seeing his mother put on the slippers.

'It's like being bare-foot,' she exclaimed time and again, putting them on and walking a few steps, then removing them to inspect the workmanship. Yannis watched with a smile on his face, which turned to amazement when his mother produced a gift for him from the cupboard. There were tears in Yannis's eyes as he thanked her. Two soft, warm sweaters in lamb's wool represented weeks of work, they were a real labour of love.

'I couldn't have asked for anything better,' he said as he kissed her. 'I shan't have a cold the rest of the winter if I wear these.'

'Try them on,' insisted Maria. 'I had to guess how much you'd grown.'

Yannis removed his jacket and pulled a sweater over his head.

'What's that?' asked Anna, pointing to the lump on his neck.

'Just my gland.'

'Ugh,' she shuddered. 'It looks all horrid.'

'Let me see.' Maria was on her feet, examining her son's neck. 'What's happened to it?'

'The doctor took a sample from it when he took the stitches out of my head.'

'What did the doctor say it was?'

'He said he would send it to the hospital and if there was any problem they would write to me. I haven't had a letter from them, so there's nothing wrong.'

'Does it hurt?'

'Not a bit, in fact I'd forgotten about it,' he replied cheerfully. 'Maybe if I grow a beard everyone will forget it'

Maria shuddered. 'Not a beard, only priests have beards.'

'It would be nice not to have to shave. That reminds me,' he ran a hand over his chin. 'Yes, I did shave before going to church.'

'I should hope you did! I hope you cleaned the mud off your shoes as well.'

Yannis senior clicked his worry beads impatiently. 'Pour me some more brandy. It's Christmas, even if I am laying here with a broken leg.'

'Not for me, Pappa. I have enough trouble getting up. Any more to drink and I'll stay in bed all day.' The work in the fields was exhausting Yannis.

'I have presents for you all,' Maria spoke shyly. 'They're only little things. I did them during the summer when we had time to laze around. I'll get them.'

She returned with two sheets of cardboard whish she laid carefully on the table. Between them was a collection of sketches she had made of each member of the family engaged in a task. At the bottom of the pile was a poor attempt at drawing her head and shoulders.

'How did you do that?' asked Yannis.

'I kept looking in the mirror. It was very difficult and I haven't done it very well.' She seemed embarrassed and went to replace the cardboard.

'I like it. Could I have it to take back with me?' asked Yannis and was surprised to see a look of horror in his sister's eyes.

'No! Oh, no, Yannis. Not this one. I'll do another for you. A better one, if you want me to.'

Yannis was amused. 'Who's this one for?'

Maria blushed as scarlet as the scarf Yannis had given her. 'A friend.'

'What's his name?' teased Yannis.

'I'm not saying.'

'It's Babbis,' said Anna, without looking up from the cat's cradle she was playing. 'You know he's courting her.'

Yannis did know, in fact the whole village knew that Babbis visited Maria. 'I like Babbis, I'm pleased for you, Maria.'

'He's a good worker.' Yiorgo measured everyone's merit by their ability to work. 'He's really built that place up since his father died. Worked all hours and weathers.'

Maria returned the cardboard container to her bedroom. It was embarrassing to have Babbis spoken of in such a way. Yannis senior pursed his lips. He considered his oldest daughter too young to marry yet. Besides, once she had married he would have Anna pestering him to let her do the same.

Stelios and Anna were sent to bed, whilst the other three played a game of cards. Yannis found it hard to concentrate and lost game after game until he finally pushed them away from him. 'I can't tell one card from another. I'm too tired.' He picked up the two new sweaters. 'Thank you, Mamma.' he said as he kissed her. 'I'm off to bed. Don't forget to wake me, Yiorgo.'

'I'm not likely to forget,' Yiorgo assured him and Yannis knew that was true.

The days merged into each other for Yannis. Every morning Yiorgo would shake him into consciousness as soon as it was light. He would trudge up the track to the fields, shivering in the early morning chill and toiled under Yiorgo's instruction until the sun rose to give them a little warmth. Yiorgo hardly rested and Yannis struggled to keep pace with him. By the evening Yannis was exhausted and stumbled back home, longing for his comfortable mattress, hardly able to eat the food his mother placed before him. Added to his fatigue was the continual worry about the amount of schooling he was missing. He had written to Yiorgo Pavlakis explaining that his father had met with an accident and that he would have to stay at Plaka to help until his father had recovered. He had also asked him to visit the High School and museum on his behalf. The letter he wrote to Annita he was able to send by a fisherman and she had answered him promptly, full of sympathy for his father.

1927 – 1930

It was four weeks after Yannis senior had fallen that the Widow appeared at the house with a pair of crutches tucked under her arm. Yannis and Yiorgo lifted their father to a chair and watched as he tried to stand.

'Only one foot,' screeched the Widow. 'You mustn't put the other to the ground. It won't be ready yet.'

Yannis senior was obedient. He went in great awe of the Widow, whom he had known since he was a boy. He had faith in her as a healer, but was not entirely sure that she wouldn't curse anyone who displeased her, and when she was in the house he watched her warily.

'I'll be able to get to the fields tomorrow,' he was more cheerful than he had been for days. It was good to be able to move around again, albeit slowly.

'Any more talk like that and I'll take them back with me,' the Widow warned. 'It's one thing walking across your living room; it's another when you try to walk outside. If you tripped you'd be back in bed again, probably worse off than before.'

Despite her threats, once she had gone, Yannis struggled out to the yard. He leaned against the wall, drawing deep breaths of air and looked longingly towards his fields. By the time he had reached the yard gate he realised there was no way he would be able to negotiate the rough ground without an accident. Reluctantly he dragged himself back into the house where Maria was baking bread. Wiping her hands on her apron she decided this was a good time to approach her husband.

'What's happening about Yannis?' she asked.

'How do you mean?'

'He should have been back in school three weeks ago. He's worrying about it, that's why he's so tired.'

Yannis senior snorted. 'I think town life has softened him. He gets more tired than Anna out in the fields. A few more weeks would toughen him up.'

'A few more weeks could ruin his chance of going to University,' observed Maria shrewdly.

Yannis was thoughtful. 'Well, he can't go yet,' he decided. 'Spiriton will be here in a few days for this month's contract. Yiorgo couldn't manage without him.'

'I could help now you're able to get about,' suggested Maria.

Yannis shook his head. 'You're not going back to the fields. You did enough up there when we first started. Besides, you have enough work to do here.'

Secretly Maria was relieved. She had no wish to return to the fields during the winter months. She had a pang of guilt that her daughters were expected to help each day, but consoled herself that they would come to no more harm than she had as a child. Maria even seemed anxious to go each day, but her mother had an idea that Babbis was coming to visit her so they could snatch a few moments together. Now it was cold they were unable to stroll down the village street together and sit outside the taverna. Babbis had to spend the evening with them and he was obviously ill at ease when he visited.

When their father told them Spiriton would be calling again Yannis's heart sank. He had hoped he might be able to leave at the end of the week. Yiorgo was worried. It had been all they could do to complete the work before.

The weather decided it had been kind to them for too long and changed dramatically. The sun stayed hidden behind the sullen black clouds that hung over the distant mountains, rumbles of thunder reaching their ears, which made them look up anxiously. The first drops of rain were felt when they were loading their third trip to the quay. They could see Spiriton waiting for them, impatiently scanning the hillside.

'It seems pointless packing in this weather,' remarked Yannis to his brother. 'It will be spoilt by the time it gets there and they'll have to throw most of it away.'

'That's their problem. Pappa said to pack as much as possible.'

'What about the crate?'

'This trip.'

Yannis shivered. That meant he would have to stop packing to help lift the crate onto the cart. 'Why don't we stay down and do the vegetables next? It would be quicker than this and we should be able to catch up a bit. The girls can stay up here and we'll come back to help as soon as we can.'

Yiorgo turned the suggestion over in his mind. 'We'll try it.'

Munching a roll each they negotiated the track with the donkey. The rain had made it slippery and Yannis had to pull on the cart to stop it from rolling too far forward. Once in the yard they were faced with a further problem. The crate was too heavy for them to lift between them.

'There's nothing for it. We'll have to ask Spiriton to send a couple of his men to help.' Even Yiorgo knew his limitations.

'I don't want to do that,' Yannis said stubbornly. 'There must be a way.' He looked at the miscellany of objects strewn around the yard. 'I know, help me unload.'

Yiorgo stared at his brother crossly. 'What for?'

'We can tip the cart and push it on.' Yannis had already set to work, stacking the boxes in a neat pile.

'It would have been more sensible to take these down to Spiriton first,' grumbled Yiorgo. 'That way we'd only do the job once.'

Yannis had to admit that Yiorgo was right and was about to

start replacing the boxes when his brother began to help unload. Even with the cart tipped back it was a tremendous struggle for the two boys to push the crate on, the rain was falling faster now, numbing their hands and stinging their faces. The boxes replaced they slithered down to the quay where Spiriton was waiting.

'We'll be as quick as we can,' promised Yiorgo as the boat drew away.

'I'll go on ahead. It doesn't need both of us to walk with the donkey.'

Yannis set off, slipping on the greasy mud, glad he had taken his father's advice and worn the old pair of boots that stood by the back door. At least his feet were warm and dry, which was more than he could say for the rest of him. When Yiorgo joined him he was busily sorting potatoes and placing them in sacks.

'Not like that,' Yiorgo remonstrated immediately. 'Use a spade.' He began to shovel potatoes in at break neck speed.

'A lot of those are rotten.'

'Makes no difference; so are the lepers.' Yiorgo continued without a break in his rhythm. 'Don't touch those over there. They're for us.'

Yannis obeyed. He had been right; filling sacks with produce, which could be shovelled in, was far quicker than packing boxes. By the time Spiriton returned they had the cart loaded and sacks standing by ready for the next trip. Yiorgo went down to the quay on his own, trying to guide the donkey and control the cart at the same time, praying that no mishap would befall them, whilst Yannis stayed shovelling. He was not sure whether the moisture that was trickling down his face, neck and back was rain or sweat. Another load was ready by the time Yiorgo returned, and so it went on for the next two hours, back breaking toil from which they dared not take a rest. The potatoes exhausted they retraced their steps up the hill.

'You were right, Yannis,' Yiorgo had to admit. 'Making up the sacks was quicker. The girls should have a load of boxes ready for us and then there are only three more trips and we've finished.'

'There's still tomorrow,' groaned Yannis.

'We'll try it the same way. Clear as many boxes as we can, then when we're running behind we'll go down and sack up carrots. That way we can catch up again.'

Yannis nodded. He really was past caring. All he wanted was to get home, rub his wet, cold, body with a towel, drink some of the hot soup he knew his mother would have prepared and sleep. Stelios arrived with a jug of hot soup and they took it in turns to stand under the dripping trees to drink. They worked frenziedly, Yiorgo taking a load down to Spiriton, whilst Yannis stayed to help his sisters.

'We're not going to manage it,' remarked Yannis gloomily. 'It will be dark soon.'

'Yes we will.' Maria spoke with determination and attacked the shrivelled cabbages viciously with her knife. 'Just throw them into the boxes, and Stelios can cover them.'

By the time Yiorgo returned the next load of boxes were ready. He grinned as four wet faces looked at him questioningly.

'He says it's too dark to take any more. We've got to take this load down and leave it on the quay ready for the morning.'

Maria rose from the ground. Her knees were muddy, her skirt soaked and her hands chapped with the cold rain. 'We've done it.'

They all helped to load the cart and Yiorgo slapped the unwilling donkey. 'Come on, old girl, then you can go home as well.' She looked at him reproachfully with her dark, soft eyes and shuffled forwards.

'Home you go, girls. Tell Mamma we're on our way.' Yannis collected their tools and began to follow them down. He felt elated, and the feeling shocked him. Was he becoming accustomed to working in the fields that he should be so pleased with the day's accomplishment?

He dumped the tools inside the yard and continued down to

the quay. Yiorgo would need some help with the final unloading and then they could walk back together to finish off the jobs in the yard. He need hardly have bothered, by the time he arrived there were only a few boxes remaining on the cart and Yiorgo appeared to have as much energy as when he had started that morning. Unexpectedly Yannis sneezed.

'Go home,' advised Yiorgo. 'Get some dry clothes on.'

Yannis shook his head. 'I'm all right.' He would sink even lower in his father's estimation if he returned home at the first sneeze and left Yiorgo to rub down the donkey and feed her. Wearily the two boys and donkey plodded home. The cart was unhitched and pushed into the shed, the donkey led to her stable where she was rubbed down and left with an armful of hay and a pail of water.

'Now our turn; I'm so tired.'

Yannis looked at his brother in surprise. 'I've never heard you say that before. It's always me who's complaining of tiredness.'

'You were marvellous today, Yannis. You had the strength of ten men.'

Ruefully Yannis shook his head. 'Thanks, but I still can't keep up with you.'

They stripped off their sodden clothes in the kitchen and took turns in stepping into the wooden tub that their mother had filled with hot water.

'Oh, that feels so good!' remarked Yannis, as he sluiced hot water over his shoulders. 'There was a time when I thought I'd never be warm again.'

Yiorgo nodded. 'This is what keeps me going on a bad day. I know Mamma will always have a hot tub ready for me.'

Yannis dipped his head under the water and pushed back his dripping hair. 'I must get this cut as soon as I get back to Heraklion. It's far too long.'

They towelled their bodies dry and donned warm sweaters and trousers, finally ready to go into the living room where the rest of the family were sat round the table. Immediately Maria left her meal to get theirs.

'Did you manage, boys?' asked their father.

Yannis nodded, leaving Yiorgo to explain to their father how they had worked and managed to complete the trips.

'I'm coming up myself next week,' Yannis senior announced to the surprise of his family. 'I'm getting about quite well now. If I sit on the back of the cart there and back I should be able to manage.'

Yannis swallowed hard. 'Pappa, if you're going up to the fields next week will you be needing me any longer?'

His father looked at him sadly. 'You can't wait to go, can you?'

Yannis flushed miserably. 'I'm worried about missing school.'

'I know, I know.'

'I'll stay as long as I'm needed,' promised Yannis. 'I'm not a lot of help, but I'm willing.'

'You've been a good boy. I'm proud of all of you, especially you, Yannis. You could have insisted on returning to Heraklion at the start of the term and I wouldn't have blamed you. Instead you stayed to help, and you did so uncomplaining. You go back when it suits you.'

'Thank you, Pappa, but I'll only go if you're sure you can manage.'

Yannis calculated rapidly. Today was Tuesday, and he must help Yiorgo tomorrow. If he returned to Aghios Nikolaos on Thursday he could catch the Friday bus to Heraklion. It was so important that he returned to school. He had missed four whole weeks!

Thursday arrived with a thin drizzle. He trudged along the cart track that was called a road between the two villages, wishing Yiorgo would be at the canal to meet him. His bundle grew heavier as the rain soaked through. In Elounda he entered a taverna where it was warm to the point of stuffiness, and dropped his burden to the floor.

He delayed his return to the cold drizzle as long as possible, lingering over his roll and coffee, before shouldering his bundle and leaving. As the wind began to blow the rain into his face he hunched himself down into his coat, pulling up his collar as far as he could and hoping his aunt would be able to dry it before morning in readiness for his bus journey. It was mid afternoon before the house he was seeking came into view and encouraged him to walk a little faster.

'Yannis! Yannis! It is Yannis!'

Yannis dropped his bundle and clasped his cousin to him. 'I'm so pleased to see you. Everywhere looks deserted.'

'Do you wonder in weather like this? Have you walked all the way? You must be frozen. Let's get home.'

Gratefully Yannis followed Andreas. 'Look who I've found,' he called as he opened the door.

Elena rose from her chair with an exclamation of pleasure. 'Yannis! We weren't expecting you. Did you write?'

Yannis shook his head. 'I had no time. Pappa said I could leave, so I want to catch the bus to Heraklion tomorrow. May I stay the night?'

'What a question! Of course you may. Take off that wet coat and come and get yourself dry and warm. Did you walk all the way?'

Yannis stretched out his hands to the welcome fire. 'I swear the road grew with the rain – it seemed to last for ever.'

Elena went to heat some soup for her unexpected visitor. Andreas sat in her chair and looked at his cousin.

'Are you all right?'

'Of course, just a bit damp and tired.'

'You look drained. Did you have to work terribly hard for your father?'

Yannis nodded. 'I'd never realised how hard he works. He has a contract to send food over to the island every month. Yiorgo and I slaved. Even the girls and Stelios were up in the fields in the pouring rain.'

'How did your father break his leg?'

'He slipped over in the yard. It was lucky I was home at the time, but goodness knows how much work I've missed. I'll probably do awfully badly in the next exams.' Yannis sighed deeply.

'It's a shame Annita isn't here. She had her day off yesterday.'

Yannis felt a pang of guilt that he had not asked after her, which was also tinged with relief.

Elena returned with a bowl of hot, thick soup. 'That will warm you. I wish Yiorgo would hurry up.'

'He's probably taking it slowly. There's a stiff breeze blowing and you can't see further than your nose.'

By the time Yiorgo arrived, soaked to the skin, even Yannis was beginning to be concerned about his safety. He was surprised to see Yannis at his fireside, but Elena insisted he changed his clothes before he talked.

'Why were you so late? We were all worried about you,' she asked him anxiously.

'Wind was against us. There's quite a sea running now. We tried to hug the arm for shelter, but didn't dare get too close.' Yannis and Andreas made room at the fire for him and he drank his soup noisily. 'What brings you here, Yannis? Your father well enough to leave?'

Yannis nodded. 'He said he could manage once we'd finished the island contract.'

Yiorgo nodded, a slight smile on his lips. 'It's a good thing, that contract.'

'That's what Pappa said. He'll be able to give the girls good dowries.'

'How long are you staying?'

'Only tonight; I must be back at school on Monday, so I'll catch the bus tomorrow.'

They chatted over the supper Elena produced, and Yannis was about to excuse himself and go to bed when Andreas rose. 'I have to go.'

Yiorgo and Elena nodded, but Yannis looked up in surprise. 'Go? Go where at this time on a night like this?'

Andreas flushed, looked down at the floor, then at his parents.

'Go on, or you'll be late. I'll explain to Yannis.' Yiorgo nodded to his son. He leaned forward on his seat. 'Andreas is contemplating entering the church. He goes along each evening for instruction.'

'Why didn't he tell us?' Yannis was puzzled and a little hurt.

'He felt you might laugh at him. He made his mother and I promise to tell no one until he was quite certain.'

'I won't say anything,' promised Yannis. 'It explains his mysterious disappearances. I often saw him coming out of church and yet I never guessed, even when he said a prayer for Aga.'

Yannis was so tired that Andreas coming to bed did not disturb him and Elena left him to sleep as long as she dared before he would be in danger of missing the bus. She insisted on waiting with him until it left. 'Come back soon,' she said as she kissed him goodbye. 'Annita will be sorry to have missed you.'

'I'll write to her as soon as I get back,' promised Yannis.

The driver made good use of his horn, frightening babies and startling the donkeys, gears ground and the engine laboured as they struggled up the first steep incline and out of town. The journey to Neapolis over, they climbed steadily higher before dropping down to the winding track towards the sea to continue on relatively flat ground to reach Heraklion. They passed through Eleftherias Square and crawled down the hill to the waste ground, which was called the bus terminal. Yannis was grateful to rise from the hard, wooden seat and be free from the shuddering and jarring he had endured for the past hours.

He made his way to the taverna by way of the harbour. It was good to see the familiar sights and know he was truly back in the city. As he pushed open the door of the taverna he thought Louisa was going to faint. Her face paled and she halted in the act of polishing a glass.

YANNIS

'Yannis? What are you doing here?'

Yannis frowned. 'I've come back to stay, to continue at the High School.'

Louisa had recovered her composure. 'We didn't think you were coming back. You should have been here four weeks ago.'

'Didn't you get my letter?'

Louisa shook her head and Yannis groaned.

'I wrote to Yiorgo. I explained that my father had broken his leg and I had to stay in Plaka to help on the farm. I asked him to let them know at the High School and at the museum.'

'Yiorgo didn't think to go to the post office. He was elected to the local government, and what with that and getting married soon he's been so busy.'

'Married?' Yannis could not believe his ears.

Louisa nodded. 'Yiorgo and I are to be married.'

Yannis felt confused. A few weeks ago Louisa had been declaring vehemently that she had no intention of marrying Yiorgo.

'I'm very pleased for you. What made you change your mind?'

'That's my business.'

'You can tell me. I shan't say anything to Yiorgo.'

Louisa looked at Yannis, finally deciding she could trust him. 'Do you swear?'

'I swear.'

'I'm pregnant.'

'You're what?'

'You heard. I'm pregnant.'

'Does Yiorgo know?'

Louisa gazed at him scornfully. 'Of course not, and you swore not to tell him.'

'But you can't marry him just because you're pregnant - or is it his?'

'I can, I will and it's not.' Louisa looked at Yannis defiantly.

'Whose child is it?' Yannis felt a cold chill creeping over his heart.

'What's that to do with you?'

'I thought, maybe, it was possible......' he faltered to a halt.

'Who knows? It could be, couldn't it?'

'Please tell me.'

'Why? So you can boast to your friends? Or would you want to marry me to make an honest woman of me?'

'No, I couldn't, but I'd be relieved to know it wasn't mine.'

'I'm sure you would! Annita wouldn't like to think her Yannis had been a naughty boy.' Louisa's voice was mocking.

Yannis shrugged. The parentage of Louisa's child was not his business. 'I'm going up to unpack. May I take a bottle of wine with me?'

Louisa nodded. 'Do you want something to eat?'

'Not yet; I'll have something later.'

Louisa watched him go up the stairs. Maybe she would tell him when she was safely married; she did not want him doing anything impetuous to spoil her plans.

Unpacking was a tedious chore, but Yannis decided to complete it before writing a letter to Annita. He told her how hard they had all worked and how he had left the farm as soon as his father gave him permission. He related his visit to her parents, but remembered his promise to Andreas and did not tell her the boy's intention of becoming a priest. He also vented his annoyance to her that Yiorgo had not been to the post office and consequently had not received his letter, but then excused him by saying how busy he had been, getting elected to a government position and also making wedding plans with Louisa. By the time he had finished he knew the post office would be closed and he placed it on his table to take the following day.

He ran his hands through his hair. He really must get it cut tomorrow. His fingers stopped, along his neck and up behind his ear he could feel a series of small lumps. He rubbed them with his fingertips; they didn't hurt. He had probably been bitten whilst he was working in the fields.

YANNIS

Yiorgo returned to the taverna and was as surprised as Louisa had been to see Yannis. He kissed Louisa passionately, revelling in this new pleasure she allowed him. He pushed back his lock of hair and ran his hand down his trousers.

'I am sorry, Yannis. Of course I should have thought that you would write. I've been so busy. Did Louisa tell you I'm a member of the government now?'

Yannis nodded. 'Congratulations. She also told me you are soon to be married.'

Yiorgo beamed. 'Isn't it wonderful news? The most beautiful girl in the world has agreed to marry me. Bring a bottle, Louisa. Yannis should celebrate with us.'

Despite Yiorgo's elation at his forthcoming marriage, his thoughts were all on his election success. 'I've had some posters printed. I make my first speech next week so I want to have a good turn out. Pavlos and I are going to distribute them tomorrow. You wouldn't like to help us, would you, Yannis?'

Yannis frowned. 'I will if I have time. I want to go to the museum, post a letter and get my hair cut.'

'If you could deliver some on your way to the post office it would be a great help. Now, would you like to hear what I'm speaking about?'

Yannis felt obliged to show an interest and spent the rest of the evening thoroughly bored. He had enjoyed the meat balls Louisa had made for them, drunk a bottle of wine and was having a job to stifle his yawns. 'I really must go to bed. I'm still catching up on my rest after all the hard work on the farm.'

Yiorgo nodded sympathetically, not really listening. 'And then I plan to say …'

Yannis rose. 'Tell me tomorrow, Yiorgo. I'm going to bed.'

Yiorgo looked crestfallen. There was no one else in the taverna to act as his audience.

Yannis lay in bed, revelling in the luxury. There was no point in getting up too early, as the post office would not be open, or the museum. He could get his hair cut first, but that would mean carrying around the bundle of posters that Yiorgo had asked him to deliver. He pulled his blanket up to his chin and lay there happily for a further hour.

Each shop he entered he had to explain to the owner why he wanted a poster displayed and he wished he had started earlier. By the time he reached the post office there was a queue and Yannis stood impatiently in the line. He paid for the letter to be sent to Annita and asked if there was any mail for Yiorgo Pavlakis. His own letter was returned to him and he sighed deeply.

'There's one for you.'

Yannis looked at the brown envelope first in surprise, then in horror. It was a letter from the hospital. He pushed it deep into his pocket, unsure whether he wished to open it. He could feel a cold sweat breaking out on him as he mumbled his thanks and on shaking legs left the building.

He turned into the first taverna he came to and took a seat by the door. With trembling fingers he tore open the letter and read the contents in disbelief. He was to report to the hospital immediately for further tests. Inadvertently his fingers went to the nodule on his neck. It did not hurt, but his fingers contacted a damp stickiness that made his stomach lurch.

The coffee he had ordered grew cold as he sat and tried to marshal his thoughts. If the doctor had thought it was something serious he would not have let him return to school. The hospital outpatients would be closed until Monday, so he might as well visit the barber and have a haircut and a shave, then go on to the museum as he had planned. He drank his cold coffee, pulled the neck of his pullover a little higher and left.

He joined the queue at the barber's and when his turn arrived he requested a shave followed by a haircut. The barber nodded and went to drape a grubby towel around his neck.

'I'll do it.' Yannis placed it over his pullover, but made no attempt to tuck it down, holding the ends firmly between his fingers.

YANNIS

A close shave made him feel considerably cleaner and he sat up ready to have his hair trimmed. 'Not too short, please.' He indicated a line with his hand.

The scissors snipped, removing the long hair that was beginning to form straggly curls. 'How's that, sir?' The barber stepped back and held up the mirror for Yannis to inspect the finished effect. None of the bites showed.

'That's fine.'

Before Yannis could stop him the barber had removed the towel and pushed down the neck of Yannis's jumper to brush away the ends of hair. As he did so an open nodule was revealed on his neck. The barber recoiled from him, visibly shaken.

'Get out. Get out quick and don't ever come back here.'

'It's nothing,' Yannis tried to explain, but the barber gesticulated towards the door.

'Out! I don't deal with lepers.'

Yannis's face blanched. 'I'm not. The .....'

'Out!' The barber was backing away from him.

'I haven't paid you,' protested Yannis.

'I wouldn't touch your money. Get out.'

The two men who had come in after Yannis rose and slipped through the door. There were plenty more barbers in town that lepers did not frequent. As Yannis stumbled through the door they spat at him, a globule hitting his face. Yannis wiped it away with his sleeve. Hot tears were stinging at the back of his eyes. He was not a leper, he could not be. Slowly, the tears forcing their way down his cheeks, he returned to the taverna. It was no use thinking of going to the museum. He would stay in his room for the weekend until the hospital opened on Monday. After his visit there he would go on to school and pick up the threads of his life again.

Miserably he pushed open the door. Louisa looked out from the kitchen. 'You were quick,' she remarked. 'I thought you were going on to the museum.'

Yannis swallowed hard. 'I thought I ought to catch up on my reading ready for school on Monday.'

She nodded, not really interested. Yannis helped himself to a bottle of wine, feeling in his pocket for the coins and retreated to his room. He examined his neck in the mirror and shuddered. The nodule was raw and open, the skin at the sides cracked and dry. With a sick fascination he explored it with his fingers. Nowhere did it hurt. Maybe if he covered it no one would remark upon it and it would heal up. He clung to the thought that the doctor had allowed him to return to school, so he could not be ill. He tried to read, but could not concentrate, his mind continually returning to the scene in the barber's.

Yiorgo knocked his door and entered. 'Did you finish delivering the posters?'

Yannis nodded. 'It took longer than I'd expected.'

'Are you coming down? We could have a drink and a game of cards when Pavlos returns.'

'No. I have a lot of reading to catch up on. Do you think I could have a tray up here? I can read whilst I eat then.'

'I'll ask Louisa.' Yiorgo was only too ready to return to the taverna where he could watch Louisa's every movement, still hardly able to believe that she had agreed to marry him. He had drunk half a bottle of wine by the time Pavlos returned.

'Did you finish?' asked Yiorgo eagerly.

'Yes, but what a time it took. I heard a strange story when I was out. People were saying there's a leper in town.'

Yiorgo and Louisa looked at him in amazement. 'A leper? There aren't any lepers around now. You must have misheard.'

'No, I didn't.' Pavlos was indignant. 'Elias told me that Dimitrakis had told him that Andreas, the grocer, had sat next to him in the barbers.'

'What was he doing there?'

'How do I know? Having a shave, I expect, or a haircut.'

'I'll go and ask Yannis. He said he was going to the barbers.'

Yiorgo ran up the stairs and knocked again on Yannis's door. 'Yannis, do you know anything about the leper?'

There was a moment's silence. 'What leper?'

'The one who went to a barber. We wondered if you'd seen him.'

'No. I really am busy, Yiorgo.'

With that Yiorgo had to be content. He returned to the taverna and shrugged his shoulders at Louisa and Pavlos. 'He said he hadn't seen him.'

Disappointed they began to eat their meal, and little information could be gleaned from the customers during the evening. It was always someone else who had told them. His description varied from an old man with one leg, to a young man with one arm, but despite all the rumours no one seemed to have any definite knowledge of the incident.

Yannis was hungrier than he had realised. He tried to convince himself that he was being foolish, but the thought that a customer in the taverna could once again brand him a leper horrified him. Time and again he rose and looked in the mirror, hoping he would see signs that his neck was healing.

He undressed and lay in his bed. Cold fingers seemed to be touching him as he tried to reason his fears away and sleep. Twice he gave up the struggle, re-lit his lamp and tried to read, but nothing could allay his terrors. Dawn came, finding him still sleepless. He rose stealthily, dressed quietly and made his way downstairs.

How could he spend the day? If he stayed in his room they would think he was ill, but he dared not sit in the taverna, certain that he would be recognised as the man who had been branded a leper by the barber.

Sounds from above decided him. He slipped out of the taverna into the chill morning, walking hurriedly away and round the corner. Where could he go? If he stayed in the centre of the town he was certain to meet someone he knew. He gazed around, as if lost, looking at the still sleeping houses. The tolling of a bell startled him. He smiled to himself, how silly to jump when a church bell sounded. The church! That was it, he would go to a church, and maybe there he could find some peace of mind.

Turning in the direction the sound had come from, Yannis walked through the back streets until he reached the plain, low building, the bell still swinging gently between the supports. He hesitated. Would he be questioned about his presence? He hurried down the steps and slipped into the dark interior, relieved to find few people inside. Taking a place at the back in the darkest corner he could find, he tried to concentrate on the service. He dared not light a candle for fear that he would be recognised. Kneeling, his mind rejected the words that fell from the priest's lips. The same sentence was repeated over and over again by him in a frenzied prayer.

'Please don't let me be a leper. Please don't let me be a leper.'

So engrossed was he that the few people leaving did not disturb him. A hand, placed on his shoulder brought him to his feet. 'I'm sorry. I must go.'

'There is no need to go. God's house is open to everyone at all hours. Maybe I can help a little.'

'No one can help me.' Tears coursed down Yannis's cheeks.

Gently the priest pushed him onto a chair and sat beside him. 'Tell me your troubles, then we'll decide if no one can help you.'

Yannis sobbed, his head on his arms. 'Don't touch me.'

'I shan't touch you.' The priest placed his hands in his lap. 'It's very cold in here. Would you consider coming to my room? There's a fire in there.'

Yannis shook his head. 'I can't. I can't go anywhere.'

'I have invited you. Whatever your problem, whether you wish to tell me or not, it would be more bearable if we were warm. I cannot leave you here in this distressed state and I do not wish to freeze to death. I haven't eaten yet and you're keeping me from my breakfast.'

'Go then.'

The priest shook his head. 'Not without you. Come and sit by my fire and have some breakfast. You don't have to tell me anything.'

Reluctantly Yannis followed the priest across to his house and into a small room, sparsely, but comfortably furnished with two rocking chairs, a low sofa, table and glowing fire. Still shaking with sobs, Yannis huddled down before the fire. Saying nothing the priest poured coffee for them both and placed a cup beside Yannis. Taking a seat in the rocking chair he picked up a sheaf of papers and began to read. The silence between them continued unbroken, until the priest rose.

'I have the next service to take. I doubt I shall be more than half an hour. Have more coffee if you wish.' With a swirl of his robes he was gone.

Yannis stayed huddled by the fire, his sobs gradually abating. The warmth was making him feel drowsy. With a sigh he stretched his cramped limbs and turned so he could rest his head on the chair behind him. Within a few minutes he was asleep.

The priest returned, looked at Yannis's sleeping form and sat down in the opposite chair. He studied the boy carefully. He looked well dressed and well fed. What could have happened in such a short life to cause such obvious distress? He poured more coffee and sipped at it slowly. He ought to tell his housekeeper there would be one extra for lunch. The fire was dying rapidly and he placed another log on the embers, making sparks fly out onto the threadbare rug. He stamped them out with his boot, gazing anxiously at the sleeping figure that stirred slightly. The poor boy was obviously exhausted. In the kitchen he found his housekeeper preparing his lunch.

'Can you manage a few more vegetables?' he asked. 'I think we may have a guest.'

She pursed her lips in disapproval. Nearly every day there was a 'guest', every parishioner knew they could have a meal with the priest whenever they were short of money. He was too kind hearted for his own good. Before she could answer him he had re-filled his empty coffee pot and was gone. He returned to the small sanctuary where Yannis still slept and attempted to read his next service through. Every movement or slight sound Yannis made distracted him and he felt unprepared when he had to return to his duties in the church.

At the end of the service he found Yannis just stirring. Taking his place in the chair opposite he smiled at the boy. 'Feel better now?'

Yannis nodded. 'I've been asleep.'

'For a while; It's nearly lunchtime. I hope you'll join me. I've told my housekeeper there will be one extra.'

'I can't.'

'Oh.' The priest seemed genuinely surprised and disappointed. 'I'm sorry. It will be wasted. My housekeeper will be upset.'

Yannis wavered. He had not eaten since the previous evening and his stomach felt empty. 'Maybe I could have a little, here in your room.'

'Of course,' the priest smiled broadly. 'I'll go and fetch it in about half an hour.'

Yannis rose from the floor and sat in the chair. 'Don't you mind me being here?'

'Why should I? I'm glad of your company. Being a priest can be very lonely.'

'My cousin wants to be a priest.'

'Really? That's good to hear. Does he live locally?'

'No.'

'Then I wouldn't know him. I know most of the novices who live here.'

'He's still at school.'

'He's very young to recognise his calling,' observed the priest.

'We should have guessed long ago. He said a lovely prayer for Aga.' Yannis's voice was wistful. 'She was our donkey. She died in the summer. Andreas insisted on saying a prayer for her.'

'He was very fond of her?'

Yannis shrugged. 'He hadn't known her long, but we were all fond of her. She was so good-natured, not like the one we have now who'll only walk for Yiorgo or Pappa.'

The priest nodded. The boy had a father, probably a brother and a cousin. At least he was not alone in the world, whatever his trouble was. 'You live in the country, then?'

'I used to. I live here now.'

'Do you like the town?'

'Very much.'

'Do you have some work?'

For the first time Yannis smiled. 'More than enough.'

The priest rose. 'I'll get our lunch.'

He had at least started the boy talking; maybe a meal and some wine would loosen the boy's tongue a little more. They ate their lunch in silence, the priest wondering how best to get Yannis to talk again.

'Did you go back to the country for Christmas?' he asked.

'Yes.'

'Your people were pleased to see you, no doubt.'

Yannis nodded, his eyes suddenly filling with tears.

'How is your mother keeping?'

'Fine.'

That was not the problem then. 'And your father?'

'He's a lot better now.'

'Was he ill?'

'He broke his leg.'

Again a blank. 'How about your brothers and sisters?'

'They're fine.'

'What do you do with yourself here that you're so busy?'

'I'm studying.'

'What for?'

'I hoped to go to University.'

The past tense was not lost on the priest. 'Did you fail your exams?'

'No.'

'Then why do you say "hoped"?'

Yannis buried his face in his hands. 'It's all gone wrong.'

The priest pushed his tray onto the table and leaned towards the distressed boy. 'Tell me about it. I may be able to help you.'

'You can't. No one can.'

'You don't know that. Some things seem impossible to us, then when we tell someone else they see the solution immediately.'

'No one can help me.'

'How can you be so certain?'

Yannis pulled down the neck of his pullover to expose the ugly wound on his neck. To his surprise the priest did not recoil in horror, but came closer and examined it carefully.

'What is it?'

'What does it look like!'

'I know what it looks like.'

Yannis turned his stricken face towards the priest. 'I'm a leper, aren't I? Now you'll want me to leave.' He began to rise from the chair.

'Sit back down. You've no need to go. I'd like to talk to you some more. What makes you so sure it's leprosy? Have you seen a doctor?'

'I went before Christmas. I'd had a fall and needed some stitches in my head. When he took them out he saw my lump and took a sample. He said if there was anything wrong the hospital would contact me. The letter was at the post office waiting for me yesterday.'

'Why hadn't you checked before?' The priest frowned.

'I only arrived back in Heraklion on Friday. I had to stay home longer than I'd planned because of my father's leg.'

'I don't think you should condemn yourself until you've been to the hospital. It could be a localised infection.'

'I've got some more lumps coming up.' Yannis lifted his hair.

'Yes, you do have a few.'

'What can I do?'

The priest sat back in his chair. 'I think that depends upon you. You can sit and fret and worry until you see a doctor or you could use your time constructively. Have you written to your parents to say you have arrived safely?'

Yannis shook his head.

'That could be your first task. You don't have to mention your worries or fears. Then you could try to catch up on some of your schoolwork. You must be behind.'

'I can't concentrate.'

'A letter does not take a lot of concentration. Do your letter; then set yourself some homework. What are you studying?'

'History and Literature.'

'Then you must have plenty of reading to do.'

'I tried to read yesterday.'

'That was yesterday. Today you can make a fresh start. Read one of my books if you want. I have another service fairly soon. When I've gone, choose a book or there's pen and paper on the table.'

'You're very good to me.'

'You're very good for me. I feel it is part of my duty as a priest to help people. I don't often have the chance. If I can help you through a bad twenty-four hours then I feel I'm fulfilling my calling. I'll bring some coffee back with me when I return.'

Yannis smiled at him gratefully. 'I'll try a letter whilst you're away.'

'Good. I'll be about an hour.'

Yannis did manage to write to his parents in the priest's absence. At first it was difficult. He wanted to blurt out his fears, ask them if he could go home and work on the farm, tell them how frightened he was. Instead he described his journey to Aghios Nikolaos, said he had been unable to see Annita, told them about the bus journey and then added Mr Pavlakis's news. He made no mention of his own doings, except to say that he was going to try to catch up on his reading. He had just finished when the priest returned.

'You wrote your letter?' His face lit up with a smile. 'Good. Now, shall we talk or would you rather read?'

'I'd like to talk,' admitted Yannis. 'I'd like to talk about you.'

'Coffee first, then we'll swap stories. I'm not very interesting, I'm afraid. The first thing you're going to ask is why did I become a priest, yes?'

'Oh, no; I know why you became a priest. It's obvious, you're so, so, oh, just so right. I was going to ask your name.'

'I'm Father Minos, and your name?'

'Yannis. Yannis Christoforakis.'

The priest held out his hand, for a moment Yannis looked at it doubtfully, then extended his own. 'I'm pleased to meet you, Yannis.'

Yannis looked at their clasped hands. 'Aren't you afraid to touch me?'

'No. Why should I be?'

Yannis hesitated. 'I might be contagious.'

Father Minos shrugged. 'I go to people who are dying. Many of them have something contagious. I can't refuse to give absolution to someone because I'm frightened that I might become ill. I have faith in my God. If it is his will that I catch a disease so be it. Until that time I'm immune, so why should I worry about touching you?'

'Do you really believe that?'

'I most certainly do,' replied Father Minos firmly. 'I believe that every obstacle that is put in our way during our lifetime is put there for a reason. We may not be able to see that when a misfortune occurs, but we have to have faith, faith in someone who is greater than all of us put together. If you are ill there must be a good reason. At the moment no one knows how you catch certain diseases, and it's only through studying those who are sick that the doctors eventually find out. There are many diseases for which there is no known cure; again, doctors need to try various medicines until they find the right one. Nothing is in vain, Yannis. You could be the person who helps them find the cure.'

Yannis shifted uncomfortably in his chair. 'I wish I had your kind of faith. There are hundreds of sick people in the world. I doubt if I'll make any difference. It just seems so unfair, so pointless.'

Father Minos shook his head. 'Always remember there is a purpose, even if we can't understand it. We're only a very small part of an immense pattern, but the tiny segment that is ours is essential to making the whole complete. But why are we talking like this? Tell me about your life on the farm.'

Yannis talked. He described his family and the years he had spent on the farm, followed by his schooling in Aghios Nikolaos. Father Minos led him on to talk of his hopes for University, watching the boy's eyes light up with enthusiasm when he spoke of the pottery he had found and the work he was doing in the museum. When Yannis finally finished reminiscing Father Minos rose.

'I have another service to take. Do you fancy joining me?'

Yannis hesitated, then agreed and followed the tall, dark figure into the dimly lit church, taking a place near the door. The service seemed interminable to him as he sat there; wishing he were back in the small, warm room. Try as he might to follow and join in, his thoughts drifted continually to his own worries and as soon as Father Minos returned to his house he hurried after him.

Once again Father Minos collected a tray from his housekeeper and they ate and drank together. The priest began to talk about his own life, how he, too, had lived in a village and wanted to be a bookkeeper. He had even taken his first examination at University before he decided that his real calling was in the church and plucked up enough courage to tell his father.

'What did he say?' Yannis was curious.

'He cried. He was so happy for me that I felt guilty for not telling him before,' smiled Father Minos.

'What did your mother say?'

'She was dead. She died when I was ten.'

'I'm sorry.' Yannis felt embarrassed.

'You don't have to be. I was terribly upset as a child, but now I see it for the best. Had she lived she would have been an invalid, confined to her bed for ever.'

The conversation began to flag and Yannis realised he had taken up most of the priest's day.

'I ought to go. I've taken up enough of your time.'

Father Minos smiled. 'I've enjoyed talking to you. You're welcome to visit me whenever you wish. Where are you going now?'

'Back to the taverna. I have to go back. All my belongings are there.'

'Have you told your friends?'

Yannis shook his head. 'I've told no one, only you.'

Father Minos laid a hand on Yannis's shoulder. 'Keep it like that. No need to worry them unnecessarily. Come and talk to me again tomorrow when you've been to the hospital.' Beneath his hand the priest could feel Yannis tremble. 'Have faith, Yannis. I'm always here if you need me.'

'Thank you, Father.' Yannis choked on the lump in his throat and turned away up the street.

Father Minos watched him sadly. He wondered if Yannis would visit him again and wished he had asked the name of the taverna so he could have enquired for himself.

Contrary to his expectations, Yannis slept well, not stirring until the sound of rain beating on his window aroused him. He shivered as he dressed, resolutely refusing to look at or touch his neck. The kitchen was cold when he entered and he lit the stove before looking for some coffee. As his water came to the boil Louisa appeared.

'You're early,' she remarked.

'The rain woke me,' explained Yannis. 'May I take some hot water up with me?'

Louisa shrugged. 'If you wish.' She sat down on the stool Yannis had just vacated and placed her head on the table.

'Are you all right?'

'Yes, just a bit queasy. It will pass.'

Yannis nodded and left her, balancing a roll on top of his coffee and carrying a jug of hot water. Once back in the privacy of his room Yannis decided to eat and drink before shaving. He realised he was delaying the moment when he would have to look at his neck in the mirror. Finally he picked up his razor. It was more with revulsion than curiosity that he undid the buttons on his shirt and looked at his neck. There was an ugly, disfiguring raw area, where once there had been a small, white lump. Gingerly he touched it, still surprised not to feel any pain. He shaved carefully, cursing as he nicked his chin, bringing blood to the surface. Re-fastening his collar and pulling on his pullover, he picked up his jacket and took a last look round as he left. Where was the letter he had written? He felt in his coat pocket, then his trousers, before remembering that it was lying on the table in Father Minos's room. He shrugged. He had promised the priest he would return to tell him the doctor's diagnosis, so he could collect it then.

Louisa was looking better when he re-entered the kitchen and was able to greet him with a smile. 'More coffee before you go?'

'No thanks.' He was about to enquire after her health when Yiorgo entered, pulling the girl to him and kissing her affectionately.

'Goodbye,' called Yannis, crossing the taverna rapidly and leaving before either of them could question him.

It was too early to go to the hospital and Yannis wandered

down to the harbour. He wanted to avoid any chance encounter with any of his friends from High School and stood watching those fishermen who had been out during the night unloading their catch. The heavy rain had lessened to a misty drizzle and Yannis shivered. Finally he hunched his shoulders and wandered into the town, turning into a taverna, resisting the urge to squeeze himself in beside the stove and two old men who were playing backgammon. He ordered coffee and lingered over it, until the owner began to cast suspicious glances in his direction.

Unwillingly Yannis dragged himself to his feet and slowly walked in the direction of the hospital. He took his place in the waiting room, surreptitiously studying each person who was already there and those who entered after him. Each time it was his turn to enter he let another patient go before him, until he was alone, sitting on a hard, upright chair.

'Are you coming in?' The doctor was standing in the doorway of his room.

Yannis swallowed. 'Yes, please.'

Yannis followed the white-coated figure into his room and sat in the proffered chair. 'What can I do for you?'

'You sent me a letter, asking me to attend the hospital.'

The doctor frowned. 'When?'

'I'm not sure. I only received it on Friday, but it may have been sent before Christmas.'

'Give me your name.'

'Yannis Christoforakis.'

The doctor removed a ledger from his shelf and began to run his index finger down a list of names, finally finding Yannis's. He read the information entered against it and looked at the boy carefully.

'Remove your shirt, please.'

With trembling fingers Yannis did so, trying to keep the afflicted side of his neck turned away from the doctor, who took up a stance behind him.

YANNIS

'Ouch!' Yannis jumped.

'Hmm.' The doctor continued to poke his neck, sometimes hurting him considerably and finally returning to stand in front of him, tilting Yannis's head first to one side and then the other. At last he returned to his seat and began to write.

'Put your shirt back on.'

Yannis sat, impatient for the doctor to finish writing, yet not liking to interrupt him.

'When did you first notice this condition?'

'I was about nine, I think. I had mumps.'

Almost imperceptibly the doctor raised his eyebrows. 'Why have you waited so long before coming here?'

'There was no need. It was only a little lump.'

'Did you ever see a doctor?'

Yannis nodded. 'He said it was a blocked gland and nothing to worry about.'

Leaning forward the doctor raised his voice. 'Tell me the truth, boy. You've known for years. Who's been hiding you? Your parents?'

'No sir, it's the truth.'

'Luckily for you it appears to be a localised infection.'

'It isn't leprosy?' Hope soared in Yannis's heart.

'Oh, it's leprosy, but after the years of neglect it could have spread to other parts of your body and it doesn't appear to be anywhere else. We'll take you in and give you a course of treatment. Have you got your things with you?'

Yannis shook his head. 'I'll have to go and fetch them. How long do I have to stay?'

The doctor shrugged. 'That depends. Months, maybe longer.'

The colour drained from Yannis's face.

'Give me your address and we'll send a cart for you.'

'No!' Yannis's voice was full of pent up emotion. 'I walked here this morning, I can walk again.'

'It's the law. All lepers are collected by cart.'

'Not me. I'll be back this evening.'

'You can't......'

The doctor's voice tailed away as Yannis slammed the door, his footsteps sounding loud in his ears as he ran down the corridor and out through the heavy wooden door. He continued to run until his breath came in gasping sobs and he was forced to rest in a doorway. He hated the doctor, with his hard, probing fingers. He wouldn't go back. He would go….. His thoughts failed him. Where would he go? There was nowhere to go. His parents would look after him, but at what cost? They would be ostracised by the rest of the village, maybe catch the disease themselves.

Certainly if the villagers found out he was a leper he would be driven out into the hills to fend for himself until the authorities finally found him and sent him to Spinalonga. He shuddered. Anything would be better than that. He could not return home, he could not stay at the taverna. There was no choice but to return to the hospital.

Slowly he regained his breath and began to plod miserably along the wet streets. The rain had stopped, but the sky was a sullen grey, promising to rain again shortly. By the time he reached the taverna Louisa had lit the oil lamps in an effort to attract customers and also add a little cheer to the day. For the first time Yannis wondered how he was going to explain his leaving. Ignoring her greeting he mounted the stairs to his room.

Systematically he sorted through his belongings and placed his books in the bottom of the sack he had unpacked such a short while ago. He added his underclothes, three good shirts, two pairs of trousers and the two pullovers his mother had knitted for him. His razor he wrapped carefully in a piece of newspaper and placed it in the pocket of his jacket, along with his collection of pens and pencils.

He stood in the middle of the room and looked around, tears coming into his eyes. It looked bare and deserted without his belongings strewn about. He would have to explain his sudden departure, but there was no way he could tell them the truth. He chewed the end of a pencil as he tried to think of an excuse.

Finally he wrote, "I have to leave on personal business. You can let my room if you wish. Thank you. Yannis." He read the note over and thought they would probably assume he had returned home. With a sigh he placed it on the table and weighted it with a book that belonged to Yiorgo. If he could leave unseen they might not find it until the next day.

Sadly he closed the door behind him and made his way quietly down the stairs, wishing his sack was not so heavy and did not bump against each step. Holding it in front of him he walked through the taverna, feeling Louisa's eyes on his back.

Once outside he breathed more easily. The rain was falling now, a strong wind blowing it in his face. Head down, the sack on his back, he made his way towards the church to keep his promise to Father Minos. The church was in darkness and Yannis knocked at the door of the house, waiting until an elderly woman whom he took to be the priest's housekeeper, opened it to him.

'May I see Father Minos, please?'

She shook her head, setting her large gold earrings swinging. 'He's out. He had a message this morning to say that old Dimitris was dying and could he go to him. As far as I know he's still there. You can wait for him if you like, although I don't know how long he'll be, or I can direct you to their house.'

'It doesn't matter.' Yannis turned to go.

'Can I give him a message?'

Yannis hesitated. 'Could you tell him it was Yannis on his way to the hospital.'

'Of course. God be with you,' she called after him as he walked along the wet street.

The sack grew heavier, the ground seemed slippery beneath his feet, and three times Yannis lowered his burden to regain his breath before he saw the bare walls of the hospital loom up in front of him. He leaned against the doorway, shivering from the cold as well as the fear inside him. He felt the door give beneath him and stepped aside hurriedly.

'Are you waiting to go in? There's no need to knock. The door's open.'

Yannis passed through into the hall and walked down the passage to the room where he had seen the doctor and knocked tentatively on the door.

'Come in and wait.'

He stood just inside the room, his sack on the floor beside him, and waited. After an interminable time the doctor looked out from his inner room.

'Well, well, I was certain I'd not see you again for a few weeks.'

'I said I would come back. What do I do now?'

'A few formalities, and then I'll take you to the ward.'

Yannis nodded. He no longer cared very much. Emotionally he was drained and exhausted. He sat down on the chair opposite the doctor and waited.

'We'll need the name of your family and their address.'

'Why?'

'They will have to be checked. You could have caught it from them or given it to them.'

Yannis thought rapidly. 'I have no family.'

The doctor frowned. 'You told me earlier you went home at Christmas.'

'I went to my home.'

The doctor looked at him suspiciously. 'And where is that?'

'Thrapsano.' Yannis named the first town that sprang to his mind.

'We can check up, you know.'

Yannis shrugged. 'Do so.'

'Have you any money to pay for your treatment?'

'How much does it cost?'

'That depends how long it takes. If you hand over what you

have I'll give you a receipt. When you leave your expenses will be deducted.'

Yannis pulled a bundle of notes from the top of his sack and placed them on the table in front of the doctor. The doctor counted the notes quickly, wrote the amount down on a piece of paper, signed it and handed it to Yannis.

'Keep that, it's your receipt. Now, if you'd like to follow me.'

Yannis pushed the piece of paper into his pocket and followed the doctor from the room, down a maze of passages and up a flight of worn stone steps until they stopped before a stout door that had a grill inset at eye level. Taking a bunch of keys from his pocket the doctor unlocked the door. Curious eyes studied Yannis as he entered.

Yannis gazed back. Everyone had a look of resignation, but none of them looked ill. The doctor indicated a bed at the end of the ward and Yannis walked towards it. The doctor took a last look round, nodded and left the ward, locking the door behind him. Yannis sat on the bed, not knowing what to do next.

'I should take your things out of that wet sack,' advised a voice.

'Yes, yes, I will.' Slowly Yannis began to remove his clothes, followed by his books. As he laid them on his bed they were picked up, thumbed through, commented upon and placed back again.

'Please, leave them alone.'

'We're not hurting them.' A book was tossed back carelessly and Yannis stretched out his hand to prevent it falling to the floor.

'Is there anywhere I can put them?'

'Your box is there.'

Yannis looked where the finger pointed. At the head of the bed stood an open wooden box. 'Do I put everything in there?'

'Where else?'

For the first time Yannis took stock of his surroundings. At the end of the ward there were two washbasins and a small, screened area that he took to be the lavatory. The beds were placed a few feet apart against the walls, each having a box at its head. Running down the centre between the beds was a long table with upright wooden chairs. Light filtered in through grimy windows set high up in the walls, but now oil lamps, making the shadows of the patients look like giants, lighted the ward.

As he placed the last of his belongings into the box he heard the key turn in the lock. An orderly pushed a trolley containing food into the room, called "supper" and withdrew, locking the door after him.

'May as well see what it is. Come on.' The man who had advised Yannis to unpack had stood watching his every move, now he pushed Yannis before him towards the trolley.

'I'm not very hungry,' protested Yannis.

'You will be if you don't eat,' remarked Yannis's new acquaintance as he helped Yannis to a spoonful of a doubtful looking mixture from a large bowl.

'What is it?' asked Yannis.

'I've no idea. Doesn't taste too bad.' He licked the finger he had dipped into the mixture; then ladled some onto his own plate. 'Take plenty of bread.'

Seating himself next to Yannis he proceeded to introduce himself and the other occupants of the ward. Hardly registering their names Yannis nodded in acknowledgement, wishing his companion would stop talking and leave him with his own melancholy thoughts. Finally he turned to Yannis, laying down his spoon and fork.

'Are you always this unsociable?'

'I'm sorry.'

'You will be, unless you loosen up. You haven't even told us your name!'

'I'm Yannis. I don't mean to be rude. I can't quite get used to the idea that I'm in hospital.'

'You will. Everyone does in time.'

'How long have you been here?'

'Some months. They say I'm responding to treatment, so it may not be too much longer.'

Yannis nodded. 'What about everyone else?'

'Various stages of treatment. Different people respond differently.'

'What happens if you don't respond?'

'I've no idea. We've about an hour before the lamps will be burnt out. Would you like a game of backgammon?'

Yannis shook his head. 'I'd rather read; if you don't mind.'

'All the same to me.' Vassilakis returned his plate to the trolley.

Yannis sat at the table, his book before him. The words danced before his eyes and he soon gave up any pretence of reading and gazed furtively around the room. There was laughter and talk, games of dice, backgammon and cards being played. Men looked back at him, some curiously, some friendly, some disinterested, but to his relief none of them looked ill. If they did not look ill, he reasoned, they were obviously not seriously ill. If they were not seriously ill, he could not be either. The thought gave him comfort. If Vassilakis was responding to treatment he would respond also and his stay would only be of a few months duration.

Yiorgo Pavlakis read the note left by Yannis and frowned. 'How strange,' he remarked to Louisa. 'What could have been so urgent that he had to leave without saying goodbye?'

Louisa shrugged. She had her own ideas why Yannis had left and she had no wish to discuss them with her fiancé.

'I suppose his father needed him,' continued Yiorgo. 'Why come back at all? He had most of his belongings with him. We could have packed the rest and sent them down to him, or even given them to my old landlady to give to his relatives when she comes up for our wedding. Oh, Louisa, I am the happiest of men. I can hardly believe that in a few weeks time I'm to be your husband.' He dropped a kiss on her hair and caressed her cheek with his hand.

'I hope you'll not be disappointed.'

'I shall never be disappointed in you,' he assured her.

Louisa's eyes flickered upwards. 'I shall remind you of your words if necessary.' She spoke quietly and Yiorgo imagined the words held a hidden threat. He looked into the unfathomable depths of her eyes; then kissed her passionately.

'I shall always love you, Louisa,' he vowed.

Father Minos eyed the letter that sat on his table. What should he do? The boy had not come back. A whole week had gone by without a sign of him. He sighed. The hospital must have declared him well, so he had no further need of comfort from a priest. It was a sad fact of life that he was gradually accepting, but he had thought Yannis to be different from the usual distressed people he tried to help. Obviously he had been wrong. The boy was the same as anyone else.

He picked the letter up and tapped it against his hand. Should he send it? There was probably little point. Yannis would have written another by now. He had it in his hand when his housekeeper appeared with his tray.

'He didn't come back,' observed Father Minos as he placed the letter back on the table and took the tray.

'Who?'

'The boy who was here last week.'

A look of consternation came over the old woman's face. 'I forgot!' Her hand went to her mouth in horror. 'I've never forgotten to give you a message before.'

'What did he say?'

The woman's brow wrinkled. 'I'm not sure now. I think he said his name was Yannis and he was going home.'

Father Minos smiled. 'I'm very pleased for him.'

'It won't happen again. I never usually forget to give you a message.'

'I know you don't. This one wasn't important. No need to

worry.' He glossed over her mistake and turned his attention to the tray.

Maria was worried. Why had Yannis not written to say he had arrived safely in Heraklion? Her husband assured her that Yannis would be too busy to write, he would be catching up on the work he had missed at school.

'He's always written before,' grumbled his mother.

'I'll write to him, Mamma,' promised Maria. She sat and wrote a long letter to her brother, explaining that they had not heard from him, maybe a letter had gone astray in the post, and her mother was worried. She told him how their father was progressing, how she had sold another drawing, and that Yiorgo was working very hard in the fields, finishing by sending him love from all of them.

The letter sat on the shelf for three days before Maria remembered to go down to the general store and pay for it to be taken to Heraklion. Smiling contentedly she returned home, hoping her brother would write soon to put her mother's mind at rest.

Annita wrote to Yannis each week and waited anxiously for a reply. She had received his first letter to say he had arrived; then there was silence. At first she excused this by saying he must have work to catch up on, but she began to feel resentful. What was more important to Yannis; spending time socialising with his friends and working at the museum or writing a letter to her? She became convinced that he had succumbed to the charms of a girl from Heraklion and spent her nights tossing and turning, tormented by her own miserable thoughts.

Finally Annita confided in her brother and persuaded him to make her a promise. A promise that he hoped fervently he would not have to keep. He had arranged to spend the Easter holiday at the monastery at Ierapetra, now he had promised Annita that if she had not heard from Yannis by then he would visit Heraklion and talk to him, finding out the reason for his silence.

As Easter drew nearer he was beset by a further problem. He would need money to stay in Heraklion. His parents would give him sufficient for his fare, ostensibly to Ierapetra and a little over, but even that might not be sufficient to take him to Heraklion. He approached Annita, and she gave him the ten drachmas she had saved since starting work at the hospital. With this Andreas had to be content.

The journey was uneventful to the driver, but every mile was a delight to Andreas. At times there was a sheer drop down to the sea and the road seemed far too narrow for them to travel safely. Rocks had fallen from the bank that rose up steeply and in some stretches the driver had to take the vehicle sickeningly close to the edge to avoid hitting them. Andreas rose to leave the bus as they coasted into Malia.

'Thought you were going to Heraklion?'

'I thought we were there,' explained Andreas feeling foolish.

'Not yet.'

The driver accelerated and Andreas was almost catapulted onto the floor. He gripped the edge of the seat, feeling excitement beginning to build up inside. He tried to suppress the emotion, reminding himself that he had deceived his parents.

The bus ground wearily up the hill towards the town and then hurtled dangerously down the other side to stop abruptly, once again nearly shooting Andreas from his seat. The driver jumped out, followed by the few other passengers who had joined them during the journey. Andreas waited until last, not wishing to repeat his earlier mistake.

He looked around him. Which way should he go? He pulled the scrap of paper from his pocket and studied the address of the taverna before approaching the bus driver.

'Can you tell me the way to this address, please?'

The driver shook his head. 'Can't help you there. I suggest you go to a taverna and ask.'

Andreas shouldered his bundle and made his way up the hill. He had expected to find the town busy, but Heraklion appeared to have most of the world's population milling in Eleftherias Square. He stood and watched, fascinated, as the people moved about their business. Deciding that the middle road would lead him to the centre of the town he began to weave his way through the people, donkeys, carts and small, three-wheel trucks. On reaching the road he felt more bewildered than ever, and realised the suggestion from the bus driver made sense. A boy, probably not as old as he, asked what he wanted, and reeled off a list of food and drink that made his head spin.

'I'd just like some directions, please.' Andreas pulled the crumpled piece of paper from his pocket. 'Can you tell me the way to that address?'

Screwing up his eyes the boy looked at it and shook his head. 'I'll ask inside.'

Fidgeting, Andreas looked after him, hoping he would return with the information quickly and not forget. It was like being in the centre of Aghios Nikolaos, but with many more people. The same activities were going on all around him, but with more speed, a hurried intensity seemed to emanate from everyone as they pushed, jostled, shouted, laughed and talked. Diving in and out amongst them were men of various ages with swinging trays of coffee, stopping only long enough to collect their few coins before returning to a taverna for further supplies.

'You go along the main road here, past the market,' the voice made Andreas jump, so engrossed was he in the scene before his eyes. 'Then about four or five roads on you turn to your right. Better ask again then. It's in one of the side roads.'

Following the waiter's instructions he joined the throng on the main road. The market was not hard to find and it seemed that most people he was walking with were destined for that area.

Not sure how many roads he had crossed he looked around for someone to ask. On the corner stood a man with a cart loaded with oranges. Andreas approached cautiously, half expecting to be knocked over by someone racing round the corner, but his only encounter was with a bent, old lady who pushed past him and began to handle the fruit.

Andreas waited until she had shuffled away; then produced the dog-eared piece of paper again. 'Please can you tell me how to get to this address?'

'What does it say?' The orange seller peered at it.

Andreas read the address out to the man who shrugged. 'Could be anywhere. Who runs it?'

'A brother and sister.'

'Sounds like Louisa's place. Turn down there.' A grubby finger pointed to a narrow alley. 'About half way along turn right, then turn left at the end of the road and sharp right again. If you get lost ask for Louisa's. Everyone knows her place.'

Thanking him Andreas started off down the alley and took the appropriate turns. After the bustle of the main streets the area appeared deserted. At the far end of the street an old woman, dressed in the habitual black of a widow, was sitting in her doorway.

'Excuse me, ma'am, can you tell me the way to Louisa's please?'

Rheumy eyes looked at him. 'Round the corner. She's not there now, though.'

Andreas thanked her and hurried round the corner where he could see the taverna. He pushed at the door, which did not yield, then hammered on it, standing back to see if anyone had heard him.

'What do you want?' A voice called from the opposite side of the road.

He spun round gratefully. 'Is this Louisa's?'

She nodded. 'You're at the right place, but there's no one in.

Pavlos has gone to work. He'll be back this evening. His sister's away.'

Andreas felt deflated. 'Thank you, I'll come back later.'

He wandered down the narrow street and to his surprise found he was close to the harbour. He gazed at the fishing boats in delight. He would surely find a fisherman who knew his father and would be willing to give him a bed for the night. As he neared them he was surprised. Not a single fisherman was mending a net or swilling down his deck. Andreas was puzzled. At home there was always a certain amount of activity. Further out in the sheltered bay was a large ship, a white flag with a red cross fluttering from the mast. By screwing up his eyes Andreas could see there were people aboard, moving slowly about their business.

Losing interest, he walked on, admiring the fort that stood guarding the harbour entrance, wondering if Yannis had visited it. Vaguely he wondered where the museum was and if Yannis was there. As the thought struck him he cursed himself for being foolish. Of course Yannis would be there. He hurried along to the waste ground where the bus had deposited him and back up the hill to the Square, entering the first taverna he saw. Breathlessly he asked for directions to the museum.

'Over there.'

He walked over to the dingy building. The door was locked. Of course, it was Monday. Museums and libraries were always closed on a Monday. He leaned against the wall and took stock of his surroundings. He might as well explore the town. The road curved, following the contours of the massive stone wall that ran as far as he could see. He guessed it was the old boundary wall of the city so he was hardly likely to walk far from the centre. The further he went the poorer the area seemed to be, the houses more neglected, the occupants gazing at him curiously, children running after him and begging for a coin, young women leaned from their doorways and smiled and beckoned to him. He looked around wildly as he quickened his stride; there seemed nowhere he could go to avoid the undesirable neighbourhood without turning back. A priest left a house a few doors away and Andreas called to him, panic in his voice. 'Father. Please, Father, wait for me.'

The priest turned, expecting to see one of his parishioners and to his surprise a young boy who was a total stranger to him stood there. 'Did you want me?'

'Please may I walk with you? I'm a stranger here and I've wandered away from the centre and lost myself.'

'Certainly you may walk part of the way with me, then I'll direct you.'

Andreas breathed a sigh of relief and walked in silence beside the man who called out a greeting or waved to many of the people as they passed. A bell in the distance began to toll mournfully and the priest quickened his pace. Andreas kept up with him, noticing people were following behind them. The priest hurried into a side road where the street widened to form a small square. Drawn up outside the double doors of a building was a large, open cart, half loaded with boxes. The bell seemed to be ringing inside Andreas's head and he realised it was placed on the roof of the building.

'What is it? What's happening?' Andreas turned to the priest for enlightenment.

The priest had sunk to his knees. 'They're moving the lepers.'

Andreas gazed in fascination, tinged with fear, as the men came out in single file and climbed into the cart. They none of them looked particularly ill, just somewhat shabby and apprehensive.

Andreas felt the blood freeze in his veins. His head swam in disbelief as he clutched at the priest's sleeve. The crowd, which had gathered, were hissing and hurling whatever missile they could lay their hands on. The last man to climb into the cart looked around, unable to believe the sight before him. For a split second his eyes and those of Andreas met.

YANNIS

'Yannis!' The exclamation came from the priest and Andreas at the same time. Recognition reached Yannis's brain as the rock thrown from the crowd hit him on the temple and he fell unconscious amongst the occupants of the cart.

Father Minos was the first to recover. 'You know him?'

'He's my cousin.' Andreas almost choked on the words.

'May God forgive me.' Father Minos crossed himself. 'The poor boy! All this time.'

'Where are they taking him?' Andreas was wild eyed.

'To the ship. They'll take them to Athens.'

'We must stop them.' Dragging the priest by the arm Andreas began to follow the cart.

Father Minos resisted. 'I've no power to stop them. You must understand that. They're going to the hospital over there.'

'I must speak to him. There must be some mistake.'

'We'll go to the harbour. Follow me.'

Father Minos gathered his robes in his hand and began to hasten away from the hospital, Andreas following him, his breath coming in panting sobs. They reached the quay as the cart drew up. Father Minos started forward.

'I wish to speak to one of the men. He was a parishioner of mine.'

The crowd had grown and it seemed to Andreas that the whole population of Heraklion must be at the harbour. Father Minos pushed his way through to where Yannis had been placed on the ground and knelt beside him.

'Yannis, can you hear me? It's Father Minos. I didn't get your message. Yannis, can you hear?'

The inert figure made no response. Andreas bit back his sobs. 'He's dead. They've killed him.'

Father Minos shook his head. 'He's not dead, just stunned.' He turned to the guard. 'May I take this man? I'll look after him and be responsible for him. I believe there may have been a mistake.'

The guard shook his head. 'There's no mistake. He's to go to Athens with the others.'

Andreas tried to lift Yannis's head. A hail of stones surprised him and he lay across Yannis's face to try to prevent further injury. Father Minos pulled him back.

'I told you there was nothing I could do. You must look to yourself. They'll send you as well if you're not careful.'

Andreas realised the truth of the priest's words as those nearest to him began to draw back and whisper "leper". The priest pulled the boy into a kneeling position and began to pray, Andreas joining him fervently.

As the boat drew away the people began to disperse and Andreas looked around furtively. He waited until Father Minos rose and followed suite. The priest looked at him anxiously.

'I think you should come back to my house for a while. We can get to know each other better and I'd like to hear more about Yannis.' Not waiting for a reply he led the way up the hill and away from the port. Andreas followed him obediently. Once inside the priest's house he sank down gratefully in a chair whilst Father Minos opened a cupboard and returned with two glasses of brandy.

'Drink this,' he ordered. 'It will make you feel better. It was most unfortunate that you had to witness that ugly scene.'

Andreas sipped at his glass and screwed up his face. 'That's horrible.'

'It's brandy – for medicinal purposes,' smiled Father Minos as he emptied his glass. 'Sip it slowly. It will calm your nerves. Tell me, is that young man really your cousin?'

Andreas nodded. 'I came here to look for him. He wrote to my sister to say he had returned safely and we've not heard a word since.'

Father Minos looked at the boy speculatively. 'Do your parents know you are in Heraklion?'

Andreas flushed. 'No one knows I'm here except Annita. She's betrothed to Yannis. I promised her I'd come if we hadn't heard from Yannis by Easter. He always stayed with us before going on to Plaka. What's happened to him?'

Father Minos spread his hands. 'I don't know all the facts. I met him when he'd just returned to Heraklion and was rather worried about a letter he'd received from the hospital. We spent a day together. I feel I know you all so well.' Father Minos poured himself another brandy. 'I failed him. I shall never forgive myself.'

'You failed him?' There was curiosity in Andreas's tone.

Father Minos nodded. 'He agreed to come to tell me what had happened at the hospital. I wasn't in when he arrived and my housekeeper muddled his message and gave it to me a week later. I should have enquired at the hospital.' He drained his glass a second time.

'What will happen to him now?'

'He'll go to Athens for specialised treatment.'

'How long will it take?'

'I've no idea. I'm not a doctor. Had you no idea he was sick?'

Andreas shook his head. 'We just thought he was busy catching up on his studies. I was going to the taverna this evening to see if I could find him. There was no one in earlier.'

'Strange that they should not have contacted his family,' observed the priest. 'His schoolteacher lived there also, I believe. He must have known why Yannis left.'

'I don't know. I may have been at the wrong taverna anyway.' Once again Andreas pulled the scrap of paper from his pocket and handed it to Father Minos.

'We'll go along together.'

'I couldn't think of anywhere else to go for information.'

'Why didn't you go to the museum? Yannis said he spent most of his spare time there.'

'I did, but it's closed today.'

'Monday, of course it's closed. Do you feel sufficiently recovered to go to the taverna now?'

1927-1930

Andreas nodded; then looked round the room. 'My bundle? Where is it? I dropped it when they were stoning Yannis.'

'I expect they loaded it with the boxes. What was in there?'

'My clothes. I'll have to tell Mamma where I've been and what has happened. Once I've done that I doubt she'll be very worried about a few shirts.'

'You're probably right. Have you eaten since breakfast?'

Andreas shook his head. 'I've had a coffee.'

'We'll see what they're serving at that taverna.'

They left together, Andreas wishing he could linger in the church for a while. 'When do you take a service?'

'Later this evening. This is really my day off. I only take two services then, one in the early morning and the other in the late evening.'

Andreas nodded, determining to return for the evening service. They walked through mean, narrow streets until they arrived at the taverna Andreas had seen earlier in the day. Pavlos greeted them impersonally and brought the bottle of wine that Father Minos requested.

'I should like to talk to you for a short while. Please, have a drink with us.'

Pavlos accepted and perched on the edge of a chair.

'I'd like to talk to you about Yannis. He lived here I believe.'

Pavlos nodded. 'Until Christmas, then he went home.'

'Didn't he return?'

'Arrived on the Friday and left on the Monday. He left a note saying we could let his room. He went back home.'

'I understand his teacher lived here with him. Didn't he say goodbye to him?'

Pavlos wrinkled his forehead. 'Not that I know of. Yiorgo seemed as puzzled by his sudden departure as I was. He didn't even ask for his father's money back.'

'Do you still have the money?'

Pavlos shifted uncomfortably in his chair. He wished he had

not mentioned the money. 'Not all of it. My sister was married last week.'

'It's not important.' Father Minos looked at Pavlos. 'I have to tell you that we saw Yannis this afternoon. He was being sent to Athens on the hospital ship.'

The glass Pavlos had been holding slipped from his hand and crashed to the floor. His face became ashen and although his mouth worked no words came. There was only one reason why people were sent to Athens on the hospital ship.

'I had no idea.' Pavlos looked at them with terror in his eyes.

'Did your sister know?'

'I'm sure she didn't. She would have told me. We would never have let him a room.'

Father Minos sighed. 'Yet before you knew of his affliction you were quite happy to take his money?'

'Please, understand,' Pavlos defended himself, 'a leper living in a taverna! No customer would ever go there again.' His eyes swivelled round the empty tables. 'We would be ruined. Just as we were getting back on our feet! Please, I beg you, tell no one that he stayed here.'

'Your sister must be told, and his teacher.'

'Yes, of course,' agreed Pavlos. 'But no one else; please tell no one else. I'll return his father's money. I had to give my sister a dowry, you understand. We'll work hard when my sister returns.' Suddenly craft took the place of fear in Pavlos's eyes. 'If word should get around we would be quite unable to pay anything. We'd have to keep it as compensation for our ruined business.'

Father Minos looked at the young man with contempt. 'You don't think Yannis's father might need compensation for the loss of a son! Come, Andreas.'

They left the taverna, Pavlos still pleading with them for secrecy, walking in silence until they turned the corner. Father Minos placed a hand under Andreas's elbow to steady his swaying gait.

'You need some food, but I thought it better not to eat there after all.'

They threaded their way through the dark streets until they reached a taverna by the harbour. 'They serve a reasonable meal here,' he remarked. 'Not a great selection, but wholesome.' He held up two fingers to the waiter who nodded and began to prepare a salad.

Having eaten moussaka with salad and three hunks of bread Andreas felt considerably better. Father Minos regarded the boy's healthy appetite with something approaching amusement. He leaned across the table towards him.

'Now you're feeling better I think we should have a talk. Where do your parents think you are?' Father Minos did not want a runaway on his hands.

'At Ierapetra.'

'What should you be doing there?'

'I asked if I could stay at the monastery for a week.'

Father Minos raised his eyebrows. 'A strange request.'

Andreas shook his head. 'I want to enter the church,' he felt the colour flooding his face. 'I've wanted to do so for some years now. I have instruction from my local priest, but I wanted to spend some time living in seclusion before I decided.'

'Decided on what?'

'Which I should finally become, a priest or a monk.'

Father Minos nodded understandingly. 'So your parents will not be worrying about you?'

'No, but I think I should go back tomorrow, not wait until the end of the week.'

'Of course; do you feel capable of telling them?'

Andreas looked at the priest in surprise. 'Capable? I hadn't thought about it. They have to be told, so do Yannis's parents. Someone has to do it and I'm the only one who knows.'

'It's a great responsibility for one as young as you. Would you care for me to come with you?' As soon as the words were out Father Minos regretted them. His responsibilities lay here in his parish, not miles away with a family he did not know. The look of relief, which flooded Andreas's face, was thanks enough for him.

'Would you be able to come? What about your duties here?'

'I can ask a colleague to take over for a few days. I feel that I failed your cousin in his hour of need, I don't wish to fail you in yours.'

Andreas felt as though a weight had been lifted from him. He had accepted the fact that he had to be the bearer of bad news to his own family and his cousin's, but he had been dreading the moment. 'I shall be forever in your debt. They will probably,' he searched for the right word, 'Understand better if it comes from you.'

Father Minos knew exactly what the boy was thinking. Priests were trusted and whatever they said the people believed. He rose and paid their bill, hoping as he did so that he would have enough money in his box at home for the journey to Aghios Nikolaos and back. He shrugged, the Lord would provide, he always had in some miraculous way.

Andreas studied the congregation whilst his friend took the service. Everyone looked poor, far poorer than a farmer or fisherman at home and he wondered why that should be. He had always thought that people who lived in the town would be wealthy. He wondered how Father Minos managed to live if the poverty of the people was reflected in the amount of money they gave to the church. It was well known that the pittance allowed them by the government would have left them to starve and 'borrowing' from the collection frequently paid outstanding bills.

Father Minos explained to the people that he had an urgent errand out of town and would be unable to be with them for the Easter services. An audible sigh went round, making Andreas feel guilty. As they left he saw them each say a personal farewell, pressing small gifts into the priest's hands and wishing him well.

Andreas rose to leave last, intending to thank Father Minos and arrange to meet the following day, but the priest would have none of it.

'You'll stay here. I have a spare mattress.'

Once again Andreas felt deeply indebted to the priest, but accepted gratefully. His experience during the day had unnerved him more than he realised. Before finally retiring Father Minos insisted he had another glass of brandy to help him sleep. He woke whilst it was still dark and wondered where he was. Stretching out his hand he groped for the familiar feel of a wall beside him and nearly rolled off the mattress. Memory flooded back to him and he laid still, the fingers of fear clutching at his body.

Ironically he remembered that he had lost his bundle and that in all probability it was with the lepers. He hoped Yannis would have it, if Yannis were still alive. The thought came unbidden to his mind and he drew in his breath sharply, biting his lip to stop himself from sobbing aloud, whilst he felt the tears running down his cheeks. Unable to check himself any longer he turned his face down towards the mattress and allowed full rein to his grief.

At last he slipped from the mattress, pulled on his clothes and crept to the door. As he had hoped the church was unlocked and he made his way to the picture of the Virgin. Kneeling on the cold, hard stone before her, he sent up fervent prayers. How long he had been there before Father Minos found him he had no idea, but his self-control had returned. There was no need to explain his actions to his priest, who knelt beside him for a while, then announced it was time for them to eat. Automatically Andreas followed him from the church and was surprised to see an old woman seated at the table with them.

'My housekeeper,' explained Father Minos and began to extol her virtues.

Father Minos ate heartily, but Andreas was only able to toy

with the roll in front of him. 'I must have eaten too much last night,' he excused himself.

The bus journey was uneventful, although over too soon for Andreas. He swallowed nervously as they alighted in the town and stood beside the bus as though uncertain of his bearings. Father Minos's hand on his shoulder gave him a degree of comfort and he was extremely grateful for his support.

'Pappa may not be at home.'

'We will see. You live in a remarkably pretty town.'

Andreas nodded. He led the way silently, unable to speak now the dreaded moment was so near. The door yielded to his touch and he stood aside to allow the priest to enter.

'Andreas! I wasn't expecting you.' She bobbed a curtsey to the priest. As she straightened up her son flung himself into her arms and began to sob. 'What is it? What's wrong?' She looked at the priest for enlightenment.

'I suggest we all sit down.' Father Minos took a chair from beside the table. 'I regret to say that we have some very distressing news for you.'

'Annita?'

Father Minos shook his head. 'To the best of my knowledge she is well. It's her cousin.'

'They've sent Yannis away.' Andreas lifted his tear stained face.

'Away? Away where?'

Father Minos frowned at the boy. 'May I tell you from the beginning? Andreas, maybe you could find your father.'

Andreas nodded, scrubbed his face with his sleeve and ran down to the quay.

'This has been a great shock to your son, madam. You may find he has some difficulty in finally coming to terms with the facts.'

Elena's face was white, the lines showing taut with fear.

'Please tell me what this is all about. I thought Andreas was in Ierapetra, now he's here.'

'He arranged with his sister to visit Heraklion and find his cousin. I had met Yannis some weeks earlier. By coincidence I met your son, he'd lost his way and I offered to direct him. On our way we passed the hospital as they were moving the patients down to the ship. Yannis was amongst them.' Father Minos leant back and waited.

Elena looked at him puzzled. 'I still don't understand. Is Yannis ill?'

'I believe he is very ill. They've taken him to hospital in Athens.'

Realisation dawned on Elena. Her hand flew to her throat. 'It can't be. There must be some mistake.'

Sadly Father Minos shook his head. 'There's no mistake. When he came to me and showed me the sore I knew what it was, although my medical knowledge is very scanty. I still blame myself.' He slapped his fist into the palm of his hand. 'I should have looked after him.'

The door opened and Andreas stood there with his father. Judging by the pallor of Yiorgo's face he had been told on his way up from the harbour.

'Is it true?'

Elena nodded. 'They've taken him to Athens.' Her voice broke. 'The poor boy, the poor, poor boy.' Instinctively her hand went out to her own son as if to protect him.

Yiorgo crossed to the cupboard and reached for glasses and a bottle, pouring liberally and handing a glass to everyone. Andreas coughed as the fiery mixture caught at his throat. He had not sampled whisky before.

'Tell me.'

Father Minos repeated the story to Yiorgo who listened attentively until he stopped speaking.

'So what do we do? Which hospital have they taken him to in Athens? How long will he be there?'

'I don't know the name. It's just spoken of as 'the hospital'.'
'Then we must find out. How did he look when he left?'

Before the priest could answer Andreas had said the one word. 'Dead.'

'Dead?' Both Yiorgo and Elena turned on their son in surprise.

'They stoned them! The people stoned them! Yannis was hit on the head and fell down.'

Elena's eyes filled with tears. 'They're wicked, wicked, wicked,' her voice rose and Yiorgo slapped her smartly on her cheek.

'Control yourself. This is no time for hysteria.'

'I'm quite sure Yannis isn't dead,' Father Minos assured them. 'He was only stunned.'

'But why stone them?' Elena looked at the priest in horrified disbelief.

'Haven't you ever thrown a stone at a leper to drive him away?' asked Father Minos.

'Yes, but Yannis …..'

'Yannis is a leper,' the priest finished the sentence for her. 'You have to face that fact. He's not welcome anywhere.'

'Suppose,' a germ of an idea was forming in Yiorgo's head. 'Suppose I took my boat over to Athens? I could bring him back with me.'

'Out of the question.' Father Minos shook his head. 'The hospital could be anywhere in Athens. You'd have to carry a certificate of clean health from the doctor before they would let you take him, and besides, Yannis went to the hospital voluntarily. He could have run away to the hills and hidden, or even stayed on at school until his affliction became more obvious. If they've held out hopes of a cure for him he wouldn't thank you for taking him away.'

Yiorgo stroked his chin. Had he known a priest was coming he would have shaved that morning. 'You think he will be cured?'

'I pray that he will. He's young. In all other respects he appeared healthy, so there is hope.'

'Elena, some food for us,' Yiorgo turned to his wife who was twisting her glass of whisky between her fingers. 'Elena,' he spoke more sharply. 'Some food for our guest.'

With a start Elena looked at Yiorgo. 'I was just thinking of Yannis.' She took a gulp of the whisky and choked, handing the glass to her husband. 'I don't want any more of that.'

Yiorgo turned back to the priest. 'I haven't thanked you for coming to tell us, also for looking after my son.'

Father Minos spread his hands. 'That was a pleasure. We have much in common. Andreas says he has a desire to take up the religious life.'

'We are very proud of him.'

'My father was of me. I regret I failed him.'

Andreas and Yiorgo looked at the priest in surprise.

'He expected me to rise to the top, become wealthy with vast estates, a figurehead to grace a church once a week. As it is I am poor, my parish is poor. I spend seven days a week in church and as a rule I am available to anyone at any time. Maybe I would have been better suited as a monk. I would certainly have been no poorer or spent more time in devotions.' His eyes took on a dreamy look. 'I still feel I am being called. God has something else in store for me yet.'

Elena returned, bearing rolls, cheese, olives and tomatoes. 'We have only very plain fare at mid-day,' she explained.

'As I like it,' Father Minos assured her. 'With a glass of wine to wash it down it is food fit for a king.' He looked ruefully at his empty glass and Yiorgo rose hurriedly to offer a choice of wine or whisky. Father Minos chose the whisky, making sure the bottle stayed near him. Another would not come amiss later.

The meal was eaten in silence, only Father Minos really doing justice to the food. Andreas was the first to push his plate away. 'I wonder what Yannis has had to eat.'

'Much the same as us, I expect.' Father Minos spoke reassuringly. He was beginning to feel completely out of his depth and was annoyed with his shortcomings. He should know to which hospital the lepers were taken, of what their meals consisted, how long their treatment lasted and the chances of complete recovery. He determined to find out once he was back in Heraklion. He tipped the bottle that stood near his elbow and refilled his glass. Andreas went to do the same and his father laid a restraining hand on his arm.

'No more. I'll need your help this afternoon.'

'What for?' Surely his father was not going fishing!

'We have to go to Plaka. We'll be quicker if we go through the canal.'

Maria sat in her chair, clutching the arms. She seemed to be falling to one side and if she did not hold tightly she would fall out altogether. The buzzing in her ears made her deaf to the voices of her family who were clustered around her in consternation. She tried to speak, to say she wanted air, but only a strange gurgling noise came from her parted lips.

'Get the Widow.'

It was an order that Andreas obeyed, running as fast as he was able over the cobbles and mud that made up the village street, and hammering on the door as if to break it down.

'Come. Come quick. Maria's had a fit or something. I think she's dying.'

The Widow peered suspiciously at him. His face was vaguely familiar. She sniffed. Maria had been perfectly well that morning. She shuffled her swollen feet into her wooden clogs.

'Are you sure, boy?'

'Yes, hurry, please hurry.'

'Where's my shawl?'

'Here.' Andreas draped it round her shoulders.

'I'll need my stick.' Still she sat in her chair.

Andreas picked up the stick from beside her. 'Let me help you.' He almost pulled her from her chair in his anxiety.

'Not so fast,' she grumbled as he propelled her across the room. 'I'm not as young as I was.'

Still grumbling she allowed him to help her along the uneven road, annoyed at being called out on a fool's errand. As she entered the cottage she was taken aback to see a priest there. Was Maria that ill so suddenly? The family, who had been clustering around the chair of the stricken woman, fell back before the waving of the old woman's stick.

'Let me get to her. What happened? Did she fall?'

Father Minos acted as spokesman. 'It was my fault. I had to break some distressing news to her. I did it rather clumsily.'

In truth he had broken the news gently, step by step, offering hope all the time of a mistaken diagnosis or a rapid cure before finally mentioning the word 'leper'.

The Widow stood back from her patient. 'Best get her to bed. She's had a shock. Give her some brandy. It will help her sleep.'

Yannis nodded. They had all had a shock, followed by another when his wife had collapsed so dramatically. He poured out a glass and offered it to Maria, whose fingers seemed to curl tighter round the arms of the chair. Anna, seeing her father was at a loss to know what to do, took the glass from him and held it to her mother's lips.

'Drink this, Mamma. It will help you feel better.'

Once again the strange gurgle from her lips. Didn't they understand that she could not move? Anna tilted the glass so that a little of the liquid entered her mother's mouth, most of it running out at the side.

'Mamma, please,' Anna whispered, thoroughly frightened. 'You must try to swallow it.'

A gurgle again, but a little of the liquor went down her throat. Anna persevered, not knowing how much her mother was swallowing or how much was running down her neck.

The Widow hobbled back to her own cottage, leaving the two girls to look after their mother as best they could. Yannis sat with his head in his hands. His son, the clever boy with the brilliant future before him, was as good as dead. Maybe he would be better dead. Maybe they would all be better dead. His leg was crippled; his wife looked half dead, his son a leper, what was going to happen to them? He took another swig from the brandy bottle. He had given up using a glass.

Father Minos looked at the drunken farmer. This was getting out of hand. He took the bottle away from Yannis and called to Andreas.

'Get one of the girls to make some coffee. Strong.'

Andreas looked at his cousins and decided it would probably be made more quickly if he did it himself. He returned with the steaming pot and the plain white cups his aunt always used for visitors. Father Minos insisted Yannis drank the strong brew, until most of the pot had been consumed, by which time he made a rush for the yard. Father Minos was relieved. That was one problem averted. He turned to Yiorgo.

'Could you help me place this poor woman on her bed? I'm sure her daughters could make her more comfortable there.'

Together they lifted Maria. Anna appeared to be taking charge, ordering her sister to remove her mother's shoes, apron and shawl, whilst she arranged the pillows, putting one down each side of her mother to hold her in a sitting position.

Yannis returned from the yard and stretched out his hand for the bottle of brandy.

'No more.' Firmly Father Minos removed the bottle from the farmer's hands. 'It will do no one any good to have you incapable. Your wife needs you.'

Yannis nodded. His head was throbbing as though he had been clubbed. 'Yannis? Tell me again.'

Patiently Father Minos explained. This time Yannis listened quietly and as the priest stopped speaking a large tear crept slowly down the side of his nose, which he tried to brush away with his sleeve. Yiorgo cleared his throat and left the room for a turn in the yard, signalling to his son and the girls to join him. Left together the priest took the big man into his arms, feeling his chest heave with emotion as he sobbed like a baby.

Yiorgo returned from the fields, leading the donkey and giving her a flick with a twig every so often to relieve his feelings. His father had promised to return to help him load up the cart as soon as he had discovered uncle Yiorgo's errand. Now, no doubt, they were sharing a bottle of wine and had completely forgotten him. He turned into the yard and was surprised to find the silent group standing there.

'What's wrong?'

Andreas was about to answer when his father frowned at him. 'Best see to the donkey, then come in.'

Hurriedly he tethered her and followed his uncle into the house, a feeling of foreboding coming over him. He took in the scene at a glance, his father and the priest sitting at the table, his mother lying in her bed.

'Mamma? She's dead?'

'No, no, she's had a shock, but she's all right.'

'What is it then?' His eyes were wide with fear. 'Why's the priest here?'

Again Father Minos told his news, awaiting a reaction of horror and disbelief. Yiorgo stood perfectly still, then took a deep breath.

'Where's Stelios? Does he know yet?'

Yannis lifted blood shot eyes to his son. 'He went over to Babbis's farm and he's not back yet. Your Mamma has taken it the hardest.'

Yiorgo nodded. 'She would. He was her favourite – and she was so proud of him. We were all proud of him.' Yiorgo turned on his heel and left the room. 'I must see to the donkey,' he called back over his shoulder by way of an excuse.

Stelios had enjoyed walking over the fields with Babbis. He

seemed to know so much about the countryside. Yiorgo only knew about farming the land, Yannis only knew how to find pottery in the soil, but Babbis knew where certain animals and birds lived and fed. He kicked at a stone idly as he walked.

'Look, there's uncle Yiorgo's boat. I wonder what he's doing here?' He pointed to the little bay; then took to his heels.

Babbis followed more slowly, hoping he might be able to spend an hour with Maria before returning to his own home.

Stelios rushed through the door shouting. 'Mamma, Maria, Babbis is here.' A stony silence met him. 'What's the matter?' He looked from one to the other, his gaze finally resting on his father. 'What's happened Pappa?'

Yannis stretched out his hands to his son. 'We've had some bad news. Yannis is ill.'

Stelios looked at the priest. 'Is he dead?'

'No, but he is very ill.'

'Is that why the priest is here?'

'Partly. He came to break the news to us.' Stelios looked at his father whose red-rimmed eyes betrayed his grief.

'What's wrong with Yannis?'

'He's gone to the hospital in Athens.'

'What's wrong with him,' repeated Stelios.

The words seemed to stick in Yannis's throat. 'He has leprosy.'

Babbis, standing just inside the doorway, felt his heart lurch. Slowly he backed out of the door, then took to his heels and ran back up to the hills.

Stelios stood there, biting his thumb. 'How?'

His father rounded on him angrily. 'What do you mean "how"? I don't know how you get leprosy.'

Stelios's lower lip trembled. 'I mean did he get it in Heraklion? He was all right when he left here.'

Yannis made an effort to control himself. 'He may not have been. We don't know. In fact he probably did have it before he left here.' He was trying hard to come to terms with the facts.

'You mean we may all have leprosy?'

'No, no, of course not.' Yannis hastened to reassure his son.

'Why not, if Yannis had it when he was here?' persisted Stelios.

Yannis shook his head. He had a great desire to hit Stelios really hard to stop him continuing with his questioning. Father Minos interrupted.

'The disease doesn't seem to work like that. Some people have it and others don't, even when they've been living in the same house.'

'And sleeping in the same bed?'

'And sleeping in the same bed,' Father Minos assured him.

'What's happened to Mamma?'

'It came as a shock to her. She's just resting. Best not to disturb her yet.'

Stelios nodded soberly. 'I'll go for a walk, if you don't mind.'

No one tried to stop him as he left the room.

Yiorgo and his son were thankful to leave the unhappy house and walk down to the quay, accompanied by Father Minos. It was as Yiorgo was about to cast off that he spotted Stelios. The boy was standing on a small promontory, shaking his fist, shouting and throwing stones as far as he could into the sea.

'I'll go.' Father Minos clambered from the boat and slipped and slithered his way over to Stelios. The string of obscenities that reached his ears surprised him in a boy so young.

'What good is that going to do?' he asked sternly.

Stelios whipped round. 'I hate them. Yannis hated them. They should all be dead.'

'Steady now. Who do you hate?'

'The lepers; out there on the island.'

Father Minos looked for the first time at the tiny island that guarded the inlet. 'That island?'

Stelios nodded. 'That's where they go. Good thing too. Nobody wants them around.'

'Wouldn't you like your brother around?'

'That's different. He's my brother.'

'They are all someone's brother or son. You're very lucky. You have another brother and sisters, suppose you had no one? Yannis has no one now.'

'He will come back, won't he?' Stelios turned imploring eyes to the priest. 'I want him back.' Tears began to pour down his face.

Father Minos crouched down beside him and tilted his chin upwards. 'You've got to be brave. Your mother and father need you. Can you believe that it's even worse for them than it is for you? You must have faith that one day your brother will come back, but until then you have to be brave for your parents' sake.'

Once again Father Minos hated himself for holding out false hope. He cursed his ignorance of the disease and vowed again that he would discover as much as possible on his return to Heraklion. He stood and watched as Stelios threw a last stone into the sea before turning and walking away. There was no farewell called on either side and Father Minos slithered his way back to the waiting boat.

'He'll be better now. His anger has mostly gone.'

Yiorgo trimmed the sail, turning the boat towards the canal.

'Before we leave could we sail a little nearer to the island?' asked the priest.

Yiorgo and Andreas looked at him in surprise. 'It's a leper island.'

'I know. Stelios has just told me.'

Yiorgo steered nearer. 'Thank God Yannis was sensible and didn't try to hide. They send them here when they find them.'

Father Minos scrutinized the island as they sailed past. The cliffs, sheer and straight, the spray breaking at the foot, were topped by the massive construction of a Venetian fort.

'Where do they live?'

Yiorgo shrugged. 'Inside the fort, I suppose.'

The island had an air of desolation and despair, which seemed to reach out to them. Yiorgo steered the boat further out to avoid

the sharp rocks that lay just beneath the surface of the water.
'Seen enough?'

Father Minos nodded. He too, thanked God that Yannis was safe in hospital and not on that desolate island.

Father Minos returned to Heraklion a subdued and worried man. During his bus journey he had turned the problem over in his mind. He was a failure. He admitted he was able to give comfort to the dying and their families, he never refused to give help of any kind if it were within his means, and he was a friend to everyone who lived in his parish whether they attended the church or not, but he had to face the unpleasant truth. The one time he had been tested he had failed miserably. He was totally ignorant of the treatment for leprosy, not even knowing the name of the hospital in Athens and quite unable to give any comfort to the family of the poor afflicted boy.

By the time the bus reached the waste ground by the harbour he had decided to ask for a release from his Holy Orders. Set in his decision he climbed the hill to the Square and walked the short distance to the church of Ayios Titos. He could ask for an audience there and renounce his calling. The church was deserted and it seemed only fitting that he should say a prayer asking forgiveness for his shortcomings first. He knelt, feeling the cold, hard stone through his cassock and bent his head. When he raised it his face held a look of bemused mysticism and it was with trembling hands that he lit a candle in thanks. The voice had spoken so clearly, yet it was not of earthly origin.

"Find the answers to your questions. You cannot heal, but you can help."

He walked from the church, no longer seeking an audience of the priest. A weight seemed lifted from his mind. He could continue in the church, but in work that would bring its own reward. First he would consult the doctor at the local hospital and find out all he could about the disease. He would ask for the name of the hospital in Athens and write to the authorities there for news of Yannis, then visit the family again and try to comfort them.

The doctor, at first, was reticent. He could discuss his patients with no one. Father Minos persisted. Day after day the doctor would find the priest quietly waiting for him at the end of a queue of patients and gradually the reluctance was overcome.

'Do you spend time talking to them?' asked Father Minos.

The doctor spread his hands in a gesture of resignation. 'How can I? I have little enough spare time. Besides, who would sit and talk with a leper from choice?'

'I would,' replied Father Minos stoutly. 'That boy, Yannis, who came to you a few months ago, he came to see me the day before his illness was diagnosed. He was distraught. At first he would tell me nothing, but within a few hours I knew his life history.' Father Minos sighed deeply. 'And still I failed him.'

The doctor regarded him curiously. 'Do you really mean that you would sit and talk to a man you knew to be a leper?'

'All men are equal in the sight of God, whatever their affliction.'

'Would you be willing to go into the ward and talk to the patients?'

'I most certainly would. Do their families visit them?'

'Of course not! They disown them. The most loving wife becomes a terrified woman longing to be a widow once her husband has been admitted.'

'Then may I visit them?'

'Suppose you contract the disease? What then?'

'If I become a leper it is by the will of God. I feel,' Father Minos struggled for the right words. 'As though I had been sought out and called to help them in some way.'

'You would have to sign a paper to absolve me of any blame.' The doctor looked dubious.

'Willingly. Have it ready for me by tomorrow. I shall be back – and thank you for giving me a chance.' Father Minos rose. He had learnt long ago that persistence usually got him what he wanted.

Annita sat on the cliff overlooking the natural pool that lay at the foot. She had taken the news of Yannis's affliction with an air of calmness and no show of emotion at all. As her mother had tried to take her in her arms to comfort her she had turned away and walked out of the door. Now she looked down at the water far below. The last time she had been up there Yannis had been with her. As she looked down now the water looked menacing, yet attractive. She edged herself forward a little. Strong hands gripped her shoulders and wrenched her backwards. She looked into the grim face of her brother.

'You were too close to the edge. It might crumble.' He spoke defiantly, still holding her.

'How did Yannis look when you saw him?'

'He looked fine, a bit bewildered, but fit and well.'

'What can I do?'

'There's nothing any of us can do, except pray for his speedy recovery.'

A look of scorn came over her face. 'Of course you would say that. What good is prayer to him?'

'If I were ill I'd like to think someone was praying for me. Come and sit down, Annita.' He led her further away from the edge and pushed her down on the grass.

'Tell me about it, Andreas. Did you speak to him?'

Andreas shook his head. 'I wasn't able to, but I think he saw me.'

He related to his sister the events leading up to the meeting with Father Minos and finally seeing Yannis go out to the hospital ship. He omitted to mention that Yannis had been rendered unconscious by a stone. Throughout Annita sat hugging her knees and when he finished she appeared deep in thought. Eventually she broke the silence between them.

'I'll go there too.'

'Don't be silly. You can't go. He's in hospital.'

'I'm training to be a nurse.' she spoke fiercely. 'I'll ask to be sent to Athens and they won't be able to refuse me, because I'll be their best nurse. Once I'm there I can nurse Yannis.'

Andreas did not answer. Hard work would help her pass her time without brooding.

Maria moved like an automaton. Apart from her mother she seemed to have been affected most by the shattering news that Father Minos had brought. For some days the family had moved around the house quietly, as though in mourning, looking at each other with fear in their eyes. Maria tended her mother, cooked and cleaned, looking eagerly for Babbis in the evening, but he did not arrive.

They had not mentioned Yannis's illness to anyone. When callers came to express their sorrow over Maria's stroke and offer help they were not told the reason behind it. Although eyes looked round curiously and probing questions asked, everyone was given the same information – it had happened suddenly, hopefully she would recover soon. Yannis senior, his face drawn and haggard, had called his children together and forbidden them to mention his son's illness to anyone.

'If people ask you must say he's studying in Athens. No one must know.' His gaze raked them all and each nodded solemnly. 'We have to carry on. Maria, you'll have to look after your mother and the house. Anna and Stelios will have to help more in the fields, taking Maria's place.'

Again the children nodded dutifully.

'How long will Mamma be sick?' asked Stelios, his lower lip trembling.

'We don't know.' Maria drew him to her. 'We must be happy

and brave in front of her. She can hear everything we say, she just can't talk very well or move one side. If we're cheerful she'll get better far more quickly than if we're miserable.'

Maria tended her mother carefully, being rewarded with a lop-sided smile and almost indistinguishable words. She spent long hours with her, talking about the cooking or her embroidery. She would ask advice, couching her questions in such a way that they could be answered by a nod or shake of the head. It was tiring and Maria began to lose weight and look older than her years.

It was an evening when she was sitting on the yard wall, gazing at the hills behind the farm, when a shadow fell across her. 'Babbis!' she started up in delight.

'Stay there, please.' He held up a warning hand, standing a few feet away from her. 'How's your mother?'

'A little better, maybe, it's hard to say.'

'How's Yannis?'

'Yannis?' Wariness entered Maria's eyes. 'He's fine.'

'Where is he?'

'Studying in Athens.'

'Is there any hope for him?'

'What do you mean?' Maria felt herself alternately flush and pale under his scrutiny.

'I heard, Maria. I'd come back with Stelios. The priest was here and I heard.'

'What did you hear?' Maria gazed at him defiantly.

'Yannis is,' Babbis hesitated, 'ill.'

Maria lowered her eyes.

'You don't have to deny it to me,' Babbis continued. 'I heard the priest say it. I haven't told anyone, Maria.'

'Thank you.'

'Is there any way I could help?'

Maria hesitated. She longed to say, "Yes, hold me, comfort me, make me feel wanted by you," but she did not dare. Instead she shook her head.

'I'll be on my way, then.' He turned towards the hill, a short cut to his farm.

Maria watched him go, her heart beating wildly. 'He doesn't care,' she thought bitterly. 'Because Yannis is a leper Babbis no longer loves me.' She leaned against the wall to steady herself, watching the figure disappearing into the distance. At the brow of the hill she saw him turn and look back.

Common sense deserted her. She raced up the track, her breath coming in frantic sobs as she reached the summit. There was no sign of Babbis. She stood there bewildered. Even if he had run after looking back at her he would not be out of sight. Breathing deeply to refill her lungs she looked around. He must have seen her coming and hidden. Anger welled up inside her.

A slight sound came to her ears, a muffled groan. He must have fallen and hurt himself. Compassion took the place of anger and she moved forward carefully. Behind a low wall she could see Babbis lying on the ground, his hands beating the earth.

'Babbis.' She knelt beside him. 'What is it? Are you hurt?'

His body stiffened beneath her touch. 'Go away, Maria.'

'I'm not going anywhere until you tell me what's wrong. Please Babbis.'

She heard his swift intake of breath, but had no idea of the struggle that was taking place within him. 'Are you sure you're all right, Maria? You're not sick?'

'Of course I'm all right.' She knew she had lost a little weight, but she did not think she looked ill.

'Truly?'

Realisation dawned on her. 'You mean you think I might have leprosy?'

'It's possible. I keep seeing you horribly crippled,' he buried his face in his hands and his shoulders began to heave. 'I can't bear it.'

Maria slipped her arms around him. 'Babbis, do you honestly think I'd touch you if I thought it was possible I was infected?

I've looked at myself all over and I haven't a mark, not a single mark that could be the beginning of it.'

'Why has Yannis got it?'

'I don't know.' She shuddered. 'I'm glad Yannis has gone to the hospital to be well looked after and not tried to hide.' Tears ran down her face. It was the first time she had been able to cry ever since the news was first brought to them and now it seemed she was unable to stop. At first they sobbed together in each other's arms, then Babbis began to kiss her, gently at first, then with an increasing urgency, finally pushing her down on the grass as he fumbled to undo his belt.

Maria pushed her damp hair out of her eyes and looked at Babbis in fear. 'What have we done?' she whispered. 'What will Pappa say?'

Babbis looked at her, shame-faced. 'It was my fault, Maria. Maybe it will be all right. We'll get married anyway.'

Maria shook her head. 'I can't leave Mamma. I can't get married.' Her tears began to flow again.

Babbis took her in his arms. 'There'll be a way. I love you so much, Maria.'

Yiorgo Pavlakis returned from his honeymoon in a state of euphoria. He considered himself the luckiest man in the world to be married to such a beautiful and charming girl. To be greeted by Pavlos with a worried look in his eyes was a shock. His relating of their sea trip and sightseeing was cut short.

'You can tell me later. I've something important to tell you. I had a visitor whilst you were away.'

'Yannis?' asked Yiorgo.

Pavlos shook his head. 'It was Father Minos. He had Yannis's cousin with him. He'd come up here looking for Yannis and met up with the priest.'

'I don't know where the boy is. I thought he'd returned home.'

'He's a leper. They've......'

YANNIS

A noise in the kitchen made both men jump to their feet. Louisa lay slumped on the floor unconscious. Between them the two men lifted her into a sitting position and Yiorgo began to rub her wrists, talking to her gently. Pavlos opened a bottle of vinegar and held it beneath her nose until her eyes flickered open. Yiorgo fussed over his wife, insisting that she went up and rested, assuring her that she was tired from their journey and should not appear in the taverna that evening. Louisa smiled at him weakly. She had been able to keep her pregnancy a secret from him during their honeymoon. Maybe she would now lose the unwanted child due to the shock she had just received and the fall she had sustained.

Pavlos was waiting impatiently for Yiorgo to return to the taverna, hoping no one would come in before he had the chance to tell the full story. He sipped a glass of wine morosely. As Pavlos feared a customer came in asking for a meal and he was forced to retire to the kitchen. Yiorgo returned and insisted on taking some soup up to Louisa.

'I need to talk to you,' growled Pavlos.

'Later. I shan't be long.'

This time he returned fairly quickly, bearing the empty bowl with pride. 'She managed all of it and is going to sleep for a while.'

Pavlos nodded. 'I'll just take this out. Stay in the kitchen. We have to talk – privately.'

Yiorgo waited until he returned. 'Well?'

'You heard what I said just before Louisa fainted? About Yannis.'

'I heard. Where is he?'

'According to the priest they shipped him off to Athens. That's not the point, no one must know he stayed here or I shall be ruined, and there's the money.'

Yiorgo Pavlakis held up his hand. 'You're going to fast for me. Who knows he stayed here?'

'The school, the museum, his friends, lots of people.'

'But do they know where he has gone?'

Pavlos shrugged. 'I don't know. I don't think so. I think everyone believes he returned to his village at Christmas and never came back.'

'Then there's no problem. Leave it at that.'

Pavlos eyed his brother-in-law doubtfully. 'What about the money? His father paid a year's board and lodging for him.'

'Well, send it back to him.'

'I can't. I haven't got it.'

'You haven't got it?' Yiorgo could hardly believe his ears.

'I was hoping you might be able to lend it to me,' mumbled Pavlos. 'I used it to pay for Louisa's wedding, most of it, anyway.'

'What else did you use it for?'

'A few card games, just occasionally, when I felt lucky.'

'And were you lucky?'

Pavlos shook his head miserably. 'No. Can you lend it to me? I'll pay you back, I promise.'

'I haven't got it to lend you. I spent money on my political campaign, and I used the remainder of my savings to take Louisa to Athens.'

Pavlos pressed his hands to his head. 'What can I do? Suppose he asks for it?'

Yiorgo shrugged. 'I don't know. I think you'll just have to wait a while and see. In the meantime I suggest you start saving.'

'Saving! Trade has dropped off. It's almost as though people knew and were avoiding the place.'

'Don't be foolish. It's probably because you've only been open in the evenings whilst Louisa hasn't been here.'

'Maybe.' Pavlos sighed deeply. 'I can't sleep, worrying over this,' he lied. 'I'll have to talk to Louisa. She'll know how to bring the customers in.'

* * *

YANNIS

Yannis's eyes flickered open, then closed. His head hurt intolerably. He raised his hand and touched his temple gingerly, there seemed to be a large bump. He tried to think. The pain in his head made thinking difficult and the stench in his nostrils made him want to vomit. He opened his eyes and tried to focus.

'You've decided to wake up, then?'

Yannis swivelled his eyes to one side. A young man of about his own age stood there. Full consciousness was returning. 'Where am I?'

'In hospital.'

'Hospital?'

'You arrived a few hours ago with the others. Don't you remember?'

Yannis closed his eyes again. Did he remember or was it a nightmare? He had been told to collect his belongings, he was going to Athens, walking down the corridor and out through some massive doors to a cart, waiting to climb in, seeing Andreas. He was sure he had seen Andreas, but that was the last thing he remembered. He flexed his arms and legs, they seemed sound; it was just his head.

'Am I in Athens?'

'Of course.'

'Was there an accident?'

'Not that I know of.'

'Then why am I in hospital?'

'The same reason as the rest of us.' There was bitterness in the reply.

'What's wrong with you?'

For a moment the young man was taken aback by Yannis's ignorance. 'Leprosy, of course.'

Yannis sat bolt upright, his face ashen. 'There must be a mistake....' His voice tailed away. There was no mistake. He remembered now. He had been in hospital before. They had sent him here for further treatment.

'You'll soon get used to it. Don't upset yourself. You've a hell of a bump on the side of your head.'

Yannis struggled for self-control. 'Is there something I could drink?'

'I'll get you one.'

The young man shuffled away and Yannis dared to shoot a swift glance at his immediate surroundings. On an iron bed next to his lay something that was making a noise like a kettle on the fire, hissing, wheezing and bubbling. The "thing" moved just a little and an aroma of fetid decay wafted up. Yannis turned his head away, fighting the nausea that was rising in him.

A bandaged hand passed him an enamel mug of water. Yannis took a mouthful and shuddered. He had difficulty in swallowing the brackish liquid.

'When does the doctor come?'

'Tomorrow, maybe, the day after, next week, who knows!'

'How long have you been here?'

'About a year, I think.'

'Don't you know?'

'You tend to lose track of time.' He yawned and took the cup away from Yannis, placing it on the floor by the bed. 'Feeling better now?'

'A little.'

'Well enough to go visiting?'

Yannis shifted his position on the bed. His head still throbbed. 'I'm not sure I want to.' He allowed himself to look round the ward. The iron bedsteads were placed no more than two feet apart down the length of the wall on each side. Down the centre, placed head to head, ran two more rows. On most beds a body sat or lay, small groups of men were passing the time by playing cards, dice or backgammon. 'What's the smell?'

'Smell? Oh, you get used to that. It's the toilets,' he lowered his voice, 'and some of the people.'

Yannis's eyes went involuntarily to the bed at the side of him.

Cautiously he placed his feet on the ground and let them take his weight. The room swam for a moment or two and Yannis sank back.

'Lean on me. I'm Spiro, by the way.'

'Yannis.'

He took the arm gratefully. Gently and slowly Spiro propelled him across the ward. 'Meet Manolis.'

Dutifully Yannis held out his hand, averting his gaze from the torso and looking into the friendly brown eyes.

'Excuse me for not shaking hands.' He held up a clawed appendage and a stump.

'My mistake.' Yannis felt embarrassed.

'Yannis has come to stay with us for a while.'

'You don't look that bad to me.' Manolis eyed the boy up and down. 'You're in better shape than most of us,' he grinned at his joke. 'Sit down and tell us about yourself.'

Yannis perched on the end of the bed.

'Plenty of room; don't mind the feet.' Manolis grinned again. 'Spiro always finds the new comers and brings them over to meet me. I don't get about much myself. Lack of transport.' The claw flicked an olive into the grinning mouth, chewed the stone clean, and then spat it on the floor. He sniffed the air. 'Food on the way.'

'Come on.' Spiro was making his way to the door.

Yannis hesitated, then realised that most of the occupants had left their beds and were pushing their way to the end of the ward. The door swung open and a man in a dirty white overall, facemask and gloves stood there. From his wrist swung a wooden truncheon.

'Back, back,' he shouted, waving his weapon threateningly. Cowed, the foremost patients shuffled back, giving room for a trolley to be wheeled in. Immediately the orderlies left the ward the lepers swarmed towards it, grabbing, screaming and pushing. Yannis hung back until most had taken all they wanted. He was disheartened by the remnants that appeared to be his meal. Two slices of bread, a handful of olives and a squashed tomato. As he looked at it a hand with one finger and a partial thumb scooped up the scraps from the other side. Yannis stepped back, returning miserably to Manolis's bed.

'Did you get some?' Spiro had taken a stand beside the bed and was sharing out the food with Manolis.

Yannis shook his head. 'I'm not hungry.'

'There'll be nothing more until tomorrow,' warned Spiro and pressed a piece of bread into Yannis's hands.

Yannis lifted the crust to his mouth and began to chew slowly. It was hard and stale. 'Is the food always like this?'

'It varies. Tonight we had meat and it didn't walk in on its own.'

'Why do they carry truncheons?'

'To keep us away from them. They're frightened to death that they'll end up in one of the beds.'

'Not next to me, I hope.' Manolis rolled his eyes heavenwards. 'It would be a fate worse than death.'

Yannis stared at him curiously. 'How can you joke like that?'

Manolis looked hard at the young man. 'I had my illness diagnosed five years ago – look how quickly it's overtaken and crippled me. Death would be a blessing. If I didn't joke, I'd cry. Even if the disease does halt, what kind of life do I have? Without my friend Spiro I'd soon be dead from starvation and neglect. My family wouldn't want me; they'd prefer me to die. My wife would certainly like me to die. She'd be able to marry again, this time to a man who has two legs and two hands that he's likely to keep. Are you married?'

Yannis shook his head. He felt humbled before the badly crippled man. 'I'm betrothed to my cousin. I'd planned to marry her when I'd finished University.'

'We have a scholar in our midst.' Spiro whistled through his teeth. 'You must meet Aristo. What was your subject?'

'History and Classics.' Yannis felt close to tears.

'Then you must certainly meet Aristo. He used to lecture in Theology. Does your cousin know you're here?'

'I don't know. I don't know anything any more.' Yannis sobbed unashamedly. His new friends did not try to cheer him, but let his grief take its course.

Maria gripped Babbis's hand tightly. 'Pappa, Babbis wants to speak to you.'

Yannis smiled. He had been expecting Babbis to come to him for some time now. When the news of his son's illness had first been brought to him he had felt uncertain of the young man. For weeks Babbis had been nowhere near the family, then he had become a familiar sight in their living room each evening. He sat back in his chair, his glass in his hand.

'Talk to me, then, Babbis. I'm listening.'

Babbis swallowed nervously. 'I should like to marry Maria.'

Yannis smiled more widely and nodded. 'Good. I couldn't wish for a better son-in-law.' He frowned. 'You could have a betrothal party in a week or two and be married next year.'

'No, Pappa.' Maria's voice was harsh and strained. 'We want to get married now.'

'Now? That's impossible. Who would look after your mother and the house? No, you'll have to wait until Anna can take over your tasks.'

'Pappa, we have to get married now.' Involuntarily Maria laid her hand on her stomach.

Her father gazed at her in disbelief. 'You have to get married? Now?'

'Yes, Pappa.' She lowered her eyes.

'You slut! You harlot! Was there ever such an unfortunate man as me! Out! Get out! You're no daughter of mine. Get your belongings and go.' He ignored the strangled pleading that was coming from his half-paralysed wife, rose from his chair and walked through to the yard.

Maria held her mother in her arms. 'I'm sorry. I'm sorry,' she sobbed. 'I didn't mean to. It just happened and then…..' a fit of sobbing tore at her, stopping the words.

Her mother struggled to speak, wanting to comfort her daughter.

'I have to go, Mamma.' Maria pulled herself away. 'Pappa means it. I'll get my clothes and go with Babbis. He'll look after me. I'll come to see you when Pappa's in the fields.' Choking back her sobs she ran up the stairs and hurriedly gathered her few possessions, stuffing them into a sack and returning to kiss her mother. 'I'll come every day. I promise, Mamma.'

'I'll look after her well,' vowed Babbis. 'She'll want for nothing, nor will,' he hesitated, embarrassed, 'the baby when it comes.'

Without a backward glance Maria hurried out, pulling Babbis with her. The moment she had been dreading was over. When she had first discovered she was pregnant she had cried and suggested that she went to the Widow Segouri, but Babbis would not hear of it. 'We'll ask your Pappa if we can get married.'

Maria had agreed, but she had known what her father's reaction would be. It had been two weeks before it had been possible to speak to him without her brothers or sister being present, now the ordeal was over. Babbis took the sack from her and together they walked up over the hill, away from the small farmhouse she had called home for the last sixteen years, towards a new house and a new life. The nearer they got the slower her steps became. Babbis squeezed her hand gently.

'There's nothing to be frightened of. I've talked to my mother.'

Maria shot a glance at him. 'I doubt that she was very pleased.'

Babbis shrugged. 'She has enough sense to know that she's gaining a daughter.'

'Oh, Babbis.' Maria began to cry, the tears trickling down her face and making her sniff.

Babbis stopped and swung her round to face him. 'We'll have

none of that. What's done is done. I love you and I don't want to start our life together with you snivelling and wishing you were back home with your parents.'

'I won't, Babbis. I'm just frightened of meeting your mother.'

'You don't have to be,' his voice had become gentle again. 'Remember when you were little and used to come to our house? She always had a biscuit for you.'

Maria nodded. 'But I'm not a little girl coming visiting any more. I'm walking into her house for ever.'

'I hope so.' Babbis's voice was gruff with emotion and he held Maria tightly to him. 'I love you very much, Maria. Do you love me?'

'You know I do.'

'Then there's nothing to worry over. Come on,' he released his grip on her and picked up the sack again. 'Mother's been waiting to welcome you for more than a week now.'

With a wan smile Maria allowed herself to be led along the dusty road to the farmhouse. Arriving at the door Babbis gave her hand a final squeeze.

'We're here,' he called out cheerfully as he pushed his way through to the room that served as both kitchen and living room for them. Rising from her seat at the table Babbis's mother came forward, a smile of welcome on her face, and Maria felt her fears dissipating.

'Maria! I've missed your visits, but we can make up for lost time now. How's your poor mother? Is there any sign of improvement? Sit down, now, dear, you must be tired after your walk over the hills.'

'No, I'm fine,' Maria assured her, sinking gratefully into the chair that was pushed towards her. 'Mother's much the same. She has some days when she's better than others.'

'Babbis, you take Maria's belongings upstairs for her,' commanded his mother. 'Then you'd better get along outside to see that everything's ready for the night.'

Babbis winked at Maria. 'I'll be back soon.'

Once her son had left the house Mrs Andronicatis leaned forward to Maria. 'How far are you?'

'Almost three months, I think.'

'Have you seen the Widow?'

Maria shook her head. 'There's plenty of time before that.'

Mrs Andronicatis pursed her lips. 'Best go along and let her have a look at you soon. Prepare her as well as yourself. How are you keeping?'

'I feel a bit sick in the mornings.'

'That's natural. It will pass. Now, we have to come to some arrangements.'

'Yes?' Maria looked up timidly.

'Whilst you're able I'll expect you to help me with the vegetables and fruit. You'll also do your share of the cooking and cleaning. You'll do the washing for yourself and Babbis, and your own mending,' she added. 'I also expect you to nurse me if I'm ill and look after me when I'm too old to work.'

Maria nodded. 'Yes, ma'am.'

'You can stop calling me ma'am straight away. My name is Kassianai; I suggest you shorten it to Kassy as most people have done all my life. There's just one very important thing for you to remember,' Kassy leaned even closer to Maria. 'I'll not interfere between you and my son, but it'll be no good you running to me for sympathy the first time you have a cross word. You're each other's responsibility now.'

Maria nodded again. 'Thank you,' she began, 'I appreciate your kindness.'

'You're not a bad girl,' Kassy smiled. 'You were just a bit unfortunate. There are others who do much worse in their lives and get away with it.'

'I promised my mother I'd visit her every day. I don't see how I can if I have to help you all the time. I can't go in the evening as my Pappa will be there then.' Maria's eyes filled with tears at the memory of the recent painful scene she had endured.

'You can go off and see your mother each day. You're young and strong and at the moment you should be able to work fairly fast, besides there'll be two of us doing the job I managed to do alone for a number of years. Don't stay over there for too long, though. Your place is here now.'

'Thank you,' Maria said again. 'I expect Pappa will come round in time.'

'I'm sure he will.' Kassy smiled grimly. She knew a few things about Yannis Christoforakis that he would rather keep secret from the villagers. It would not be very difficult to ensure a change of heart towards his erring daughter.

Louisa carried her baby along the road towards the town, finally stopping at the house of the woman who had agreed to look after the child during part of the day. Louisa laid the baby on a bed the woman had prepared for her and gazed at the sleeping form. She bore no resemblance to anyone except her mother, for which Louisa was greatly relieved. She had been lucky so far. Yiorgo had accepted his daughter's premature birth and considered the child to be his own. Her only blemish was the red birthmark, which ran from just above her left ear to the top of her shoulder blade.

Before she had become too large and unattractive she had used her time well during the day, raising her price a little and being available for as long as she dared before Yiorgo returned. Only half the money earned each day went into the till, and by this foresight she had managed to make the taverna look prosperous up until the time of her confinement. For two months now the takings had been low and she must appear to build the business up again.

Louisa smiled to herself as she continued towards the harbour, hoping a ship would have docked with at least one sailor hungry for a woman. Yes, she had been very clever and managed the situation extremely well to her own advantage. She felt confident she could deal with any other difficulties that arose. Yiorgo was so besotted with her, and she would make quite sure he stayed that way.

The time had come, Kassianai decided, to face Yannis and make him come to his senses regarding his daughter. Each day the girl hurried over the hills to visit her mother, scrambling over the low walls and running over scrub land that could trip her at any moment. As she had become larger and heavier both her husband and mother-in-law had prevailed upon her to use the track, which was less hazardous, and she had finally agreed. Even that was becoming tiring now, and Kassy would feel happier if her son could accompany his wife.

She chose her time carefully. What she had to say was for his ears alone. She watched as Maria set out along the dirt track that led down to the village, having admonished her to be very careful not to slip on the damp ground. Waiting until her daughter-in-law was out of sight, she wrapped her shawl over her head and shoulders. Not only was it chilly out now, but also there was a good chance that Yannis would not recognise her until she was face to face with him.

Yannis was working on one of the higher slopes, clearing away the tangled growth. Kassianai was standing next to him before he realised there was anyone else in the field.

'Yannis Christoforakis, I want a word with you.'

He jumped visibly and spun round on his heel. When he realised who was accosting him he spoke angrily. 'I've nothing to say to you. Get off my land.'

'I'll not go until I've had my say. You're a wicked man, a hard man; you don't deserve that sweet girl that you've disowned for the past few months.'

Yannis snorted and turned to go back to his work.

YANNIS

'You've no right to treat her the way you have.'

'No right! No right! After the way she repaid me for all the years I'd looked after her and loved her.'

'Some love it is when at the first fault you get thrown out of your home, denied access to your ailing mother.'

'She did wrong. She knew that. I'd brought her up to know right from wrong.'

'I'm sure you had. Who would know right from wrong better than you, Yannis?'

Yannis sucked in his breath. 'What do you mean?'

'Do I have to tell you? Have you forgotten Olga?'

Yannis's face paled under his tan. 'What are you talking about?'

'Olga, old Nikos's daughter, no better than a cheap town girl. Every man hereabout knew Olga.'

Yannis shrugged.

'Who gave her the money to go to the town, eh? Who wanted her out of the way so he could court a respectable girl?'

'It was a long time ago. How should I know?'

'You should know better than anyone else. How much did you give her to go away and get rid of your brat in secret?'

A dull red suffused Yannis's neck and cheeks. 'What makes you think it was mine? It could have been any one of a dozen's.'

Kassy nodded. 'It could, but it was you she went to for the money when the Widow said she was too far gone for any of her remedies, and it was you that gave her the money that killed her.'

'I didn't kill her,' protested Yannis vehemently.

'You killed her as sure as if you stuck a knife in her.' Kassy shook her finger at the man in front of her. 'She wanted money to go to the town and make her way there. We all know what way that would have been, but you persuaded her that if she went to the town she would find a doctor who could solve her little problem. She'd be able to come back to the village with her head held high and nothing trailing at her skirts to hamper her.'

Yannis's mouth opened and shut.

'Had you left well alone and let her go her time she'd be with us now, a comfort to her father in his old age, despite her waywardness. But no, you wanted her out of the way so you could court your Maria who thought the sun shone out of you.'

'You don't know what you're talking about.'

'Oh, yes, I do. I was with her. It was quite by chance. I'd gone to Aghios Nikolaos to buy the material to make my wedding dress and there she was. Too close to death for anyone to save, squatting in the gutter of a back street, her life blood all but gone. They tried, at the hospital, but it was too late. I stayed with her and she told me. She told me all about you and her.' Kassianai paused for breath and also to see what affect her words were having on the farmer.

'You're an evil old woman,' he spat at her.

'Evil! Me! I could have put paid to your hopes with Maria years ago. I kept my silence. What was the point of blackening your name? The poor girl was dead and gone and I had nothing to gain by pointing the finger at you. But I have now. You make your daughter welcome in your house, and her husband and child with her, or I'll tell the village what I know about you. They might shrug and say it was a long time ago and best forgotten, but I doubt old Nikos would be so forgiving. He'd have his shotgun out for you. You think on that one, Yannis Christoforakis, and be thankful that your girl is a good girl and my son saw fit to do the right thing by her, not like some.'

Kassy turned and began to walk back the way she had come. She was trembling with the violent emotion she had felt during the unpleasant scene, but she also felt triumphant. She would give him a few days to mull over what she had said and if he had not seen his daughter by the end of a week she would try again.

The days passed monotonously. At fairly regular intervals the door was unlocked. Each morning the cleaners would arrive with mops and buckets of water. Within a few minutes they had mopped the floor carelessly from end to end, completely ignoring the occupants of the beds. An hour or so later stale bread, hard cheese and jugs of water were brought in and called breakfast.

At mid-day tomatoes, olives and cucumber accompanied the bread, cheese and water and some evenings a small amount of meat and rice came on a separate dish. Yannis noticed that for each person who was completely bed-ridden there was an ambulant leper looking after his welfare, feeding him if necessary.

Long hours were passed talking to Manolis and Spiro, the two men he felt closest to in the ward. He tried to talk to the orderlies when they entered, but was waved away with a menacing truncheon. Each day when his name was called he hoped he would be free to leave, but it was only to hand him the two capsules that constituted his medication.

The first time Yannis saw a leper die he was moved to both tears and fury. Dimitris had been a living torso in the bed next to him. The smell that arose from his gangrenous body kept most people away from him and he would shout abuse and curses at them. The night he died he was calm, asking for various people to go up to his bed and say farewell to him. Some did as he requested, others were unable and called out to him, yet others that he asked for had died earlier.

'Can we say a prayer for Dimitris?'

Beside each bed a leper knelt, those who were legless sat with heads bowed respectfully. For some unaccountable reason Yannis found he was crying, and as he rose Spiro's eyes looked suspiciously moist. He gave a weak grin.

'Lucky man. He deserves heaven after all he's been through.'

'Is he very old?'

Spiro shrugged. 'I've no idea.'

'Is he really dying?'

Spiro nodded. 'I expect so. Somehow people seem to know.'

'How many people have died here?'

'About thirty, I think, since I've been here, anyway.'

Yannis felt the skin on the back of his neck prickle. 'I think I'll go to bed.'

For the rest of the evening the ward was quiet. No one played dice or cards, groups chatted together in undertones, everyone glancing at Dimitris from time to time. The white haired man stayed by his bed in a continual attitude of prayer. Sleep did not come easily to anyone, least of all to Yannis who seemed to hear the slightest sound. The dawn light was filtering through the high, grilled window when Yannis heard a sound that made his hair stand on end. The shrill keening of women came to his ears, making him shiver. Groping his way to Spiro's bed he shook his friend awake.

'What's happening?'

Spiro propped himself up on one elbow. 'They've told his wife.'

'Where is she?'

'In one of the other wards.'

'What? Are there women in here as well?' Yannis's eyes widened in horror. 'He would have wanted his wife with him at the end.' The dirty sheet had been pulled up over Dimitris's face.

The keening and wailing continued well into the morning, until Yannis felt his teeth on edge and his head throbbing. 'When will they stop?'

'When they've been told the body's been taken away.'

'I wish they'd hurry up!'

'It's not a pretty sight,' warned Spiro.

Yannis shrugged. 'I've not seen anything in here yet that could be described as pretty.'

Spiro was right. The disposal of Dimitris's corpse was sickening. Two orderlies arrived and threw a sack at the first inmate they saw. He held out his deformed hand and was tapped by a truncheon. 'Get on with it.'

Unwillingly he made his way towards Dimitris's bed and an

orderly beckoned two more men over. The first held the sack open whilst the others placed the bodily remains inside. They tied it securely and dragged it to one side of the ward. The orderly unlocked a trapdoor set in the floor and the body was unceremoniously pushed through.

'Where does it go?' asked Yannis in a whisper.

'I'm not sure,' answered Spiro, 'probably to an incinerator. They treat us like rubbish whether we're dead or alive.'

'Can't we do something? We're people. We can't help being ill. If we spoke to a doctor wouldn't he do something?'

'Yannis, you have to realise that once you're in here you can do nothing. If you complain to an orderly he'll just give you a cosh.'

'Suppose we forced them to take notice of us?'

'How?' Spiro was scornful. 'What shall we do? Stage a protest march or go on hunger strike?'

'I'm serious.'

'Yes, Yannis, and so am I when I say there's nothing we can do.' Spiro walked away.

Yannis followed him. 'Let's talk to Manolis. Maybe he can think of something. He's been here longer than us.'

Spiro sighed. 'You don't give up, do you?'

Manolis was as scornful as Spiro had been. 'I suggest we break up our beds and attack the orderlies with the iron bars, then we can walk out of the doors and return to our homes. Stop dreaming, Yannis. I thought you'd come to terms with it by now.'

Yannis tilted his chin defiantly. 'I'll never come to terms with it. I may have to put up with indignities, it doesn't mean I have to accept them.'

He left the two men together and returned to his bed. It seemed strange not to have his noisy, putrefying companion next to him. He had grown used to the bubbly breathing and the nauseas smell.

'I'm getting like the others,' he though miserably. 'I'm beginning to accept these conditions and even be grateful for them.' He banged his fist on the mattress. 'I won't! I won't!' he vowed. His head cleared. 'I won't what? I won't lay here day after day, growing steadily more neglected, then what am I going to do?'

Dimitris's bed was filled before the week was out. A middle-aged man, whose eyes held a wild, hunted look was allocated to it. Yannis spoke to him gently, introducing himself and asking the stranger's name. The eyes stared at him and two well-shaped and manicured hands fluttered at him, pointing to his mouth.

'Can't you speak?'

The man shook his head.

'Can you hear?'

The man's hands fluttered again and he nodded.

Yannis crossed his legs under him and sat on the man's bed. 'I'll talk and you can nod or shake. Understand?'

For almost an hour Yannis sat communicating with the dumb leper, when he left him he felt more depressed than usual.

'You know,' he said to Manolis, 'I can almost envy you. He can't speak and he has trouble eating. I dread to think what the inside of his mouth is like. He ought to have special foods and milk to build up his strength.'

Manolis looked at Yannis in despair. 'What's the point of fattening him up? It would be better to starve him for a few days so he could die.'

'Have you seen his hands?' asked Yannis. 'He was a musician and he has the most beautiful hands you've ever seen.'

'Some of us would just like hands,' remarked Manolis dryly. 'You have to accept, Yannis, that the people who enter these four walls are here to die, and most of us would be grateful to get it over and done with. You seem to have some wonderful idea that we'll all get better. Face facts, Yannis. We're the living dead. There's no hope at all for us.'

Manolis turned away, but Yannis took him by the shoulder and rolled him back to face him. 'I've been thinking and I've got a plan. I want to know what you think.'

Manolis sighed. 'I think you're crazy.'

'No, seriously, listen to me. Suppose we attacked the orderlies, no hear me out,' Yannis remonstrated as Manolis threw back his head and laughed. 'If we overpowered them, took their truncheons away, and held them here until the authorities agreed to treat us properly.'

'They'd probably shoot us! For a start we aren't able to fight them. We're all of us sick and most of us are crippled, and if by any chance we did manage to overcome them they'd only send more to take their place. You must just put up with it, Yannis, like the rest of us.'

Yannis shook his head. 'I'm sure if the hospital authorities knew how we are treated they'd do something. Conditions weren't as bad as this in Heraklion. The food wasn't very good, but it was edible. The doctor came to see us once a week. Here I've never even seen a doctor. Let's give it a try.'

Manolis looked at Yannis's flushed face and bright eyes with suspicion. He was probably running a temperature. 'We'll talk to Spiro. Call him over.'

As Spiro approached Manolis shook his head at him. 'Yannis has been thinking and wants to put an idea to you.'

Spiro sat on the end of the bed. 'I'm listening.' He winked at Manolis.

'I want to attack the orderlies and make them take us to the administrator. He'd have to listen to us.'

'Would he? Why?'

'He'd have to listen because we'd only make reasonable requests. I've thought it all out carefully.' Yannis settled himself on the end of Manolis's bed. 'We'd ask them to provide more water, so we can wash properly,' he began to tick them off on his fingers. 'We'd ask for more food, so we don't fight over it like a crowd of animals, and fresh food, not scraps and stale left-overs.'

Spiro nodded. 'That sounds reasonable enough.'

'Then we'd ask for clean sheets and clean clothes more often. Once a month isn't enough. We all smell. Think of those who have open sores, their clothes and sheets stick to them. We could include in that clean bandages, every week at least.' Yannis paused for breath.

'I don't know. They could make it worse for us.' Spiro was doubtful.

'Worse! How could it be worse? They hit us, underfeed us, leave us in the kind of filth you wouldn't keep an animal in and dispose of our dead like sacks of rubbish.'

'Does it matter when you're dead?'

Yannis rounded on Manolis. 'It may not matter to you when you're dead, but you know the effect it has on the rest of us. God knows we have little enough dignity whilst we're alive, why shouldn't we have a little when we die?'

Spiro shifted uncomfortably. 'I know you're right, Yannis, but I can't see it working.'

'Let's try. How many others are there as fit as us?'

'I don't know, ten, twelve maybe.'

'Then let's ask them. If they all say no I'll forget it, but if the majority are with me, let's give it a try.' Yannis's eyes gleamed with enthusiasm, the first he had shown since he arrived.

'We'll see,' Spiro was cautious. 'I'll talk to some of the others.'

Manolis thumped his stump on his mattress. 'You're mad, both of you. If you manage to overpower the orderlies, and if you manage to get to the administrator's office, and if you manage to get him to listen to you, what do you think he's going to do?' Spiro and Yannis looked at him. 'Nothing! Absolutely nothing.'

'Then we'll do it again, and again, until he does do something.'

'Count me out.' Manolis turned away from his friends. Spiro raised an eyebrow to Yannis and jerked his head. They walked over to Yannis's bed.

'Take no notice of him. He's having a bad day.' Spiro leant his head on his hands. 'I love Manolis like a brother. He kept me sane when I first came here, but how I wish he would die!'

Yannis hardly heard him. 'Spiro, who's the most respected man in here?'

'I don't know. Whoever's managed to survive the longest I should think.'

'I don't mean like that. I mean by profession. The priest, what about him?'

'Maybe, but he isn't really a priest. He was a monk.'

'Anyone else? Yiorgo, the doctor?'

'He's all right with cuts and bruises, but he's not a doctor. He was a butcher before he came in here. Still is, according to his patients.'

'We need someone who'll be listened to. Someone that even the authorities will respect. Think, Spiro, you know them all better than I do.'

'There's Andreas, but he can't walk. He was a lawyer.'

'We could carry him.'

'That would mean using more men who were fit. I'm not sure if we'd have enough.'

'You're with me, then?' Delighted Yannis clapped his friend on the back. 'We'll do it, I know we will.'

'I wish I had your confidence.'

Yannis gazed at Spiro earnestly. 'I've got to do something. I'll go mad soon. There's nothing to do, no books, not even a newspaper. Anything could have happened in the world and we wouldn't know. Do you even know what day it is?'

Spiro considered; then shook his head. 'Yannis, I fretted like you when I first came here. It takes a while to settle down and accept. If you continue to get yourself so worked up you will go mad.'

'I will not accept this life, this existence. You were a farmer before you were brought here. Don't you miss being out in the fields, smelling the soil, picking your crops?'

To Yannis's surprise tears filled Spiro's eyes. 'Of course I miss it. Sometimes I dream I'm back home and I wake up smelling the soil or the grapes. When I was first diagnosed I shouldn't have agreed to treatment. I should have hidden and let my family care for me.'

'You'd have been found and sent to the island.'

'What island?'

'Opposite my village there's an island. They send all the lepers there that they find hiding in the caves or begging.'

'Have you been there?'

Yannis remembered his night visits. 'I've sailed round it with my uncle. We used to send food out to them, usually the poorest of the crop. Now I'd insist that my Pappa sent them the best of everything.'

'Do your parents know you're here?'

Yannis shook his head. 'No one knows.'

'Won't they have worried and looked for you?'

'Probably, but I can't do anything about it now. That's another thing we could ask the administrator for – paper and pencils so we could write to our relatives.'

'Please, Yannis, give up this scheme of yours.'

'I thought you agreed with me?'

'I do, but I can't see it working.'

'We won't be any worse off if it doesn't work,' Yannis replied stubbornly. 'If you don't want to do anything yourself introduce me to Andreas and let me ask him to speak for us. Point out the men you think are the fittest and let me approach them. If everyone disagrees with me I'll accept that I'm wrong and forget the whole idea.'

Spiro gave up. 'Very well, after supper we'll talk to Andreas.'

The old man listened carefully to Yannis. 'My boy,' his voice was thin and weak. 'I agree with you. Something should be done, something must be done, but I can't help you. I haven't the strength.'

'We could carry you, sir,' Yannis offered eagerly.

YANNIS

Andreas shook his head. 'I shan't be here much longer. By the time you needed me to speak for you I could be dead, then your efforts would have been for nothing. You must find someone stronger.'

'We need someone they would listen to, he must be a lawyer or solicitor.'

'Costas is the man you want. He was a politician in Athens. They'd listen to him. Call him over, Spiro, and you can tell him all you've told me.'

Spiro looked around until he saw the man. Wearing an incredibly dirty, old, grey suit, a middle aged man sat on the edge of his bed. His clawed hands hung down between his knees; altogether he presented a picture of apathy.

'I'll get him.' Spiro threaded his way through the beds to the other side of the ward. At first Costas shook his head, then finally Spiro persuaded him and he rose slowly and shuffled over to them, sitting on the end of Andreas's bed.

'Come closer,' ordered Andreas.

Obediently Costas moved nearer and Andreas repeated to him the conversation he had shared with Spiro and Yannis.

Costas shook his head. 'It won't work. They won't listen.'

'It's worth trying,' insisted Yannis. 'Will you speak for us?'

'You'll make it worse for all of us,' he sniffed dolefully.

Yannis tried to be patient. 'You don't have to touch the orderlies. We only want you to talk to the administrator for us. There'd be no trouble for you.'

Still Costas shook his head. 'It won't do any good. They won't listen.'

'No wonder you failed as a politician!' Andreas almost spat the words at him. 'I'm a dying man, but I'm willing to help. I'll be your spokesman if this coward is too frightened.'

'It won't do any good,' repeated Costas dully. 'They won't listen. Can I go back now?'

The three men nodded and he shuffled back to his own bed,

sitting on the edge as he had before, his shrivelled hands hanging uselessly between his knees.

'He's losing his mind,' remarked Spiro.

'Did you mean it?' asked Yannis of Andreas.

The old man nodded. 'Arrange it as soon as you can and I'll do my best to be around to help you. Organise it properly, each man to have his own job, and two standing by to carry me. You'll only get one chance.'

Spiro looked around. 'We'll start now. Come on, Yannis. We'll ask them to come to a meeting, then we'll only have to say it once.'

'Talk to Elias first,' Andreas advised them. 'He knows the men and he might be able to persuade any who are doubtful.'

It was from Elias that the suggested time of the meeting came. 'I'll hold the service on Sunday evening as usual and you can hold your meeting behind us.'

Over the next few days all the ambulant lepers were approached and their general health was inquired after and discussed. Finally Yannis and Spiro selected fifteen men who appeared to be fairly fit and strong. Yannis wished Andreas was stronger. Each time they talked his voice seemed thinner and weaker.

On Sunday Yannis was in a fever of impatience. The time between each meal dragged interminably. Finally supper arrived and Yannis and Spiro spoke to those they had selected and asked them to gather at the back of the ward when the service started. Each was somewhat surprised, but none refused.

The trolley with the dirty dishes was eventually collected. Yannis and Spiro sat and waited for half an hour, then they walked to the end of the ward. Elias took his cue and called out that he would be holding the usual Sunday service. With sideways glances at their fellows certain of the inmates slipped to the back of the little congregation and as a prayer was intoned Yannis spoke to them quietly.

The men exchanged doubtful glances, some shook their heads; two turned away and joined the service. Yannis looked at Spiro desperately.

'Listen, friends,' Spiro included them all in his outstretched arms. 'Think about it, talk to each other, then come and tell me if you are with us. There has to be ten of us at least, more if possible. Remember we have nothing to lose and everything to gain.'

Hope shone in eyes that had been dull with despair and one man shouted "I'm with you," and Spiro hushed him quickly.

'Don't shout about it. We chose you all because you're the fittest. Others may want to help and they may not be well enough, then they'd be in the way.'

Yannis could not sleep that night. If he dozed off he awoke, startled by another's noise. Each time he closed his eyes he saw a scene of massacre where the orderlies had fought and maimed each attacker. He wished he had never thought of the idea.

Sleep came eventually and he was jolted awake as the cleaner banged against his bed. He growled a complaint and shifted his position, scratching his head as the lice irritated his scalp. If only they could have their hair washed and cut it would help. The tangled, unkempt mass of hair that hung around him was disgusting. That could be another thing they could ask of the administrator.

For the rest of the day Yannis fretted. Two patients came over to speak to him, both refusing to participate. He had seen three go to Spiro. There were not going to be enough men to carry out his plan. In despair he lay on his bed, his eyes closed, feigning sleep.

'We're there,' Spiro hissed in his ear. 'With you and I there are nine willing.'

Yannis opened his eyes. 'It's not enough.'

'It has to be. All we have to do now is arrange the day and the time. We have to go through with it, Yannis. Too many know and are depending on us. Even those who won't join us are hoping it will make things better.'

'What about Andreas? Is he still willing?'

'I expect so. Come with me and tell him.'

Andreas appeared to be asleep as they approached his bed and Yannis was struck anew by his frailty. They sat each side of him as he listened carefully.

'You can do it,' he said at last. 'The others will rally round once you start. Decide on your day quickly before they lose interest.'

Yannis and Spiro exchanged glances. 'Tomorrow – lunch time.'

Andreas nodded. 'It's probably the best time. Go and tell them, Spiro, whilst Yannis and I talk. I want to be quite certain I remember all we want.'

Yannis ran through the list again, Andreas nodding as he did so. Finally he smiled at Yannis. 'You're a good boy, plenty of courage. Don't expect miracles, will you?'

'I can hope for them. Rest now. We want you fighting fit tomorrow.'

The time dragged and Yannis wished they had arranged to act that day. He sat with Manolis, hoping he would be in one of his humorous moods and distract his thoughts.

'Pity I haven't any nails,' he remarked, regarding his claw like hand. 'I could bite them to pass the time away. Dice or cards?'

'Dice.' Yannis chose instantly. He could still not beat Manolis. Somehow the deformed hand had a way of flicking the dice that gave him the numbers he required with unfailing regularity. They played until the oil lamps burnt down and it was too dark to see. That was another thing, they should ask for, more oil for the lamps. He must tell Andreas.

Unpredictably Yannis slept soundly, waking as usual when the cleaner swirled his mop under the bed and bumped the leg. He stayed where he was until the water arrived and as usual he pushed and elbowed his way to the barrel with his basin. Breakfast was the usual fare of stale bread, by arrangement the conspirators took as much as they were able. They would probably miss their lunch, and food, however unpalatable, was necessary.

YANNIS

The waiting became almost unbearable. The nine men circulated slowly around the ward, telling the other patients of their plans. Many pursed their lips and shook their heads in apprehension, yet wishing for their success. Others told them not to be foolish, whilst more had no real comprehension of the proposed incident and grinned inanely. Yannis took it upon himself to tell the dumb musician and was surprised by the reaction he received. Hope blazed in the man's eyes, he shook Yannis's hand firmly; then began to whirl his fists around. Yannis grinned. He should have thought of asking him.

'You're with us?'

An emphatic nod answered him.

As the lunch hour approached the ten men made their way towards the end of the ward, waiting for the doors to be opened and the trolley pushed in. They formed small groups and tried to behave normally. The orderly entered and looked around suspiciously before beckoning to those behind to bring the trolley in. As the patients moved forward slowly and uncertainly Yannis shouted. In vain the orderlies hit out with their truncheons, hampered by a man hanging on each arm.

'Close the doors!' Manolis roared at them from the other end of the ward, wishing he were closer and could see exactly how they were faring. A crippled man pushed each door closed, wincing with pain as the hard wooden cosh caught him a glancing blow on his kidneys.

It seemed an age to Yannis that he twisted and turned the man's arm, trying to release his grip on the weapon and it was doubtful that he would have succeeded had Aristo not come to his aid. The orderlies were clearly petrified of the lepers touching them, continuing to fight with fists and feet until they were firmly pinned to the floor. Panting and sweating Yannis rose to his feet.

'Listen to me! We don't want to hurt you. We want you to take us to the administrator. We've a number of complaints we want to put before him. If you take us to him we won't lay a finger on him.' He poked at a man with his foot. 'You, get up slowly, and lead us to him. We'll keep your friends here for insurance.' Sulkily the man scrambled to his feet. 'Those two can sit in the corner until we get back. Watch them, though. At the first sign of trouble let them feel a cosh.'

The two captives shuffled into a sitting position into the corner, wrinkling their noses at the smell from the latrines that were near by, a semi-circle of lepers pinning them in.

'Fetch Andreas,' called Yannis.

The old man eased himself onto the mutilated hands that were to carry him and placed an arm around each neck. 'Not too fast,' he muttered. 'I don't feel very safe.'

'Don't worry. I'll walk behind you.' It was a patient who had refused to join them until the fracas started.

Moving slowly for the sake of Andreas they were led down two long corridors until they came to a halt before a door marked "private". Yannis placed a hand over the orderly's mouth. 'One sound out of you and I'll hit you so hard you'll never wake up,' he threatened.

Stark fear showed in the man's eyes, but Yannis did not consider that it was due to his threat of violence. In a swift movement he swung the door wide and the administrator looked up from his meal, wondering who was invading his privacy so rudely. As he took in the little group his face purpled.

'What is the meaning of this?' he swallowed nervously.

The orderly was pushed to one side to make room for Andreas to be brought before the desk. 'We want to speak to you,' explained Yannis. 'We believe we are within our rights and have asked Andreas as a trained lawyer to be our spokesman.'

'Rights! You have no rights! You're lepers!'

Yannis advanced towards him, seeing the fear flickering in his eyes as he tried to back away. Yannis stretched out his hand until it was no more than an inch from the man's face.

'I won't touch you provided you listen to us.'

YANNIS

The administrator had started to sweat; he moved his head back a little and eased his collar. 'I'll listen, just move back.'

Yannis dropped his hand, but stayed standing where he was.

Andreas began in his frail voice. 'I have been asked to speak on behalf of all the lepers in my ward. We would like our conditions improved. We are kept like animals, not sick people. We want proper medical treatment, examinations by the doctors and clean bandages. We want proper food, not stale scraps, enough for each man so there is no need for us to fight each other for a portion. We also want a decent burial for those who die. The way a body is removed and disposed of is disgusting. We deserve a proper burial like any other man. We also want newspapers, books, pens, paper, so we can pass the time and write to our relatives.' Andreas paused, wondering if he had forgotten anything. 'And water. We want more water. Often there is not enough for us to wash.'

The administrator had recovered from his shock and decided to appear conciliatory. 'There was no need for this,' he waved his hand towards the orderly. 'You should have approached me properly, asked for an interview.'

Yannis bent forward. 'How are we to approach you, sir? The orderlies won't speak to us, so how do we get a message to you? If we try to speak to them they beat us back with truncheons.'

'They have to have a means of controlling you. Look at the way you have behaved today! How will I find people willing to work here if you attack them?'

'We don't want to attack them,' persisted Yannis. 'We just want to live decently, with enough food and water and to be able to pass the time by reading or writing.'

'You cannot have books or paper. You would contaminate them.' The administrator skilfully evaded the main issue.

'We could have books that we keep in the ward. It wouldn't matter if they were contaminated.'

'There is no money for luxuries.'

1927-1930

'When I agreed to be admitted in Heraklion I was given a receipt for my money and told that my expenses would be deducted. There must be enough money in my name for us to have one newspaper a week.'

The administrator looked at Yannis coldly. 'How long are you staying with us? You don't know, I don't know; so how can you say you have enough money for a newspaper? You are in a hospitable for the incurables and I expect that is where you will stay for the rest of your life. I doubt very much that you can afford anything.'

Yannis felt his legs buckling beneath him. He had refused to admit he was incurable.

'Go back to your ward. I can promise you there will be changes.'

The lepers exchanged delighted looks. The two men who were carrying Andreas were flagging visibly beneath his weight and Spiro went to relieve one of them as they made their way back to the ward. They pushed the doors open and signalled to the other lepers to allow the hostages to leave. Andreas was deposited gently on his bed where he lay back with his eyes closed.

'We saw the administrator,' shouted Yannis, 'and he has promised us changes.' Delighted he clasped Spiro to him. 'We've done it, we've really done it.'

As he spoke he heard the heavy doors swing to and a key turn in the lock. Disappointment showed in his face.

'You must have expected that!' Spiro saw the look. 'They couldn't let us just wander; we might interfere with other patients. Come and tell Manolis what happened.'

Yannis followed his friend to the bed in the centre of the ward. 'We should have made the administrator come here and spend the afternoon. I don't think he understands how bad it is. Did you see what he had for lunch?'

'Spiro grinned. 'I bet he hasn't eaten it now.'

Manolis gave them the bread they had saved from their

breakfast. 'Sorry, dolmades were off, moussaka was off, roast lamb was off, bread was on. It was pretty stale to start with, it's even worse now.' He listened to them gravely as they related the details of the interview. 'I bet they're petrified they'll be in here with us. They'd soon be pressing for better conditions if they were.' He leaned back against his thin pillow. 'If only there was someone who really understood. To know what it's like just to lay around all day when you've been used to working. They have a garden here, you know. To me it would be bliss to sit out there and feel the sun.' A tear crept down Manolis's cheek, which he brushed away impatiently. 'Leave me alone for a while. I'm obviously overtired, been over exerting myself again, no doubt. Go and talk to Andreas.'

Spiro and Yannis left. When melancholy overtook Manolis he was best avoided for a while. Andreas appeared to be asleep as they approached him, but as they stood beside him his eyes opened and he smiled.

'I thought you were marvellous,' said Yannis. 'You managed to say everything in so few words. If I'd had to do it I'd still be asking for a decent meal.'

Andreas leaned back closing his eyes again. 'I'm so tired now, but it was worth it.'

Spiro gazed at the old man anxiously. 'Are you all right, Andreas?'

'Very tired,' he murmured, hardly audible, 'But worth it.' His head rolled to one side, his mouth falling open.

'Get Elias,' Spiro ordered Yannis as he looked around the ward for Yiorgo.

The monk hurried over and after one look began to pray. Yiorgo felt Andreas's heart and took his pulse. He dropped the limp arm and shook his head.

'He's dead. The exertion was too much for him.'

The ambulant lepers crowded round, asking for information. One of them turned on Yannis. 'This is your fault. It was your idea to take him to the administrator. You should have left the old man alone.'

Spiro came to Yannis's defence. 'He knew he was dying. He wanted to do it. With his dying breath he said it was worth it.'

Elias laid a hand on Yannis's shoulder. 'You mustn't blame yourself. He'd been longing for death, always said it couldn't come too quickly for him once he was bed-ridden.'

Yannis shook off the monk's hand. 'It was my fault,' he said sadly and walked to his bed, Spiro following him.

'Don't be a fool, Yannis. He knew what he was doing and the risk he was taking by exciting himself.'

Yannis lay on his bed, his head throbbing. He blamed himself, despite the comforting words from Spiro and Elias. The afternoon dragged on and his head ached more with each passing hour. When the supper trolley was finally wheeled in he could not move; the pain in his head was so intolerable. Spiro brought him over some bread, cheese and a little meat, but Yannis pushed it away.

'I couldn't – my head – it feels as if it will burst.'

Yannis spent the night racked with pain and tortured by nightmares. Visions of his parents, brothers and sisters appeared before him, each one horribly mutilated by disease. Intermittently he felt someone lift him, mop his brow and press some water to his lips, then he would lapse back into a fevered frenzy from which there was no escape.

It was three days before Yannis had any semblance of consciousness. He opened his eyes and groaned. Spiro was beside him, urging him to try to sit up a little and drink. Gratefully he clutched the mug and swallowed some water, sighed and fell back on his mattress to sleep dreamlessly. When he awoke he felt decidedly better. He looked around. Most of the occupants were clustered round a trolley. Cautiously he swung his legs over the side of his bed and took his weight on his feet. The ward swayed violently before his eyes and he dropped back into a sitting position to save himself from falling.

YANNIS

'I've got some for you.' Spiro's voice came from far away. 'Lay down for a while, then sit up slowly when your head clears.'

Yannis did as he was instructed, then opened his eyes. Concern was written all over Spiro's face. 'Feeling better? You've had a bad few days. It happens to us all at times.'

'My head; I thought it was bursting.'

'You'd over done it. You'd been all tensed up and excited; then you collapsed like a pricked balloon. Take it easy for a few days and you'll be all right again.'

Memory came back to Yannis. 'Has anything happened? Have things improved?'

Spiro scratched his head. 'Nothing's changed, but things are happening.'

'Tell me.' Yannis began to devour the meat and bread hungrily.

'Not too fast,' Spiro cautioned him. 'They send in guards when the orderlies and cleaners come in. They just stand there by the doors and look at us, truncheons at the ready. They're all great big, ugly brutes. We'd never stand a chance against them.'

'Andreas said we'd only get one chance.'

'They came in yesterday and measured the ward. When we asked what they were doing they didn't answer. Maybe they agree we're overcrowded, or are going to put in some more basins or toilets.'

'That would be an improvement.' Yannis was beginning to feel distinctly better. 'It's a start. I wonder how long it will be before we know. I need some more to drink, Spiro. My throat feels parched.' Yannis put his hand up to his neck; then withdrew it, damp and sticky. Eyes wide with fear he looked at Spiro. 'What's happened to my neck?' he whispered.

Spiro looked carefully. 'It's spread a bit. I expect you scratched at it when you were delirious. You certainly said some things then! Who's Louisa?'

'Louisa?' Yannis frowned. 'She owned the taverna with her brother, where I lived in Heraklion. She must be married by now.'

'Should have been a long while back if what you were saying was true. What was she like, Yannis?' Spiro leaned forward eagerly.

'Very beautiful.'

'No, you know what I mean.'

'No I don't.' Yannis could feel himself redden as he lied. 'Goodness knows what nonsense I talked.'

Spiro grinned. 'Have it your way. I'll get you some more water, then I'll tell Manolis you're with us again.'

Despite having slept naturally for most of the day, Yannis had no difficulty in sleeping that night, born up by the hope that improvements were about to be made to their ward.

The matron in charge of the trainee nurses was concerned about Annita. She worked harder than most of the other girls but rarely smiled and would only answer when spoken to, which did not make her popular. She became as near a recluse as possible in the busy hospital, gaining a reputation for being weird and totally friendless. She passed her examinations with ease and finally approached the matron.

'I should like to request a transfer to another hospital, please, ma'am.'

The matron regarded the slim, white-faced girl. 'Aren't you happy with us?'

Annita gave an imperceptible shrug of her shoulders; the movement was not lost on the matron. 'I wish to move to Athens.'

The matron shook her head. 'It's not possible for me to authorise a transfer for you. The most I could do would be to write a letter of recommendation.'

'I would be grateful if you would do so. I'd like to move as soon as possible.'

Annita sighed. It should have been so easy. Now she had to face her parents.

It was more than a month since Yannis's recovery when change did come to the ward, and in a way no one had visualised. As soon as the cleaners had left the guards ordered each man to move his bed closer to his neighbour, leaving just enough room to walk between them. The work took all day and was exhausting for those who had four reasonably healthy limbs. By the time they had finished they crawled onto their beds, too tired to bother to eat. Manolis, unable to help at all, lay and pondered over this latest whim of the authorities. He shuddered. It was bad enough normally to have so little privacy, but now he could touch the man next to him if he stretched out his arm.

They were left to speculate for a further week, when once again the guards arrived, pushing bed after bed into the ward and ordering the inmates to place them in position. Manolis lay and counted. They were obviously not intended to have new beds or the old ones would have been removed, it could only mean they were having a number of new patients. The ward had previously held forty-six beds, now it held sixty-seven.

Although exhausted again that evening the men did not go to their beds, but gathered in little groups and speculated. They all came to the same conclusion, more patients were being sent into their ward. Sideways glances were directed at Yannis. This was his fault. In his misguided attempt to help them he had made things worse. Their ward was going to be overcrowded so that the air would be more fetid, there would be even less privacy and their inadequate toilet facilities would be unable to cope.

Yannis sat miserably on his bed and Spiro decided he would try to convince him that he was not responsible after they had eaten, but his intention was thwarted by the arrival of the new patients. Bales of bedding were thrown into the ward and the patients were instructed to make up the beds. Resentfully they did so, each wishing they could have a new mattress or extra blanket. By the end of the morning the beds were occupied and Spiro approached the one nearest to him.

'Which ward have you come from?' he asked an elderly man.

The man looked puzzled. 'We arrived this morning from Thessaly.'

'Thessaly!' Spiro was amazed. 'That's miles away.'

'I know. They suddenly shipped us all out. Now there's no hope at all.' The man spoke sadly. 'I always dreamed that one day I'd be cured and able to go home. Now I know I shan't.'

'That's the wrong way to think,' said Spiro firmly. 'You didn't ask to come here, so when you're cured you ask to be sent back where you belong. Do you all come from Thessaly?'

'I think so. There were about a hundred of us, but we were split up and sent to different wards.'

Spiro's brain was spinning. 'Come with me and tell someone else about those in other wards. It could really put his mind at rest.' Obediently the new arrival followed Spiro to Yannis's bed. 'Meet a new friend. He's come all the way from Thessaly to bring us some news.'

'What do you mean, Spiro?'

'What I said. They've sent a load of patients from Thessaly. There are more of them in the other wards.'

'Is it true?' Yannis propped himself up on one elbow and looked from one to the other of the two men. 'I'm Yannis, by the way.'

'Panicos. There were over a hundred of us in the hospital and they suddenly decided we were to be moved here. They left about six behind, those they didn't think would make the journey.'

'What does it mean?' Yannis was as puzzled as Spiro. 'Why should they send lepers from one end of the country to the other?'

'Maybe the treatment is better here?' suggested Panicos.

Yannis and Spiro snorted with laughter. 'There's one thing for certain,' gasped Spiro. 'It couldn't be worse. Come and introduce some of the others to us, then we'll take you to meet Manolis.'

The day passed more quickly for Yannis than any other for a long time. It was good to have some fresh faces around and a few new voices, to be able to talk about different topics. The supper was scanty with barely enough for everyone; Panicos had gazed at his meagre portion with dismay.

'Obviously they weren't expecting so many of us at once and their catering's gone haywire. I hope there'll be a little more to eat tomorrow.'

'You know,' Yannis was speaking almost to himself. 'We live on hope in here. We hope there'll be more food, more water, clean clothes, a cure. They're lucky we're able to dish ourselves up liberal helpings of hope each day or they'd have a ward full of dead men.'

Yannis spent a good deal of time with the new arrivals, asking about conditions in their previous hospital. He came to the conclusion that life was much the same wherever you were and suggested to Panicos that they should once again try to take the guards and orderlies prisoner and force the administrator to make improvements.

Yannis sat on his bed trying to calculate how many ambulant lepers would be willing to join them and risk the consequences. Spiro calling urgently for Elias and Yiorgo caught his attention. In a moment he was beside his friend.

'Manolis. He's dying.' There was a break in Spiro's voice and Yannis put an arm across the man's shoulders to comfort him.

'You know it's for the best. He's suffered so much.'

Spiro was sobbing openly. 'I know, but now it's happening.'

Elias was kneeling beside the bed, saying a prayer. A silence had fallen on the ward. The laboured breathing stopped and Yiorgo shook his head. He could no longer feel a pulse. Spiro buried his head in Yannis's shirt and allowed himself to be led back to his own bed where he lay, face down, grieving. Elias pulled the soiled sheet over Manolis's remains and made his way to Spiro in the hope of comforting him. Yannis felt superfluous and wandered back to his bed. What did it matter if they improved their conditions? They were all bound to die ignominiously in the end. Manolis had always been there to cheer him when he had felt like this before. There could be no one to take his place. The lunch trolley came in, but Yannis did not bother to move; maybe he could starve himself to death.

'Move over. I've brought you some food.'

'I don't want it,' he muttered sulkily.

'Suit yourself.' Panicos rose to go.

'I'm sorry. I'm just rather upset. Manolis was such a good friend.'

'He must have been. Most of the ward appears to be mourning him.'

Yannis raised himself on his elbow. It was true. Usually at meal times there were little gatherings and a certain amount of laughter mixed with the general conversation, but today the men ate silently.

'What was so special about him?' asked Panicos.

'He was always so cheerful and had ways to make us laugh. He was often in a lot of pain, but he never complained.' Tears filled Yannis's eyes again. 'I wish it had been me who died.'

'A lot of us feel like that.' Panicos's words were heartfelt.

Yannis nodded. Spiro was sitting motionless on his bed as though in a trance. His mind was blank with misery and despair. All Elias's comforting words and his own common sense could not take away his feeling of loss and loneliness. He showed no sign of acknowledging Yannis and Panicos as they sat on his bed.

'We want to talk to you, Spiro,' began Yannis gently. 'We know how much Manolis meant to you. He meant a lot to all of us, but he wouldn't have wanted any of us to grieve for him.'

'They'll put him in a sack! They'll put him in a sack!' Spiro's voice began to rise.

Yannis looked at Panicos in despair. 'I'll stay with him until he's feeling better.'

The afternoon dragged. The patients sat around listlessly, yet there was an air of tension about them that Yannis could not understand. The silence was broken by a key grating in the lock, as two orderlies and a guard entered. They carried the familiar black sack with them, which they threw at the nearest bed.

'Put him in,' ordered the guard.

The man picked up the sack and advanced slowly towards Manolis's bed.

'No!' Spiro jumped forward and barred the way. 'I won't let you. He was my friend. He must have a decent burial.'

Men were moving slowly and purposefully towards Manolis's bed. Instead of pushing Spiro out of the way they formed a silent ring around it. The orderlies looked at each other helplessly, then at the guard who was frowning.

'Put him in, and be quick about it,' he shouted.

'No.' A chorus of voices answered him.

The guard spoke to the orderlies who moved forward hesitantly. Yannis waited until they were nearly in the centre of the ward.

'Now!' he called and launched himself at the nearest orderly. To his surprise the other lepers joined in immediately, grappling the two men to the ground. Panicos took in the scene at a glance and launched himself into the melee. The guard blew his whistle desperately, hoping to be heard by the other guards. His whistle clenched between his teeth he began to lay about indiscriminately with his truncheon, and although he left a trail of cut and bloody heads the numbers did not seem to decrease.

Yannis fought for all he was worth, trying to bring the guard down. Twice the guard lunged at him and missed, but the third attempt found its mark. Blackness invaded Yannis's brain as he collapsed on to the ground like a rag doll.

Yannis stirred. His head hurt. He tried to lift his hand to it, but found he could not move his arms. He tried to speak, but only a feeble groan came from his dry lips and parched throat. Everything was dark and a smell was clogging his nostrils, making him retch violently. The retching increased the pain in his head, sending stabbing, red-hot knives from his temple to a point above his eyes where they broke into thousands of piercing needles. He sank back, trying to take the shallowest of breaths, lulled back into oblivion by the swaying motion that seemed to be inside his head.

How long he spent drifting in and out of consciousness he had no idea. When he next opened his eyes the pain in his head had subsided a little, it no longer stabbed viciously with every breath he took. He tried again to move his arms, realising they were pinned tightly against his body. He struggled violently, panic sweeping over him, ignoring the pain in his head.

'Sit still, can't you.' A harsh voice came from the side of him.

'I can't move my arms,' croaked Yannis, hardly able to speak the words, his throat was so dry.

'Nor can any of us.'

Yannis sat still for a while. 'Why can't we move?'

'They put us in strait jackets. Some crazy bastard set about the guards.' His informant spoke bitterly.

'Where are we?'

'How the hell do I know? At sea somewhere.'

Yannis was silent again. Why were they at sea? Were they going to be thrown overboard and drowned? He shivered at the thought. No one would ever know what had become of them. He renewed his struggles, ignoring the protests of his nearest companions until sweat began to pour off him, adding to the vile stench that surrounded them.

'Save your strength. You may need it later.' The warning voice was familiar.

'Spiro? Is that you?'

'Of course it is.'

'What are they doing to us now?'

'I don't know. They must have been prepared for trouble. They called the army in.'

'The army!' Yannis was aghast. 'What for?'

'To control us. They made a pretty little speech before they took us out. Told everyone they were removing us to ensure the safety of the other occupants.'

'Where are they taking us?'

'They didn't say. I just hope we arrive fairly soon. We've been given nothing to eat or drink.'

'How many of us are there?'

'Thirty or so.'

'All from our ward?'

'I think so.'

Yannis was thoughtful. It seemed unlikely they would drown such a number. 'Maybe we're going to another hospital,' he suggested hopefully.

'I don't care where it is provided we get out of this stink hole soon.'

Fully conscious now Yannis was even more aware of the disgusting smell of unwashed humanity, excreta and vomit. He found he was praying; the same words over and over again were hammering inside his brain. 'Please let me die, please let me die.'

A violent rocking of the ship threw them against each other, a tramping of feet was heard overhead and a voice shouted instructions. The frightened men sat silently, trying to make some sense out of the different sounds they heard, then the door swung open, almost blinding them as the light flooded in. The four men nearest the door were hauled to their feet and dragged from the hold. The remainder sat motionless, tensely waiting for the door to open again.

As Yannis stumbled out into the sunlight he recoiled in horror. 'No! Please, God, no. Not here!'

His pleas were ignored as he was manhandled into the waiting boat and rowed the few yards to the quay along with the other occupants. He was dragged out of the boat and dumped unceremoniously onto the hard concrete. He seemed to lie there for hours as the rest of the lepers were disembarked by the same rough method, followed by boxes and sacks. Finally the guards released half a dozen men from their strait jackets and ordered them to release the others, before they rowed swiftly back to the waiting vessel.

Yannis sat up and rubbed his arms to restore the circulation. He blinked in the bright sunlight and looked at the familiar faces around him. Everyone looked bewildered and uncertain. What was expected of them now? One by one the men rose to their feet and stretched their limbs and Spiro walked over to Yannis.

'Come on, you can't sit there all day.'

Yannis did not answer.

'Yannis, come on, move,' urged Spiro.

'I can't.'

'Why not? Are you hurt?'

'We're in hell.'

Spiro placed his hand on Yannis's head. 'Are you running a temperature? We're sitting on quay, out in the open air. We've been released.'

Slowly Yannis shook his head. 'We're on Spinalonga. There's no hope for any of us here.'

Spiro frowned and looked around. Across the bay was a village, close enough to see people working in the fields and the fishermen in the harbour. 'You're wrong, Yannis. Look across the bay and see for yourself.'

'I'm not wrong. This is the island I told you about, that's my village over there.'

'Then it's not so bad. You told me they had water sent out to them and the local produce. We ought to find the hospital. At least we'll get a drink there – and I don't think I can last much longer without one.'

'You go then.'

'I'm not going without you,' replied Spiro stubbornly. 'If you're going to sit on the quay and die from thirst and malnutrition then I will also.'

'Don't be so stupid.'

'You're the one who's being stupid! Come with me to the hospital. Most of the others have moved off and we want to get a bed for the night.'

Yannis felt too weak and despondent to argue. He allowed Spiro to help him to his feet and followed him through the stone archway and up a ramp strewn with stones. At the top Spiro hesitated. There was no sign of their companions or anyone else, just a collection of half-ruined houses and a concrete path.

'Which way?' asked Spiro.

Yannis shrugged. He did not care which way they went.

Spiro struck off to the left. The path narrowed and the bank rose considerably after a few yards and if a voice had not called to them they would have missed the man. As they turned towards the direction of the voice, they found themselves looking into the eyes of a legless leper, a large piece of wood clutched in his hand.

'Who are you?' he asked.

Spiro was the first to regain his composure. 'We've been sent here from Athens. You wouldn't have any water, would you? We've not had a drink for hours.'

The eyes regarded them suspiciously. 'You're criminals.'

'Criminals?' Spiro could not believe his ears.

'You were sent here in strait jackets. You must be criminals.'

Spiro laughed mirthlessly. 'If being a leper is a crime, if asking for better living conditions and respect for the dead is a crime, then we're criminals. Please, just tell us where we can find some water.'

His eyes never leaving them he groped for a jug that stood nearby and handed it to Spiro who drank noisily before passing it to Yannis.

Spiro breathed a sigh of relief. 'Can you direct us to the hospital?'

'Hospital?' The man chuckled. 'Ruin, more like.'

'Where are we expected to live?'

'Wherever you fancy.'

'Where do you live?'

'Here.' The leper indicated the tiny wooden shelter, open on two sides.

Spiro looked at him doubtfully. 'What do you do in the winter or when it rains?'

'Someone usually takes pity on me and carries me to the tunnel or the church.'

'Why don't you live in one of the houses?'

'Most of them aren't safe. Those that are have people living in them already.'

Spiro took a deep breath. 'You mean we're expected to live out in the open? If there's no hospital what happens to the really sick people?'

'They die, same as anywhere else.'

'Please, could I have another drink?' Yannis spoke for the first time. The jug was handed to him and he drank again greedily. 'Where's your water supply?' he asked, realising he had almost emptied the jug.

'By the tunnel; there's an old fountain in the wall.'

'You wouldn't have any food, I suppose?' asked Spiro, his stomach had been growling with hunger for some time. 'We haven't eaten for twenty four hours.'

A piece of bread was handed to each of them, followed by a hunk of cheese, which Spiro wolfed down quickly, pleased to see that Yannis was also eating.

'Where do you get your food from?'

'You help yourself from the storehouse down by the quay.'

Yannis slumped down beside the bank. 'I told you this place was hell. You didn't believe me.'

'What do you know about it?' asked the legless leper.

'I used to live in Plaka.'

'What's wrong with you, Yannis? It's not so bad here. We'll find somewhere to live,' Spiro assured him. 'It can't be worse than the hospital.'

'I wish they'd thrown us over-board in our strait jackets. At least it would be over by now. God knows how long we shall survive here and in what misery.'

Spiro shook his head in despair. 'Well, I'm going to take this jug and find the water fountain. Then I'm going to the storehouse to see what food there is. Are you coming, Yannis?'

'No. I'll stay here – if you don't mind?' he looked at the man above him.

'Come on up. There are some steps lower down.'

Yannis climbed the steps and found he was on the catwalk of the old fortress; running down the centre was a low tunnel, which culminated in a square, open chamber.

'What's that?' Spiro heard him ask.

'It catches the rain. Come and sit by me and tell me about yourself. What's your name for a start, I'm Kyriakos, Kyriakos the legless.'

Spiro was distinctly worried. For five years he had lived in the close confines of the hospital ward, dirty, un-kempt, ill-fed and bored, but sheltered from the elements and receiving rudimentary medication. How would he and the others fare now? The next few months, if they were lucky, would be tolerable, but what would happen to them when it rained for days on end? How would they keep warm during the winter months? At the entrance to the quay he hesitated, then decided he would fetch the water first. Lining both sides of the path were houses, lacking doors, windows, roofs, some hardly more than a wall with a heap of rubble behind it. In a little knot stood the lepers who had recently arrived, looking frightened, bewildered, hoping someone would come and tell them what they should do or where they should go.

'Hey, Spiro.'

'Panicos.'

The two men embraced sombrely. 'What's your opinion?' asked Panicos.

'There's nothing here. There's some water down by the tunnel and food in a room by the quay and that's it.'

Panicos paled. 'I thought someone would come and take us to the hospital.'

'There is no hospital. Yannis and I have been talking to a man further up. He says most of the buildings are dangerous, so they live in the open. When it rains they take shelter in the church or a tunnel.'

'What are we going to do?'

'I don't know.' Spiro rubbed his knuckles over his forehead. 'Yannis feels pretty bad.'

'Ill?'

'No, I don't think he's ill. He just feels responsible for us being sent here. He used to live somewhere nearby and knows the island by reputation.'

Panicos frowned. 'Where are you off to now?'

'To fetch some water and food.'

'I'll come with you. I think most of us came down this way and found the water. I'm not sure about the food. We'll pass the word as we go back.'

Spiro agreed readily. He felt uncertain wandering around alone. As they passed people melted into the shadows of the buildings or glared balefully at them from where they were sitting. The waterspout was set into the massive wall of the fortress, which towered above them. A few feet away a dark entrance yawned, whilst opposite a flight of steps cut into the hillside led to the battlements above. Behind them there was a house, which appeared to be in reasonable repair, and they could feel eyes watching them, making their skin prickle. The jug almost full, Spiro manoeuvred it carefully away from the spout and looked towards the house, smiling and waving his hand.

'What do you think?'

'Worth a try,' agreed Panicos.

Together they went to the doorway. 'Hallo, there,' called Spiro. From the dark interior a man enquired their business roughly.

'We've recently arrived and wondered if there was any shelter available.'

The man hesitated, and then limped forward to lean against the doorpost. 'Are you lepers?'

'Of course.'

'You were brought here like criminals.' The man was suspicious. 'We don't want criminals here.'

'We're not,' Spiro assured him. 'It's a long story. We had a fight at the hospital, but we're not criminals.'

'There's no room anyway.' The man spat on the ground. As Spiro's eyes had become accustomed to the interior gloom he could see the man was speaking the truth. There seemed to be bodies everywhere.

'I believe you, friend. We'll look elsewhere.'

They felt eyes following them as they returned towards the quay. 'It explains a lot if they thought we were a band of thieves or murderers sent amongst them,' remarked Panicos. 'I thought it odd that no one came to look at us out of curiosity. They're all busy protecting whatever few possessions they have in the mistaken belief that we're here to rob them.'

'Let's get some food and be done. This jug's heavy and I'm tired.'

Spiro half expected to find the food under guard, but there was no one. The high stone room was littered with crates and boxes, haphazardly placed on the earth floor. High, open windows allowed the light to penetrate and they began to examine the containers.

'Figs!' Spiro crammed one into his mouth. 'I just love figs.'

Between them they gathered bread, cheese, olives, tomatoes

and figs, putting it all into one of the empty boxes they found in a corner.

'I hope we haven't taken too much,' observed Spiro, popping another fig into his mouth.

'I'm sure we'll soon be told if we have!'

The two men returned to the sunlight, Panicos putting his hand on Spiro's arm. 'What were those boxes and sacks they off loaded? Whilst we're here we may as well have a look. It could be more food.'

They placed their burdens in the shade and walked through the arch onto the quay. Panicos opened the neck of the first sack and looked at Spiro in surprise.

'It's clothing! We can have some clean clothes!'

Spiro pulled a box towards him. Daubed on the top in white paint was a name, the sack next to it was also named.

'Wait a minute.' He moved more of the containers; on each there was a roughly painted name. 'These are our belongings.' He began to sort through them frantically until he found one bearing his name and undid the neck of the sack eagerly. 'It's mine,' he announced in satisfaction.

Panicos found a box that belonged to him and dragged it to one side. 'We can't manage these and the food. Let's go back and get Yannis to come and help.'

They retrieved the food and water and walked slowly back up the slope to the path, following it until they came to Kyriakos's shelter. Yannis was lying asleep in the sunshine.

'Wake up, lazy, see what we've got.'

Kyriakos frowned at them. 'Let him sleep. He's had a bad time.'

'We've all had a bad time,' replied Panicos dryly. 'Stir yourself, Yannis. We need your help.'

Yannis opened a sleepy eye. 'What?'

'When they dumped us ashore they also dumped our belongings. There are boxes and sacks down there with our names on. We found ours, but couldn't manage to bring them back this trip.'

Yannis sat up, suddenly more interested. 'Tell me.'

'We went for the water and spoke to a man in one of the houses. He said there was no room, and it was true. There were people everywhere. Then we went down to the quay and made up a box of food. Panicos remembered the boxes and sacks that had been put ashore and we went to have a look at them. They've all got names on, so we found ours. Yours must be there somewhere.'

Kyriakos was steadily eating the figs. 'I suggest you go and get them before someone else does. Bring them back here, they'll be safe with me.'

Reluctantly Yannis rose to his feet, took a long drink from the jug and prepared to follow his friends. It would be good to change into some cleaner clothes. When they reached the quay the pile of belongings was considerably diminished, men were carrying bundles and pushing boxes back up to the path. Panicos and Spiro checked that their possessions were where they had left them and began to help Yannis search for his. Finally they returned up the slope carrying their belongings.

Once back with Kyriakos they unpacked eagerly, Yannis delighted to find that in the bottom of his box was his treasured collection of books that he had not seen since leaving Heraklion. Each man changed his clothes and Yannis turned to Kyriakos.

'Is there somewhere we can wash these and maybe have a bath ourselves?'

Kyriakos chuckled. 'You can use the old laundry, down by the quay, but there's only sea water for a bath'.

Panicos and Spiro exchanged glances, whilst Yannis picked up his discarded clothing. 'It's better than nothing. Are you coming?'

The three men went down to the quay, with their dirty clothes bundled into their arms. One sack was still sitting there and Yannis approached it curiously. His name showed clearly and he began to undo the neck, wondering if it did belong to him. Yannis began to remove articles of clothing that looked vaguely familiar, but were certainly not his. At the bottom of the sack was a small prayer book, which he opened carefully. Written on the flyleaf was the name "Andreas Mandrakis".

'I don't believe it. It's not possible.' Yannis sat with the prayer book in his hands. 'This belongs to my cousin. Is he a leper?'

Spiro shook his head. 'I've no idea, but if he's on this island we'll soon find him. Put it to one side and we'll take it back up with us.'

They immersed their bodies in the sea, before using a shirt from the sack to dry their wet bodies. Despite the salt, which stung their open wounds, they all felt considerably cleaner than they had for years. They rubbed at their old clothes to remove the dirt and carried them back to Kyriakos, spreading them on the ground to dry. Yannis looked again at the prayer book; then placed it carefully in his box with his books.

He felt more relaxed, and he realised with something of a shock that he was more comfortable than he had been for a considerable amount of time. He stretched out his hand for the last fig and Kyriakos shook his head.

'You'll spoil your supper.'

'What supper! We'll have to go down and get some more bread and cheese before it gets dark.'

Kyriakos smiled to himself 'Be patient for a while, you could have a surprise.'

Panicos and Spiro suggested a game of cards and Kyriakos accepted eagerly, whilst Yannis preferred to sit and read one of his books. He read slowly, revelling in each word. He had not realised just how much he had missed reading. A savoury smell teased at his nostrils and he looked around curiously. Coming towards them was a young girl carrying a large basket. Kyriakos waved a hand at her.

'Come and be introduced, Phaedra.'

She smiled at the newcomers and placed her basket on the ground. 'I hope there's enough. There's plenty of bread to go with it.' She placed earthenware bowls on the ground and filled each one with meat and vegetables.

Yannis ate hungrily; wiping his bowl round with bread, and wishing there was more. 'That was magnificent,' he smiled at Phaedra. 'I don't know when I last enjoyed a meal so much.'

'She's a good girl,' Kyriakos praised her. 'She makes sure I have a proper meal each day and does her best with whatever is sent over.'

'Where do you live?' asked Panicos.

'Further up the path.'

Panicos moved a little closer to her. 'Is there anywhere to live? I mean, a proper building where you're sheltered from the elements?'

'Not really, most of the houses are falling down.'

'Why don't you repair them?'

Phaedra looked at him scornfully. 'You haven't seen the island yet, or the people. I'll take you on a tour tomorrow. That will answer all your questions.' She gathered up the bowls and replaced them in her basket. 'Is there anything you want, Kyriakos?'

'No, these young men can refill the water jug and settle me down for the night.'

'How about a walk?' suggested Spiro, 'we ought to see how the others have fared.'

Reluctantly Yannis agreed. Despite the fact that it was still light he would have liked to curl up on a mattress and sleep. Panicos yawned hugely, and Yannis guessed he felt the same.

It was only a short walk back to where the waterspout was situated, and that also seemed to be where most people lived. The new arrivals were still clustered together in an apprehensive group and looked relieved when they saw Yannis and Spiro arrive.

'Have you eaten?' was the first question Yannis asked and was gratified to find that everyone had made a meal of sorts, although it was doubtful that any of them had eaten a meal as good as his.

Panicos was shaking his head and he called to Yannis to join him. 'Talk to them, Yannis. They want to insist the occupants make room in their homes for them to shelter for the night.'

'What am I going to say?'

'I don't know, but we must keep them calm or there could be real trouble. We've no idea how many people there are on this island or how physically strong they are. If we upset the inhabitants we could be set upon and probably wouldn't stand a chance. You know this island, you're the best one to speak to them.'

Yannis sighed wearily; then raised his voice. 'Listen everyone. Listen.' He waited until he had gained their attention. 'We are all newcomers over here. We want to be friends with the inhabitants, but it will take time on both sides. When we arrived they thought we were criminals because of our strait jackets. We have to prove that we are no different from them, ordinary people, who just want to live as best we can. It won't hurt any of you to sleep in the open tonight. Put on an extra pullover, you've all received your boxes. Tomorrow we'll look around and see if there are any empty houses we can occupy. We need to ask permission, we're newcomers here, we mustn't take other people's homes.'

The men listened in silence, grudgingly agreeing that Yannis was right, and dispersing in twos and threes to find a wall to huddle against for the night.

Yannis soon found the piece of concrete he was laying on became cold and hard. He had donned two pullovers and placed all his other spare clothes beneath him, but it seemed to make no difference. Despite being huddled against Spiro he felt chilled to the bone and thoroughly miserable. Maybe if he went for a walk he would become warmer. Stealthily he rose to his feet and stood for a while rubbing his legs to restore the circulation. Moving slowly he groped his way down the steps and tiptoed along the path. Within a short space of time the outer wall of the fortress curved inwards and the concrete gave way to dirt.

Yannis leaned against the wall and strained his eyes in the

darkness. Across the bay pinpricks of light could be seen, and even as he watched they were being obliterated as the people retired to their beds.

'I'm so sorry, Mamma.' His hand went to the charm she had given him.

'What are you doing?'

The voice made Yannis start. 'Who's there?'

'Only me, Phaedra. What are you doing?' she repeated.

'I couldn't sleep. I thought I'd walk around.'

'You'd better go back and wait until the morning before you start walking around. A bit further on the path narrows and there's a dangerous drop.'

Yannis shrugged. 'No doubt if I'd fallen people would say it was what I deserved. It's all my fault they've been sent here.'

'And is it?'

'I don't know. I caused trouble, but I only wanted to make things better, not worse. I never thought they'd send us here.' Yannis spoke miserably.

'What's so bad about being here? You said I'd given you the best meal you'd tasted in years, you have your belongings and you can do as you please. Go back to your friends and get some sleep.'

'Coffee?' Panicos pushed an enamelled mug of the hot brew into his hands.

Yannis sniffed at it. 'Is it real coffee?'

Panicos nodded. 'Phaedra gave it to me.'

Yannis sipped at the mug. It tasted good. 'Is there anything to eat?'

'There's a bit of bread.'

Yannis dipped the bread into his coffee to soften it and munched slowly. 'Kyriakos,' he said finally, 'who's in charge of this island?'

'How do I know? The government, I suppose.'

'No, I mean who amongst you runs the island? Who decides how much food you have and where you live?'

'No one. You just find somewhere and call it yours.' Kyriakos shifted his position slightly. 'If there'd been just one or two of you, you could have been squeezed in somewhere. As it is there are too many of you.'

'So what can we do?'

'Talk to Antionis.'

'Will he be able to help?'

'I don't know.' Kyriakos shut his eyes.

'Where will I find him?'

'Down by the water fountain.'

Yannis looked at Panicos and raised his eyebrows. 'Shall we try to find him?'

'Nothing to lose.'

'Bring back some water,' Kyriakos called after them and Panicos picked up the jug.

'Where's Spiro?'

'He said he was going down to get some food. We can meet him down there.'

Yannis looked across the bay and felt a lump come to his throat as he saw people moving in the fields. They must be his family. 'Come on,' he said gruffly and led the way down the steps.

When they reached the domed building Spiro was sitting outside talking to Phaedra.

'There's no food,' he announced. 'Phaedra said the boats would start coming over soon.'

Yannis nodded, remembering the routine. 'I'm glad you're here, Phaedra. Kyriakos suggested I spoke to Antionis. He said he lived by the fountain. Can you show us his house?'

Phaedra looked at the men doubtfully. 'It would be better if only one of you went or he might feel threatened.'

'You go,' said Panicos to Yannis. 'It was your idea. I'll stay with Spiro.'

YANNIS

Yannis followed Phaedra, remembering to thank her for providing him with coffee. 'We only ever had water in the hospital. It was wonderful to smell and taste coffee again.'

'I said you were better off here. Treat Antionis gently, won't you? He's an old man.'

'Of course I will. I'm not a ruffian, despite whatever Spiro may have said about me.'

Phaedra smiled to herself. 'He didn't say you were a ruffian. Here we are.' She rapped smartly on a door. 'Antionis! One of the hospital men wants to speak to you.'

The door opened, sightless eyes peered out into the sunshine. 'Where is he?'

Phaedra took the old man by the arm and led him towards Yannis. 'He's here.'

The old man eased himself down onto the ground and Yannis squatted beside him.

'What do you want?'

'Kyriakos suggested I spoke to you.' Yannis struggled for the correct words. 'I want everyone to know that we want to be friends. All we want is a fair share of the food and somewhere to shelter.'

Antionis did not reply and Yannis began to wonder if the old man was deaf as well as blind. He began to repeat himself. 'We want to be friends....'

Antionis held up his mutilated hand. 'I heard you the first time.'

Yannis fell silent and waited for the man to speak.

'You will have food, when food is sent to us. There is usually sufficient, unless the weather is too bad for the boats to land. Shelter is different. There's very little shelter. We are sick, very sick. You're all much fitter than we are. If you want shelter you must make your own.'

'Make our own!' Yannis was horrified. 'How can we?'

'When I had my sight I saw many houses that just needed to

be cleared of rubble and strengthened. They won't have disappeared.'

'How long have you been here?'

'Who knows? When the world goes dark about you day and night become as one. Time no longer means anything any more.' Antionis fell silent and Yannis wondered if he was asleep. Quietly he rose to go. As he did so Antionis's hand reached out and clawed at his trousers. 'You will rebuild. Promise me.'

'I don't know. I can't…..'

'Promise me.'

'How can I?'

'Promise.'

'I promise' Yannis crossed himself as he said the words, hoping his vow would not be held against him at a later date.

Yannis looked for Phaedra, but she had disappeared. He walked slowly along the concrete path to the quay where he had left Panicos and Spiro. He would have to talk to them.

'Well?' Panicos looked at him eagerly.

Yannis shook his head. 'Antionis said we would have to build our own shelters. He said there were plenty of places that just needed repairing and cleaning up.'

'Can he take us to them?' asked Spiro eagerly.

'He's blind,' said Yannis simply.

'How long has he been blind?'

'I don't know; he doesn't seem to know.'

'So these buildings that he says can be repaired may no longer be standing! Who else could we ask?'

'Why don't we go and look?' suggested Spiro.

'Phaedra was going to show us the island today.' Yannis looked round, hoping to see her. 'Shouldn't we wait for her?'

'Why? I doubt that we'll get lost.'

'Let's walk up to Kyriakos; we need to take him the water. She may be with him,' suggested Yannis hopefully.

There was no sign of Phaedra so the three men continued up

the path until it petered out to become a dirt track. Yannis did not mention that he had already explored that far. A projection of cliff appeared to bar their way, but as they reached it they looked down a steep, rocky bank that led to a catwalk, littered with stones and rocks. Yannis shuddered. No wonder Phaedra had been concerned. Had he fallen down there in the darkness he could well have ended up with broken bones. The path continued, a narrow track with sheer rock rising above them and also falling down to the sea below. There was nowhere that would be suitable to build and no signs that anyone had ever attempted to do so. The path curved again and as they rounded it Spiro stopped in surprise.

'Well, who would have thought there would be a church round here.'

Set back into the hill, the path once more concreted and widening considerably, the church looked sad and neglected.

'I'd like to go in. Will you wait for me?'

Without waiting for their answer Yannis walked to the door, which yielded under his touch, and he found himself in the bare interior. Leaving the door open he walked to where the altar would have been placed and fell on his knees. His jumbled thoughts could hardly have been described as prayers, but as he left he felt vaguely comforted and at ease. He smiled at his companions.

'Shall we continue?'

The path became steeper and they passed a house, the roof had gone and most of the walls. 'Built for the view!' observed Panicos, as they looked out across the open sea and back to the bay, clearly visible on the mainland were the villages of Elounda, Olous and Plaka.

Yannis looked away. He did not wish to be continually reminded how close his home was. 'What's up there?' He pointed to some steps, broken and overgrown with weeds, which led up to the outer wall of the fortress.

Silently they climbed upwards, passing heaps of rubble, the

way becoming steeper once the steps petered out until they were climbing over slabs of granite rock to reach the heart of the fortress. A final large, slippery block brought them to the foot of a wall, far too high for them to climb. Cautiously Yannis edged his way forward until he saw a small opening and they were able to file through and stand on level ground. Around them the walls rose, almost undamaged over the years, but no vestige of a roof. Passing through an arch they looked on to the catwalk, which could be reached by a short flight of steep, stone steps. Beneath the walk itself were the shallow archways that had originally held the canons.

'May as well go back.' Panicos felt disheartened. He had hoped that part of the old fortress would be habitable. 'You wouldn't get much shelter up here.'

Yannis looked around. 'Is there no way out from here? The Turks and Venetians wouldn't have scrambled up the way we came to man the guns.'

'The only way out would have been over there.' Spiro pointed to a fallen archway and a tangle of masonry that barred their way.

'Back we go then.' Yannis began to negotiate the slippery granite to regain the path and ended up by sliding down. He held out his hand. 'I don't recommend that! It was painful. Come down as far as you can, then hold on to me.'

They retraced their steps and regained the main path, following it down to a small beach, sheltered on both sides by the wall of the fortress. Turning right they entered a tunnel and immediately began to choke at the smell that rose to their nostrils. Their eyes became accustomed to the gloom and they were able to step over and around the worst of the debris. Once outside they drew deep breaths of fresh air.

'I will never, ever, shelter in that place, however desperate I might be,' vowed Spiro.

They had exited into the little square where the water fountain was situated and looked at each other with sinking hearts.

YANNIS

'So!' Panicos let out his breath. 'That is the extent of the island. No other water, no buildings, no shelter of any kind. Now we know why they live huddled together in that collection of ruins.'

'There must be some other houses. We just haven't found them,' said Yannis stubbornly.

Spiro took a long drink from the water fountain. 'I'm exhausted,' he admitted. 'All the exercise I've had in the last few years has been walking around the hospital ward. I'm going back to Kyriakos to have a sleep.'

'Maybe some food has arrived,' suggested Yannis hopefully. 'I'm hungry.'

'We'll call in on the way.'

They made their way back to the storeroom and helped themselves to a variety of foods, eating as they walked back towards Kyriakos. Yannis tried to ask him about the buildings Antionis had mentioned, but Kyriakos only grunted and said 'Ask Alecos' before closing his eyes more firmly against the mid-day sun. Resigned, Yannis settled himself down to sleep along with his friends, forced to admit that his legs ached from the unaccustomed exercise.

He was unable to settle, the rhythmical breathing of the others annoyed him, rather than soothed and he finally gave up the attempt. He looked for the water jug, and found it was empty. He would have to walk to the fountain for a drink. Silently he left them and walked between the sleeping men and women who lined the path to the square. He slaked his thirst and wondered what to do, maybe if he went for a swim from the small beach it would ease his aching legs and he would be able to sleep.

Taking a deep breath he picked his way carefully through the gloom of the tunnel until he stood again in bright sunlight looking at the sea. The idea of a swim no longer seemed so attractive and he turned to the left, taking the path that led to the deserted church and pushed open the rickety door.

How long he spent on his knees with his hands clasped he did not know. The word 'rebuild' was hammering in his head, becoming Antionis's voice saying, 'You can rebuild' and getting louder and stronger each time it was said. Involuntarily Yannis put his hands over his ears and shouted. 'No!'

The voice seemed to answer more strongly than ever. 'You can rebuild.'

'I can't! I can't!' Yannis rose and stumbled back out into the sunshine. He almost ran up the slight incline, only stopping and drawing his breath when the path narrowed dangerously. He walked more leisurely to the promontory and as he rounded it the village of Plaka came into view. The sight made a lump come into his throat and he looked around desperately. His experience in the church had unnerved him completely and he had no wish to return in that direction. He looked upwards. Just above his head the rock shelved. Placing his foot in a niche he pulled himself up and looked in surprise. Stretching out before him was a path, very narrow, which twisted and turned out of his sight between the scrub and bushes that clung precariously to the rock.

Cautiously Yannis moved forwards, climbing steadily, until the path suddenly widened into a flat rock and he was on the summit of the island. Below him stretched the Venetian fortress and many ruined buildings. He turned to face the open sea and watched the sunlight dancing on the ripples, trying hard to empty his head of the thoughts that were plaguing him. His legs were trembling with the unaccustomed exertion and he lay down on the hot rock and folded his hands beneath his head.

A lizard running across his leg wakened him with a start. Sleepily he sat up and looked around. His mouth was dry and he licked his cracked lips. He made a conscious effort to avoid looking across to Plaka and gazed instead down onto the ruined buildings. There was something wrong. From his vantage point there seemed to be many more ruined structures than there were when you followed the path round the island. Yannis forgot his thirst as he began to concentrate on the layout displayed below him.

Maybe he should speak to Alecos as Kyriakos had suggested. Judging by the position of the sun in the sky most of the inhabitants should be awake by now and he might be able to find the man. As he rose to his feet he realised just how stiff his legs had become and clambered back down the narrow path carefully. He made his way first to the fountain and joined the queue of those waiting to refresh themselves after their siesta. Once satisfied he knocked on the door of the first house and asked where he could find Alecos.

'Third house, over there.'

Yannis thanked him and walked to the house he indicated. He knocked on the door, but there was no answer, he asked a woman who sat outside and she shook her head.

'He's somewhere around.'

Yannis tried the next person and was told the same. Frustrated he stood in the middle of the square.

'Alecos!' he shouted and jumped violently when a voice at his elbow answered him.

'You looking for me?'

'Are you Alecos?'

The man nodded.

'Is there somewhere we could sit and talk? Kyriakos said I should speak to you.'

Alecos walked over to a patch of shade offered by the fortress wall. 'Well?'

'I spoke to Antionis this morning. I wanted to know if there was anywhere we could shelter at night. He said we would have to build our own and there were places that just needed clearing up and repairing. We walked all round the island this morning and couldn't find them. Kyriakos said I should speak to you.'

'It's been a dream of his since we first arrived. He was so sure it could be done, but no one would listen to him.'

'Tell me about it,' urged Yannis.

'Antionis was one of the first to be sent here. There were

only a handful of them and they moved into the most habitable houses. As more arrived the houses became overcrowded and more dilapidated. He continually urged them to do some repairs and rebuild, but they were apathetic. No one had any hope or incentive. They were all convinced they would die soon and there seemed no point in expending their energy. For a while they managed, enough died to make space for the living, then they seemed to live longer, but we were still able to manage. Now that you've arrived something has to be done. You're all fitter than we are. Now's the time to do it, before you become too old or ill to work.'

'Is there anyone here who was a builder? Who could tell us if the walls were safe before we started or how to put a roof on?'

'Two or three – if they're willing.'

'Why shouldn't they be willing?'

Alecos shrugged. 'They wouldn't do it for themselves, why should they do it for you?'

Yannis considered the problem. 'I'll talk to my friends, then I'll come back and speak to you again.'

Alecos nodded. 'You know where I live.'

Panicos, Spiro and Kyriakos were playing cards when Yannis returned. He waited until the hand was finished and sat down beside Spiro.

'I've just been talking to Alecos. He said Antionis has been telling them for years that they must do some repairs and there are some builders here amongst them. The snag is that they wouldn't do it for themselves and he doesn't think they'll do it for us.'

'We only need them to tell us how to do it. We can do the work.'

Panicos frowned. 'Wouldn't they expect to have their houses repaired?'

'I expect so.'

'Then we offer to do theirs first.'

'That would probably leave us outside all winter.'

'We'd have to bargain with them. If we repaired their house some of us would have to be allowed to live in it with them.'

'Even so, how many helpers could we muster?'

'Thirty of us came over.'

Panicos laughed shortly. 'I'll be interested to see if they all volunteer.'

Spiro tapped his teeth with a playing card. 'All right, Yannis. Have it your way. Everyone is going to rebuild houses, but what with? We've no tools or materials.'

'Whilst you were all sleeping the afternoon away, I climbed to the top of the island. There's a narrow track and when you get to the summit you can see for miles. There are many more ruins than you can see from down here. There should be plenty of wood and stone laying around.'

'And the tools? Are they just lying around? Forget it, Yannis.' Spiro picked up the rest of the pack and dealt a hand to each of them. Yannis pushed them away.

'Count me out. I'm tired.' He rolled a pullover beneath his head and turned his back on his companions. He felt unreasonably annoyed and frustrated with them.

'Supper time.'

The voice seemed to come from far away and Yannis thought he was dreaming. He stirred and tried to rise, falling back as his head throbbed violently and a feeling of nausea overtook him. Trying to speak, his voice came in a hoarse croak and Phaedra reached for Kyriakos's water jug, holding it to Yannis lips. He raised himself slowly and allowed her to support him as he drank thirstily. The water did nothing to ease the pain and dryness of his throat.

'Lay back, you've probably done far too much.'

Yannis obeyed, realising he had no choice. Pain was shooting up the side of his head from his ear and breaking like thousands of fireworks behind his left eye. He felt someone mop his brow and wash his face with cold water and realised he was being covered with Kyriakos's old rug in an attempt to stop his shivering.

For three days Yannis lay, racked with pain in his head and throat, shivering and sweating alternately, tended by Phaedra and an anxious Spiro.

'Don't worry,' she assured him. 'It will pass. It often happens to newcomers. They don't realise the energy they're using and exhaust themselves.'

Whatever their conversation, it always returned to the pressing problem of where they could shelter. 'I had an idea just before I was ill, but I can't remember what it was.'

'Don't try to remember. It'll come back if you don't try to force it,' advised Spiro. 'We've been waiting for you to get well so we could talk to you.'

'Have you had any ideas?'

'We've been talking to the others. Between all of us on the island we have a multitude of talent. There are four men who used to be builders, two carpenters, two barbers, a solicitor, three school teachers, five musicians, a tailor and goodness knows how many fishermen, farmers, taverna keepers and shop keepers. There's only one snag. Two of the builders are blind, one has hardly any hands left and the other has only one leg. One carpenter is too old and sick to do anything and the other only made furniture.'

'Fantastic! The men who could really help us aren't able to.' Yannis felt unreasonably depressed.

'There's one good point, though, apart from getting to know the people. Have you seen my hair?'

For the first time Yannis took stock of his friend. 'You've had a haircut. It looks marvellous.'

'I persuaded one of the barbers. I bargained with him and he finally agreed to do it for a leather belt.'

'I wonder what he'd do mine for? I've the clothes from Andreas's bundle. Would they be of any use to him?'

'I shouldn't think so,' chuckled Spiro. 'He's enormous. I think everyone must barter their food in exchange for a hair cut.'

'Is there any food? Proper food? Not that awful coddled mess Phaedra's been making me eat.'

'There's plenty in the storeroom. A boat came out this morning with some mattresses and blankets. There was almost a riot; everyone wanted one. Panicos and I stood on the quay and would only let those from our ward in Athens have them.' He winked at Yannis. 'I did manage to get an extra one, though. I've given it to Kyriakos.'

'That was kind of you.'

'He was kind to us when we first arrived. I just repaid the favour.'

Yannis rose to his feet, realising just how unsteady he was as he swayed dangerously for a moment. 'I'm going for some food, and then you can introduce me to the barber. Whilst I'm there do you think you could locate the one-legged builder? I'd like to talk to him.'

'You're at it again.' Spiro sighed and shook his head.

'What do you mean?' Yannis took Spiro's arm gratefully as he descended the steps to the path.

'Dashing around, trying to do three things at once. You've plenty of time, Yannis. You'll wear yourself out again.'

'I promise I'll be more sensible in future.' He frowned. 'If we do start to rebuild we'll have to limit our working time, just a few hours each day until we've built up our strength. Point out the barber to me, then you go and find this builder and Antionis.'

Yannis leaned against the fortress wall and gazed across the bay. A lump came into his throat as he looked at his home village and visualized his family. Two whole years! Anything could have happened in that time. For a while he toyed with the impossible idea of swimming across to the mainland and pretending to be a beggar. Would they recognise him? He touched his face with his hands. He had not seen his face since he was in Heraklion. Apart from his abundant hair growth his skin felt bubbly, but whole. Feeling the hair reminded him he was supposed to be going to the barber. He shuddered, remembering the last time he had visited a barber and been chased from the shop, abuse ringing in his ears. At least that would not happen this time.

Unwillingly he dragged himself to his feet and returned to the man whom Spiro had pointed out to him. Just before the arch leading into the square, a fat man sat, his legs stretched out before him for a modicum of comfort. Yannis sat down beside him, regardless of the scowl that greeted him.

'I understand you're a barber. Would you cut my hair for me, please?'

Tiny eyes, sunk deep into rolls of fat, took stock of Yannis. 'What for?'

'Because it's dirty and untidy.'

'What do I get for doing it?'

'What do you want?'

The man shrugged. 'What have you got?'

Yannis sighed in exasperation. 'Very little; a few clothes, some books.'

The fat man thought. 'Books are no good to me. I can't read.' He wiped his nose with the back of his hand. 'Do you have any socks? I get through a lot of socks.' He pointed to his misshapen feet.

'I've got a pair you could have.'

The barber nodded. 'Bring them along and I'll see what I can do for you.'

'What? Now?'

He nodded again. 'I like to have the goods in my hand. I can't go chasing after you to remind you.'

'I won't be long.' Yannis rose and walked back up the path. Kyriakos waved to him.

'Come and talk to me now you're feeling better. I've done nothing for the last few days but play cards with Panicos.'

'What did you lose?'

Kyriakos grinned. 'Two pairs of shoes; they weren't a lot of good to me.'

Yannis had to agree with him. 'I can't stop and chat now. I'm going to have a hair cut.' He rummaged in his box and produced a pair of socks. 'The price of a haircut.' He held them up to show Kyriakos.

'He needs them, poor devil. He can't put a shoe on either foot now.'

Yannis hurried back down the path to where the fat barber sat. He thrust the socks into the grasping hands. Slowly the barber unrolled and inspected them. 'They're good ones. Haven't even been mended.' He smiled broadly. 'Help me up and we'll get started.'

Yannis allowed the heavyweight to lean on him as he hauled himself to his feet, finally propping himself against the wall and instructing Yannis to kneel before him. From his pocket he took a pair of scissors and began to snip away at the long locks. By the time he had finished Yannis's knees were numb and when told to stand he rose stiffly, rubbing the life back into them.

'That feels better.' He ran his hand along the back of his neck.

'Do you want to see?'

'Can I? Have you got a mirror?'

From his back pocket the barber pulled a small square of glass and held it out. Yannis studied his face carefully, pretending to look at the haircut. His skin felt worse than it looked. He tried to screw his head round to look at his neck, but the scrap of mirror was too small.

'That's fine. Thanks a lot.' He handed the mirror back and continued down the path in search of Spiro.

A heated argument was taking place between Spiro and the one-legged builder, whilst Antionis sat and listened. Yannis decided to intervene.

'What's the problem?'

Spiro struck his leg in disgust. 'Christos says it can't be done.'

'Why not?' Yannis sat down beside them.

'A number of reasons. There's no one fit enough here to build a house. It's hard work, heavy lifting, climbing up scaffolding, work that we can't do. Even if we could where would we get the materials from?'

'We can work.'

'That's what I'm telling him,' insisted Spiro.

'All we want is your advice. We want you to tell us if a wall is safe, how to put the roof on and hang a door.'

Christos shook his head.

'Suppose I said I know a way for us to have plenty of water?' Yannis waited for the effect of his words to sink in.

Christos hauled himself to his feet, placing a prop of wood under his armpit. 'You're mad. Talking about building and having water!'

Yannis watched him limp away in disappointment. He shrugged and was about to walk away when Antionis's soft voice cut through the silence.

'Tell me about your idea for more water.'

'It's quite simple. You just collect rainwater and save it.' Yannis spoke sulkily.

'How would you collect enough and where would you store it?'

'The same way as the Venetians did, make channels for it to run down the roof, catch it in a barrel and store it until it was needed. You need roofs to make channels,' Yannis ended bitterly.

'Yannis,' the old man turned his sightless eyes towards the youth. 'You'll have to do it yourself. Once they see it can be done they'll follow you. You can rebuild.'

Yannis looked at Spiro. 'He's right, you know. If we showed that one house could be made habitable they'd be only too pleased to help us. It's just a question of showing them it can be done.'

Spiro shook his head. 'We were dreaming. It's like Christos said, we need materials.'

'We've got the materials.'

Spiro looked at Yannis scornfully. 'Broken walls and doors and windows. They'll make fine materials! Where are the hammer, nails, and screwdriver? Even a ladder would help.'

'We'll make them or manage.'

Spiro snorted in disgust and disbelief and began to walk away. At first Yannis started to follow him, then changed his mind. He would investigate the possibilities of the ruins he had seen from the summit of the island. Turning away from the concrete path into a narrow, overgrown walkway next to the main church building, he pushed his way through the scrub and low bushes that were growing there. Thorns clutched at his clothes, but he forced his way, all the time Antionis's voice ringing in his ears. He reached the first of the crumbling walls. It was built with one stone on top of the other; the gaps plugged with slithers of rock, and stood about two metres high.

Yannis pushed against it with all his might, expecting it to tumble over and add to the fallen masonry, but it stayed solid under his strength. He had helped his father build similar structures to retain the earth on the sloping terraces. He searched amongst the fallen blocks for one of a reasonable size, finally lifting it on to a slight depression. Another appeared to fit beside it; he tested it with his hand to ensure the two flat sides were together. It rocked very slightly and Yannis searched amongst the smaller, broken pieces for a wedge.

He became completely engrossed, following the line of the standing wall and adding a row of stones to make it a little higher. One side of the doorframe was still in position, the other having fallen some time in the past. Calculating that he would need at least two more rows of stones to reach the top of the frame he moved to the other side of the wall in his search for materials. The stones were more plentiful on that side, the wall having fallen inwards originally, and he found he was progressing quite quickly. Oblivious to the damage he was doing to his hands, he tugged, pulled, heaved and lifted the stones into place, the sweat pouring from him until he had to rest.

Sitting on the ground he admired his handiwork. He had raised the wall by at least a metre. Elation with his accomplishment turned to despair. The wall he had tackled was the highest, even if he managed to build up the other three, how would he fit windows, door and a roof? He tried to think logically, timber was needed. He would have to collect it from the other ruins and hope it would serve. He scanned the three lower walls. It would take at least a week to raise them to their former height and whilst he was doing that he could consider the problem of fixing a roof.

Wearily he made his way back to the quay and washed his face and hands in the sea before returning to the square of concrete where Kyriakos sat. He felt restless for the remainder of the day, yet dared not return to the ruined house. A re-occurrence of his high temperature and inability to move was the last thing he wanted. Pretending to read he planned carefully. He would clear the scrub as best he could round all the ruins and then decide which ones to rob of timber. Each time the wind blew he wondered if his wall would still be standing when he next went there and he longed for the morning to come. A disturbed sleep saw him hollow-eyed and Phaedra became concerned.

'I'm perfectly all right,' he snapped. 'Just leave me alone.'

'Where are you going?' she asked as he rose abruptly and began to walk away.

'To be alone.'

'Leave him, Phaedra,' advised Spiro. 'He's going through a bad patch.'

Father Minos decided he could no longer avoid visiting the family in Plaka. It was his duty to tell them he knew the name of the hospital where their son had been sent for treatment. They could at least write to him, although it was doubtful that he would be allowed to write back. Descending from the rattling bus in Aghios Nikolaos he hoped he would be able to find the fisherman's house. It was over two years since he had accompanied the young boy to his home to break the news. He ate a leisurely lunch before walking down to the quay where he spotted a solitary fisherman mending his nets, and he picked his way over the debris of boxes, floats and containers to reach his side.

'Excuse me.' The fisherman looked up and crossed himself hurriedly. 'I'm looking for a fisherman, maybe you can help me.'

'What's his name?'

Father Minos racked his brains. What was the man's name? 'He has a son, Andreas.'

'You must want Yiorgo. He went out for the day.'

'Could you direct me to his house?'

A thumb jerked over his right shoulder. 'Up there, fourth house.'

'Thank you.' Trusting that Yiorgo's wife would be in he crossed the road and counted the houses until he reached the fourth where he knocked on the door.

'Come in,' called a woman. 'Come straight through. I'm making pastry.'

Father Minos obeyed her instructions, stopping in the doorway and giving a little cough. Elena whirled round, her hand going to the crucifix she always wore.

'Yiorgo?' Her voice was hoarse with fear.

'There's nothing to be alarmed about. I'm Father Minos who called on you once before. May I come in?'

Elena nodded.

'When I came before I brought bad news about your nephew.'

'Yes?' There was a sudden eagerness about her. 'Have you any news?'

'I've no news of him, but I do know which hospital he was taken to in Athens. Your daughter was betrothed to him I believe. I thought she might like to write to him, if there is no other young man, of course.'

'There's no one else. She hopes that one day he'll be cured.'

Father Minos pursed his lips. 'Have you talked to her? Tried to make her understand that it's most unlikely.'

'She doesn't talk about him. Maybe she would talk to you.' Elena looked at him hopefully.

'I'll speak to her if you wish, but .....' Father Minos spread his hands.'

'Thank you, Father.' Elena bent and kissed his hand. 'She'll be home later. She works at the hospital as a nurse.'

'Really?' Father Minos encouraged Elena to tell him more about her daughter.

'She passed her examinations very well. They're so pleased with her that when she asked to leave they tried to persuade her to stay.'

'Leave? Why should she want to leave?'

'She plans to go to Athens.' Elena smiled sadly. 'I think it's a mistake. She wants to look for Yannis; she hopes to nurse him. I feel she'll be more hurt. Better to stay here and look for someone else who could make her forget.'

'I will talk to her,' promised Father Minos. 'Tell me, how is your son?'

This time Elena beamed with pleasure. 'He's been accepted as a novice. He's a good boy. With him it is a calling.'

Father Minos listened as Elena talked about Andreas. He would like to meet that young man again. There had been a certain strength about him that had attracted the priest. Gradually he turned the conversation to the family living at Plaka, distressed to hear that Maria was little better and her eldest daughter had been forced to marry in haste.

Yiorgo arrived, smelling strongly of fish. He rubbed his hands down his pullover and advanced towards Father Minos. 'It's good to see you again. Do you have any news?'

Sadly the priest shook his head. 'Very little, I'm only able to tell you the name of the hospital where they took your nephew.

YANNIS

You could try writing to the authorities there and ask them for news of his progress.'

Yiorgo looked doubtful. Writing was not one of his accomplishments. 'My daughter's going to Athens soon. Maybe it would be better if she made the enquiry direct.'

'Maybe. She could then let you know if there is any improvement.'

'You should go and wash, Yiorgo,' Elena admonished him. 'You're making the whole house smell of fish, and Annita will be here soon.'

Yiorgo agreed that he did not smell very wholesome. 'You'll stay and eat with us?' he asked of the priest.

'I would be delighted. I would also like to beg a favour of you.'

'Of course, anything.'

'Would you be able to take me to Plaka tomorrow? I feel I should speak to Yannis's parents, but I'm not very sure of my route. You took me by boat before.'

'It will be my pleasure,' beamed Yiorgo. It was an honour to be asked a favour by a priest.

Annita was late. For a while Elena waited before serving their meal, then unwilling to let the priest wait any longer, she served up succulent bowls of fish soup with hunks of bread, which they dipped into the liquor. By the time Annita finally arrived the meal was over and her father and the priest were sipping whisky. At the sight of Father Minos she stopped and crossed herself.

'What's happened?'

'Nothing has happened. Father Minos is just paying us a visit.'

'Oh!' Annita relaxed visibly. 'Are you a friend of Andreas, then?'

'I like to think so. You must be Annita.'

She nodded and slipped into her chair at the table. 'Is there any supper left, Mamma? I know I'm late, but I couldn't help it.'

Elena went into the kitchen, returning with a bowl of fish soup and warm bread for her daughter. 'What kept you? Was it matron or a patient?'

'Neither,' replied Annita. 'I'd lost an earring and I wasn't leaving until I'd found it.'

Father Minos looked at the girl in surprise. Annita saw the look on his face and defended herself immediately. 'They were my betrothal gift.'

'I see. They are very precious to you, then?'

'Yes.' Annita fingered her ear lobe. 'Are you here to see Andreas?' She thought it would be a good idea to change the subject.

'Not exactly, although I would be delighted to spend some time with him. I came partly to see you and also to visit a family I know in Plaka.'

Annita had paled as he spoke. 'Have you got some news of Yannis?' Her eyes searched his face, pleading for the words she wished to hear.

Father Minos shook his head. 'I have no news at all of him. I can only give you the name of the hospital in Athens and suggest you write. I doubt if he could write back to you, but I'm sure he would enjoy reading your letters.'

Tears had sprung into Annita's eyes. 'Will he get better?'

Father Minos shook his head. 'I'm not a doctor. I wouldn't like to hold out any false hopes. I hear you are a very good nurse, you must know more about the treatment of the disease than I do.'

Annita shook her head. 'We don't nurse lepers,' she spoke the words defiantly. 'They're sent to the hospital in Heraklion, then on to Athens. Have my parents told you I'm going to Athens as a nurse?'

'Yes, they did mention it. Don't you feel you're needed here?'

'Nurses are needed everywhere.'

'I fear you may be very disappointed.' Father Minos was picking his words carefully. How could he tell the girl that lepers received no nursing? 'One hospital must be very similar to another.'

'Probably.'

'Would you consider working at the hospital in Heraklion, just for a short time?'

YANNIS

'Why? As you said, one hospital must be very like another.'

Mentally Father Minos saluted her astuteness. 'I merely thought it would not be so far to return home if it did not come up to your expectations.'

'I have no intention of returning home. My parents know this and understand. I want to go right away where no one knows me. I'm sick of being pitied by my family and sneered at in the hospital because they think Yannis has jilted me.'

'You are a very determined young lady,' Father Minos smiled at her gently. 'When do you propose to go?'

'Two more weeks.' A spark of enthusiasm lit her eyes for a moment.

'I'll give you my address in Heraklion. If you wish to visit me you are very welcome.' Father Minos passed two pieces of paper over to Annita. 'There's my address and also the address of the hospital in Athens. Will you be able to visit your relatives in Plaka tomorrow?'

'No, I have to work. Please give them my love.'

'What about Andreas? Would he be able to come? I'd very much like to meet him again.'

'That should be possible. Annita could walk along and ask permission when she's finished her supper.' Yiorgo refilled the glasses and stuck his feet out before him. The whisky was making him feel lethargic.

'Yes, Pappa.' Annita sighed to herself. She had been on her feet since six that morning and wished for nothing more than to go to bed. It would take her at least an hour to go to the outskirts of Aghios Nikolaos, talk to Andreas, wait for him to obtain permission from his superior and return. She wiped the bowl round with the last of her bread. 'I'll go now.'

Her tiredness was dispelled by the pleasure her brother displayed on seeing her, and to her surprise she was invited inside to wait in a tiny parlour whilst he went to obtain the necessary permission. When he finally returned he had his jacket with him.

'I've been told I can have forty-eight hours at home.'

'You sound as though you're in prison,' remarked Annita dryly.

Andreas smiled. 'I can leave at any time I want. That's not being in prison. I'm glad I chose to be a priest rather than a monk, though. I don't think I'd want to spend the rest of my life hemmed in by high walls and silence.'

Annita smiled at him, tucking her hand into his arm and together they sauntered along the cobbled streets.

'Did Father Minos say why he had come to visit us?'

'He just said he had the address of the hospital where Yannis had been sent and I could write if I wanted. Maybe he'll tell you more.'

'Maybe. What did you think of him?'

'I'm not sure. I felt that he is a very good man, kind, well meaning, but I wouldn't want to go against him. I should think he could be quite determined to get his own way, almost ruthless.'

Andreas grinned. 'I'd like to think I could be like him. He has such strength, inner strength. You can almost see it round him.'

'Andreas, you're talking rubbish. How can you have inner strength that can be seen! Come on, let's hurry. I'm tired and I have to be up early again tomorrow.'

By the time they arrived back at the cottage Father Minos and their father had almost finished the bottle of whisky. A makeshift bed had been prepared for Andreas, as Father Minos was to occupy his.

Father Minos gradually dispelled Andreas's initial shyness and within a few minutes they were talking as old friends. Annita excused herself and retired to her bed. Yiorgo opened another bottle of whisky and settled back to listen to the conversation whilst Elena continued with her embroidery. She was relieved when the men finally decided to go to bed, giving Father Minos an oil lamp to light his way.

Yiorgo groaned as he lifted his head from his pillow. He had been a fool to drink so heavily the night before. He had planned an early start for the visit to Plaka, hoping for an early return and some afternoon fishing. If the priest felt as he did, it was unlikely that he would rise for another hour or two. Yiorgo could hear movement in the kitchen and to his surprise he saw Annita sitting at the kitchen table deep in conversation with Father Minos.

'You're early,' he remarked, on his way out to the yard.

Annita smiled at the priest. 'I'll get Pappa some coffee. He probably needs it.'

Yiorgo returned and sipped at the scalding black coffee gratefully. 'Where's Andreas?'

'Still at the church. We went down together, but he wished to stay a little longer,' explained Father Minos.

Yiorgo nodded. He was used to Andreas forever being inside a church. Annita held out her hand to the priest. 'Thank you, Father. I shall never forget how you have helped me.'

'It was nothing.' Father Minos held her hand for a moment. 'You have my address should you ever need me?'

Annita tapped her pocket. 'Goodbye, Pappa. Give Mamma a kiss for me when she wakes up and say goodbye to Andreas for me.' Taking her shawl from the hook behind the door Annita left and Yiorgo looked enquiringly at the priest.

'What did you say to her? She seemed happier than she has for a long time.'

'What I usually say to people who have been deeply hurt,' replied the priest evasively. 'I expect you've said the same to her, but somehow people will accept comfort from a man of the cloth, when they reject it from those who love them most.'

Yiorgo studied the man over his coffee cup. What made men like this priest and his son? He felt very ignorant when in their presence and shifted uncomfortably in his chair. 'We should be off soon. I hope Andreas won't be much longer.'

As if in answer to his words the door opened and Andreas entered, smiling contentedly. 'Are you ready, Pappa? It's a beautiful morning. Which way do you plan to go? Through the canal or round the island?'

'We'll see what the wind is like.'

With Andreas's help he cast off and rowed away from the quay. Curious eyes followed their progress and Yiorgo guessed that Elena would have a number of visitors that morning, asking why her husband and son had gone fishing with a priest. The wind decided their route and Yiorgo set a course for the open sea.

'We'll place some lobster pots as we go.' The day need not be completely wasted.

Andreas nodded and Father Minos watched as the boy expertly baited the open, bell-like cages, roped them at intervals and threw them over the side each time his father raised his hand, all with the tiller tucked under his arm.

'Have you had any news at all of Yannis?'

Father Minos sighed. 'Nothing. When I left you I felt I had failed dismally in my calling. I was about to relinquish my parish.'

Andreas looked at him in surprise. 'Whatever for?'

Father Minos spread his hands. 'I couldn't tell you where your cousin had been taken, what his treatment would be, how long he could wait for a cure. I couldn't tell you anything that you did not already know. I felt I was a complete failure.'

'What made you change your mind?'

'I thought about it very carefully and decided to do something a little more constructive than running away.' Father Minos could not bring himself to tell Andreas of his experience in the church. Even he, looking back, could not be certain he had not imagined the voice that had spoken to him so clearly. 'I decided I would go to the hospital on a regular basis and visit the lepers whilst they're there.'

'Yes?' Andreas's eyes were alight with interest.

'It was a little difficult at first,' a smile played round the mouth of the priest. 'The doctor was most unwilling, but I finally overcame his objections. I go in every Thursday and I think they appreciate it.'

'What do you do?'

'I spend some time talking to each of them. If I know their families I take messages back and forth. I make small purchases for them and take them news of the world they have left behind. I try to make sure they have a few comforts that otherwise they would lack.'

'Don't their relatives visit them?'

'They're not allowed visitors. The risk of infection, you know.'

'But they allow you?'

'Only after a lot of negotiating with the authorities.' Father Minos smiled, remembering the long, wordy battle he had finally won. 'Each time I go I have to change my clothes and disinfect myself before I leave.'

'I hope there's someone like you in Athens. I should like to think that we could hear how Yannis was keeping. Do you think his condition will be cured?'

Father Minos looked Andreas in the eyes. 'Do you want the truth?'

'Yes, I'm not a child any more.'

'He's been sent to the hospital they use for the incurables. It's most unlikely he'll ever leave Athens.'

Andreas turned his head away, unwilling for the priest to see the tears that had filled his eyes. 'Did you tell Annita there was no hope?'

'Not in so many words, but she is a nurse, you know.'

Andreas nodded. 'I think that makes it worse for her. You won't tell my aunt and uncle there's no hope, will you? I think that would probably kill my aunt.'

'I shan't tell them.' Father Minos sighed. 'Maybe I'm wrong, but I never tell anyone there's no hope. Miracles still happen.'

'I like to think so.'

Father Minos leaned towards him. 'I can assure you they do.

When you least expect it something occurs and afterwards you recognise the event for a miracle.'

'You speak as though you have witnessed one,' Andreas smiled

'Are we nearly there?' Father Minos obviously wished to change the subject.

'Nearly. We round this promontory and slip through the channel between the islands, then it's just across the bay.'

Father Minos gazed at the tiny island as they sailed past the high walls of the Venetian fortress that was built into the rock. They passed the archway that led up from the quay and began to head towards the tiny village on the opposite shore. An idea was forming in Father Minos's mind, it was so stupendous that even he could hardly grasp the implications at first and sat in silence as they glided over the rippling water to tie up at the jetty.

He followed Yiorgo and Andreas along the dusty road until they stopped at the door of the farmhouse and after knocking they entered unannounced. Maria sat in her chair, a rug over her knees. She extended her hand to her cousin and slurred words of greeting came from her lips. Anna appeared from the kitchen, wiping her hands on her apron, the smile of welcome freezing on her lips as she saw the priest.

'I'll fetch Pappa.'

'There's no need.' Father Minos laid a hand on her arm. 'I'll walk up to the fields and see him for myself.'

'You don't bring bad news?'

Father Minos shook his head. 'Nor do I bring good news. This is just a friendly visit as I was in the vicinity.'

Anna gazed at him doubtfully. 'I'll fetch some coffee.' She returned to the kitchen, Andreas following her.

'It is bad news, isn't it? He wouldn't have come otherwise.'

'No, Anna. He arrived at our house yesterday and gave us the address of the hospital where Yannis is. He has no news of him at all. How is your Mamma and Maria?'

'Are you telling the truth, Andreas?'

'I swear I am.'

He took the jug from the hook and went out to the yard to fill it from the pump. Anna prepared a tray, adding a plate of homemade biscuits, and waited for Andreas to return.

'How's your Mamma?' he asked again.

'Much the same. I don't think she'll ever be well again. Her speech seems a little clearer recently, or maybe I'm getting more used to it.' Anna stirred the coffee carefully.

'And Maria?'

This time Anna smiled. 'She's very happy. It won't be much longer now. She was over earlier this morning.'

'How are you managing?'

Anna looked at her cousin from under her thick lashes. 'I'm enjoying myself. I love looking after Mamma and the house.'

Andreas nodded, unable to comprehend how anyone could enjoy spending their day cooking, cleaning and nursing. 'Shall I take the tray in?'

'Just a moment.' Anna placed the dirty coffee saucepan on the stone floor. 'Could you take a letter back to Annita for me?'

'Of course. Is it ready?'

Anna shook her head. 'I didn't know you were coming, but I've been thinking about writing it for some time.'

Andreas led the way through to the living room where Father Minos was talking earnestly to Maria. Yiorgo had lit a cigarette and was wondering if he should offer to go up to the fields and fetch Yannis. He took his coffee from the tray and smiled at Anna. She was becoming a beautiful young girl and he speculated what would happen to his cousin when she met a young man. If Yannis knew what was good for him he would welcome any suitor into his house with open arms.

'Would you like me to prepare some rolls for you to take up to the fields? You could eat up there with Pappa and Yiorgo.'

Father Minos looked at Yiorgo. 'That would suit me very well, but I have to be ruled by my friend. Do your fish call, or do we have time to spend an hour with your relatives?'

'We have time. I am at your disposal for the rest of the day. I want to talk to Yannis myself. Andreas can stay and help you, Anna. He can bring the food up to us which will save your legs.'

Anna shot him a grateful glance. It was easier to make rolls than to cook a meal at such short notice and if Andreas was to stay and help her it would be quicker still.

'I need some onions pulled and cleaned,' she instructed him. 'I'll do the rest.'

Deftly she sliced tomatoes and cheese, filling the rolls and adding the onions as Andreas handed them to her. 'I'll write the letter whilst you're gone,' she said.

Andreas wrapped the rolls in a cloth and began to make his way towards the hills whilst Anna returned to the living room and collected the dirty cups and glasses.

'I'm going to write a letter to Annita, Mamma.' She had formed the habit of talking continually to her mother in the belief that hearing words would improve her mother's speech. Maria nodded. She was feeling tired and wished to sit and think about her recent conversation with the priest. Rummaging in the cupboard Anna found an old piece of paper and began to write:

"Dear Annita,
I am worried about Maria. It will not be much longer before she has her baby. The Widow Segouri is going to help her if she can get there. She has become all crippled up in her joints. What do I have to do?"

She felt relieved when she waved goodbye to the three men that afternoon. It had been good to see her uncle and cousin for a short while and know her letter would reach Annita, but her mother now seemed so very tired. She hoped she had not over-taxed her meagre strength. She did not want her to relapse into the vegetable existence they had taken such pains to draw her from.

Yiorgo sat silently in the boat. Yannis had accepted eagerly when he had suggested that Stelios go to Aghios Nikolaos and attend the school there as his other son had done. Father Minos's soft voice broke in on his thoughts.

'Could we sail to the island, do you think?'

Yiorgo looked at him in surprise. 'The island? Whatever for?'

'I should like to speak to the people who live there.'

'But only lepers live there.'

'I know. That's why I wish to speak to them.'

Yiorgo shrugged. 'I'm not landing.' It was one thing to creep onto the island at night when everyone was asleep, but it would be entirely different during the day when everyone would be moving around and likely to touch him. He manoeuvred the boat into the shallow water and Father Minos stood up, steadying himself by holding a rope and began to call loudly.

'Hello. Hello. Is there anyone there?'

Someone at the storehouse looked towards him and stared, then called to someone unseen. Gradually, consumed with curiosity, people began to appear until a small crowd had gathered.

Father Minos called across the water. 'I am Father Minos. I would like to speak with you. Do you have a priest on your island?'

Confused muttering answered him; then one man limped forward and raised his voice. 'Do you come from the authorities?'

'No. I come as a friend. Do you have a priest with whom I could talk?'

'We have no priest! We have nothing!' The man answered bitterly.

'Nothing?' Father Minos was puzzled.

'Nothing except the food sent by the villagers.'

'Where is your doctor?'

'We've no doctor. We're lepers. We're dead men. Why should we need a doctor?'

Father Minos seemed taken aback by the reception he was getting. He turned to Yiorgo. 'Please, go in closer. Let me land.'

Yiorgo shook his head. 'They'd tear you to pieces. They're animals. They lived in caves before they were sent here. We'd do well to go.'

'Not yet.' Father Minos turned back to the shore. 'My friends, I have to leave you. Before I go would you care to kneel and say a prayer with me and receive a blessing?'

The lepers looked at each other, uncertain what their reaction should be. One or two turned away, others knelt. A woman called something unintelligible. More people were crowding onto the tiny quay, those without limbs being carried, those who were sightless being led, a gathering of humanity, which defied description in its deformities and suffering. Andreas sucked in his breath. This was a horror past all his worst imaginings. Father Minos was stretching out his hands to the populace, asking for God's blessing on the afflicted, for a relief to their suffering and a betterment of their lot. Andreas felt hot tears stinging his eyelids as the faces, disfigured with pain and disease, took on a look of hope and mutilated hands were stretched out towards the priest.

The press of people on the quay made the foremost step into the water and they began to walk slowly towards the boat.

'Row, Andreas, row. Fast as you can.'

It took a moment for Andreas to appreciate the threat that was nearly upon them.

'Row, before they reach us.'

Andreas bent to the oars and pulled with all his might, the tiny boat shooting rapidly forwards, nearly toppling the priest overboard. A sigh went up as the boat drew away. Father Minos waved. 'I shall be back,' he called. 'I shall be back, my friends.'

Yiorgo growled as he plied the oars. 'Not with me, you won't.'

Andreas sat silently, trying to sort out his emotions. He had been repulsed by the people he had seen living on the island, yet he felt guilty that he could do nothing to help them. Thank God his cousin was not amongst them, but in a hospital. No doubt he was being looked after properly.

Father Minos had fallen to his knees, his head bowed in prayer. He had no wish to show the fisherman and his son how shaken and moved he was by the people's plight. For the rest of the journey back to Aghios Nikolaos he sat with his head bowed, wrestling with the problem in his mind. These people were desperate for help. The voice came back to him, so loud and strong that he thought his companions must have heard it also.

'You cannot heal, but you can help.'

'I will, I will,' he muttered fervently, his head still bowed.

Yannis inspected his handiwork of the previous day with a critical eye. He pushed at the wall, nothing shifted and he smiled in delight. Rolling up his sleeves he began to select his stones, making a pile of larger ones before starting to try to place any of them. This time he plugged the gaps after every sixth stone instead of each one as he had done before and was convinced he was working more quickly. After two hours he stood back and surveyed his handiwork. The wall had risen no more than half a metre, but it was longer than the one he had tackled previously.

He forced himself to stop, looking at his damaged hands ruefully. His nails were torn and two of them were bleeding. He wished he had thought to bring some water with him, and decided to visit the fountain for a drink. Having slaked his thirst he dived into the tunnel and hurried through to the fresh air on the other side. The blue sea, lapping gently against the shore, looked inviting and Yannis plunged his arms in up to his elbows, washing away the dust with the salt water as best he could, soaking his shirt and trousers in the process. Damp and tired he toiled back up the hill and lay down in the shade of the half-built wall to rest. He slept far longer than he had intended, waking with his tongue feeling like fur in his mouth. He would remember some water in future. He returned to the fountain and drank deeply. He debated whether to return to his building or leave it for that day. His empty stomach influenced his decision and he hurried along the road. As he reached the port he was surprised to see most of the islanders gathered there.

'What's happening? More arrivals?'

'We had a visitor. A priest came to have a look at us.'

'I wish I'd known,' Yannis sighed regretfully. 'I'd have liked to have received a blessing.'

A tall figure stood on board a boat, his hand raised in farewell, just discernible in the distance. Sadly Yannis gazed after him. He turned into the food store and took the opportunity to stuff two rolls into his pocket along with a lump of cheese. Munching slowly he returned to the sunlight and began to walk along the road where Spiro caught up with him.

'Where were you? A priest came to the island. He wasn't allowed ashore, but he talked to us and gave us a blessing. He wanted to know how we lived and he's promised to come again.'

Yannis looked at his friend wearily. 'What did you tell him? That we exist, without proper shelter, that the chronically sick have no medicine, that we all pray for a speedy death?'

'What's wrong with you? You're so bitter! Of course we told him.'

Yannis threw himself on the ground beside Kyriakos. 'It's everything. You're still revelling in the novelty of fresh air and being able to walk around as you wish, but what have we got? Nothing. We're dependent upon the villagers for everything. The priest was not allowed to land! Why not? Are we animals? We wouldn't have touched him.'

'The priest wanted to land. He said he wasn't frightened, but the boatman wouldn't hear of it.' Spiro tried to placate him.

'It doesn't matter,' Yannis spoke resignedly, 'once you're a leper. If only they realised.'

YANNIS

'Realised what?'

'That we're human. Having leprosy doesn't stop you thinking and feeling the same as anyone else.'

Spiro was silent. He had heard Yannis speak like this before and he had no way of comforting him or distracting his thoughts. It was with relief that he saw Phaedra coming, her arms loaded with food.

'We ought to help her.'

'You can. I'm tired.'

Spiro glanced at Yannis crossly. What had he been up to that he was too tired to carry an armful of food for a few yards? For the first time Spiro noticed the stains on Yannis's clothes and his damaged hands.

'What have you been doing all day?'

'Poking around.' Yannis laid back and closed his eyes.

Yannis slept well that night, but groaned as he sat up. His arms felt as heavy as lead. Yawning, he rose and left his companions still sleeping. He visited the port and helped himself to some food, purloining an old jug that had lost its handle and filled it with water. He carried it carefully to his half built walls and placed it in the shade.

For the first hour Yannis spent his time searching other ruined buildings for items he could use. He had taken a door from its resting place on the ground and as near as he could judge it would fit his opening. Various lengths of timber were lying where they had fallen when their support had collapsed and Yannis hauled them all back painstakingly. The work was arduous and he drove himself to exhaustion point before stopping to rest, determined to fix the window openings.

He sat in the shade he had created and contemplated his achievement so far. Two more walls needed to be brought up to the same height as those he had completed; then the problem of a roof would have to be solved. He tried to think how to fix supports, but was unable to concentrate. Closing his eyes he drifted into a sound sleep. When he awoke the sun was high in the sky and he cursed himself for sleeping for so long. It was unlikely he would be able to finish one wall, far less both of them and the windows as he had planned. To add to his problem he was running out of large, suitable blocks of stone. He moved further afield and began to collect and move the largest he could find, stacking them in an untidy pile. Very weary he finally decided to abandon his project for the day. His craving for a drink had become the most important objective in his life at that moment, he had finished the jug he had brought with him long ago.

Despite the enthusiasm with which Yannis started each day his progress seemed to become slower. Trying to build a row of masonry above the window openings proved impossible until he removed the original timbers and replaced them with longer crosspieces, taking him two days to reconstruct. The roof was the most time consuming and exhausting of all. Having found the longest timbers that were lying in the ruins he had to haul them back and prop them against the completed walls. Piling large blocks of stone at the foot of the wall gave him a narrow and unsteady catwalk and enough height to manoeuvre the unwieldy pieces of wood into position. Try as he might, they would not lie parallel and he just hoped the roof tiles would bridge the wider gaps.

Scrambling up on the catwalk he tiled as far as he could reach on each side, leaving the centre open to the sky. The most testing time of all arrived when he had to place his weight on the half-completed roof and trust the supports would bear him. Feeling his way carefully he placed the tiles, overlapping them carefully.

'That is fantastic!'

Yannis almost fell off the roof. He twisted his head to see Spiro gazing up at him admiringly. Carefully he climbed back down to the ground.

'It isn't very good,' he said modestly.

YANNIS

'It's wonderful! How did you do it?'

Together they sat on a block of stone whilst Yannis described how he had toiled at the building.

'No wonder you were coming back exhausted each day. We thought you were going through a bad patch and wanted to be left alone. Why didn't you say? I'd have helped.'

Yannis laughed derisively. 'After the way you mocked me and said it couldn't be done! I had to do it on my own to prove to you, prove to all of you, that it was possible.'

Spiro clapped him on the back. 'You've certainly done that.' He wrinkled his brow. 'Do you really think it can be done with the others?'

'I'm sure it can. It's just a question of convincing people and getting them to help. I can't repair them all myself.' Yannis grinned, his exhaustion disappearing as Spiro's enthusiasm became contagious.

Spiro dragged Yannis to his feet. 'Come and tell them.'

'Who?'

'Anyone who'll listen, and if they don't believe you we can bring them up here and show them.' Spiro began to drag Yannis down the hill.

'I'd like to tell Antionis first.'

'If you like. Then we'll tell Christos.'

Slipping and sliding they hurried downwards and along the path to the square. Yannis went first to the fountain and took a long drink whilst Spiro hammered on the door of Antionis's house. The old man hobbled to the door.

'Who is it?'

'It's me, Yannis. I've something to tell you.'

Antionis allowed Yannis to take his arm and steer him towards a wall where he lowered himself down carefully.

Yannis swallowed. 'I've built a house,' he mumbled.

'Say it again. My hearing's not so good now.'

'I've built a house,' Yannis repeated.

A slow smile spread across the old man's features. 'I said you could rebuild. I knew you could do it.' He searched for Yannis's hand and squeezed it. 'You're a good boy, Yannis. You can rebuild.'

Yannis felt a lump come into his throat. 'I wish you could see it.'

'It's enough for me to know you've done it. Now they'll believe you, Yannis. They'll help you. They believed me once.' He turned his sightless eyes towards Yannis. 'I failed them. You won't. You can rebuild.'

'I'll try. I'll try for you,' promised Yannis.

'No,' Antionis shook his head. 'It's too late for me. Do it for them.'

'If they'll help me.'

'I'll talk to them. You go and rest. Remember, you have to take care. Too much too soon and you'll suffer. Take it slowly. Pretend you're old, like me, and take life slowly. When I first came here I couldn't wait for each day to pass. I saw my friends die and I still lived. Living with nothing to live for! Now I want to live and there is little time left. Take it slowly, Yannis.' Antionis's head sank down onto his chest, his last words becoming so faint that it was difficult for Yannis to hear them. He released his hand from the old man's grasp and stood up.

'Thank you, my friend.' As he walked away with Spiro he was not sure whether Antionis called after him or the words 'you can rebuild' were ringing inside his head.

'Do you think Antionis will tell the others and get them to help?'

Yannis smiled to himself. 'I believe in him.'

'You're two of a kind! Idealists.'

'No.' Yannis shook his head. 'Realists. I know that if I have to live here then I have to live with a degree of decency. That decency begins with having somewhere to call my own, where I can shut my door and say this is my home.'

YANNIS

Spiro looked guardedly at Yannis. He had hardly changed since his arrival at the hospital; he obviously suffered more mentally than he did physically.

'I think you should rest,' persisted Spiro. 'You're far more tired than you realise.'

Yannis smiled at him wearily. 'You're probably right.'

Spiro settled him beside Kyriakos, with a jug of water. 'Now, tell me exactly how you managed it.'

Yannis related how he had heightened the walls and searched for timber and tiles. 'You know, Spiro, I was so pleased with myself, but it isn't really very successful.'

'Why ever not?' Spiro stared at Yannis in disbelief.

'I didn't know how to fix a door or think of a chimney, so you couldn't have a fire in there.'

'I don't think that matters. You've proved a house can be built. If the others help we'll figure out other ways of doing things.'

Yannis closed his eyes. He felt deflated. His grand accomplishment was not really so great. Anyone at all could have managed to construct the hovel. It was meaner than any peasant's hut on the mainland. Spiro looked at the prone figure and rose silently. He would go and inspect Yannis's handiwork properly. As he approached the house he was surprised to find quite a gathering there. Christos had managed to haul himself up the slippery path with the help of his crutch and was surveying it critically.

'Well?' Spiro grinned. 'Not bad for an amateur.'

'I doubt if it will stand up to a mistral. He hasn't tied his corners in or rebated his rafters deeply enough.'

'If you'd helped us as we asked it could have been more professional,' snapped Spiro, unwilling to have Yannis's work belittled.

Christos shrugged. 'Did you help him?'

Spiro shook his head. 'He did it entirely alone.'

'Are you both going to live up here?'

'Yannis didn't mention living in it. He wants to repair some of the others.'

'Better tell him to take advice or he'll do more harm than good.'

Spiro took a deep breath. He had an overwhelming urge to drive his fist into the sneering face. 'Will you advise us?'

'I might. If it was worth it to me.'

'What do you mean?'

'I'd want my home done first.'

Spiro nodded. 'I see. I'll tell Yannis and let you know what he says.'

Christos slithered back down the path, leaving Spiro to listen to the admiring remarks of the others who had come to inspect the accomplishment. He decided there was no time like the present to try to rally support. Mounting one of the blocks of stone Yannis had used as a catwalk he shouted at the tiny gathering.

'Listen to me, listen all of you. You've seen what Yannis has done here. He did it all alone. No one helped him. Think how many houses could be rebuilt if we all helped. Wouldn't you like to have somewhere to call your own?' Spiro jumped down and caught the nearest man by the shoulders, spinning him round to face him. 'You could shut your door and be alone when you wanted. You could put your books on a shelf, your clothes in your chest and know they would be there the next day. No one could borrow them without knocking on your door and asking your permission.'

'What door? There is no door.' The man swung away from Spiro's grasp.

Spiro looked about him helplessly. The people who had come up to look and gasp in admiration were now dispersing back down the hillside, smiling and tittering about the lack of a door.

'Fools!' shouted Spiro after them. 'I laughed at him and said it couldn't be done and he proved me wrong. You've seen it can be done and still you laugh. Don't you want a roof over your heads? Do you enjoy living in the open? Please, help us. You don't do anything all day except sit in the sun.'

'I'll help.'

Spiro turned, a smile spreading across his face. Behind him stood a girl, she looked about fourteen, thin and pale, the upper part of her left arm was badly ulcerated and dirty.

'What could you do to help?' he asked her gently; she looked hardly strong enough to stand, let alone work.

'I'd bring water up to you, and food if you wanted it.' She looked up at him eagerly, hoping her offer would not be ridiculed.

'You would? It's a bargain.' He placed his hand on her shoulder and she beamed with pleasure. 'I've got one volunteer,' he called after the others. 'Lazy bastards,' he growled, as they continued downwards without looking back at him. 'You ought to keep your arm wrapped.' He twisted the limb towards him, the ulceration spread from below her elbow almost to her shoulder.

She pulled her arm away. 'I tried wrapping it, but it didn't seem to do much good, so now I'm leaving it unwrapped. The sun might help to clear it.'

'It ought to be wrapped,' Spiro spoke firmly. You never know when you might get some dirt in it, then it would get a lot worse.'

She shrugged. 'I'll wrap it when I'm working. When do we start?'

'Come back with me and meet Yannis. Where are you sheltering?'

'There's a tower further up. It's small, but it has a roof.'

Spiro was silent. They had passed the small structure on many occasions and never considered it as a place to shelter. The doorway was so low you would have to bend double to enter and it was doubtful that you could lie down once in there.

Yannis was still asleep when they reached the shack, Phaedra sitting beside him. Spiro spoke to her quietly and she helped herself from the sack of clothes that were too large for Yannis bringing out an old shirt. She ripped the side seam open; then with the help of her sharp little teeth she tore it into strips and handed them to Spiro.

'Hold out your arm,' he ordered. He dabbed at the raw patches on Flora's arm with a little clean water on a wad of cloth, ignoring the way she winced and tried to draw away from him. Finally satisfied that it was as clean as possible he wound the makeshift bandage around and tied it securely.

'At least that will keep it clean.'

'Is he going to wake up?' She pointed to Yannis.

Spiro shrugged. 'He's tired. He'll probably be full of ideas when he does wake. Why don't you help Phaedra get a meal whilst you wait?'

Flora followed Phaedra and after a while Spiro could hear them laughing together. It was the first time he had heard Phaedra laugh. He laid himself down and closed his eyes. It occurred to him that he was sleeping far too much. When it became dark he slept until dawn, then most of the afternoon. He was either more ill than he thought or becoming very lazy.

'I'll soon find out,' he thought. 'I'll have to try to keep up with Yannis,' and grimaced at the idea.

Maria cradled her baby gently in her arms, studying the tiny, wrinkled face with pride. Babbis sat beside her, his arm around her shoulders, smiling fatuously. Kassy bustled around, tidying away the soiled sheets ready for washing, pausing every now and again to have another look at her first grandchild.

'I wish I could take her to show Mamma,' Maria remarked wistfully.

'Time enough for that when she's a little older and you've got your strength back.' Kassy was not having the girl get any wild ideas about walking over the hills the following day. It had become easier for her after her father had called and asked after her health a few weeks earlier. Babbis had been able to walk over with her in the evenings and it had been a weight off Kassy's mind to know that her daughter-in-law was safe. 'Besides,' she added, 'Anna will tell her how beautiful she is.'

Maria smiled. 'Wasn't she wonderful? Who would have believed that my little sister could have been so efficient?'

'Good job she was,' snorted Kassy. 'The Widow is past it, and I know nothing. Without Anna it could have been a difficult time for you.'

'It was difficult anyway. I had no idea it would take so long.'

'Nor had I,' agreed Babbis. 'I ran like the wind for Anna and the Widow and I thought they would be too late the time it seemed to take them to get here.'

Tears began to roll down Maria's cheeks.

'What is it? What's wrong? Do you hurt?' Babbis was all concern.

Maria shook her head. 'I'm just so happy,' she sobbed. 'She's so beautiful and perfect.'

'Then why are you crying?' Babbis was way out of his depth with his wife's unpredictable behaviour.

'Leave her alone,' his mother advised him. 'It's only natural she should cry. Mothers often do so. She's tired and relieved that it's all over and that both she and the baby are all right. Let her have her cry out and she'll feel better. Then it's a good sleep she needs.'

Babbis held her to him whilst she sobbed, waiting until she had stopped before he spoke again. 'What are we going to call her?'

'I don't know.'

'After you and your mother?'

'No, it gets too confusing, everyone having the same name.'

Babbis sat silently. Dare he suggest it or would Maria laugh at him. 'Do you like the name Marisa?'

'Marisa?'

'You don't like it. You choose what we call her.'

'Marisa,' repeated Maria. 'I do like it.'

'It's half your name and a bit of my mother's, but if there's something else you'd rather call her I don't mind.'

'There's nothing I'd rather call her. She's Marisa, and it isn't to be shortened.'

Babbis kissed his wife's forehead. 'May I hold Marisa for a short while? Then I think you should get some rest.'

Maria handed the precious child to her father and lay back on her pillows as he handled her inexpertly. Life was so good to her. She had a wonderful husband, a kind mother-in-law; her father had forgiven her and now this incredibly beautiful baby. She sighed with contentment. What more could one ask from life?

Yannis sat inside the house he had constructed. The floor of beaten earth felt cold and damp to the touch and the wind blew through the window and door opening unceasingly. Huddled beneath his blanket he felt more miserable than he had for months. This was only the beginning of winter. He shivered. His hopes and dreams of rebuilding had fallen on stony ground despite the enthusiastic reception of his first house building attempts.

It had taken weeks of begging and pleading with the mainlanders who brought over supplies before they finally agreed to bring a ladder to the island. Having the necessary elevation it proved impossible to climb the ladder carrying the heavy blocks of masonry and unwieldy tiles. Yannis eventually designed a sling that he would haul up with the necessary materials, but the work was arduous. Christos had propped himself against a wall, his crutch under his arm, and criticised everything Yannis tried to do.

'It's no good,' Yannis finally declared to Spiro. 'It's impossible to do some things without tools.'

'Then we must get some.'

'How are we going to do that? Pop over on the next boat and buy them? What do we use for money for a start?'

YANNIS

Spiro shook his head. 'Don't talk foolishly. We have to beg them, the same as we begged for the ladder.'

'How long is it going to take?'

'Probably quite a long time, but if you can think of a better idea I'm willing to listen.'

'I'm sorry, Spiro. It all seemed so easy when I talked about it at first and managed to build this. I can't even hang a door without a saw to cut the wood and a screwdriver to drive the screws home.'

Spiro and Phaedra had taken it in turns to sit on the quay and plead with the boatmen to no avail; it was little Flora who was most successful, returning one day with a hammer. She had presented it to Yannis as if it was made of gold and he had thanked her in like vein. From that day she had taken it upon herself to be the one to sit on the concrete jetty and beg from each boat as it arrived. The sickly looking waif who accosted them, asking for nails, screws, hinges and tools intrigued the regular suppliers.

At first they had laughed at her, but finding her continually huddled in the same place and making the same requests they gave in and would bring a handful of nails or a couple of hinges which they had scrounged from a local store. Manolis would appear regularly and always had something for her. The gifts were not always items she had requested, but she would thank him gleefully, whether it was a nail or some homespun wool that he threw across the water to her.

Despite her apparent success their stocks grew slowly and winter was almost upon them when Yannis nailed the final tile on the roof of Christos's house. Having examined the repair from inside Christos declared himself satisfied, but demanded that Yannis should also replace the shutters which had fallen off and lay rotting on the ground. Reluctantly Yannis agreed and used some precious pieces of timber he had been saving for his own house, despite criticism of his actions by Spiro.

'You've got to stand up to him, Yannis. Tell him that is the last thing you'll do for him.'

Yannis shook his head. 'It's not as easy as that. We need his knowledge and the only way we're going to get it is by doing everything he asks.'

Reluctantly Spiro had let the matter rest and watched whilst Christos's house became waterproof ready for the winter. Now, sitting in his miserable hovel, Yannis realised the sense of Spiro's words. He had enough wood for one shutter, it was cut to size, but it would be impossible to fix until the rain stopped. There was no sense in getting his clothes soaked; they would take weeks to dry. He would just have to be thankful that he had four walls and a roof that he and his friends could use as a shelter.

'Next year it will be different,' Yannis promised himself. 'Somehow I'll make them help me.'

Next year! The thought suddenly hit home. He was beginning to accept that this was where he would stay until the end of his days. He groaned aloud. Kyriakos shifted uncomfortably on his mattress and Yannis looked at the old man. He should be somewhere warm and dry, not in this dank hut. Spiro returned from the storehouse, shaking drops of water from himself like a dog as he entered.

'That's all there is. The bread's hard and the cheese is mouldy, but it's food.'

Yannis shrugged. He had eaten worse in the hospital, but at least you knew there would be something each day, however unpalatable. Now unless a boat arrived soon they would all starve. The knowledge added to his misery and depression.

'I think it's easing off,' Spiro tried to cheer him. 'If it does I'll help you fix that shutter.'

Contrary to Spiro's optimism the weather did not improve for a further two days. By that time their clothes and mattresses were soaked and the food exhausted, despite severe rationing on their part. Spiro had lost his cheerfulness and lay, like Yannis, huddled against Kyriakos for warmth, trying to ignore the gnawing pains in his stomach that craved for food.

YANNIS

Silence woke Yannis and he struggled up stiffly from his mattress to look out of the open doorway. From beneath ragged wisps of cloud a pale sun was trying to emerge. With a resigned sigh Yannis realised that although he felt weak and miserable he was not going to die from deprivation. A boat would probably arrive that day bringing supplies which would fortify them all ready for the next spell of bad weather and enforced starvation.

Slipping and sliding down the path that was a sea of mud and exposed rocks Yannis reached the main path. He passed the patch of concrete and the wooden shack where they had passed the summer months and continued on beyond the ammunition tower. There he staggered across the bare, slippery rock to the Venetian wall and stood looking down at the sea, which sucked menacingly at the rocks below. Across the bay he could see the farmhouse where he had spent his childhood and he screwed up his eyes to try to discern any movement. He would have liked to see his mother once more before he died.

'What are you doing, Yannis?' He felt clawed fingers in his belt.

He stared at Phaedra blankly before sinking to the ground at her feet, shivering violently. 'I can't,' he stammered back at her. 'I can't.'

'You can't what? You can't face a few days of being cold and hungry?' she spoke scornfully. 'Some of us have faced it for years. It will happen more than once before the winter's out. You just have to get used to it and accept it.'

'I can't,' repeated Yannis.

'You don't have a choice,' she answered him curtly. 'All the time it's warm and you have food you're full of grand ideas. The moment things become difficult you're prepared to give in. The winter doesn't last for ever.'

'The house is cold and wet. The rain blew in on everything.' Yannis tried to excuse himself.

'That's your fault. You shouldn't have done so much for Christos. He's quite capable of looking after himself.'

'I have to help Christos if he's going to help me,' reasoned Yannis.

'How much help did he give you when you repaired his roof? He watched you struggling and criticised from the ground. Did he ever tell you how to place the tiles, or even bother to thank you when you'd finished?'

Yannis shook his head. 'I just placed them where the old ones had been.'

'So what did you need him for?'

'Nothing really,' Yannis had to admit. 'But we shall need him if we are to repair things properly.'

Phaedra shook her head. 'That's rubbish. You proved that when you repaired the house where you are now.'

'He says I haven't fixed the roof or corners properly. He doubts if it will last the winter.' Yannis spoke miserably.

'Then you'll have to repair it as you go and prove him wrong. It's not raining now, you and Spiro could fix that shutter you've been talking about.'

'The rain will still come in the other window and the doorway.' He shivered as he spoke.

'Then go and find some more wood. Don't be so defeatist, Yannis.'

'I'm just so cold and hungry.'

'I'll make you a hot meal as soon as the boats have unloaded,' she promised.

'Have they come over?'

'They're almost here.'

Yannis breathed a sigh of relief. 'I thought we were going to starve. I'll find Spiro and see what he thinks about fixing that shutter.' Yannis rose to his feet and shivered again. 'We might get a bit warmer if we were able to work.'

For a week Yannis lay on his bed alternately sweating and shivering with a chill. He was frustrated by his enforced inactivity, but had to admit that Spiro was right when he forbade Yannis to go out in the rain. Spiro and Phaedra tried to persuade Yannis to stay inside for another week, but he refused. 'I want to see Panicos. I want to talk to him.'

Spiro shook his head. 'If you go wandering out to meet him you'll probably get chilled again.'

Yannis argued. He was well now and it would not hurt him to go out for a short while now it was no longer raining. He had to speak to Panicos urgently. Finally Spiro agreed to compromise.

'I'll go and ask Panicos to come up here. He hasn't been well either.' With that Yannis had to be content, although Spiro seemed to be in no hurry to fulfil his errand.

Yannis noticed immediately how hollow-eyed and thin Panicos looked. 'I hear you've been ill.'

'Haven't we all.'

'Are you still in the church?'

'There's nowhere else to go and it's reasonably warm and dry.'

'How many of you are there?'

Panicos shrugged. 'I'm not sure, probably about seventy.'

'Seventy!' Yannis was horrified. 'In that tiny church! Don't you mind?'

Panicos turned troubled eyes towards Yannis. 'I hate it. We all hate it, but we have no choice. It's worse than it ever was in the hospital. There's no room, no air, the smell is beyond description,' he shuddered,

'How many are bed-ridden?'

'About twenty.'

Yannis sat thoughtfully. Panicos stirred uncomfortably and coughed.

'Is that all you wanted to talk to me about?'

'No, don't go. I wanted to come down and see you, but Spiro thinks I should be wrapped in cotton wool. I've had an idea.' Yannis waited for a reaction that did not come. 'How is Christos keeping?'

'He seems to be all right.'

'Why do you think he's keeping well when the rest of us appear to have been ill?'

'How should I know? I'm not a doctor.'

'You don't think it might be because he has a dry, waterproof house?'

'We're dry and waterproof in the church.'

'But you're overcrowded.'

Panicos nodded. 'What are you getting at, Yannis?'

'I want to try to persuade people to repair the houses and if they're suffering now it could be a good time. Whilst the summer is with us it doesn't matter if you're living in the open. Now they've spent part of the winter herded together the idea of having your own house could be appealing. You know them better than I do. If I come down to the church who should I talk to first?'

Panicos coughed again. 'I'm not sure.'

'Will you help me?'

'How?' Panicos was suspicious.

'Talk to them; tell them how much better it is up here.'

'Is it?' Panicos looked around critically.

'It doesn't smell.'

'That's because there's only three of you.'

'Exactly. If the houses were repaired small groups could live in them and they'd be healthier.'

'Maybe.'

'I know this isn't perfect, but it's better than being in the church. As soon as the weather improves I'll be working on it again. By this time next year you'll see a difference,' boasted Yannis.

'Maybe,' repeated Panicos.

'I thought you'd be enthusiastic.' Yannis's disappointment was reflected in his voice.

'I'm sorry, Yannis. I'm too tired. I agree with you, but I just haven't got your energy.'

'When the sun shines you'll feel better. All I want you to do is talk to them, persuade them how much better off they would all be. You mustn't give in,' Yannis urged his friend.

Panicos sighed and rose to go. 'I'll try, but don't expect too much. You're a more persuasive talker than me.'

Spiro returned and Yannis forestalled any speech on his part by asking him a question as soon as he entered. 'Is it very bad down there?'

'What do you think?'

'Is that why Panicos is ill? What are the others like?'

'I haven't stayed inside long enough to find out. I just looked for Panicos and got out as fast as I could.'

'I must go down there.' Yannis began to search for his shoes.

'Why? That would be foolish of you. Heaven knows what you would catch.'

'Does it matter?' Yannis gave a wry smile.

'It does to those who have to nurse you,' replied Spiro. 'Besides, I've been talking to Kyriakos and he says that over-exerting yourself makes you ill.'

'Over-exerting myself! I don't think a walk to the church could be called over-exertion.'

'I don't mean that. He says that when you try to do things, physical things, like house building, it wears you out and you become ill more frequently until your heart stops.'

Yannis looked at Spiro scornfully. 'Do you really believe that?'

'Well, it seems to make sense.' Spiro shifted uncomfortably.

'Have you got something wrong with your heart?'

'Not that I know of.'

'So why should you have a heart attack?'

'He's not talking about an ordinary heart attack. He's saying that you make yourself more and more sick until your heart isn't strong enough to beat any more.'

'How long does this take to happen?'

'I don't know. He didn't say.'

'So,' Yannis considered, 'if I sit here and do nothing I'm likely to live for another forty or fifty years.'

Spiro nodded.

Yannis rose with alacrity. 'In that case I'll start working on something immediately. I don't want to live another forty years, not even one more year. If working will bring me slightly better living conditions and an early death, that's what I want.'

'But, Yannis….'

'But Yannis nothing! Do you want to go on living in this misery for years and years? Wouldn't you rather die? I certainly would.'

'I don't think you're well enough to think about doing very much yet.'

'Then with luck I shan't have to do very much for very long. I'm going down to the church. You can come if you want or stay here.' Yannis stood with his hands on his hips, daring Spiro to challenge him and attempt to bar his way.

'I'll come, if only to find out what hare-brained scheme you have in mind.'

Silently Spiro followed Yannis to the church, knowing he would be expected to support his friend. Yannis pushed open the door and almost recoiled from the smell of decaying flesh and excrement that met him. Curious eyes followed him as he stepped cautiously around the mattresses spread over the floor and the assortment of debris that surrounded them. By the time he reached his objective a silence had fallen amongst the occupants and Spiro looked around uneasily. Yannis appeared unperturbed and began to speak, his voice cracking as he tried to pitch it loudly enough for everyone to hear.

'My friends, I want to talk to you. You all thought I was crazy when I suggested we repaired some of the houses to live in during the winter. I made a house with my own bare hands. It isn't very substantial, but it is better than living crowded together down here. Do you enjoy living like this? Wallowing in your own filth? It's not your fault. You have to shelter from the elements. Imagine how much better it would be if you had a shelter of your own, just three or four of you living together. If we work together you could all have a home of your own by next winter. I'll leave you to think about it. I'll come back tomorrow.'

Yannis was beginning to feel that he would vomit if he stayed in the fetid atmosphere very much longer. He began to pick his way carefully to the door, ignoring those who tried to stop him. Spiro followed him, shouting. 'Yannis is right. You should listen to him,' every few steps.

Once outside Yannis leant against the wall and took deep breaths of fresh air. 'Do you think it did any good?' he asked Spiro anxiously.

'I don't know, but they must realise they can't live like that each winter. I'll be surprised if they manage to survive this one without all of them suffering from dysentery.' Spiro glanced at the overcast sky. 'Which houses do you have in mind to start with?'

'Whichever are in the best repair. We haven't a lot of choice. Our tools and materials are somewhat limited.'

'Why don't we have a look?'

Yannis grinned. He felt he had won a major battle by managing to imbue a little enthusiasm into Spiro. They pushed open the rickety door of a house that stood a few yards from the storehouse and peered inside.

'The back wall seems sturdy enough,' observed Spiro.

Yannis nodded. The wall had at one time been plastered over to hide the rough stones and apart from patches that were peeling, there seemed no evidence of collapse. The sidewalls were almost as good, but the roof was non-existent.

'It seems it's only the roof that needs renewing. That's easy enough.'

'Oh, yes?' Spiro was sceptical.

'Yes,' answered Yannis firmly. 'We need timbers that are the right length and tiles.'

The next house they ignored, the back wall having crumbled

to below window level and the sidewalls showing signs of falling at any moment.

They moved down the path slowly, entering each house and studying as best they could the damage and discussing the easiest way to affect a repair. Out of the dozen houses they visited Yannis decided that four would be fairly simple to repair, two others were possible, but would take longer and the rest presented a very real challenge.

'If it's dry we can start tomorrow,' decided Yannis. 'We can collect timber and tiles. There are plenty of complete ruins up the hill. Between us we could move down what was needed, then gradually do some repairs and when a house is ready Panicos could offer it to three or four of them.'

Spiro grinned. 'What about your own house? I thought you wanted to work on that.'

'I thought so too, until I saw how much better one of these could be. I'd rather live down here, wouldn't you?'

'Yes, if we stay together.'

Yannis looked at his friend in astonishment. 'What do you mean? I thought we would always stay together.'

'You might want to get married.'

'Me! Married! Don't be silly.' Yannis felt distinctly uncomfortable. 'Besides, you might get married.'

It was Spiro's turn to look uncomfortable. 'I'm all right as I am. Until either of us changes our mind we stick together, yes?'

'What do you think?' Yannis rested his arm across his friend's shoulders.

Kyriakos was sitting propped against a rock and he waved and called to them. 'Boat coming.'

Spiro and Yannis looked across the bay to see a small boat sailing towards them.

'I'll go,' said Spiro. 'I'll see what they've brought and ask for some nails.'

Yannis nodded. He still avoided being on the quay when a

boat put in for fear of being recognised by anyone from his village. Spiro came back smiling.

'Potatoes and goat meat. Phaedra said she would make us a stew tonight.'

'Did you ask for some nails?'

'They said they'd try to bring some next time.'

'Fine. Let's go up there and see what we can find.' Yannis pointed to a house that had fallen completely and they proceeded to sort tiles from lumps of stone and pull lengths of timber to one side until the first drops of rain fell.

For the next few weeks, whenever the sky lightened, they were out. If the buildings were too wet to work on they went searching for the materials they needed. It was a slow and laborious process, but eventually Yannis declared himself satisfied with the first house they had tackled. The ambulant occupants of the church had taken to stopping to watch their progress whenever they went down to the quay, commenting on the work that was taking place. Now the time had come for them to offer the property to someone they were faced with a problem.

'I think the bedridden should have it,' said Spiro.

Yannis disagreed. 'It would be better to have the healthier people there. They might even manage to do some running repairs. You can't expect those who are crippled to replace a tile.'

'I don't think any of the fitter deserve it,' argued Spiro. 'Not one of them has even passed a nail up to us.'

'What about the women?'

Spiro thought about it. 'That's a better idea, but which ones?'

'We'll see Panicos.'

Yannis insisted that Panicos met him outside the church, the air had grown fouler with the passing months and he did not think his stomach would be able to contain itself if he went inside. Panicos looked more haggard and shrunken than the last time Yannis had spoken with him and the pitiful sight changed Yannis's intentions.

'We've repaired a house,' he announced. 'Would you like to see it?'

Sighing, Panicos nodded. He had planned to spend the morning trying to sleep. Dutifully he shambled along beside Yannis and Spiro until they stopped and opened the door, ushering him inside.

'What do you think?'

Panicos looked up at the rafters. No chink of light came through, or through the walls. The shutters and doors fitted tightly, the earthen floor had been stamped down to make it as hard as concrete. 'You've worked hard.'

'It's yours.'

Spiro sucked in his breath as he heard Yannis make the offer. This was not what they had planned. Panicos looked at Yannis with sad eyes and shook his head.

'It's a wonderful thought, Yannis, but I can't live here.'

'Why not?'

'It's where Yiorgo lives in the summer.'

'Is Yiorgo crippled?'

'Pretty much; walking is difficult and he has only one hand.'

'Then he comes with you. Has anyone else got a claim to it?'

Panicos coughed and they had to wait until he had regained his breath before he could reply. 'Probably about ten other men.'

'Are they crippled?'

Panicos wrinkled his brow in an effort to think. 'One of them is for certain, but the rest of his cronies seem fairly fit.'

'Did they offer to help repair this house?'

'No, you and Spiro did it.'

'So the way I look at it, that gives us first claim and a say as to who we let live here. I say you live here and Yiorgo, his crippled friend and one other who must be fit.'

Still Panicos shook his head. 'There'll be trouble.'

'If there's any dispute I'll raze it to the ground,' threatened Yannis. 'Go and talk to Yiorgo. We'll wait outside and move your things when you're ready.'

YANNIS

Standing outside the church waiting for Panicos to reappear Spiro rounded on Yannis. 'I thought we were going to offer it to the women?'

'I know, but I hadn't the heart when I saw him. He needs a doctor.'

'We all need a doctor! You're stirring up a hornet's nest, Yannis. Giving away a house that someone has considered their own for years is going to upset everyone.'

'It might just make them realise that I'm serious about repairing them. If they think I'm going to do it and then hand them over they're mistaken. If I do the work, I say who lives in it. If they bestir themselves and repair their own that's fine by me.'

They stood in silence waiting for Panicos to return. When he did so he had a wry smile on his face. 'Yiorgo has agreed. The two of us, Costas and Lambros.'

Yannis clasped Panicos's hand. 'We've made a start, we've really made a start.' He turned to Spiro and held out his hand. 'Thank you, my friend.'

'Dare we go in and collect your mattress?' asked Spiro, masking the sudden emotion he felt.

A bought of coughing delayed the reply. 'There's no time like the present,' Panicos tried to joke.

The mattresses were heavy and unwieldy, but between them the two men managed to manhandle them out of the confined space and towards the door. Once outside they paused for breath.

'Where are your boxes or sacks?' asked Yannis, dreading that he would once again have to enter the evil smelling interior.

'We can manage those,' Panicos assured him, 'But Lambros needs to be carried.'

'Bring everything to the door whilst we move the mattresses. We can help you with it when we return.' Yannis and Spiro set off, a mattress carried between them. 'I feel so happy,' remarked Yannis. 'All that work was worthwhile.'

Spiro shrugged. He was still not convinced that Yannis's high-handed action was right. It was with pride that Yannis pushed open the door to show off his handiwork for a second time. Lambros, hardly more than a torso, was laid gently on a mattress. Beside him Panicos placed his meagre belongings and covered him with a blanket. With tears in his eyes the old man began to mutter his thanks, but Yannis cut him short.

'I want to talk to you before I go.' He squatted down at the foot of Yiorgo's mattress. 'I've been told there will be trouble with the others for mending your house and then giving you the opportunity to live in it. I say that if I've done the mending I have the right to give it to whom I please, but I want something in return.'

The four men eyed him suspiciously. Now the time of reckoning had come. To all of them it had seemed to good to be true.

'Lambros must be well looked after, kept clean and fed. Panicos is ill and needs rest and good food if he's to recover his strength. I shall expect Yiorgo to see to most of that. Costas I shall expect to help Spiro and myself.'

Costas looked at Yannis. 'Help you do what? Repair another house?'

Yannis nodded. 'If you don't want to then someone else can take your place here and you can go back to the church.'

'I don't know the first thing about repairing a house. I was a clerk in an office, and, besides, I have no head for heights.'

'You can learn, the same as Spiro and I did. There's plenty of work that can be done from the ground. You can soon learn how to fix a door or shutter.'

Costas shook his head. 'It won't be possible. Yiorgo can't turn and lift Lambros on his own, nor can he be expected to keep the place clean, go to the store and cook. He's only got one arm, remember.'

Yannis frowned and Spiro nudged him. This was a time for compromise. 'All right, you spend the morning helping Yiorgo, then you come to help us.'

Sulkily Costas agreed and Yannis rose to go. 'The arrangement starts tomorrow.' Once out of earshot Yannis took a deep breath. 'I never thought that would work.'

Spiro gazed at him with respect. 'That was clever, Yannis. You've got us another helper.'

'A somewhat unwilling one, I'm afraid. Still, he'll be better than nothing. I am tired.' Yannis yawned and Spiro looked at him anxiously. Was Yannis wearing himself out with his obsession with rebuilding?

The following day was one of enforced idleness for Yannis as he sat on his mattress and listened to the rain falling outside. He felt miserably chilly, although he was fully clothed and had a blanket round him. He tried to envisage the repairs he would make to the next house until a shadow in the doorway woke him from his reverie.

'What's the problem?' asked Yannis anxiously as Costas entered, fearing the man would say the roof had fallen in during the night.

'Nothing. You told me I was to come and help you in the afternoon and here I am.'

Yannis nodded. There was nothing they could do in the rain, but he was unwilling to turn the man away. 'Come and sit down. I want to work out how to build a fireplace.'

Costas sat down obediently on the end of Yannis's mattress. Costas and Spiro sat in silence. Costas was unable to add anything constructive to the conversation and Spiro usually let Yannis finish thinking aloud before putting forward any suggestions of his own.

For the next hour Yannis tried to work out to his own satisfaction how the fireplace should be built and finally gave up. He would need to have the necessary materials on hand and experiment. Costas rose to go, he could have spent the afternoon playing cards with Yiorgo instead of listening to Yannis trying to build fireplaces.

'I'll expect you tomorrow,' Yannis called after him. 'If it's too wet to work we'll collect materials.'

It was with surprise that Yannis found two men on his doorstep the following afternoon. Costas looked a little sheepish. 'This is another Costas. He's come to help.'

It was too wet to attempt any construction and the two men spent the afternoon pulling lengths of timber from a fallen building and stacking tiles at the side. To Yannis's surprise they worked hard and willingly until he called a halt to their efforts for the day.

'We'll take this lot down and stack it; then we can make a good start tomorrow. We'll ask Flora to meet any boats and beg for some more nails and screws.'

Once back in the privacy of their hut Yannis smiled triumphantly at Spiro. 'We're going to win, two helpers now. Maybe it will be four tomorrow.'

'Maybe it won't!' Spiro was sceptical. 'I'd take a bet that Costas has told the other Costas that if he helps he can have first claim to the house.'

'I don't mind. All I ask is for them to help themselves a bit. They seem quite resigned to sitting around until they die. They just don't seem to care. It's their whole attitude, it's pathetic.'

Spiro slipped away. He had heard Yannis talking too many times about the attitude of the other islanders to wish to hear it all again. He stopped to visit Panicos and was pleased to note that the only smell in the house was that of food. Panicos looked a little healthier, his skin less sallow and his eyes brighter. Costas was lying on his mattress, snoring gently, exhausted from the day's exertions.

Panicos jerked his head towards the sleeping figure. 'He's becoming quite enthusiastic, kept talking about fireplaces last night.'

'That was Yannis. He's trying to work out how to build them.'

'He's a good man. Don't let him wear himself out.'

'You know how determined he can be.'

Panicos smiled wryly. 'It's probably a good thing when it rains. It forces him to stop.'

Costas stirred in his sleep, muttering. 'That's long enough.'

Spiro grinned. 'I'll go. Better not to disturb him, besides, the smell of your supper is making me hungry.'

The next day dawned dry, but windy, which filled Yannis with enthusiasm. 'We can work today.'

Spiro yawned. He knew that meant unceasing labour until mid-day, when they would eat a roll, sit for a short while, and then return to the exhausting work until Yannis decided they had reached their objective for that day. He pulled on his pullover, looking ruefully at the snags and holes that were appearing. It was to be hoped that Yannis had solved the problem of fireplaces by next winter or he was going to suffer badly from the cold.

The second house proved far more difficult than the first and they were glad of the help offered by Costas. By building a series of steps on each side of the building Yannis and Spiro were finally able to sit astride the walls whilst Costas had the unenviable job of passing up lengths of timber to them. By the time the other Costas arrived most of the rafters were in place and the three men were taking a well-earned rest.

'What do you want me to do?' he asked cheerfully.

'Start on the fireplace,' was Yannis's immediate rejoinder.

Costas's face fell. 'How?'

'You and Costas go and find the largest blocks of stone you can and bring them back here.'

'Where are you planning to put it?'

'There.' Yannis pointed to the back wall. 'Come on, we'd better make a start.'

Spiro waited until Yannis was safely astride the wall before he began to hand up the roof tiles. The first few were painstakingly slow, until Spiro was able to balance more tiles on those already laid and the work progressed a little faster. Once the two Costas returned with large blocks of stone, which they were only just able to manhandle, Yannis climbed down. Between them they moved the blocks to the far wall, then looked at the effect.

'What do you think?'

'A bit more that way if it's going to be in the centre.'

They moved the stones and regarded the wall critically. 'It looks right now.'

'Then leave those two blocks where they are. When you've collected some more we'll try building it up.'

The remainder of the afternoon was spent with Yannis and Spiro working on the roof whilst the other two men collected the largest blocks of stone they could find, all four ending up exhausted. Despite all Yannis's careful plans and rebuilding of the fireplace each time they tried to light a fire they were nearly choked by the smoke that billowed out into the room. They stood outside; waiting for the smoke to clear and Yannis finally admitted defeat.

'We need cement. We'll never be successful without it. We may as well give up.'

'What do you mean? Take it all down again?'

'No, it may as well stay. If we can get some lime and sand sent over we could try giving it a coat to fill the cracks.'

The knowledge that they had been unsuccessful depressed all four men.

'It's still a house,' observed Spiro. 'Some will be grateful.'

Costas was looking with pleading eyes. 'I'd be grateful.'

'I know you deserve it, but there could be others who need it more.'

The house would sleep six people easily, but Yannis suddenly found there were ten who claimed it as their right as they used it during the summer months. He scanned the four women and six men and decided he could use the situation to his advantage.

'The women can have the house and choose two companions. Who they choose makes no difference to me. Whoever isn't chosen will help to repair the next one and they can have that.'

The group disagreed; they wanted to stay together. Why should some of them not have to work? Yannis gave them an ultimatum.

'You decide by this evening or I'll offer the house to someone else. We built it, so it's up to us. Draw lots if you like, but I'll expect all six men to make up a work party; two of you because you're grateful and the others because they want somewhere to live. Does that seem fair?'

Grudgingly they had to admit that it was and Yannis left them to decide whose mattresses should be moved. He felt fairly confident that by the following day he would have ten people working on the buildings. He felt sorry for Costas, who had worked so willingly, but he dared not upset too many people at one time or the tightrope he was walking would snap beneath him. He was surprised the next day when two of the women joined the little work party.

'It doesn't take four to make a meal for six,' said Penelope. 'We can probably fetch and carry for you.'

Yannis agreed they would be useful, although he racked his brains how he could use them. They would not be strong enough to carry heavy loads, but Spiro thought of a solution.

'Why don't we put them to sorting? We often spend hours moving bits out of the way to get at a piece of timber or some tiles. They could do that and also sort out the rubbish.'

Yannis grinned. 'I don't know what I'd do without you.'

The system worked well, and the amount of work they accomplished in one day astonished them all. With more workers they were able to tackle three buildings at the same time and within two weeks they were habitable.

'Yours, Costas.' Yannis waved a hand to the furthest house. 'Yours, Makkis. Go and choose your companions, but tell them if they're fit they'll be expected to work. The other house has to go to the barber. It's not very big, so I think it only fair that we limit the occupants to three.'

Costas shook Yannis by the hand; he was delighted and felt a great sense of accomplishment each time he looked at the house he had been instrumental in repairing. It was no more than half an hour before a straggle of men made their way down from the church with their mattresses and meagre possessions. Yannis looked at them with interest. All except the barber appeared to be reasonably fit, and Yannis automatically counted them as extra hands for building.

The dry, crisp spell they had taken advantage of gave way suddenly to torrential rains and once again Yannis fretted at the delay. Every day he braved the elements to visit each house and ask if there were any leaks and was relieved to report to Spiro that they were watertight. What Yannis did not know was that the occupants had made good use of the wet days. Shelves, balanced on large stones had been placed between the unusable fireplaces and the wall, and now held an assortment of articles. Costas had visited the church and harangued the occupants for their apathetic and lazy way of life. He boasted of the space, the air, the cleanliness of his dwelling and told them repeatedly how he had helped. At first they listened disinterestedly, then first one and then another would ask a question, wondering if they would be capable of the same efforts.

The barber cut hair and trimmed beards that for months had gone unattended, finding that he had not lost his touch, despite a stiffening of his fingers. When Yannis visited him on the third day of unrelenting rain he was invited inside.

'Would you like a hair cut?'

'Yes, I would, but I've nothing to give you in return.' It was many months since the barber had last cut his hair.

'I'm in your debt, Yannis. Come and sit over here and I'll try to do a fair job for you.'

It was some time before the barber declared he was satisfied with his handiwork and gave Yannis the small square of mirror to check for himself. Yannis took it and held it up. Was the face looking back at him from this tiny piece of glass really his? The skin was mottled with small, white lumps from his ear to his nose on the left side of his face. He tilted his head and looked at the lump on his neck. It was still an open, running sore. He looked again at his face. He would never have been called handsome before, but now he could imagine how people would shudder if he went among them.

'Thanks,' he said quietly and handed the mirror back. 'You've done a fine job.'

Once outside he wandered back down the path, away from the house he had intended to visit. Did he really look like the image in the mirror? Sadly he climbed the hill to his own humble dwelling, hoping only Kyriakos would be there. He was disappointed. Inside was Spiro and at least another dozen men and women, all of whom looked slightly embarrassed when Yannis entered.

'What's going on?' he asked.

'It was to be a surprise for you when the weather improves.'

'What was?'

'Workers.'

'Workers!' Yannis could hardly believe his ears. 'You mean you're all willing to help?'

'I've never done anything before. I was a jeweller.'

'I'd only just left school.'

'I was a seamstress.'

'It doesn't matter what you did before,' Yannis assured them. 'I'd never done any building before. We can learn as we go along.'

Yannis's face was alight with enthusiasm as he extended his hand to each person as he or she left and murmured 'That's our agreement,' as they shook it. He felt strangely deflated when he was finally left alone with Spiro and Kyriakos. At last the people were beginning to come round to his way of thinking, he just hoped they would be willing to work together and not spend all their time arguing about the jobs they would be asked to do.

1931 – 1939

Father Minos was elated. It was nearly a year since he had visited Doctor Kandakis and requested permission to visit the island of Spinalonga. He had talked to the doctor for over an hour, trying desperately to persuade him, meeting the whole time with refusal. Finally Father Minos had taken his leave, disappointed but determined to pursue his objective. He composed long, persuasive letters to the doctor, waiting eagerly for a reply, only to receive an abrupt refusal.

Eventually he declared his intention of approaching the Government, hinting that the continued refusal on the part of the doctor could be an attempt at covering up possible malpractice. The letter had the desired effect and now Father Minos held in his hand the piece of paper which said he could make a visit of one day's duration to the island, calling on the doctor before his departure and on his return which must be no later than seven in the evening.

No one was in sight on the quay when Father Minos arrived at Aghios Nikolaos and he felt vaguely disappointed. He turned up into the tiny huddle of houses and knocked on the blue door, hoping he had remembered correctly, but received no reply. Wearily he retraced his steps down the cobbled road and up over the hill to where the doctor lived. Patiently he sat and waited until the last of the sick had departed, then he asked to be admitted.

Father Minos waited for the doctor to complete his paper work before opening the conversation. 'Good morning, doctor. I have your letter giving me permission to visit the island. I thought you might be able to tell me a little about their way of life over there.'

Doctor Kandakis shrugged. 'I can tell you nothing.'

'You mean you don't visit them?'

'I go over once a year. There is no need to go more frequently. They are incurable. My services are needed here.' He did not add that he received additional income from the Government to treat the islanders.

'I see.' Father Minos was completely nonplussed. It was quite unbelievable that the doctor went only once a year to the island. 'Would you care to accompany me tomorrow?'

'Quite out of the question, I'm afraid. I have a full day of appointments. Besides, there's no point in wasting time on them.'

'They are people,' Father Minos pointed out gently.

'They are also lepers.' Doctor Kandakis glowered at the priest from beneath his eyebrows. 'How would my patients feel if they knew I was visiting the island and possibly bringing back the disease to spread amongst them?'

'Don't you feel it is your duty? I have been going amongst them for the last three years and I have no sign of the disease. My parishioners know this and respect me for it.'

'Your profession is somewhat different from mine.' The doctor rose, indicating that the conversation was at an end. 'I will arrange for a boatman to take you across tomorrow. Be on the quay at eight in the morning.' The doctor held the door open and Father Minos had no option but to leave.

Deep in thought he returned to the waterfront. He found the whole attitude that emanated from the doctor disturbing. He turned into the nearest taverna for a meal and also to ask for news of Yiorgo and Elena. The owner of the taverna was garrulous and quite willing to sit and chat with his customer, informing the priest that they had set off in their boat the day before, probably going to visit their relatives in Plaka. Their son would be at the church if that would help.

Father Minos thanked the man and decided he would certainly visit Andreas and see how he was adapting to his calling and when he planned to take his final vows. The young man's face lit up with pleasure when he saw the priest.

'Mamma and Pappa are away for a couple of days. They went to Plaka yesterday. Will you be able to wait and see them when they return?'

'I'm not sure. Much depends upon my visit tomorrow.'

Andreas looked at him curiously. 'Where are you going?'

'Spinalonga.'

Andreas drew in his breath. 'May I come?'

'You? Why?'

'I'm not sure I can answer that. I just want to be with you when you go.'

Father Minos frowned. 'I don't know. I have a letter giving me permission, besides, what would your parents say?'

Andreas shrugged. 'I have no way of asking their permission, but I doubt if they would object to me accompanying you anywhere.'

Father Minos thought differently, but the pleading in the boy's eyes won him over. 'We'll see what the boatman says.'

With that Andreas had to be content. He introduced Father Minos to the other novices with whom he shared instruction and also to the three priests who served the town. He begged time off from his instruction and devotions to accompany Father Minos around the town and also on his impending visit the following day, returning with the necessary permission to his tiny room where the priest had waited for him.

'Shall we go?' he asked.

'Go where?'

'Wherever you like. There's a fine view from the top of the hill above the pool.'

They toiled up the hill together until they stood on the summit of the steep cliff, looking at the vista that was unrolled before their eyes. In front of them the sea stretched in an endless shimmering blue, below them the lake looked small and insignificant, the hills rising on the far side of the huddle of fishermen's cottages below. Behind them the countryside spread out in a variety of colours, whilst on the other side the houses of the town were clustered together, high and low buildings crowding in on each other, jostling for supremacy.

'It's worth the climb,' admitted Father Minos, distinctly out of breath.

Andreas grinned. 'I often come up here when I need to think. It gives me a feeling of closeness together with privacy.'

They stood in silence until Andreas began to lead the way back down the hill.

'Everyone needs a place like that. You're lucky to have one so near. I have to walk to the outskirts of Heraklion and sit on a deserted beach. What news do you have of your sister?'

Andreas wrinkled his brow. 'She went to Athens, but they wouldn't let her work at the leper hospital. They don't have nurses apparently.'

Father Minos raised his eyebrows in surprise. 'Who looks after them?'

'She was told they look after each other. She's working at the ordinary hospital, so she might as well have stayed here.'

'Is she happier?'

'I don't know. She's very reticent about her private life in her letters.'

'Maybe she will come back. What about the rest of your family? Your aunt at Plaka?'

'Much the same. Sometimes she appears to be improving; then she seems to lapse back again. Anna is so good with her. She should have trained to be a nurse.'

'And the others?'

'Uncle appears to be keeping well, he still limps, of course, but he doesn't have any pain. Maria's fine. She's so happy. She's expecting another child. They're hoping for a boy this time.'

Father Minos smiled with pleasure. 'Has her father forgiven her?'

'Everything's fine between them now, and he loves his granddaughter.'

'I'm so glad. Family rifts are always so unpleasant and hurtful. It's much better to accept misfortunes head on. They have a strange way of righting themselves. Shall we find a taverna?' suggested Father Minos. 'I could do with a drink after such unaccustomed exercise.'

They sat until the bell tolled from the nearby church, calling parishioners to worship. Automatically the two men rose to go, each lighting a candle as they entered and kneeling to say their own private prayers before moving closer to the altar to listen to the exhortations of the priest. Father Minos wondered if he should take some candles to the island with him. Would there be a church there for him to conduct a service or would he have to work in the open air as he had done before? It was something akin to a shock that he realised he was not listening to a word the priest was saying, all his thoughts were occupied with his projected visit to the island. Automatically he knelt at the altar rail to take communion and after a final prayer left the church.

'Now where?' he asked Andreas.

'A meal and then bed. I'd like to go to the early service which will mean being up at five.'

Father Minos agreed and followed his companion into the taverna where they had passed most of the afternoon. Andreas ordered for both of them, including a bottle of wine.

'I don't drink much,' he spoke almost apologetically, 'But the food here deserves an accompaniment.'

The boat that suddenly rounded the side of the island and began to nose in towards the tiny jetty took Flora by surprise. Usually the boats came over from the villages and she saw them long before they were within hailing distance. She scrambled to her feet, the words of greeting dying on her lips; then she hurried up the rough path towards the building where she expected to find Yannis.

'Yannis, Yannis, come quick.'

From his precarious position on top of a wall Yannis looked down at the excited girl.

'There's a boat. It has two priests in it.'

Carefully Yannis climbed down to the ground. 'Are you sure?'

'Of course! They must have come from Aghios Nikolaos. I didn't see them until they were almost at the jetty. Come quickly, Yannis. They must be tied up by now.'

Following Flora back down to the quay Yannis's heart felt heavy. Somehow it seemed even worse when men who had led a good and blameless life were afflicted by a disease that would make them outcasts. Yannis stood at the top of the steps and waited for the two men to approach. They seemed hesitant, their eyes fixed on the ground before them. As they came level with the archway they lifted their eyes and Yannis felt the world spinning before him.

'Andreas!'

Suddenly the two men were in a close embrace, tears pouring down the faces of each of them, whilst Flora looked on in surprise. Finally the two drew apart, trying hard to smile and compose themselves. In silence they mounted the steps to the main road, Yannis trying to think of words of comfort for his cousin and Andreas wondering how to ask about Yannis's welfare. Flora smiled at Father Minos who appeared at a loss.

'Have you come to stay?'

'No. I've been given permission to visit for the day. I promised you I would come back. Maybe you'd like to tell some of the others that I'm here.'

Flora scampered off; shouting to everyone she saw and curious men and women began to approach from all sides. Father Minos turned to Andreas.

'No doubt you and your cousin would like some time to talk. I'll hold a service for those who wish it and meet up with you later.'

Andreas nodded. 'Come on, Yannis. Take me to your house.'

Yannis shook his head. 'It would be better to sit out in the open.' He led the way to where he had sat for many hours with Kyriakos and Spiro. 'We shan't be disturbed. How did you know I was here?'

'I didn't,' admitted Andreas. 'Father Minos managed to get permission from Doctor Kandakis to visit for the day and I just came along.'

'How did you meet him?'

'In Heraklion when I was looking for you.'

'Looking for me?'

'We were all worried about you. You hadn't answered any of Annita's letters so I agreed to go to Heraklion to see if I could find you.'

'Only to find I had disappeared.' Yannis's mouth set in a straight line.

'I found you, thanks to Father Minos, but it was too late. You were just coming out of the gates of the hospital to go to Athens. The crowd turned nasty and threw a few stones; one of them hit you and knocked you unconscious just as I called you. I thought you were dead.'

'Then it wasn't a dream! Somewhere lurking at the back of my mind was your face and someone calling me. I just didn't think it could be true. Is that how I ended up with a bundle of your belongings?'

'Probably. We followed you down to the port and at some point I dropped my bundle. I expect they thought it was yours.'

Yannis sighed. 'I thought you must be a leper too.' He shifted a little further from his cousin. 'You shouldn't be here. You might catch it. You're taking a terrible risk.'

'Have you forgotten that we used to share a mattress? If I was going to catch it I'd have done so then.'

'How's Mamma?'

Andreas shrugged. 'As well as can be expected.'

'What do you mean?' Yannis gazed at him, his eyes wide with fear.

'I'm sorry. I forgot you wouldn't know. Father Minos returned to Aghios Nikolaos with me and then we went to Plaka to tell your Mamma and Pappa. Your Mamma took it hard. It was such a shock to her.'

'What happened?' Yannis's voice was harsher than usual with his emotion.

'She had a slight stroke. She's much better now. Anna looks after her.'

'Anna? Why not Maria?'

'Maria's married. She married Babbis about two years ago and has a little girl and another on the way.'

'Maria, married, a mother! It's hard to believe. Pappa, Yiorgo and Stelios, what about them?'

'They're all fine. Stelios is doing well at school.'

'What about Annita?' Yannis could feel his heart beating just that little bit faster.

'Annita's gone to Athens to be a nurse.'

'Why? Why didn't she stay in Aghios Nikolaos?'

Andreas hesitated. 'She thought she would be able to nurse you.'

Yannis gave a snort of derision. 'Lepers don't have nurses. They're just left to die.'

'She was refused a place at the leper hospital and works at the ordinary one.'

'Just as well, it's no place for a woman. It's no place for anyone!'

'How did you get here? We all thought you were receiving treatment in Athens.'

'It's a long story. Let's just say I made myself pretty unpopular and they decided it would be a good thing to get rid of me, along with some of the others.'

Andreas studied his cousin. He no longer looked like the young, carefree boy he had been at school with. His skin bore the unmistakable white marks, nodules and sores of the disease, his eyebrows had thinned considerably and deep lines were etched in his face.

'It's been pretty tough?'

Yannis nodded. 'Just a little.'

'Do you want to talk about it?'

Yannis shook his head. 'It isn't something you can talk about. I don't think there's anyone here who could put into words what they've suffered over the years.' The sound of voices raised in the chanting response to a prayer made Yannis look towards the port. 'We ought to join them. I missed him the last time.'

They reached the gathering just as Father Minos was saying a final prayer followed by a blessing. The cripples began to rise to their feet, some being helped upright and others lifted and carried. Instead of dispersing they crowded closer to the priest, besieging him with questions.

'Yannis, do something,' Andreas caught at his cousin's arm. 'They're mobbing him.'

Shouting as loudly as he could Yannis began to order the crowd to move back, elbowing his way through to get near to Father Minos with Andreas following him. Once at the priest's side he held up his hands for silence and to Father Minos and Andreas's surprise was instantly obeyed.

'Move back, friends,' he called. 'Give Father Minos room to breathe; he'll talk to all of you.'

Spiro shouldered his way to Yannis's side. 'You didn't tell me you knew the priest.'

Yannis grinned at him. 'I didn't know myself. This is my cousin, Andreas.'

Spiro looked down at his deformed hands. 'I'm pleased to meet you, but I won't shake hands.'

'I'm pleased to meet you. How long have you been here?'

'Yannis and I came together, not by choice. The hospital was bad enough, but here…' His voice tailed off.

'Tell me,' Andreas encouraged him softly. 'I talked to Yannis about his family. Tell me what it was like when you first arrived.'

'Well, they took our strait jackets off after we had left the ship and …'

'What?' Andreas was aghast.

'Didn't Yannis tell you? We were sent over here as prisoners for causing trouble in the wards.' Spiro grinned to himself. 'We must have given them a bit of a shock. Anyway, they dumped us here and left us to get on with it.'

'So where do you live?'

'We're still up on the hill, but we're gradually getting the houses repaired, then we'll move down.'

Andreas was puzzled. 'I'm not understanding this. You'll have to explain.'

'Well,' Spiro took a breath, 'Everywhere was in ruins. Certain people had laid claim to them over the years, but they were only fit to shelter from the sun, hardly a roof between them and crumbling walls. Yannis realised what it was going to be like in the winter and tried to persuade everyone to rebuild.'

'And did they?'

Spiro spoke scornfully. 'Of course not! They all thought he was out of his mind. They just didn't believe it could be done. Yannis proved it, though. All on his own he rebuilt the little house where we are. It's not marvellous, but it keeps the rain out. A couple decided to join us, and it's just escalated since then. Now they realise they can do it they all want their own house rather than being crowded into the church for weeks on end.'

'And the villagers bring you the materials, I suppose.'

'No, they've given us some tools. Flora's wonderful at wheedling things out of them, but it took us weeks to get a screwdriver.'

'So where do the materials come from?'

'From here, the island. Many of the buildings are past repair so we take whatever we can from those.'

Andreas gazed around. From where he was standing he could see little of the work that had been taking place prior to his arrival. On the far side of the road the church stood, silent and neglected, in front of him was a sea of heads and behind them a few houses could be seen, all looking as though they would tumble to the ground at any moment.

'Where do you get your cement from?'

'We don't. We just balance the stones up, like farmyard walls, and block up the cracks.'

Andreas pursed his lips. 'It doesn't sound very safe.'

'It's safer than it was, and it's all thanks to Yannis.'

Andreas looked over to where his cousin was standing next to the priest, listening quietly to the questions and answers that were passing between the islanders and Father Minos.

'How is Yannis, in himself?'

Spiro shrugged. 'Who knows? He's had his bad times, but at the moment he seems pretty fit. He's been less depressed since he's managed to persuade people to rebuild. Let me introduce you to some of his friends.'

Pushing and shoving Spiro led the way to where Flora and Phaedra were standing, trying hard to listen to the interchange that was taking place. Flora smiled and nudged Phaedra.

'This is Andreas. He's Yannis's cousin,' explained Spiro.

Phaedra looked at him. 'Did you know Yannis was here?'

'No. I was with Father Minos when he spoke to all of you from the boat. I've lived near here all my life and I thought it about time I visited to find out the truth for myself.'

'What truth? That this is the best place for lepers, abandoned on an island?'

'No, no.'

'Where would you put us, then?'

'How about some food for our guests, Phaedra?' Spiro came to Andreas's rescue.

Phaedra turned away with Flora following her. It was almost as if their going was a signal for the rest of the company to disperse. Quietly they began to slip away, murmuring an excuse to the person next to them until Yannis and Father Minos stood alone on the path. Passing his hand over his brow Father Minos sat on a low wall. His whole frame seemed to sag from weariness.

'I would never have believed, never,' he muttered to himself. 'Yannis, what can I do?'

Yannis looked at him in surprise. 'What could you do?'

'Maybe the authorities would listen to me.'

Yannis shook his head. 'I doubt it very much. They were only too pleased to get rid of us, so they're not likely to welcome us back.'

'There must be something.'

'Don't worry about it. To be quite honest with you, Father, now we're becoming a bit more organised I'm beginning to think we're better off here.'

Father Minos shook his head. 'But no medicine, no proper homes, little water; it's not right, Yannis. Something must be done.'

'We could do with some more packs of cards,' grinned Spiro. 'Some of ours are so worn we can hardly see the spots. Come and see if the girls have some food ready for us.'

Slowly they escorted Father Minos and Andreas to the patch of concrete where they sat with Kyriakos. He was already there, having been carried back from the port and propped against the wall and waved gaily to them.

'Come and talk to me. I could hardly hear you down there.'

Father Minos sat beside the crippled man. 'How long have you been here?'

'For ever.'

'You were one of the early arrivals?'

Kyriakos nodded. 'I was a young man when they first sent me. I had my legs.' He looked down ruefully. 'We were most of us young then. I've seen some changes.'

Father Minos cleared his throat; he had a delicate question to ask. 'When one of you passes on,' he hesitated for a moment to see how his words were being received, 'What happens to the body?'

'It goes into the tower.'

'The tower?'

Kyriakos nodded. 'When we've eaten they can take you on a tour of the island. There isn't much up this end, just the cliffs and the fort. Go down the other way and you'll see the houses Yannis built, then round through the tunnel and you'll see the other church and the tower.'

Father Minos was not sure he wanted to see the tower, but felt he would be a disgrace to his calling if he did not go and say a prayer for those poor souls whose bodies had been disposed of so casually.

'Do you use the churches?'

'Only for shelter in the winter.'

'We'll start to use them properly soon,' interrupted Yannis. 'Once everyone has a house there'll be no need to use the church. Then we can clean it out thoroughly and use it for its proper purposes.'

'Do you have a priest here?' asked Andreas.

'No. For a moment when you arrived I thought you were both sufferers who'd been sent here.'

'Who's the little girl with you?'

'That's Flora. She's a plucky little thing. She was the first person who volunteered to help us. She can't do much with her arm the way it is, but she's quite invaluable in cadging. We wouldn't have half our tools if she hadn't spent time persuading the fishermen to give them to her.'

'What's wrong with her arm, apart from the obvious?' asked Father Minos.

Spiro looked round to make sure the girl could not hear him. 'It's very badly ulcerated. It could easily go gangrenous. She ought to have it amputated.'

His words were received in a shocked silence.

'I had no idea,' murmured Yannis.

'Don't tell her,' warned Spiro. 'I make sure she doesn't see it.'

'Don't you mind touching it?'

Spiro shrugged. 'Someone has to do it for her. I've seen worse sights.'

Yannis remembered from the hospital how Spiro had nursed Manolis devotedly until the man had finally died.

'What's keeping those girls?' Spiro was feeling hungry. 'I'll go and help them carry it down.'

'I don't know what they're preparing for you. I doubt if it will be very elaborate, but they certainly do wonders with what we're sent.' Yannis was beginning to feel somewhat uncomfortable, the conversation had lapsed and the questions he wished to ask were private. It was with relief that he saw the little procession coming down the path and went to the side of the bank to take the plates and bowls from them.

Without any hesitation the two visitors ate with relish everything that was placed before them and declared it tasted as good as the meal they had eaten the night before in the taverna, lacking only the bottle of wine.

'Now, that would be a luxury,' smiled Yannis.

The four men walked back down to the port entrance and Yannis led the way onwards to where most of the repaired houses were situated. A barrage of questions regarding construction or shouts proclaiming the successful completion of a task greeted him.

'You should have seen it six months ago,' boasted Spiro. 'They were just ruins, not only unfit to live in, but unsafe as well.'

To Father Minos and Andreas the buildings still had a somewhat dangerous aspect, some walls propped with timbers, no cement holding any of the stonework in place, one or two having sagging balconies which, as yet, had not been touched. Both men tried to hide their horror at the conditions in which so many of the sick men and women spent their time.

'It's much better now,' Yannis assured them. 'When it's warm everyone stays outside. It was during the winter when there were so many of them crowded into the church that it was almost unbearable, even they realised that at last. Come and meet Panicos. He's been very sick, but he's on the mend now.'

Father Minos remembered the man from the crowd that had surrounded him. The sunken eyes, sallow skin and persistent cough all spelt out tuberculosis amongst his other problems and the priest thought it most unlikely that he was recovering. He sat beside the emaciated man and chatted whilst the others waited outside for him. When he finally emerged he looked at Yannis speculatively. The boy he had met in Heraklion had been petrified by his illness and the consequences. This young man seemed to have come to terms with every obstacle that was continually put in his way. First Spiro had given all the credit for rebuilding to Yannis and now Panicos had said the same. He wondered what had happened to bring out this hidden strength and leadership from a very ordinary person. From Panicos he was taken to visit Antionis.

'He had such faith in me,' explained Yannis. 'He was convinced that the houses could be repaired. Whenever I was about to give up in despair I could hear his voice encouraging me.'

Father Minos bent over the frail old man as he lay on his mattress, his unseeing eyes staring at the broken roof of his house. A withered, wrinkled hand touched the cloth of the priest's robes and a smile of contentment settled on his face.

YANNIS

'Father, would you hear my confession?'

'I would be honoured.' Father Minos put his head down close to Antionis and listened to the weak voice as he told of misdeeds in his youth, taking an apple from a stall, forgetting to shut his father's chickens in for the night, the lie he told his wife about leaving her for another woman when he first found out he was ill. For each small sin Father Minos gave him absolution and when the list finally ended Antionis smiled again.

'I feel at peace now. Thank you, Father. I doubt we shall meet again. Look after Yannis, won't you? He's needed here. I'm tired, so very tired.'

Father Minos rose. He was more moved than he cared to admit by the old man's confession and stood in the dark interior to regain his composure before joining his companions. He wondered how many more of these pitiful victims had died without gaining absolution for their sins. It was wicked that there was no one on the island who could comfort them in their last hours.

'He asked me to confess him,' said Father Minos by way of explanation for his long absence. 'He hasn't much longer and knows it.'

'They always do,' remarked Spiro. 'He's a strange old man. Refused to let us touch his house. Said he wanted us to leave it as it was, wanted to remember it that way. He's been blind for years so he wouldn't have been able to see the repairs anyway. The others won't move back in with him now, they're still in the church.'

Yannis led the way up the steep path and pointed out the tower where the bodies of those who died were flung and left to disintegrate. Almost opposite, but some distance away was another tiny church.

'Is there anyone in there?'

'There's no roof.'

They moved on, the path narrowed and they had the high walls of the fort on their left side and a steep drop down to the rocks and sea below them on their right. Andreas shuddered and averted his eyes, relieved when the path widened out to show an old catwalk of the fort below them, the drop appearing less formidable. Rounding an outcrop of rock they arrived almost opposite an ammunition tower and walked on down the path to the patch of concrete where Kyriakos sat awaiting their return.

'Well?' he called. 'What do you think of our island?'

Father Minos smiled sympathetically. 'I couldn't describe it as paradise.' He looked at the sun. 'We mustn't stay much longer. I was told to report back to the doctor at seven. I don't want to be late. He might not let me come again.'

Yannis looked up in delight. 'Do you really plan to come again?'

'I most certainly do. I have a number of plans for the immediate future and returning here is one of them. Would you like us to take any messages to your family?'

'You won't tell them I'm here!' Yannis looked at his friend in horror.

'I think your family would be far happier knowing you're here, in reasonably good health, than not knowing whether you're alive or dead. The news could work wonders for your mother.'

Yannis considered. 'I suppose so. You'll make sure they know I'm all right, won't you?'

'You've no need to worry on that score. I think you look remarkably fit and well, don't you, Andreas?'

Andreas nodded in agreement. 'I'll write to Annita and let her know where you are. She could send a letter to me and I could get a boatman to bring it over.'

Yannis shook his head. 'There's no point in her writing to me. Tell her that I release her from our betrothal agreement and that I wish her well.'

Andreas shrugged. 'If that's what you want.'

'I do,' confirmed Yannis.

Father Minos rose to his feet. 'Should we tell the people we're leaving?'

'Of course, they'll all want to wave you off. Before you leave I'd like to say thank you. It's meant more to me than I can say to see you and Andreas.'

'Now we know you're here we'll do something about it. There are a lot of improvements that could be made. We won't rest until you have all you need over here to live a decent life.'

Yannis smiled, the words were comforting, but he saw no way that either Father Minos or Andreas could put them into effect. It was more convenient for the authorities to forget them.

Crowded together on the quay they waved farewell as the tiny boat edged gently away from the island into deeper water where it could turn and navigate the treacherous channel that led to the open sea. Once out of sight Yannis found his legs gave way beneath him and he sank to the ground.

'I can't believe it. They did come, didn't they, Spiro. I didn't dream today, did I?'

'They came. What a wonderful man Father Minos is. He never flinched whatever he saw, he never once shuddered and looked away.'

'Nor did Andreas,' Yannis defended his cousin. 'Do you think they will be able to help us?'

'I know they'll try. I'm going along to Antionis now. Coming?'

'No, I just want to sit and think.'

Spiro nodded. 'I understand.'

He walked away, leaving Yannis to shed bitter tears as he remembered all the details of his life with his cousin and family, details he had fought so hard to obliterate from his mind.

No word was spoken between Father Minos and Andreas on the journey back to Aghios Nikolaos; each was immersed in their own memories of the day. Once ashore Father Minos thanked the boatman and took Andreas to one side.

'I have to see Doctor Kandakis. When I've finished with him can I meet you somewhere? I think we should talk.'

Andreas nodded. 'I'll be at the taverna where we ate last night. I'll have to get permission, but that should be easy.' Andreas watched as the priest walked swiftly away to the doctor's house and wished he could be present at the impending meeting.

Father Minos hammered on the doctor's door and without waiting for an answer he swung it open and entered. No one was waiting in the small room, but the doctor opened the door of the surgery to investigate the noise. A look of annoyance crossed his face when he saw his visitor.

'Was it you making all that noise?'

'I'm afraid it was. I was taking out some of my anger and frustration on your door.' Father Minos strode over to the doctor, standing almost a head taller. 'What kind of man are you? What sort of doctor do you call yourself? No wonder you didn't want me to go over to that island. I've seen sights there today that would make men weep. Have you any idea how they survive? When did you, you who are supposed to be looking after them, ever do a single thing for them?' Father Minos paused for breath and the doctor backed away from him.

'I think you should sit down and explain yourself a little more calmly. Come, take a seat and share a glass of wine with me.'

Father Minos hesitated. It was no good antagonising this man too far. 'Very well, but I'll say what I wish and then leave.'

Doctor Kandakis poured two glasses of wine and sat heavily in the chair behind his desk. 'Now, what is it you wish to consult me about?'

'Don't you think that as a doctor you should know about the conditions that exist over there?'

'It is hardly my business. The Government send them there.'

'I see, so if I told you they are dying through neglect, lack of decent housing and sanitation, poor food and no medicine, you would just shrug and say it was none of your affair?'

'I find what you say rather difficult to believe. Many of them have lived there for years without complaint.'

'Without complaint! Who can they complain to? No one is allowed to land except the boatmen to offload supplies. They would not take a letter back to post for them, even if they had writing materials. They have little water, ruined houses to live in and you feel there is no need for you to do anything because they have not complained.' Father Minos banged his fist down on the desk. 'I insist you do something.'

'You insist! How dare you insist! You have no idea how debased those people on the island really are. No doubt they behaved themselves for you today, but I'm sure the boatmen could tell a different story.'

Father Minos took a deep breath and tried to calm himself. 'I spent seven hours on that island. I sat and talked with educated men. Men who calmly bandage an arm that is gangrenous and realise that amputation will eventually be the only way to save a life. I talked with men who are trying hard to repair the buildings to give them some reasonable shelter during the winter because they realise that to be exposed to all weathers is harmful and to be crowded together is a way of spreading disease. I gave absolution to an old man who knew he was dying and wanted to confess his sins before his soul departs and his rotten carcass is thrown into the tower to finally disintegrate. The sights I've seen over there today defy description.' He covered his face with his hands. 'I shall never forget, never, and you,' he looked venomously at the doctor, 'you would just wash your hands of them and say they're not your responsibility.' The priest leaned back against the upright chair and took a deep shuddering breath. The face of the doctor had at first purpled with rage under the onslaught, but now he had paled, a greenish tinge about his mouth.

'It is God's will that they are outcasts and therefore suffering,' he tried to defend himself.

Father Minos rose and drew himself up to his full height. 'It is God's will, but I am God's messenger on earth and God has told me that the time has come to help them.'

Doctor Kandakis's mouth opened without any words coming from him as the priest stalked across the room, his glass untouched, and slammed the door behind him. Once outside he cursed himself for a fool. Losing his temper with the doctor was no way to get the help he so much needed. He leaned against the wall of the house, the cool night air a balm to his over heated brow as he fought to regain his composure.

Andreas was waiting for him at the taverna and raised his eyebrows in an unspoken question as the priest approached. Father Minos shook his head.

'I made a terrible mess of that. I lost my temper.'

Andreas said nothing, but poured a glass of wine and pushed it towards his friend who drained the glass and pushed it back to be refilled.

'Would you believe that he says being a leper is God's will and therefore not his responsibility? How can you talk to a man like that?'

'I don't know. I haven't got your experience of life and people,' Andreas leaned forward. 'I know what I want to do, but that's probably impossible.'

'Tell me.'

'I'd like to buy the materials and medicines they need and send them over with the boatmen. I told you it was impossible.'

Father Minos smiled. 'I've thought the same, but it's a question of money. I'm sure if we spoke to the villagers they would send whatever they could, but medicines and building materials,' he pursed his lips, 'that's a different matter.'

'We could try, though, couldn't we?' Andreas spoke eagerly. 'If I spoke to my father and uncle they could ask the other villagers. They don't have to know Yannis is over there. They can say a priest visited and he is appealing on their behalf.'

Father Minos shook his head. 'It wouldn't be fair. Yannis's father would beggar himself trying to help his son. The Government should take the responsibility.'

YANNIS

'They do pay the farmers for sending their quota over. We could do something about that. I remember helping to pack crates when I stayed on the farm. They always send the worst of the crop, the grapes that would have been trodden into the ground as fertiliser, or the olives, which haven't ripened properly, vegetables that have been blighted. You put a few decent ones on top so they look all right.' Andreas's eyes gleamed with enthusiasm. 'I know uncle Yannis will always send the best in future and he could try and persuade the others to do the same. They wouldn't make so much money, of course.'

Father Minos nodded. 'That's certainly something that would help. I'll visit Yannis's father tomorrow. I hope the shock won't be too much for his mother. Do you think I should tell her or ask her husband to break the news?'

Andreas considered the question carefully. 'I think you'll have to tell her. The moment she sees you she'll know you've brought some news.'

'You're right.' Father Minos sighed. He was not looking forward to his mission the following day. 'Are you able to come with me?'

'Not tomorrow, if only I were still a novice it would be easy for me to have time to myself.'

'Have you any plans for when you are finally ordained?'

'Not really, I expect there'll be an opening for me somewhere.'

Father Minos, sitting in the boat that was taking him back to Aghios Nikolaos, ruminated on the reaction he had received from the family he had just visited.

Yannis's mother had cried, the tears rolling unchecked down her cheeks, Anna joining her. His father had hidden his emotion by rummaging in a cupboard for a bottle of brandy, Yiorgo had shaken his hand and thanked him gruffly before returning rapidly to the fields, but Stelios had stared at him blankly, turned on his heel and left the room without a word. They had wanted to know every detail of his visit and how their son had looked, did he have a decent bed to sleep in, were his clothes in good repair, was he eating properly, what did the doctors say about his chances of recovery?

Father Minos had sipped his brandy slowly and thought carefully about his answers. He did not want to upset Maria more than necessary, yet he had to impress upon them the need for action.

'It's not easy for them over there. They are totally dependent upon the food and water that's sent to them from the mainland. I've heard that the produce sent is not always the best, maybe you could persuade those who send it to improve the quality?'

Yannis shifted uncomfortably. 'What else do they need?'

'Everything; cooking utensils, bedding, clothes, building materials, the list is endless. They're trying to rebuild the houses to make them fit to live in. They need sand, cement, lime, nails, screws, timber, and tools. Their clothes are in tatters, just rags hanging from their backs. There's no medicine for them, no disinfectant or bandages. Nothing.'

Yannis refilled the priest's glass. 'We thought the Government looked after them.'

'The Government wants to forget them.' Father Minos leaned forward and spoke softly to Yannis's father. 'I'm not sure what happened at the hospital. Yannis didn't say very much, but from what I gathered from his friends he caused some trouble over there, him and a group of others. They were sent to the island as a punishment. It's hardly likely the Government would do anything for them. They consider themselves better off on the island than they were in Athens.'

Yannis shook his head in despair. 'What can I do?'

'You could send them some old clothes, pots and pans, maybe a blanket or two. Anything would help.'

Yannis rose and rummaged once again in the cupboard,

bringing out a small cloth bag, tied securely at the neck. He handed it to Father Minos. 'Buy what they need.'

'Yannis wouldn't want me to take your savings.' Father Minos tried to push the bag back to the farmer.

Yannis regarded him sternly. 'My son is suffering on that island. I can't go out and buy goods to send over there. People would wonder and question and before long they'd guess. I've a sick wife. I can't afford to be thrown out of the village.' He lowered his voice. 'I'm not a poor man. I paid for Yannis to go to Heraklion to study. I'll do the same for Stelios and the others won't want. Take it, just don't mention who gave it to you.'

Father Minos tested the weight of the bag gingerly. It was not very heavy. 'Was this the money returned to you by the taverna owner where Yannis was staying?'

'I'd forgotten about that. I expect Yannis took it back from him.'

Father Minos shook his head. 'When I visited the taverna, he hadn't returned it. I'll speak to him again. Where do you suggest I go for my purchases?'

Yannis considered. 'We have the local store, but you'd probably do better in town.'

'There's just one other thing, would you have a goat you could spare?'

Yannis looked at the priest in amazement. 'One goat wouldn't go very far between them.'

Father Minos smiled. 'I'm not planning that they should eat it. One of them has tuberculosis. Fresh milk could help him.'

'Yannis?'

'No, one of his friends. It was just an idea.'

Yannis nodded. 'I have one in kid. I'll see that it's sent.'

'It's for Panicos,' explained Father Minos.

'Remember that, Anna. You can write a label for its neck.'

'May I write a letter to Yannis also?'

'Certainly not!' her father snapped. 'Do you want to tell everyone where your brother is?'

Anna tilted her head defiantly. 'I'm not ashamed of him.'

'He's a young man to be proud of,' agreed Father Minos, 'but your father is right. It could mean problems for your family.'

'Then I'll wave to the island every day. Only Yannis will know I'm waving to him.' Tears filled her eyes again. 'I wish I could see him.'

Father Minos laid a hand on her head. 'Be thankful he's so close. Many of them are miles away from their families and will never see a sister wave to them.'

The priest took his leave of the family, promising to send them any news he had. Anna stood on the shore and Father Minos could see her waving a red scarf and knew it was not meant for him. Maybe a boatman could let Yannis know. He gazed at the young man as the boat sailed far closer to the island than was necessary and watched as the fisherman raised his hand in salutation and blew a kiss to the girl standing on the jetty. He grinned at the priest and Father Minos realised he had an ally.

'Do you know her well?'

'Not really, she's always asking us to take something over. Odd things. She asked me for a ladder a few months back. I usually take her a little present when I deliver.'

'I'm sure she appreciates it. They live very Spartan lives over there. I plan to buy some supplies for them in Aghios Nikolaos,' continued Father Minos. 'Would you be willing to deliver them?'

'Of course, what are you buying?'

'Sand, cement and lime to start with.'

'What?'

Father Minos smiled at the young man's amazement. 'They need it to repair their houses. When you deliver could you pass on a message for me?'

'Who to?'

'The girl on the jetty will do. Ask her to tell Yannis that Anna is waving.'

Father Minos was longing to count the money that was in the

little cloth bag, but thought it unwise in front of the young boatman. He leaned back, lulled by the gentle movement and closed his eyes.

Having moored he arranged to meet Manolis the following day to pass over his purchases and went in search of the doctor. This time he knocked and waited politely.

'I've come to apologise for my conduct yesterday. I was somewhat overwrought,' he began.

Doctor Kandakis looked at the priest. He had hoped he had seen the last of him. He began to push the door closed, but Father Minos held up his hand. 'May I come in? I wish to talk to you.'

'I've very little time. I'm a busy man.'

'I understand. I'll be as quick as possible.' Father Minos stepped just inside the door. 'I was unforgivably rude to you yesterday, but that doesn't alter the facts. Everything I said about the people on that island is true. I've come here now to ask if I can buy some bandages and medicines from you to send over to them.'

The doctor eyed the priest suspiciously. He could probably make a fair profit from the man. 'How much do you have to spend?'

'One hundred drachmas.'

'It's not a lot.'

'According to my calculations it will buy a thousand rolls of bandage and a case of disinfectant.'

Doctor Kandakis swallowed. The man even got his sums right! 'I don't have those kind of stocks here. You'll have to ask at the hospital.'

'Very well.' Father Minos had been expecting that. 'Do you have any medicines I could buy from you?'

'I am not allowed to sell any medicine without first seeing the patient.'

'I'm quite prepared to hire a boat for you to visit the patients.' Father Minos looked at the doctor steadily.

'I do not have the time. Now, you really must excuse me.' The door was opened and the doctor stood back to allow the priest to leave.

'Good day, Doctor. I doubt we shall meet again.'

Doctor Kandakis did not deign to reply. He hoped never to see the meddling priest again.

Yannis could hardly believe it. During the last week the goods that had arrived on the island were beyond his wildest dreams. Manolis had arrived, grinning delightedly, and off-loaded sacks of sand and cement, calling to Flora that Anna was waving to them. Flora had shrugged. Who was Anna? She had called excitedly to Yannis who waited for Manolis to sail out of sight before he came hurrying down to examine the sacks.

'It's wonderful! It must be due to Father Minos. There's only one problem, I've no idea what kind of quantities I should mix and I've nothing to mix it with.'

'I'll ask Manolis for a spade,' Flora promised him. 'He said he'd be over tomorrow with some more things. He asked me to tell you that Anna was waving.'

Yannis pulled the girl to him and kissed her on the forehead. 'That's one of the most wonderful things I've ever heard.' He released her swiftly and ran up the path to where he had a good view of his village. He waved wildly, screwing up his eyes to try to discern any figure on the opposite shore. Disappointed when he saw no one he turned away to find Flora standing behind him.

'What are you doing?' she asked curiously.

'I thought I might see Anna waving.'

'Who is she? Your girl?'

Yannis smiled. 'No, my sister.' He leaned against the fortress wall and looked across the bay. 'I used to live over there, in that farmhouse. When I first came here I couldn't bear to look across the water.'

YANNIS

'Are you happy here, Yannis?'

'Happy! What a question! How can you be happy here?'

'I'm not unhappy. You've made it so much better over here.'

'Not just me, the others have helped.'

'It was your idea.' Flora gazed up at him admiringly. 'I don't know what we'd do without you, Yannis.'

'I'm sure someone else could have done just the same.'

'You won't leave us, will you, Yannis?'

'Leave you? How can I?'

Flora squirmed uncomfortably. 'I just thought that as you had friends who were priests and a family nearby that somehow you might be able to go.'

'No,' Yannis sighed. 'I'm here forever, the same as everyone else. It's just a coincidence that one of the priests is my cousin and I used to live near here as a child. I used to be so frightened of this place.'

Flora giggled. 'You are funny, Yannis. You, being frightened.'

'It's true. I was.'

Flora was no longer listening to him. 'Antionis,' she gasped and fled from Yannis's side. Yannis followed her; his ears picking up the thin wailing from the women that announced the death of the old man.

Yannis pushed his way to the bedside and took the cold hand in his own. Spiro rubbed his eyes from lack of sleep. 'He didn't wake up, Yannis. He went peacefully.'

'Thank you, Spiro.' Yannis turned away, dejected. He would have liked to have spent a few moments to say goodbye, but he had no time to dwell on Antionis's death, the bags of cement had to be moved from the quay and stored where they would stay dry until they were able to use them.

Each day Flora called to Yannis to come and witness the new goods that were arriving, sacks of lime, bundles of new clothes, blankets and shoes. Delightedly people rummaged through, selecting whatever fitted and they needed. The whole atmosphere had changed; from despair and acceptance of their lot had sprung hope. Life was improving.

Every morning Yannis would stand and stare across the stretch of water, hoping to see Anna, but until now he had been disappointed. This morning there seemed to be more activity than usual on the beach and Yannis screwed up his eyes to try to see more clearly. Goods were being loaded and someone was struggling. Some poor sufferer was being sent to the island. Yannis hoped it was not one of his relatives and craned forward to try and see.

'Be careful, Yannis.'

'I'm just watching the action over there. I think we're having a visitor.'

Phaedra leant by his side. 'Who is it? The priest again?'

'Judging by the struggle they were putting up I would say it was a fellow sufferer. Look! Look!' Yannis grabbed Phaedra's arm. 'It must be Anna. She's waving.'

Frantically Yannis waved back. 'Wave! Wave!' he shouted at Phaedra who raised her hand obediently.

Slowly the boat drew away from the shore, but still Yannis continued to wave to the tiny figure until his arm ached. Abruptly the waving stopped and the person turned, making their way back up the rough path, followed by a taller figure.

'It was Anna.' Yannis's eyes were alight with pleasure. 'That must have been Pappa with her.'

Phaedra pulled at Yannis's arm. 'Come on, let's see who's arrived.'

Yannis, Phaedra and Flora watched the boatmen from the top of the steps. The first thing that came off was a goat, still struggling frantically, until her feet were untied and she was set upright on the ground. The men chased her up the ramp to where the trio stood and Yannis caught her deftly. Holding her by the string that was round her neck he stroked her gently, trying to calm the frightened creature.

'What does it say?' Flora had spotted the label.

Yannis turned it towards him. '"For Panicos." Well, he'll have a good meal tonight.'

'You can't eat her.' Flora spoke in horror.

'Why not?'

'She's having a kid.'

Yannis looked at the distended belly of the animal. 'You're right there. Pretty soon by the look of things.' He looked at the label again and turned it over. 'I'm pretty stupid,' he announced. 'For milk.'

Flora giggled. 'Poor little goat! Let's take her to him.'

Once over her first fear the goat was docile and walked sedately between them until they reached Panicos's house and pushed the animal inside.

'It's for you,' explained Yannis. 'So you can have some fresh milk.'

'Where from?'

'I'm not sure. It doesn't say. I suspect that Father Minos had a hand in it somewhere. Who else would know you needed milk?'

'That man's a saint.'

Privately Yannis agreed with him. The crate of bandages that had arrived two days earlier was the most welcome sight that any of them had seen. At last they would be able to change their soiled rags. The food sent from the mainland had improved; no longer was there a sodden, pulpy mass at the bottom of a box of grapes, or carrots full of small holes where the maggots had made a meal. Yannis wished there was some way he could repay the priest, as he was sure everything was due to him.

Father Minos had been shocked when he opened the moneybag and discovered the amount it contained. He counted note after note, then stowed them safely away again. He would make a list of essentials and budget carefully. To send too much at one time would invite wastage and he doubted if he would ever have such an opportunity again. He negotiated with the hospital for bandages and disinfectant, buying all they could spare and warning them that he would want the same again in a few weeks. He bought every blanket the local shops had to offer and found time to consult with Yiorgo and Elena. Yiorgo assured him the money given by Yannis's father could well be spared, matching it with a sum almost as great and winking conspiratorially at the priest.

Father Minos could not see how farmers and fishermen could possibly make such a good living that they could hand over a thousand drachmas and insist they had plenty more. It amounted to a sum greater than any he could hope to save in his lifetime. By the end of the week the priest had a reputation for being an eccentric millionaire and the townsfolk were talking of little else apart from the philanthropist who was sending goods to the island to help the lepers who lived there. When he departed he left the balance of the money with Andreas, instructing him to purchase items that Manolis said the islanders needed, and it was with a feeling of accomplishment that he finally boarded the bus to return to Heraklion.

Having settled back into his routine in the town he had the opportunity to visit Pavlos. He called during the day and found the taverna closed, but was assured by a neighbour that it was open each evening. When he returned Pavlos was behind the counter and Father Minos approached him with a smile.

'Good evening, do you remember me?'

Pavlos glanced at him quickly. One priest was the same as another. 'Should I?'

'I called when your sister had just married. It was regarding Yannis and a small matter of the rent.'

Pavlos frowned as he tried to bluff his way out of the difficult situation. 'That was a long while back. I really can't say I remember. So much has happened since then; the birth of my little niece, and Pavlakis becoming a town governor. Maybe it's him you wish to speak to?'

'Oh, no, it's quite definitely you.' Father Minos leant his elbows on the counter. 'The young student, Yannis, had been staying here. He was taken ill and left rather hurriedly. I came here and broke the news to you. His cousin was with me. I understood that his father had paid you for a year's board and lodging and the boy was only able to avail himself of half of that time.'

'It was a long time ago,' repeated Pavlos. 'It must have been repaid by now.'

Father Minos raised his eyebrows. 'Do you have a receipt? When I was speaking to his father last week he was under the impression that it was still owing to him.'

'I'll have to speak to my sister. She does the accounts.'

'Please do. I can wait.'

'She's not available at present. She has a small daughter.'

'I have the whole evening at my disposal. I'm sure she will be able to spare a few moments sooner or later.' Still smiling amiably Father Minos sat down at a table. 'I should like a glass of wine whilst I wait.'

Pavlos brought over a bottle and two glasses. Maybe he could ply the priest with drink and make him more amenable. 'I'll speak to her. Do you have any idea of the figure involved?'

'I have it exactly.' From his pocket the priest drew a sheet of paper. 'Sixteen drachmas a week, inclusive of all meals and laundry, for six months is three hundred and eighty four drachmas. I understand Yannis's father paid you eight hundred. He'll be happy to receive four hundred back.' Father Minos raised his glass.

'It's a lot of money for a poor taverna owner to find.'

'It's a lot of money for a poor farmer to lose. I feel sure that his need is greater than yours. His poor son; whom he relied upon to repay him when he had completed his education; never to be seen again; his wife an invalid, needing their daughter to look after her. Just him and a second son to work the farm and try to make a living.' Father Minos shook his head. 'It's very hard.'

'It's not easy here,' Pavlos protested. 'We do our best, but there's not the patronage.'

'I understand you are working and your brother-in-law is a teacher. The taverna should be a nice little addition to your income.'

'Yiorgo has a position to keep up. Now he is a governor he has to have suits, attend functions, it takes most of his salary.'

'I'm sure. It would not be advisable for it to be known that his brother-in-law owed a large debt, would it?' Father Minos refilled his glass. 'Or, for that matter, that a very sick boy lived here; that could be bad for your business, even after all this time.'

Pavlos pushed back his chair. 'I'll fetch my sister.'

From the bottom of the stairs he called to her frantically. 'Louisa! Louisa, I need you here.'

Frowning with annoyance Louisa descended the stairs. 'Can't you be quieter? I've only just got her to sleep.'

'It's that priest. The one who came asking for Yannis's money. I've tried to stall him, but it's no use. He's threatening to tell people that we owe and Yannis was sick when he stayed here.'

Louisa bit at her lower lip and thought rapidly. 'How much does he say we owe?'

'Four hundred.'

'Tell him I'll be down to talk to him.'

Pavlos returned to where the priest was sitting, drinking steadily. 'I've spoken to my sister. She'll be down shortly.'

He heard the thin wail of his sister's child and to his surprise she entered almost immediately, holding the girl in her arms. 'You'd better start the cooking, Pavlos.' She slid into the vacant seat. 'I understand Mr Christoforakis thinks we owe him some money?' She smiled sweetly at the priest.

'I've explained to your brother. A year paid in advance and the room used for less than six months means that half the money is due to be returned,' repeated Father Minos patiently.

'I'm sure if you were able to speak to Yannis he would have

no wish for the money to be returned. He would probably ask his father to send some more – for his grand-daughter.'

Father Minos stared at the brazen girl before him; then shook his head. 'I don't think that very likely. Yannis was a fine young man, not a philanderer, besides, your husband? What would he say?'

'Yannis was a hot-blooded young man. I don't think that he would deny that he was the father of my child.' Louisa looked into Father Minos's eyes. 'My husband is a good man who took pity on an innocent girl who had been molested with disastrous consequences.' She leaned forward confidentially. 'I have never divulged the paternity of my daughter before and I trust you as a man of the cloth not to tell anyone. For her sake and for my dear husband.' Tears glistened in her eyes as she spoke.

Involuntarily Father Minos reached out and patted the girl's hand. 'Of course, my dear. Perhaps, under the circumstances, rather than embarrass anyone, it would be better to forget my visit?'

Louisa smiled. 'I would be very grateful.'

'I'll tell Mr Christoforakis that at present you are unable to repay him.'

Louisa nodded and rose. 'It has been a pleasure to meet such an understanding man.' She held out her hand. 'Please come again at any time.'

Father Minos touched her hand briefly. 'The pleasure has been mine, my dear.'

'Pavlos, can you leave your cooking to say goodbye? The Father is leaving.'

Pavlos appeared from the kitchen area, looking anxiously at Louisa.

Father Minos smiled at him. 'We've settled everything for the time being.' He placed some coins on the table. 'For my wine.'

Before Pavlos could refuse he had left the taverna and Louisa sank back into her chair, hugging her daughter to her and laughing.

'What did you say to him?'

Louisa shrugged. 'Just told him a sad story.' She was not prepared to tell her brother the nature of the conversation. 'Don't mention it to Yiorgo, it would only upset him.'

Pavlos smiled at her. 'I'm not likely to tell him.'

He was beginning to dislike his brother-in-law who continually returned to the taverna with a following of men who made up the government. They would sit until the early hours of the morning, consuming food and wine, without adding to the day's takings. When he had approached Yiorgo regarding the matter of the bills for them he had met with a refusal, Yiorgo insisting that the money he gave Louisa should cover the cost. It was necessary for him to entertain and where more natural to do so than in his own home.

Father Minos left the taverna saddened by the secret Louisa had shared with him. He knew her reputation and wished he knew the truth of the situation and able to call her bluff. He wondered if he dared ask Yannis such a personal question. He would decide the next time he visited the island. The more he thought about Spinalonga the more he was drawn towards the island. He could visualise it in a few years time, the houses repaired and their occupants living a decent life.

Doctor Kandakis banged his fist on the desk. It was all the fault of that meddling priest! He should never have given him permission to visit the island. Now he had a direct order to visit immediately and report back his findings to Athens. How he wished he knew if Father Minos had written to them. How could he say everything was fine if the priest had said otherwise? He tried to console himself. Surely they would take his word as a doctor; or would they? For years he had accepted the responsibility of being the doctor for the island and taken the addition to his salary. If the authorities found out that he only went over once a year, stood on the quay and left a meagre supply of Chaulmoogra Oil capsules he would not only be asked to repay the money, but be disgraced. He had no option. He would resign.

YANNIS

He could plead his advancing years and increased workload on the mainland and hope that would be the end of the matter.

Maria lay on her bed, trying hard to breathe deeply and keep the excruciating pain at bay. If only Babbis would come back with her sister. She let out a low moan. This must be a big baby. Her little Marisa had not hurt so much. Kassy was worried. The first baby had been so easy, but this one was going to be a different matter, already Maria was in a lot of pain. She stared out of the window, trying hard to penetrate the darkness in the hope of seeing her son returning.

It had all happened so suddenly. Maria had been fit and well in the morning, helping as usual, then late in the afternoon she had clutched at her stomach and collapsed in a crumpled heap on the floor. Panic stricken Kassy had run to the fields for her son, leaving little Marisa sitting on the living room floor, hoping she would not get into mischief. Babbis had raced back to find his wife semi-conscious. The time it took for his mother to return seemed unending.

'What shall I do? What shall I do?' he asked as she entered.

'Get her on the mattress,' advised Kassy.

Between them they lifted the heavy figure as gently as possible, then Kassy sponged the clammy forehead and held a vinegar soaked rag before Maria's nose. Babbis stood by the bed, his daughter in his arms, his gaze riveted on his wife, praying silently that she would open her eyes and smile at him.

'Best go for Anna,' his mother urged him.

Reluctantly he dragged his eyes away from the bed and handed Marisa to her grandmother. 'I'll be as quick as I can.'

Now Kassy was pacing the floor, Marisa wriggling in her arms, and Kassy remembered the child was probably hungry. Heating some milk and feeding her would take her mind off Maria, and with luck the child would be asleep by the time Anna arrived.

Maria did not open her eyes, her face had a greenish hue and her lips, parted with her laboured breathing, had a bluish tinge. Anna took the scene in at a glance.

'Hot water,' she demanded of Kassy and then turned to Babbis. 'Go to my Pappa. Ask him to bring the Widow up here on the donkey. I'll need her help. Quick now.'

Babbis nodded. He had great faith in his sister-in-law, young and untrained as she was. Anna went to Maria and took her pulse. It was far too rapid and she did not like the colour of her face and lips.

'I'll need more light,' she called to Kassy. 'Bring all the lamps you have.'

Silently Kassy obeyed until Maria laid ringed in light. Anna loosened her sister's blouse and then removed her skirt and under garments, covering her legs with a rough blanket. Gently she placed her hand on the enlarged stomach; then pushed downwards, following the contours of the baby's body. She frowned, her eyes meeting those of Kassy's.

'It's breach,' she announced.

Kassy wrung her hands. 'What can you do?'

'I don't know.'

Anna bit her lip. She had gleaned as much knowledge as possible from the Widow and knew that breach babies could be turned by careful manipulation. She was now faced with a dilemma. Should she try to effect the turn and in her ignorance do more damage, or wait for the Widow, by which time it could be too late to do anything? Maria groaned again and Anna decided to wait no longer. Pressing down firmly once again on each side of the distended stomach she attempted to persuade the child to move. Something soft and damp touched her arm and she straightened her back.

'Hold a lamp,' she ordered.

Kassy obeyed and Anna examined her sister. 'Too late,' she announced. 'There's a foot born.'

Kassy replaced the light. 'What can we do?' she whispered.

'Pray.' Anna's voice was harsh with emotion. The labour was going to be lengthy, the most difficult part coming at the end when Maria would be exhausted. She knew how dangerous such a situation could be.

Babbis arrived back alone. 'How is she?'

'It's going to be a breach birth. It will take time. Put some water on for coffee. It's going to be a long night.'

Silently Babbis went into the kitchen. Never again would he risk Maria's life in this way. She was far too precious to him. He returned to the living room, hardly daring to look at his wife. He sat with his head in his hands, wishing there was some way he could help. Anna noticed the dejected figure.

'Come and hold her hand. She'll need something to grip later.'

Babbis moved next to his wife, taking the limp hand into his own and raising it to his lips. Once again Anna felt the weight of the responsibility that rested on her. If only the Widow would arrive.

Maria drifted in and out of consciousness. Faces appeared before her as if in a dream, her father, sister, husband, mother-in-law and the Widow, most of all the Widow, speaking sharply to her, giving instructions which she tried her hardest to carry out. A faint cry penetrated her confused mind. They must see to Marisa. She tried to raise herself to tell them. A strong hand held her down.

'Lay still. Try to sleep. It's all over now.'

Babbis sat by his sleeping wife, still holding her hand. His face was drawn and grey. The Widow sat huddled in a chair, a rug over her, needing rest as much as the young mother. Kassy nursed the tiny baby, the cause of so much distress. Anna washed her sister gently and examined her for tears and bruises. She hoped fervently that the internal damage was not as bad as the external appeared. She tapped Babbis on his shoulder and beckoned him to a corner in the room.

'She needs to see a doctor. I've done my best and so has the Widow, but we haven't the knowledge. Go and ask Pappa if you can borrow the cart to take her to Aghios Nikolaos.'

Babbis looked at his wife and back again at Anna.

'Go on,' she urged him. 'I'll look after everything here.'

Still Babbis hesitated.

'What is it?' Anna was becoming impatient.

'I haven't any money for a doctor,' he mumbled.

'Ask Pappa. He'll not refuse, and Babbis, tell Mamma that I'll be back soon.'

Babbis nodded and went out into the chill of the morning whilst Anna turned back again to her patient.

It was left to Anna to break the news of Maria's death to her mother. She tried to do so as gently as possible, but the invalid sat unmoving for days afterwards and Anna was frightened she would have another stroke. She was desperately tired herself. Sleep was a luxury. She would lie for hours wondering if she could have done more to save her sister, although Babbis had returned from the town assuring her she had done her best. No one could staunch the massive internal bleeding that had taken its final toll on her weakened heart. He appeared to be sleep-walking most of the time, working long hours in the fields, arriving home exhausted and collapsing into his lonely bed to find solace in a few hours slumber. Kassy was trying hard to cope with the house, her morose son and a bewildered toddler who asked for 'Mamma'. The new baby had been just too much for her to tackle and Anna had offered to look after the child for a while. He was demanding. When she finally fell into an uneasy sleep he would wake, crying for food and comfort. Stelios complained bitterly about his disturbed nights, but her father and Yiorgo said nothing.

Now Anna rose as the dawn streaked the sky and crept from her room. Maybe the child would sleep for another half an hour and she would be able to prepare a meal for Yiorgo and her father to take to the fields with them. It would save her time and energy if they could take the food when they left instead of her having to trek up the hill and find them at mid-day. Maybe, if Yannis slept on, she could wash her mother and get her comfortably settled in her chair before he demanded more attention.

The days merged together and they did not seem to get any easier. Babbis would visit them once a week and nurse his son in melancholy silence, but did not offer to take him back to his own house. The one time that Anna had broached the subject of the baby's return Babbis had seemed embarrassed and made the excuse that his mother would not be able to manage. Marisa was such a little handful and his mother was not young. By the time Yannis had reached six months old she accepted the fact that her brother-in-law had no intention of relieving her of his son. Gradually she had worked out a routine and was managing a little better now the baby slept most nights. She had written to Andreas and asked him to pass on the sad news to both Annita and Yannis. If little Yannis were awake when she waved to the island she always held him up, hoping her brother would see his tiny namesake.

Her father had long given up protesting at her daily ritual of waving and had even stood beside her on one or two occasions when a figure could be seen waving back. Yiorgo took little notice. He had problems of his own. The farm was gradually becoming neglected and was likely to become more so. Stelios had no interest in the fields at all and was leaving for Aghios Nikolaos in the autumn, Anna had no time to help, his mother was unable and his father was still troubled by his lame leg. However long Yiorgo worked he never seemed to make any headway and he was wondering if he should suggest to his father that they sell some of the land.

Doctor Stavros read the letter through a second time. It did not make sense. Why was he being asked to visit Spinalonga? Doctor Kandakis was in charge of the island. Much as he disliked the idea he supposed he would have to find out what was expected of him. There was no urgency; he would leave it until after his annual holiday. A few days in Sitia would do him good. He might even visit the oculist whilst he was there. His headaches had definitely worsened over the past six months and a new pair of spectacles was probably the answer.

The week passed pleasantly and all too soon he returned to his duties. Within two days his holiday was erased from his mind. Back into his usual routine the time passed swiftly, holding his small surgery in the front room of his house and visiting his hospital patients took up most of the day. It was on one such visit to the hospital that he encountered Doctor Kandakis and remembered the letter. Holding the door as the doctor emerged he smiled, hoping he would be recognised.

'Excuse me, may I have a quick word?'

'If you're ill come to the surgery.'

'I'm Doctor Stavros. I wish to speak to you about a letter I've received.'

Doctor Kandakis grunted. 'I'm in a hurry.'

'Quite. I was merely puzzled as the letter was from the Medical Authorities requesting that I visit the island. I understood you were in charge of it.'

'I have resigned. Excuse me.' Doctor Kandakis pushed his way past, leaving Doctor Stavros bewildered and annoyed. Now he would have to answer the letter.

He tried to compose a suitable reply that afternoon and finally gave up, deciding to take a stroll along the waterfront. He always enjoyed the bustle of the quay and once or twice a fisherman, who was still feeling grateful for medication received, would offer him the pick of the catch. He felt lucky, and fancied a nice plump mullet for supper.

As usual the waterfront was a hive of activity, even more

interesting was a young fisherman who was loading his boat with sacks until his fragile craft appeared in danger of sinking. Curiosity getting the better of him, Doctor Stavros moved closer.

'What's in there?' he asked.

A flash of white teeth answered him. 'Sand and cement.'

'Sand and cement,' the doctor repeated stupidly.

'For the island.'

'What do they need that for?'

The fisherman shrugged. 'The priest told me he'd arranged for supplies to go over regularly and pays me for taking them.'

Doctor Stavros raised his eyebrows. 'Do you go to the island?'

'Only to unload on the jetty.'

'So you don't see the people?'

'Sometimes, from a distance, and I see Flora.'

'Who's Flora?'

'She's always on the jetty. Asks the boatmen for all sorts of things.' The fisherman grinned again. 'Hammers, nails, screwdrivers; all sorts of stuff. Never anything for herself, but I take her a few trifles sometimes, you know, a hair ribbon or a comb when I can get it.'

'Is she very ill?'

'How should I know? I'm not a doctor.' He heaved the last sack aboard. 'I'm off now. Any message for anyone?'

'No. Should there be?'

'I thought you might know someone over there. I'm always willing to give a message to Flora. She'll pass it on.'

Doctor Stavros shook his head. 'No, I've no message.'

He watched as the boat sailed slowly out towards the open sea. Why would sick people want building materials? What was it the fisherman had said? The priest had arranged it. He smiled to himself. That was the answer. He had obviously persuaded them to build a church! Doctor Stavros moved on slowly, many fishermen waved to him, but none came forward to offer him a fish.

1931-1939

Entering the general store he purchased a bottle of raki and was about to leave when a small brown envelope was handed to him. He turned it over and across the back was the medical authorities stamp. He tapped the letter against his fingers speculatively; then ripped it open. A quick glance at the contents made him realise he had to read it carefully.

Once home he read the direct instructions. A further fifty patients had been sent to the island and more were on their way. He was to visit the island and send back a report on the general health of everyone living there. Now that Doctor Kandakis had resigned he was to be solely responsible. There would be a small fund at his disposal to pay for a boatman and he could requisition supplies from the hospital. The letter was couched in terms that brooked no refusal.

Yannis sat with the letter from Andreas in his hand. It was unbelievable. His sister dead in childbirth! What had they done to her? How could it possibly have happened? He had been so thrilled when Flora had handed it to him, saying Manolis had brought it over. Now his pleasure had turned to bitterness and misery. He had assumed the girl waving to him with a child in her arms to be Maria, but maybe it was Anna. He beat his fists on the ground in frustration. If only he knew what was happening to his family. Andreas's letter contained little information other than the salient facts. Maria had given birth to a son. The birth had been difficult. Anna had done her best, but Maria had been taken to hospital in Aghios Nikolaos where the doctors had been unable to save her.

Phaedra sat beside him, saying nothing. She could sense that Yannis had received bad news and thought that in all probability his mother had suffered another stroke.

'It's so unfair,' he said finally. 'She never hurt anyone and he loved her so much.'

'Your Mamma?'

'My sister. Phaedra, how do women die when they're having a child?'

Phaedra shrugged. 'I don't know. It just happens.'

'Everything 'just happens'! My sister 'just happens' to die, my mother 'just happens' to have a stroke, I 'just happen' to have leprosy. It isn't fair, Phaedra.'

'Life isn't, Yannis. There's nothing you or I can do about it. Did any of us ask to be sent here? I was fine living in a cave on the mainland. I wasn't harming anyone.'

Yannis looked at the girl in concern. 'I'm pleased you're here and not in a cave miles away. I always have someone to talk to. I rely on your common sense.'

'You take everyone's problems onto your own shoulders and think everything's your fault. You must learn to shrug and walk away.'

'I'm not like that. I wish I were. What makes you so wise, Phaedra?'

She shrugged her thin shoulders. 'I'm not wise. I just see everyone turning to you, taking all their problems to lie at your feet, blaming you when things don't go right, relying on you. It's too much. I just feel I want to scream at them to go away and leave you alone. To give you some peace.'

Yannis looked down at her earnest face. 'When I come to you, you never shrug and walk away.'

'That's different, besides, you're the only one who brings their problems to me,' Phaedra was embarrassed.

'In my book that says you're a friend; a very special, precious friend.'

Phaedra was still looking up at him. Gently Yannis bent and kissed her, softly at first, then with mounting passion. After her initial response Phaedra pulled herself away. Yannis felt himself flushing with confusion.

'I'm sorry,' he apologised. 'That became rather too friendly.'

Phaedra touched her lips with her fingers. 'I've never been

kissed before,' she spoke almost in a whisper.

'Never?'

'Not by a man. I've always avoided the men over here.'

'Why?'

'They frighten me.'

'Do I frighten you?'

'No, of course not.'

Yannis slipped his arm round her waist. 'I'm glad of that. I don't want my favourite girl to be scared of me.'

'I thought your cousin was your favourite girl?'

'That was a life-time ago – and before I met you.'

'Would you still like to marry her?'

Yannis shook his head. 'I haven't seen her for years. She will have changed in that time and I certainly have. She probably has some other young man paying court to her. Andreas said she was in Athens.'

'Does it hurt you to talk about her?'

'Not now; I've accepted the fact that I'll never see her again. I know she's all right. She has her parents and brother to look after her. I would like to see my mother again.' Yannis held up the little eye he always wore on the silver chain. 'My mother gave me this when I first went to Heraklion. It was to bring me good luck.' He laughed mirthlessly. 'Some luck it brought me, or her for that matter.'

It was a bright, clear morning, with just the hint of a breeze. Doctor Stavros cursed silently. He had hoped there would be a mistral blowing and his trip postponed. Manolis was waiting for him on the quay, his boat loaded as heavily as he dared, and he greeted the doctor with a dazzling smile.

'We should make good time if the wind holds,' he assured his passenger.

'I'm not a very good sailor,' the doctor warned him, not adding that he was petrified of the sea, having once suffered a long and arduous crossing between Heraklion and Athens.

Manolis screwed up his eyes. 'Shouldn't have any problem today.' He cleared a space for the doctor to put his feet, cast off and jumped aboard. As the island loomed into view the doctor regarded it curiously. It was smaller than he had imagined and the high wall of the Venetian fortress that ran around the perimeter gave it a secluded and forbidding appearance. On the jetty there was a young girl, who leapt to her feet and waved a greeting to them.

'That's Flora,' announced Manolis, waving back to her. 'She'll go and tell the others I've arrived. You go ashore and walk up the steps. Someone will soon see you.'

'How many people are there on this island?'

'I've no idea. Two or three hundred, judging by what the priest said.'

'Three hundred?' gasped the doctor. He would never be able to visit everyone in a day, let alone examine and prescribe. 'I'll be some time. Will you wait for me?'

'Sure. I'll do some fishing and chat to Flora.' He grinned again as the doctor clambered clumsily out of the boat. What landlubbers these doctors were!

Doctor Stavros walked along the quay and through the arch. The air immediately seemed oppressive and he hoped he was not going to have one of his headaches. At the top of the flight of steps a young man appeared and the doctor felt more than one pair of eyes was watching him. He cleared his throat.

'Good morning, I'm Doctor Stavros and have been asked to come here by the authorities.'

'Why?' Yannis did not move. 'What do they plan to do with us now?'

'I believe they want to ensure there is enough accommodation for those who have been sent over recently. They wish to send some more sufferers to join them.' Doctor Stavros passed a hand over his forehead. 'Maybe if I saw the island and where you live, then visited the hospital cases.'

Yannis raised his eyebrows. 'My dear doctor, we are all hospital cases!'

'Oh, yes, yes, of course. I meant those who are bedridden.'

Yannis smiled grimly to himself. 'We'll go this way,' he said and turned up the slope towards Kyriakos.

Doctor Stavros looked at the legless man. 'How long have you been disabled?'

'I don't remember. Years.'

The doctor placed his bag on the ground. 'May I examine you?'

Kyriakos shrugged. 'Why? They're not going to grow again.'

'Of course not, but I might be able to put your mind at rest about the progression.'

Kyriakos gave a sour look towards Yannis. He was sensitive about showing his disfigurements.

'I'll see if Phaedra's around.' Yannis walked away and did not return until he saw the doctor pick up his bag.

'Who looks after that man?' he asked Yannis.

'He looks after himself, more or less. We make his meals and carry him if he wants to go anywhere.'

Doctor Stavros shook his head. 'I mean who washes him and changes his bandages?'

'He does that for himself. Most of them do. If we go round this way you'll get an idea of the island.' Yannis led the way past the overhang, pointing out the catwalk they did not use and continued down the narrow path towards the church.

'That's dangerous,' remarked Doctor Stavros. 'Any one could fall over there to the rocks below.' He made a note on his pad.

'We all know it's there. We don't often come round this side.' Yannis dismissed the precipice as unimportant. 'Do you want to see the tower where we dispose of the dead?'

Doctor Stavros stopped in his tracks. 'Dispose of the dead! Don't you bury them?'

YANNIS

Yannis looked at him. Was it possible that any doctor could be so naïve? 'We live on a rock. It's somewhat difficult to dig a hole, besides, we'd soon have no space to live on.'

'I don't think I need to see the tower. I'll not be able to do anything for the occupants.' He followed Yannis through the tunnel. 'Wouldn't they be better off inside?' asked the doctor, waving his hand towards the various groups who were sitting or lying around at the side of the path.

'All the houses are occupied, and there aren't enough anyway.'

'Can't they go into the hospital?'

'The hospital is a ruin.'

Doctor Stavros shifted uncomfortably. 'Is there somewhere we could sit and talk for a while? I seem rather confused.' He rubbed his hand over his forehead; his head was throbbing.

Yannis nodded. 'We'll go back up to Kyriakos. I've asked Phaedra to include you for lunch.'

As the doctor followed Yannis, he was conscious of the suspicious glances that were directed at him and felt distinctly uncomfortable. He doubted the wisdom of eating or drinking anything on the island, but some food might help his headache, and he certainly did not want to offend this strange man. Feeling completely out of his depth he sat silently as mutilated hands tore bread into pieces and passed cheese, olives and tomatoes to him. Yannis tried to converse with him, but the doctor was evasive. He had been sent to the island to compile a report for the authorities, say how the new arrivals had settled and requisition essential supplies from the hospital on the mainland, he had no other instructions.

'No, I'm sure you haven't! Out of sight, out of mind, that's what we are.'

'I'm sure they have your welfare at heart,' insisted Doctor Stavros. 'I had a letter saying I was to visit and be responsible for you, medically speaking.'

Yannis's eyes gleamed. 'So what are you going to do?'

'I don't know. I'm confused. That's why I wanted to talk to you. You seem to be in charge.'

'There's no one in charge, as you put it. We just live from day to day as best we can.'

'How many of you are living here?'

Yannis shrugged. 'Three, maybe four, hundred.'

'As many as that!' Doctor Stavros gasped, and wrote the figure down on his pad. 'Is there sufficient accommodation?'

'Of course not.'

'So where do you live?'

'In the houses and the church. The men are gradually rebuilding.'

'You're doing it yourselves?'

'Well, not building, more repairing.'

'So, if you're able to build your own house you can live in it, if not you're condemned to the church.' Doctor Stavros shuddered.

'Not at all,' Phaedra was quick to correct him. 'Yannis insisted that the first houses were occupied by at least one sick person who needed to be looked after, and the others had to help him with the next houses. Those who are in the church are the recent arrivals. You could go and talk to them, then you could visit the houses with Yannis.'

Doctor Stavros rose; he had eaten sparingly, but shared the jug of water with his companions, wiping the edge carefully with his sleeve before he placed it to his lips. He walked over to the church and pushed open the door. The heavy atmosphere of unwashed bodies, excreta and vomit met him like a wall. The people inside eyed him suspiciously, pulling their few, pathetic possessions towards them protectively.

The truth of the situation suddenly dawned on him. People were not sent here to survive. They were sent in the hope that they would die. His head was spinning and he felt as though it would burst as the full realisation penetrated his throbbing brain.

YANNIS

He stumbled out of the door, leaning against the jamb. This was against all humanity, worse than a jail, and these people had done nothing wrong. They were the innocent victims of illness and disease, victims he had sworn by his Hippocratic oath to serve to the best of his ability. As the mist before his eyes cleared he saw Yannis watching him.

'How long will those people stay in there?'

Yannis shrugged. 'That depends upon them. If the fittest are willing to help with some repair work it will only be a matter of weeks. If they think we're going to do it all for them they'll be there for ever.'

'It's a breeding ground for disease.'

'Tell them. They took no notice of me.'

'Then I doubt if they'll listen to me.' The doctor looked inside the church again. 'I can't work in there. If they want to see me they must come outside. In the meantime I'll visit some houses – if I may,' he added.

At each house the doctor knocked and waited until he was asked to enter and Yannis had to admit that his preconceived opinion of the man was changing. He seemed genuinely concerned with all he saw, asking for bandages to be unwrapped, probing for the amount of live nerve tissue in a limb, wanting to know if the symptoms had worsened recently. After each discussion he would make notes on the pad that he slipped in and out of his back pocket with regularity. Finally he admitted defeat.

'I can't possibly see everyone in one visit. Is there anyone who's in urgent need of a doctor?'

'What is the point of you seeing any of us? You'll go away, write your report, return again next year and ask us if we're feeling better.'

Doctor Stavros shook his head. 'You have my word that won't happen. I'm going to tell the authorities that you need medicine and more. You need a doctor over here permanently, a hospital, proper sanitation. It may take time, but I shan't let this rest when I return. You are people and the government has to treat you as such.'

A slow smile spread over Yannis's face. 'I wish you every success. I doubt very much that any one considers that we're people. As far as the rest of the world is concerned we no longer exist.'

Doctor Stavros spent three days writing a long and impassioned letter to the authorities, retiring each night exhausted in mind and body, appreciating his soft mattress and warm cover. Inadvertently he thought of those less fortunate on the island. He wondered how they kept themselves warm in the winter when he usually lit his stove or sat before the open fire in the kitchen, and where did they wash and dry their clothes? Questions ran riot in his brain each night until he finally slept, only to awake heavy eyed and tired.

Each time he visited the island he discovered fresh horrors that demanded a further letter of appeal to be sent to the authorities, stressing the need for urgent action. Despairing of ever having a reply he took his letter saying he was responsible for the island to the hospital and confronted the matron who looked at him curiously.

'The other doctor never had supplies from us. They must have been sent directly to him. We don't hold any great quantities of anything, in fact we've hardly any bandages since the priest bought so many.'

Doctor Stavros frowned. Who was this priest he kept hearing about? 'Where can I find him?' he asked.

'I've no idea. He just arrived one day, paid me an enormous sum for bandages and said I was to send to Heraklion for more and keep them until he called again.'

'You can't tell me any more about him?'

'He wasn't from round here. I think he said his name was Minos.'

YANNIS

Doctor Stavros felt he had come to a dead end. 'Are you able to let me have anything at all? You can mark it out to me and requisition for more to replace it.'

The matron cast her eyes down the list. 'I've some aspirin and a little morphine. I'm waiting for disinfectant. Would methylated spirits be any use?'

'Yes, anything that cleanses.'

'I'll get the caretaker to get a parcel ready for you. Come back tomorrow.'

With that Doctor Stavros had to be content. He must now decide which day he was going to visit the island each week and make a regular arrangement with Manolis. He sat on the sea wall and looked out across the bay, watching other fishermen return, sort their catch and hang their nets up to dry. There was no sign of Manolis and his boat was missing from its usual mooring place. A priest walked past, his companion not yet ordained, and scanned the boats eagerly.

'He's not back yet.'

'I can't wait. I'll have to get back or I'll be too late to beg for the day off tomorrow.'

Father Minos smiled. 'I'll arrange a time with Manolis and see you later.'

Father Minos sat on the wall and waited. There was nothing more he could do. It was far too late to think of going out to the island that day, better to wait for the fisherman to return and make an early start the following day. The man in the suit who was sitting a few yards away had taken a great interest in their conversation.

'Good day.' The man moved closer after Father Minos had greeted him.

'Good day to you. I couldn't help overhearing. I understand you are waiting to speak to Manolis, the fisherman?'

'I am.'

'Would you, by any chance, be the mysterious priest I keep

hearing about? The one who bought bandages from the hospital and who has sent out sand and cement to the island?'

Father Minos smiled. 'There's nothing mysterious about me, but I have had some dealings with those unfortunate people.'

Doctor Stavros held out his hand. 'I'm pleased to meet you. I'm Doctor Stavros. I've been placed in charge of the island.'

Father Minos shook the doctor's hand vigorously. 'You don't know how pleased I am to meet you. I went to Doctor Kandakis and he all but threw me out. All I wanted was permission to visit the island.'

'You've been before?'

'Twice. The first time I held a service from the boat, the second time I went ashore and met the people. They are so brave. My heart went out to them.' He watched the doctor cautiously. 'I have a dream, an ambition, but maybe it's not possible.'

The doctor looked at the priest enquiringly. 'Do go on.'

'I want to live with them, as part of their community, helping them with their daily life, giving comfort where I can.' The priest's face seemed to glow with an inner resolve.

'How does the Bishop feel about your ambition?'

'I've not approached him yet, but I intend to do so as soon as I return.'

'Have the medical authorities given you permission?'

'I thought I should ask the doctor in charge of the island first.'

Doctor Stavros shrugged. 'Who am I to say yes or no? If you have the necessary permission from the authorities I'll not stand in your way. In fact, you could be quite useful to me over there.'

'Useful? I know nothing about medicine,' Father Minos hastened to assure him.

'A priest has the confidence of his people. I've only visited the island a few times, and I was appalled at their conditions, but they seem somewhat hostile towards me. I want to do my best for them, but to do that they have to trust me. Maybe you could persuade them?'

YANNIS

'I could never betray anything told to me during a confession.'

'I would simply ask you to convince them that I have their welfare at heart.'

A boat rounded the headland and both men sprang to their feet and went to the edge of the quay. Manolis frowned as he moored his craft, expecting trouble.

'What's wrong?'

'Nothing,' replied Doctor Stavros. 'I merely wished to make an arrangement with you to take me to the island every Thursday.'

Manolis shrugged. 'If you wish.' He wondered if he dared to ask for an extra drachma each time he took the doctor, although he was being paid to ferry across the goods that Father Minos had ordered. He decided it was a legitimate request, as he would have to await the doctor's convenience before returning. 'I'll have to ask you to pay me for waiting time.' He flashed his teeth in a cheeky smile.

'How much?'

'I'll take you over and back for nothing, it will be one drachma for waiting for you.'

Doctor Stavros smiled. Manolis could have named a far higher price. He shook his head. 'I can't afford that every week. It's not my money, you understand. I have to account for everything I spend to the authorities and I don't think they've included a travelling allowance.'

Manolis pretended to consider also. 'It's my time. I may have to wait all day for you as I did before. Whilst I'm waiting I can't be earning.'

'We could arrange a time for you to come back for me. You could then go and fish.'

'Maybe, but suppose you wished to leave earlier?'

'I'd just have to wait. Fifty lepta, you drop me and collect me. No need to sit and wait.'

'Very well.' Manolis shook hands to seal the bargain. 'In advance.'

'In advance,' agreed the doctor, 'although where I would run away to I do not know.'

Father Minos was amused at Manolis's audacity, knowing he was being paid a drachma each time he took out a load of goods, and that left him ample time for fishing.

'I presume the same fee holds good for me? I'd like you to take me out tomorrow.'

Manolis grinned. He had charged a drachma before and the priest had not demurred. 'You drive hard bargains,' he complained. 'I'm only a poor fisherman.'

'At this rate you'll soon be a wealthy fisherman,' commented the doctor.

'I'll see you at seven. My young friend will be with me. Are you going to charge me extra for him?'

For a second Manolis dared to hesitate as if considering. 'Out of the goodness of my heart I shall pretend I did not see him.'

Father Minos shook his head in assumed despair. 'Seven,' he reminded Manolis and began to walk slowly along the quay. Doctor Stavros hurried after him.

'Please, come back to my house. I should like to talk to you.'

'Very well.' Father Minos had nothing more pressing to do and a few hours would have to elapse before he could meet Andreas again. He followed the doctor between the rows of fishermen's cottages and up the slight rise of the hill.

The island loomed into view, looking deserted as always when one approached, and to Manolis's surprise Flora was not on the quay to greet them. Father Minos and Andreas stepped ashore and walked through the arch. People looked up as they approached, shouting to each other that the priest was there and someone should tell Yannis.

'Where is he?' asked Andreas.

'Down by the fountain.'

They followed the path down to the square where they found

YANNIS

Yannis labouring with a mix of cement, the sweat pouring off him and the muscles in his arms straining. Andreas called to him.

'Yannis, what are you up to?'

Yannis grinned. 'What does it look like? I'll be with you when this mix is ready.' He continued to labour for a further quarter of an hour before wiping his face with his shirt and throwing himself onto a pile of sacks full of sand. He scanned the building where two men were applying a skin of cement to the stones that made up the side of the house.

'No, not like that,' he leapt to his feet. 'It must be thin.' He took the trowel from the man's hand and spread the cement out, covering twice the area, then handed it back. 'If they put too much on at once I'll be mixing again in no time.'

'How's it going, Yannis?'

'Slow and tiring. I shan't be able to make another mix for a couple of hours. You need two hands to work the shovel, so I'm a bit limited in my choice of workers. It's the same with everything we try. We haven't got the stamina. So many of them have a useless limb that I can't ask them to climb a ladder, so most of the harder work falls on the few. But we're winning. Come and see what we've done over here.'

Yannis led the way to a tall house that was still bare masonry interlaced with timber and sticks, the gaps plugged with slivers of stone. The windows were still open and the house unoccupied. Yannis led the way inside.

'Look,' he pointed towards the ceiling where joists had been laid to provide an upper floor. Father Minos and Andreas examined the structure. The room had been divided into three small units with the walls providing resting places for the thick timbers.

'We didn't have any longer lengths so we thought we'd try doing it this way. When we get some boards we'll floor it over and there'll be living quarters for about six.'

Father Minos nodded in appreciation. 'What made you think of doing that?'

'I'd been thinking about it for ages, but I didn't know how to go about it. We've just had some new friends arrive and a couple of them are going to be invaluable to us,' his eyes glowed with enthusiasm.

'Is that what you call new arrivals? Friends?' asked Andreas.

'Why not? We have to call them something. Come and see Panicos. He seems a good deal better since he started having goat's milk.'

They followed him to where Panicos was sitting in the early morning sun. He attempted to rise and they hurriedly motioned him to stay where he was. Father Minos sat down beside him; the man did look far fitter than when he had last seen him. By his side nestled a kid, Panicos stroking its head fondly.

'How's Mamma?' Yannis took the opportunity to ask Andreas.

'About the same; I haven't seen her myself, but Pappa goes each week.'

'Why so often?'

Andreas shrugged. 'I've no idea. Business he says. Did you get my letter?'

Yannis's face saddened. 'Poor Maria; poor Babbis, too. Why is life so unfair to some people?'

'I wish I knew the answer to that, Yannis.'

'What's happened to the baby?'

'I thought I said, Anna's looking after him.'

'Anna? Why? What's wrong with Babbis's mother?'

'He says it would be too much for her. Personally I think he blames little Yannis for Maria's death and can't come to terms with the child yet.'

Yannis pursed his lips. 'Poor little boy! Why did they call him Yannis?'

'It was Maria's choice. After you – and your Pappa,' added Andreas.

Yannis felt sentimental tears come into his eyes. 'Babbis didn't mind?'

'If Maria had asked him for the moon he would have tried to get it for her.'

Yannis nodded. 'He's a good man. How's Anna coping?'

'It's been hard, with your mother and the rest of the family to look after.'

'Poor little Anna! Her whole life has become one long round of looking after people.'

'She does enjoy it,' Andreas assured him. 'She's highly thought of in the village, now the Widow can't get about much.'

'Oh, well, so long as she's happy.'

'Stelios is going to school in Aghios Nikolaos in September.'

'Really? I hope he enjoys it and does well. What's happened to Mr Pavlakis - and Louisa?' he added.

'Father Minos would know more than I do about him.' Andreas beckoned and the priest walked over to them. 'Yannis was asking about Mr Pavlakis.'

Father Minos raised his eyebrows and looked quizzically at Yannis. 'He's quite a public figure now. A member of the local government and aiming to rise higher.'

'And Louisa?'

'She appeared well. She has a child, you know.' Father Minos watched Yannis's reaction to his words.

'Only one? I would have expected another by now,' answered Yannis calmly. 'Does she still work in the taverna?'

'So I understand, her brother's still there also.'

Yannis nodded. 'It all seems so long ago. Come up to Phaedra and Kyriakos. They'll be pleased to see you.'

'Where's Flora? Manolis seemed quite downcast when she wasn't there to greet us.'

Yannis's face became grave. 'Spiro's with her; she's very sick.'

'Her arm?'

'It's spread so suddenly. Spiro says it's only a matter of time. The silly little girl said nothing, and she must have been in pain for weeks.'

'Didn't the doctor see her when he came?'

'He doesn't have time to see everybody and she avoided him. I wish I knew what was going on. We're left alone for God knows how long, then suddenly a doctor visits us.' He turned to Father Minos, a look of terror in his eyes. 'What are they planning to do with us?'

'Do with you? Why, nothing.'

Yannis looked at the priest in disbelief. 'There's something going on.'

'If there is I hope it's for your good. When I left here I went to Doctor Kandakis. He was most unhelpful, so as soon as I was back in Heraklion I wrote to the authorities. I heard nothing, so I wrote again to the doctor who did not reply. I visited him yesterday and he said he'd resigned his responsibility for the island and had no idea who was in charge. I was waiting for Manolis to return when I bumped into Doctor Stavros.'

Yannis still did not appear convinced. 'I suppose Doctor Stavros talked about building hospitals, latrines and burial grounds?'

Father Minos smiled. 'He did and he's right. He thought I'd sent over sand and cement for you to build a church! He's a good man, Yannis, he has your interest at heart.'

'I thought he was just going to write another report for the authorities. I was surprised when he came again.'

'He's going to come every Thursday. I was there when he arranged it with Manolis.'

'Maybe he'll have some medicine for Flora when he comes,' suggested Andreas.

'Maybe. Let's go and have a look at her.'

The young girl was lying on a mattress in the house she now shared with Phaedra. Spiro looked up as the figures blocked the doorway.

'She's still delirious. You can't confess her until the fever breaks.' He mopped her forehead again with a damp rag.

Andreas plucked at the priest's sleeve. 'The doctor - Manolis would go.'

'Manolis has probably gone fishing.'

'I'll go and see. If he's still there I'll tell him he must fetch the doctor.' Without waiting for an answer he was gone, running up the path and down through the archway to the port. Manolis's boat was bobbing gently at the quay and Andreas gave a sigh of relief.

'Manolis! Manolis!'

His head turned, he had waited, hoping Flora would put in an appearance.

'We need the doctor,' gasped Andreas. 'You must get him. Tell him it's urgent.'

Manolis did not stop to question Andreas regarding his mission. He raised his hand as he cast off, hoping the wind would hold and wishing he had a motor engine. Andreas watched as the boat rounded the island and was lost from view. Slowly Andreas walked back to the house where the sick girl lay.

'He's gone,' he announced. Father Minos was on his knees beside Flora, holding his crucifix in his hands and praying fervently. Andreas joined him in his intonation, whilst Yannis crossed himself and left the house. He could be more useful elsewhere.

Phaedra climbed to the top of the island and scanned the horizon. She had reckoned without Manolis's common sense as she looked across the open sea. Manolis had started on the usual route and then remembered the canal. It was hard work taking the sails down and manoeuvring the shallow water on his own, but it would take almost an hour off his journey. He returned the same way, urging the doctor to lower his head to clear the concrete bridge.

He had repeated Andreas's message and urged him to hurry, fretting at the delay whilst the doctor visited the hospital to collect the parcel of medication that had been promised to him. To the doctor's enquiry regarding the patient Manolis could not help. He had no idea who the patient was and the doctor had a horrible suspicion that there had been an accident.

Phaedra stumbled down from the rocky plateau where she had been keeping watch and hurried down the path to where once again Yannis was supervising the cement skin to a house. 'There's a boat coming. It could be Manolis.'

This time Yannis did not hesitate, but followed Phaedra down to the quay where Manolis was just mooring. The doctor scrambled ashore, waiting until Manolis could hand up his bag and push a box on to the jetty for him.

'Who's my patient?'

'Flora. She has gangrene.'

'Flora!' Manolis face had paled and he leapt ashore. 'Where is she? Show me the way. Why didn't anyone tell me when I arrived this morning?'

'You can't go to her. She'll be all right. The doctor's here.'

'I'll show you. Follow me.' Phaedra pushed her way between the men and Manolis followed her gratefully.

'Tell me about this girl.'

Yannis picked up the box Manolis had left on the quay. 'Is this yours?' The doctor nodded and Yannis continued. 'She's not very old, maybe fifteen or sixteen. Her arm's been getting steadily worse, then her temperature shot up a couple of days ago and this morning she was delirious.'

'You're sure it's gangrenous?'

Yannis nodded.

'Why didn't you tell me? I'd have made her a priority when I was here. She's the little girl who greets the boats, isn't she?'

'She seemed all right and never complained.' Yannis pointed to Phaedra's house. 'She's in there. Spiro's with her.'

'I expect Manolis is also in there,' remarked the doctor grimly. He strode through the doorway and waited until his eyes became accustomed to the dim light. Removing his jacket and rolling his sleeves up above the elbows he knelt down on the earth floor and unwrapped Flora's arm. Spiro continued to sponge her forehead and Manolis was holding her other hand. Father Minos rose, signalled to Andreas and left the house for deep breaths of the fresher air outside.

'I can't see a thing,' complained Doctor Stavros. 'We'll have to carry her outside.'

Half dragging, half carrying the girl on the mattress they manoeuvred their burden through the doorway and deposited it on the ground outside. Examining the offensive arm in the sunlight the doctor was appalled that such neglect had been allowed to continue for so long. He looked around helplessly. Never before had he been confronted with such a situation. He walked over to where Yannis stood with Father Minos and Andreas.

'What do you want me to do?' he asked.

Yannis looked puzzled. 'Don't you know what to do? You're supposed to be a doctor.'

Doctor Stavros regarded him steadily. 'I know what to do, medically speaking. I can't guarantee she'll survive.'

'And if you leave her?'

'Maybe a week.'

Yannis rubbed his cement-caked hands down his trousers and looked at the priest, then to Manolis who was kneeling beside Flora, talking to her softly, although it was doubtful if she could hear him. Yannis swallowed hard.

'If it was me I'd like you to take the risk.'

The doctor nodded briefly and turned back to his patient. He lifted Flora's arm and she moaned in her delirium. The blackness of the dead flesh had spread above the elbow and down to her wrist. The discolouration giving way to a greenish bruising streaked with red.

'I shall need hot water, plenty of it.'

'I'll get Ritsa to help me. It will take some time.'

'Get it started,' the doctor answered Phaedra tersely. He

opened the box that Yannis had carried up from the quay and sucked in his breath. Only one bottle of morphine! He would need at least two for the operation. He examined the rest of the contents, two bottles of methylated spirits, six rolls of bandages, two bottle of iodine and a dozen bottles of aspirin.

'Has anyone any medication on this island?'

Yannis shook his head and the doctor sighed, wishing he had a bottle of raki with him. 'Go and wash, all of you,' he included Andreas in his directive. 'I shall need help.'

Doctor Stavros walked over to Father Minos. 'Father, tell me I'm doing the right thing.'

'My son, it's always right to try to save a life. You are the judge of your own capabilities, but God will guide you. The poor little girl is in His hands.'

'Pray for her.'

'I've done nothing else since we sent for you.'

The two men sat and waited until those who had gone to wash returned. Finally Phaedra returned with a shallow bowl of water.

'I need more than that, much more.'

'There's more coming. We haven't any large containers.'

'I need a stick, about that big, or a fork, that would be better.'

'I'll get one.' Phaedra re-entered the house and emerged holding a fork with a missing prong. The doctor eyed it suspiciously. It would have to do. Flora moaned and Doctor Stavros looked at her warily. Was her system strong enough to withstand the shock?

He gazed at the concerned faces before him. A short distance away a crowd was gathering. Word had spread that the doctor was going to save Flora and everyone wanted to witness the miracle.

'Father, take the people lower down and conduct a service, anything, just keep them away from here, Manolis also.'

The priest nodded, relieved. He had no wish to witness the operation that was about to take place. He had a sneaking feeling that his stomach would betray him. Andreas made to follow him, but the doctor called him back.

'I need your help, and you two,' her pointed to Yannis and Spiro. He waited until Phaedra had deposited two more bowls of water and was out of hearing before he continued. 'I'm going to amputate her arm. There's no other way. I don't know if I'll be successful, but it's her only chance.' He held up the bottle of morphine. 'I've only one bottle. It's not enough.' He looked at the three men, trying to sum up their strengths. 'You'll have to hold her.' His eyes rested on each of them in turn, their eyes looking back showing the fear they felt. 'You must do exactly as I say when I say. It isn't going to be easy.'

He received no answer, just three pairs of eyes gazing steadily back at him. Through the fear there was now determination showing. Doctor Stavros rolled up his coat and knelt on it, he then opened his bag and began to lie out an assortment of implements. Finally satisfied that all was ready he washed his hands in the boiled water.

'You,' he spoke to Spiro, 'at her head. You,' he pointed to Yannis, 'on that side and hold on tight, both hands. You,' he pointed to Andreas, 'hold her legs. If she really starts to buck you'll have to lay across her.' Silently the three men moved into the positions allocated to them. 'You'll do the morphine,' the doctor pointed to Spiro. 'Like this.' He gave a demonstration, then passed the bottle over. 'Start now and count to ten each time.'

Deftly the doctor tied a tourniquet around Flora's arm and inserted the fork. From his implements he selected a small surgical saw, holding it in the water along with a knife, reminding Yannis of a butcher. Calmly the doctor sliced through the skin on the upper arm, turning the fork swiftly as the blood welled to the surface. At the first cut Flora had stiffened and Spiro rapidly administered more morphine.

Doctor Stavros examined the raw flesh and shook his head. He placed the tourniquet higher up and re-inserted the fork. Again he cut into Flora's arm and examined the edges of the wound. This time he appeared satisfied and continued to cut more deeply. Despite the tourniquet the arm was bleeding freely and Doctor Stavros bit his lip. He should have had someone else to help.

'Hold that,' he ordered Yannis, who stretched his arm obediently across. He cut again, this time through muscle and sinew that was tougher than he had expected. Precious minutes were being wasted.

'How much is left?' he asked of Spiro.

'About half.'

Doctor Stavros nodded. As he had thought, it would not be enough. Reaching the bone he placed the knife in the bowl and took up the saw. The rasp of the blade set Yannis's teeth on edge and the effort brought out beads of sweat on the doctor's forehead which he wiped away impatiently with his arm. The grating noise continued and Yannis head began to throb in rhythm with the sound. Flora moaned and Spiro shook the bottle.

'That's it,' he announced.

'Hold her,' commanded the doctor.

He cut as swiftly as he could through the mass of pulpy flesh. Flora screamed. An ear-splitting, shattering, inhuman scream and it took all their strength to hold her. Each time she tried to wrench herself away the doctor had to stop and wait until she had calmed herself a little. Yannis was talking to her, he appeared to be telling her about his childhood, but the doctor was not really listening. With a sigh of relief he sliced away the last remnant of skin and tossed the limb aside. Liberally he applied methylated spirits to the raw area, which diluted the red blood, making it trickle away in pale pink rivers. Pinching together the open ends of the artery and veins he inserted stitches to keep them closed.

Between each stitch Flora sobbed and each time the needle was inserted she screamed and tried to drag herself away from the burning pain. Releasing the tourniquet Doctor Stavros watched carefully to see how much blood she was likely to lose, thankful to see very little seeping through. Once again he doused the wound with methylated spirits, pulled the ragged edges of skin together and sewed as rapidly as he was able. He removed the tourniquet completely and watched for any sign of bleeding. Satisfied that there would be very little blood loss he made a pad from a bandage, soaked it in iodine and placed it over the stump, bandaging it firmly into place.

As he finished he was suddenly conscious of eyes watching him and he looked up to see that he was ringed by silent lepers, Father Minos had been unable to keep them away from the scene any longer. Doctor Stavros rose to his feet.

'That's it. Ask one of the girls to give her a wash, then we'll take her back inside.'

Andreas moved slowly from his position at her legs, he felt stiff and cramped, thankful the ordeal was finally over. Yannis was finding it impossible to leave; Flora was holding his hand so tightly he could not release himself. Manolis came to his aid, prising the girl's fingers up, releasing Yannis and taking his place. Yannis rose, staggered to the side of the path, pushed his way through the silent watchers and was violently sick. He leant his head against the building, clutching his stomach and sweating.

Doctor Stavros picked up his jacket from the ground and looked at it ruefully. It was completely ruined, creased and covered in blood. He looked at his shirt and trousers. They were in the same state and would have to be thrown away; no amount of sponging would get the stains out. The throng of watchers still stood silently.

'Say something,' Father Minos hissed in his ear. 'They're uncertain of you.'

Doctor Stavros felt an insane desire to laugh rising up in him. They were uncertain of him! He took a deep breath to quell his hysteria. What could he say? What did they want from him? 'My friends,' his voice sounded weak and shaky. 'I have done my best.'

1931-1939

The crowd murmured sympathetically, then Christos's voice could be heard.

'Cut her up like a piece of meat on a butcher's slab.'

Doctor Stavros went white. 'I did what I had to do.'

'Poor little devil! I heard her scream. A butcher, that's what you are.'

Helplessly Doctor Stavros stood as people moved away from him and Christos, leaving them facing each other. Doctor Stavros dropped his eyes. He did not have the energy left for a confrontation.

'You don't deny it, then, butcher?' Christos limped forward.

'I did my best with what I had,' the doctor defended himself.

'Did your best,' sneered Christos. 'You cut off her arm whilst she was conscious and say that's your best! Why didn't you go back and get more morphine? Why didn't you take her back to the hospital with you, where she could have been treated properly?'

Doctor Stavros ran a trembling hand across his forehead. He lifted his head and looked at the menacing figure before him. 'I couldn't get any more morphine, that was all the hospital could spare.'

'Why didn't you take her back for proper treatment?'

'They would not have admitted her. Please, I'm very tired.'

'How would you like your arm cut off?'

'There's no need.' The doctor wished he had put away his knife and saw. He would be helpless in their hands. The grin on Christos's face and that of his cronies was most unpleasant. The doctor took a step backwards and felt a hand on his arm. He wheeled round to find himself looking at Spiro.

'Leave him to me.'

Doctor Stavros watched in horror as he saw Spiro advance, the knife that had been used earlier to sever the girl's arm in his hand. He waved it in Christos's face.

'Go home. Go home, or I'll cut your arm off and when I've

done that I'll cut off your leg. You won't get any morphine, not a drop. By the time I've finished with you, you'll be pleading with me to cut your throat!'

Christos held up his hand. 'Hold on, now. I didn't mean it.'

'Then apologise.'

Christos looked round for his friends, they had moved further back as Spiro approached. Spiro ran his deformed thumb along the blade.

'Apologise.'

By way of an answer Christos spat at Spiro's feet, turned and began to hobble away. In a flash Spiro had darted forward and kicked the crutch away from under Christos's arm, sending him sprawling. A string of obscenities came from his mouth as he struggled to rise and a ripple of amusement went through the watching people, removing the tension from the scene. Spiro walked back to Doctor Stavros and handed him the knife.

'Thank you,' he said quietly. 'I'll see to Flora now, then you'd better tell me what I have to do for her each day until you can come back.'

'Yes, of course.' Doctor Stavros was visibly unnerved by the recent scene. He looked down at his hands, still stained with blood. 'I'd like to wash.'

'Come with me.'

Yannis joined them. He had hurried down to the port as Christos had limped away and rinsed his hands and face in the sea. He removed his shirt, still covered in blood, and threw it to one side, sitting down beside the doctor.

'I'm sorry about that,' he apologised. 'I should have warned you that I haven't a very strong stomach.'

Doctor Stavros looked at him puzzled and Yannis went on to explain. 'I was sick.'

'There's no shame in that. I was sick the first time I saw an operation.'

'Really? I didn't think it affected doctors that way.'

'It's far worse to watch. When you're doing it you're concentrating and haven't time to think what it looks like. I doubt if I could have held her whilst you operated.'

'Will she recover?'

'I can't say. She won't die from gangrene, but she could easily die from shock. She was very brave.'

'She was conscious once the morphine ran out. She must have suffered agonies.'

'What were you talking to her about?'

Yannis frowned. 'I've no idea. I was just talking. I was probably trying to calm myself as much as her.'

'I have to apologise also.'

The doctor looked at Father Minos. 'Whatever for?'

'I couldn't keep them. As soon as she screamed they left me.'

'Human nature,' smiled Doctor Stavros.

'What are we going to do about Manolis?' Father Minos looked first at the doctor, then at Yannis.

'Who's Manolis?' asked Yannis, pursing his lips and looking up at the sky.

'Oh, you mean the boatman who went off fishing.' Doctor Stavros spoke very deliberately.

Father Minos sighed with relief. 'I'm so glad he spent his time profitably.'

'What would happen if the authorities knew?' asked Yannis.

'I've no idea. I shall send them a full report, telling them how Manolis came for me and then waited until I was ready to return.' Doctor Stavros rose. 'I'll look at my patient; then I'd like to return to the mainland. I do have other patients over there that I need to visit.'

Yannis rose with him. 'We do appreciate you coming so quickly – and what you did.'

Doctor Stavros smiled. 'That's what I'm for. Just don't make a habit of it. Save your problems for a Thursday, please.'

On his subsequent visits to the island Flora was his main concern. For ten days she had lain in a state of shock from which she appeared unlikely to recover, then she had murmured her first words to Phaedra, who had hardly left her side.

'My arm hurts.'

'It will a little, just at first.'

Phaedra was not sure if Flora had understood as she closed her eyes and appeared to be asleep. The next time she woke it was to complain of the pain in her fingers and Phaedra was seriously worried. The girl had no fingers to give her pain. When Doctor Stavros arrived that week he removed the dressing gently. The skin, pink and puckered, appeared healthy. He spoke to Flora gently.

'Can you hear me, Flora? Are you awake?'

Her eyelids fluttered open. 'It hurts,' she whispered.

'It will hurt, my dear, for another week at least, but the hurt will get less and the pain will go away as you get well.'

'What did you do? It hurt so much?'

'Your arm was badly infected. I had to remove the infection.'

Flora appeared to accept the explanation and closed her eyes again whilst her stump was re-bandaged. Doctor Stavros left the house with a feeling of accomplishment. The amputation had been successful and all the signs were that the girl would make a complete recovery from her ordeal.

Despite the fact that he had been successful in his treatment of Flora, two other women died, the disease creeping into their lungs until they could no longer breathe. Doctor Stavros could not get the incidents out of his mind. He had witnessed both deaths and their subsequent disposal, and for him it had been a horror that far surpassed anything else he had seen so far on the island. He wished he could talk to Father Minos, but the priest had returned to Heraklion, not mentioning again his desire to live on the island.

Flora continued to progress slowly and had become something

of a celebrity. Manolis sneaked onto the island to visit her whenever he could, ignoring her missing arm and assuring her she looked healthier than she had before. He brought her little presents, a scarf, handkerchief, a comb for her hair or a bunch of wild flowers. She thanked him for each one, delighting in his attentions, but the flowers enraptured her.

'They're beautiful,' she exclaimed, burying her nose deep into the posy. 'I hadn't realised how much I miss flowers.'

'Why don't you grow some?' suggested Manolis.

'Where would you grow flowers? There's nowhere on this rock that you could plant a seed and expect it to grow.'

'I'll bring you some every week,' Manolis promised. An idea had taken hold of his mind. He knew the other fishermen would laugh when they saw, but he would ignore that if he could bring pleasure to the crippled girl.

The sacks of sand and cement were no longer being sent over. Yannis had called a halt as the winter was approaching, not wishing to risk damaging his precious building materials, instead he had sent a message to Andreas to ask if more mattresses and blankets could be sent out. He inspected the houses thoroughly and declared himself satisfied that they should be watertight during the worst of the rain.

He consulted Spiro and Panicos about an idea that had come to him one night when he had been unable to sleep. He sat between the two men and spoke softly; he wanted no eavesdroppers.

'Suppose we asked each house to take an extra person for the winter? They'd have to be fit enough to help repair a house we haven't touched yet, and it would ease the congestion in the church.'

Panicos considered. 'Some of them could probably take two.'

'I don't want to push too hard. If they offered that would be different. It's the very sick no one really wants to be responsible for, not that I blame them. I wouldn't want some of them with me for very long. What do you think, Spiro?'

'I think we should forget building houses for a while.'

Yannis turned to him in amazement. 'Are you ill? I thought you'd become as enthusiastic as I am.'

Spiro grinned at him. 'It's hard not to be, but I think we ought to repair the hospital.'

'And who would look after the patients?'

'I would. Some of the others would probably help.'

'You're serious, aren't you, Spiro?'

'We'd be able to use the footings and a good deal of the masonry. If we could manage to get somewhere habitable to put all the chronically sick before the winter sets in it would give us a few more places in the houses. No one wants to be cooped up with someone who can't control their bowels, but they'll make room for someone who can look after themselves.'

Yannis viewed the sprawling ruins. 'If we did rebuild, how many do you think we could house?'

Spiro squinted; the sunlight was beginning to hurt his eyes. 'At least twenty, maybe thirty.'

'And how many chronic sick do we have? At least sixty! It seems a bit pointless.'

'No building will ever be pointless here! If we could get thirty in it would mean that the church was available for the rest and the conditions would be a lot better.'

Panicos had sat silently during the discussion. 'Do I count as chronically sick?' he asked.

'Of course not,' Yannis assured him.

'How ill do you have to be to be classed as "chronic" by you?'

'Someone who cannot move from their bed to perform nature's necessities, someone who has become blind and cannot manage to look after themselves, or someone who's mind has gone making them incapable.' Spiro ticked them off on his deformed hands before Yannis could answer.

'Then I think you should try to do it before the winter. If you tell people that the church occupants are going to be placed in their houses unless they help to build a hospital for them you'll have more volunteers than you can use.'

'More likely to have a riot on our hands,' Spiro was sceptical.

'We've left it late,' sighed Yannis. 'It's already September. The rain will start soon; then we shan't be able to move. Maybe it would be better to wait until spring.'

Panicos leaned forward. 'Yannis, think. The chances are that we shall have another six weeks of good weather. If you can get enough help you can finish the outside and have the roof on in a month. If you leave it until next spring there are going to be so many deaths from pneumonia and dysentery that people are going to ask if there's any point in building it at all.'

Yannis would not be convinced. 'Conditions were terrible last year. There was hardly any shelter at all. This year we're much better off.'

'And we could be better off still. How many are there working regularly on the houses?'

'Between thirty and forty, depending on how they're feeling.'

'Then that's at least thirty to work on the hospital.'

'It's not that simple. If we take all the men off the houses some of the necessary repairs won't be done before the winter, which means that some of the houses we'd counted on for shelter won't be available. Also, thirty people trying to work on one building would be falling over themselves, particularly at first.'

Spiro smiled. 'You're right there. I've got another idea. Why don't we call a meeting and explain that we want to repair the hospital and ask for volunteers? I'm sure most of the newcomers would help. Most of them are fitter than us anyway,' he ended with a touch of bitterness.

'Maybe we could ask Doctor Stavros to give them a medical and declare them fit enough,' smiled Panicos.

Yannis smiled with him. 'Actually that's not a bad idea. We could ask him to decide which are sick enough to need hospitalisation when the time comes and that would weed out the lazy who'd like to be waited on and looked after.'

'It would also make those go in who were stubborn and convinced they could still manage on their own.'

'So tomorrow we'll call a meeting,' insisted Spiro. 'We can start spreading the word tonight and have it early tomorrow morning.'

Yannis looked at the sea of faces before him. He was standing on a large block of stone that he and Spiro had pushed into the square. His mouth felt dry and he licked his lips nervously.

'Friends,' he began.

'Louder,' hissed Spiro.

'Friends,' he repeated. 'I asked you to come here so I could ask for your help. The winter will soon be here, and although some of you have houses that are weatherproof, a good many of you have not. There are two ideas I want to put before you. If you agree with both of them I'll ask you to move to this side.' Yannis indicated with his hand. 'And if you don't agree move to the seaward side.'

'What happens if we only agree with one?' called out someone.

'Stay in the middle,' called out Spiro.

'The first thing I want to ask for is volunteers to help repair the hospital for those who are unable to look after themselves.' Yannis waited for them to grasp the implications. 'The second thing I'm asking for is lodging. If each of you who have a watertight house could take one, maybe two extra people during the winter it would ease the situation in the church. In return your lodger would be expected to help with the maintenance or cleaning or something,' he finished lamely.

'How many would the hospital hold?'

'I'm not sure. We're aiming at thirty.'

'Who'd look after them?'

'Spiro has volunteered, and I hope some of you would be willing to help him.'

'Who would go into the hospital?'

'That would be decided by the doctor.'

The questions ceased and there was a shuffling in the square. To his delight he saw that most people has drifted to the left hand side and others were standing in the middle. Only Christos and his cronies had moved to the seaward side. Spiro had taken in the situation at a glance and began to go amongst the people standing in the centre asking them their objections. Whatever their concern he seemed to reassure them and gradually they moved to join their comrades. Yannis waited until Spiro returned to his side, then called again to his audience.

'I need volunteers to help with the hospital building. Not those of you who are working on the houses down here. We can't stop that yet.'

Yannis sat down upon the stone whilst the discussion was taking place. 'What was their problem?' he asked of Spiro.

'They seemed to agree with repairing the hospital, but they were a bit worried about who would be lodged in their house. I assured them they would be able to choose their companions.'

Yannis nodded. He wished Spiro had not told them they could choose whom they housed. It could lead to trouble later, although it had solved the present indecision. He felt weighed down by problems that he had never considered in the first flush of enthusiasm. He rose wearily from his seat.

'Come on, we may as well start.'

Leading the way up the hill Yannis wished with all his heart he could make the short trip across the water to his home, curl up in comfort on his mattress and sleep. The prospect ahead of him was daunting. A month to repair a building suitable to house at least thirty sick people! The men and women who had followed him looked at him expectantly, awaiting his directions.

'It would probably be easiest if you split into groups. Each group collecting stones and making piles here, there and there. As soon as you have a reasonable quantity you can start building

YANNIS

the wall. Remember you have to leave spaces for windows and the door, but it will take a while before you get that far. Have any of you built anything before?'

'I have. I was a builder.'

Yannis turned to him in delight. 'Thank goodness. Could you be in charge, do you think? You must know far more than I do.'

'I probably do, and I'll make sure this is the best building on the island, but I want something in return.'

'If it's possible,' promised Yannis.

'I want one of the ruins as my own house. I'll repair it, but I want it to be mine alone, no lodgers.'

Yannis frowned. 'That's a bit of a hard bargain when there are so many who need shelter.'

'I've a good reason.'

'So have the others for objecting to the arrangement,' argued Yannis.

The man's mouth set in a stubborn line. 'No house, no work.' He folded his arms and stood looking at Yannis defiantly.

'I'll talk to the others. It can't be my decision alone.'

'I thought you were in charge?'

Yannis shook his head. 'No one is in charge. We make decisions together.'

'That's not what I've heard. It's all 'ask Yannis, Yannis will tell you, Yannis knows'.'

Yannis walked back to Spiro. 'I've got a problem. Our friend over there, whose name I still have to find out, wants a house of his own, without lodgers, in exchange for his work.' Spiro pursed his lips and Yannis continued. 'And what's more, he says everyone considers that I'm in charge. I don't like that.'

'You have become sensitive suddenly,' grinned Spiro. 'Someone has to tell them what to do, so why not you?'

'I think it would be better if other people made decisions as well. I only see my side. They would see things in a different light and would probably come up with some good ideas.'

Spiro nodded. 'I can see what you're getting at, but it could mean hours of wrangling before anything ever gets done. At least if it's just you it saves time and energy.'

'I don't want to be a dictator, and it appears I've become one,' remarked Yannis gloomily.

'Cheer up. We can talk about this later. We ought to solve the immediate problem first. Give the chap a house. By the time he's finished repairing it we probably shan't need to ask anyone to take in lodgers.'

'That's possible. You think it's all right, then?'

'We want a hospital, don't we? He wants a ruin; let him have it. If he's as good as he says we will get the best of the bargain.'

Yannis returned to where the man stood waiting. 'It's agreed. You can have a house, but you have to supervise the building of the hospital in return.'

'That's fair,' he grinned. 'I'm Takkis.'

'Well, you know who I am. Shall we start?'

'I'm in charge, you say?'

Yannis nodded. 'You're the builder.'

'Then I suggest you go back down to the main area and supervise whatever's going on down there. You'll be more use there than up here carting stones. If I come across a problem I'll let you know.'

Yannis turned away. He felt crestfallen and subdued. Takkis had made it more than clear that he was not needed.

Father Minos was annoyed and frustrated. For three years now he had been writing to the medical authorities requesting permission to live on Spinalonga. His first letters had been ignored, then finally he received a reply that told him he was free to visit Spinalonga whenever he wished, but on no account could he stay over night. It was explained to him in very simple wording that if he were given permission to live there others might want to do the same and those who were free from the disease could not be forbidden the mainland, hence the island would no longer be an isolation colony and the disease would spread unchecked. He screwed the letter up in disgust and threw it towards his rubbish bin. He could not envisage anyone else wanting to make a home on the island. If only he could convince the authorities that the people there needed him. Feeling dejected he walked into his church and knelt before the altar. He let the peace spread over him until he felt suitably composed to go to the hospital on his regular weekly visit.

Sadly he wandered down the mean back streets, passing the time of day with those parishioners he met, admiring a new baby, inquiring after the health of a relative he knew was sick. He was obviously destined to spend the rest of his life in this dull routine that at one time had seemed so attractive. His ministrations to the sick finished he began to retrace his steps towards his home. His attention was caught by a woman who stepped from a doorway and approached a passing youth who smiled at her and shook his head. She caught at his arm and seemed to be trying to persuade him; again he refused, pulled his arm free and walked on. She spat after him in derision and looked along the street to where a middle-aged man stood, obviously trying to get his bearings. It was obvious to Father Minos that the girl was prostituting herself and he hurried forward. He must talk to her; try to persuade her that there were better ways to earn her living. The words died on the priest's lips as he recognised the woman before him.

'You're Louisa, surely, from the taverna.'

She gazed back at him defiantly. 'What is it to you?'

'I couldn't help noticing that you were stopping men who walked this way.'

'Is that a crime?'

'That could depend upon your reason for stopping them.'

Louisa smiled. 'What a very suspicious mind you have for a

priest! I was merely asking if they had seen my husband.'

Father Minos raised his eyebrows. 'Have you lost him? He's quite a public figure these days.'

'I need to give him a message.'

'What made you think he might be in this area of the town?'

'I've looked everywhere else.' Louisa shrugged her shoulders and began to stroll down the road. She might as well return to the taverna. By the time she had shaken off the priest it would be time to collect Anna from the old woman who looked after her during the day. 'I could ask why you are in this part of the town,' she shot a glance at the priest.

'I've been to the hospital. I visit regularly to give what little comfort I can to the sick.'

Louisa nodded. She was not really interested in his purpose; she wanted to turn his attention away from herself. 'I'm sure they appreciate you.'

'I like to think so. I feel I could do more good elsewhere.'

'Why is that?'

'There are a number of priests here who could take over my duties. They have no priest on Spinalonga.'

The word seemed to send an icy hand to clutch at her heart. 'That's where they send the lepers, isn't it?' She knew the answer to her question, but felt obliged to feign ignorance.

'Yes. I'm surprised you should be uncertain. Your husband must talk to you about the role he plays in the government. It was quite a big issue in Athens when the inmates of the hospital rebelled. I'm sure your husband must have told you of the decision to send a number of them to the island of Spinalonga.'

'He probably did, but I doubt if I took much notice.'

'I'm surprised. The last time I spoke to you I was under the impression that Yannis was the father of your child.'

Louisa lowered her eyes. 'He may be.'

'Have you ever taken her for a blood test?'

'Anna is perfectly healthy.'

'I'm glad to hear it. It does leave one little problem, I think. If Yannis is not Anna's father, as you assured me he was earlier, then there is a bill due to his father. Would it be convenient for me to call for it tomorrow?'

Louisa bit her lip. She was trapped. She thought rapidly. 'Yannis is Anna's father. I have just preferred to forget the whole incident, hence my lack of interest in the whereabouts of Yannis. I would not want my daughter tarnished by the association.'

Father Minos nodded. 'I understand. In fact I am much clearer in my mind about the whole situation. I am so pleased I met you. I turn off here, but I will escort you a little nearer to the centre if you wish.'

'There's no need,' Louisa assured him. 'It's possible that my husband has returned home by now. It was foolish of me to think I would be able to find him. He could be anywhere.'

'Of course; good day.' Father Minos watched as she hurried round the corner. Her plausible excuses had done nothing to allay his suspicions that she had been accosting men for her own purpose that afternoon. He accused himself of being un-Christian, yet he could hardly visualise Yannis forcing himself upon the girl as she claimed.

Thinking of Yannis turned his thoughts back to the island. Maybe if he approached Yiorgo Pavlakis he could get a little nearer to his goal. The medical authorities could not refuse him if he had permission from the local government. He hoped his housekeeper had not tidied his room and thrown away the letter he had discarded so thoughtlessly.

Yiorgo Pavlakis read again the crumpled letter from the medical authorities. 'I don't understand why you can't be content with this.'

Father Minos sighed. 'Most people meet their death in the early hours of the morning. That's when I am most needed. If I was declared the official priest I would be able to live on the island tending to the people's spiritual needs daily.'

Yiorgo Pavlakis pushed back the lock of hair that persisted in falling into his eyes. 'You would have to get that concession from your Bishop.'

'I know that, but if I had an endorsement from the local government it could help my plea.'

'Suppose you accepted this as a temporary measure? You could move to the vicinity of the island and continue to write to the authorities.' There must be a simple solution to the problem that would satisfy the priest and send him happily on his way.

'How would I live? I would have to pay for my accommodation and food without the income from a parish.'

'Your friends on the island would surely pay for you if they are in such need of a priest.'

'They have no money.'

'Surely, between them, a small contribution each.'

Father Minos shook his head. 'They have no money. I mean literally nothing. The first time I visited the island I was appalled that human beings should be expected to live like – like – animals.'

Yiorgo frowned. 'I feel sure you are exaggerating. How do they buy their food if they have nothing?'

'The Lasithi prefecture pays the local farmers to send out produce. They are entirely dependent upon charity.'

'Why don't they write to their relatives and ask for help?'

'How can they? They are not allowed to write letters. The boatmen unload the produce on the quay and when they have left the lepers come down to collect it.'

'Then surely one could take a message to their families?'

Father Minos sighed in exasperation. Was the man being difficult or was he just stupid? 'Many of them come from mainland Greece. It would be impossible.'

'I really do not see that giving you permission to live on the island would make a great deal of difference to these miserable people. I respect your calling. It is a very honourable thing you have in mind, but somewhat impractical.' Yiorgo held up his hand, as the priest was about to interrupt. 'You say these people have nothing. Have you considered that you might be a liability to them? The food sent by the government would have to be shared with you. A house would have to be built and furnished for you. Why should you have a house if they are living in ruins? You would soon lose their good will if you were treated differently from them, yet you are not a leper so the government would have to treat you differently.' Yiorgo sat back with a smile. Surely this naïve priest would see the sense of his argument.

Father Minos shook his head. 'I would not expect to live differently from my neighbour. The houses are being rebuilt or repaired. I would be content to wait my turn.'

'How are they rebuilding? I thought you said they were penniless and sick?'

'Some are reasonably fit, but will gradually deteriorate as the disease progresses. The fittest are working on the repairs.'

'And where are these people getting the money for materials? Their labour may be free, but it costs money to build a house.'

'A good deal is being re-used. They are dismantling some of the unsafe buildings and using the stones and timber.'

Yiorgo Pavlakis pushed back his hair. 'Very creditable and ingenious. Do they get all their requirements from these ruins?'

'Most of them.'

'And the others?'

'They are bought from the mainland.'

Yiorgo held up his hand. 'You said 'bought', did you not?'

'Yes.'

'Suddenly penniless people are able to buy things. That is interesting.'

'I did not say they were buying them.'

'Then who is?'

Father Minos took a deep breath. 'When I visited the island I found Yannis had been sent there. It's due to him that they're rebuilding. He's done wonders for their morale. As soon as I told his family he was there his father gave me a sum of money. I used a good deal for bandages, but there was some left over.'

'Yannis? The Yannis I taught? Who lived here?'

Father Minos nodded.

'What a waste! What a waste of a brain and a career.' Yiorgo shook his head sadly and pushed back his hair. 'Is there any way I can help him?'

'By obtaining permission for me to live there as their priest.'

Yiorgo Pavlakis threw back his head and laughed. 'We've already been through that, and I asked how I could help Yannis, not you.'

'By helping me you would be helping Yannis, and everyone else on the island.'

Yiorgo shook his head. 'I doubt that my word would carry very much weight. I feel it would be best for you to approach your Bishop; he could probably apply more pressure than I. What I could try to do is gain a small allowance for you.'

'I am in no need of an extra allowance.'

'I did not mean for you personally. I was thinking of an extra allowance that could be used for the sick. To provide them with some small luxuries.'

'Luxuries!' Father Minos could hardly believe his ears. 'Didn't you hear a word I said? They don't want luxuries, they want what you and I accept as necessities - a pair of socks or a blanket. To them a luxury would be a cigarette or a glass of wine.'

Yiorgo had paled under the vehemence of the priest's outburst. 'But surely the government provides them with those essentials along with their food?'

Father Minos shook his head. 'From the money Yannis's father and uncle gave me I've been able to buy blankets and mattresses, but as fast as I purchase them they need more. I can't keep pace. They need cooking utensils, clothes, soap, you name it, they need it.'

'Have none of them any money?'

'When they entered the hospital they gave all the money they had for their treatment. None was ever returned to them. Their belongings were sent with them, but no money.'

Yiorgo Pavlakis pushed his hair back from his eyes and wiped his hand down the side of his trousers. 'It was probably used up in medical expenses.'

'I'm sure a good deal of it was, but what of the remainder? Maybe you could make a few enquiries?'

'Have you made any?'

'I've tried to trace some that I thought could be owing to Yannis or his father.'

'Did you have any luck?'

'No.' Father Minos did not think he should mention that it was Yiorgo's wife and brother-in-law who owed the money in question. 'The hospital might be a little more forthcoming with you than it was with me.'

Yiorgo nodded. 'I can certainly try for you. It may take a little time. I'm rather a busy man, you know.'

'Of course, and I've already taken up far too much of your time today. I appreciate your offer of help. Maybe if I came again in a month?'

Yiorgo Pavlakis nodded absently. He was wondering just how much of the money would have been used in medical expenses and how much he could expect to be recompensed for finding the residue. Political campaigns were always in need of funds. There was another election due in six months and he very much wanted to be in charge of the prefecture, maybe, with sufficient funds at his disposal, he could present himself as a philanthropist and gain the votes of the people.

He sat gazing morosely into his glass of wine. He needed something that would endear him to the people of Heraklion, something that would ensure they elected him their Mayor. Maybe if the populace thought he was concerned with the welfare of the lepers they would be impressed. Many of them would have relatives who were suffering and it would hearten them to know they had voted for a man who had promised to alleviate some of their misery. He called to Louisa to come and sit with him and told her of his idea. She shrugged as he tentatively put the outline of his plan before her.

'I can't see why you want to concern yourself with them.'

Yiorgo twisted his glass between his fingers. 'I feel somewhat guilty that I didn't try to find Yannis when he disappeared so suddenly.'

'If he'd wanted us to know he would have told us.'

'I don't think he wanted to put us in an embarrassing position. He wanted to spare us that. I gathered from the priest that they are completely destitute, dependent upon the government for every necessity.'

'Why can't their families look after them?'

'From what I understand in many cases their families don't even know they've been sent to the island. They're not allowed to send letters or have any visitors except the priest.'

'I can't imagine anyone wanting to visit them!'

'Wouldn't you want to visit me if I were sent there?' Yiorgo reached for his wife's hand. 'I'll talk to Father Minos again and see if he can give me any idea of the best way to approach the problem. Tomorrow I'll see if I can find any trace of the money he mentioned.'

Louisa looked at Yiorgo sharply. 'What money?'

Yiorgo waved his hand airily. 'He said they had given money to the hospital when they were admitted, but had never had any returned to them. I promised I would look into the accounts, but I doubt that I'll find anything amiss. Now, I shall need you down in the taverna this evening. I've some important people coming to talk to me and I'd like Pavlos to join us.'

With a resigned sigh Louisa agreed. She had planned an early night, expecting Yiorgo to be out, now it was doubtful if she would be able to retire before the early hours of the morning.

The men, when they arrived, were unknown to her. They sat quietly at the tables whilst she served them and waited until she had retired to the kitchen area before they bent their heads closer and conversed in undertones. Three times Yiorgo called to her for further supplies and each time she approached with the bottles the conversation stopped. To her surprise they began to take their leave early, slipping away in ones and twos, until only her husband and brother were left. She collected the glasses and began to wash them noisily.

'You had no need of me,' she complained to Yiorgo. 'I could have left the bottles on the counter for you to help yourselves and washed up in the morning.'

'I wanted my friends to see that my wife supported me. It was more important than you realise.'

'Who were those men, anyway? They weren't your usual friends who come to talk politics with you.'

'I can't tell you that. Forget that you saw any of them. Go to bed now. It's late and I have more work to do.'

Sulkily Louisa retired to their room. Since their marriage, Yiorgo had become more engrossed in politics, and although still enamoured of his wife, spent less time with her. Normally his neglect did not worry her, but she objected to being shown off and made to stay up without being told the true reason. Sleep had still not come to her when Yiorgo arrived, undressed quietly and slipped into bed beside her.

'Who were those people, Yiorgo?' She asked again.

Yiorgo smiled in the darkness. The curiosity of women! 'They are people I work with, they're all interested in the present European scene and we wanted to discuss its implications.'

'What do you mean?'

'We have heard some disturbing reports from Germany, the trouble there seems to be rippling outwards. It will probably not reach us, but we want to be ready should it do so.'

'What will you do then?'

'That, my dear, you need not concern your pretty head over. I've already told you far more than I should have done. I'll be late for work if you don't let me get some sleep now.'

With that Louisa had to be content. As she lay in the darkness Yiorgo's rhythmical breathing turned into a snore and she realised he was in a deep sleep.

Yiorgo was up and had left the taverna before Louisa was awakened by their daughter. He made his way to the home of Father Minos and slipped a note into the box beside the door, announcing his intention to call that evening. He must obviously appear to be more interested in the prospect of improving conditions for the lepers than in furthering his career.

Father Minos greeted him with a glass of wine and offered olives and nuts before sitting and waiting for Yiorgo to tell him the purpose of his visit.

'I've been thinking about the lepers. I'd like to know more.'

Father Minos raised his eyebrows. 'With what purpose in mind, may I ask?'

'I may be in a position to send aid, but I would have to lay as much information as possible before a committee to persuade them of the necessity of such an action.'

The priest nodded. 'What kind of help did you have in mind?'

'That's where I need your help. You would have to tell me what they needed most. I'm talking of something of a permanent nature that would benefit everyone, not a crate of wine or consignment of cigarettes.'

'I see. What you really want is to send something that will always be associated with your name.'

'Oh, no, no,' Yiorgo assured him hastily, feeling the priest had the ability to look inside his mind. 'When I say something permanent I mean of permanent benefit to them all, that will continue for them long after I'm gone and forgotten.'

Father Minos placed the tips of his fingers together. 'So many things spring to mind, but none of them of a permanent nature exactly. You could guarantee a supply of bandages for a specific number of years, or a mattress and blanket for everyone, but I feel that's not quite what you have in mind.' Father Minos refilled his guest's glass. 'Maybe you would care to visit the island as you wish to become a benefactor?'

Yiorgo paled visibly. 'I'd not thought of going there myself. I have a wife and daughter to consider.'

'I don't think any great harm would come to you if you visited. You spent a number of years in Yannis's company with no ill effects. You see, if you visited the island I think it could give the people there a tremendous boost. They would know that the outside world had not forgotten them, that there were men like yourself willing to improve their conditions, and you would also be able to judge for yourself the kind of aid you would most like to give.'

Yiorgo hesitated and the priest pressed home his advantage. 'Remember, when you ask for other people to support your idea you will be able to speak with first hand knowledge.' Again Yiorgo hesitated, allowing Father Minos to press his point further. 'I'm sure the people of this town and the surrounding area would be impressed with a leader who puts the welfare of others before all else. They will know they can have faith in you to have their best interests at heart and will trust you.'

'I hadn't thought of it like that.'

'Then you should. There is nothing like personal example.'

'That's true.'

'Then shall we arrange a little trip together? I'd planned another visit in a few weeks. Provided I can give my parish enough notice the date is immaterial to me.'

Yiorgo felt himself trapped. He took a little black notebook from his pocket and consulted it. 'I have many pressing engagements. Maybe five weeks from today?'

Father Minos consulted his own little book. 'Excellent. Shall we enter it as a definite arrangement? I'll contact you before then to see if you have made any progress regarding the money taken to the hospital. Maybe you could take them some very good news if you were able to locate any funds due to them.'

The day of the proposed visit dawned all too soon for Yiorgo Pavlakis. The weather was overcast, threatening rain and he hoped it would be too rough for them to visit the island. He sighed. No doubt the priest would insist upon staying down there until the weather changed. As he kissed Louisa goodbye he felt a pang of conscience as he lied to her.

'I hope to be back tomorrow. I have to visit Rethymnon with some of my colleagues. Don't worry if we're delayed. Rest assured I'll hurry back to you as soon as possible.'

'I'm sure you will.' Louisa lifted her face to receive his embrace dutifully. Two whole days with him away could make quite a difference to the savings she was gradually accumulating. There was sure to be a ship in and those who had been denied shore leave would queue up for her and pay double her usual asking price.

Travelling down to Aghios Nikolaos with the priest brought back memories to the schoolteacher. He wondered if he should visit his old landlady and decided not to bother. He had invited her to his wedding as he had promised, but since then he had ignored her.

The weather worsened during the bus journey and Yiorgo thought it most unlikely they would be able to visit the island that day and return to Heraklion the next. By the time they drew into the terminus it was raining and gusty winds were driving the occupants of the town under cover. Yiorgo Pavlakis drew his overcoat closer to him and shivered.

'We might as well return on the next bus,' he complained. 'It's doubtful if we'll get over there today, or even tomorrow by the look of this.'

'We'll see. You know how fickle the weather is here. It could clear in an hour.'

Yiorgo followed the priest down the familiar streets to the quay. To Father Minos's delight and Yiorgo's dismay, Manolis's boat was in its usual mooring. The priest looked around for the young man who was nowhere in sight. Father Minos moved from boat to boat, Yiorgo following miserably in his wake, until he ran the boatman to earth playing cards in a cabin. He gave them a delighted grin.

'You want me to take you over? Give me five minutes to finish winning this hand and I'll be ready.'

Yiorgo Pavlakis, standing in a position where he could see Manolis's hand of cards, thought his chances of winning slender indeed. It was with good grace the fisherman pushed his money across the box that was serving as a table and accompanied the two men back to his boat.

The journey was rough, although they went through the shallow canal, keeping in the shelter of the land for as long as possible before sailing across the bay to the island. Yiorgo looked with interest as they approached, trying to ignore the knot of fear that had settled in the pit of his stomach.

'I only wish to talk to Yannis,' he told Father Minos. 'I'm not interested in a tour of the sick.'

Father Minos nodded. He was beginning to wonder if he had made a mistake in bringing the school master politician to the island in the first place. The quay was deserted and Father Minos led the way through the arch. Once on the pathway he stood and called loudly until Ritsa appeared.

'I've brought someone to see Yannis,' Father Minos explained. 'Do you know where he is?'

'Probably in his house if he has any sense. You know where it is.'

Father Minos nodded and led the way to the tiny house that Yannis still shared with Spiro and Kyriakos. He knocked on the door and Yannis appeared, a look of disbelief on his face when he saw his former teacher and friend. Having been assured that Yiorgo was only visiting, he apologised for the spartan interior and offered Yiorgo a place on his mattress, whilst Father Minos went to visit the islanders.

'This is a pleasure. I never thought to see you again. How are you – and Louisa?'

'We're fine.' Yiorgo sat down gingerly on the mattress. 'How are you?'

Yannis shrugged. 'As well as can be expected.'

'Why didn't you tell us?'

'How could I? I could hardly believe it myself. I didn't want anyone to know. I was so ashamed and frightened. Why have you come?'

'I've been talking to the priest and he suggested I might be able to help you. I carry some weight in political circles now.'

'Me personally, or all of us?'

'All of you.'

Yannis smiled. 'I'm glad of that. I couldn't accept help just for myself. We're like a family here, most of us. We try to share what we have and help each other.'

For a few minutes the two men looked at each other in silence. Yiorgo noticing the blemishes and nodules that stretched from ear to brow of his ex-pupil where the disease was spreading unchecked, Yannis saw little difference in Yiorgo, a few grey hairs, but apart from those he was unchanged.

'What kind of help do you have in mind?'

'I need you to tell me that.'

Yannis turned to Spiro. 'Any ideas?'

Spiro joined them on the bed. 'I think we need a few more details. Do you have any money at your disposal? Do you have any sway with the medical authorities?'

Yiorgo shook his head. 'The answer is no to both those questions. As a politician I can approach the medical authorities and suggest, possibly even pressurize a little, but I've no power at all. What I have in mind is a project of some sort that would find favour with the ordinary people so I could squeeze some money from the treasury.'

'What kind of figure are we talking about?'

'I can't tell you that. It would depend upon what you wanted. It would be no good asking for too much, I'd be turned down out of hand.'

'Let's list the things we most need; then you can take your pick. Visits from our family and friends would be first on my list.'

Yiorgo shook his head. 'I can't see me being able to do anything about that for you. What about those who come from Greece? Who would pay for them to visit a relative or friend? Besides, you said you wanted something everyone could share or benefit from. Some people might not have any relatives.'

'I haven't.' Kyriakos spoke for the first time.

'What about books?' suggested Yiorgo.

'Some people can't read,' Yannis pointed out.

'New clothes?'

'That could be difficult. We're all different sizes. Some of us need trousers, others pullovers. If we asked for clothes they'd probably send dresses for the women and nothing for the men.'

'We could ask a boatman to buy them for us from the mainland,' Spiro pursued the idea.

'What are we going to buy them with?' asked Yannis. 'You know what it's like to get money back from the government. They would have to wait months before they were sent any money, by that time we'd probably need something else.'

'That's it.' Yiorgo slapped his knee and pushed back the lock of hair from his eyes. 'Money. I ask the government to give you a sum of money.'

Yannis and Spiro looked at him puzzled, whilst Kyriakos muttered something unintelligible beneath his breath.

'They'd never agree. There are about four hundred of us here.

What kind of sum are you thinking of? Even five drachmas each would come to an enormous amount – and five drachmas wouldn't go very far.'

Yiorgo shook his head. 'I'm not talking about that kind of money. I'm talking about a regular amount, every month, that you could spend or save as you wanted.'

The three men sat and considered the idea. 'It sounds good,' Yannis agreed cautiously. 'How would you go about it?'

'I haven't worked out the details. I'll need time to think and plan.'

'Are we sure everyone would want it?' asked Spiro.

'Why not? It's the best idea we've come up with and it would benefit everyone.'

'I think we ought to give it more thought, maybe ask some of the others.'

'No, it's Yiorgo's idea and I think we should leave it at that. If we start to ask everyone we'll never get anywhere. I don't think we should even tell them until we hear that it's definite. It would only raise their hopes and cause unrest. Think what it could mean to us. We'd be able to ask the boatmen to buy us what we wanted, or we could save it, or even gamble, but it would be ours to do just as we pleased with.'

'Yannis is right,' agreed Kyriakos. 'I hate beans. Think how many times I have to eat them because nothing different is sent. I'd be able to buy courgettes.'

'I shall need some facts. How many of you are living here, your names and ages, probably which hospital you came from originally.'

'That should be easy enough. Send a message to my cousin when you want them, he'll pass it on to Manolis who'll bring it to us. We could make a start and have the information ready for you.'

Yiorgo nodded. 'I can't promise anything, you realise that, but I'll do my best. Has the weather improved at all? We should be getting back.'

'I doubt if either of them will be ready yet. Father Minos always sees everyone, if only for a moment, and Manolis would stay for ever.'

'Why?'

'Well, Father Minos feels it's his duty and having made the journey he wants to feel it was worth his while I suppose.'

'No, I mean, the boatman. Why should he want to stay?'

'He's somewhat keen on one of the women,' smiled Yannis.

'A leper woman!' exclaimed Yiorgo in horror.

'Why not?'

'Well, it's not right.'

'Why shouldn't it be? If she had anything else wrong with her you'd admire him for ignoring her disability. Tell me about Heraklion,' said Yannis, more from a desire to change the subject than from any true interest. Heraklion seemed so far removed from him that it could have been the other side of the world.

Yiorgo launched upon a description of his latest political ideas for the betterment of the community until Yannis regretted ever asking his original question.

'How's Louisa?' he managed to ask at last.

'Louisa? Oh, Louisa's fine. She is so beautiful. Each time I look at her …'

'And your baby?'

'She is as beautiful as her mother. The same nose and eyes. I can't wait for her to get a little older. I plan to teach her to read and write. I'm sure by the time she is old enough they will be accepting girls at the University. She will not only be beautiful, but well educated also.'

'How old is she now?'

'Old? Oh, five, I think. I'm not very good on things like that. Her mother reminds me when it's birthday. Now, as I was saying ……'

'Please, Yiorgo, don't talk to me about politics. I never did follow them and we're so cut off here that they're no longer relevant. Talk to me about Knossos, or the museum or school. Things I can relate to.'

Yiorgo looked at him puzzled. 'I haven't had time to go to Knossos or the museum. There's nothing of interest to talk about regarding the school.'

'What about the friends I had when I was there? Do you ever see any of them? What are they doing now?'

'I've no idea.' Yiorgo was unhelpful and beginning to feel uncomfortable without his cushion of politics upon which he depended for conversation. 'Do you think we should find the priest? Maybe he's ready.'

Yannis smiled. 'I'm sorry, Yiorgo. It's just that life over here is so – so –' he searched for the right word, 'isolated, self-contained. We're far more concerned about a new eruption on our skin than we would be about the fall of a government. One affects us, the other doesn't.'

'No, no, it's my fault. I tend to become so absorbed and I forget that not everyone else has the same interest.' Yiorgo's eyes roved around the small building. 'Do you all live in houses like this?'

'No. Most of us live in the old Turkish or Venetian ones that we've patched up. I just happen to have this one.'

'Yannis built it himself.' Spiro grinned with pride in his friend.

'You built it? Whatever for if there are others?'

'It was to prove a point.' Yannis was embarrassed and frowned at Spiro who ignored him.

'Yannis built it to prove that we were a lazy, idle lot of ruffians and also that it could be done. He's far too modest. He's gone so far as to say that he will live here until the last man and woman has a house of their own.'

'I know which one I want eventually. It has great potential. I'll show it to you as we look for Father Minos.'

Yiorgo rose. That was all he had wanted to hear for over an hour. 'I'd like that.'

'This way,' Yannis directed.

'The priest is up there,' Yiorgo indicated the dark robed figure.

'I was going to show you the house I'm interested in.'

Yiorgo stopped, but did not follow Yannis. 'Which one?'

'That one,' Yannis pointed.

'Very nice,' murmured Yiorgo. 'Very nice, I'm sure.'

Yannis felt deflated. From where Yiorgo stood he could hardly see the house. Silently he led the way to where the priest was standing, surrounded by people, despite the rain and the cold wind that blew gustily. Yiorgo pulled the collar of his overcoat closer to his neck.

'Why don't they put their coats on?' he asked. 'They'll catch their deaths if they stay out in this for long.'

'They don't have coats.' Yannis looked Yiorgo straight in the eyes as he made his statement. 'And some of them would probably be quite pleased to go to their deaths.'

Yiorgo shifted uncomfortably. 'We should go,' he muttered. 'It could be too rough to make the return journey soon.'

Yannis nodded. At least Yiorgo was right about that. 'Stay here. I'll find Manolis.'

Manolis was not difficult to find. He was with Flora, talking to her urgently whilst she bit at her lip in indecision. Yannis cleared his throat.

'The weather's worsening, Manolis. You ought to leave whilst you can still get back.'

With a resigned shrug of his shoulders Manolis rose, bent and kissed Flora's hand. 'I'll talk to you the next time I come over,' he promised.

He called Father Minos to join him, pointing to the sea and sky by way of explanation. Yannis watched as they made their way over to the shelter of the mainland, the tiny boat being tossed like a cork as the wind caught her sails until Manolis finally lowered them and began to row. Involuntarily Yannis shivered. He would never forget the first time he had been caught in a storm with his uncle, how sick and knotted his stomach had been with fear. He turned to see Phaedra waiting by the steps and walked towards her.

'Who was that man?'

'The schoolteacher I shared lodgings with. We were good friends, could talk for hours about history. Now all he can think about is politics. Even when I asked about his wife and baby he was hardly interested.'

'So what did he want?'

'I'm not sure. He said he wanted to help us, but I felt there was more to it than that, something he wasn't telling me. I probably imagined it.' Yannis put his arm round Phaedra and squeezed her. 'He's laid a ghost for me. I'd kidded myself that one day I would be able to return and everything would be just the same. Now I know it wouldn't be, and I'm not so sure about wanting to return.'

'You ought to go in and get dry,' Phaedra warned him, wanting to distract him from a dangerously depressing train of thought.

Yiorgo Pavlakis sat at his desk in the schoolroom and scowled at the children. It seemed hardly any time at all since Yannis had been an eager face amongst such a crowd. Yiorgo had been proud of him for gaining the scholarship, so delighted to be the bearer of such good news to his family, and now the brilliant scholar sat in a make-shift hut on a wind swept island, shunned by all except his fellow sufferers. He pushed his hair back and wiped his hand down his trousers.

He found it difficult to keep his mind on the lesson he was giving. His thoughts continually reverted to the island and he shuddered inwardly. Whatever he managed to do for them he never wanted to visit that island again. By the time he had finished teaching for the day, eaten and made his way to the Town Hall where the meeting was to be held, he had a plan clearly in his mind. It would need all his cunning to get his fellows to agree to his proposals before the full implication of his plan was realised. He shuffled his papers and cleared his throat nervously.

'Fellow councillors,' he began, 'Some most disquieting information has come to me, something which is in our power to rectify immediately, and in rectifying it we shall earn the respect of our fellow men for ever more.' He pushed the lock of hair from his eyes. 'I should like you to imagine for one moment that your wife, your son or your daughter was declared an incurable. What would be their fate? As it is unlikely that this terrible illness has ever crossed your path you will not know.' Yiorgo glanced round his audience, noting those who were avoiding his eyes or biting their lips in concern.

'I would never have known myself, had it not been for a priest who is well-known in this town for his merciful deeds. Father Minos came to me, not to beg for the unfortunate or the destitute, he came to ask me if I could persuade you to give him permission to live on Spinalonga.' Each and every man drew in his breath. 'He has permission from the medical authorities to visit whenever he wishes and I suggested that he moved to Aghios Nikolaos and visited daily. It was not the simple solution I had thought. The only income he has is from his parish, so he could not afford to live away from it. I suggested his friends on the island contributed to his keep, but that again is not possible.' Yiorgo paused to gauge the effect his words were having. 'He told me those who had been sent to the island do not have a lepta between them. Their food is sent over from the villages, paid for by the government, and that is all. I found it hard to believe, thinking Father Minos was trying to gain my sympathy, but it is true. I have seen with my own eyes the way these sick and suffering people live.'

Yiorgo raised his voice. 'I visited the island, in the company of the priest, and I was appalled.' He spread his arms wide. 'It was wet and windy. I had on my overcoat. I asked why those people were not wearing theirs and I was told they do not have any. They do not have an overcoat! Think about that. It is as cold and wet there as it is here, yet they do not have a coat!'

His audience shifted uncomfortably. They did not want to be reminded that a group of people had been virtually abandoned for the misfortune of falling prey to a disease. Yiorgo held up his hand.

'Now, I'm not asking you to send them all overcoats. I am asking something far simpler. When these unfortunate people were admitted to hospital, either here or in Athens, or Thessalonica or wherever, they handed over all the money they possessed, borrowed from relatives, lent to them by friends, or saved diligently during their healthy, working years, to pay for their hospital treatment. When they were sent to the island that money was not sent with them!' Yiorgo leant across the table and looked at the assembly of men. 'What I am asking is, if that money was not sent with them, where is it now?'

He waited for his words to take effect. 'I know where it should be. It should be in the hospital safe, the amount duly recorded and the amount taken for expenses during the patient's stay also recorded, but it is not. All the money was taken by the government to pay for sending food to the island. Some of those admitted handed over vast sums, far in excess of their needs, and where is it now? Distributed amongst various accounts that bear no relevance at all to the sufferers. Used by the government to balance their accounts wherever there was a shortage. This is a criminal misuse of hospital funds and I feel sure that if it reached the ears of some people there could be an outcry that would topple the government both here and in Athens.

I suggest that we act before such a disaster occurs. I do not want to use this money to buy all those on the island an overcoat. I have a far better idea. The money should be placed in a bank account where it will gain interest over the years, and from that money I want to send each of these destitute people a small remittance for the rest of their lifetime. They will be able to buy their own overcoats!' Yiorgo resumed his seat and waited.

'How much money is there?'

'We would never be able to get it back.'

'If there is any to get back!'

'How can we find out?'

'We can ask to examine the hospital account books. We are within our rights to do so.'

'The medical authorities will claim they're owed money for treatment. We'll never get a lepta from them.'

Yiorgo rose to his feet again. 'I agree with you. I am sure that the books will balance and requesting an examination would only cause trouble for us. What I am suggesting is that we run a lottery. We advertise that it is to provide comforts for the incurables and also appeal for anonymous donations. I'm sure people would give a little if they knew it would help a member of their family and there was no risk of their name being mentioned. We can then present it as a gift from the government.'

The men around the table murmured together, some making little calculations on the notepads before them, until one finally looked up.

'I propose that we accept this suggestion, but before we decide how much we are able to give to each person, we would need to know the numbers involved. We can't make promises until we have all the facts. I also propose that we only distribute so much per month. In that way the capital can stay in the bank earning interest.'

Yiorgo Pavlakis nodded. 'May I propose that we take a vote on the idea?'

The men nodded their assent and raised their hands.

'I should like it minuted,' Yiorgo spoke to the clerk. 'Mr Y. Pavlakis proposed etcetera and it was decided etcetera.' The clerk began to write assiduously. 'Now the next item I have on my agenda again concerns Spinalonga. It is a request by Father Minos that he may be given permission to live on the island, to give what little comfort he can to the sick and dying.'

'Who would pay for that?'

A silence fell. Yiorgo cleared his throat and pushed back the lock of hair. 'No doubt his friends would find accommodation for him and he would be able to have a share of the food that was sent out, apart from that, I suggest he has the same allowance as is finally decided upon for the other occupants of the island.'

'Sounds fair! If he wishes to live with them he should be prepared to live like them.' The elderly man spoke with a conviction that brooked no disagreement.

'Wouldn't we have to ask the Bishop over this one? He probably has the final say.'

'Only a fool would want to go there!'

'He must surely stand more chance of catching it if he's there all the time.'

'Maybe we should send him there anyway.'

'Why?'

'He could already have it and be passing it around the city.'

They nodded in agreement.

'I propose that Father Minos be granted his request to live on the island of Spinalonga, subject to the approval of the Bishop.'

'I'd like to amend that. He must stay on the island permanently, otherwise he risks contaminating others.'

Again the men nodded in agreement.

'May I tell the priest of your decision?'

'Better to avoid the man.'

'We'll send him a letter. Phrase it formally.'

The clerk nodded. He hoped there would be no reply that he would have to handle.

'Now, the next item…..'

Father Minos sat in the vestibule, nervously awaiting his audience with the Bishop. He had the treasured letter recommending that he took up residence on Spinalonga in his pocket. All he needed now was the permission of the Bishop. He rubbed his hands down his long black robe, hoping the sweat would not show. It seemed an age before the secretary opened the door and beckoned him into the presence of the eminent man. Father Minos made an obeisance before him and stood silently, waiting for permission to speak.

'You requested an audience of me?'

'Your Lordship, I crave your indulgence whilst I speak.'

The Bishop nodded permission.

Father Minos swallowed hard. 'Some few years ago a young man came to me. He was in dire terror and distress. When I had calmed him he confessed that he thought he was an incurable. I persuaded him to visit the hospital for diagnosis. I did not hear from him again. I dismissed him from my mind as a forgetful youngster, whose fears, once allayed, had forgotten me. It was only later when his young cousin, also a church man, came searching for him, that I discovered he had been admitted to the hospital for treatment.'

'Yes, yes.'

'Please, your Lordship, I have to tell you the whole story. I went to the sick young man's parents and told them the sad news. On the very day that I had discovered that their son had been admitted to hospital he was being transferred to the hospital in Athens. I could not tell them the address or any other details. I felt I had failed my fellows in my calling.' Father Minos bowed his head.

'You require absolution?'

'No, your Lordship. I atoned for my sin of negligence by visiting the hospital here and taking whatever succour and comfort I could to the unfortunate sufferers. I found out the name of the hospital in Athens where they were sent, but once again I was too late. The young man in question had been moved once again. This time to the island of Spinalonga. I visited the island and I cannot describe to a man of your sensibilities the conditions I found there. They defy description! To say it is Hell on earth falls far short of the truth.'

The Bishop shifted uncomfortably in his chair. This was beginning to sound suspiciously like a plea for the return of this young man to the mainland.

'I have visited the island on a number of occasions, taking whatever comfort I can to the poor souls who have been condemned to live out their earthly life there and I have become determined upon a course of action. I have been called, called as clearly as I was when I first turned to the Holy Church for orders. I actually heard a voice,' Father Minos's eyes began to glow with enthusiasm. 'I was praying for guidance when a voice spoke to me so clearly that for a moment I thought I was not alone.'

'And what did this voice say, my son?'

'He, it was Him, said, "You cannot heal the lepers, but you can help them". He spoke the truth to me. I can help them, I beg of you to let me help them.' Father Minos fell to his knees, prostrating himself before the Bishop. 'I wish to go to the island; to live amongst them, as one of them, to help them with prayer and faith to overcome their misery and despair. This is my calling. I have permission from the medical authorities, I have permission from the government, but I need your permission, my Lord.'

The Bishop relaxed. If only all his priests were to make such simple requests. 'My son, when did you first hear this voice call you?'

'Some years back now. When the young man was first sent to Athens and I felt I had failed in my calling.'

'And you did nothing?'

'I went to the hospital. I spent long hours listening to the confessions of those who were too sick to be moved to Athens and trying to comfort those who did not wish to leave Crete.'

'And this is not enough for you?'

'It is no longer sufficient when I know there are others in greater need. Any priest could take comfort to those patients who are hospitalised, but I wish to share their privations and discomforts. To be truly one of them.'

'Do you still bear a feeling of guilt for failing this young man when he needed you?'

'Yes, your Lordship.'

'Is this your way of setting yourself a penance? A penance that once undertaken can never be taken from you?'

'I do not see it as a penance. My penance is to have to live here, in comfort, whilst they have so little materially and nothing spiritually.'

'And have you given any thought to who would carry on your good work here if I allowed you to leave us?'

'Your Lordship, I am sure that anyone could fulfil my duties.'

'I am not so sure. You have a high standing in the town.'

'You will consider my request?'

'I will consider it, my son, and I shall expect you to abide by my decision.'

Father Minos bowed his head. He was under oath to obey his Bishop.

'Call upon me again in a week, when I have had time to consider your request.'

Father Minos kissed the Bishop's outstretched hand and bowed his way from the audience chamber. He had not expected an immediate decision. He tried to fill his mind with the problems of his parish, but found he continually lost his train of thought and was once again re-living his interview with the Bishop, cursing himself for the mistakes he had probably made. He felt more nervous than he had the previous week as he waited once again in the vestibule to be called for his audience. As he crossed the room he tried to read the answer in the face of the Bishop, but, as usual, the man was quite inscrutable.

'My son, are you still of the same mind?'

'I am, your Lordship.'

The Bishop sighed. 'I have thought over carefully all you told me last week. I can find no fault with your motives, they are worthy of your calling, but I cannot give you my blessing.'

Father Minos felt his heart sink. His voice sounded strangled as he tried to ask the reason.

'Your work in this city is too valuable to be discarded. Maybe if you had a novice working with you, learning your ways and willing to take on your responsibilities, I could have considered your call and given you leave. As it is,' the Bishop spread his hands. 'I cannot allow you to go. Your flock would be left without a shepherd to guide them.'

Father Minos struggled for words. 'That is the only reason, my Lord?'

The Bishop nodded.

'If I could find someone willing to take over my parish, someone acceptable to yourself and the parishioners, could that alter your decision?'

'If you were able to find such a priest.' The Bishop smiled kindly at the unhappy man before him. 'I am sorry to have disappointed you, my son.'

'Thank you, your Lordship.' Again Father Minos kissed the outstretched hand and left the room. He felt frustrated and unreasonably annoyed with the Bishop. His steps led along familiar roads to his tiny church and he looked at it with distaste, immediately feeling guilty. He hurried inside and knelt on the hard stone before the altar, asking for forgiveness for the wicked thoughts that had entered his head and also for a peaceful heart. An hour later he rose, calmer and resigned to staying in Heraklion. He passed the afternoon composing a letter to the council members, explaining that much as he wished to comply with their recommendation to move to Spinalonga as soon as possible, his Bishop had refused permission. He permitted himself a wry smile. No doubt he had upset their plans in some way.

He resumed his duties, trying hard to put his disappointment firmly to the back of his mind and concentrate on the many problems that surrounded him. A visit to the hospital brought back poignant memories of the island, of Yannis, Andreas .... Andreas! Of course! Cursing himself for a fool he hurried from the hospital. There was still time to make arrangements to visit Aghios Nikolaos that afternoon.

Andreas looked at Father Minos in disbelief. 'You are serious, aren't you?'

Father Minos nodded. 'I was never more serious. You're the answer to my prayer.'

'What happens then if the Bishop does not agree?"

'Then there's nothing lost. You'll have gained some valuable experience. You can still return here, taking your turn with the others to take a Mass or visit the sick, until such time as they feel you're ready for a parish of your own. These things can take a long time. You can be ready, but there's not always a vacancy for years.'

Andreas considered. 'If the Bishop did accept me, what would I have? I don't mean to sound mercenary, but I've no money of my own and I don't want to ask my father for an allowance.'

'I thought your father was reasonably affluent, for a fisherman?'

Andreas smiled. 'He is. He's lived frugally and worked hard.'

'Is he still planning to visit your sister in Athens?'

Andreas shook his head. 'I wrote to you. Annita visited us for a week and persuaded Manolis to take her over to Spinalonga. She said she didn't go ashore. Yannis waved to her. She was very quiet for a few days, then just as she was leaving, she told Mamma and Pappa she was getting married and going to America.'

'What!' Father Minos could not believe his ears. 'I haven't received your letter.'

'It's true. I had a job to believe it myself. Two weeks ago we all went to Athens and she had a splendid wedding.'

'Who did she marry?'

'She's been working with a microbiologist who is researching into leprosy. He's been given a scholarship in America. That's why I don't want to ask Pappa for an allowance. He gave Annita a good dowry, paid for us all to go to her wedding and paid my keep whilst I was a novice. He and Mamma have also mentioned going to America.'

Again Father Minos raised his eyebrows. 'For a holiday?'

'No, to live, once Annita is settled. I think they hope she will have children and they don't want to miss them.'

'What about you? Would you plan to join them?'

Andreas shook his head. 'I could never leave Crete. It's my home. This is why I'd like to accept your offer. I'm sure my parents would be happier to know I was settled. They must be free to leave if they wish.'

'I'm not offering you a fortune.' Father Minos smiled. 'There's my small house, and a large, poor parish. You'll suffer from lack of sleep, and always want more hours in the day and an extra day in every week. I live fairly simply and find the income sufficient.'

'May I talk it over with my Bishop and my parents and let you know tomorrow?'

'Talk it over by all means, but I can't wait until tomorrow to hear your answer. I have to return by the bus that leaves this afternoon.'

'Do you have anyone else in mind?' Andreas could suddenly see the opportunity slipping away from him.

'No. You were my only thought. Let me know what you decide.'

Andreas knocked vigorously on the door, a broad grin on his face. 'Is Father Minos here, please?' he asked of the housekeeper.

She shook her head. 'You've missed him. He left for the hospital a while back.'

'May I leave my things? He's expecting me. I'll go to the

hospital and find him there.' Andreas placed his bundles in the hall and raised his hand to her. 'I know where it is. I'll be back later.'

He found Father Minos sitting beside the bed of an elderly man, listening to the tirade that poured forth against the government who had finally found him hiding in a cave and removed him forcibly to hospital. Andreas waited until the man lay back against his pillow, worn out by the strength of his emotions.

'You must not be bitter. In here you will be looked after. Imagine how you would have suffered had your wife fallen ill and been unable to bring you food. Relax, my friend. I'll visit you again next week and I'm sure by then you'll consider yourself fortunate.'

'Father.'

The priest turned. 'Andreas! It's good to see you. Why didn't you write?'

'I decided it would be quicker to come in person. I've left my belongings at your house.'

'You're coming?' Father Minos seized him in a fervent embrace. 'I'm so happy, so very happy. What did your parents say?'

'They were pleased, relieved almost. They feel they're free now to make whatever plans they wish.'

'And your Bishop?'

'He was very kind. He gave me his blessing and said I'd be welcome to go back if I changed my mind.'

'Come and meet the patients.' Father Minos remembered his reason for being at the hospital. 'We can talk later.' He led the way from bed to bed, introducing Andreas and explaining that the young man would be visiting whilst he took a holiday. Andreas looked at him questioningly.

'It's better if I say that,' he explained. 'There'll be no premature goodbyes and if the Bishop refuses me permission we neither of us lose face.'

Andreas tried to take in all the details of each person they spoke to. He sympathised with those who complained of pain, promised to take messages to families and joined Father Minos in the communal prayer. Once outside he took a deep breath.

'I feel I've been more useful this afternoon than I have for the last six months. They're all so lonely and worried.'

Father Minos nodded understandingly. 'Have any of them asked you to take messages to their families?'

'A couple.'

'We'll do that tomorrow. I always try very hard not to let others know who are in the hospital. If I visit a dozen parishioners tomorrow two or three of them will have relatives in here, but no one can point the finger.'

'I have a lot to learn,' Andreas admitted. 'I would have gone rushing straight off. You'll have to show me your way of doing things so I don't offend people.'

Father Minos smiled indulgently. 'I'm sure you won't offend. I'll show you my way, but I'm sure you'll want to make changes.'

Andreas followed the priest as he led the way around his parish, pointing out various landmarks that could be used as boundaries.

'Never refuse a supplicant, wherever they may be from, but never knowingly encroach on another's parish. Remember, the size of your congregation makes a difference to your life style. You wouldn't want someone to entice half your parish away or you would end up starving.'

'I'll remember that. Will your housekeeper stay with me? You'll have to tell me how much to pay her. I've never had anything like that to do before.'

'Don't worry. I doubt if I'll be able to get another audience with the Bishop for months. By then you'll know everything there is to know about living in this town.'

To Father Minos's surprise his request for a further audience was granted more quickly than he had envisaged. Within a month he and Andreas stood waiting to be admitted. They approached the door together, but only Father Minos was allowed to enter.

'My son, I understand you have come to repeat your former request.'

'Yes, your Lordship.'

'The young man you propose is fully ordained?'

'Yes, your Lordship.'

'Why do you consider him suitable as your successor?'

'He is young and has enthusiasm and energy. He is devoted to his calling, sympathetic to others and has a maturity beyond his years.'

The Bishop nodded. 'Why doesn't he want to go to Spinalonga? I understand he has visited the island with you.'

Father Minos realised that whatever information he gave about Andreas the Bishop would already know, having investigated him thoroughly.

'His cousin is on the island. Although he is in sympathy with them he feels that such a relationship in the community could cause problems. He also feels that he does not have the experience for such an undertaking.'

'Yet he feels capable in taking over from you?'

Father Minos thought rapidly. 'He knows he has other priests around whom he could consult should a problem arise.'

'And who will you consult if a problem arises?'

'I would apply to you, your Lordship.'

The Bishop shook his head. 'I have had a letter from the government. They are in favour of you going to the island and staying there. Once you are committed to living with the lepers you will be subject to the same restrictions.'

'You mean – for life?'

The Bishop nodded slowly. 'Have you really thought this through? Had you imagined you would be able to take a holiday whenever you wished? Visit friends? Come to me to solve a problem? You have to understand that if I grant this request it will be more like a sentence than a favour. There will be no way you can ever return.'

Father Minos stood in an agony of indecision. He knew that if he failed in his resolve now it was most unlikely he would be given another opportunity, yet to be on the island forever. Was he strong enough to carry that burden?

'I understand, your Lordship. It is still my wish to be permitted to live on Spinalonga.'

The Bishop smiled and Father Minos realised the interview was at an end. He returned to the vestibule whilst Andreas took his place in the audience chamber. The waiting seemed interminable until he was finally recalled, his heart thumping loudly beneath his cassock as he bent his knees and kissed the Bishop's hand.

'I have decided this young man should be given a chance to prove himself. If he does not fulfil the promise he has shown to you or fails in his duty then I will have no choice but to replace him. That would not mean that you would be recalled. If you are still determined to take this course then you are taking a further vow which will bind you for the rest of your life.'

'I could ask for nothing more,' Father Minos's voice was husky with emotion.

'Then provided you fully understand the commitment you have made, you have my blessing. May God keep you safe and healthy.'

Again Father Minos kissed the Bishop's hand and Andreas followed his example. Once outside Father Minos led the way to the nearest taverna.

'This calls for a glass of wine to steady my nerves. I never thought he would agree.'

'Nor I! The questions he asked me! He wanted to know why I didn't want to live on the island to be with my cousin.'

'What did you say?'

'That I didn't have the experience that you did in dealing

with people. I thought I'd said the wrong thing. He looked at me with those beady little eyes of his and asked if I had so little experience of life how did I possibly think I could cope with a parish.'

Father Minos sucked in his breath. 'That was a mistake.'

'I managed to extricate myself. I said I had plenty of experience of life and dealing with people, but that I didn't have enough experience to be isolated on an island.'

'He accepted that?'

Andreas nodded. 'I think he had already made up his mind to let you go. The interview was just a formality.'

'Maybe. Just be very careful if he sends for you again to ask after your progress. If you go in full of confidence he'll probably confront you with mistakes and failures you'd not even noticed, and if you go in hesitantly he'll ask when you're going to mature and grow in confidence. You have to tread very warily when dealing with a Bishop.'

Andreas considered the advice. 'I don't see how I can please him, then. I'll just have to take a chance if he sends for me again. Let's forget him and really celebrate.'

'Not here, it's much too close to his residence. You don't want a reputation as a drinker before your start. We'll return home, have a meal and see what my cellar has hidden away.'

Yannis read the letter Manolis had brought him from Yiorgo Pavlakis. He frowned in consternation.

'I can't cope with this. Most of the information he asks for I don't have.'

'What does he ask?' Spiro was bandaging the stump of Kyriakos's left leg where an ulcer was infected and suppurating.

'He wants to know our names and ages, when we were first admitted to a hospital, which one, where we came from and what work we did, information about our relatives, the list is endless.'

'What do we get if we answer all those questions?'

Yannis turned to the next page. 'I'm not sure; he's not specific about anything. He says the idea of a regular sum of money for us has been agreed in principle, but he needs the information he has asked for so the council can work everything out.' Yannis threw the letter to one side in disgust.

'So what are you going to do about it?'

'I don't know. He says that once all this information is on file it can easily be kept up to date and he won't have to ask again.'

'That sounds logical enough.'

'I don't see why we can't just count heads and leave it at that,' grumbled Yannis. 'I don't want to tell the government where my relatives live. How do I know what they'll do with the information? They could send people there to take skin and blood tests and make their lives a misery. Do you think they'd do it quietly and tactfully? I don't! They'd ask the first person they saw to direct them to the house and tell them what they wanted with the family. Before the day was out my parents would have been driven from the village.' Angrily he tore the letter across.

'Don't be so hasty,' Spiro retrieved the pieces. 'Why don't you write back and say we're not prepared to give them any information about our families and explain why.'

Yannis shook his head. 'It's a trick. A trick to enable the government to persecute our families,' he insisted.

'You can't be sure of that.'

'I feel sure.'

The argument raged back and forth between the two men, Kyriakos's bandages forgotten, until finally Yannis rose. 'I'm going for a walk.'

Miserably he wandered along the path and up the slight incline. He had believed Yiorgo Pavlakis when he had first spoken of helping them all. Now it appeared that instead of helping the lepers he was going to help the authorities to carry out a witch-hunt on their families. Sadly Yannis gazed over the expanse of water to his home. His family were in danger. Of all those on the island Yiorgo knew exactly who his parents were and where they lived.

'What's wrong?' A small hand was slipped into his and he turned to find Phaedra looking at him with concern.

'I had a letter from that schoolmaster friend of mine. He's also a politician and he wants to persuade the government to give us some money.'

Phaedra smiled. 'That sounds good, but where would we spend it?'

Yannis smiled back at her. 'We'd ask people to bring us what we wanted from the mainland and pay them.'

'You mean we could choose things?' There was wonder in her voice.

'If you wanted a red dress or a blue one you'd be able to choose, then pay when it was sent over to you.'

'No more fighting over bundles of old clothes? It would be wonderful, Yannis.'

'It would be if it were that simple. He wants to know the name of everyone who lives here and where their relatives live. It would mean that the government could find our families. Soon all the neighbours would know who was over here, and you can imagine what that would mean.'

Phaedra nodded. 'Do you have to tell him? Suppose people don't know where their family lives?'

'I expect the government would send someone to make enquiries. Even if they'd moved on they would probably trace them eventually.'

'Why don't you ask Orestis?'

'What good would that do?'

'He was a solicitor before he came here. He might be able to advise you.'

'Phaedra, you're wonderful. I can always rely on you to know what to do.'

Phaedra reddened with pleasure. 'It was just an idea.'

He returned to his own house where he found the torn letter placed carefully on his bed by Spiro. He read it through again before making his way to the house where Orestis lived. Yannis knocked on the door. 'Stir yourself, Orestis. I've some work for you to do.'

Orestis ignored the voice, hoping he would be left in peace to read his book.

Yannis tried again. 'I'm not going away. I'll continue to knock until you open your door.' There was no reply and Yannis wondered if the house was empty. He raised his voice. 'I need your help as a solicitor. It's a legal matter I want to talk about.'

The door opened and Orestis stood there smiling. 'Why didn't you say so in the first place? I thought you'd come to ask me to haul stones around.'

'This is more important.'

'I thought nothing was more important to you than your precious buildings.'

Yannis ignored the taunt. 'I want you to read this letter and then give me your professional advice.'

'Who tore it up?'

'I did,' admitted Yannis. 'I was somewhat annoyed.'

Orestis read in silence, turning to Yannis when he finished. 'So what do you want my advice on?'

'Do we have to supply all the information he asks for?'

'Well, that depends. It's a logical request when he asks for the name of everyone over here and which hospital admitted them.'

'So we've got to do it?'

'It looks like it, if we want to accept this offer of money. How much is he trying to get for us?'

'He doesn't say. It probably depends how many of us there are.'

Orestis nodded. 'I'd suggest you ask him why he needs all the details he's asked for. He may have a good reason, or as you seem to think, it may be a way of tracking down our families and causing them embarrassment. I, for one, wouldn't want it generally known that I was over here. My wife knows, but she told the children I'm in France, working for the government. I'll tell you what, Yannis, I'll write this letter. I'll go through, point by point, and put forward our objections to certain questions. You realise, though, it may mean we don't see any of this promised money?'

'It all seemed so easy when we talked about it,' sighed Yannis. 'He said he just wanted a list of the people who live here and left me some paper so I could make it.'

'Nothing is easy when it has to go before politicians. Your friend is either very new to the game or he's managed to only get very simple issues through so far. Alternatively, of course, he could have the makings of a very wily politician. One of those who promises you the earth for nothing and when you've swallowed the bait you find you've sold your soul to the devil.'

Yiorgo Pavlakis waited impatiently for the answer to his letter. The date of the mayoral election would be announced any day and he wanted to be able to point to his accomplishment of a pension for the incurables as an example of his charitable outlook in the hope of winning the majority of the votes. He had a vision of himself on the platform, cheered by the crowd as the chain of office was placed round his neck, and a smiling, beautiful, Louisa at his side.

When the mail was brought to his office he tore open the envelope eagerly, his enthusiasm gradually ebbing away as the sheets inside were covered in a hand entirely unknown to him. He read the missive through slowly and thoroughly, a flush coming to his cheeks as the words of truth struck home and pricked his conscience. As Orestis pointed out, there was no necessity for their relatives to be involved if the money was coming from the government, therefore their town or village of residence prior to their admittance was entirely superfluous information. Their previous occupation was also irrelevant, and their age could be ignored, leprosy often advanced more quickly if it attacked the young than if it were diagnosed in later life. Yiorgo Pavlakis had no option other than write back and agree to those questions being temporarily waived, but a list of the islanders was essential.

It was with trepidation that Yiorgo faced the council to read Orestis's letter and as he anticipated they smiled openly and made remarks behind their hands to one another. Yiorgo cleared his throat, pushed back his hair and addressed them. 'I propose that we proceed with our idea regardless of their lack of co-operation. When they see we are prepared to keep a bargain they will have more confidence in us, then will be the time to press with the other questions.'

'How much did you have in mind for them?'

'They can't need very much. They have everything sent to them.'

'They'll simply smuggle it back to their families.'

'Or gamble.'

'You still haven't said how much you have in mind to give them.'

Yiorgo shrugged his shoulders. 'I really don't know how to assess it. As you say, they have their essentials sent to them, this is just to give them a modicum of independence.'

'Load of rubbish.'

Yiorgo heard the undertone and seized upon it. 'How would you feel if everything you ate and wore was sent to you by charity? You wouldn't think it a load of rubbish then.'

'How much?'

'Yes, how much? We're straying from the point. We can't make any decision until we know the sum involved.'

Yiorgo cast around desperately in his mind for a figure he hoped they would find acceptable. 'Twenty drachmas?'

'A year?'

'Oh, no, that would do them no good at all. I was thinking of twenty drachmas a week.'

'Twenty a week!'

The whole body of men catcalled and whistled in derision.

'They'd soon be millionaires!'

'I'd go there myself if I was paid that for doing nothing.'

'First time I've heard of people being paid for being ill.'

'Ridiculous!'

Yiorgo waited until the noise had subsided. 'How much then?' he asked, sulkily.

'One. One a day – and that's being generous.'

Yiorgo looked round the assembly. They all seemed to be nodding in agreement.

'Very well, one drachma a day.'

'How many are on the island?'

'Four hundred and twenty seven.'

'How do you know that figure is correct? They may have added some.'

'We have to trust them.'

'Trust? Outcasts! How can you trust them?'

Yiorgo had an inspired thought. 'The priest, they wouldn't lie to him, and he wouldn't lie to us. When he's established over there we'll ask him to check the numbers.'

A young man leant forward with his notebook in his hand. 'If we take the figure you gave as correct and we are going to give them a drachma a day that is twelve thousand, eight hundred and ten a month, amounting to one hundred and fifty three thousand, seven hundred and twenty per year. I can't see one lottery bringing in that kind of money.'

Yiorgo looked at him helplessly. 'Finance is not my province.'

'This means a good deal to you, doesn't it?' He held up his hand as Yiorgo was about to reply. 'I won't ask why it means so much. It might embarrass you.'

'I have no relatives on the island,' Yiorgo hastened to assure him.

'I'll take your word for that, but I have a suggestion to make. I have an acquaintance who has a good deal of money, honestly come by. If we fall short on the lottery, I suggest we ask him for an interest free loan, placed at my father's bank.'

Yiorgo shook his head. 'It wouldn't work. His money couldn't last forever. The money has to come from government funds; either raised from lotteries or increased taxes.'

'Of course! How short sighted of me! Maybe we could keep the idea at the back of our minds should we need extra funds in the future?'

'Can we get the motion down on paper?' Yiorgo licked his dry lips. He must not let this opportunity slip away from him. 'Are you ready, clerk? "The proposal from Yiorgo Pavlakis to give the lepers dwelling on Spinalonga a pension of one drachma per day for the rest of their natural life to help to alleviate some of their suffering was passed unanimously" – today's date.'

'Suppose we're not able to raise the money and have to withdraw it?'

'They won't know the wording,' Yiorgo assured them. 'For all they know it could depend upon whoever is holding office at the time.'

Dimitris slapped his notebook down on the table and grinned. 'I understand now. Who do you think will be in office, Yiorgo?'

'That will depend upon the outcome of the election.'

'And whoever stands for election would like to be able to point to a public service and say "Look what I have done for those unfortunate people." Very clever, Yiorgo, very neat; we were slow not to realise you had something up your sleeve.'

A silence had fallen and all eyes were turned upon Yiorgo.

'Even without an election pending I would have put forward this suggestion. Having seen these people with my own eyes and the appalling conditions under which they live I feel it is every citizen's responsibility to try to better their lives.' Yiorgo tried to defend himself.

'I would like to believe you,' sneered Dimitris.

'And I should like to believe that you had their welfare at heart when you proposed a friend to provide some of the money and it to be handled by your father's bank. The deposit of such a sum would no doubt have helped to increase your lending power and bring you more profit.'

Dimitris rose to his feet. 'That is an insult to my honesty and integrity.'

'It was meant to be,' snarled Yiorgo. 'You are a jumped up young puppy.'

'Young puppy I may be, but at least I have all my wits about me, not like some who spend most of their life in a cloud of dreams and don't see what's going on under their nose.'

'Gentlemen, gentlemen.' Two of the committee rose to try to restrain the politicians who appeared about to fly at each other's throats.

'Apologise. Apologise.' The call began to be taken up by each and every member.

Dimitris looked at Yiorgo. 'I'll not apologise. What I said was the truth.' He turned on his heel and walked towards the door. 'Please accept my resignation.'

Spiro greeted Doctor Stavros at the door of the hospital with a smile of pride. 'It's not bad, is it? I've persuaded some of the women to come up on a regular basis and we have Roula. She used to be a nurse. She's marvellous, she seems to know when a patient needs attention before they know themselves.'

Doctor Stavros looked at Spiro carefully. 'I think it would be a good idea if you worked out a system so that each of you had a free day once a week.'

Spiro shook his head. 'That's not possible. We're only just managing.'

'Then you'll have to find some more to help you. Impress upon them the necessity of helping here. I'm insisting that you all have a day off once a week. You'll be ill otherwise. Let me see your charges and how they're faring.'

Spiro led the way into the ward. The mattresses were laid a few feet apart, the patients each covered with a blanket, another by their side, which could be rolled and placed under their head or on top for extra warmth. The floor was clean, the patients clean, their bandages freshly attended to and there was only a slight smell of decaying flesh and excrement to offend his nostrils. At the far end sat Spiro's helpers, preparing vegetables for the mid-day meal, chatting and laughing together, evidently quite at ease and happy to be there. At each mattress the doctor stopped and examined the occupant. Finally he went and sat with the group on the floor.

'I'd like to congratulate you all. You're doing a fine job here. I was talking to Spiro earlier and we've agreed that you'll have one free day each a week. Spiro is also to have a day off.' He looked at Spiro, daring him to contradict. 'I'd like to see you all a bit more comfortable. I'll try and get a table and some chairs sent over, some cushions, so you can prop your patients up more easily when you feed them, and I want to know how many more you can cope with.'

The women looked at each other doubtfully, until Roula spoke firmly. 'We can't. I don't even see how we can have a day off unless there are more of us helping.'

Doctor Stavros sighed. 'Then one of you must spare the time to persuade others to join you. With the care these poor sufferers are getting they could live for a considerable time, but that won't save others from needing your attention. Some of them may have to come in permanently, others just for a short while when they have a relapse. It isn't just to make life easier for the few who look after the sick outside; it's to boost their confidence when they're ill. Knowing there are people to look after them will help them to recover more quickly. Now, I must be off. When I come next week I'll expect to see a list of days off and a few more recruits.'

The remainder of the morning and afternoon passed all too quickly for the doctor and he had still not seen Flora. Finally he ran her to earth down by the tunnel and greeted her with a smile. 'I've been looking for you everywhere, Flora.'

'Why?'

'I just wanted to have a look at your arm. I like to admire my handiwork from time to time.'

Dutifully Flora extended her stump and the doctor examined it. The skin was healthy wherever he looked. 'Don't watch,' he ordered as he took the pin he always carried from his lapel and began to touch her gently with it. Each time she gave a little start of pain. Beaming, Doctor Stavros replaced the pin and took her hand. 'Have you noticed any signs anywhere else on your body? Anywhere at all?'

Flora shook her head. Her eyes were frightened and her whole attitude told the doctor she would run from him at any moment. 'Sit down and let me look at your feet.'

Flora obeyed, still watching the doctor warily. Finally he straightened up. 'I'm very pleased with you, Flora. I'll give you a complete examination the next time I'm over, maybe take some tests as well.'

Flora sat where she was, a solitary tear trickling down her cheek.

'There, there, my dear.' He patted her shoulder. 'You mustn't think the worst each time I ask to look at your arm.'

Flora shook her head, unable to speak, and with a last pat to her head he lifted his bag and made his way down to the quay. It was there that Phaedra found her some time later when she went for water from the drinking fountain.

'What's the matter, Flora? Manolis asked me where you were. He wanted to talk to you.'

'I don't want to talk to him.'

'Why not? He's been so good to us all.'

Flora did not answer and Phaedra tried again. 'He seemed very miserable and worried about you.'

'He doesn't have to worry. The doctor says I'm all right.'

'That's good news.'

'It makes no difference. I'm still a leper.'

'Manolis doesn't take any notice of our illness.'

'He's got to. Talk to him, Phaedra, explain to him that we're contagious.'

Phaedra looked at her in surprise. 'He knows we are. What's wrong, Flora? You two were good friends.'

'Manolis wants to marry me.' Flora's voice was no more than a whisper.

'Oh, Flora!' Phaedra's heart went out to the young girl. 'Do you love him?'

'Of course I do. I know it couldn't be a proper marriage, but I want to. That's why I'm hiding away from him. We mustn't. He's clean. He's not a filthy leper like me. I want him to stay clean. What would people say back on the mainland? He'd be an outcast like we are, and worse. They'd drive him away, then I'd never see him again.'

'Have you told Manolis how you feel?'

'I've tried, but he won't listen. It's better if he just forgets me. Tell him that for me, Phaedra. Tell him to forget and find some nice girl on the mainland who can be a proper wife to him and give him healthy children.' She turned her tear-streaked face to Phaedra. 'Promise me, Phaedra.'

Father Minos stood on the quay waiting for Manolis to appear for his daily journey to the island. It was going to be hot, already he could feel the warmth of the ground penetrating his sandals, inviting him to dabble his feet into the cool water. He smiled.

What would people think if he gave way to the urge? A priest, holding up his robes, paddling in the sea! Before he had time to take his fantasy further Manolis appeared, his face lighting up in a grin as he saw the priest waiting for him.

'This is a surprise. You've got a mountain of stuff with you. Good thing I'm not too loaded. Usual price for the round trip?' He began to heave the sacks aboard the boat.

'Half price for a one way trip.' Father Minos held out the coin.

Manolis frowned and straightened his back. 'What do you mean? One way?'

'I'm not coming back. I have a new parish.'

'Are you ill?'

Father Minos shook his head. 'No. I've been given permission to live on the island.'

Manolis opened his mouth to ask a question and then thought better of it. This was not the time.

Father Minos watched as Aghios Nikolaos disappeared from view and wondered if he would ever see the town again. It was too late for him to have second thoughts and doubts now. He sat quietly until the island became clearly visible and the priest felt his heart leap as it always did when he first saw it. 'I'm coming home,' he murmured to himself.

He was greeted on the quay with pleasure, which turned to disbelief when he announced his intention of staying.

'There's nowhere for you to live.'

'I'm sure there's somewhere I can store my belongings. This time of year it will be no hardship to sleep out of doors.'

Still Yannis looked perplexed. 'If you'd let us know you were coming we could have had somewhere prepared.'

'I don't need anywhere prepared,' insisted the priest. 'I've come to live with you as one of you. No special treatment.'

'You're not ill, are you?'

'Not that I know of; I've come here because I want to be with you all.'

1931-1939

Yannis looked at the man in disbelief. 'You want to be with us? You must be mad.' He picked up one of the priest's bundles and began to walk up the path. 'You'd better bring your belongings to my house for the time being. There's room now Spiro's living up at the hospital.'

Father Minos looked in bewilderment at Yannis's back. He was not usually so unwelcoming. He picked up two of his sacks and followed in Yannis's wake. The heat seemed even greater on the island than it had when he waited at Aghios Nikolaos. He reached Yannis's house and dropped his burdens gratefully.

'May I come in?'

'Of course.' Yannis was sitting on the end of his mattress. 'Put them where you like.'

'The hospital's finished, then?'

Yannis nodded. 'Takkis had it habitable well before the worst of the weather. Spiro and Doctor Stavros keep thinking of improvements they want to make so I doubt if it will ever be finished.'

'I'd like to see it later. What else has been happening since I was last here?' Father Minos sat down beside Yannis.

'Not much. Pavlakis wrote asking for a load of personal information which we refused to give him, Doctor Stavros visits us regularly, and more people have been sent out.'

'Is that why you're so depressed?'

Yannis shrugged. 'I don't know. It could be.'

'Is that all that's on your mind?'

Yannis rose abruptly and walked to the other side of the tiny room. 'I'm sick of living here. I was so proud of this hovel when I first built it, now I hate it.'

'So why don't you move into one of the other houses? There are plenty of them.'

'I made a promise to stay here until everyone had a decent house to live in. Only then was I entitled to have one. I know which one I want. It will take a lot of repair work, but one day I'll move in.'

'You're lonely, aren't you?'

'I miss having Spiro around.'

Father Minos shook his head. 'It's more than that. It's an inner loneliness. You should get married.'

Yannis laughed harshly. 'You're not allowed to marry if you're a leper.'

'So who's going to stop you? How many of the men and women who live together over here are legally married to each other? Not a single one. No one condemns them and I'm sure God doesn't.'

Yannis looked uncomfortable. 'Let's go up to the hospital and tell Spiro you're here to stay.'

Word had already spread around the island that the priest had come to live with them and all the way to the hospital they were stopped and asked if the news were true. It took almost an hour to cover the short distance and Spiro was waiting impatiently for them. After a brief greeting Father Minos began to make a round of the mattresses spaced out on the floor.

'Is he really going to stay?' asked Spiro.

'So he says. He's brought his belongings and they're in my house. It was the only place I could think of at such short notice.'

'Fine. He'll be company for you.'

'What makes you think I'm not happy living on my own?'

'It's not natural. I think you should take a look at things as they really are. We're stuck here for life. God knows how long that will be for some of us, but it could be a long time for you. You're young and in pretty good shape. You can't live like a monk forever. Take a look around and see what's staring you in the face.'

Yannis shook his head. 'I haven't the faintest idea what you're talking about. How's it going up here?'

'Not bad, I'll probably have a spare mattress by the end of a week.' Spiro indicated with a slight nod of his head. 'Thanassis is just sinking into oblivion. Ritsa sat up with him last night. She was convinced he would go then.'

Yannis allowed his eyes to wander over the still form. 'I'm glad she was wrong. At least Father Minos is here now.'

Spiro frowned. 'That could cause a problem. Will the priest accept placing him in the tower?'

'There's no alternative. He knows that.'

'He may not feel he can condone it, though. Why has he come? Is he sick?'

'Apparently he wants to be with us.'

Spiro snorted. 'The man's mad. Still, he'll be useful.'

'How do you mean?'

'Once the novelty has worn off he'll be bored to tears and only too willing to help with anything. He could even be an encouragement to some of the lazy devils who are only too willing to sit in the sun and say they're not fit enough to lift a finger.'

Yannis grinned. 'Maybe we could get him to preach a sermon about the lazy being made to toil for ever after their death, whilst the industrious live a life of idleness in heaven.'

Yiorgo Pavlakis raised his glass. 'Let us drink to our success.' Obediently his friends raised their glasses. 'Bring some more bottles, Louisa.'

'Haven't you had enough?' muttered Louisa beneath her breath.

She placed the bottles beside her husband, wishing the party would break up and she could go to bed. Since the result of the election had been posted outside the Town Hall Yiorgo had been celebrating steadily. He would no doubt pay for it the following day with bleary eyes and a headache that would make him surly and lethargic. A thin wail from the upper floor drew her attention.

'I'll have to go; you've woken Anna.'

Before Yiorgo could stop her she had left the taverna and was on her way up the stairs to their daughter's bedroom. The child was hot and wanted a drink. With a sigh Louisa retraced her steps downstairs and collected a cup of water. The child was a nuisance. Her earnings were dwindling and Pavlos kept urging her to earn more money to help him pay his heavy gambling debts.

Wearily Louisa returned to the taverna. The men were still there, huddled close together and talking quietly. Despite the number of glasses they had consumed they showed no sign of intoxication. She sat on the high stool and leant against the wall, closing her eyes.

'Louisa, more bottles.'

She stumbled into the taverna carrying the bottles by their necks.

'Bring a glass for yourself and join us.'

Sullenly she did as he bade her, knowing that if she refused the honour of drinking with the men, Yiorgo would take it as a personal insult to himself and to his friends. She raised her glass. 'To my successful husband, of whom I am very proud.'

Yiorgo beamed with pleasure. 'To my beautiful wife. Could any man be more fortunate than me?' He glanced round, daring anyone to contradict him.

Louisa sipped at the wine. As she had been invited to join them it meant the party was ready to break up. She would leave the washing up until the morning. The overflowing ashtrays and litter of bottles could wait also. The conversation was desultory, obviously the men had talked themselves out, one by one they drained their glasses, stubbed out their cigarettes and left. With a sigh of relief Louisa called goodbye to the last one and made for the stairs.

'Louisa.'

'Yes, Yiorgo,' her voice was flat and emotionless.

'Come and finish the bottle with me and I'll tell you about this evening.'

'I'm going to bed.'

'Louisa, I want to tell you.'

Louisa shook her head. 'Yiorgo, I'm tired. I'm going to bed.

Tomorrow I'll be delighted to listen to you, but not now.'

As she had predicted Yiorgo rose late, complaining of his head and remembering that his wife had refused to stay up any later listening to him. He began to complain vociferously. It was her duty. She had promised to honour and obey her husband, so when he asked her to sit and listen to him she should do so.

Louisa ignored him. Anna was fretful, having wet her bed and met with a sharp slap from her mother. Pavlos had risen late and left unshaven and unkempt, berating his sister for not calling him earlier. She washed the glasses, leaving them to drain whilst she stacked the empty bottles in the crate and wiped over the tables to remove the slops and cigarette ash. No sooner had she finished than Yiorgo sat at a table and lit a cigarette.

'Bring me an ashtray.'

'I'm washing them.'

'I need an ashtray. There isn't one out here.'

Louisa wiped her hands on her apron and picked up the wet ashtray that promptly slipped from her hands, shattering on the stone floor. 'You'll have to wait whilst I clear this up.'

Yiorgo sighed and let the ash fall to the floor. 'I'm going out.'

'Go – and good riddance,' muttered Louisa beneath her breath. At least she should be able to finish cleaning before anyone arrived expecting a meal.

Yiorgo walked through the narrow streets until he reached the main road. He would buy Louisa a present, a present to celebrate his success. He paused and looked in the jeweller's window. What should it be this time? She wore only her wedding ring, saying that any stone would be ruined in no time. She had her bracelet that he had given her as a betrothal present, her earrings for giving birth to Anna, and a pendant when he had first been elected to the local government. This time it should be something suitably ornate to fit the occasion. His reflection stared back at him, the lock of hair falling over his forehead and he pushed it back automatically. Behind him was reflected the face of a young man that seemed vaguely familiar.

'It is Mr Pavlakis, isn't it?'

'Yes.'

'I'm Andreas, well, Father Andreas now.'

'Yes?'

'Don't you remember me? I was at school in Aghios Nikolaos. My sister and cousin were in your class. I was younger.'

Yiorgo Pavlakis was struggling with his memory. He had taught so many young people and promptly forgotten them the moment they left. 'And you have taken Holy Orders, I see.'

'I always wanted to. I've been very fortunate. I've taken over Father Minos's parish. He's gone to the island.'

Memory suddenly clicked into place. 'I hope you'll be very happy fulfilling his duties.' Yiorgo began to walk away.

'I'm sure I shall.' The young priest stepped in front of him. 'Actually it's fortunate for me meeting you like this. I had planned to call.'

'You would be welcome.' The familiar cliché fell from the politician's lips.

'I would like to think so. It concerns money and many people find that distasteful.'

'You want a donation for the church?' Yiorgo's hand went to his pocket.

'No, although, of course, anything given is always welcome. It's the matter of the pension agreed upon for the islanders.'

Yiorgo shot him a quick look. 'It will all be paid through the proper channels. The books will be open for inspection at any time.'

'I'm quite sure they will. Father Minos had an idea regarding the distribution and administration which he asked me to discuss with you.'

'There are a good many details to be worked out before the operation can commence.'

'That is why I wish to speak with you. The idea is simplicity itself.'

Yiorgo pulled his precious timepiece from his pocket. It was already eleven. 'I could be free at three thirty if you would care to come to my home.'

He turned back to look in the jeweller's window, but the idea had palled. He would return to the taverna and admire his beautiful wife whilst she busied herself, maybe he would find time to play with little Anna. Having decided he strode out quickly.

Louisa scowled as he opened the door. 'I thought you were going out?'

'I have been out. I have made an appointment for this afternoon to discuss business.' Yiorgo sat down at the nearest table, taking his cigarettes from his pocket. 'Where's Anna?'

'She's asleep. Move your feet.'

'Asleep? Why?'

'She had a disturbed night.' Louisa looked at him scathingly.

Yiorgo shrugged and sighed. 'I have so little time to spend with her.'

'Whose fault is that?'

'Louisa, you must understand. I have to be at the beck and call of everyone. A man in my position has to snatch his family pleasures when he can. I would love to spend all day with my family, but what can I do? The moment I step outside the door someone wishes to speak to me.'

Louisa sniffed derisively. 'And you love it.'

Pushing back his hair from his forehead Yiorgo gazed at his wife in concern. He had discovered her sharp tongue within a few weeks of their marriage and excused it as due to her pregnancy. Maybe that was her problem now. He looked at her again. There were no obvious outward signs, but there had not been before until she was just over a month. He had never ceased to marvel that a girl so slight had managed to carry such a large baby that she had been forced to give birth prematurely.

'Louisa,' his voice was soft. 'Come here, my dear.'

YANNIS

Louisa obeyed. Usually when he spoke in that tone of voice he had a present for her. She propped the broom up against the counter and walked over to him smiling. Yiorgo reached out and took her hands, pulling her down onto his knee.

'Is there anything you wish to tell me?'

'Tell you?' Louisa's brain raced. What had he heard? Had someone mentioned her name to him? She tried to be discreet, going down to the port or meeting only long standing and trusted acquaintances when she was certain Yiorgo would not return unexpectedly.

Yiorgo nodded. 'Do you have a little secret you should share with me?'

Louisa bit her lip. 'What makes you think that?' she fenced.

A broad smile crossed Yiorgo's face. He ran his hand lightly across her stomach. 'I remember how shy and hesitant you were to tell me about little Anna. For days you blamed the sea, the sun, the different food, then you realised and once you shared your secret with me you stopped feeling so ill, and I, Louisa, was the proudest man in all Greece.' He raised her hand to his lips.

Louisa had an overwhelming desire to laugh. The relief made her feel quite light-headed. She had no reason to believe she might be pregnant, but it would not hurt Yiorgo to think she might be. 'It's possible.'

Yiorgo beamed with pleasure. 'You see, you cannot keep secrets from me. I know you far too well.'

Louisa smiled also, this time with genuine amusement. 'Let me go now. I must finish clearing up before anyone comes in.'

Reluctantly Yiorgo released her and watched as she finished sweeping the floor, pushing the chairs deftly back into place with her foot. After almost eight years of marriage he could still hardly believe the beautiful girl was his wife.

Andreas arrived promptly and Yiorgo poured him a glass of wine. 'We have some business to discuss, my dear, and you should be resting.'

Louisa ignored him, moving to the doorway where she could watch Anna playing outside and overhear the conversation. Yiorgo raised his glass to Andreas.

'Well, let's hear this idea.'

Andreas sipped cautiously. The wine was cheap and tasted sharp to his palate. 'The simplest way of keeping account would be to have all the names written in a ledger, entering each amount monthly and deducting the appropriate amount when necessary. The lepers could make a list of the purchases they want, the shopkeepers present their bills to the agent who draws the total sum from the bank and pays each one of them whatever they are owed.'

Yiorgo looked at the young man. The idea was incredibly simple. Why had he not thought of it? 'It might be possible.' Yiorgo emptied his glass. 'There is one problem. Who would be willing to act for them on the mainland? It would mean dealing with the lepers.'

'Father Minos suggested one of the boatmen, Manolis, should be asked. It doesn't worry him to go over there and talk to them. He knows most of them anyway, as he takes the doctor as well as supplies.'

'I'll think about it. I'll even put it before the council.'

'I'll let Father Minos know. I must go. I have a service to take. Thank you for your time.' Andreas rose, leaving his glass half full on the table. 'I hope the council will agree to the idea.'

Yiorgo nodded and held out his hand. 'It might work.' His attention was caught by his wife; she was shaking her head as she spoke to a thick set, fair young man. He pushed his way past the priest. 'What is the problem, my dear?'

'There's no problem. The gentleman was asking if I knew where he could rent some cheap accommodation for a few nights.'

Yiorgo frowned. The man looked more like a sailor than a tourist. 'Try the waterfront. There's usually accommodation to be had there. If you follow the road round...'

'I know my way.' The stranger cut him short and strode away.

YANNIS

Yiorgo took hold of Louisa's arm. 'You are not to stand in the doorway. It looks improper.'

Louisa did not answer. She would be able to find the man easily enough the following day.

Anna contemplated the young man as he sat with his head in his hands across the table from her. It was a month now since he had returned to his home to find his mother lying dead on the kitchen floor. It was time he took himself in hand and thought of the children.

'Babbis,' she spoke more sharply than she had intended and his head jerked up in surprise. 'Babbis, I have to talk to you.'

'Yes?'

'What are you planning to do?'

'Do?' he repeated stupidly after her.

'Babbis, you have two small children. You have to think of them. You have a farm that needs attention. You must pull yourself together. I know the death of your mother was a terrible shock, it was a shock to all of us, but you have to come to terms with it.'

For a moment Anna thought he was going to cry. 'What can I do? I can't look after the children, a house and a farm on my own. I need my mother.' He turned anguished eyes to her.

'You could get married again.'

Babbis shook his head. 'No one could take Maria's place.'

'If you sold the farm and moved to the town, maybe you would meet someone.'

Again Babbis shook his head. 'What would I do if I moved to the town? I'm a farmer.'

Anna tried again. 'What about the children?'

'I hoped you could look after them a little longer.'

'Babbis, I've had Yannis since he was born. He looks upon me as his mother and he's far more than a nephew to me. Looking after the children is no burden for me. It's you I'm concerned about.'

Babbis shrugged. 'I'll manage. I may go up tomorrow.'

Anna brought her fist down on the table with a force that made her wince. 'You will go up tomorrow. For days you've been saying maybe. If you don't go up tomorrow you'll find these doors barred against you.'

Babbis looked at his sister-in-law. 'You really mean that?'

'I mean it, Babbis. I'll go up with you.'

Anna gazed after him as he left the room. Maybe she had been too hard on him. It was only a month after all.

Stelios gazed across the sea towards the island. His heart yearned for his older brother whom he had loved and admired. A slight movement caught his eye and he turned away. He hated lepers, even if his brother was one. It was through him that his mother was confined to a chair, that his sister was dead and his other sister no more than a slave. A surge of unreasonable hatred against all his family made him bite his lip and drained the colour from his face. He could hardly wait to return to Heraklion. One more year, provided he worked hard, and he would gain a scholarship to Athens University and then he would show everyone. He would not contract any incurable disease and end up exiled on an island. He would rather die.

Die! That was the answer. When he went to Athens and was asked about his family he would say they were dead. No one would question him, they would be sympathetic over his loss and he would say he did not wish to talk about it. No taint would ever spread to him, he would make sure of that. He looked towards the island again. There were people moving around on the quay. Someone was waving. It must be Yannis! Stelios turned his back on the sea. Anna was standing there, the two children by her side.

'Wave to Uncle Yannis,' she instructed them and they dutifully held up their hands and waved in the direction she indicated.

'You're sick,' he commented bitterly as he walked past her.

'I'm taking the children up to see Babbis. Do you want to come?'

'I've better things to do with my time.'

'Come along.' She took the children's hands firmly in her own and began to walk away. If Stelios was in one of his black moods she did not want to bandy words with him.

'It's about time Babbis faced up to his responsibilities,' he called after her. 'Let him look after his own brats.'

Father Minos found Yannis was correct in his forecast that people would offer their help when they had thought over all he had said to them upon his arrival. In ones and twos they sought the priest out, others went to Spiro offering their services. His surplice and cassock removed, dressed in an old pair of trousers and ragged shirt, Father Minos worked beside them, digging, moving blocks of stone that tore at his finger nails, hammering bent and rusty nails straight so they could be used again. Each night he lay on his mattress, his muscles aching from the unaccustomed exertion, and fell into a deep sleep.

Manolis had told Doctor Stavros that the priest was living on the island, but he was totally unprepared for the sight that met his eyes when he made his weekly visit. Struggling with a block of masonry was an unkempt figure; the only thing distinguishing him from the other men on the island was a large cross hanging round his neck. Wiping the sweat from his eyes the priest held out a calloused hand.

'I would never have recognised you!'

'Only practical, besides, I'll need my robes when I take the church services. No point in ruining them.'

'You really plan to stay indefinitely?'

'I have no choice. The Bishop made it quite clear that I would not be welcome to return.'

'You're a brave man.'

'Foolish is probably a better word,' smiled Father Minos. 'The only difference between us is that I stay the night and you don't.'

Father Minos watched as the doctor walked up to the hospital to check on the clean and well cared for patients. From the hospital the doctor moved from house to house, examining ulcers, nodules and eyes, making a note of his findings in his notebook ready to be transferred to the ledger he kept on the mainland. He wanted to speak to Yannis before he left for the day and somehow he seemed to be elusive on this occasion. He finally found him inside the church, scrubbing the floor with vigour.

'What's this for?'

Yannis straightened up and grinned. 'We plan to use the church again. The last of the people have finally been found accommodation, some of it is only temporary, but it means we can clean the church out. Father Minos is getting quite excited. He wants it ready by Sunday for a service.'

'I'm pleased for you. Everyone housed. That's a fine accomplishment. Where's Father Minos living?'

'He's staying with me until there's another house ready.'

Doctor Stavros smiled. 'It's time you stopped working for others and did something for yourself. I'd rather you didn't spend another winter in that shelter.'

'So would I! The last time we had a mistral I thought I was going to take off. I lost some of the roof.' He walked from the dim church into the sunlight and blinked. 'That's bright,' he said as he sat on the ground to take a well-earned rest.

Father Minos read the letter joyfully and went in search of Yannis. The priest waved the letter at him. 'Mr Pavlakis has had a bill passed. You're to get thirty drachmas a month.'

Yannis's face lit up. 'You mean he's really done it without us having to give him all that stupid information he asked us for originally?'

'Read the letter.'

YANNIS

Yannis brushed his hands down his trousers. 'Let me see.' He scanned the words eagerly, then read the letter again more slowly. 'They've given it to us in theory, but there's still a problem. If we have the money over here no one from the mainland will accept it as payment for anything and if we keep the money on the mainland how are we going to pay anyone? We'll be no better off.'

Father Minos smiled. 'I hope by now Andreas has seen Mr Pavlakis and laid a simple solution before him. Your names are entered into a book and the amount you are paid. Whenever you wish to purchase something from the mainland the cost is deducted. All the deductions are added together, an amount withdrawn from the bank and the individual vendors are each paid whatever is due to them. That way the money doesn't leave the mainland, yet you can buy whatever you wish.'

Yannis considered the idea. 'That's fine, but who does all this buying and paying and keeping the books.'

'Manolis.'

'Manolis! He's just a fisherman. He's never done any bookkeeping.'

'We have two on the island who can show him how to do it, besides, it will give him a good excuse to be over here most of the day.'

'You approve of him and Flora, then?'

Father Minos shrugged. 'Who am I to judge? I feel desperately sorry for both of them. I pray for a solution.'

'Doctor Stavros doesn't approve.'

'How could he? He's a doctor. Doctors say lepers shouldn't marry because it speeds up the disease.'

'But you've married couples since you've been here.'

'Of course! If they're living together a blessing on their union isn't going to affect their illness, but it can give them an easy mind.'

Yiorgo Pavlakis cleared his throat, pushed back his hair and looked around the council chamber.

'I hoped that today we might be able to finalise the details about the pension for the lepers who live on Spinalonga.' He paused, hoping no one would start to ask questions. 'I have worked out the book keeping for the project and it should be quite simple to instigate and run. A large ledger, maybe two, will have the name of each person on a separate page. The date and the sum given entered. When anyone wishes to purchase goods from the mainland the bill is given to the bookkeeper. He will deduct the amount from the balance. The total expenditure is added up and the amount withdrawn from the bank to pay the bills.'

'Who would be responsible for keeping the ledgers?'

'I have been told that there are two trained book-keepers on the island.'

'Who would make the purchases and pay the bills?'

'I understand that the young boatman who ferries the doctor across would be willing to undertake both purchases and payment. May I have your approval for the suggestion?'

Hands were raised and Yiorgo sat back well satisfied. Thanks to Father Andreas this had been simple. 'Motion passed,' he announced to the clerk. 'Now,' Yiorgo shuffled his papers. 'We must discuss the real purpose of our meeting. I have received a communication ....' His voice droned on and the council members settled into their customary positions with their eyes open whilst mentally they allowed their thoughts to wander.

Yannis looked across the bay towards his home, fighting down the surge of longing that was threatening to overwhelm him.

'What is it, Yannis?' Phaedra was at his side.

'Just homesick; how far do you think it is from here to the mainland?'

'I've no idea. A long way.' Suddenly she became fearful. 'No, Yannis, you mustn't try to swim that far.'

'I don't intend to, but I could probably float that distance quite easily.'

'Please, Yannis, you'll be drowned.'

'When I first came here I would have drowned myself with pleasure, but not now. I'll get there safely, but it may take a little time for me to get back.'

He explained to her his idea of using one of the wooden bathtubs that the doctor had procured for them. The current should take him near enough to the opposite shore for him to swim to land. Once there it was just a question of walking into the village and waiting until his family rose at dawn.

'How will you get back?'

'I'm sure I'll find a way. You don't need to worry about me.'

Phaedra did worry. She was filled with dread should Yannis drown or decide to stay hidden near his family, and tried to persuade him to take her with him.

'Now that's being silly,' he chided her. 'You've told me that you can hardly swim. If it did capsize you could drown.'

'How long will you be gone?'

'I can't say for certain. I'll go at night, but it depends where I manage to land and how far I have to walk to Plaka. I expect I'll be at least three days.'

Phaedra pursed her lips. 'I wish there was some way you could let me know you were safe.'

'That's easy. I'll ask Anna to wave her red scarf to let you know I'm there.'

With that Phaedra had to be content. 'When are you going?'

'Tonight.'

She swallowed quickly. 'Are you sure, Yannis? Wouldn't it be better to wait awhile?'

'There's no moon tonight. I'm going to speak to Takkis and Spiro now as I'll need some help.'

Phaedra listened whilst he outlined his plan to the two men. They were full of enthusiasm and encouragement, eager to help him carry his bathtub down to the jetty, offering advice about currents and the shortest distance to the shore.

'Couldn't Manolis take you over?' asked Phaedra.

Yannis shook his head. 'If the authorities found out he'd have his boat impounded. It wouldn't be fair to put him in that position. If he lost his boat he wouldn't be able to come to see Flora.'

Spiro and Takkis grinned. 'I just wish he'd stop bringing her geraniums. The whole place reeks of them. Couldn't she have a fancy for marrows or onions? At least they'd be useful.'

Yannis waited until the cooking fires began to glow, then he, Spiro and Takkis picked up his bathtub and marched openly down to the jetty. From beside the storehouse Yannis took a length of wood and climbed into the bobbing tub.

Spiro looked at the flimsy craft in apprehension. 'You're running a risk, you know, Yannis. It all sounds easy, but you could end up miles out at sea.'

'It's not likely,' he assured Spiro with more confidence than he felt. 'If the current does double back I'm more likely to be sitting by the island tomorrow than on my way to Rhodes.'

Once away from the shore it was darker than Yannis had envisaged. He felt panic rising in him and tried to reason with himself. All the time he stayed afloat he was in no danger at all. The mainland was a dark mass in front of him and he used the length of wood as an improvised paddle to speed his slow progress. He shifted his position cautiously, the tub rocking wildly as he did so, bringing a return of the panic that had assailed him earlier. The sky darkened and he cursed himself for his stupidity for trying the trip on a moonless night. He could no longer see the landmass in front of him and had to rely on his instinct and the current to take him towards his goal.

He felt a grating and shuddering beneath him as he skimmed across a submerged rock, tilting dangerously for a moment or two before rocking on his way. With a sudden lurch that nearly threw him into the water the tub stopped, stuck fast between two rocks. Without any hesitation Yannis slipped over the side. The water was deeper than he had anticipated and almost up to his neck, he floundered, slipped and swam across the rocks until he reached the shallows and was able to walk on dry land.

Now that the time had come Yannis felt strangely nervous. Stifling his fears he walked quietly along the road to the farm where he had been born, realising with a shock that he had tears running down his face. He longed to push open the door and rush inside. Instead he crept into the yard; then risked drawing attention to himself by pulling the handle on the pump and plunging his head under the cold water. It trickled down his throat and made him gasp. The kitchen door opened and a wavering oil lamp was held aloft.

'Who's there? Who is it?' The oil lamp began to move closer.

'Yiorgo?'

'Who are you?'

'I'm Yannis. Your brother Yannis.'

'How did you get here?'

'It's a long story. How's Mamma?'

'Much the same.'

'Can I come in and see her?'

Yiorgo hesitated. 'I'll ask Pappa.'

'I'll understand if he says no. If I can't come in could you bring me some dry clothes and some food?'

Yannis did not see Yiorgo nod in the darkness; the sound of the door closing told him he was once more alone. Yiorgo eventually returned.

'Come into the kitchen.'

Yannis walked inside the door and looked around him. It was exactly as he remembered. A chair was thrust towards him and he sat down wearily. His father studied his appearance. The disease was quite apparent in his son now. His eyebrows were missing, one side of his nose flattened where the bone had been absorbed, the whole side of his face covered in white nodules. Yannis tore a chunk from a loaf of bread with hands that were clawed and masticated noisily.

Yiorgo turned away. This was his brother, his brilliant brother whose future had been destroyed along with his health and his looks. The man sitting before him looked old beyond his years, careworn and pathetic. Yiorgo cleared his throat.

'Before you see Mamma I think we ought to smarten you up a bit.'

Yannis smiled ruefully at him. 'I didn't wear my best for the trip. I must look like a beggar. My clothes are soaked.'

'What did you do? Swim?'

'Only the last few yards, I borrowed one of the bathtubs.'

'I'll find you some clothes.' Shaking with emotion Yiorgo left the kitchen and Yannis senior gazed at his son.

'What have they done to you?'

'Nothing. I took a bit of a beating when I was in hospital, but that was a long while ago. I'm fine now.'

A silence fell between the two men.

'I'm sorry, Pappa.' Yannis put his head on his arm and sobbed brokenly. 'I shouldn't have come here, but I wanted to see Mamma.'

His father watched, a lump in his throat. He took a bottle from the shelf and poured a generous measure into a glass. 'Drink that, you'll feel better.' He put the bottle to his own lips and took a long pull, wiping his mouth with the back of his hand. 'Go on, drink it.'

Yannis lifted the glass and allowed a little to trickle down his throat. He choked as the fiery liquid slipped down, then took another small sip. 'I haven't tasted brandy in years. I'd forgotten how strong it was.'

Yannis sat down opposite his son. 'Did you get permission to come here?'

Yannis shook his head. 'I floated over in a bathtub.' He took another cautious sip of the brandy. The initial shock and emotion having passed he felt better now.

'What made you do a foolhardy thing like that?'

'For years I've looked across at this farm, wondered what you were all doing, how you were keeping. I didn't know about Mamma until Father Minos visited us, and I didn't know about Maria until Andreas was able to send a letter to me. Finally I had to come myself.'

Yiorgo entered with a bundle of clothes in his arms. 'These should fit you – and I don't need them,' he added, thrusting them at Yannis.

'I'm grateful for anything.'

'Where are you going?'

Yannis looked at his brother in surprise. 'Going? Nowhere.'

'You can't stay here.' Yiorgo spoke more sharply than he had intended.

'I know. I'm an outcast. No one wants a leper in their midst. Even the hospitals treat you like a criminal. I didn't ask to be ill. It's not my fault.'

'Then where are you going?' Yiorgo repeated the question.

'I came to see you, particularly Mamma. I'll leave again tomorrow and get back to the island.'

'How?'

'The bathtub is down amongst the rocks. I can go back in that.'

Yiorgo shrugged. 'There are some caves up in the hills.'

Yannis shook his head. 'How long could I stay hidden before someone saw me and told the authorities? I don't want to be hunted like an animal. When I've seen Mamma and Anna I'll get back as best I can.'

'Where will you spend the night?'

'In the stable, I've slept in worse places. I could do with some more to eat, though.'

Yiorgo handed him another small loaf and a jar of home made brawn.

'Any tomatoes and olives?' asked Yannis hungrily and Yiorgo produced them. His father and brother watched as he munched and chewed, sipping intermittently at the brandy.

'When can I see Mamma?' he asked.

'In the morning. I think it might be wiser if we talked to Anna first and she prepared Mamma. We mustn't give her too much of a shock.'

Yannis was forced to agree, anxious though he was to see her. 'I'll wait until you call me.'

He slept well, curled up on the straw next to the donkey, not stirring until long after dawn. When he first awoke it took a moment for him to realise where he was, then the donkey, stamping her feet, reminded him and a smile of pure pleasure spread across his face. He was at home. Impatiently he waited until he heard footsteps in the yard and the door was thrown open.

'Anna!'

She threw her arms round his neck, burying her face in his shoulder. 'Yannis, oh, Yannis, it's so good to see you.'

Gently Yannis disentangled her hands and held her away from him. 'I'd love to hug and kiss you, Anna, but it's better not. I don't know how infectious I am. No one seems to know and I don't want to risk giving it to you. Have you told Mamma I'm here?'

Anna nodded. 'I'm not sure she believed me. She kept nodding and smiling and saying "he's a good boy, a clever boy," as though you'd just returned from High School. You'll see a great change in her, Yannis.'

'She'll see a change in me too, so we'll just have to accept each other.'

Anna led the way across the yard and into the kitchen. 'I'm so pleased to see you.'

'I don't think Pappa and Yiorgo are.'

'They are really. They're just worried in case someone sees you. If you were found here they'd probably take us all for tests.'

'Then we must make sure I'm not found.'

Yannis gazed at his mother, slumped slightly to one side in her chair. She looked far older than he remembered her. 'Mamma.'

YANNIS

'Come here, Yannis, let me look at you.' Her words, although slurred, were quite distinguishable.

Yannis stood before her. She studied him for a long time before she spoke again.

'You look well enough – considering.'

'I am – considering. How are you?'

'I'm useless.' She pointed to her withered hand. 'No more embroidery or cooking.'

'You deserve a rest. You always worked so hard.'

Maria hardly seemed to hear him. 'I have Anna. She's a good girl. Sees to everything, even little Yannis. Maria's gone. Gone forever. I couldn't say goodbye to her. She wasn't a bad girl, just unlucky, impatient, couldn't wait. Babbis blames himself. Won't take much notice of little Yannis. Reminds him of his poor Maria. Bad luck has hit this family. We've been cursed. First Yannis broke his leg; then you were taken away, then I became ill, then Maria. What's to become of us?'

'I'll always be here, Mamma,' promised Anna.

'Yannis's come back, Anna. He's come to visit us now he's better.'

'Mamma, I'm not better. Not yet. I have to go back later today.'

'Go back? Go back where?'

'I live on the island. I'm a leper.'

Maria nodded slowly. 'That's what they told me. My Yannis, a leper.' She sucked in her breath. 'You're still my Yannis; my clever Yannis. Who brought you over to see me?'

'No one, Mamma. I floated over in a bathtub.'

'Clever Yannis; always had good ideas.' Maria's head sank down and she appeared to be asleep. Anna turned to Yannis.

'Come and sit over here and tell me about the island.'

Yannis smiled at her. 'It isn't a very pleasant subject.'

'I want to know just the same. Everything Yannis. From when you were first ill in Heraklion and went to hospital there.'

'Father Minos will have told you all about that.'

'I want you to tell me,' insisted Anna. 'Tell me now, whilst Mamma sleeps.'

Capitulating to his sister's wishes, Yannis related how he had first been diagnosed and the help the priest had given him, then his short stay in the hospital in Heraklion before being sent to Athens.

'That was the first we knew, when Andreas and the priest came here. It was a terrible shock. Did they give you all the latest treatment in Athens?'

'The treatment they gave us there was worse than you can possibly imagine. We were treated like criminals. Locked up, half starved, beaten if we protested.'

Anna's eyes opened wide in horror. 'I'm glad you're not there now.'

'I'm glad too. I wasn't at first. I thought we'd been sent to the island to die. I suppose we were in a way. No one seemed to care until Father Minos came.'

'What was it like when you arrived? Tell me truly, Yannis.'

Yannis smiled grimly. 'Derelict, dirty, stinking – you name it.' Yannis described the island as he had found it when he had first landed. He painted a sad picture of the crippled occupants, trying to live on decaying food and sheltering in derelict buildings.

'It's much better now,' he assured his sister. 'I'm sure Father Minos has had something to do with better food being sent over.'

Anna shook her head. 'It was Pappa. He threatened to report to the government anyone who sent rotten food.'

'I'm surprised they worried about that threat. The government doesn't care. You should have seen some of the food in the hospital.'

'I think they guessed Pappa has a reason.'

'You mean the villagers know I'm there?'

Anna nodded. 'Why should I suddenly start waving to an island occupied by lepers, or Pappa send out a goat and insist that the food was fresh? He'd never bothered before.'

YANNIS

'Waving!' Yannis clapped a hand to his forehead. 'I'd forgotten. I promised Phaedra I'd let her know I was safely here by asking you to wave your red scarf.'

'Who's Phaedra?'

'One of the women out there.'

'Is she your girl?'

Yannis laughed. 'Hardly. No girl is likely to look at me. We're just friends.'

Anna did not believe him. He was far too insistent that she must go and wave immediately. She teased him for a few more minutes, then took her red scarf from behind the door and went down to the beach. As soon as she had left Maria opened her eyes.

'You've had a hard time, Yannis.'

'I thought you were asleep, Mamma.'

'I was listening. I knew you wouldn't tell me the truth as you would Anna. I'm proud of you, Yannis. You were always the clever one. I shan't grieve for you any more. You've found your purpose in life. Ill or not, you were sent there to help them.'

Yannis looked at his mother. 'Do you really believe that?'

'There's a reason behind everything. We can't always see it, but you were needed there, and the only way you could go was to be sick yourself.' Maria closed her eyes again. 'You're a good boy, Yannis. I often sit here and they think I'm asleep, but I'm really listening. I hear their arguments and I think "what would Yannis have done, or said?" and I let my thoughts drift away. I hear much more than they realise. You stay with your Phaedra. If you're good friends now you always will be. Yiorgo, now, he never looks at a girl. Always busy on the farm. Loves the land too much to be interested in anything or anyone else. Anna, well, maybe, but not yet, poor child. She won't leave me, but when I go there's Babbis. It's poor Stelios I worry over. He worshipped you, Yannis, tried to be like you in every way. Now he's changed; he's very bitter. Won't talk about you. Father Minos tried to talk to him, but he wouldn't listen. I think he's frightened that he will have it and be sent to the island.'

'I know how he feels. I hated that island. When I found I'd been sent there I was petrified. Gradually I realised it wasn't as bad as the hospital had been. I've some very good friends there, usually we have enough to eat, and we're not prisoners in one large room, watching each other decay and die.'

Maria nodded. 'And you have your Phaedra. I don't doubt that you've chosen the prettiest and cleverest girl on the island.'

Yannis shook his head. 'You're a crafty old lady, Mamma. You've gone far ahead of me. I would be lost without Phaedra; she's been a good friend to me. She's not particularly pretty, and she can neither read nor write.'

'Then why don't you teach her?'

'Teach her?'

'There's probably a good few over there that have either never learned or have forgotten. Why don't you teach them? Keep you occupied.'

'Oh, Mamma, you always did want me to be a teacher if I wouldn't become a doctor.'

'So now's your chance, Yannis.'

'Maybe,' Yannis agreed cautiously. 'In the winter.'

'Have you got your books, Yannis?'

'Most of them. I often wish...' Yannis's voice tailed off as Anna burst through the door.

'Yannis, they've found the bathtub. They're looking for you.'

Yannis's face paled. 'Who are?'

'The fishermen. If they don't find you they're going to inform the authorities so they can start a full scale search.'

'I must go. I can't let them find me here. I'll walk on towards Elounda and if they find me I'll say I'm making for Aghios Nikolaos to see my girl.'

Anna's eyes filled with tears. 'I wish you could stay, Yannis.'

'I wish I could too. Don't cry. I'll come again.'

YANNIS

Yannis turned to his mother who stretched out an arm to him. 'Kiss me goodbye, Yannis. I may not be here the next time.'

Yannis hesitated. 'Come along,' insisted Maria. 'You're my son, Yannis, and I want you to kiss me goodbye.'

'Oh, Mamma!' Yannis cradled her head against his chest and kissed the top of her head. The talisman to ward off the evil eye that she had given him years ago when he first went to Heraklion bruised her face.

'You still have it, then. Not that it did much for you, but it could have been far worse. Keep it always and it will keep you safe.'

'Yes, Mamma,' he promised. 'I must go. Bless you, Anna and keep waving.'

Anna watched as Yannis left by the kitchen door and began to make his way up over the hills, using the track that led to Babbis's farmhouse. At the ridge she saw him turn and look back, then he was gone from her sight. He moved as fast as he could, trying to take advantage of the sparse cover of olive trees, carob and vine. He could see his father and Yiorgo working hard a short distance away and wished he could stay and spend the day with them. He picked his way over the uneven ground towards them.

'Where are you off to?' asked his father.

'I've come to say goodbye. They've found the bathtub. The fishermen are looking for me, so I want to try to get to Elounda before they catch up with me.'

'Best get onto the cart then.'

Yannis looked at his father in surprise. 'The cart?'

'Be quick about it.'

Yannis scrambled up and laid flat as his father ordered whilst Yiorgo began to fork grass and vine cuttings over him. Yannis pushed his head clear. 'I can't breathe.'

'Make a hole for your mouth and keep still.'

Yannis felt the donkey being hitched between the shafts and he began to jolt over the grassy track until they reached the flatter surface that served as a road between the two villages. For an interminable time Yannis jolted along getting hotter, and wishing he could push away the grass that was tickling his neck and making him itch. Yiorgo whistled tunelessly as he guided the donkey and Yannis began to feel quite light-headed. Abruptly the donkey stopped, backing into the shafts and jerking Yannis alert.

'What's the problem?' he heard Yiorgo ask.

'There's a leper about. Seen anyone on the road, Yiorgo?'

'Not a soul,' replied Yiorgo truthfully, and smacked the donkey on the rump to make her continue.

'Just a minute.'

The cart stopped. 'Cover his foot up, Yiorgo. Word's got round. They'll be looking everywhere.'

'Thanks.'

They moved again and Yannis pushed some grass away from his face. 'Yiorgo.'

'Keep quiet and stay hidden.'

'No. I want to get off.'

'Wait until we're the other side of Elounda.'

'No, now.' Yannis threw off the grass and leapt down. 'I'll make for the hills.'

'Pappa said to take you all the way.'

'If you take me much further they'll want to search the cart, then they'll know I've been home. Mamma and Anna could suffer. Thank Pappa for me. Tell him you took me wherever you please. And Yiorgo – thank you.'

Without waiting for his brother to answer Yannis scrambled up the bank and down into the ditch out of sight. Yiorgo stood in the middle of the road and scratched his head, not at all sure what he should do. Yannis sat where he was until Yiorgo had rounded the bend in the road, then emerged and began to walk openly to Elounda. To his surprise he had reached the far side of the village before he was challenged. Once stopped a small crowd

517

began to gather and before Yannis could explain or defend himself a stone flew through the air and landed at his feet.

'Better move.'

A stick prodded him in his back and Yannis started his ignominious walk to Aghios Nikolaos. The whole way he was followed by men, women and children who jeered and threw stones at him at intervals that made him duck and weave. On the quay Yannis could see Manolis whittling at a piece of wood and breathed a sigh of relief. At least he would not have to wait around for the boatman to return before he could escape the hostile crowd.

Manolis scowled at him. 'You, is it? I might have guessed when they told me to wait around. Get in. Up to the prow.'

Silently Yannis took his place and Manolis cast off. They were well away from the land before the boatman spoke to him. 'Did you make it to your family?' Manolis asked eagerly.

Yannis nodded.

'Good for you! What was it like, drifting over there in a tub?'

'Pretty nerve racking.'

'There was quite a panic when your tub was found. Messages were passed between the boats and to all the villages. I was told I couldn't go over to the island until you'd been found. Can't think why not!'

'They may have thought I'd arranged for you to pick me up from one of the coves.'

Manolis struck his head with his hand. 'Fool that you are! Why didn't you ask me to do so?'

'Because if they'd found out you would have had your boat taken away and that would have been the end of your living.'

Manolis grinned. 'If we'd brought the bathtub back with us they would probably never have known you'd been away.'

Yannis smiled with him. He had a strange feeling of relief to know he was on his way back to the island. No longer must he hide or face a howling, jeering mob. He saw the island growing larger as they approached and wondered if Phaedra would be waiting on the quay or if he would have to search for her. His mother's words throbbed in his ears. "You have your Phaedra."

Phaedra could hardly believe her eyes when Yannis stepped from Manolis's boat. Despite Yannis's assurances regarding his return she still thought he might decide to stay hidden close to his family. To see him return so soon filled her with relief and pleasure. She managed to wait until the little crowd that surged round him fell back; then she walked down the ramp.

'Welcome back.'

'It's good to see you.'

They walked in silence, a strange uneasiness between them.

'Did you see Anna wave?' asked Yannis finally.

'I was beginning to get worried. I'd been watching for hours. How's your Mamma?'

Yannis smiled. 'She's a naughty old lady. She sits there pretending to be asleep and really she's listening to everything that's going on. I must say she was a pleasant surprise. I hadn't quite known what to expect. She can't walk without help or use one arm, but apart from that she's fine.'

'And Anna?'

'Poor Anna, she looks after Mamma and the house as well as Maria's children. She has no life of her own at all.'

Phaedra shrugged. 'At least she has a family. Not like us.'

'We're like a family over here.'

'But we don't belong to anyone. We're all separate people from all different parts of Greece who just happen to be on an island. When someone dies we all feel sad, but no one grieves for them, no one is that close.'

'What about the couples who are living together? They would grieve if one or the other died.'

'I suppose so. I can't really explain what I mean. Tell me all about your trip. Did you have to swim?'

Yannis related to her how dark and frightening it had been with just the slap of the waves against the tub and no idea if he was still going in the right direction. 'Next time I'll go when there's a moon.'

'Next time?'

'Of course, if I can do it once I can do it again.'

'You may not be so lucky a second time.'

Yannis laughed at her fears. 'There's really nothing to it.'

'Suppose a storm blew up and you were wrecked?'

Yannis shrugged. 'It's a chance you take. Everyone has to go one day and to be drowned would be no worse than mouldering here.'

'Please, Yannis, don't talk like that.' Phaedra shivered. 'I'm going to church to say thank you for your safe return.'

'Do I mean that much to you?'

Phaedra began to scramble to her feet. Yannis caught at her skirt and pulled her back down beside him. 'Answer my question.'

'I don't remember it.'

'Yes, you do. Stop teasing. I want an answer.' Yannis put his arm around her waist and pulled her closer to him. 'Do you care about me, Phaedra?'

'Of course, I care about most of the people over here.'

'But not especially about me?'

'Why should I?' Her chin tilted defiantly.

'Because I realised when Manolis was bringing me back that I care a good deal about you. I wanted to be back here, with you. You're very special to me.'

'Do you mean it, Yannis?'

By way of an answer Yannis kissed her, pushing her back onto the hard ground, cushioning her head on his arm. 'I'd like to feel that you belonged to me, Phaedra.'

Stelios opened the letter he had collected from the post office. It was a good deal longer than Anna's usual notes, telling him all was well at Plaka and urging him to work hard at school. As he unfolded it the words seemed to jump from the page before his eyes.

"There was a great commotion on the island a few days ago. When I went to wave to Yannis there were a lot of people milling around and waving, they seemed to be shouting something, but I couldn't hear what it was. I asked one of the boatmen and he said there was going to be a wedding, a proper wedding, in the church on the island. I felt so happy for them, yet at the same time very sad that they couldn't have all their friends and relatives with them.

I asked Davros to wait and asked Pappa if we could send something. He was a bit unwilling, but finally said I could send them half a dozen chickens. By the time I'd caught them and tied their legs Davros was getting impatient, but he loaded them and promised to deliver them to the groom. I was just leaving to go up to Babbis when Davros returned. He waved to me and called that Yannis and Phaedra said thank you.

My heart missed a beat and I nearly fainted. Isn't it wonderful for him? I'm so happy. I ran inside and told Mamma and she cried and cried. Pappa wished he'd sent more than six chickens and is wondering if they had any wine or brandy for a celebration. I do wish I could go over and meet my new sister-in-law. I'm sure I'd like her."

And so the letter ran on, making Stelios grit his teeth as he read, until he finally crumpled the sheets of paper and stuffed them into his pocket. 'Disgusting,' he muttered. 'Disgusting. Revolting. Filthy lepers, it shouldn't be allowed.'

He turned into a taverna and ordered a brandy. The owner eyed him with suspicion, the boy did not look old enough to be a brandy drinker and he wanted no trouble or mess to clear up. 'You'd be better on wine at your age.'

'I've had a shock.' A small glass was placed in front of him and he downed the contents in one swallow. 'Another.'

Doubtfully the bar tender poured a second glass and hovered

until he had been paid. This time Stelios drank more slowly, not sure whether the burning sensation in his brain was due to the liquor or his emotions. He deposited the glass on the bar top and made his way unsteadily towards the door. He would never return to Plaka.

Yannis kissed Phaedra gently. 'I'm glad I'm home and you're here waiting for me.'

'Don't be silly. You're never very far away. I often see you half a dozen times a day.'

'I still appreciate coming home to you. Tell me what you've been doing.'

Phaedra giggled. 'You know what I did. You kept seeing me.'

'I want you to tell me.'

'Well, I swept the floor and tidied the bed, collected two buckets of water, then decided what I would cook for your supper. I prepared that and left it whilst I went up to the hospital to see Panicos. Spiro told me Elena hadn't arrived so I went to find her. I came back down to get some vegetables for the patients' meals and I saw her chatting to Apostolos. When she saw me she said she was feeling better and was on her way up. I didn't believe her. She looked far too guilty so I gave her the vegetables and a message for Spiro to say I'd be back later, so she had to go.'

Yannis grinned. 'What did you do then?'

'I looked for Flora and talked to her until Manolis arrived.'

'What did Manolis have to say?'

'Very little. I thought it best to leave them alone for a while so I went to find Father Minos.'

'Where was he?'

'In the church. You know, Yannis, it really is nice in there now. He always has a candle burning and some little ones kept by the door so you can light one when you go in. I lit one,' Phaedra's face was glowing with enthusiasm. 'I'd love to see a proper church, one on the mainland. Father Minos says there are always lots of candles burning in them and pictures all round the walls.'

'I like ours the way it is.'

'Why? Don't you like pictures?'

'Yes, I do, in the very big churches. In the little ones they make you feel, well, as though you're being watched to make sure you behave properly. What did you talk to Father Minos about?'

'A lot of things, we went from one thing to another. He said he wanted to talk to Doctor Stavros the next time he came over. You don't think he's ill do you?'

'I hope not. He's made such a difference to us. I'll go and talk to him myself after supper.'

Phaedra pouted. 'I thought we could have an evening at home.'

'We have plenty of time to have evenings at home. I shan't be long.'

Yannis forced himself to eat slowly and make conversation to his wife, although her words had disturbed him and he longed to go to the priest.

It was nearly dark when he left their house, but he needed no light to guide him on the familiar path round the island. Father Minos was not at the church, nor at the house he had helped to repair and now occupied. Yannis cursed under his breath. He would have to search from house to house now.

No one seemed to know the whereabouts of the priest and Yannis was becoming increasingly worried. He retraced his steps down the path, returning again to peer into the church. Finally he trod warily through the tunnel and began to climb the slope on the seaward side of the island. There he almost collided with Father Minos.

'I've been looking for you everywhere!'

'What's wrong? Does someone need me?'

'I only wanted to talk to you. I was worried when I couldn't find you.'

Father Minos smiled in the darkness. 'Come with me, Yannis. I'd like your opinion.'

Yannis followed until they stopped at the little church and Father Minos opened the door. Yannis crossed the threshold whilst the priest lit an oil lamp and held it aloft, showing the roof almost repaired.

'Looks better, now, doesn't it? I've been coming here whenever I had a chance. This is a church also, and it seemed wrong to renovate one and neglect the other.'

'So what will you do? Hold services alternately?'

'I want to use this church just for burial services.'

'It's closer to the tower.'

'I don't want to use the tower.'

Yannis looked at the priest puzzled.

'Just across from here is a small patch that isn't rock like the rest of the island. There are a few feet of soil. I thought we could make it into a proper cemetery.' Father Minos's eyes were gleaming with enthusiasm. 'Don't you think it's a good idea?'

'Father, of course it's a good idea, but there's so much that still needs to be done for the living. Once a person's dead you can do nothing for them.'

'Nothing for their body but there is still their soul to be considered. How would you feel when you knew your last moments were near and there was nothing to look forward to except being thrown into a tower amongst other bones and rotting flesh? No burial rites, no grave where someone could say a prayer for you. You just become another pile of bones, indistinguishable from all the rest.'

Yannis swallowed. The memory of the sack that had been thrust into the hospital ward for a body to be placed inside and disposed of as rubbish came back to him vividly.

'It was the lack of burial rites that started the fight at the hospital.'

'Then I'm surprised some of you haven't thought of it before.'

'We've been rather busy trying to keep alive.'

'I know, Yannis, and I'm not blaming you. I just want to know what you think of my idea. What did you want to see me about?'

'I'd almost forgotten. Phaedra said you wanted to see Doctor Stavros when he next came over and I wanted to ask why. I'm not just being nosey, Phaedra was worried in case you were ill.'

'I've never felt better, Yannis. I want to talk to him about a burial ground. He may come up with a medical reason why it isn't feasible.'

The doctor was disturbed by the hospital. Spiro had moved the mattresses closer together and there were six more patients than before. 'I did the right thing by bringing them in, didn't I?' he asked anxiously.

'You did quite right. I'm just worried about space. You've hardly room to move with so many mattresses and you could do with a couple of extra helpers.'

'I have them,' Spiro assured him. 'Whenever I need extra help I tell Roula. She seems able to conjure up helpers from thin air.'

'She's a wonder. I'll have a look at Panicos again before I leave. He's very low.'

'He didn't want to come in. Said he was quite fit enough to stay where he was. The truth was he didn't want to leave his goats.'

'Who's looking after them now?'

Spiro grinned. 'They're tethered round the back. When it's milking time we bring them in so he can pet them. Wish we had a few more.'

'Could you cope with more? There's not much for them to eat except food scraps and they tend to chew at anything.'

'We could manage. They'd be worth it for their milk.'

'I'll ask Manolis to see to it.'

Father Minos was waiting outside the hospital for the doctor. 'I'd like to talk to you for a while. Can you spare a few minutes to walk round the other side of the island with me?'

'Of course. Are you consulting me professionally?'

'Very much so, but not personally, I've had an idea and I want your medical opinion.'

Doctor Stavros raised his eyebrows. 'Are you about to present a medical discovery to me which has been under my nose for years?'

'Not at all. Mind how you go. We really should get this path repaired here and maybe a small wall built. It would be such a nasty drop if anyone missed their footing. I'll have a word with Yannis and see whom we can ask. Now, do you remember the little church on this side of the island? I want to start using it again.'

The doctor nodded. Had he been asked to walk the long way round just to be shown a church?

'At the moment,' continued the priest,' When someone dies I say a few words over them, then we carry them down through the tunnel and throw them in the tower with half a bucket of lime. Not a very illustrious way to depart, you must agree.'

Again the doctor nodded. Their method of disposing of the dead revolted him, but he had no better solution to offer.

'I thought it might be nicer to have a separate church where we could hold a proper service and then use that bit of ground over there to bury them.' Father Minos indicated with his hand to the space between the tower and the walls of the fort.

'How are you going to dig through the rock?'

'Ah,' Father Minos's eyes gleamed. 'That looks like rock, but in truth it's compacted earth. That's what I want your opinion about. It only has a depth of about four feet – would that be deep enough for a burial?'

'It would, but you'd have to contain the body in something. You can't just bury people. Before you knew it bones would be coming to the surface, natural earth movement at that depth.'

Father Minos frowned. 'I knew there had to be a catch. I thought it was such a good idea.'

'It is. I thoroughly approve, but you'll have to place them in something.'

'I'll work on it,' Father Minos smiled. 'Thank you for your time.'

Yiorgo Pavlakis collected his papers together and went in search of Andreas. The priest was not at home, but the housekeeper assured him he would be back for the mid-day service and would be able to see him directly afterwards. There was no alternative for Yiorgo but to return to the taverna and wait for the time to pass. He was not unduly despondent; it would give him an hour to spend with his daughter. Now she was older and no longer behaved like a baby he was beginning to dote on her.

He held the child on his knee, turning over the pages of a picture book.

'What's that, Pappa?'

'Let me see.' Yiorgo pushed the cloud of dark hair back from where it hung over the page. Anna pulled it back. 'No, darling, Pappa can't see with all your hair there.' He held the heavy hair back with his hand. 'That's the golden fleece that Jason set out to find. You remember the story?' He looked up at her and the smile froze on his lips. Her birthmark seemed to have spread considerably. He forced himself to speak normally. 'You tell me the story of Jason.'

Anna shook her head. 'No. You tell me the story of Theseus. I like it when he fights the monster.'

Yiorgo smiled. 'All right, now, let's see, how did Theseus get to Crete in the first place?'

'As one of the boys and girls who were sent every year.'

Yiorgo and Anna sat with their heads close together, each telling a little of the story and pointing to the pictures. Anna was laughing as Yiorgo pretended to be the Minotaur when her mother walked in. Immediately the laughter stopped and she looked at Louisa warily.

'Time for lunch, Anna. Go and wash.'

'Yes, Mamma.' Obediently she closed the book and slipped off Yiorgo's knee. 'Thank you for the story.'

'I must make sure I have more time at home with you, then we can have more stories.' He waited until Anna had left the room. 'Louisa, when did you last take Anna to the doctor?'

Louisa shrugged. 'I don't remember. She's always well, besides, doctors cost money.'

'Her birthmark seems to have got considerably bigger.'

'Of course it will. As she grows so will the mark. She's lucky her hair hides it.'

'I'm not happy with it. I don't care about the cost. It's Anna, our daughter; nothing is too good for her. I'll take her tomorrow if you don't have the time.'

The doctor was unknown to Yiorgo. 'What can I do for you?' He smiled blandly from behind his desk.

'I should like you to examine my daughter.'

'What's wrong with her?'

'She has a birthmark. It seems to have grown considerably larger over the last few months.'

'Birthmarks grow with the child.'

'Of course, but I'd be grateful for your opinion.'

With a sigh the doctor rose. 'Can you show me your birthmark?'

Anna pulled back her hair.

'I see. Does it hurt or itch?'

'No.'

He ran his hand over the raised, red skin. 'I can see nothing to worry over. As you say, it's a birthmark. It may grow for a while; it could also diminish as she becomes older. She's fortunate to have most of it covered by her hair. Is there any other problem?'

Yiorgo shook his head.

'I charge five drachmas for a consultation.'

Yiorgo took the money from his pocket. To have his mind set at rest was worth the extortionate amount.

'You're just the man we want,' called Father Minos as the doctor approached. 'Phillipos is a carpenter. He says he would be able to make coffins if the wood were available and he had the tools.'

'Good.' Inadvertently the doctor looked down at the man's hands. They were cracked and bruised, two fingers almost missing and the others clawed. It was doubtful if he would have the skill left. As if reading his thoughts the carpenter held up his hands.

'I won't be able to do the job as well as I'd like, but I could manage something reasonable.'

'I'm sure you could. Maybe someone could help you?'

'I've trained plenty in my time. Not for coffins, mind, we made tables, chairs and the like. Nothing fancy, but good, solid stuff.'

Doctor Stavros nodded. 'Where's the timber coming from?'

'Would the government pay for it? Timber like that is costly.'

'There's no need to involve the government. We'll have our pensions. Anyone who wants to be buried will have to pay for a coffin.' Yannis frowned. 'Mind you, by the time the government get round to sending it we shall probably all be dead.'

'I'm sure it won't be much longer now.'

'I think they're doing it deliberately,' complained Yannis. 'Every delay will mean less money for us.'

'Why worry? You'd never thought of money until the pension was suggested.'

Yannis shrugged impatiently. 'It's the principle.'

Phillipos grinned. 'You'll never be satisfied, will you? Since you've been here we've got houses, water, better food, bedding, medicine, a doctor and a priest. What more do you want?'

'Do you really want to know? I'd like to see the hospital enlarged and a doctor on the island permanently, day and night, to cope with emergencies and not be dependent upon the weather to get across.'

'It doesn't happen often,' protested Phillipos.

'One time it will be crucial to have a doctor and he won't be able to come. We need electricity, too.'

'Electricity?' The men looked at him in amazement.

'Like they have now in the hospitals on the mainland. Suppose the doctor had to operate on an emergency in the evening? He wouldn't be able to see what he was doing with our poor oil lamps. It could be a matter of life and death.'

Doctor Stavros and Father Minos exchanged glances. Yannis was completely serious.

'It would take years for us to get those things,' laughed Phillipos.

'That's why we have to keep on pressing. As soon as we get one thing we ask for another.'

Father Minos smiled at Yannis's flushed face. 'You haven't been so vehement about anything for a long while.'

'I have my moments. I'm serious about all of them. If we just sit back and wait for the government or medical authorities to give us anything we'll wait forever. We have to be persistent, even to the point of being a nuisance so they give in to our requests just to keep us quiet.'

'I'm with you, Yannis. Just let me know when you want me to be a nuisance,' Phillipos declared.

1940 – 1945

Pavlos sat drinking morosely. He had been unfortunate again. The cards had definitely been running against him. The more he had increased his bets in an effort to recoup, the greater the eventual loss had been and now he was desperate. None of his card-playing friends were willing to lend him even a lepta and he knew Yiorgo never had any spare money. He would have to ask Louisa yet again.

He studied the customers. They were a motley collection. Two elderly men, who came in every evening, had a bottle of wine between them and played dominoes, were sitting hunched over their table. Four young men, obviously students, were at another, eating voraciously. His brother-in-law was deep in conversation with two of his fellow councillors.

Pavlos felt an unreasonable anger against all of them rising within him. What a waste of an evening. No money to go out and enjoy himself and having to wait until his sister finished working to beg money from her. He lit another cigarette and waited. Even Yiorgo was making life difficult for him that evening. On previous occasions he had been able to hear every word Yiorgo was planning to say at the next council meeting and had sold the information for a good price. Tonight he had his back towards him and the talk was low and confidential. He waited until his sister was washing the glasses and offered to scrape the plates for her. 'Louisa, are you able to do me a small favour?'

'How much?' She did not even look at him.

Pavlos wetted his lips. 'Five hundred drachmas.'

'What!'

'I went down heavily the other evening and they're after my blood.'

'Be a good job if they had it.'

'Please, Louisa,' he wheedled. 'I am your brother.'

'I haven't got that kind of money.'

Pavlos took her arm in a vice-like grip. 'I think you can find it. I need it by tomorrow. Remember Yiorgo thinks he's the proud father of that little bastard who's asleep upstairs. What would he say if I told him you had no idea who her father was? Told him that his beautiful Louisa was the town's best known prostitute?'

'You wouldn't!'

Pavlos grinned. 'That depends upon your co-operation. I need five hundred now, unless you'd rather I had a word with Yiorgo.'

Louisa stared at him coldly. 'He'd never believe you.'

'Oh, yes, he would. I can be very convincing.'

'He'd kill you.'

Pavlos shook his head. 'He'd be more likely to kill you, my dear. Once I've told him, everything would fall into place. The premature birth of his beloved daughter, the rather excessive income from a somewhat seedy and run-down taverna, the number of seafarers who forsake the waterfront bars to come here. You probably have far more than that hidden away. I'm only asking for five hundred.' He twisted her arm up her back.

'Then you'll have to keep asking. I can let you have three.'

'That will do for a start.' He released her arm and she rubbed it to restore the circulation. His debts were in the region of two hundred so he would have some remaining money to use for another game next week when he was sure he would be luckier.

Yiorgo Pavlakis sat at the head of the table and tried to listen attentively. If only they would say exactly what they meant, not try to hedge everything around with meaningless phrases. He banged on the table with his fist.

'Can we take a vote? Those for joining Greece first.'

Hands were raised and he counted them carefully, calculating the result as he did so.

'Those who think it is better for Crete to stay out of the conflict?'

Again hands were raised, but the result did not add up to a clear-cut decision as he had hoped. A young man jumped to his feet.

'Permission to speak, sir, and put forward another motion?'

Yiorgo Pavlakis frowned. He had prepared a speech ready for this moment and he was sure that his logical thinking would sway every member to the decision that he thought was a solution. He pushed back his lock of hair and wiped his hand down his trousers.

'Is it relevant to the matter under discussion?'

'Very, sir.'

'Go ahead, then.' Yiorgo sank back into his seat, hoping it would not prolong the proceedings for more than half an hour. As he listened he shook his head in disbelief. No more than two days ago he had spoken those words as he had rehearsed his speech for tonight, and now here was this young man repeating them, almost verbatim, as his own.

Yiorgo gazed fixedly at the young man as the council members clapped. This had been his speech. He was the one who deserved the applause and the credit for thinking so calmly and with foresight. 'Do you wish to vote again?' he asked.

Hands were raised. 'Very well. Those for joining Greece first.'

Three hands began to rise, hovered, withdrew or scratched an ear or nose.

'Those who think it better for Crete to stay neutral for the present time.'

Hands were raised and smiles exchanged with neighbours. It made sense now it had been explained.

'Motion carried.' Yiorgo was about to add the final thrust of his speech, but the young man was too quick for him.

'There is just one more thing. Although we have passed a motion for non-alliance I think we should consider the European implications very seriously. Although we are not going to actively aid Greece we are not going to be obstructive, and this could bring the wrath of other nations on our necks. We should prepare ourselves, take precautions should anyone try to interfere with our policies and draw up contingency plans.'

As he stopped speaking the silence that followed was like a thick, enveloping mist.

'Do you really think that is necessary?'

'I think we should consider the necessity. No panic decisions, but we must be aware and prepared. I should like to propose a motion, sir. All those who would like a further meeting to discuss future policy to raise their hands.'

Yiorgo nodded and watched as the men raised their hands. He had been robbed!

Yannis approached Doctor Stavros. 'Just a plain gold one; I've got fifty four drachmas according to the ledger and you can spend as much of that as you need.'

'Why are you asking me? Manolis does the shopping.'

'I trust you.'

The doctor raised his eyebrows. 'You don't trust Manolis?'

'I trust him with the money, I just don't trust his taste.'

'It may take a while. I can't promise to have it for a week or so.'

'Could you manage to have it three weeks on Wednesday?' asked Yannis anxiously.

'Probably.'

Yannis smiled. 'It's just that we'll have been married for two years and I thought it would be nice to give it to her on our anniversary.'

'You try very hard, don't you, Yannis.'

'Try? How do you mean?'

'You try to pretend you're not ill and life is no different here from the way it would be if you lived in a village on the mainland.'

Yannis shook his head. 'I don't try to pretend. Phaedra can hardly remember what it's like to live a normal life, a home; a family. I want to give her as much as I can. She accepts having our food delivered instead of going to the market, or even into the garden to pick vegetables. I can't alter that. I'm trying to give her a home, to give her a feeling of belonging, the knowledge that someone cares for her. I want her to believe that life here is the same as it would be anywhere else. I know it isn't, but she doesn't.'

'I still think you're doing it to fool yourself. One day you'll have to come to terms with your illness.'

Yannis's mouth opened and shut. 'We don't have to come to terms with it as you put it. There's no way we can get away from it. We see it around us all day long, and there's nothing wrong in trying to live like a decent human being, even when the rest of the world has declared you deserve no more from life than a miserable animal gets. Once you've been sent to this island you come to terms very quickly with the fact that you aren't wanted anywhere on earth and never will be. If we can make life more bearable over here, why shouldn't we?'

Doctor Stavros turned on his heel. 'I'll bring you the bill.'

The small gold ring glittered in the box and Yannis looked on it in delight. 'Thank you; I really appreciate you getting it.'

The doctor held out the bill, which Yannis did not even glance at. 'Give it to Manolis, he'll settle up with you.'

Doctor Stavros cleared his throat. 'I took the liberty of having it engraved.' The doctor pointed to the tiny letters inside. YANNIS – PHAEDRA and the date they had been married.

'That was a wonderful idea. How much extra do I owe you?'

'Nothing. Take it as a belated wedding gift.' The doctor walked rapidly away up the path towards the hospital. After a long talk with Father Minos he had been forced to agree that it was preferable for the lepers to consider themselves legally married than move from one partner to another. He could not enforce celibacy any more than the priest.

Yannis waited until they had eaten their evening meal before drawing Phaedra to him and telling her he had an anniversary gift for her. At first her face lit up, then she blushed.

'Wait a moment. I have something for you. I didn't like to give it to you before in case you'd forgotten and I made you feel guilty.'

'As if I could forget anything as important as our anniversary.'

He pulled the box from his pocket. 'Close your eyes.' He slipped the ring onto her finger.

'Oh, Yannis, it's beautiful.' She turned her head from side to side, admiring the slim gold band.

'Doctor Stavros had it engraved with our names and wedding date.' He held her hand and admired it with her.

'Have your present, Yannis.'

'What is it?'

'Open it and see.'

Phaedra watched as he did so. She knew what he had dreamt of having for so long and she had made Manolis promise that if Yannis asked him to buy him a watch he would delay the purchase with excuses. Yannis handled it reverently, listening to it tick and showing Phaedra how the hands moved around to show what time of day it was. He could see by her puzzled frown that the mysteries of telling the time by a small mechanism were beyond her, but she was delighted at his pleasure.

Yannis sat with Spiro and Father Minos, waiting for their reaction to the idea he had placed before them.

'I don't know how people will feel about being charged for things they've always had given in the past.'

'I think it would be good for them. It would give them a modicum of self-respect,' argued Yannis.

'But what do we have to sell?' asked Father Minos.

'That's part of the challenge. Those who have a trade, like a barber and a carpenter, could charge for their services. We could grow our own vegetables and herbs, buy some more goats and sell the milk. Someone could open up a taverna and we could meet there in the evenings. Once you start to think about it the list is endless.'

'What about those who are in hospital?' asked Spiro.

'They have a pension, the same as the rest of us. From a given date they'll be asked to pay you for being looked after. From that money you keep a little for yourself, and pay those who help you with the work.'

Spiro scratched his head. 'Suppose some of them don't want to do anything?'

'They wouldn't have to. It will be entirely up to the individual.'

Father Minos leaned forward. 'What kind of prices do you have in mind, Yannis, and, more important, where would the money come from?'

'I'm talking about a few lepta. You go for a hair cut and pay two lepta, the barber goes to the taverna and buys a glass of wine. The next day he fancies an egg so he goes to whoever keeps chickens and buys one. It's a circular motion. All we have to do is ask Manolis to bring some money over with him.'

'Would the government allow it?' asked Spiro.

'Are you going to ask them? I'm not. I think it would give us some pride, even our pension is a form of charity.'

'I think you have something there, Yannis, but it would have to be carefully planned. We couldn't just rush into this. There would have to be a limit to the number of barbers or tavernas opening.'

'That's where people like Orestis come in. If you wanted to open a business you'd have to pay him to draw up a proper agreement, giving you the right to trade.' Yannis's eyes began to glow with enthusiasm.

'What I suggest,' Father Minos looked at the two men, 'Is a discussion with Orestis. If he can't find anything against the idea then I'll call a meeting and put it to everyone else.'

Doctor Stavros was delighted. The change that had come about in the last few weeks was remarkable. Patients who had claimed his attention each week were feeling considerably better now they had an incentive. Discussions and meetings were taking place in every house; arguments were frequent until an agreement could be reached. Everywhere he went he was told about plans the person had for earning a small amount of money to supplement their pension.

Takkis had gathered a small group together and they were to become the official builders, Antonis had laid first claim to being a barber, whilst Vassilis and Stathis were arguing which of them was to open the first taverna. Louisa had a notice in her window saying she was a dressmaker, and Elena was ordering lengths of material through Manolis. Phillipos had been asked to make furniture for the taverna and refused, saying it would take him too long and would be easier bought from the mainland. He had agreed to take two men as apprentices for a small weekly sum, mainly to make cupboards and counter tops for those who planned to open shops. Father Minos had sent for more candles from the mainland, hoping by the end of the year to have made enough money to purchase a bell to hang in the tower of the church, and everywhere there was an air of purpose and excitement.

Phaedra was elated by the idea of earning money. 'I've never had any money before. When I bought your watch it wasn't like having money. I just asked Manolis to get it and then I had to sign my name for him – and I did it right,' she added proudly.

'Of course you did.' Yannis smiled at her.

'Some of them couldn't'

'Not write their names?'

Phaedra shook her head. 'They couldn't, truly.'

'Well I'm glad you can.'

'Only because you taught me.'

Yannis nodded slowly. 'How many do you think can't write their names?'

Phaedra shrugged. 'I don't know. There were four when I was there.'

'I'll have a word with the book-keepers.'

'What for?'

'It could make a little job for me. How would you like a school master for a husband?'

Phaedra looked at him in amazement. 'A teacher?'

'You said yourself some of them can't write their names. I could teach them, and how to read and write properly.'

Phaedra shrugged. 'What's so important about reading and writing anyway? You read things from the newspaper to me and I can write my name.'

'Wouldn't you like to read the paper for yourself? Am I reading things that interest you?'

'I don't know.'

'Exactly. If you could read for yourself you would know. Everyone should be able to read. I'm going to see Father Minos. I'll be back later.'

'But your lunch is ready,' protested Phaedra.

'It will keep. This may not.' Without stopping to pick up his jacket Yannis left the house, ignoring Phaedra calling after him.

Father Minos was enthusiastic. 'It's a good idea, Yannis. I'll try to encourage them. It will be confidence they need at first. Once they find out it's not as difficult as they'd thought I'm sure they'll enjoy it.'

'I wonder if I will!'

'Not getting cold feet, are you, Yannis?'

YANNIS

Yannis grinned. 'No, just thinking how we treated poor old Yiorgo Pavlakis when he taught us.'

Andreas opened another letter from Father Minos. They arrived regularly, each one asking for something from the government, which Andreas was supposed to be able to procure immediately. He felt irritated by the continual demands. He had enough to do in the parish, set in the worst area of Heraklion. Each day he walked the mean streets, talking to the young girls who solicited unashamedly from their doorways, trying to persuade them to change their occupation. So far he had met with little success, they agreed with him that their life was degrading, but nothing he could say could make them leave the streets. His services were always well attended, and after his mid-day devotions there was always bread and cheese for the unfortunate. It never failed to amaze him how many unfortunate families there appeared to be in that part of the city.

His housekeeper, inherited from Father Minos, grumbled, but she could not stop him continuing with the charity. Two afternoons were regularly spent at the hospital, talking to the sick, and then he had various house calls to fit in and the occasional wedding, baptism and funeral. Sometimes he would spend an hour or more whilst someone poured out their problems. On top of this he was supposed to spend long hours persuading Yiorgo Pavlakis that the demands from the island were essential improvements and necessary to the occupants' health and conditions.

He read the latest letter from the priest again. Permission was being asked for relatives to visit them. Andreas sighed. He could well imagine the scene this would cause. Yiorgo Pavlakis would argue that such a thing was out of the question due to public health regulations. He would have to insist it was their right and minimise the possibility of infection. He wished he could pass the irksome task on to someone else.

When Yiorgo saw him waiting patiently outside the school he frowned. Almost every week the man was there. He was both an embarrassment and a nuisance. He tried not to let his annoyance show.

'Good afternoon, Father. I can guess what's brought you here. Shall we find a quiet taverna?' Yiorgo led the way a few doors along the road and chose a table towards the back. 'What do they want this time?'

Without answering Father Andreas handed the letter over, watching Yiorgo's face redden as he read it. Silently he handed the letter back, pushed the hair out of his eyes and lit a cigarette, drawing on it deeply. 'It's out of the question, of course.'

'Why?'

Yiorgo shrugged. 'It's obvious. Carrying infection. If we allow them to have visitors they'll be asking to visit their homes on the mainland and before we know it everyone will be contaminated.'

Father Andreas shook his head. 'I disagree. There's no evidence to show how the disease is transmitted. I find it hard to believe that it can be caught like measles or mumps. If that was the case whole families would be living over there by now.'

'Then how do you suggest it's caught?'

'I don't know. I'm not a doctor, and even doctors don't appear to know.'

'All the more reason for keeping them isolated.'

'None of the boatmen who deliver there have caught it.'

'They don't go near the occupants.' Yiorgo smiled triumphantly.

'Father Minos hasn't caught it.'

'There are always exceptions.'

'I haven't caught it, and I spent a year sharing a mattress with Yannis. You, also, spent a good deal of time with Yannis, yet you show no signs.'

Yiorgo Pavlakis crossed himself hurriedly. 'I did not kiss and hug him!' He leaned forward. 'Imagine the scene – a boat arrives, out steps a mother, sister, wife, arms are thrown about each other's necks, their tears are mingling between their kisses, without doubt they'd bring it back with them.'

'I think you're exaggerating the possible danger. If it spreads as you suggest I'm amazed that we're not all suffering from it. I visit the hospital regularly and if there are lepers waiting to be moved to the island I mix with them freely.'

Yiorgo shrugged somewhat sulkily. 'I disapprove of the idea.'

Andreas smiled. This was the time to appear to accept defeat and press for something else instead. 'So you're not prepared to suggest such a move to the government?'

'Certainly not.'

Andreas sighed. 'At least, if you'll not let them see each other, give them permission to write to their families and have a letter sent back to them.' Andreas watched Yiorgo purse his lips. 'There can be no cause for concern there. Letters leaving the island can be sterilised. The doctor is sure to have a machine and he could do that before posting them. It would be so simple and such a comfort to those who are so far from their relatives.'

Slowly Yiorgo nodded. 'If it was strictly controlled, every letter would have to bear a stamp to say it had been sterilised.'

'Of course,' Andreas beamed. 'I'll write today and say they can use the postal system. Now, do you remember the other letter I had, asking for better equipment in the hospital?'

Yiorgo nodded. 'I put it before the government and they agreed the doctor could order almost anything he wanted. All he had to do was to send us a list and the cost before he bought anything.'

'And he sent you a list and you agreed to every item he'd asked for. You were incredibly generous. Doctor Stavros wrote to me and said how very grateful they were. I understand some of the goods have started to arrive now.'

'Good, good.' Yiorgo was wondering where this sudden show of gratification was leading.

'There's only one problem. Some of the equipment that has

been sent has to be run by electricity, and, of course, they don't have a supply.'

Yiorgo let the words sink in slowly. What a fool he had been not to realise that 'arc lamps for operating' would need a power source. 'Then why were they foolish enough to ask for such equipment?'

'They thought when you passed the items that you were going to supply them with a generator.' Andreas spread his hands. 'I know they should have asked for that before the lights, but,' he shrugged eloquently, 'there is also the X-ray machine. I know the doctor thinks it essential to find out how much of the bone in a limb is infected before he considers amputation, but again he can't use it at present.'

'They've managed without until now.'

'Very true, but you promised them better conditions. Such equipment would help their treatment considerably. If they don't have it their conditions can hardly be said to have been bettered.' Andreas smiled gently.

'So are you suggesting that I ask the government to pass an order for a generator? Have you any idea of the cost?'

Andreas nodded. 'Without a generator the expensive items dispatched to the island are useless – a terrible waste of money. Why not just add the generator to the top of the list?'

'It's a question of cost. I'm sure the government can afford the equipment, but a generator!'

'Can the government afford not to provide a generator?' queried Andreas. 'They would be a laughing stock once it became known that a good deal of money had been spent on items that are totally useless.'

Yiorgo slammed his glass down on the table and rose angrily to his feet. 'You've tricked me. You and those scheming lepers.'

Andreas rose with him. 'It was a misunderstanding.'

'I still say you tricked me. It won't happen again.' Yiorgo walked away, leaving the wine half finished on the table.

YANNIS

Father Andreas had hardly expected his triumph over the generator to be so easy. He had not mentioned that a generator would have to be fixed and wired by trained electricians and they would have to come from the mainland. Once that hurdle had been overcome he would re-open the question of visitors to the island.

Stelios sealed the letter he had written to his family. He smiled to himself. They had every reason to be proud of him. He had finished University and obtained good grades, good enough for him to be accepted into the army as a trainee clerical officer, where he had worked hard, gaining experience and the respect of his fellows. Now he had been given a promotion and by the time the letter reached Plaka he would be installed in an office in Athens, independent of his family forever.

Louisa pushed the cutlery into the tray and wiped her hands on her apron. She was tired. Yiorgo had spent until the early hours of the morning arguing and drinking with three companions from the government, whilst she had run back and forth with bottles of wine and providing mezedes. She heard the taverna door open and looked out from the kitchen.

'Can I help you?'

'I am looking for Louisa.'

'I'm Louisa.'

A smile spread across the good-looking, fair face. 'I was told you run the best taverna in town.' He examined her with cold, blue eyes.

Louisa shrugged. 'This taverna is popular. Whether it is the best ....'

'Maybe I could sample some of the delights I am told you offer, then I could judge for myself.'

'If you please.'

The man nodded. 'I do please.'

Louisa removed her apron and locked the taverna door.

'Why don't you Greek girls do something with yourselves?'

'Do something?'

'Yes, dress your hair, wear colours instead of the continual black of which you seem so fond.'

'Black is a very serviceable colour. If you don't like Greek girls why do you bother to seek us out?'

'When sent to a country you have very little choice of companionship. We are wasting time. Bring a bottle of wine with you.'

He pushed open the door that led to the upper floor of the taverna and walked noisily up the wooden stairs, waiting at the top for her to join him. 'Which room?'

Louisa pointed and he opened the door with a flourish, standing back for her to enter. He gazed around the whitewashed walls, noting the full-length mirror, the cheap brush and comb on the table along with the water jug and bowl and shuddered.

'It is understandable that you all wear black if you all live like this. Where is your comfort?' He looked disdainfully at the rag rug that covered a portion of the floor, then walked to the bed and pulled back the cover. 'At least it's clean.'

Louisa stood, uncertain, holding the bottle and two glasses.

'Well, come on, girl, pour it out.'

He removed his clothes and sprawled back across the bed. Louisa handed him a glass and he sipped and grimaced. 'Poison, absolute poison.'

He sipped again as Louisa stood hesitantly beside him. He reached out his hand and ran it from her breast to her thigh. 'Undress,' he commanded.

Louisa placed her own untouched glass on the table and untied the drawstring of her blouse. 'Do you wish to help me?' she asked.

'No.'

YANNIS

Louisa pulled her blouse over her head and then let her skirt drop to the floor so she stood naked before him. Still he lay on the bed unmoving.

'Move the mirror.'

'Where to?'

'Closer to the bed.' Louisa pulled first at one side, then the other. 'Closer, turn it slightly. That's right; now stand in front of it. Turn round.'

Slowly she turned round; then faced him again.

'Stand there and brush your hair.'

The knuckles of her hand stood out white as she gripped the handle of the brush and began to apply it slowly down the length of her hair.

'Come here. I will do it.'

He pulled himself up into a sitting position and she took her place beside him. He placed an arm firmly round her waist and began to pull the brush vigorously through her hair, tugging her head backwards with every stroke until she cried out for him to stop. By way of an answer he pulled her closer, moving his hand from her waist to her breast, his finger nails digging into the soft flesh, whilst he continued to wield the brush. From the position of the mirror Louisa could see her face contorted with pain and the satisfied smile on her assailant's face, making the white scar on his face stand out prominently.

'Stand up.'

Bemused she did as she was told, only to receive a stinging blow on her buttocks from the brush. Almost before she had time to cry out another followed it, and another. Sobbing she tried to pull away, but he had a firm grip on her hair and she was unable to move. Finally he flung the brush to the floor and still holding her hair, began to explore her body with his free hand, all the time watching her reaction in the mirror.

A final twist of her hair had her lying on her back on the bed, his weight pressing her down as he took his time satisfying himself. To her surprise she found herself responding to his body and enjoying what had become a mundane and boring experience for her. She abandoned her usual caution and gave herself up to the pleasure of the moment. The man's appetite sated he pulled himself away from her and smiled.

'I'm forced to agree that you run the best taverna in town. Where else would one find such a delicacy?' He ran his hands over her body gently. 'A beautiful gem in such an ugly setting! You are worth so much more than this. Properly dressed every man would turn to look at you, to admire and desire you. To envy the man who held your arm and helped you along the road. Those eyes, one look and a man could be enslaved forever. Skin like alabaster; no wonder the Greeks have always been such great artists. With models like you how could they not be? Why don't you answer me?'

'How can I answer you?'

'You could say that I am the most accomplished and handsome lover you have ever had.'

'You are the cruellest.'

'You are not used to being beaten? It's good for a woman to be beaten. It shows her the man is the master at all times, and besides,' he ran his hand the length of her body again, feeling the tremors he created in response, 'it heightens the senses. What for you is an everyday occurrence suddenly becomes an experience you will never forget. Now, drink your wine and tell me about yourself.'

With a wriggle Louisa settled herself beside him, explaining that the only reason she was willing to entertain was for the sake of her brother who gambled heavily and relied upon her to settle his debts. Her husband was the local Mayor and as such no breath of scandal should ever touch him. He was important. She boasted of his accomplishments, and his latest proposals for Crete to avoid being dragged into the conflict that was taking place in Greece and throughout the rest of Europe. The blue eyes narrowed as he listened intently, asking questions which she answered freely, although her knowledge was limited.

'I should like to meet your husband. He sounds an interesting and intelligent man. Are there many more like him in the government?'

'They are all like him, teachers, doctors, lawyers. They would not have been elected to the government otherwise, but Yiorgo is the leader.'

'And your brother? He had no political ambitions?'

Louisa laughed gently. 'I don't think my brother has any ambition at all now. He used to want to be a hotel manager.'

'Really? It's just possible I could help him.'

'Are you in the hotel business?'

'No, I have a very uninteresting occupation. I'm a surveyor.'

'Is that why you're over here?'

'Not for much longer, thank goodness.'

'Don't you like Crete?'

'There is nothing here that attracts me.'

Louisa pouted. 'Don't I attract you?'

'Not any more. How much do I owe you?'

'Twenty drachmas.'

He raised his eyebrows. 'You put a high price on yourself.'

'It's not every day I have to put up with a beating.'

He shrugged, rose and commenced to dress, plunging his hand into his trouser pocket and pulling out a handful of coins, which he threw on the bed. Louisa gazed at the money, not sure if she was supposed to take it all or count out the amount she had asked for.

'Will I see you again?'

'Probably.'

Louisa watched as he laced his shoes, then he straightened and took her hand, bending over to kiss it as he bade her farewell.

Pavlos was gazing anxiously at the cards he held in his hand.

The luck that had been running with him during the last two hours now seemed to have deserted him. His last few games had taken all his ready money and now he was playing on credit, hoping to recoup his earlier losses. The gold teeth opposite him flashed in a smile as their owner played his cards and Pavlos threw down his hand in disgust.

'I'm going,' he announced. 'I'll be back later with what I owe you.'

'Play another hand. Your luck could change again.'

Pavlos hesitated. If his luck returned it would be worth his while to stay and play off his debt, but should he lose again he would be forced to go to Louisa.

'One more hand? Double stakes?'

The temptation was too great. Pavlos nodded and sank back into his seat. He eyed the cards warily as he turned them over. They seemed better than before. He placed a pair of queens on the table for his opponent to immediately take with a pair of kings. They were replaced by a run of low cards, leaving only the aces he had wanted to save. Biting his lip he laid them and pulled the cards to his side of the table. A flicker of amusement showed in the other player's eyes.

'My lead,' he said. A run of higher cards was placed on the table and the man smiled, showing his empty hands. 'My game, I believe. Two hundred drachmas you owe me, unless you'd prefer to work off the debt?'

'How?'

'We want some information on a man. He arrived here three days ago and we'd like to find out a bit more about him. He hired Alkis to take him into the countryside and took a number of photographs. According to Alkis they're not the usual snaps a tourist would take and he didn't go to any of the sites. He seemed more interested in the plains and coastal areas.'

Pavlos studied the photograph that was handed to him. 'Where's he staying?'

YANNIS

'Alkis isn't sure. He picked him up and dropped him on the corner of Eleftherias Square. There are a number of hotels close by and he could be at any one of them. Alkis is collecting him again today at twelve. I suggest you hang around and see if you can spot him coming out of anywhere, or wait until they return and follow him back.'

Pavlos nodded. 'Can I keep this?'

'For the time being, but we shall want it back later. Any information about him will be welcome.'

Pavlos pocketed the photograph and left to walk to the Square. He lounged where he had a good view of the main road and waited. It was just before twelve when he spotted the man he was looking for drinking coffee outside a taverna. Pavlos hurried over and sat at the table behind. He took out a cigarette.

'Excuse me, would you have a light?'

A box of matches was passed to him. 'Keep them.' The man rose and walked across the Square to the corner and waited for Alkis to appear with his battered taxi.

'Coffee?' The waiter stood at Pavlos's elbow.

'Who's that man who was here? Any idea?'

The waiter shrugged. 'Never seen him before.'

Pavlos sat and thought. There was something odd about a man who ordered a taxi on a regular basis, yet did not ask it to go to his hotel. He sipped at his wine; it was just possible his sister could help. There should be plenty of time to return to the taverna and back to the Square before Alkis brought his passenger back. He swallowed the rest of his wine, left a few lepta on the table and hurried away.

Louisa looked out from the back room as she heard the taverna door open. She frowned. Pavlos did not usually return during the day unless he wanted money from her. He sat down at a table and called to her. 'Get yourself ready to go out.'

'Out where?'

'Up to the Square; I want you to get into conversation with a man.'

'What kind of man?'

'Just a man.' Pavlos was beginning to feel exasperated. 'Get a move on. I don't want to be away too long or I might miss him.'

Pavlos hurried his sister along to the taverna he had so recently left. He drew the photograph of the man from his pocket and passed it to her. 'He went off with Alkis in his taxi a short while ago. When he returns I want you to get talking to him.'

Louisa gave the snapshot a cursory glance. 'I saw him earlier today.'

Pavlos raised his eyebrows. 'Did he tell you what he was doing here?'

'Not really. He said he hoped he wouldn't be here much longer, that he didn't like Crete.'

'Why did he come here, then?'

'I had the impression he'd been sent here by his company.'

'How much did you charge him?'

'Ten drachmas.'

Pavlos smiled. 'Did he complain about paying you double?'

'He just said I was expensive.'

'Did he arrange to come again?'

Louisa shook her head. Pavlos lit a cigarette and they sat in silence until the waiter hovered into view and Pavlos ordered baklava for them both.

'How long do I have to wait here?'

'Until he returns.'

With a sigh Louisa settled herself back into the chair. What a waste of time. She would just close her eyes for a short while and think about the fair skinned man she had entertained that morning. She felt a little shiver go through her and wished he had arranged to visit her again.

'There he is.'

Louisa opened her eyes and alighting from the taxi she saw her acquaintance of the morning. 'What now?' she asked her brother.

'Come with me. Speak to him, introduce me, invite him for a meal.' He took her arm and propelled her to where the man was paying Alkis.

'Why, hello, what a surprise.' Louisa smiled widely. 'I certainly didn't expect to see you again so soon. I am pleased, now I can introduce you to my brother.'

For a moment the man looked at her blankly, then realising it would be of no use denying their earlier association he smiled also. 'How do you do?' He held out his hand.

Pavlos grasped it. 'I'm pleased to meet you, Mr ….?'

'Dubois.'

'Mr Dubois. My name is Pavlos. Louisa has told me that you spent some time chatting together this morning and how very interesting you were.'

'Really?' Mr Dubois raised his eyebrows in surprise.

'Louisa tells me you are a surveyor. Are you working for an historical society, looking for a new site?'

'Yes, exactly that.' Mr Dubois answered quickly.

'Have you had any luck?'

'Who knows? I only look and photograph. It is up to the specialist to decide whether the features shown are worth investigating.'

'I would enjoy talking to you. I worked for a while on the excavations at Knossos,'

'I am not interested in the known sites.'

'Maybe you'd care to tour the town with me, I could show you anything you wished to see, then we could go to my taverna and Louisa would have a delicious meal prepared.'

Mr Dubois hesitated. It could be advantageous to be shown around by a local and he would very likely be able to extract some useful information from him at the same time.

'That is very kind of you. I would not dream of taking up your time.'

'It would be my pleasure. Louisa, you return to the taverna and make us a delicious surprise whilst I show Mr Dubois our fine city.' Pavlos took Mr Dubois by the elbow and steered him towards the taverna they had recently left. 'First, let us have a glass of wine together.'

Louisa watched as the two men walked off. She had not been needed at all once the first introduction had been made. It had been a completely wasted afternoon for her and now she would have to busy herself preparing a meal that would impress the Frenchman.

Pavlos drained his glass. 'Now, my friend, where would you like to go first? Are you interested in churches? We have a number of very fine buildings.'

'I am in your hands.'

'Very well, we will first of all go down to the waterfront. You will see our fine fortress and the remains of the Venetian arsenals, from there we can walk through and view the Morosini Fountain and the Venetian Loggia, we will then turn back to the main road and you will see the Fondaco. I know a number of short cuts so we can view other fountains and buildings on our route.'

Mr Dubois nodded. He was not interested in fountains and churches. He accompanied Pavlos, listening carefully as he pointed out various places that he thought might interest the stranger.

'Now we will make our way back up the hill and you will see the Venetian Loggia and all our new public buildings. Here we have our post office and the banks.' He stopped outside the Venetian building for Mr Dubois to admire it. 'Now we take a short cut through here and you will see the Morosini fountain.'

'Where is your police station?'

Pavlos grinned. 'All in good time. The police station, the army barracks, the Town Hall, you see, you did need someone to show you the town.'

Mr Dubois smiled politely. 'You are quite invaluable as a

guide. I only wish I had met you earlier. I am sure that rascally taxi driver took me the longest way to everything.'

Pavlos shrugged. 'Where did you ask him to take you?'

'The plain of Lassithi, Rethymnon, Chania.'

'I doubt that you'd find much in those areas. Tomorrow I could take you to more likely places.'

Mr Dubois shook his head. 'I have to leave tomorrow. There is a boat to Athens that I must not miss.'

'There'll be another.'

'There will, but by then I will have missed my connection. I wish to get home.'

'Where is home?'

'Paris.'

'I've heard that it's been ravaged, that much of France has suffered.'

Mr Dubois shrugged. 'That is war.'

'Poor Greece is suffering also. We are fortunate to be an unimportant island.'

'Fortunate indeed.' A smile played across his lips. 'What is that building?'

'The back of the Court House; we will walk up the side road so you can see the front.'

Mr Dubois followed his guide up the narrow road, stepping carefully over the holes and loose stones. 'I wish you people would repair your roads.'

'Why? We have little traffic. The main roads are well surfaced, but the side roads are only used by pedestrians.'

'Many of the roads I travelled on were like ploughed fields!'

'You reached your destination and returned again, so there was no problem.'

Mr Dubois shook his head. How could people accept such things without protest? The Cretans were barbarians, their plumbing was almost non-existent, their roads were appalling and their standard of living was totally abhorrent to him. They would certainly benefit once they had settled down under their new rulers. He followed Pavlos around the centre of the town, dutifully admiring the churches and monuments of which his guide was so proud, mentally mapping where the most important of the public buildings were situated and often stopping to take a photograph.

'These are my own souvenirs,' he explained.

Pavlos nodded. Photography did not interest him. 'When we reach the end of this road we shall be close to the old Venetian walls of the city. I'll take you back through some of the older streets until we reach the taverna. How did you find it this morning?'

'I was recommended and directed there by a sailor from the waterfront.'

Pavlos nodded. 'Our humble taverna has a good reputation.'

Mr Dubois did not deign to reply. He just hoped the delicious surprise that Louisa was preparing for them would not be too oily. His stomach was beginning to protest. They walked together through the mean streets, which had nothing to attract Mr Dubois. 'I see that all your public buildings are concentrated in one area. Most old towns have them dotted around everywhere.'

'There was a considerable amount of rebuilding in the late eighteen hundreds and the planners of the time decided it would be wisest to group buildings together, hence most of our public buildings are in one street.'

'Very sensible and convenient.' Mr Dubois eyed Pavlos speculatively. A strange young man, not one that he would trust. They reached the taverna and once again Mr Dubois took out his camera. 'I would like a photograph of you and your sister, to remember your hospitality.'

Smiling broadly Pavlos called to Louisa. 'A family group,' announced Pavlos, as though it had been his own idea. 'Fetch Yiorgo and Anna, Louisa.'

Louisa obeyed, returning after a few moments with Yiorgo, who had replaced his stiff collar and donned his mayoral chain of office, and Anna, whose hair she had hurriedly brushed. They stood against the wall, smiling vacantly into the camera and feeling foolish. Mr Dubois made no comment, returned his camera to the leather carrying case and hung it over his shoulder. Yiorgo eyed him enviously. He wished he had possessed a camera when he had visited Athens and Rome. He would not have bothered with photographs of taverna keepers and their families. He sighed; the days when he had time for ancient history were gone. He poured a glass of wine for their visitor and tried to open up the conversation.

'Do tell me about Paris. I've often longed to visit such a beautiful city.'

Mr Dubois looked bored. 'I can tell you nothing about Paris that you cannot read in a book. I live on the outskirts and visit the centre rarely.'

'But the buildings, those that were spared by the French Revolution, surely they must be worth visiting?'

'So they tell me. I prefer open spaces myself. I am not interested in looking at brocade and marble, topped with silver and gold plate. I found your countryside far more attractive than your towns.'

'We have a very beautiful country, such difference in scenery within a few miles. We have the coastal strip, some natural harbours, and then a fertile area before the mountains begin to rise. Did you venture into the mountains?'

'I did not feel that my transport could be relied upon for such a journey.'

Yiorgo smiled. 'The best form of transport in the mountains is a donkey, unless you enjoy walking. You were wise, even with a guide it's easy to lose your way and it wouldn't be pleasant to spend the night in one of the caves.'

'Caves?'

'The mountains are riddled with them. Some are supposed to be the homes of Greek Gods and many of the villagers would not dream of going near them once it was dark. During the daylight hours many are visited and treated as healing shrines. Even now people will take an offering and pray for the cure of a loved one.'

'Superstitious nonsense.'

Yiorgo spread his hands. 'Who can say? Some people have more faith in the mountain spirits than in modern medicine.'

'They must be illiterate peasants.'

'I would call them people who have a simple faith in the stories that have been handed down to them over the generations.'

Mr Dubois sipped at his wine. It was better than the girl had given him in the morning. 'Tell me about the other side of the island. My travels have been very limited.'

'I don't know the other side of Crete at all,' admitted Yiorgo. 'I imagine it's very similar to this coast. There are no large towns on that side, one or two archaeological sites and some Venetian forts. For some reason this side of the island always appears to have been more popular.'

Mr Dubois tried to hide his impatience. A government official who had no idea what the other side of his home country looked like! 'Do you not have to travel there in the course of your duties?'

'Oh, no, I'm only a local government official. The Prefecture of Heraklion is my domain. That includes the town, the suburbs and the country area which surrounds it.'

'I am surprised. By the way your wife spoke I imagined you controlled all of Crete.'

'I apologise for her. She has no great understanding of politics.'

'You are still an important man, though?'

'No more so than my colleagues, despite being the mayor.'

Louisa laid plates in front of them and her husband turned to her. 'What have you prepared for us this evening, my dear?'

'There's roast lamb with garlic and cheese, stuffed courgettes or moussaka. You can have whichever you please.'

'It will be lamb for me, which would you prefer Mr Dubois?'

'The lamb sounds very acceptable.' His heart sank at the thought of the inevitable salad that would accompany it.

'I'll have the same,' said Pavlos and smiled complacently as his sister waited on them.

To Mr Dubois's surprise the lamb was surprisingly succulent and certainly the meal was one of the best he had eaten since arriving on the island. Having complimented Louisa he turned to Pavlos.

'Your sister told me you had ambitions to be the manager of a hotel?'

Pavlos laughed harshly. 'It was a dream I had when I was younger.'

'I do have various influential friends who might be able to help, if you were still interested. I would obviously need some more information about you, some of it might be quite personal, but it would be treated confidentially, I can assure you.'

'What would you need to know?'

'Just the usual data. I will give it some thought this evening and send a letter to you before I leave. When you have answered it to your satisfaction you can send it on to me at an address in Athens.'

'I thought you were returning to France?'

'I am, but only for a short while before I return to Athens for some negotiations with the government. Rather than have your letter chasing me around it would be easier to have it sent there. Now, I have to ask you to excuse me. I have to be up early tomorrow and I have just promised to do some work before I leave.'

'Where is your hotel?' asked Pavlos. 'I'll walk there with you.'

'You are very kind. I am staying at the 'Xenia'.'

Pavlos hoped the surprise did not show on his face. The 'Xenia' was the best hotel in the whole of Heraklion, probably the whole of Crete. Politicians or visiting dignitaries stayed there, not ordinary people. 'It's just along the road from here.'

He took Mr Dubois's arm and steered him along the side roads, across the Square and into a narrow road, through a passage way and to the entrance. Bidding the Frenchman farewell he hurried off into the meaner district of the town to report to his gambling partner that he had repaid his debt. The gold teeth flashed as he related all he had been told by Mr Dubois and slowly a slip of paper was withdrawn from the wallet and torn in two.

The news coming from Greece was disconcerting. Yiorgo spent long hours poring over despatch boxes that arrived in Heraklion. After the stand that had been taken in Greece to repulse the Italian invasion an air of complacency had settled on the population of Crete. Now the Germans had invaded Greece, breaking the central sector of the Metaxas Line, which everyone had thought to be impregnable. The loss of life had been great on both sides, but still the Germans had pressed relentlessly onwards through the country, and Yiorgo was more worried than he cared to admit, despite the troops that had been sent to guard the three airfields on the north side of the island.

There would have to be an emergency meeting of the council. There was no longer time for talking; this had to be a time of action. He re-packed the boxes carefully, placing various papers into his briefcase to take back to the taverna to read again. He must be sure of his facts and have his arguments well prepared. He wrote a hurried note, which he pinned to the front door of the Town Hall and with his case under his arm walked homewards.

'Louisa,' he called. 'I wish to talk to you.'

With a sigh she left the table she was mopping and walked over to her husband. He stood aside to let her pass into the kitchen, his face drawn and tired.

'What have you ready that I can eat?' he asked.

'There's some moussaka. I can heat it up for you.'

'That'll do. No need to heat it. I've got to get back for a

meeting.' He reached out and took her hand. 'I want you to go away, Louisa.'

'Go away? Where? Why should I?'

'I want you and Anna to be safe.'

'What's happened Yiorgo?'

'I'm not sure myself. The messages are confusing and there are so many rumours. All I know is that the Germans are much further into Greece than we ever thought they would be. I don't want you and Anna to be around if they decide to land here.'

Louisa looked both surprised and scornful. 'How can they land? There are Australian troops everywhere.'

Yiorgo pushed back his hair. 'This is no time to argue with me. I want you and Anna to go down to Aghios Nikolaos. Go to my old landlady there. I'll feel happier if you're well away.'

'Why should we be any safer there than we are here?'

'An invading army always makes for the capital of a country. They have to take control of the seat of communications. If they seize Heraklion it's doubtful that they'd bother with the country areas.' Yiorgo was trying hard to be patient with his wife. 'I'll go to the bank and draw out all I can. There'll be enough for the journey and to live on for a few weeks. You take whatever money is in the till.'

Louisa stood there dumbly as Yiorgo helped himself to the cold moussaka and began to eat, still giving her instructions. 'Stay open as usual this evening, then get packed. Don't say anything to Anna tonight, there's no need to alarm her, and you can leave on the first bus tomorrow morning.'

Louisa felt a moment of fear. 'What about you?'

'I have to stay here. You'll be quite safe if you do as I say.'

'Suppose the Germans don't come here?'

'We'll know their intentions in a few weeks. If they don't invade you and Anna can come home.'

Louisa sniffed. 'I'd rather stay here.' She had been making a good deal of money with the influx of troops.

'You'll do as I say. If not for your own sake or mine, think of Anna.'

Louisa opened her mouth to argue, then thought better of it. She crashed the dirty dishes into the sink and began to wash them vigorously. Yiorgo added his to the collection and put his arm round her, resting his face against her own.

'I don't want you to go, Louisa, believe me, but I couldn't bear it if anything happened to you and Anna.'

For once Louisa did not resist him. 'We'll be all right,' she assured him. 'As you say, no one will bother to go into the country areas, and even if they did they wouldn't be interested in a woman and child. It would be soldiers they would look for.'

Yiorgo did not disillusion her. For a few moments he held her tightly, then turned away. 'I'll go to the bank.'

Louisa finished washing the dishes, wiped her hands down her apron mechanically and sat down at the nearest table, surprised to find that her legs were shaking. The talk she had heard from the army had not alarmed her and she had considered their presence on the island not only a boost to trade, but also as a deterrent to the Germans. She thought Yiorgo had probably been exaggerating. With this comforting thought she smiled. It would be like a holiday to be away from the taverna and Yiorgo for a week or two. She wished she did not have to take Anna with her. The child would be a nuisance. She emptied the contents of the cardboard box that served as a till and was half way through counting the money when the taverna door opened and to her surprise Pavlos stood there.

'Are you adding or taking away?' he asked coming close to her.

'Yiorgo wants me to go away for a while. The Germans have pushed well into Greece apparently and he's worried that they'll try to land over here.'

Pavlos whistled. 'Have they!' His eyes roamed round the empty taverna until they alighted on Yiorgo's briefcase. 'Let's see where they've got to, shall we?'

'No, you mustn't. That's government business.'

Pavlos pushed her away. 'If it's a question of saving our skins it's our business. The government won't care for the likes of you or me.' He pulled out a sheaf of papers and began to scan them. He raised his eyebrows. 'I'll say they've pushed down! They're almost at Corinth. It's time to go, little sister.'

'That's why Yiorgo is sending us to Aghios Nikolaos.'

Pavlos smiled mockingly. 'When I say go, I mean really go. How much have you got upstairs?'

'A couple of hundred.'

'Go and get it.'

Louisa hesitated. 'Where will you go?'

For a moment Pavlos seemed uncertain of himself. 'Mr Dubois is going to arrange for me to go away. Probably America.'

'Mr Dubois!'

Pavlos nodded. 'He promised to pay my fare to somewhere safe if I did a few odd jobs for him here, to save him having to come over himself.'

'What kind of jobs?'

'Oh, just descriptions of places and how to get there. Nothing very much.'

'Yiorgo says we'll be safe if we leave town.'

'Yiorgo has always lived in a dream. I've no intention of waiting around to see if it's safe in this country. Go and get the money.'

Still Louisa hesitated until Pavlos advanced towards her menacingly, then she fled up the stairs. Dragging a shawl from the back of the drawer she fumbled to untie the knot. The coins cascaded out, rolling across the floor. She collected up those she could see and thrust them into the pocket of her apron. Breathlessly she returned downstairs to find Pavlos stuffing papers from Yiorgo's briefcase into his pocket.

'What are you doing?'

'These could be more use to me than to Yiorgo.'

Louisa paled. 'I don't think you should touch those.'

'You mind your own business. Now, how much are you able to give me?'

Louisa handed him the money from her pocket and without counting it he transferred it to his own. 'You have been working hard. I shall be eternally grateful for having the most beautiful and profitable sister in the world. It's a shame I can't take you with me.'

'I wouldn't want to go with you,' Louisa spoke defiantly.

'What a way to say farewell,' he mocked her. 'Now, a few items from my wardrobe and I'll be off.' He scooped the money from the till and added that to the change in his pocket.

'I was supposed to have that for my journey,' protested Louisa.

'My need is greater than yours, dear sister. My journey is longer.'

His feet pounded on the wooden stairs and Louisa could hear him moving about overhead. She stood as if rooted to the spot until he returned. Gone were the old trousers and pullover and he wore a smart pin-stripe suit, a mackintosh draped over one arm and a light case held in his hand. As he passed her on the way to the door he lifted his trilby hat politely.

'Good bye, take care. If I ever return to Crete I'll look you up.'

Louisa watched the door close behind him. A feeling of desolation swept over her. Over the years the love she had felt for her brother had waned to nothing, but the man who had just left the taverna was a total stranger to her.

Yiorgo returned to the taverna flushed and anxious. It had taken longer to withdraw the money from the bank than he had anticipated. Whilst in the midst of negotiations he had remembered the briefcase thrown to one side in the taverna. The papers in it were confidential and he had carelessly left it on a chair. He had hoped Louisa had moved it to the back room, but now he saw it was where he had left it, but on inspecting the contents he could tell at a glance they had been tampered with. 'Has anyone been here since I left?' he asked.

'Only Pavlos.'

Yiorgo swallowed hard. He tried to comprehend the messages that were coming to his brain from all directions. Pavlos had read and taken the papers. Pavlos had heard his practised speeches. Pavlos was responsible for informing his rivals of his every move. He emitted a low groan. 'Where is he now?'

'I don't know,' Louisa answered truthfully. 'He went out again.'

Yiorgo shook his head and sank down onto a chair at the nearest table. When he looked up at Louisa she was touched by the pain and weariness in his eyes. She slipped into the seat next to him. 'Don't worry, Yiorgo. It will be all right. We'll soon be back with you.'

Yiorgo groped for her hand. 'Louisa, always remember how very much I loved you. You and Anna.' He spoke gruffly and Louisa was embarrassed. She could not reply with the same sentiments. She searched her mind carefully for words.

'I shall always be grateful to you, Yiorgo.'

He squeezed her hand. 'I've very little time. Find me some paper and I'll write the address of my old landlady for you.'

Louisa stumbled back upstairs. The look of utter defeat on Yiorgo's face had touched her far more than his slavish devotion to her had ever done. For the first time she felt concerned for him. How would he manage whilst she was away? She handed him a sheet of paper. 'Yiorgo, suppose we just sent Anna to the country?'

Yiorgo shook his head. 'I want you to be there with her. She'd be frightened on her own.' He bent over the paper and wrote rapidly. 'I'm sure she'll do her best for you.'

Silently Louisa folded the paper and looked at the address. 'How will I find it?'

'Ask at the bus station. Anyone can tell you, it's a small place.'

'We'll manage.' She smiled at her husband.

Anna pushed open the door and looked inside the taverna warily. Yiorgo and Louisa exchanged glances.

'Come here, my little one.' Yiorgo held Anna closely to him, stroking her hair. Anna wriggled; fond though she was of her father an excess of affection embarrassed her.

'Go and wash,' ordered Louisa and obediently Anna went through to the yard.

Yiorgo turned to Louisa again. 'I must go. Don't wait up for me. The meeting could go on all night. I'll try to get back before you leave.' He took her face in his hands. 'Promise me, Louisa, even if I'm not back in time you'll take Anna and go.'

'I promise.' She watched as he took up his briefcase and with a last look at her left the taverna. She shook her head sadly. Poor Yiorgo. She had more feeling for her husband at this moment of crisis than ever before.

'Supper's ready,' she called to Anna. 'I want you to have an early night. You've been late all week. Have your supper and then into bed.' Louisa did not want to waste precious time in the morning arguing with a tired child.

'I saw Mr Dubois when I was coming home. I'm sure it was him. He has that funny white line on his face.' Anna referred to a scar.

'What was he doing?'

'Talking to uncle Pavlos.'

So that explained Pavlos's hurried departure. 'He may come and see Pappa later.'

Anna wrinkled her nose. 'I don't like Mr Dubois.'

'You'll be in bed anyway,' Louisa reminded her and Anna hurried to comply with her mother's orders.

Long habit made Louisa wake at the usual time. She dressed rapidly, placed a few last minute items into her sack and put the water on for coffee before waking Anna.

'Get dressed quickly. We're going on a visit.'

Anna's sleep-filled eyes stared at her mother uncomprehending. 'Pappa wants us to visit an old friend of his. I've packed your spare clothes. Hurry yourself.'

Bemused Anna did as she was told. The smell of coffee wafted up to her, made her feel hungry, and gave her the incentive to hurry.

'Where are we going, Mamma?'

'I told you, to a friend of Pappa's in the country.'

Anna eyed the bags that were sitting in the kitchen. 'How long are we staying?'

'A few days. Eat your roll. We have to be at the bus station in good time.'

Obediently Anna ate. There was something strange happening that she did not understand. By the look of the bulging bags and the empty chest in her bedroom, they were going forever, not a few days.

Pavlos flipped his cigarette end out of the window. The outskirts of Rethymnon looked the same as Heraklion. He had enjoyed the journey. There had been none of the irksome stops to pick up passengers as there would have been had he made the trip by bus. The truck swung round a corner and drew to an abrupt halt before a dilapidated building.

'In there,' announced the driver, his first words since leaving Heraklion.

'Thanks.' Pavlos eyed the building warily. 'Who am I meeting?'

There was no answer, already the driver had released the hand brake and was moving. Pavlos pushed open the door and entered the dim hallway.

'Good evening.' A man stood in the darkness.

'Mr Dubois! I didn't expect to see you here.'

'I arrived by car a short while ago. Do come in.'

1940-1945

Pavlos was ushered into a room and a hand waved towards a seat. 'Sit down, my friend. Here we can carry out our business in private. You said you had some information which I might find helpful.'

'I want something in exchange.' Pavlos licked his dry lips. 'You're not really a surveyor, are you? You're working for the Germans.'

'How very astute of you!'

'I've known from the start,' boasted Pavlos. 'I was given the job of finding out about you.'

'Really. I would be interested to know what you told your friends about me.'

Pavlos smiled craftily. 'I told them your name and where you were staying whilst you took photographs for a firm of surveyors and they cancelled my gambling debt in exchange for the information. You offered me the opportunity to go away and start afresh in a new country if I did a little work for you. I decided you'd made me the best offer.'

'And you think the time has come to take up this offer?'

Pavlos nodded. 'I had access to my brother-in-law's papers.'

'Maybe you would like to tell me why you think they would interest me.'

'They said that Thermopylae had been lost and the Germans were being held at the Molos Pass. They thought it would be doubtful if there would be enough men to hold Athens.'

Mr Dubois smiled. 'Was that all? I feel that hardly warrants the cost of bringing you to Rethymnon.'

Pavlos shook his head. 'There were all sorts of details regarding an invasion of Crete. The beaches they would probably use and where to deploy the greatest number of troops for their defence. I have the papers here.' Pavlos took them from his pocket.

Mr Dubois looked at the man. 'Does it not worry you to betray your country?'

'I won't be here, will I?' Pavlos relaxed in his chair.
'Exactly.'
The bullet reached Pavlos's heart and he died with a look of amazement on his face.

Anna was bored and unhappy, Louisa discouraged and sulky. Her money was fast disappearing. There had been no one at the address Yiorgo had given her and she had been forced to trail around the streets in search of lodgings. The landlady had insisted she paid a month in advance and all meals had to be eaten out. There had been no word from Yiorgo and the newspapers reported only setbacks and defeats for the allied armies. Aghios Nikolaos was full of troops who had been hurriedly evacuated from the mainland, spilling out from Heraklion when resources were too strained to cope with them. Now she sat and watched the uniformed men passing by, their foreign tongues grating in her ear, and she tried to shut out their harsh voices by concentrating on her newspaper.

'Excuse me.' Louisa turned to see a middle aged officer standing beside her. 'May I borrow your newspaper when you have finished with it?'

Silently she handed it to him. By his accent he was obviously a foreigner and she wondered if he could read the language. She watched as he folded it and ran his fingernail down the column, which listed the movement of the various battalions who had been evacuated from Greece. He turned to her again. 'Can you tell me how far Chania is from here?'

Louisa looked doubtful. 'I'm not sure. Quite a long way, it's past Rethymnon.'

'How far is Rethymnon?'
'A morning's drive from here.'
'Is there anywhere I can buy a map?'
'Try a book shop.'
He touched his cap and moved off down the street where he

stopped and leant against a jeep and mopped his forehead. He and the driver seemed to be arguing and Louisa watched them idly. Finally he climbed in and sat disconsolately beside his companion. As Louisa and Anna walked past both men raised their caps to them and Anna giggled.

'Why are they here, Mamma?'

'I don't know. They seem to be everywhere these days.'

'How much longer do we have to stay here?'

'Until Pappa sends for us.'

'How can he do that?'

'He'll write a letter and we'll catch the bus home.'

Anna eyed her mother doubtfully. 'They say the buses aren't running. There's no petrol. It's all been taken by the army for their vehicles.'

'Who told you that?'

'I heard some of the local people talking.'

Louisa bit her lip. 'What else did they say?'

'They were complaining that they couldn't get any news of their sons or visit their families.'

Louisa stopped. 'Wait here for me,' she commanded and walked back to the stationary jeep. She smiled at the occupants who straightened themselves from their slumped positions and touched their caps.

'My daughter has told me that the buses are no longer running between the towns. I have to get back to Heraklion to see my husband.'

'Impossible at the moment, far better to stay here.'

'It's very important. He's a member of the government.' Louisa wrung her hands.

The two men exchanged glances. 'We shall be moving that way in an hour or so.'

Louisa looked from one to the other eagerly. 'Would you take me? At least part of the way, I could walk the rest.'

'What about the girl?'

'She can stay here. I can make arrangements.'

The two conversed rapidly in their own language whilst Louisa stood waiting anxiously, for the outcome. The man who spoke Greek turned back to her.

'We'll take you to the outskirts of Heraklion. Sort the girl out and start walking out of town. We'll catch up with you.'

Louisa walked back to where Anna was waiting. She took her arm and steered her along the road, round the corner and to the far end of the lake. 'I'm going back to Heraklion,' she announced.

Anna's face lit up with a smile. 'It will be lovely to go home.'

Louisa shook her head. 'I can't take you. I've managed to get a ride in the jeep part of the way and after that I have to walk. You couldn't do that.'

'Yes I could.'

Louisa continued as if the girl had not spoken. 'You're to stay here and I'll be back in a day or two.'

Anna's lip trembled. 'Where am I to stay? I don't like that old woman.'

'I'll give you some money for your food and the rent is paid.'

'Suppose you're not back before the money runs out?' Anna was frightened, trying hard to think of something that would stop her mother from leaving her.

'I shall be. I'll get another lift and be back in a few days. You'll be all right.'

She opened the drawstring bag and pulled some notes from it, which she stuffed inside her blouse before handing the bag to Anna. A sudden impulse made her pull her daughter to her and kiss her. 'Be a good girl. I'll be back as soon as I can.'

Anna watched as her mother began to walk across the bridge on her way out of the town. She felt unable to move, deserted, abandoned in a strange town with no one to turn to. Tears crept down her cheeks and she sniffed as she tried to stem the flood by brushing them away with her hand.

Louisa found the journey to Heraklion quite enjoyable in the company of the two soldiers. In his heavily accented Greek one had kept up a steady stream of conversation with her, translating her replies to the driver. As they neared Heraklion he quizzed her regarding the routes available to them, but she was ignorant. She was asked to leave the jeep at least a mile from the outskirts, allowing herself to be helped down and offering both men the hospitality of the taverna in Heraklion when they next passed through. The message relayed to the driver set him laughing and they waved cheerily to her as they accelerated away.

'They'll never believe us when we tell them that we brought the most famous prostitute in Heraklion all the way from Aghios Nikolaos and didn't lay a finger on her.' The driver guffawed again. 'Pity we couldn't take her all the way with us. We could have had some sport tonight.'

Louisa walked in the dust at the side of the road, her heel chaffed by the back of her shoe, which was gradually splitting, until she finally removed them, wincing as the small stones pricked her feet. It was further than she had imagined and she was doubtful that she would reach the town before it grew dark. She walked on, her mouth dry from the late afternoon heat and the dust that hovered around her. As she reached the crown of the hill she espied Heraklion sprawled before her, before night engulfed it in total blackness. There was not a light to be seen and the darkness seemed intense as she trod wearily along the unfamiliar streets. She had no idea of the time when she finally inserted her key into the door of the taverna and entered into the dark room. She groped for a lamp; then screamed in terror as her arm was grasped and twisted up behind her back.

'Who are you? What do you want?'

'Yiorgo, Yiorgo, it's me.'

Her arm was released immediately and she rubbed it ruefully. 'Light the lamp, Yiorgo.'

In the darkness Yiorgo shook his head. 'It's not safe. Come upstairs.'

He moved over to the taverna door and dropped the latch, then felt his way to the inner door. Louisa followed him up the stairs and into their bedroom where he pulled down the heavy blind before lighting the lamp and turning to look at his wife. She was struck by his haggard appearance.

'What's happened, Yiorgo?'

'The Germans have landed. It was an airborne attack and we were expecting them to come by sea. They've suffered heavy losses, but I don't know if we can hold them.'

Louisa felt her throat constrict. 'What will happen if they get to Heraklion?'

'I don't know. I didn't want you here. Where's Anna?'

'She's safe enough. I left her at our lodgings.'

'You should have stayed there yourself.' Yiorgo pushed back his hair from his forehead. 'Why have you come back?'

'I was worried. I'd heard nothing from you, and I was running out of money.'

'You could have worked in a taverna.'

'There's hardly anywhere open.'

'Why didn't you sell your jewellery? You've got it all with you. You must be on the first bus back tomorrow.'

'There are no buses running, Yiorgo.'

'No buses? Then how did you get here? You didn't walk?' He looked down at her dirty, unshod feet.

'Some of the way, I had a lift in an army jeep to the outskirts.'

Yiorgo groaned. 'Louisa, anything could have happened to you. You must never do such a thing again. How am I going to get you back?' He rubbed his hand across his head.

'I'll stay here until the buses start to run again. I can open up the taverna and bring in some money.'

Yiorgo shook his head in despair. 'Don't you realise that the situation here is dangerous? If our lines don't hold, the

Germans will be swarming all over the town.'

'They won't trouble us, though, will they?'

'Louisa, I don't know. I've enough problems without having you as well. I thought you were safe and now you turn up here. I can't cope, Louisa.'

Louisa pouted. 'I thought you'd be pleased to see me.'

'Under different circumstances; I only came back for a clean shirt and something to eat.'

'You're going back to the Town Hall?'

'I have to. You must stay here and keep the door locked. Don't open it to anyone, understand?'

Louisa nodded; Yiorgo's fear was suddenly contagious.

'I'll be back as soon as possible. You're not to show a light or go out anywhere.'

'But Yiorgo....'

'I mean it, Louisa. No one knows you're here, make sure it stays that way.' Yiorgo bent and kissed her. 'When this is over and the world becomes sane again we'll go away. I'll give up politics and become just the local school teacher again.'

Louisa smiled. Yiorgo's sincerity she did not doubt, but she thought it highly unlikely that he would remember his intentions later.

'Don't forget, no lights, don't undo the door and don't go out. I'll be back as quickly as possible. Then I'll see about getting you back to Aghios Nikolaos. You should never have left Anna alone down there,' he admonished her.

'She'll be safe enough,' Louisa assured him.

Yiorgo held her hands, reluctant to leave. He kissed her again. 'I have to go.' Quietly he made his way back down the stairs and across the dark taverna.

The noise in the street below woke Louisa. Curiosity overcoming her caution, she pulled back the blind. In the street she could see people carrying all manner of objects, a bundle of stones, a kitchen knife, an axe, even old rifles and shot guns had been taken down from their resting places. Yiorgo's instructions to stay in were impossible to obey. She had to know what was happening. Dressing rapidly she hurried downstairs and out into the street to catch up with the stragglers.

'What's happening? Where are you going?'

'To the city gates.' The woman waved her knife in the air. 'The Germans are coming.'

'What are you going to do?'

'Defend the city, of course.'

'The soldiers will do that.'

'What soldiers? They've all been sent out to the airfield and they couldn't hold it.'

'If the soldiers couldn't stop them what hope do you have?' Louisa looked at the rabble, which was rapidly disappearing into the distance.

'We're going to the old gates. They'll never get over the walls and the openings are narrow. We'll hold them back.'

Louisa fell into step beside her, realising she had brought no weapon with her. They stood in a growling mass, waiting for the first spark to set their raw emotions alight. It seemed to Louisa that they stood there for hours before the noise in the distance reached them and they fell silent. This was what they had been waiting for. Now they would show the Germans what Cretan people were made of.

The noise grew louder, impossible to distinguish one sound from another and then they came into sight. Louisa sucked in her breath sharply. Shambling towards the archway was a motley collection of tattered men, some limping, their arms round a companion's shoulders, others being led, their makeshift bandages slipping from their eyes, yet others being carried on light stretchers. Silently the throng parted to make way for them to pass, then closed in again to block the access. Pitifully small numbers of soldiers began to arrive, taking up their stand before the mob, and all the time there was noise. It reminded Louisa of the mistral which blew with an unending shriek, but this was more like an unending groan, dragged from the very heart of the people. She felt her cheeks wet with emotion, an emotion she had not felt for many years, sadness, pity, a love for her fellows, and she took to her heels and ran.

Sobbing for breath Louisa leant against the Morosini fountain. Now she was able to understand Yiorgo's fear for her. If the townspeople were prepared to defend their city with their bare hands the bloodshed would be indescribable, and if they failed in their defence she dreaded to think of the reprisals that would take place. Slowly she regained her breath and her head stopped reeling. Peering anxiously around each corner as she went, she made her way back to the taverna.

Numbly she gazed around. The whole place had an air of neglect. More for something to occupy her than a desire to restore order, she ran some water into a bowl and began to mop the tables. The slightest sound made her start, yet she dared not go out to investigate lest she be caught up in the carnage that she was certain was taking place. Of Yiorgo there was no sign.

She wondered if the market was functioning. On inspecting her cupboards she had found the salad items in a slimy, mouldering mass, bread covered in a green film and cheese that was as hard as a rock. The smell when she opened her meat safe sent her reeling back and she slammed the door shut hurriedly, unable to face cleaning it out. The only food that was eatable was a bag of rice and another of sultanas. At least she would not starve. She cooked an unpalatable mess of rice and managed a little, washed down with wine, of which she had a plentiful supply, all the time watching through the taverna windows for any sign that her neighbours were returning. The silence was oppressive and she moved restlessly round the room once she had finished eating.

She jumped, and then stiffened in fear as a muffled booming

came to her ears. Anxiously she peered through the windows. If only someone would pass by! As if in answer to her prayer an elderly man staggered round the corner, clutching at the wall and window frames for support. In an instant Louisa had unlocked the door and was at his side.

'What's happening? Tell me what's happening.'

He pointed to his leg where the sticky, red blood was oozing through his trousers. 'Butchery. That's what's happening. Bloody butchery!'

Louisa supported his weight. 'Come in. I'll bind up your wound.'

Half-fainting and unresisting he allowed her to lead him across the room and sank gratefully into a chair. She passed him a bottle of wine with a trembling hand. She had little idea what she should do apart from clean the wound and bandage it, hoping she would not faint whilst doing so. 'How did it happen?'

'Bayonet.'

'Can you remove your trousers?'

He dropped his trousers to his knees and Louisa felt the bile rising in her as she looked at the gaping flesh. Sweating with fear and revulsion she mopped the blood away from the damaged skin.

'I can't do much,' she admitted. 'You'll have to get it stitched. I'll bandage it up as best I can. Can you try to hold it together?' she asked.

Wincing, he pushed the two flaps of skin as close as he could whilst she used a grubby tea towel as a makeshift bandage. She passed him the bottle of wine again.

'Tell me what's happening.'

'You must be the only one in town that doesn't know!'

'My husband told me not to go out and not to let anyone in. I saw a crowd go past this morning, but they haven't come back yet.'

'Doubt many of them will! We were trying to hold the wall, but it's hopeless. We haven't got the weapons. I was at the

Chanion Gate, but it can't hold much longer. There's dead and dying everywhere.' He took another mouthful from the bottle. 'I must get home. My wife's on her own; you can come with me if you want. I don't live far and my wife won't mind.'

Louisa felt tempted; then she remembered Yiorgo's instructions. He would be quite distraught if he arrived home to find she was missing. 'I can't,' she said. 'I promised my husband I'd wait here.'

He limped to door and turned back. 'God keep you safe.'

She shut the door and watched as he made his way painfully and slowly down the road until he turned the corner and was out of her sight. Without his presence the muffled booming assaulted her ears again and she remembered that she had asked him for no explanation of the noise.

Another mess of rice and sultanas, accompanied by half a bottle of wine and Louisa felt a little better. By the morning everything would surely be back to normal. She sat where she was until the light went and darkness enveloped the street. It was then that she heard the neighbours returning, scuffling, dragging their feet, some groaning, she could hear them going by at intervals. It was over then. The injured man had been wrong and the defence of the gates had been successful.

Feeling incredibly weary she climbed the stairs in darkness, remembering Yiorgo's instructions that she must not light the lamp unless she were certain it would not be seen from outside. The oil was low and it gave off only a dim flicker. She must remember to refill it. Maybe she would be able to get some decent food tomorrow. Her stomach growled angrily, upset by the mixture of rice and wine. No doubt Yiorgo would be able to leave the council offices in the morning and he would insist that one of the general stores sold them provisions. With this comforting thought she fell asleep.

She was not sure what it was that woke her. It was still dark and she lay, listening. Footsteps. It must be Yiorgo. She sat up, waiting for the door to open, but when it did the light of a torch blinded her. She shielded her eyes as best she could, trying to avoid the merciless beam.

'Well, well, all alone.' The voice was mocking and familiar.

'Mr Dubois!' The delight sounded in her voice. 'Give me a moment to light the lamp.'

'There is no need. Stay where you are. I hoped to find your husband here. I wanted to ask him for a few names, so that we know which men to seek out and ask advice from.'

'What men?'

'Those who are on the council.'

'I know some of them.'

'Then you could help me.'

'Has my brother left Crete? He said you were going to help him to go away.'

'He left some weeks ago, my dear. You need not worry over him any longer. Maybe you would like to join him some time? Now, the names.'

Louisa began to reel off the names she knew whilst Mr Dubois listed them.

'And where will I find these men if they are not in the council chamber?'

'I know where some of them live.' Again Louisa was as helpful as her memory would allow. 'Mr Lenakis is a doctor. He's probably at the hospital as so many people seem to have been wounded.'

'Most unfortunate.' His tone belied the words. 'I see you are as unblemished as ever.'

Louisa smiled. 'I've only recently returned from Aghios Nikolaos. Yiorgo sent me down there – in case the Germans came.'

'Why did you come back?'

'I needed some money.'

Mr Dubois threw his head back and laughed derisively. 'You needed money? You could have made plenty.'

'The town was deserted.'

'Poor Louisa, unable to make money the only way she knows how. No doubt you will make plenty now. I'll mention your name to some of my friends.' Mr Dubois eyed her in the light of the torch. 'Whilst I'm here I might as well take advantage of the situation. It could be a considerable time before I find another beautiful young girl who is so willing and accomplished.'

He snapped the torch off and in the darkness Louisa could hear his clothes falling to the floor. A smile of pleasure on her face she moved over to allow him room beside her.

The city of Heraklion simmered during the hours of darkness. Sporadic fighting erupted on street corners as the inhabitants met their invaders, other families cowered in their darkened homes, hoping they would not be noticed; yet others nursed their wounds or mourned their losses. With daylight people regained their courage and gathered in small knots before their houses, talking in hushed voices, hoping to obtain news and reassurance. Louisa had woken to find herself alone and she crept down the stairs to the taverna. After two glasses of wine she began to move around disconsolately, doing odd jobs, but unable to settle for very long at any task, wishing Yiorgo would return. It was nearly mid-day when he walked in, looking considerably older than his years due to lack of sleep and worry.

'Have you eaten?' asked Louisa.

'I had something earlier. I just need to sleep.'

Louisa nodded. 'What's happened?'

'The Chanion Gate gave, the others are holding at present. It depends upon our allies. If they can get through to relieve us we'll manage.'

Louisa opened her mouth to ask more questions, but Yiorgo was already through the door and mounting the stairs. Late in the afternoon, after a plate of boiled rice, he insisted on returning to the Town Hall.

'I have to find out the latest developments,' he argued with Louisa. 'It's my duty. There's nothing for you to worry over. I'll walk with you to the corner shop and insist they sell us some food. You can't continue to live on rice.'

At Yiorgo's insistence the shop allowed them to have some stale bread, a little meat and vegetables and two eggs. There was no milk to be had, only a few spoonfuls of coffee and six oranges. Louisa sniffed at the meagre allowance, but did not refuse.

When Yiorgo returned in the evening his face was grey and haggard. 'There's nothing we can do. Greece can't help us. The allies that were sent over to us have little ammunition and nothing but light arms. Maleme has fallen and the troops are trying to get back to help defend Heraklion. It's a shambles.' Yiorgo shook his head in despair. 'I wish you'd stayed in Aghios Nikolaos.'

Louisa also wished she had stayed. 'Don't you think they'll go down there?'

'First they'll want to make sure of Heraklion; then they'll start fanning out. By the time they reach Aghios Nikolaos you and Anna could have taken a boat over to Egypt and been safe.'

'Why don't we try to go now? You say there's nothing you can do here.'

Yiorgo shook his head. 'It's impossible to leave Heraklion. You'd never get past the troops outside the gates.'

Louisa had to admit that he was probably right. She would just have to bide her time as patiently as possible and see if Mr Dubois could help her as he had Pavlos.

For days the position was confused inside the town. The Chanion Gate, having been forced by the Germans, had been retaken and was holding. Food supplies were dwindling. The country folk dared bring nothing to the city, as they knew it would be seized and used to feed the invading army. The townsfolk were unable to leave, due to the soldiers camped just outside the walls, their rifles and machine guns at the ready. The steady bombardment of the port continued, the muffled booming sometimes giving way to the crash of masonry falling. The sky was continually black with aircraft as they harried all those who tried to relieve the island. The tolling of church bells attracted people to the streets, fearing the worst. The bells were intoning a mournful note. Surely if the Germans had withdrawn they would be ringing joyously?

Louisa joined the throng in the streets, taking a stand on the fringe of the crowd and waited. From each church a priest emerged. The people genuflected reverently, then stood in silence. Something important was obviously going to be announced. Yiorgo Pavlakis stood in front of the Town Hall, his council members behind him. Everywhere the same message was given to the people of Heraklion; 'We have surrendered the city to the Germans.'

A stunned silence greeted the announcement, then the women began to wail, keening and beating their breasts as they did at funerals, holding their children close to them, whilst the men wiped away surreptitious tears. Before the people had time to return to their homes a new sound smote the air and the crowd moved aside to make a passage for the marching ranks. The keening and wailing gave way to a stony silence. The hatred in the air was both oppressive and volatile. Louisa watched and accepted their presence philosophically. They were men who were far from home and would be lonely. It could be a good thing after all that she had returned to Heraklion.

Anna wandered desolately through the streets of Aghios Nikolaos. Her mother had not returned as she had promised and she had used the last of her meagre funds to buy a roll for her supper two nights before. No one seemed to take any notice of her as she wandered around. She was becoming quite adept at slipping items from stalls into her pocket as she passed by and eating them when she had moved far enough away not to be challenged, but the problem that concerned her most was the rent. By the end of the week the elderly woman would be demanding her money. She dawdled along the streets, smiling at the various shopkeepers who greeted her as a familiar figure. She was not feeling hungry yet and her mind was on other things apart from food.

She entered the greengrocers and sidled over to where he kept the box for his money, holding a lepta in her hand. 'Could I have an apple, please?'

He turned to take it from the pile and quick as a flash she had taken a handful of coins, stuffing them into her pocket. It had been easier than she had envisaged when the idea had first come to her. Once out of sight she examined her haul and was disappointed to find the small change was worth little over a drachma. She shrugged. There were other shops. She counted out some change carefully and returned to the bakers.

'May I have a roll, please?'

Again her hand dipped into the box, her fingers curling round a note this time.

'Oh, no you don't!'

Her wrist was caught in a vice-like grip, forcing her fingers to drop the note and coins. Anna had been concentrating on the baker's back and failed to see his wife standing almost directly behind her. She struggled, but the grip was firm. The baker looked at her sorrowfully. She was a pitiful little figure. 'Let her go. She'll not try that trick on me again.'

His wife shook her head. 'She's nothing but a thieving little beggar and her sort should be punished.'

'She's only a child.'

'A gypsy child, well taught to steal and lie. Where are your folks?'

Anna looked at them, only half understanding what was expected of her. The woman shook her. 'Where are your folks?' she asked again.

'I don't know,' whispered Anna. 'Mamma went back to Heraklion to find Pappa and get some money for us.'

'When did she go?'

'Three weeks ago – I think.'

'You mean you've been left on your own? No one looking after you at all?' The baker and his wife exchanged glances. Taking advantage of the situation Anna struggled frantically and tried to kick the woman's shins.

'That's enough of that!' Anna felt a grab at her hair and the woman pulled her head sideways exposing her birthmark. 'There's a place for girls like you.'

She was dragged unceremoniously along the street until they reached the police station. Eyebrows were raised as Anna was pushed inside the door and the irate woman began to insist they did something with the girl.

'Now, let's just quieten down a minute.' The policeman held up his hand to stem the tirade that was spilling from the woman's lips. 'Have a seat and we'll get to the bottom of it. What's your name, girl?'

'Anna Pavlakis.'

'And where are you from, Anna?'

'Heraklion.'

'What are you doing here?'

'My Mamma brought me.'

The policeman leaned forward. 'So, tell me, Anna, where's your Mamma now?'

'She went back to Heraklion.'

Slowly the story was dragged out of her. The policeman sat back and looked at the baker's wife. 'Don't you think a little charity could be in order – under the circumstances?'

'If she were an ordinary child I'd take her in,' the woman assured him. 'As it is there's no way I could give her shelter.'

The policeman raised his eyebrows in surprise. Why should an ordinarily kind-hearted woman suddenly be so adamant about the girl? It was not a great deal of money that she had tried to steal. The woman lifted Anna's hair and exposed her neck. The policeman recoiled, then looked again.

'Are you sure?' The policeman pursed his lips. Should he fetch the doctor? He would like to be rid of the girl as soon as possible if she was a leper. 'I want you to wait in here,' he said gently. 'I'll make some arrangements for you to be looked after until your Mamma returns.'

He pushed her into a bare little room and shut and locked the door. Anna hammered on the door in panic whilst he tried in vain to calm her, finally asking the baker's wife to stay and talk to her whilst he was gone.

First he went to the house occupied by Doctor Stavros and of whom there was no sign, then to Doctor Kandakis. After lengthy explanations the doctor grudgingly agreed to return to the police station to make an official diagnosis. He looked through the grill at the young girl, shivering in the corner of the cell.

'Come here, girl, and show me your neck,' he ordered.

Anna did not move.

'Confirmed.' He turned to go. The policeman and baker's wife looked at him in surprise.

'You didn't examine her.'

'There's no need. I'll send in my bill.'

'But surely you should look at her.'

'My advice to you is to get rid of her as soon as possible – and don't forget to disinfect the cell afterwards.' He marched from the police station, thoroughly annoyed that his afternoon siesta should have been disturbed.

'I'll be off, then.' The baker's wife adjusted her shawl and made for the door.

The policeman scratched his head. This was completely outside his experience. He dragged a chair over to the cell door. Anna was huddled in a miserable heap

'Don't be frightened,' he said gently. 'No one will hurt you. It's just somewhere for you to stay until I can make some arrangements for you to be properly looked after. Are you hungry?

Look, my wife put me up some brawn. Would you like to share it with me?' He held up a meat-filled roll temptingly. 'There's far too much for me, and I'll only get a scolding if I take some back home.'

Anna eyed the roll greedily. She was indeed very hungry.

'Come on,' he urged her. 'We'll have a bite to eat, then I'll make some coffee.'

Anna turned her head away. He tried again. 'I have a little sister about your age. I wouldn't want to think she was feeling hungry. Have a roll.'

'Let me out.' Anna spoke in a dull, flat voice.

'I can't do that,' he shook his head. 'If I unlocked that door you'd take off like lightning and that would be the last we'd see of you until you were found somewhere out in the wilds dead from starvation. What I'm going to do,' he waved the roll temptingly in the air, 'is wait until a friend of mine arrives back. He's a boatman. I'm going to ask him to take you over to the island. You'll like it there and they'll look after you properly. There's the doctor and the hospital. I don't know how long he'll be,' he scratched at his head again. 'That's what worries me, not knowing how long he'll be away and thinking of you being hungry and refusing to share my lunch.'

'I'm not ill. I don't need to go to a hospital.'

The policeman winked. 'Between you and me I don't think you're ill either. That doctor,' he lowered his voice, 'he's a pompous old fool. He didn't want to come and see you in the first place. What is that mark on your neck?'

'A birthmark.'

'Well, then, you take my advice. Have something to eat now; then when my friend takes you over to the island you'll see the doctor there and as sure as anything he'll say 'take her back' and Manolis will bring you back again. I'll be waiting for you and you can come and stay with my wife and I until your Mamma comes back for you. How does that sound? There's just one condition, have a bite to eat, because it's going to take a while and you might not get another chance for a few hours.' He held the roll through the grilled window to her and this time she took it, cramming it into her mouth greedily. He sighed with relief. At least he appeared to have gained her confidence. That would make everything a good deal easier. 'There's a good girl.' He looked at her in mock horror. 'Would you believe it! My wife has put three more rolls in here. You'll have to eat another.'

This time Anna needed no further urging and stretched her hand through the grill to take the roll. 'You've got a nice wife,' she remarked.

'I'm a lucky man. She's only got one fault, thinks I need feeding up.' He rubbed his paunch and grinned. 'I'll make some coffee.'

The afternoon passed slowly for both of them and after eating another roll and managing to swallow her third cup of bitter coffee, her gaoler announced that he would go in search of his friend. He scanned the water anxiously, a number of boats could be seen returning to the port and he hoped one of them would contain the doctor and Manolis so he could discharge his burden. Half an hour later he was about to give up when Manolis arrived alone.

'Where's the doctor?'

'Had to stop off at Elounda. Some emergency.' Manolis jumped ashore.

'I've got a problem for you. The baker's wife caught a child stealing. Hauled her along to me. I was going to give her a lecture and let her go, then the woman pulls back the child's hair and says she's a leper.'

Manolis whistled through his teeth. 'Poor little devil! What have you done with her?'

'She's in one of the cells.'

'I can't do anything without the doctor's diagnosis.'

'Doctor Kandakis has confirmed it.'

'Is she bad?'

'Not that you'd notice, it's mostly hidden by her hair.'
'Does she know?'
'Says it's a birthmark. She's a stranger round here. Says her Mamma brought her down here to get away from the Germans; then went back to Heraklion to get some more money. It's my guess that the mother knew and abandoned her.'

'You want me to take her over?'

The policeman nodded. 'I've told her you'll take her over tonight and the doctor will examine her when he visits. If he's happy that it's a birthmark you bring her back and the wife and I will look after her.'

'Better get on with it, then.'

Most of the journey across the water was conducted in silence until the island was no more than a few yards away. Manolis cut the engine and looked at the pathetic little girl who sat in the stern of the boat.

'Cheer up. I'm going to ask a very nice lady to look after you. We'll ask the doctor to have a look at you the next time he's over and within a few days I expect I'll be taking you back.'

'Take me back now, please.'

Manolis shook his head. 'I can't do that.'

'My Mamma won't know where to find me,' she turned large, frightened eyes on Manolis who smiled cheerfully at her.

'That's no problem. As soon as your Mamma can't find you she'll go to the police. He'll tell her where you are. Look, there's Flora. Give her a wave.' He cupped his hands to his mouth and called. 'Find Yannis. I want to talk to him.'

Flora scampered away and Manolis took his time tying up until both Flora and Yannis appeared. He jumped from the boat and helped Anna out.

'I've brought a visitor for you. She probably won't be staying long, just a day or two; then I'll take her back to Aghios Nikolaos. I thought you'd look after her, Flora.'

Dumbly Flora nodded. She had no experience of looking after young girls. This was an entirely new situation to her – a girl come to stay for a few days! She opened her mouth to ask Manolis more, but he forestalled her. 'Take her up to your house, Flora, and make her feel at home.'

'What's all this about, Manolis?' Yannis was curious. 'Where did you find her?'

'Just a minute.' Manolis waited until Flora and Anna were out of hearing. 'I don't know much about it myself. I had to drop the doctor off at Elounda, and when I arrived back I found Nikos, the policeman in Aghios Nikolaos, waiting for me. He said he had a girl in one of his cells. Apparently she's been abandoned by her mother and was caught stealing from the baker. She thinks it's a birthmark, but Doctor Kandakis has diagnosed her as a leper.'

'That's all very well, but where's she going to stay?'

'I thought Flora could look after her.'

'Flora spends all her time with you, besides, her house is hardly suitable. There's three of them sleeping in one room at the moment.'

'It may only be for a few days.'

'I don't think it's a good idea. I'll talk to Phaedra.'

Manolis's face lit up with a grin. 'I knew you wouldn't let me down.'

Yannis looked at him in amazement. 'You had it all worked out, you crafty devil. Suppose I hadn't taken the bait?'

'Then I would have suggested it.' Manolis assured him.

Yiorgo was uneasy. For the last three days the town of Heraklion had been too quiet and appeared too normal, considering it had been invaded and wherever you turned there was a German with a rifle pointed in your direction. Louisa had reopened the taverna and each evening it was packed with off-duty soldiers, but shunned by the locals who preferred to drink in their own homes rather than fraternise. He had called for a council meeting and there had been no message from their new masters to say it was banned. For two days he had laboured over his speech, wondering if he should urge his members to stand firm and resist all German ideas, or whether they should acquiesce and allow themselves to be ruled. He had finally decided the line of least resistance would be safest. Now he knotted his tie, picked up his briefcase and with a final look in the mirror strode confidently down the street.

Yiorgo looked around the assembly room; the number of council members who had turned up was disappointingly small. He pushed his hair back and cleared his throat.

'Shall we give our friends another five minutes?' he suggested. They sat in silence until Yiorgo could hold the meeting up no longer. He shuffled his papers.

'My friends, I have called a meeting here today, not to discuss the unhappy events of the past week, but to plan our future. The Germans will not stay on Crete forever, but whilst they are here we have to live with them and obey them unless we want further bloodshed. We have to think of our families, wives and children, not how we would like to act if we had no responsibilities.'

A stony silence greeted his proposal. The older members agreeing with his policy, yet fearing they would be branded cowards by the others.

'What I am proposing is a policy of non-resistance. If we are told to do something we obey, unquestioningly, but we do not offer any help at all.'

'You're a fine one to talk,' Orestis was on his feet, shouting angrily. 'You say we shouldn't offer help, yet every night your taverna is open for their pleasure.'

'I have to live,' Yiorgo defended himself. 'I do not choose to have them in my taverna, but if they weren't there they would be somewhere else spending their money.'

'I say you should refuse to serve them.'

'Agreed! Agreed!'

YANNIS

Yiorgo looked at the angry faces before him. He had not expected this. He held up his hand for silence. 'Very well, if allowing Germans to spend their drachmas in my taverna offends you I shall see they no longer frequent it. Are we going to insist that no greengrocer supplies them with vegetables, no baker with bread, and no grocer with flour? How are you.....'

He was interrupted by the opening of the door behind him and turned, expecting to find a late council member entering. It was with amazement that he greeted Mr Dubois.

'Excuse me, Mr Dubois. We are in the middle of a council meeting.'

'You were in the middle of a council meeting, Mr Pavlakis. You are now at the end of a council meeting.' Mr Dubois beckoned and a dozen soldiers moved into the room, their rifles at the ready.

'What do you want? What does this mean?'

'You and the council are under arrest.'

Mr Pavlakis looked at his council members. 'May I know why we have been arrested?'

Mr Dubois ignored the question. 'Are all your members present?'

'Some are missing.'

From his pocket Mr Dubois drew a list. 'When I call your name, please stand.' He reeled off the names, ticking each one as they stood. He looked at the list again. 'You have more than some members missing, Mr Pavlakis, most of your members seem to be missing. I think a little visiting is in order.'

Mr Dubois spoke rapidly to the soldiers in a language Yiorgo could not understand, but recognised as German.

'You may sit, gentlemen, whilst we wait for your companions to join us.'

Uneasily the men resumed their seats, glancing at one another. Yiorgo Pavlakis cleared his throat. 'Mr Dubois.....'

'You will not talk.'

'I only.....'

A stinging blow across the mouth stopped Yiorgo from uttering anything further. He took his handkerchief from his pocket and mopped at the trickle of blood that came from the side of his mouth. The men looked at each other. This was alarming.

At intervals a soldier would return and push a council member roughly through the door, shouting the name to Mr Dubois who would tick him off the list. They slid into their seats, their eyes fearful and their hands twitching nervously. By mid-afternoon the entire council except one were assembled and Mr Dubois looked at them with satisfaction. He turned to Yiorgo and gave a little bow.

'It is comforting to know that your wife and brother-in-law have such good memories, is it not? One person missing is of no consequence. Now we will take a little walk. Stand!'

The men shuffled to their feet, rasping their chairs against the wooden floor. The soldiers jostled them into a double line and Mr Dubois gave the order to move. He led the way resolutely down the main street, passers-by looking curiously at the strange procession.

The enforced march went on and on, the soldiers showing no sign of strain, the politicians flagging visibly. Yiorgo wished his heart would stop beating so hard. He must not panic. He was still the mayor and as such must show himself to be their leader. They passed through the Chanion Gate and continued out of the town. Still there was no relief; they were made to continue at the pace set by the army without a break.

The straggle of buildings finally gave way to open countryside, flat and scrubby. Ahead a range of low hills, their rugged summits running inland from the shore without a break. The little party were marched on towards them and Yiorgo could only think they were being taken to a hidden headquarters in one of the many caves that riddled the hills. They turned abruptly inland as they reached the foothills and after a few yards were herded into a valley. The path was the floor of an old river, littered with boulders and sharp stones which cut into the men's shoes, making them slip and slide until eventually they were told to halt.

They huddled together, uncertain what was expected of them; then the rifles sent a hail of bullets whipping through the air. Instinctively each man ducked, a dozen or more fell to the ground, writhing in their agony, whilst three or four fell immobile. The rifles took aim again and more men lay on the ground, their blood mingling with that of their companions. Yiorgo opened his mouth to speak, but no sound came as the bullet reached him.

It had taken no more than ten minutes for the soldiers to complete their task. With their rifles still cocked they inspected each body and an occasional solitary shot was heard before they formed a small, tight-knit column and began their march back to Heraklion.

Louisa had prepared the taverna for the usual evening visitors. The meeting had obviously gone on far longer than Yiorgo had anticipated. As the taverna door opened she looked out from the kitchen, expecting to see him, but instead Mr Dubois stood there.

'Wine,' he called and she hastened over to the table where she placed a bottle and glasses on the table, hoping she would be asked to join him.

'Thanks to you and your brother I have been saved a good deal of time and trouble. I'm very grateful to you both.'

'What do you mean?'

'The list of names you so kindly provided for me. It made it easier for my men to find them.'

Still Louisa stared at him uncomprehending. 'I don't understand you.'

Mr Dubois poured his wine. 'The entire council of Heraklion have been annihilated. Without leaders people are prepared to do as they are told, and we shall make sure they do just that.' He drained his glass and poured another.

Louisa felt a buzzing in her ears and the room was darkening around her. Mr Dubois's voice seemed to be coming from far away. 'What have you done?' she heard herself say.

'We shot them.'

The buzzing in her ears grew louder, she could vaguely see Mr Dubois's mouth working before she keeled over to lay unconscious on the floor.

When she regained consciousness it was dark. The taverna was deserted, the door standing open. Her memory flooded back. The council members had been shot? There must be some mistake. She would go to the Town Hall and find Yiorgo. He would tell her the truth. Staggering to her feet she began to lurch like a drunkard along the road. A shout reached her ears and she turned as a stone whistled through the air to fall at her feet.

'There she is.'

'German lover.'

'Whore!'

'Death to traitors.'

Through the darkness she could hear their voices, but hardly distinguish their shapes. They must have been waiting for her to leave the taverna. She began to run, but they followed, hurling missiles at her, some reaching their mark causing her to stumble and gasp in pain. A stone caught her a glancing blow on the head and she put up her hand only to bring it away sticky with blood. Sobbing for breath she continued on whilst the stones hailed around her.

She darted into a shop doorway, hoping she had not been seen, but she was unlucky. Taking up a stance a short distance away from her hiding place the small crowd stoned her unmercifully until she finally sank to the ground unconscious, bleeding profusely from the wound on her temple. Satisfied, the mob slowly melted away into the dark streets.

Father Andreas rose from his knees and crossed himself. He had first prayed for the salvation of the town; those prayers had been followed by the more personal ones to help the bereaved. He had gone from house to house as messages had been brought to him, taking what little comfort he could to the occupants. Maybe now that the worst was over he could get some sleep. Wearily he opened the door of the church.

'Father, Father Andreas, are you there?' an anxious voice came from out of the darkness.

'I'm here. Who wants me?'

'It's me, Doctor Lenakis, from the hospital.'

'Am I needed there?'

Doctor Lenakis rubbed his hand over his forehead. 'No, I've come for myself.'

'What can I do for you?'

'I want to make a confession.'

Father Andreas opened the door of the church. 'Feel free, my son.'

The doctor knelt before the altar. 'Father, I have sinned. I am guilty of abject cowardice. I am not worthy to live now my companions have died.'

'How are you guilty of cowardice? Did you stay at home when the sick and injured needed you?'

Doctor Lenakis shook his head. 'When the Germans came for me I hid.'

'That was a very natural reaction.'

'I hid in bed with a leper who is near to death.'

'It was wicked of you to take advantage of his affliction.'

'I've done worse than that.' The voice was a hoarse whisper.

Father Andreas waited patiently whilst the doctor tried to compose himself. His voice broken with sobs he tried to explain.

'When they entered the hospital they brought money with them, to pay for their treatment and their keep. I made false entries in the books.' The doctor sank his head in his hands and began to sob openly. 'I deserved to be caught and shot along with the others.'

Father Andreas laid a hand on his shoulder. 'You have confessed, that is in your favour.'

'What can I do?' He turned an anguished gaze on the priest. 'All my friends, my colleagues, all dead.'

'Your punishment is the pain of being left behind.'

'Come with me, come back to the hospital with me so I can give the money to you,' he pleaded. 'I don't want it. It's no good to me any more.'

'What had you planned to use it for?'

'Just to live on, repair my house, buy my clothes, a bottle of wine occasionally.'

'You had your salary from the hospital. Why should you need to steal from those less fortunate than yourself?'

'I wanted to be sure of enough in my old age.'

Father Andreas frowned. 'What do you want me to do with this money?'

'Whatever you wish; use it for the church or return it to them. I don't want it.' His voice was rising hysterically.

'I'll come back with you. First let me give you a blessing so you may sleep easily in your bed tonight.'

The doctor bowed his head. He was not at all sure that a blessing would enable him to sleep well. Never would he forget lying in the bed with the leper, touching his suppurating skin, breathing his fetid smell and petrified that the Germans would discover him. Shakily he rose to his feet and allowed the priest to take his arm to help him along the road. Once inside his office in the hospital he could hardly unlock the safe, his fingers were trembling so badly. He removed a number of small bags, thrusting them into Father Andreas's hands along with a small notebook.

'They're yours,' he kept repeating.

Father Andreas hesitated at the door of the hospital. 'What are you planning to do now, doctor?'

'I am going home to sleep, blessed sleep.'

YANNIS

'I'm glad to hear it.' Father Andreas had wanted to do the same thing some hours earlier. He felt weary through to his bones. He was relieved by the man's answer. The doctor's conscience was obviously salved by handing over the money and making the confession. He had no further need of him.

Whilst she ate Anna watched Phaedra bustling around. These people were not as frightening as she had expected, in fact they seemed quite ordinary and nice. Phaedra was taking pains to set the child at ease, remembering how she had felt when sent to the island at about the same age. Yannis entered and smiled at Anna. 'Did you enjoy your supper?'

'Yes, thank you, sir.'

'You don't have to call me sir. I'm Yannis.' He sat down beside her. 'Can you tell us about yourself?'

'Not tonight.' Phaedra spoke firmly. 'She's far too tired. She can talk to us tomorrow.'

Yannis winked at Anna. 'You can see who's the boss in this house.' He took her small hand in his own. 'Goodnight, Anna, sleep well. If you wake in the night and want company Phaedra and I will be here.'

Anna bit her lip. She was not worried about sleeping on her own, but she found their kindness and concern for her so touching.

She slept well and late and when she finally opened her eyes she saw Phaedra sitting on the step in the sun. 'You're to wait here with me until the doctor arrives. When he's seen you I'll take you for a walk. There's not a lot to see, I'm afraid.' With that Anna had to be content and listened eagerly as people passed and Phaedra told her their names.

'Where are they going?'

'Various places; some help Spiro at the hospital, others will be getting their shops ready, there's a lot to be done each day.'

Anna looked at her curiously. 'Shops?'

'You'll see.'

'What does Yannis do?'

Phaedra smiled. 'Yannis does everything. He started the building here, he helped to get the hospital built, but now he spends a lot of his time teaching people to read and write.'

'Like my Pappa.'

'Your Pappa is a teacher?'

Anna nodded proudly. 'And he's the Mayor of Heraklion.'

Phaedra looked at the child. 'Are you telling the truth, Anna?'

'Of course I am. My Pappa's a very important man.'

Phaedra rose. 'Come with me. I think we ought to find Yannis so we can tell him what an important man your Pappa is.'

Happily Anna walked along the path with Phaedra. Yannis was sitting on a block of stone, half a dozen or more people sitting on the ground to one side of him, whilst he made symbols in the sandy dust at his feet with a stick. He smiled as he saw Phaedra approach.

'Have you come to join us?'

'I need to talk to you, Yannis.'

Yannis looked at his wristwatch. 'Ten more minutes, then the class will have a break. If we stop now we'll lose continuity.'

Phaedra frowned. What she wanted to talk to Yannis about was far more important than the class continuing. She opened her mouth to argue, but Yannis frowned at her.

'Doctor Stavros has arrived,' he announced and turned his attention back to his small class.

'Come on, Anna. We'll see the doctor first, then tell Yannis how important your Pappa is.'

Anna slipped her hand into Phaedra's. 'What will he do to me?'

'Nothing. He'll just look at you. There's nothing for you to be frightened about. I'll stay with you.'

Anna submitted herself to the scrutiny of the doctor. He examined her back and neck carefully. 'Do you have marks like this anywhere else, Anna?'

She shook her head.

'Who's looking after you over here?'

'Phaedra and Yannis.'

'Then I think I should talk to them next. There's nothing for you to worry about, Anna. Manolis tells me your Mamma went back to Heraklion?'

Anna nodded. 'She went back to get some money for us. My Pappa's a very important man and I expect they'll be looking for me in Aghios Nikolaos very soon.'

'She says her Pappa is the mayor of Heraklion,' Phaedra informed the doctor.

Doctor Stavros looked at Phaedra and pursed his lips. 'Where's Yannis?'

'He was teaching. He'll probably be along in a few minutes.'

'I'll go and find him.' Doctor Stavros walked back up the path, leaving Anna still holding Phaedra's hand.

Yannis, despite his allowance of ten minutes, was still talking to the class. 'I won't be a moment, just finishing.'

Doctor Stavros tapped his foot impatiently. 'I need to speak to you urgently.'

Yannis looked at the doctor's grim face and decided he must curtail the lesson. 'What's so important?'

'Where can we talk where we won't be interrupted or overheard?'

'Follow me.' Yannis led the doctor to the far side of the island and found a convenient granite rock to sit on. 'What's wrong? Is it Phaedra?'

'Have you heard any news from the mainland?'

Yannis shook his head. 'There have been rumours, nothing more.'

'Heraklion fell last week. They fought in the streets, trying to hold the Germans back, but it was no use. They were completely outnumbered and had little in the way of arms. That wasn't the worst, though.' A shudder went through the doctor. 'They took all the government ministers and marched them out of town. They massacred them all.'

Yannis drew in his breath. 'I don't believe it! Why should they do that?'

'I don't know.' The doctor sounded weary. 'Who knows why these things are ever done?'

'All of them? What about Yiorgo Pavlakis?'

'Who was he?'

'The mayor. He was my old school teacher who came over here and visited us. It was through him we used to bargain for concessions. He managed to get our pensions granted.'

'That brings me to another problem, the child.'

Yannis smiled at the thought of Anna. 'She's a nice little thing. Seems quite amenable to being here.'

'Do you know who she is?'

'She was caught stealing in Aghios Nikolaos, said her mother had returned to Heraklion.'

'She says,' Doctor Stavros took a deep breath. 'She says she's the daughter of Yiorgo Pavlakis.'

The doctor was quite unprepared for Yannis's reaction to the news. He turned white, his hands clenched and unclenched. He grasped the doctor by his shirt and his voice was hoarse with emotion when he spoke.

'Tell me that's not true.'

Doctor Stavros tried to pull away. 'What's the matter? For God's sake man, you're strangling me.'

Slowly Yannis relaxed his grip and wiped a trembling hand over his forehead. 'She can't be. It would be too cruel.'

'She says her father's the mayor of Heraklion; you say the mayor was Yiorgo Pavlakis. He was a friend of yours so you must know if she's his child.' The doctor's voice seemed to be coming from far away.

Abruptly Yannis rose to his feet and began to hurry down the path. The doctor followed more slowly, puzzled by Yannis's shock

YANNIS

at his news. Yannis stopped at the tunnel entrance where Phaedra was showing Anna the drinking fountain.

'Anna, I want to ask you about your Mamma and Pappa. You say your Pappa is the mayor of Heraklion?'

Anna nodded.

'What's his name?'

'Yiorgo Pavlakis.'

'And your Mamma is Louisa? You live in a taverna?'

Anna nodded again. 'And Pappa is a teacher, too,' she volunteered.

Yannis's voice sounded strangled. 'He was my teacher, Anna.'

Anna's face lit up. 'You know him?'

'Yes, Anna.' Yannis turned and walked away, as the doctor caught up with him.

'Yannis, what's wrong with you? You're behaving like a lunatic.'

'How do you expect me to behave?' Yannis shook off the doctor's hand and walked rapidly up the path. Yannis pushed his way through the door of the hospital and looked around. Father Minos was sitting beside the mattress of a woman who was obviously dying. There could be no help from him yet. Disconsolately Yannis sat outside and waited.

When Father Minos left the hospital he was tired and drained, quite unprepared for Yannis's wild, incoherent speech. He took his arm.

'Be quiet, Yannis. I don't understand anything you're saying. Come back to my house. I want a glass of wine to clear my head. You sound as though you could do with one as well. I've been in the hospital for nearly twenty four hours and I'm exhausted.'

Yannis hung his head. 'I'm sorry. I shouldn't be troubling you at a time like this, but I need to talk to you. I need your advice.'

Father Minos refused to talk until they each had a glass of wine and he had removed his sandals. He wriggled his toes in appreciation. 'Now, Yannis, what's troubling you?'

'A girl was brought over from the mainland last night. You were up at the hospital so you wouldn't have seen her.'

Father Minos nodded. 'I was told. She's no more than a child, I gather.'

'That's right. Phaedra and I were asked to look after her until the doctor had seen her. She says she has a birthmark.' Yannis's face took on a stricken look. 'I didn't even ask the doctor if he'd diagnosed! I must find him.'

'You can see him again later.'

Yannis ran a trembling hand through his hair. 'What am I going to do?'

'You don't want this girl to live with you?'

'I don't mind and Phaedra's delighted to have a child to fuss over.'

'Then what's wrong?' Father Minos was beginning to feel impatient. He wanted to go to bed and catch up on his sleep.

'I think she's my daughter.'

The glass fell from the priest's fingers. 'Your daughter!'

Yannis nodded. 'It's quite possible that Yiorgo Pavlakis's wife had my child.'

Father Minos waited quietly. 'Do you wish me to confess you?'

'It's too late for confession. I paid for Louisa; I feel no guilt there. She was a prostitute. When I returned to Heraklion she told me she was going to marry Yiorgo as she was pregnant.' Yannis smiled wryly.

'Couldn't it have been Yiorgo's child?'

Yannis shook his head. 'She was supposed to be betrothed to him, but refused to discuss marriage with him. She told me she was happy with her way of life. Poor Yiorgo. He worshipped her.'

'What makes you think the child was yours? You say she was a prostitute.'

'It was the way she spoke to me.'

'Let's assume the child is yours. What then?'

'That's what I wanted to ask you. Should I tell her?'

'Can you be certain she is your child?'

Yannis considered. 'I don't know.'

'Then you can't lay claim to her. How would Yiorgo feel after all this time?'

'O, God, you don't know, of course. The doctor brought some news with him. Heraklion has fallen and the Germans have shot the government. Yiorgo is dead.'

Father Minos crossed himself. 'Yannis, think for a moment what kind of effect you would have on this child. You say the man she has called 'Pappa' all her life has been killed and you're suggesting that you should tell her he wasn't her father anyway. All you want to do is salve your conscience. You should be praying that the girl has a birthmark and nothing worse. Go into church, Yannis, and spend some time on your knees. Say a prayer for the soul of Yiorgo Pavlakis whilst you're there.' Father Minos leant back in his chair and shut his eyes. So Louisa had been speaking the truth. This he would have to think about.

Anna sat by herself looking out across the sea. Below the waves pounded on the rocks, matching the pounding in her head. She was confused and felt as though she was living in a dream from which she would finally awaken and find herself back in the taverna in Heraklion. After the doctor had left Father Minos had spent a long time talking to her. He had explained that her Pappa had been killed by the Germans and that at present her mother would have no way of getting to Aghios Nikolaos to find her and take her home. She had cried, dry, shaking sobs, which had racked her body and finally fallen asleep in Phaedra's arms. Now, two weeks later, she was wondering how much longer it would be before her mother finally found where she was.

The wind was rising and Anna shivered. She rose slowly and walked to the edge of the path where there was a drop to the cruel granite rocks below. Cautiously she peered over, watching the waves as they sucked and gurgled or broke in a cloud of spray. She almost toppled over the edge when her arm was taken in a firm grip.

'What are you doing?'

'I was watching the waves.'

'There are safer places to watch them.' Flora steered her away from the edge. 'The cliff could crumble and give way at any time. You must learn where to avoid on this island.'

'I shan't be here much longer,' Anna assured her. 'My Mamma will come for me.'

'And when your Mamma does come she'll want to find you safe and well, not covered in bruises where you've slipped down the cliff. You can watch the waves from here. You should be safe enough. You ought to have a shawl around you, the wind is cold.'

'I'm warm enough. The waves are not as high here,' she complained.

'They soon will be. There's going to be quite a storm. It will be too rough for Manolis to come over so I'm going up to the hospital to help.'

'Do you like helping?'

'Not much, but someone has to. I'm not a lot of use.' Flora pointed to her mutilated arm.

'How did you do that?'

'The doctor had to cut off my arm to save my life. It was poisoning all of me.'

'Don't you mind only having one arm?'

Flora smiled. 'I'd rather have two, but I'd rather be alive than dead, so there's not a lot to mind about.'

Anna shuddered. 'Some of the people over here make me feel ill.'

Flora gazed at her sadly. 'Anna, if it makes you feel ill to look at them, think how they feel when they look at themselves. Never let them know. It hurts far more than the disease when you know people can't bear to look at you.'

'I'll be glad when I can go home.'

'I'm sure you will, but we shall miss you. We like having you here.' Flora felt a catch in her throat.

Anna stayed watching the waves for most of the morning. The scene of wild desolation matched her mood and she was glad to be alone. Hunger finally drove her back to the house where Phaedra had soup simmering and freshly baked bread from the communal oven.

'What have you been doing all morning?'

'Watching the sea.'

'You should have had a shawl with you. The wind can cut right through you. You don't want to catch a chill.'

Anna shrugged. 'I won't catch a chill. I've never had a chill,' she boasted.

'You've never lived on an island before, either. Now, have you finished the writing Yannis set for you? He wants to spend the afternoon with you.'

'Why should I have to do lessons?'

'You should be pleased that Yannis bothers. No one taught me how to read and write when I was a child.'

'I don't think Yannis likes teaching me.'

Phaedra looked at her in amazement. 'Of course he does. Yannis loves teaching. He's taught many of us to sign our names and read the newspapers.

'I can sign my name and read,' protested Anna.

'So Yannis can teach you other things. You're very lucky to have a teacher all to yourself.'

'It would be more fun with other people.'

Phaedra looked at her sympathetically. 'I'll see what Yannis says. Maybe some lessons you could join in with the others.'

Anna nodded. There was obviously no way she was going to avoid the lessons. 'I'd like to learn to sew,' she volunteered. 'Like you do.'

'I can teach you to sew in the evenings.'

'I'd rather do that in the day time than the lessons,' Anna tried again. 'When I go back home I won't be taught how to sew.'

'Doesn't your Mamma sew?'

Anna shook her head. 'She's too busy to show me. She has to work in the taverna.'

Phaedra wished she could think of a way to change the subject. 'Maybe your Mamma will let you stay with us a little longer if she's so busy.'

Anna looked at Phaedra from under her lashes. 'May I get down? I've finished.'

'You may, then get your pencils and papers.'

Anna returned and sat at the table bored. Yannis had not arrived and Phaedra insisted that she waited there for him. She began to draw, first the pot of geraniums, then Phaedra busy in the kitchen area, Father Minos as she remembered him when he had talked to her so seriously, Flora, with the arm of her blouse hanging limply, Manolis tying up his boat at the jetty. She had almost finished the picture of Manolis when Yannis entered the room.

'Practising your writing?'

Anna tried to shuffle the papers out of sight, but she was not quick enough. Yannis picked them up, holding them at arm's length; then he looked at Anna. It was the look she hated, it seemed to go right through her as though he were trying to see her heart pumping. When he spoke his voice was very quiet and controlled.

'Where did you learn to draw like this, Anna?'

Anna shrugged. 'I just draw.'

Yannis nodded. 'You're a very clever little girl. May I borrow these? I'd like to show Father Minos.'

'You can have them if you want them. I can always do some more.'

Yannis hurried to Father Minos, pushing open the door of the house without ceremony and sat down opposite him at the table.

'I want to show you something.' Yannis spread the drawings out in front of him.

Father Minos studied them carefully. 'They're not bad, not bad at all. Who did them?

'Anna.'

'In that case they're very good.'

'The last time I saw drawings like this they'd been done by my sister Maria. I know Yiorgo and Louisa couldn't draw, so she must have inherited it from my family.' Yannis's eyes were glowing.

Father Minos held up his hand. 'Yannis, it proves nothing. She could have inherited the talent from her grandparents.'

'She could, but these pictures are identical in style to those drawn by Maria.'

'How long is it since you've seen any of Maria's art? Don't you think your memory could be playing you tricks? You're seeing what you want to see.'

'I'll show you. I'll prove it to you. I won't be long.'

On returning to his house Yannis began to sort through his box of possessions, shaking his precious books until two thin sheets of paper fluttered to the ground and he clutched at them joyfully, rushing from the house and back to the priest.

'There!' He placed the drawings on the table, one of himself and the other of his sister.

Father Minos was struck by the uncanny likeness between Anna and Yannis's sister. 'This still proves nothing, Yannis. These are portraits of two young people done years ago. Even if I asked Anna to draw you it wouldn't look like this. You've changed, matured.'

'Never mind the faces, look at the lines, the simplicity. It's exactly the same style of drawing. You don't learn that, you inherit it.'

'That still doesn't prove that Anna inherited it from your family.' Father Minos handed the papers back, making sure Maria's portrait was at the bottom. 'Yannis, listen, you must give up this idea that the child is yours. It would do no one any good.

What difference would it make if Anna called you Pappa instead of Yannis?'

Yannis sighed. 'Why won't you believe me?'

'I don't disbelieve you, but I say you need to have proof, greater proof than a couple of pictures drawn by your sister and some more drawn by Anna.'

Yannis was following the interchange between Father Minos and the German with interest. It was obvious that despite the priest's pleadings they would receive no concessions at all. Father Minos was explaining that everyone on the island was totally dependent upon the mainland for supplies of food and medicine and if they stopped the fishermen from bringing it they would starve. The blonde commander listened patiently to all the priest said; then held up his hand.

'I will speak now. You people out here are lepers, yes?' Heads nodded to confirm his assumption. 'Then you are of no importance. You have been sent to this island to stop the spread of your filthy disease. You are an abomination on the face of the earth. I do not wish to know if you are sick or starving. Maybe you have enough on this island to keep you alive, maybe not. It is not my concern and I will not make it my concern. What I will not have is a seat of resistance here. It would be too easy for you to shelter men who decide to take up arms against us and disappear into nowhere when we pursue them. The solution to the problem is to ensure that no one comes here.'

'Please,' Father Minos implored. 'We are not criminals. We can't help being sick. Our government sent us here, but they didn't condemn us to death. They sent us food and water and a doctor to tend to our ailments.'

'Being contaminated with leprosy is a crime. Your government has been very lenient and forbearing. We are not inclined that way. I am leaving a battalion of Italian soldiers on the shore and they will obey my instructions. No one is to come to this island. You need not watch for boats to come out to you. Any boat that goes out to fish will have an armed escort so do not think your friends over there in the villages will be able to help you. You should be thankful that we are willing to leave you in peace on this island. If you were in my homeland at this time you would be taken off to a camp to be cleansed. We do not like illness and impurity. It is only by exterminating such things that we can rise to become a pure race of healthy people.'

'We are human beings,' protested Father Minos. 'You cannot treat a fellow human with so little compassion.'

'I see no humans. I see only lepers. Have I made myself clear? I have no more time to waste.' The commander raised his arm and the men he had forced to row the boat out from the shore began to haul on their oars.

'Please,' called the priest, 'listen to us, listen to our prayers.'

No one in the boat turned at the sound of his voice. Father Minos fell to his knees and began to pray loudly, asking for mercy and compassion. A gunshot sounded and he stopped abruptly, the silence following the report uncanny.

'You can consider yourself fortunate that I ordered my man to shoot into the air. If there is any more of this hysteria I will order him to shoot you.' He fixed the priest with a steely glare.

Father Minos stayed on his knees. 'I shall pray that the good Lord will have mercy on your black soul.'

Another shot rang out, narrowly missing the priest and scarring the fortress wall. Yannis pulled at Father Minos.

'Come. You can't reason with them. They have no feelings.'

Father Minos shook off his hand. 'If I were not a priest...'

'You are, so don't even think it!'

Silently they watched as the boat pulled away. Still they stood huddled together, saying nothing, whilst the full impact of the German's words penetrated into their numb brains. The silence was broken by Anna's piping, childish voice.

'I don't like Mr Dubois. I didn't like him when he came to the taverna.'

Yannis rounded on her. 'What do you mean? Who's Mr Dubois?'

'That man in the boat that talked to us. He's Mr Dubois. Pavlos brought him to the taverna and he took our photographs with his camera.'

'You're mistaken, Anna. That man was a German.'

Anna wrinkled her nose. 'I'm sure he's the same man. He has that funny white mark down his face.'

Yannis took her by the shoulders. 'Are you quite, quite certain, Anna?'

'Of course I am. I saw him talking to uncle Pavlos the day before Mamma and I came down to Aghios Nikolaos.'

Yannis released her. 'Poor Yiorgo, poor, gullible, Yiorgo.'

Flora sat hunched up on the quay. For hours at a time she would sit, gazing across the expanse of grey water hoping to see Manolis, despite knowing that soldiers always escorted the fishing boats and were also stationed as look-outs on both the headlands. Yannis and Father Minos were more worried than they cared to admit. The food supplies were dwindling fast, despite the fact that occasionally a boat came over from Plaka with an Italian soldier accompanying it and a small amount of food would be thrown ashore.

'There's nothing for it, Father, we'll have to ration ourselves. We'll have communal cooking. That way the food can go further.'

'I don't see how.'

'We all eat the same food, so there's no waste. Phaedra cooks for Anna and I and we often leave some. It's the same up at the hospital. There's often enough left over to make a couple of extra meals. All the vegetable leftovers could go into a pot to make soup, along with any bones when we kill a chicken.'

'I can't see that being very popular,' protested the priest.

'They'll have to get used to it. It will be easier than trying to give everyone an equal share. We'll have to ask the women to cook. One group will have to bake bread most of the time; we can eat rolls or bread for breakfast and then a soup for lunch and something more substantial with rice or pulses for supper. Once the gardens start producing we'll be able to use the vegetables.'

'That won't be for some months.'

'We can only hope it will be over by then.'

'Even with rationing the food won't last for ever.'

'I know, but we can supplement it.'

'What with?' Father Minos looked at Yannis for explanation. Where did he think more food could come from?

Yannis grinned. 'There's plenty of fish in the sea. Some of the men fish now to pass the time.'

'I don't like fish very much.'

'If we're unable to get supplies from the mainland you'll very soon grow to like it,' replied Yannis grimly. 'The important thing is that there must be no hoarding. What we do have must be shared.'

'I'll ring the bell.' Father Minos rose wearily to his feet.

'Father, you don't have to stay here, you know. You could always ask to be taken back to the mainland.'

'Don't be foolish, Yannis. I wouldn't be much of a man, let alone a priest, if I left you all now. I chose to come and live with you and like you. What little we have over here we'll share – and God preserve us all.'

Yannis clasped the priest's hand. 'I don't know what we'd do if you did leave. God works in mysterious ways, but it was certainly a miracle the day I met you.'

Embarrassed, Father Minos returned the handclasp, then hurried away to ring the bell to summon the islanders to a meeting. He and Yannis stood together and outlined their plans for survival at all costs. Alarm, despair and fear showed on people's faces. Spiro was particularly concerned.

'What am I to do about the hospital patients? They don't eat much, but what they do eat has to be nutritious. They can't be expected to have bread for breakfast. Most of them wouldn't be able to chew it!'

'For them we'll make one concession. Those who can't eat bread can have milk with the bread crumbled in it. They can also have eggs whenever the chickens lay.'

With that Spiro had to be content. He wondered how long any of them would be able to stay alive as the rations were cut time and again until the day when they finally ran out altogether. He disbelieved the assurances that the economy measures were for the winter months only and that the gardens would have sufficient produce to feed them in the spring. Even if that were true the next winter would be looming on the horizon. Gloomily he returned to the hospital. Just as they were beginning to be able to live a reasonably normal life this had to happen.

The church bell tolled mournfully as Yannis struggled into his coat. It was threadbare at the elbows and showed signs of damp in the lining, but he considered it to be his best. It hung on him, two sizes too large now he had lost so much weight, but it was still the most respectable he had to wear to another funeral. Each day, with regular monotony, the bell would sound and those who were able would attend the service and carry the light, makeshift coffin to the tower to add another body to those already there. Father Minos would say a prayer and the undernourished gathering would slowly return to their houses, each wondering which of them would be next.

This time it was Yannis who led the shabby little procession of people along the path until they reached the church on the opposite side of the island. There the coffin was lowered to the ground and Father Minos began the service. Tears coursed their way down Yannis's cheeks, whilst Anna sobbed on Flora's breast. This was the final goodbye.

Phaedra had suffered, suffered as so many had. As Yannis

had sat and watched her sinking slowly day by day he had managed to convince himself that her death would be merciful, now he felt that his last reason for staying alive had left him. He bowed his head, praying fervently that the next funeral held in the tiny church was his own. Spiro led him out and across the small graveyard, treading carefully to avoid the occupants.

'She should have had a grave. Phaedra deserved a grave.'

Spiro said nothing. He thanked God once again that he had not succumbed to the lure of marriage, but taken his pleasure as he found it, and if he died no one would mourn him as deeply as Yannis was mourning for his wife. He averted his eyes as the coffin was opened and the light body slid down into the tower to join so many who had departed before her. Father Minos intoned a last prayer and then walked over to Yannis, taking his other arm and he and Spiro helped him along the path until they reached his house. The priest opened the door and followed him inside.

'Sit down, Yannis. The experience is always distressing, but it has to be. Phaedra wouldn't want you to grieve. She was ready to go. She'd been very brave. You helped her so much. Without you and the strength you gave her she would have succumbed far sooner. You still have responsibilities, you know. You can't just give up now, Phaedra wouldn't have wanted that.'

'My life means nothing without Phaedra.'

'Phaedra wouldn't want you to give in. She loved you and it would break her heart to find out you were a coward.'

'A coward?' Yannis felt a hot flush creep over him as he looked at the priest in surprise.

'Ever since you've been on this island you've thought of others, bullied them for their own good, badgered the government to better their conditions, been their leader. Was it all an act? Are you really a frightened coward at heart who did it all to boost his own ego in other people's eyes?'

'No, I believed in all I did,' protested Yannis.

'If you believed in it then, you should believe it now by carrying on?'

'How can I? We're cut off from the mainland, cut off from everything except death.' Yannis spoke bitterly.

'The war won't last forever. Sooner or later the nations will come to an agreement. When that time comes we'll want a leader who will fight for our rights as Greek citizens. Things change during a war. Medicine will have developed. They may even have found a cure.'

'There's no cure, Father, not now or ever.'

'You don't know that. The important thing is to have you around to fight for our rights, whether there's a cure or not. It's what Phaedra would have wanted. Besides, you have Anna to think of, you must look after your daughter.'

Yannis's head shot up. 'Daughter? Anna? I thought you said it was all in my imagination!'

'Louisa told me years ago, but I saw no good reason for telling you. Anna is going to miss Phaedra a good deal. You can comfort each other.'

Yannis's face lightened a little. 'I'd like to think so, but she can't stay with me now.'

'Why ever not? Remember, she's your adopted daughter in everyone's eyes. It's only natural she should stay with you. You ought to find her and talk to her. She needs her father.'

Yannis looked at Father Minos uncertainly. 'Do you really think so?'

'I do.'

'Then I'd better take my coat off and go and find her. She should be with Flora.'

Yannis sat on the rock, his fishing line dangling into the water hopefully. A few yards away sat Father Minos. They looked like two old friends out for a day of pleasure and relaxation. Yannis wedged his rod into a cleft in the rocks and shaded his eyes to look across at the shore. There seemed to be a good deal of movement. He assumed the troops were about to harass the occupants of the tiny village and prayed silently that his family would be safe.

'I wish I could see properly,' he complained.

Father Minos scrambled over to sit beside him. 'There's certainly a lot of activity. We might see more from higher up.'

Yannis shrugged. They might, but he did not have the energy to drag his body across the rocks and maybe lose the chance of catching a fish to flavour the water that would be their lunch. 'You go if you want. I'll stay here.'

They continued to sit together, each engrossed in their own thoughts and trying to ignore the hunger that gnawed away inside them. Yannis dozed; he had ceased trying to fight the lethargy that overtook him so often due to malnutrition. Father Minos shook him gently by the arm. 'There's a boat putting out.'

Yannis was not interested. At first whenever a boat had left the shore they had been excited, only to have their hopes dashed as it sailed past them, always with a soldier on board. Now Yannis did not bother to open his eyes.

'They're coming towards us.' Still there was no response from Yannis. Boats had appeared to be making straight for the island before, only to swing to right or left. 'They're waving!'

This time Yannis did bother to open his eyes. The priest was right. He sat and watched as the boat drew closer. They were shouting something, but he could not make out what it was.

'There's no soldier with them,' called Elias weakly, from the wall above them.

Slowly Father Minos and Yannis trod cautiously back across the treacherous rocks, their bare feet slipping and sliding. By the time they reached the jetty their hearts were pounding. The boat was making for them. From nowhere people began to appear and gather below the archway, silently waiting.

The boatmen calling to them made Yannis's head spin and the words buzzed in his ears, not making any sense. He had a sensation of floating, but he could see nothing, a thick, clammy darkness surrounded him, then he began to choke as a fiery liquid hit the back of his throat. Stars seemed to be exploding in his head as he fought to regain consciousness.

'Feeling better now?' Spiro was bending over him.

'What...'

'Don't talk. You passed out, so we carried you to the hospital.'

Yannis sank back. So it was his turn at last. He had helped Spiro carry so many up the hill. It had always been the same. They had lost consciousness, Spiro had nursed them as well as he was able, but they had never recovered and when they left the hospital it was to make the final journey to the far side of the island and the tower. He felt strangely at peace. He would not resist.

'I'll bring you some broth in a short while. There's so much food we've had to put a guard on it or people will gorge themselves and become ill.'

Still Yannis lay, his eyes closed, a serene smile on his lips. He was in Heaven already. Soon Phaedra would come and he would be content. He tried to resist as he felt his shoulders being raised and a spoon forced between his lips. Why couldn't they leave him alone? Phaedra was coming soon and he wanted to be with her. Every few minutes he was disturbed again, frustration began to build up in him.

'Leave me alone,' he complained.

'That's more like it.'

Yannis opened his eyes. Spiro was kneeling beside him, a mug and spoon in his hand. 'If I prop you up a bit do you think you could drink for yourself?' he asked.

Yannis neither answered nor resisted as a blanket was pushed behind his shoulder blades. The cup was held to his lips and he took a sip of the warm liquid. Spiro was smiling broadly.

'Are you in Heaven too?' asked Yannis weakly.

YANNIS

'We're all in Heaven, the whole country is in Heaven. The war's over.'

Yannis struggled to collect his muddled thoughts. 'Over?'

'A week ago! We're going to live, my friend.'

Yannis closed his eyes again and hot tears forced themselves between the lids. Phaedra was not coming for him.

An oppressive silence seemed to follow the departure of the Italian troops from the village of Plaka. The villagers appeared to be at a loss to know how to fill their time. They gathered at the taverna and began to recount the various ways in which the soldiers had helped them, each trying to claim to have had more assistance than the last.

Marisa went about her tasks, her eyes red and swollen from crying. The memories she had of stolen moments with Victor could not assuage the deep sense of loneliness surrounding her. He had assured her of his undying love and promised to write as soon as he was back on Italian soil, but she had no idea how long that would take.

Of Yannis senior there had been no news and Anna had walked to Olous to enquire, only to return to break the news to her mother that he had died within six months of his enforced labour. Maria had crossed herself and cried, bewailing the misfortunes of war. Of Stelios there was no news to be had and both mother and daughter assumed him to be dead, although neither would admit the fact to the other.

Maria watched her daughter as she moved about the house. A weary look of resignation was on her face again as she struggled to cope with the task of running a small farm and the house. Anna never mentioned her father and Maria wondered now if she was pining for him. She tried to talk to her, but Anna would just smile and change the subject. Maria tried another tack.

'Has there been any news of Yannis?'

'He's still in hospital. I wish I could see him.' Anna spoke wistfully. 'I wish we had news of Yiorgo and Babbis as well.'

Maria nodded. She had almost given up hope of seeing any of her men folk again. 'They'll be back now the Italians have gone.'

Anna sighed. Glad as she was to see the battalion march away, she now realised how much she missed their help. However hard Yannis tried he could not do the work of a grown man. Maria patted her daughter's hand. 'Why don't you ask Davros to take you over to see Yannis?'

'Do you think he would?' Anna asked doubtfully.

'A number of villagers have been over to help them. There's no harm in you asking.'

Anna considered her mother's words. For a few days she hesitated, then found the courage to speak to Davros. 'Could I go to the island with you tomorrow, Davros?'

'If you want.' He spat his cigarette end on the ground.

'Would you wait whilst I visited the hospital over there?'

Davros scratched his head. 'You'll have to disinfect yourself.'

'I don't mind.'

'I'll be off at seven.'

'I'll be here.'

Anna watched as the shore receded, her fingernails digging into the palms of her hands as she was torn by conflicting emotions. She was looked at curiously as the boatman handed her ashore and she asked her way to the hospital. A man indicated the path up the hill and Anna walked along between the odd shaped buildings until she reached the largest and guessed it to be the hospital. She pushed open the door and stood in the dim light. Along each wall was a row of mattresses, each one occupied by a wraith-like figure.

'Yannis?'

A man shambled forward from the far end. 'Who's there?'

YANNIS

'I've come to see Yannis, Yannis Christoforakis. I'm his sister.'

The man came closer, his disfigured face wreathed in smiles. 'Welcome. He'll be pleased to see you.' Anna followed Spiro over to a mattress in the corner where her brother lay; his face towards the rough wall.

'Yannis, Yannis, it's me, Anna.'

Slowly he turned his head towards her. 'Anna?'

Anna swallowed, trying to clear the lump that had sprung into her throat at the pathetic sight before her. She sat on the ground beside him and took his hand. 'Are you very sick, Yannis?'

'Spiro says I just need feeding up a bit.'

Anna nodded understandingly. 'We've all lost a bit of weight.'

'How's Mamma?'

'She's fine.'

'Pappa?'

'They took him to work in the mines at Olous – he didn't come back.'

A tear coursed its way down Yannis's cheek. 'And Yiorgo?'

'We haven't heard from him yet.'

Spiro arrived beside them, a mug of soup in his hand. 'Maybe you could persuade Yannis to take a little more than I can.'

Anna sniffed at it. 'Did you make this?'

'No, the boatmen brought it.'

'It smells like mine. I'll be offended if you don't drink it.'

Yannis smiled weakly and allowed Spiro to help him into a sitting position. Anna was struck by his frail appearance. He took a couple of sips from the mug and handed it to Anna.

'That's not much,' she remarked.

'Later.'

'I want to see you drink it all before I go.' She handed the mug back and folded her arms.

Obediently he began to drink again. Spiro watched with a smile on his face. 'Would you be able to send more tomorrow?'

'Of course I can. What about the other patients?'

'I'm sure they'd like some, but they'll drink anything. It's only Yannis who's fussy.'

Yannis handed back the mug.

'That's better,' she commented. 'Make sure you have that much each time.'

Wearily Yannis slid back down on his mattress. The action was not lost on Anna. 'I ought to go. I have to go through the disinfecting process and I don't want to keep Davros waiting. He might not bring me again.'

Yannis held her hand. 'It was good of you to come.'

'I'll come again and next time I expect to see you up and about.' Without hesitation Anna kissed her brother's cheek. Spiro walked with her to the door where she waved goodbye. Once outside she took a deep breath to steady herself. Spiro stood beside her.

'Thank you, Anna. Your visit will have made a difference.'

'I'll come again,' she vowed. 'As often as I can.'

Yiorgo limped back into Plaka. He was undernourished and carried the scars of war. Anna was horrified by his appearance.

'Now I'm home I'll be fine again. A few of your meals will soon put the flesh back on me. Tell me your news. How's Mamma?'

'Mamma's much the same. Pappa died two years ago. He was sent to the mines and the work was too much for him. Yannis nearly starved to death because they wouldn't let supplies go to the island, and we've heard nothing from Stelios.'

'Pappa dead?' Yiorgo found the news almost unbelievable. 'I thought you'd all be safe down here.'

Anna eyed her brother warily, wondering how he would take her next piece of news. 'We were lucky really. We had Italian soldiers lodged here and they helped us on the farm.'

Yiorgo's face clouded over into a dark scowl. 'You mean you entertained enemies here? You accepted their help?'

'We had no choice. They were billeted on us. They were quite nice and kind, really. They helped in return for their meals. Victor

YANNIS

also allowed food out to the island.' Yiorgo continued to scowl. 'We couldn't have managed without their help. As it is, we've had to let Babbis's farm stagnate. They weren't all bad, Yiorgo.'

'If you'd been where I was you wouldn't have given them the time of day, let alone a meal.'

'If we'd refused we would probably have been shot dead by their German commander. Thank goodness he didn't stay. He sent Pappa to the mines and stopped supplies for the island.'

Yiorgo nodded slowly. 'We got him in the end. He was merciless. Would order people to be shot at random. "As an example to others" he used to say.'

'You met him?'

'I'd like to meet the man who hadn't! He used to worm his way into people's confidence. He spoke perfect Greek. Then when he had the information he wanted he would denounce them as traitors and have them shot. He said that if they gave away secrets to the enemy forces they were no use to either side. We finally ambushed him and made sure he'd never do any more harm. The only pity was that we did it so late. If he'd been spotted before the Germans landed the allied forces would have had a chance. As it was he knew where they were waiting and avoided them.'

Anna shuddered. 'It was a terrible time, Yiorgo. I'm so glad you're home. When will Babbis come?'

Yiorgo shook his head. 'He won't, Anna. He was part of the ambush force and didn't come back. He had a proper burial and was acclaimed a hero by his comrades.'

Anna's eyes filled with tears. 'The children,' she whispered. 'The poor children.'

'They have you, Anna. You've been a mother to them.'

'It's not the same. Yannis so wanted his father to be proud of him for the way he'd worked.'

Yiorgo held his sister to him. 'Babbis talked about you a good deal when we were away together. He was very fond of you.'

Anna sighed. 'I know.'

Yiorgo decided to change the subject. He had discovered Babbis's feelings for Anna when they had been fighting side by side, but he had no inkling of the extent of her feelings.

'When I've talked to Mamma I'll have a walk around and see what needs to be done.'

'Are you fit enough?'

'I'm just a bit thin and tired. You don't have to worry.'

By the end of the week he was striding around the farm, saddened to find it so run down. He hid his disappointment and praised his nephew, making the boy's face glow with pleasure. Yannis had taken the news of his father's death calmly.

'I knew something had happened when you returned alone.'

Yiorgo drew the boy close to him. 'I can't take his place. I won't even try. I just want you to know I'm very proud of you and there's always a home with me for you and Marisa.'

Yannis looked at his uncle. 'I appreciate that. We also have nowhere else to go should you decide to throw us out.'

'You have your Pappa's farm.'

'I don't think I'll ever go back there. We have to be sensible about it. What's the point of trying to run two houses for one family? We might as well pull the building down and use the land. That way we could run more animals. Whilst you were away I found out just how difficult it is to farm properly. You need help to get this one back on its feet. I'm willing to help and learn, but we can't run two. If we pulled down the farmhouse and fenced off the land we could run more sheep and goats. They virtually look after themselves. That way we could concentrate on growing vegetables and carob. The vegetables would feed us, and go to the island, and the carob would also bring in some money.'

'Yannis, how old are you?'

'Fourteen.'

Yiorgo shook his head. 'You sound like an experienced farmer.'

'I've had plenty of time to think how to manage on my own if you didn't come back.'

1946 - 1957

Father Andreas frowned over the letter he had received from Father Minos. It thanked him for depositing the money that belonged to the lepers in the bank and went on to say that there were few of the original claimants left. No more than a hundred of the islanders had survived, and he reminded him that their pension would have accumulated also.

The priest described vividly the hardship, suffering and deprivation the islanders had undergone during the occupation of Crete, the many unnecessary deaths that had occurred through starvation. He asked Andreas to start a campaign to compensate them for their ordeal. He suggested that labourers be sent to the island to help with the repair of the houses that had fallen, yet again, into disrepair, a modern hospital built with trained staff to run it, and all to be paid for by the government from the unclaimed pensions of the dead.

The letters went back and forth between them, clarifying the priorities until Father Andreas decided he had a feasible case to put before the hastily elected local government.

He was received sympathetically, listened to attentively, questioned, and then sent away to await their decision. Three weeks slowly dragged itself to a month and his patience was exhausted. Without an appointment he confronted the body of men when they next met and had the distinct impression that the whole matter had been shelved as of little importance.

They spoke at length, explaining to him the difficulties that the country as a whole was facing, that a mere hundred people compared with the rest of the population were too few to deserve serious consideration on their part. Anger and frustration boiled over in him and he raged and shouted at them whilst they sat and listened implacably until he quietened. Finally they suggested that he visited the island and compiled a concise report of the conditions prevailing over there. It was quite possible the lepers were being excessively demanding, there were only a few of them; maybe they could reach a compromise by doing urgent structural repairs and modernising their present hospital building?

Disappointed and disheartened by their attitude Andreas accepted. He did not doubt that Father Minos had made excessive demands and did not relish the task of convincing him that only the minimal amount could be expected by way of compensation.

It was with trepidation that Andreas stepped ashore, followed by a morose doctor. Father Minos greeted him effusively and suggested he visited Yannis before they toured the island or talked seriously about any of the problems that confronted them.

'How is he?'

'A good deal better physically, but mentally …' Father Minos shrugged. 'He took Phaedra's death very hard, but at least he had Anna. When she died he had nothing left. It was such an unfortunate accident.'

'Accident?' Andreas was puzzled. He had assumed everyone who had met their death on the island during the war had succumbed to either their disease or starvation.

'She loved to draw. Any piece of paper she could lay her hands on, then we ran out of paper and she took to carving. Yannis had forbidden her to do it for fear that she would cut herself, but she wouldn't obey him. The inevitable happened, the knife slipped and the silly child told no one. By the time she confided in Spiro it was too late. The poison had spread. He tried all he could, but there was nothing he could do without the doctor.'

'Poor little girl; such a sad life for one so young. It's a blessing that she was spared the knowledge of her mother's death.'

'Louisa? Dead? I knew Yiorgo had been massacred with the rest of the government, but not Louisa.'

Andreas crossed himself. 'Many terrible things happen during a war, but Louisa's death was particularly sickening. Her neighbours stoned her. She was a collaborator as well as a prostitute. She and her brother gave the information to the Germans that enabled them to round up the government, except the doctor. He, poor man, was so full of remorse at his escape that he took an overdose. I blame myself for his death. I should have stayed with him longer and talked until he was able to think rationally again.'

Father Minos looked at the young priest sympathetically. 'Would you like me to give you absolution?'

Andreas shook his head. 'I've received absolution from the Bishop, verbally I can excuse myself, but in my heart I'll never forgive myself.'

'You are but a man, and man is never perfect.'

'As a priest I've always striven for perfection.'

'Which is at it should be. The greatest goals we set ourselves are by necessity unobtainable. If we were able to do everything with ease we'd soon be discontented. Come and talk to Yannis. See if you can give him a goal to aim for. It's what he needs at this time.'

Andreas was appalled at the apathetic attitude that he found in his cousin. Inside the small taverna, where Anna had carved small boats on the shutters, sat a solitary figure. Across from him a group of men were playing cards and two more were passing their time in a game of backgammon.

'Cheers!' Andreas lifted his glass. 'I've been sent here officially by the government.' He had intended to make general conversation with Yannis before mentioning the object of his visit, but decided against it. 'They seem to think Father Minos is asking for the moon when he requests repairs to the houses and a new hospital. What's your opinion?'

Yannis shrugged. 'I haven't thought about it.'

'Then you should. What condition is your house in?'

'I don't know. I don't live there any more.'

'What of the others?'

Again Yannis shrugged. 'I don't know.'

'I never thought you were selfish, Yannis.'

Finally Yannis lifted his eyes from his glass. 'What do you mean?'

'Just because you have a dry roof over your head and a bed to lay on you're willing to let the others fend for themselves. I call that selfish. I was going to ask you to help me, but I see there's not a lot of point.' Andreas pushed back his chair and rose.

Yannis continued to look down. He rubbed a trembling hand across his eyes. 'I don't seem able to concentrate properly.'

Andreas's lip curled in disgust. 'I'm not surprised. It's not mid-day and you've already had too much to drink. I was not ashamed to acknowledge a leper as my cousin, but I am ashamed to acknowledge a defeated drunkard.'

He strode from the taverna, leaving Yannis fondling the glass in his hand. He was trembling with emotion. Would his harsh words have any beneficial effect or only push Yannis deeper into bottles of alcohol as he tried to obliterate his painful memories?

With pad and pencil in hand he started his assessment of the buildings. Those fronting onto the path appeared reasonably safe until you passed through the second archway. The walls on the right hand side of the first three houses were leaning dangerously and a shutter higher up was hanging on a single hinge. He must ask Father Minos if anyone was still living in them and suggest they be moved if so. He wound his way up and down the narrow paths and looked at his findings in despair. So many of the houses would need to be razed to the ground and completely rebuilt before they would be habitable again. He shivered. This would be how the island had looked to Yannis when he first arrived. No wonder he was seeking solace from a bottle. Years of hard work and energy expelled had disintegrated around him.

Sadly he made his way back past the taverna. He could see Yannis still sitting there, the glass in his hand. He went in search of Father Minos, finding him at the hospital deep in conversation with Spiro and Doctor Stavros. He waved Andreas to a seat.

'Come and join us. Ritsa is getting us some lunch. How did you find Yannis?'

'Drunk.'

Father Minos sighed. 'I'm afraid he is most of the time.'

'I was very hard on him. I hope I haven't done more harm.'

'We've tried being understanding, so a bit of plain speaking won't come amiss. His sister coming over seemed to help at first, but even she isn't able to have any lasting effect. Anyway, tell me what you thought of the buildings.'

'Pretty disastrous! Is anyone living in those by the arch?'

Father Minos shook his head. 'Panyotis is in hospital and the other occupants died.'

'What about the houses on the hillside?'

'Only one or two people have insisted on staying there.'

'So the government could be justified in refusing to help with repairs on those?'

'They could at present, but we'll have a housing problem when they start to send more people over.'

Andreas nodded. 'We'll have that to hold over them.' He turned to Doctor Stavros. 'What about the hospital?'

'It needs enlarging. The ordeal these people have been through will take its toll. It may not show yet, but it will over the next few years. Their resistance to any infection, however slight, will have been lowered. It would be nice to have some beds, make nursing easier not to have to carry out all the treatment on your knees.'

'New blankets and mattresses are essential,' interrupted Spiro.

'And there's the question of the generator. It was promised and never sent.'

Throughout their lunch they discussed the improvements they hoped the government would provide until Andreas looked at his watch. It was the only personal luxury he allowed himself and considered it essential if he wished to be punctual for his church services.

'I'm going to ask Manolis to take me over to Plaka. I'm sure I'll be able to beg a bed for the night and I want to see my aunt. I'll come over again tomorrow.'

Maria was delighted to see her nephew. Her first questions were regarding Yannis's health and Andreas replied cautiously.

'He's very unhappy, but I believe he'll overcome his problems, given time.' He spoke more confidently than he felt. 'I had a letter from Annita shortly before I left. Shall I read it to you?' Without waiting for her reply he took the letter from his pocket and began to search for the parts that would interest her.

'If Annita has servants what does she do all day?'

'She didn't say,' admitted Andreas, ' but she has the children and I assume she still helps Elias with his research.'

'What does your Pappa do with himself over there?'

Andreas lowered his eyes. 'He has a fish shop. I think he misses the sea more than he cares to admit.'

Maria nodded. 'His life was the sea. Why doesn't he come home?'

'Mamma likes to be near Annita and the children, and he would do what Mamma wanted.'

Anna greeted her cousin with surprised pleasure, whilst Marisa and Yannis looked curiously at the unknown man in the priest's robes. Anna produced a bottle of brandy from the cupboard.

'It was Pappa's best, used for celebrations. You're a good excuse for a celebration.'

YANNIS

Andreas drank sparingly. He had no wish to go to the island the following day with dull eyes and a heavy head in imitation of his cousin. They talked late into the evening until Anna yawned.

'I must go to bed, and so should you. Davros will want to make an early start.'

'May I borrow some old clothes? I don't want to wear my robes over there – too cumbersome.'

'There are some of Pappa's or Yiorgo's. Take whatever fits you best.'

This time Andreas made straight for the taverna where he expected to find Yannis. He was not disappointed. A glass was in his hand and he was swilling the red wine slowly round in it. He looked up as Andreas entered. 'I thought you might come back.'

'I had to,' replied Andreas. 'I didn't finish yesterday. I had to leave before I had time to speak to you again. I need your help.'

'Mine! The drunken cousin! You don't need my help.'

He drained his glass and reached for the bottle. Andreas was too quick for him and held it firmly. 'How many have you had?'

'Not enough.'

'Plenty for the present, you can have some more later. I want you to come round with me.'

'Round where?'

'The island; I need to know which houses were rebuilt properly and which were patched up. I need the benefit of your knowledge. What's more, I'll sit here, holding this bottle, and refusing to let you have another drink until you help.'

Balefully Yannis glared at him; then pushed back his chair. 'Come on, then. The quicker we get started the sooner we'll be finished.'

Yannis tried to turn up the hill, but Andreas steered him down to the square. With downcast eyes Yannis scuffed along beside him, a sad, shambling figure that tore at Andreas's heart.

'Right side, first house. Who lives there?'

'No one..'
'Who did?'
'Christos and his friends.'
'Did you build it?'
'No, only repaired it.'
'So what did you repair?'
'The roof, new beams, new tiles, most of that wall.'

'We'll go inside.' Andreas pushed open the long wooden door and together they walked into the gloomy interior. Yannis watched as Andreas inspected the walls, window frames and stairs. 'We'll take a look upstairs. Come up with me.'

Obediently Yannis followed and both men blinked as a shaft of light hit their eyes. There was an area of roof missing from the far corner. Andreas made a note.

Inspecting each house, inside and out, took a good deal longer than Andreas had anticipated. At the end of each inspection he would make notes in a small book. At mid-day he insisted Yannis joined him at the hospital for lunch.

'I usually eat at the taverna,' grumbled Yannis.

'Today you are with me.'

Father Minos gave an almost imperceptible nod to Andreas as Yannis entered with him and moved over slightly to allow room at the table.

'He's earned his lunch. He's been walking round the houses with me all morning, showing me the repairs and helping me to decide if those that are standing are safe.'

'No one would know that better than Yannis. How far have you got?'

'Half way up the right side. After lunch we'll start on the left and see if we can get to the same place before I have to leave.'

Yannis ate his lunch in silence whilst the other four men chatted, Doctor Stavros assuring Andreas that he would have no need to inspect the hospital as he had drawn a plan for a new one which he could show to the government. Spiro disagreed. The hospital should be inspected and repaired if necessary, as they could have to wait for some years before a new one was built. The two men argued back and forth until Andreas decided he was wasting time.

'Back to work. We have a good deal to get done.'

Yannis glowered at him, but followed. Spiro looked at Doctor Stavros. 'Do you think Father Andreas is pushing him too hard?'

Doctor Stavros shrugged. 'I'm no psychologist. Something has to shake him out of his apathy and nothing that I've tried has had any effect.'

Andreas glanced covertly at Yannis as he hurried him down the path. There was a tension about the way he was holding his body now that was inexplicable. As before his eyes were fixed on the ground and he glanced to neither left or right until they reached the square.

'First house on the left. Who lived there?'

'Achileas and Maria. Achileas died. Maria's still there.'

Andreas knocked the door and requested permission of the lame woman to inspect the house. It seemed sound, both inside and out. 'Did you do any repairs here?' he asked of Yannis.

'The side wall and most of the back, then we had to mend the roof.'

'You did a good job. Everything appears to be fine.' He thanked Maria and almost pushed Yannis out of the door. 'Come on, next one.'

'No. It's perfectly all right. There's no need.'

'I have to inspect each one.'

'This one is all right, I tell you.'

'Who lives here?'

'No one.'

'Well, who did?'

His question was met by a stubborn silence. Andreas saw the pain in Yannis's eyes. He pushed open the door. 'You have to go back sometime, Yannis.'

'No.' The sound was a strangled gasp.

'Yes.' Andreas took him by the elbow and propelled him through the doorway. Inside he stopped in surprise. Yannis's books were neatly arranged on a shelf, beside the fireplace was a workbox with two pairs of socks sitting on the lid waiting to be mended, and pinned to the wall were sketches. Apart from the dust which lay on every surface the occupants could be returning at any moment.

'Yannis.' Andreas's voice broke with emotion as he opened his arms to his cousin. 'She won't come back, she can't. You have to accept that.'

'Phaedra. Oh, Phaedra. I miss her so much.' Tears were streaming down Yannis's face and he sobbed unashamedly into Andreas's shoulder. 'I don't want to go on without her.'

'Yannis, you have to. It's what she would have wanted. You're still needed here. Everyone who's survived needs help and you're the person they look up to. They trust you. Phaedra would want you to build a new life. More sufferers will be sent over here soon, and what will happen to them if you don't take charge? They'll have no one to help them, no one to turn to when they have a problem. You created this community and you have to be strong enough to keep the community together. Everyone's life has been torn apart in these last few years and you're one of the few people able to help them rebuild.'

'Rebuild. Rebuild. Rebuild.' The word rang in Yannis's ears as it had done so many years ago, whilst he continued to sob. Andreas began to pray aloud.

'Please, God, give Yannis strength and peace of mind.'

Over and over he repeated the phrase until he felt Yannis's sobs subsiding. Slowly he released him, pulling a handkerchief from his pocket. Tears were still pouring from his eyes as Yannis mopped his face. Gently Andreas led him back to the taverna, calling for wine as they entered. He poured a glass for each of them and downed his in a single swallow, pouring another. Yannis picked up the glass and stared at the red liquid. His lip curled and he dashed the glass to the ground before he pushed his way out of the door.

Andreas let his head sink into his hands. He felt weak and with a trembling hand he lifted his glass. He could do no more today. Unwilling to move he forced himself to go in search of Yannis. He retraced his steps to the house and looked inside, then to the hospital, asking each person he encountered, until he finally discovered his cousin on his knees in the church.

Andreas genuflected. Father Minos was listening to Yannis's heart-felt outpouring of his sins and asking for forgiveness. Quietly Andreas left. He had no wish to eavesdrop on a very private conversation.

Andreas returned to Heraklion feeling far happier about his cousin. Each day he had spent on the island he was able to see an improvement in Yannis's attitude. He no longer sat in the taverna all day, befuddled by too much wine, his eyes, although filled with sorrow, were clearer and he was trying to take an interest in events around him. His parting shot to Andreas was to remind him that the generator was of prime importance.

It was a long list of requests that Andreas placed before the local government. He reminded them that Yiorgo Pavlakis had promised the generator before his death and they were under an obligation to honour the pledge. Grudgingly they agreed and then began to haggle over the other items on the list. He reminded them, gently at first, and then more forcibly that the islanders had suffered deprivation and starvation during the occupation and for that they were entitled to compensation. Subtly he pointed out that the cost of the materials and labour for essential repairs would be covered by the unpaid pensions of those who had died.

Dimitris sat, the figures on a pad before him, appearing to ignore the arguments around him. He waited for a temporary lull and then cleared his throat. 'Gentlemen, if I may speak.'

Gradually they quieted and looked towards him expectantly.

'Taking current prices for materials, labour and transportation, and allowing a margin for incidentals, by my reckoning we should have some money in hand. Before making a final decision I should like to check the figures for complete accuracy and also work out the probable time factor involved for the payment of labour. Assuming that we still come out on top I don't see how we can refuse.'

'I'd like to see it itemised.'

'We should shop around for reasonable prices.'

'I don't see how we'll get labour to work over there.'

'We'll probably have to pay them double.'

Dimitris tapped his pencil impatiently. 'Do you want me to work on a breakdown of these figures?'

Hands were raised and the decision was almost unanimous.

When the council met again Dimitris had all the necessary figures, including the time it would take for materials to be assembled and the length of time the work should take. The council searched for faults, asked questions and finally had to agree that the work should go ahead. The next problem was who should act as co-ordinator, all of them were busy men and unwilling to give up their time.

Dimitris again suggested it should be left to him to find someone both willing and able to work for them. Already he had in mind his nephew, a young man not long out of High School. Glad to shift the responsibility onto another's shoulders they agreed and Dimitris was able to tell Father Andreas that everything had been arranged.

At last Father Andreas felt he could pick up the threads of his life again. He took his responsibilities seriously and was worried by the neglect suffered by his parishioners during his absence. His flock were pleased to have him in their midst again and he was touched by the number who filled his tiny church that Sunday, lit a candle and touched the hem of his robe with their lips as they passed him. He loved them and it was gratifying to see that love returned.

He spent half an hour each morning on his knees in private devotions. The privacy and sense of communion he had at this time sustained him through the difficult and distressing times that he encountered so frequently and he was tempted to ignore the hammering on the church door that interrupted him. 'Come in, my son.'

The young man shook his head. 'They want you to come. To the hospital. Accident.' He had obviously run all the way and was panting hard. 'Urgent.'

Without ado Father Andreas followed, striding out to keep pace with the youngster. An accident could mean any thing and any number. At the heavy door he paused and breathed deeply, hoping not to appear too exhausted. He was shown into the main ward and guessed he was needed at the far end. Surrounded by screens, the body of a Greek officer lay, bleeding profusely from the temple with fluid oozing gently from his ear. Andreas crossed himself. He doubted that he would hear a confession; all he could do was give absolution and pray. The doctor acknowledged him briefly as he entered.

'Who is he?'

'No idea; found on the road.'

Father Andreas fell to his knees. The name of the victim was unimportant. His soul would be recognised. He had prayed for the souls of so many unknown young men over the past few years, yet each time it was with a sadness that gripped his heart so hard that it hurt physically. Such a waste of youth!

'He's gone.'

Father Andreas lifted his eyes to see the doctor covering the body with a sheet. He rose from his knees, staying the doctor's hand and peering at the face.

'He's not familiar to me. Is there anything in his pockets?'

Between them the two men began to turn out the contents of the trouser pockets. There was the usual miscellany of coins, scraps of paper and dust. His jacket pockets revealed little more, except, neatly folded into the inside breast pocket, was a passing out slip from the army, stamped as being issued in Athens four days earlier and signed by Commander Stelios Christoforakis. Andreas turned it over in his hand.

'Well, at least it gives us his name if anyone enquires after him. He could come from miles away.'

Andreas looked again at the signature on the paper. 'Maybe if I wrote to Athens they could let me know where he came from and I could visit the family or write to them?'

The doctor shrugged. That was the priest's affair.

'May I keep this?'

'If you wish; it's of no value to anyone now.'

Andreas pushed it into the pocket of his robes, took a last look at the shrouded body and left. He would write to Athens for information. It was the least he could do for the young man.

Yannis watched as the men struggled to get the massive generator into position. It was ugly and looked out of place against the background of the Venetian wall that rose behind it. Men arrived, rolling out thick cables and trailing them through the arch and along the road to the hospital. For days cables were rolled out, moved, cut, joined to thinner lengths and then to no more than thick wires. Ladders were placed against walls and pottery holders fixed, the wires criss-crossing from one house to another like a spider's web.

In each room a wire trailed across the ceiling and down the wall, connected to a brass switch by the door and a globe of glass that swung gently in the slightest breeze. Switches were clicked up and down and the bulbs stared at, but there was none of the promised light.

Spiro had other things to interest him. Manolis had arrived

with half a dozen iron bedsteads that had to be assembled. Yannis shuddered at the sight of them. They brought back unpleasant memories of the hospital in Athens, but Doctor Stavros was delighted.

'I'm developing corns on my knees. At least I'll be able to stand when I examine patients. It will make them more mobile as well.'

'I don't see what difference it will make to them.'

'You've never tried getting up from a mattress on the floor when you're on crutches. It's virtually impossible. What's wrong with you, Yannis? Nothing seems to please you.'

Yannis shrugged. 'I'm bored. I've read all my books until I know them by heart, I've watched the workmen and there's nothing to do.'

'You could give me a hand.'

'I know nothing about medicine and I still don't want to learn,' replied Yannis firmly.

'You could help me by reading some of the circulars I have piled up. The only benefit from the war that I can see is the advance it gave to medicine. I'll bring you some over and you can sort through them. I'm not interested in equipment, so you can dispose of those, but there's a few new drugs that it could be useful to know about.'

Yannis nodded. He was not really interested, but felt it would be churlish to refuse outright. He watched the pile growing day by day until it became inevitable that he did something about them. Most were offering adjustable operating tables, wheelchairs, unbreakable bowls and the like. A few claimed a new medicine was a miracle cure for an ailment, and one or two were treatment reports written by doctors. These he placed to one side for Doctor Stavros to peruse and discard. He had almost finished when a thin sheet fluttered out separately from a brochure.

> "Successful new treatment for Hansen's Disease (Leprosy)
> See next month's issue for details."

Yannis stared at the words. Successful! That must mean a cure. Shaking with excitement he went in search of the doctor and thrust the paper under his nose.

'Have you seen this? What is it?'

Doctor Stavros glanced at it casually. 'It's probably more about Dapsone.'

'You know about it?'

'I've read about it.'

'Is it a cure?'

'Maybe. It will need more years of testing before anyone's sure.'

'Why aren't you giving it to us?'

'It's not available in Greece.'

'Why not? It should be available wherever there's leprosy.'

Doctor Stavros shrugged. 'How should I know? I'm not a politician.'

'Well, shouldn't you write to them or something?'

'Yannis, I'm busy. I know there are less of you over here than there were a few years ago, but I'm not as young as I was, and when I get back I'm tired and I have other sick people waiting to see me. When am I supposed to have the time to sit down and write letters to politicians?'

'Have you got more information about this?'

'Probably. I'll bring it over.'

Yannis pored through the literature, understanding very little of the technical terms and confused by the tiny illustrations. He plagued Doctor Stavros until the doctor finally consented to explain the details to him.

'The government should be written to and this medicine should be demanded on our behalf,' stormed Yannis angrily. 'You could explain that we had no medication throughout the war and those of us who are left deserve the chance to regain our health.'

'I've told you; I've no time to compose letters to the government. Write it yourself. Give it to me to read through and if I agree with it I'll add a note with my signature.'

YANNIS

The more Yannis thought about it the more incensed and determined he became. A week later he handed his letter to Doctor Stavros and insisted he read it immediately.

'You feel very strongly over this, don't you, Yannis?'

Yannis nodded. 'I feel we've just been forgotten over here. No one cares, they're just waiting for us all to die so we're no longer an embarrassment to them.'

'They're spending a good deal of money on the island at the moment.'

'Our money. It won't cost them a lepta.'

'You're so bitter, Yannis.'

'Of course I'm bitter. We're over here with nothing and all the time they have a cure.'

'You don't know that.'

'We should be given the chance. I won't take no for an answer.'

Doctor Stavros tapped the letter against his fingers. 'I'll send it for you with my endorsement, but I don't know if you'll get an answer.'

Yannis's mouth set in a grim line. 'Then I'll continue to write to them until I do – and it had better be the one I want.'

Anna saw the pin pricks of light over the island and for a moment she panicked, thinking it was a fire, then she smiled. At least life for her brother was improving. She decided she would ask Davros to take her over to the island so she could see this modern electricity. It would be an experience she would surely never forget if she pressed a switch and light came into a dark room.

She was surprised when she arrived on the island to see that it looked no different from the way it had before. She was not sure what she had expected to see, but felt there should have been something. Yannis was run to earth in his own little house. It had taken a good deal of persuasion by Father Minos to make him return, to be completely surrounded by memories of Phaedra and Anna, and able to keep them in perspective. He was composing a letter to the hospital authorities in Athens, complaining bitterly that the treatment available for lepers in other countries had not been offered to them in Crete. He greeted Anna with pleasure.

'How is everyone?'

'They're all fine. Yiorgo is working hard and the farm's picking up slowly. You look a good deal better than when I last saw you.'

Yannis smiled. 'We were all of us pretty low. Had the war gone on much longer I doubt there would have been any of us left, which would have suited the authorities, no doubt. Do you know they have a new drug which can cure leprosy, yet the government haven't bothered to try it for Greek people?'

Anna looked at her brother in horror. 'That can't be true! Surely they'd try everything.'

Yannis shook his head. 'I'm writing to them now, demanding that we be given a chance.'

'Suppose they refuse?'

'I'll keep on writing. I'll write to the newspapers in Greece and also to foreign newspapers. Once they find the whole world knows of their lack of care they'll have to do something.'

'Won't they punish you if you let everyone know?'

Yannis turned incredulous eyes on his sister. 'There's nothing more they could do to me,' he said bitterly.

Somehow Anna did not feel as confident. 'Show me how the electricity works, Yannis. Everyone's talking about it.'

'I wish we'd had it years ago. When it was too rough to bring supplies over we gave all the oil to Spiro for use in the hospital. That meant we had to go to bed as soon as it was dark.' He flicked the switch down and the bulb hanging from the centre of the ceiling glowed. 'You see it better when it's dark. All the room's lit up as though the sun were shining.'

Anna stood by the door, turning the light on and off. 'May I close the shutters, Yannis, to see it better?'

He smiled indulgently at her as she played. Finally she switched it off and sat down beside him. 'Tell me more about this cure you say there is.'

'I'll read my letter to you. That will tell you all about it,' Yannis assured her.

Anna nodded. She thought it most unlikely she would understand, but if it pleased Yannis she was willing to indulge him.

Stelios crumpled the letter and threw it to one side in annoyance. He did not consider the unfortunate death of the soldier for whom he had signed a discharge warrant was any concern of his. It was even more unfortunate that it should have been his cousin Andreas who had been in attendance. Reluctantly he drew a sheet of paper towards him and wrote a curt letter. That should be the end of the matter.

He was surprised when, three weeks later, another letter arrived for him bearing a postmark from Heraklion, and he was most disconcerted by the contents. He was cross with himself for answering the first one when he could quite easily have ignored it. Finally he replied to Andreas admitting that he was his cousin, but that he saw little point in returning to Crete to visit his family. He had recently married and had no leave due to him for a considerable time. As an afterthought he added his good wishes to them all and Andreas.

As he had dreaded, his letter brought a reply, full of news and saying how delighted everyone was to know he was fit and well, and urging him to visit his mother before it was too late. He pushed the letter into his pocket and conveniently forgot about it.

Daphne eyed her husband of a few months anxiously. Recently something seemed to be troubling him and no amount of subterfuge on her part had managed to make him confide in her. She placed an arm round his neck and leant her face against his.

'I think you should apply for some more leave, darling. You're so tired.'

'I haven't any due to me.'

'You could think of some excuse.'

'Excuses have to be backed by reasons. I can't ask for more leave because I'm tired. I'm tired because I've had to work extra hours to catch up from when I had my last leave.'

Daphne pouted prettily at him. 'You could explain that we're moving to a larger apartment and you need some time to pack your belongings.'

Stelios patted her arm. 'They would ask why I'd bothered to marry a woman who was incapable of packing my clothes.'

'Then your papers.'

'I've only personal papers at home. I should be able to cope with those.'

'I could do them for you. I usually tidy up when you've left them all over the table. In fact you dropped this one when you took your jacket off.' Daphne held up the envelope.

'I need that.' Stelios made a grab for it.

'What's so important about it?' Daphne held it just out of his reach.

'I need the address. Give it to me.' He snatched it from her hand.

Daphne bit her lip. Should she tell him she had read it and knew he had a family in Crete, despite his declaration that he had no living relatives? 'I'll get the supper.' She left the room, puzzled and hurt by her husband's failure to confide in her.

Dimitris rested his arms on the table and surveyed the pile of envelopes before him. This was the penalty one paid for having a minor operation. Now he would have to spend hours reading letters and composing replies. He drew the first one towards him and slit the envelope, withdrawing a number of closely written sheets. He groaned. If they were all like this it would take him even longer than he had originally envisaged.

He skimmed through it quickly. It appeared to be full of complaints that no reply had been received to an earlier letter.

He pushed it to one side and took the next; smiling as he read the halting thanks of the widow he had helped. He began to divide them into piles, those which needed the attention of another government official, those that needed no reply, those for whom a reply was straightforward and could be left to his clerk and those he must read again.

Two hours later he decided he had done enough for one day. Leaving the letters in their various piles he returned home to be pampered by his wife and children.

For a week he sorted mail, gradually clearing the backlog, until he had no more than half a dozen that he had not opened. The first was again a letter of complaint that no answer had been received, and with an exclamation of annoyance Dimitris began to go through the pile, hoping to find the original letter. There it was, the thickest of all, and he began to read. It was tedious; there was a long description of hardships suffered over a number of years, of wartime deprivation, lack of medical facilities, and then the criminal accusation that they had all been condemned to a living death when there was medicine available for other sufferers.

Dimitris frowned. What was the man on about? He turned to the address on the first sheet. Spinalonga. The island where the lepers lived and that priest had been so insistent they should lavish money on it. He sighed and returned to the letter, glossing over the long account of their hardships and paying scant attention to the tirade of abuse regarding the lack of the latest drugs that were available in other quarters of the world. He shrugged. This man did not know what he was talking about. Anyone suffering from an incurable disease was always certain there was a miracle cure. He would pass it over to his minister for medical affairs and he could compose a placatory reply. He folded the letter and made to put it to one side. It was not folded evenly and he noticed for the first time the irregular piece of paper at the end. He glanced at it incuriously.

1946-1957

"As doctor in charge of the island of Spinalonga I can only endorse this letter and request that my patients be given the opportunity to take Dapsone."

Dimitris read the words again. Did this mean there was some cure? He started to read the letter again, concentrating this time. There were the references to various medical journals and papers with the dates when they had been written. Maybe there was something in this after all. He would have to find out. He glanced at the other letters in the same hand, they were repetitious, except that in the last two was added the information that letters of complaint about the treatment of lepers in Greece had been sent to other countries with a request that they be published in newspapers and attract public opinion.

For the first time Dimitris began to feel uncomfortable. The government was precarious. The slightest sign that it was inefficient could bring it toppling, and Dimitris was enough of a politician to know that the one thing the people needed more than anything at the moment was stability to enable them to rebuild their lives. He would find Vassilis and they could discuss this over a quiet lunch.

The two men savoured their wine, Dimitris wondering how he was to get the information without accusing Vassilis of incompetence and ignorance and Vassilis wondering what he had done that deserved lunch with the leader of the local government.

'I had a slightly disturbing letter the other day,' Dimitris began.

Vassilis looked up quickly. He had been very careful not to let too many patients go to the head of the queue. Excuses began to form themselves on his lips, but Dimitris continued. 'Do you know anything about a cure for leprosy?'

Vassilis spread his hands. 'I'm a surgeon.'

'You would receive various periodicals and papers written for your profession?'

'Of course, but I have to confess that I've little time for reading.'

Dimitris nodded understandingly. 'A man has written to me

claiming there is a cure for leprosy, he gives dates and references to various articles. He says he's also sent letters to other countries complaining that we're not interested in curing him and his like, but prefer to leave them to die.'

The blood rose in Vassilis's face. 'That is libel.'

'Libellous or not, we have to stop it. You're the medical officer for this region, so it's your responsibility. I'll leave the letters with you, and I suggest you compose a suitable reply. In the meantime I'll send a letter to tell him the government are investigating his complaints.'

Vassilis nodded. 'I'll talk to Nikos, he'll know far more than I.'

'Remind him to be discreet. We don't want this brought up at the next session or rumours spread around.'

'You can trust me,' Vassilis assured him. He took the bundle of letters from Dimitris. 'A prolific writer.'

Dimitris sighed. 'Most of them are letters of complaint, but a couple have all the references to the articles.'

'I'll sort them out. It could be as well to dispose of the others. Who wrote them, anyway?'

'Some fellow called Yannis Christoforakis. Personally I thought we'd done more than enough for them. Meet me here on Thursday for lunch and bring Nikos.'

Vassilis nodded. He hoped he was not going to be left to pay the bill. Money was short this month, as his wife had insisted on new shoes for their children.

Yannis tossed the letter aside in disgust. 'Just what I thought they'd say. "The drugs are new; they're not used in this country, we're waiting to be certain their long term effects aren't harmful". If the drugs are advertised for use they must have been tested. How long do they want to wait for long-term effects? For ever?'

Doctor Stavros read the discarded letter. 'Everything they say is quite logical.'

'It might be logical, but it doesn't help us. I'd be willing to try anything. I took Chaulmoogra Oil. Whatever their new medicine is, it can't be worse.'

'You have to see it from their point of view. Suppose they gave everyone this drug, at first it seemed to work, then in two or three years time if you became worse you'd blame them.'

Yannis turned towards the doctor. 'I'd be willing to sign a paper to say I wouldn't hold them responsible. What have I got to lose?'

'You could end up bedridden, your limbs having to be amputated.'

'I'll probably end up like that without any medicine. I'm going to write to them again. I'm going to insist that I'm given the chance. If I'm willing why shouldn't they be?'

Doctor Stavros sighed. Yannis had obviously made up his mind and it was no good trying to explain to him that the government would not listen. 'As you wish. I won't write anything to hinder you, Yannis, but I feel you may end up more bitter and disappointed.'

Doctor Stavros left him, knowing either he or Manolis would be handed a sheaf of letters to be posted from Aghios Nikolaos.

Dimitris slapped the letter down on his desk and reached for the telephone. He rang Vassilis's number and tapped his fingers impatiently as he waited for the call to be answered. He arranged for Vassilis to telephone Nikos and tried to marshal his thoughts before the two men arrived. He handed the letter first to Vassilis who read it swiftly and passed it to Nikos. Vassilis pursed his lips; this could be nasty. Nikos looked at him, his eyes wary.

'Could they do that?'

'If they could find a solicitor willing to act for them they could certainly try. There's always someone who's willing to champion the under-dog. This man Christoforakis is no fool. He probably has a relative who's in the legal profession and has already agreed to act for him.'

'More to the point, has he got a case?' Dimitris looked at Vassilis and Nikos. 'You're the medical men.'

Vassilis shifted uncomfortable. 'I know that as the medical officer for the region I should have the answer at my fingertips, but I have to confess that I don't know. I'm a surgeon. I don't bother to read the latest reports on medicines, they don't affect me, or my patients. Nikos is in a better position to answer.'

'Well?'

Nikos cleared his throat. 'I'd have to investigate.'

'Investigate what?'

'Contact the pharmaceutical firms who are manufacturing the drug, ask for their formula, request a list of all the tests they've done and the subsequent results. Very often the claims made are not strictly true, or in a few years have an adverse effect. What I'm trying to say is that if we objected to the drug we would have to prove there was something harmful in the formula. Personally I doubt that there is. We could claim that the tests that have been run are not conclusive, or the results are inconclusive, but to do that we need the information in the first place.'

Vassilis nodded. 'How long would it take to get it?'

'Who knows?'

Dimitris held up his hand. 'Can we assume this knowledge would also be essential to a solicitor acting on their behalf?'

'Of course, they'd have to have a basis for bringing the case.'

'Would they be able to obtain the information more quickly than us?'

'I shouldn't imagine so.'

'Then we've nothing to worry over on that score. I suggest you write another letter to this man, assuring him we are investigating the claims he's made for these drugs and we'll advise him of the outcome.'

'Suppose,' suggested Nikos tentatively, 'the outcome of the enquiry shows the drug is successful?'

Dimitris smiled. 'We'll think about that when and if we have to. I have to admit I was a little concerned when I first read the letter, but you've put my mind at rest. I don't think we've anything to fear from this man after all. Let's have a drink, my friends, before you return to your offices.'

Yannis put the letter to one side. 'They think themselves very clever saying they'll investigate and ask for the formula and results from the tests. By the time they've written away for them I'll be in possession of the answers.'

Spiro looked at him in surprise. 'How do you think you're going to manage that? They have access to medical papers that we'd never be allowed to see.'

'When I first came here I was betrothed to my cousin. She married a man who was researching into the disease. I can't remember his name, but Andreas told me he was given a research scholarship and they went to America. At the same time as I wrote to the government I also wrote to Andreas and asked him to write to her asking for the information.' Yannis smiled triumphantly.

'Do you think she'll send it to you?'

'Why shouldn't she? I'm not asking for anything that's secret.'

'Her husband might not like it.'

'I don't see why he should object.'

Spiro shrugged. 'Scientists can be odd about sharing their knowledge.'

'Not when it's already been published.'

'I'll still be surprised if you get what you want. You're like a dog with a bone when you get an idea fixed in your head. Be content with what you've got. Accept your life.'

'Do you accept yours?'

'Yes.'

Yannis turned away. 'I'm glad you're happy. I must go and write some letters.'

When the package finally arrived, some months later, Yannis

was surprised at the bulk. He had expected a letter, but the contents of the brown paper parcel were almost beyond belief, including a letter from Annita, hoping that his general health was good, telling him about her family and also hoping the enclosed information was what he wanted.

The letter from Elias was long and Yannis read it curiously, wondering what kind of man it was who had dedicated his life to research and persuaded Annita to share it with him. Elias expressed a wish to meet him and a desire to see the island, yet thought it most unlikely he would ever have the opportunity. He said he would be only too pleased to furnish Yannis with any information in his possession that could be of use, adding that all those who had been treated had shown no adverse signs at all, and had, in his opinion, definitely improved. He added that it was still too soon to be able to claim the drug as a cure, except in very early cases. In no way did he want to dash Yannis's hopes, but for someone who had suffered for almost twenty years and mostly without any form of treatment, he could not answer for the outcome.

Yannis smiled grimly and began to examine the contents of the parcel. There were newspaper cuttings in English, which he could not read, but each was clipped to a piece of paper and Yannis could recognise Annita's hand writing in the translation. It was the same with the reports in the medical journals, each one had been translated and often there was a note added which contained a personal opinion. Yannis sorted the information into piles on his table. First the letters, followed by cuttings, reports and papers written in Elias's own hand, describing the experiments that had been carried out and the results of each one.

It was tempting to write immediately to the government to tell them he had proof, but decided he must first write to Annita and Elias. The letter took him almost a week. He described the hospital conditions he had left behind in Athens, only to find equally as bad on the island and how they had all worked to build their houses and a hospital. He admitted his happiness with Phaedra and hoped they had found the same together. He told of her lingering death and then the sudden death of Anna, along with the decimation of three quarters of the occupants of the island and how he planned to take the government to task for denying them the medicine for so long. When he finally sealed the envelope and handed it to Manolis he felt a weight lifting from his shoulders. Now he could really start.

He made one rough draft after another, copying extracts from the papers he had been sent until he was satisfied there was nothing more he could add which would have any bearing on the way the government would act. Before he sent the letter he asked both Spiro and Doctor Stavros to read the copy he had made.

Spiro was complimentary. 'I think you've done wonders, Yannis. It's so explicit, no wasted words, just the facts and presented in order.'

'I'm sure Orestis would have made a better job of it if he were still alive.'

Doctor Stavros was unwilling to commit himself too fully, feeling Yannis would receive scant attention from the government however factual and eloquent his letter. 'I don't think you have to be trained in the legal profession to write as you've done. You needed the facts, and those were given to you. You just made a list of them.'

Dimitris opened the letter roughly, tearing at the envelope and almost spilling the contents. He recognised the handwriting. Not having heard anything for almost six months he had thought the matter over and done with, the man dead, perhaps, now here he was again. As he read the frown between his eyebrows deepened. Before he was half way through the letter his hand reached out for the telephone and he was ordering Vassilis and Nikos to meet him urgently. Whilst he waited for them to arrive he continued reading. Where had the man gathered all this information? He hoped Nikos would be able to produce counter information. This would need more than a letter to say they were investigating.

Nikos read the papers with interest, clicking his tongue occasionally, raising an eyebrow or frowning. Finally he looked at Dimitris. 'He's certainly done his homework well.'

'Is it true?' demanded Dimitris.

Nikos shrugged. 'I would expect so. Most of it's taken from medical journals and he quotes from articles written by an American researcher who professes himself willing to write to us.'

'I thought you were going to find out?' snapped Dimitris.

'I do have my work here. There's little time to go to libraries and ask them to look up medical papers. When I have managed to spend an afternoon there it's been a hopeless task. I've no reference numbers and without them I have to go through everything. There's the added problem that a great number of them are published in America and I don't read English.'

Dimitris grunted and turned to Vassilis. 'Then how has this man managed to get hold of them? He lives on an island, he has no access to any libraries and I doubt if he reads English either.'

The men looked at each other. 'Maybe someone worked on his behalf?' suggested Vassilis.

'If he's capable of getting men to work on his behalf maybe I should offer him a position in the government. He appears to have more success than I.' Dimitris glared at them. 'If he can gather this information you should be able to.'

The men shifted uncomfortably on their hard chairs. 'Do you want me to write to him again? I could say we are investigating the papers he sent and ask him to help us by telling us how he gathered the information.'

'Ask him how he did it?' Dimitris looked at Nikos in disgust. 'Make us look foolish in his eyes? No, you write to him and say we are investigating, but nothing more. I'd like to see the letter before you send it, and I suggest you do some of this investigating that you keep talking about. What you don't seem to realise is that we hold this government by a thread. If these papers are correct, and they probably are, it could cause a public outcry and then where would we be? Out on our ears.' He waited for his words to hit home.

'You mean people would take notice of a leper?' Vassilis asked incredulously.

'Since the war people have been horrified at the treatment the Jews received under the Nazis, the torture that went on to obtain information from ordinary citizens. Look at the reprisals our own people suffered! The whole world would be up in arms against us if they thought we'd mistreated or neglected sick people.'

'But we haven't neglected them.'

'We haven't exactly done anything for them either. We can gloss over what happened before, blame our shortcomings on the previous government and the war, but we can't use that as an excuse forever. Sooner or later we'll be asked what we have done for them.'

Nikos wrote to the hospital in Athens and sat back and waited. He had condensed the information from the papers so he could ask straightforward questions, hoping the answers would be brief. He wrote twice more before he received a reply. He arrived at Dimitris's office without asking for an appointment and thrust the letter under his nose.

'So now what do you want me to do?'

Dimitris read the letter slowly. It confirmed all the claims for the new drug and admitted that they had begun to use it before the outbreak of the war and were now trying to manufacture their own supply rather than have to pay the additional cost of importing. Dimitris raised his eyes and looked at Nikos. 'This must be strictly confidential.'

Nikos nodded. 'But what am I to reply?'

'I suggest you say that Athens knows of the treatment and is trying to manufacture the drug for general use. As soon as it's available we'll contact them.'

'Do you think that will satisfy him?'

'It will have to. You'll have to write back to Athens, keep in contact with them so you know how they're progressing and keep me informed.'

The letters continued back and forth between Yannis and the government. Yannis's continually pressing and urging action on their behalf, Nikos's replies placatory and urging patience. Yannis would not be satisfied, each time he wrote he added another name to the list of those who had died, and demanded that the drug should be imported for their use. Nikos began to dread the familiar envelope arriving with his other post and wrote to Athens begging for supplies of the drug to be sent to Crete. The reply he received sent him hurrying to consult with Dimitris.

'They say the patients need to have a thorough examination, blood tests and skin samples taken before they could authorise the medicine.'

Doctor Stavros frowned. There were eighty-six people on the island, most of them in an advanced stage of leprosy, and he was expected to give each one a complete medical and take blood tests and skin samples. It was not feasible. By the time he had examined the last person he would need to start again. He wrote to the government explaining that their request was impossible under the circumstances and suggested they sent a team of doctors to the island.

Nikos hesitated over the letter for almost a week, and then decided he had to show it to Dimitris. 'We can't send a crowd of doctors down there,' he protested. 'I'm pretty stretched as it is at the hospital.'

'How long do you think it would take to carry out these tests?'

'I've no idea. I don't even know what facilities they have

over there. They've electricity and operating equipment, but it's doubtful that they have a stock of specimen jars or even labels to go on them.'

'You could take those with you.'

'Me?'

'You're the local specialist. You know what tests are needed and you'll be able to get an idea of their general health by observing them as well as the facts from an examination.'

'I can't go,' protested Nikos. 'I told you, I'm over-stretched at the hospital as it is.'

'Your assistant will have to take over. You can leave him instructions for those who are in hospital and new cases would have to wait until you returned. Look, we've managed to hold off all the threats this leper has made towards us so far, but we won't be able to for much longer. If you write and say a doctor is coming as soon as possible that should keep him quiet for a bit. Take your time over there, as long as you like, maybe by then Athens will have come up with an answer.'

Nikos's protestations died on his lips. For almost two years they had delayed taking any action and Dimitris was right when he said they could not do so for very much longer.

'Maybe the doctor would be willing to put me up for a while,' he spoke desolately.

'Fine. Write to the doctor and see if you can be there in a fortnight.'

Nikos arrived at mid-day in Aghios Nikolaos and made his way to the doctor's house where he was greeted with enthusiasm and hospitality. After a leisurely lunch he sat in the room allotted to him and began to go through the book that the doctor had kept so meticulously over the years. Name, age, date of birth if it was known, headed each page. The date the patient had arrived on the island and the affected area was recorded along with the dates the doctor had examined the patient. On over four hundred pages the word "deceased" and a date was written at the bottom. All those pages Nikos skipped over, he was only interested in those who were still alive. The afternoon passed with him engrossed in the information. When Doctor Stavros finally tapped at the door and entered he looked up with bleary eyes.

'What time is it? I've been so busy I've quite lost track.'

'Six. I thought you might like a drink and we could go to a taverna for a meal later.'

Nikos nodded. 'I'd like to talk to you about some of these cases.'

'Of course, but I'd rather wait until you've paid your first visit. My information could be coloured by familiarity.' He poured wine for them both, wishing it was raki, but he thought it advisable to keep a reasonably clear head. This man was a government official as well as a doctor.

'A thing that puzzles me about these entries, so many seem to have arrived on the same date.'

'There's nothing odd about that. They were the ones who were sent by the hospital ship. In fact most of them arrived in groups. It wasn't often they came singly.'

'What do you mean?'

'They were held in the wards in Heraklion or Athens and then transferred over here. Just occasionally one would be found hiding locally and they would be sent straight over.'

'Why do you think so many of them died during the war?'

Doctor Stavros shrugged. 'I thought it was obvious. The Germans stopped all food supplies being sent over. They managed for a while, and then they were forced to live almost exclusively off the fish they could catch. I wasn't allowed to go over, so they had no medical help. There were a number of elderly who would have died anyway, and, of course, accidents.'

'Accidents?'

'One man fell off a roof he was trying to repair. He never recovered consciousness. There was the man who got drunk and thought he'd swim to safety, needless to say he drowned, a couple were shot by the Italians when they tried to get across to Plaka, Anna died of blood poisoning and a woman threw herself off the fortress wall.'

'Unfortunate.'

Doctor Stavros drained his glass. 'I'll take you to meet Manolis. He's my regular boatman and he'll take you across.'

They walked down to the waterfront and found Manolis in one of the tavernas. The doctor introduced Nikos. 'You'll be taking him over to the island every day.'

Manolis scowled. 'I go early and I return late.'

'I'll be ready and I've plenty to do.'

'Well, at least Yannis will be pleased to see you.'

Nikos pretended not to hear the remark. 'What's the food like here?'

'Pretty good.'

'I'll try it. Should I take some food over to the island tomorrow?'

'They'll cater for you as a matter of course, they always do for the doctor and myself.'

Nikos nodded. He felt a distinct outsider and wished someone else had been selected for the task ahead.

The journey took less time than he had envisaged and he gazed at the island in the distance with interest. As they drew closer the ramparts of the Venetian fort rose above them with the incongruous concrete building that housed the generator at the foot. Flora was waiting on the quay and smiled with surprise when she saw Manolis had a passenger.

'How nice to see a fresh face. I'll take you to meet Yannis and we'll find you somewhere comfortable to live. I'm sure you'll be happy here.'

'I'm not living here. I'm a doctor sent from Heraklion to examine you all.'

Flora looked at Manolis for assistance.

YANNIS

'Take him to Yannis first. He'll know where he needs to go.'

Nikos followed her up the slope, automatically noticing that apart from only having one arm, she appeared extremely fit and well, although thin. Yannis answered the knock on his door and looked in surprise at his visitor. 'What can I do for you?'

'I've been sent here by the government and hospital authorities. I'm the doctor who's going to examine you and take the tests that are needed in Athens.'

'You'd better come in then.' Yannis held the door open wide and Nikos stepped into the small, neat room. He looked around appreciatively. 'Have a seat and I'll make some coffee, or would you prefer wine?'

'No, coffee's fine by me.'

Nikos's eyes roamed round the room, noting the pile of writing paper and envelopes on the table. This was obviously the Yannis who had been writing to him. Pinned either side of the fireplace were two sketches, both of females. Nikos rose and looked at them carefully. He was still standing there when Yannis returned.

'I was admiring the art work.'

Yannis did not answer. He placed coffee and water at the doctor's elbow and sat down opposite. 'What can I do for you?'

'Are you the gentleman who has been writing to the government requesting the new drugs?'

'I am.'

Nikos nodded. 'I'm here to try to help. Let me explain. Shortly before the war America claimed to have found an effective drug for the use of leprosy patients. We were naturally interested and were waiting for more information and the results of their tests. You will understand, of course, that once we were involved in the war we were unable to proceed.'

'I know all the excuses that have been put forward.' Yannis rose and lifted a heavy file down from his bookshelf. 'I have in here all the correspondence that has passed between the government and myself, also the correspondence I received from

America. All we are asking for is our rights as sick people.'

Nikos shifted uncomfortably. 'Of course, I am just trying to explain why there seems to have been a delay.'

'You have no need to explain. I know why there's been delay. Having been abandoned on this island we were not expected to survive very long. I'm afraid we're still here to cause embarrassment and demand our rights.'

'No, please, don't think of yourselves as an embarrassment to us. We want to give you these drugs, but now we have Athens asking for health reports on all of you. It will be up to them to decide if your medical condition warrants them and if they can help you.'

'I would have thought you could have gained all the information you needed from Doctor Stavros.'

'I've gained a great deal, but I've been asked to take blood tests and skin samples and to give each of you a thorough medical.'

'And how long is this going to take?'

'No longer than it has to.'

'Where do you want to start?'

'It makes no difference provided I examine everyone.'

'Then you may as well start with me.'

Nikos opened his case. 'Very well. I'll need some details from you; then I'll do the medical and come back on Friday to take blood and skin samples. They'll be fresher if I leave them until last. Now, your full name.'

The routine questions of family background Yannis answered easily, then Nikos began to probe a little deeper. 'When was your condition first diagnosed?'

Yannis shrugged. 'Is it important?'

'Not to me, but I've got to fill in the form.'

'I was born in nineteen hundred and nine and I was in Heraklion at the High School at the time, so I would have been about sixteen, which makes it nineteen hundred and twenty five.'

YANNIS

'You went to High School?'

Yannis lifted his head proudly. 'I did. I won a scholarship.'

'I didn't mean to doubt your ability. We must have been there at the same time. What were you reading?'

'History and Classics, I had dreams of becoming an archaeologist.' Yannis smiled grimly. 'It was not to be.'

Nikos sat with his pen poised in the air. 'Say that again.'

'It was not to be.'

'No, about becoming an archaeologist.'

'It was a dream I had.'

'Did you ever work in the museum?'

'For a while, I had great plans for that, too.'

Nikos placed his pen down on the table and held out his hand. 'Yannis, don't you remember me?' There were tears in Nikos's eyes as he spoke.

Yannis frowned. 'Should I?'

'We spent a good deal of time together. You, Dimitris and I.'

Yannis frowned more deeply. 'You were my friend Nikos?'

'You just disappeared. Why didn't you write to us? Tell us what had happened.'

'You forget that we weren't allowed to communicate with the outside world. Even my family didn't know what had happened to me.' Yannis spoke bitterly. 'What did you do after High School?'

'I went on to University in Athens, finally qualifying as a doctor and staying on a couple of years to become a skin specialist. Then I had the usual struggle to be accepted and get a permanent position.'

'You're established now, though.'

Nikos shrugged. 'I gained by another's misfortunes. I was a very junior doctor before the war, due to the death of Doctor Lenakis I suddenly found myself quite important.'

'Are you married?'

Nikos nodded. 'I've a little girl and another on the way.'

Yannis nodded. 'Happy?'

'Very. That's why I don't want to spend any longer here than I can help. How about you?' Nikos looked towards the sketches.

'That was my wife, Phaedra. She died during the war.'

'I'm sorry.'

Yannis ignored the remark. 'The other is Anna.'

'Your daughter?'

'My adopted daughter. She was Anna Pavlakis, Yiorgo Pavlakis's daughter.'

Nikos's mouth gaped. 'You mean the Yiorgo Pavlakis who was shot? How did she get over here?'

'Louisa brought her down to Aghios Nikolaos for safety. She then abandoned the child and returned to Heraklion. Anna was caught stealing and sent over here.'

'Was she leprous?'

'She had a birthmark, but before Doctor Stavros could send tests off the Germans invaded. It never got any worse and she never complained of any pain from it, so it's doubtful that it was leprosy.'

'Poor child. I read Doctor Stavros's records yesterday, but I didn't associate the name. Blood poisoning, wasn't it?'

'I told her she mustn't use a knife.' Yannis sighed. 'If only she'd listened to me she could still be alive now.'

'It could be better that she died. At least she never had to know how her mother met her death.'

Yannis did not appear to be listening. He was looking at the sketch on the wall. 'She was a clever little girl. We both loved her, but to me she was very special.'

Nikos could feel a lump coming into his throat. How would he feel if his daughter met the same fate? 'Shall I start examining you?' he asked gruffly.

'For all the good it will do.' Yannis removed his coat and shirt and submitted to Nikos's probing fingers.

'You seem in good shape, considering everything. Drop your trousers.'

YANNIS

'Is that necessary?'

'I have to make a thorough examination.'

Yannis protested no longer. 'Provided the outcome is favourable.'

'It will be honest, Yannis. Whatever I find I'll report. Not just for you, but for everyone.'

For the rest of the week Nikos visited the island. He found the journey cold and miserable and longed to be back in Heraklion. He would sit hunched up in the boat watching as the island drew nearer and nearer, insisting they left in plenty of time each afternoon so there was no chance of him being at sea when darkness fell. Each day he talked to Yannis, rediscovering their old intimacy and learning about the conditions Yannis had faced in the hospital in Athens and the dereliction that had confronted him when he first arrived on the island.

On the Friday, Nikos packed the blood and skin samples he had taken carefully. He was more cheerful, the prospect of seeing his wife and daughter again uppermost in his mind. Yannis had asked him to deliver a letter to Andreas and he had it in his pocket. It was thick and the envelope only just fitted, making him wonder what Yannis could find to write about at such length.

The bus journey seemed to take an interminable time and every jolt and bump made him peer anxiously at his precious samples. He certainly did not want to take them again. Safely delivered he hurried to his house, only to find that Dimitris had left a message to say he would like to see him during the weekend to discuss his progress. He was annoyed and wondered whether he could ignore the summons, finally deciding he would visit Dimitris in his home after delivering the letter to Andreas.

He set out into the dark street and strode along briskly. The sooner the errand was over the quicker he could return home. Andreas opened the door himself and insisted he went inside.

'I mustn't stop long. I have an appointment.'

'I just wish to open Yannis's letter and see if an immediate reply is called for.' He ripped open the envelope to disclose a sheet of paper with another envelope that was full to bursting. Andreas picked it up and smiled. 'This is for my sister and her husband. The letter for me is just a request to post it. It's quicker from Heraklion.'

Dimitris furnished him with a drink and settled down opposite. 'Now, tell me about this man Yannis.'

'Do you remember our friend when we were at High School? The one who wanted to be an archaeologist and spent all his spare time at the museum?'

Dimitris nodded and frowned at the same time.

'Remember his name?'

Dimitris shook his head; then realisation dawned on him. 'You don't mean…..'

'I do. Yannis Christoforakis, the leper, is our friend from High School. A skin test he'd had taken after that fall where he cut his head open showed he was leprous. They sent him off to Athens and he created such a fuss that they packed him off to the island. He's been there ever since. He's dangerous, Dimitris, verbally dangerous.'

'So what can we do?'

'Give him what he wants.'

Dimitris shook his head. 'We can't do that until Athens gives the go ahead. It's up to you, Nikos.'

Nikos sighed. 'I had an idea it would be.'

'Well, what did you expect? I can't leave Heraklion; besides, I'm not qualified to do the job. You'll just have to delay, take your time.'

'At the rate I'm going the job will take a number of weeks anyway, and that depends upon the weather. If we get a few storms I'll be held up for days,' grumbled Nikos. 'Now I know I'm dealing with an old friend I want to help him. All he says is true.'

YANNIS

Dimitris looked at him sharply. 'True or not, you do as I say and take plenty of time over it. Go away, Nikos. Spend the weekend with your wife and enjoy yourself, exhaust yourself, so you work more slowly next week.'

At the end of a month, when Nikos had examined no more than half of the inhabitants, Yannis's patience began to wear thin. He spoke to Nikos who explained that he was working as quickly as he could, that talking to people was as important as examining them and he assured Yannis that all the information was being sent promptly to Athens.

'It's a much bigger job than I first thought.'

'If it's such a big job why don't they send people down to help you?'

'They have to be specialists, know what they're doing. There's no one else they can spare.'

'I'm going to write to Dimitris and complain.'

'I can't stop you from writing.' The threat held no fear for Nikos.

Yannis walked back to his house. He had no intention of writing to the government. If Nikos were removed due to a complaint they could have to wait months before a replacement doctor could be found and he would no doubt want to start all over again.

Nikos sought out Dimitris. 'I've finished,' he announced.

'That's what you think. I've had a letter from Athens. There's something wrong with the blood samples. You'll have to take them all again.'

Nikos stared at him disbelieving. 'What's wrong with them?'

'I don't know. I'm not a medical man. Read for yourself.' Dimitris passed the sheets of paper across the table.

Nikos read the letter twice. Attached to it was a list of names with ticks or crosses against each one. Most of them had crosses.

'They say that all the blood samples except seventeen are negative and many of the skin samples, although having lepromatus cells, show no sign of activity. I just don't believe it.'

'Can there be a mistake at their end?'

'It's possible. It's more likely that by the time they received the samples they'd changed consistency. How were they sent?'

'By ship.'

'That could account for it; could they be flown over next time?'

'I'll arrange something.' Dimitris grinned. "It's quite a good excuse to delay matters a little longer.'

'You don't have to placate Yannis,' grumbled Nikos.

Yannis was furious when Nikos told him all the samples would have to be taken again as Athens was not satisfied with the results they were getting.

'What about the medical? Do we have to go through that again?'

'No, it's only the samples and blood tests. I'll take the samples during the week and then the blood on Friday. I can have them in Heraklion by mid-day Saturday and they're going to be flown to Athens. They should be ready for them to examine first thing on Monday morning.'

Nikos worked steadily. By the end of Thursday he had completed the skin samples and on Friday morning he was syringing blood from their arms into test tubes. Yannis stood watching him.

'I do know what I'm doing,' he assured him.

'I just want to make sure you don't drop it. I'd hate you to have to do it all over again.'

'So would I! I'm beginning to be heartily sick of this island.'

'That was how we felt at first. You get used to it after about ten years.'

'You've grown so bitter, Yannis.'

'What do you expect? All I ask for….'

Nikos held up his hand. 'I know what you're asking for,

Yannis. Please believe me when I say it is none of my doing. I did my job. It was just unfortunate that it took longer than expected to get to Athens.'

'Why they just can't give it to us I don't know.'

'I may have the answer to that. It might only have been tested on recently diagnosed cases. Long term conditions could have a bad reaction and they want to avoid that.'

'If they take much longer they'll certainly avoid it! There'll be none of us left.'

Nikos shot Yannis a quick glance. His face was disfigured with nodules; his voice was soft, yet rasping, where the disease had taken its toll of his vocal cords. Apart from that he was a picture of good health and the thorough medical Nikos had given him bore this out.

'I don't think you have any cause to worry on that score. You all seem to be in pretty good shape.'

'So did Carolas, but he died three weeks ago.'

'I'd noted that his heart wasn't strong.'

'What else have you noted about us?'

'That's confidential.'

'How can it be if it's about us? It's more important to us than any faceless bureaucratic staff in Athens.'

'Yannis, I took an oath when I became a doctor. I can't tell you about the medical conditions of any of your friends. All I can say is that on the whole, most of you seem pretty fit. You can include yourself in that, if it's any consolation.'

'I'd like to know exactly about myself.'

'When we have all the results, I shall be able to tell you.'

'And when will that be?'

'When I'm able to get on with my work,' snapped Nikos. 'I'm only carrying out my instructions, Yannis. Don't hold everything against me personally.'

Nikos resumed his duties in the hospital, going confidently to his meeting with Dimitris two weeks later. As he entered Dimitris shook his head.

'Athens is still not satisfied. The results have turned up virtually the same. They want further samples in another month.'

Nikos groaned. 'I can't go back again. I've more than enough work here. There are new patients that I need to see. They could be urgent, more urgent than those on the island.'

'You really feel that?'

'I most certainly do.'

'In that case I'll write and tell them they have to wait until you've cleared your backlog of patients or they have to send a replacement.'

Nikos nodded. 'I'd be grateful. I am needed here. Maybe I could return in six months.'

'Yannis won't be very happy,' remarked Dimitris.

'Yannis will have to put up with it. I'll write to him and say Athens are investigating the results and it will be some time before we receive them.'

'Good idea. Keep him quiet for a while at least.'

Anna was worried. Maria had suffered another stroke in her sleep. She had risen to help her mother wash and dress only to find her snoring heavily and nothing would wake her. All day Anna and Marisa took turns to sit beside her, waiting for any change in her condition, until finally her breathing quietened and became regular. They exchanged glances, neither was sure if this was a good or bad sign.

'I'll try to rouse her.'

Marisa nodded, biting her lips anxiously. 'Should I fetch uncle Yiorgo?'

Anna did not answer her niece. 'Mamma. Mamma. Open your eyes and I'll give you a little drink. Come along now. You heard what I said. Don't be difficult. Marisa and I will help you sit up.'

The eyelids flickered and dropped again. 'Mamma, please try.'

YANNIS

Maria opened her eyes and shut them again. Anna breathed a sigh of relief. 'Help me,' she said to Marisa, and between them they lifted Maria up a little higher in the bed. Anna wrapped a towel beneath her chin and held a cup of water to her lips. 'Just a few sips.'

Her eyes still closed Maria tried to drink, much of it dribbling from the corner of her mouth. 'That's fine,' Anna assured her. 'You can have some more in a while. Rest now, and I'll make some chicken broth.' Maria made no sign that she had heard her daughter. She lay immobile on the pillows, appearing to be asleep.

'Come into the kitchen with me and help me make the broth, Marisa.' Anna led the way and closed the door behind them. 'I'm sure she's had another stroke.'

'What are you going to do?'

'There's nothing I can do.'

'What about a doctor?'

'He could do nothing. Strokes are not like illnesses.'

Anna spooned a little of the chicken broth into her mother's slack mouth, hoping some would be swallowed. Marisa seemed to have lost all initiative and Anna had to direct her to do the most simple and obvious tasks, until Anna insisted they changed places and Marisa tended to her grandmother whilst she organised a meal for when the men returned from the fields. Yiorgo returned early, his face strained and worried.

'How is she?'

'There's no change. Marisa's feeding her chicken broth.'

Yiorgo nodded. 'Anything you want me to do?'

'No. I'll be ready when Yannis comes in. I think we should get a message over to the island. I'll write a letter and ask Davros to take it over tomorrow.'

Yannis read the words on the crumpled piece of paper that Flora delivered to him and hurried down to the quay. 'Davros, will you take me over?'

Davros shook his head. 'Too much of a risk; I don't want my boat impounded.'

'I'd make it worth your while.'

Again Davros shook his head. 'You'd be seen, bound to be.'

'My mother's ill. It might be my last chance to see her,' pleaded Yannis urgently

'You get over and I'll bring you back. Save you the walk to Aghios Nikolaos.'

Yannis turned away dejected. It would have been so easy for Davros to take him over. Now he would have to ask Manolis if he would take the risk and if he agreed it meant waiting until early evening. By then it could be too late.

Yannis waded the last few yards to the shore, hoping no one had seen him slip over the side from Manolis's boat in the darkness. He walked up the rutted path until he reached the farmhouse and opened the kitchen door. Anna flung her arms round her brother.

'I'm so glad to see you.'

'What's the news of Mamma?'

'She had another stroke, in her sleep, two days ago. She failing fast, Yannis.' Anna looked at her brother with distressed eyes.

'What can I do?'

'There's nothing anyone can do. I just thought you'd want to see her.' Tears welled up in Anna's eyes and Yannis held her in his arms.

'Of course, Anna. You did right.'

Yiorgo looked at his older brother. 'You ought to get those wet clothes off, and have something warm to eat. You don't want to catch a chill.'

Thankfully Yannis stripped off his trousers and socks, giving them to Anna to place before the fire whilst he donned those provided by Yiorgo. He walked quietly over to his mother and looked down at her. She appeared old and worn out. He took her hand in his and sat beside her bed in silence. Anna brought him a bowl of soup and some bread.

'Come and eat,' she urged him. 'You can do no good by just sitting and looking.'

Yannis obeyed his sister, watching as she raised her mother a little on the pillows and tried to spoon some soup into her mother's mouth. He pushed back his chair and returned to her bedside. 'Mamma, can you hear me?' He imagined that her eyelids flickered just a little. 'Mamma, it's Yannis. I've come to see you.'

He tried again and again to rouse her from her stupor, until her eyes finally opened. Full recognition shone in them, along with pleasure before they closed again and Yannis bent and kissed her cheek.

Anna's eyes filled with tears. 'You've done her good, Yannis. That's more response than I've had.'

'I think she knew me.' The lump in Yannis's throat made it difficult for him to speak.

Yannis returned to the table, not noticing that his soup had grown cold. He ate automatically, his eyes fixed on the motionless figure in the bed, no longer seeing his mother, but remembering Phaedra. The pain of the memory was not as acute as it had been, more a gentle ache. He felt very much that he had lived through this before.

'You must go to bed, Yannis. You're exhausted.'

With an effort he withdrew himself from his reverie. 'I'm fine.'

'You're not. You're almost asleep sitting there. Go and lay down on my mattress. I can easily wake you if there's any change.'

'What about you?'

'I'll be staying down here with Mamma. You don't need to worry about me.'

'Are you sure?' Bed had suddenly become a very attractive idea.

Anna nodded. 'You'll feel much better when you've rested.'

1946-1957

Without any more argument Yannis climbed the stairs as he had so many times in his childhood and laid himself down fully clothed on Anna's mattress. Within a matter of minutes he was asleep.

Dawn was just breaking as Yannis felt his arm being shaken. He sat up, uncertain where he was before he woke completely. 'What is it?'

'Mamma.'

Without further ado Yannis followed Yiorgo from the room. Anna was bending over her mother's bed, Marisa and Yannis standing together by the fireplace.

Silently the three stood and looked down upon their mother. Her face, distorted by the recent stroke, seemed more peaceful than earlier, although her breathing was shallow and strained. How long he stood there looking down, remembering his mother as she had been when he was a boy, Yannis did not know. He was startled by Anna giving a choking sob and turning away. Yiorgo pulled the sheet over his mother's face and turned to comfort his sister. Yannis continued to stare at the sheet. He had seen death so many times, yet the final moment always took him by surprise. It seemed incredible that one moment you could be breathing and alive and the next you had stopped and were declared dead. In a way he could not explain he felt there should be a short while in between to prepare the witnesses for the event. He sucked in his breath.

'Is the brandy where Pappa used to keep it?' Yiorgo nodded. 'Then I think we should all have a little, then Anna and the children must go back to bed for a short while and rest.' He poured a measure of brandy for each of them and watched whilst they drank.

'To bed,' ordered Yannis.

Anna shook her head. 'I must see to Mamma first.'

Yannis poured himself another brandy that he drank quickly. 'Would you like me to help? I've helped before.'

'No, I'd rather do it alone.' She waited patiently whilst the children slipped back upstairs obediently and Yiorgo picked up the brandy bottle and followed Yannis into the kitchen.

'Anna can cope.'

'I know that. It just seems rather unfair that she should always be the one to do so.'

The brothers sat, an uneasy silence between them, as they sipped at their drinks. Yiorgo rolled a cigarette and offered it to Yannis who shook his head. 'I don't any more.'

Yiorgo drew on the thin cigarette, breathing in the acrid smoke.

'How's the farm doing?'

Yiorgo shrugged. 'It keeps us going. It's easier now I'm running so many more sheep and goats. I've taken on a couple of youngsters from the village to help me pull down Babbis's farmhouse.'

Yannis looked surprised. 'You can afford to employ?'

'We're not short of money. Pappa left us plenty. I've your share in the cupboard when you want it.'

Yannis smiled at him. 'What do I need money for? Besides, Pappa gave me more than my fair share when I went to Heraklion.'

'It will be there if you need it.'

'How much?'

About fifteen hundred drachmas.'

'What! Where did Pappa get so much money? Did he win on the lottery?'

Yiorgo grinned. 'He was a 'middle man' up until the war.'

'What might that be?'

'He stored whatever was delivered until a boat arrived. Don't you remember the heavy packing cases we had to shift when Pappa broke his leg?'

Yannis did remember. 'You mean Pappa handled smuggled goods?'

'Of course; he and uncle Yiorgo worked together.'

Yannis whistled through his teeth. 'What a simpleton I was!'

'When I returned I went through all his papers. He kept a little book. It took me a while to realise what it meant. There was always a date and a record of the amount paid to him. He kept it in a box in the cupboard. I shared it out. A portion for each of us.'

'Wasn't it really Mamma's?'

'In law I expect it was, but I told her what I'd done and she approved. I'll share hers out again amongst us.'

Yannis thought quickly. 'Whilst you're sharing hers, share mine also. I don't need it.'

'You may do one day. I sent a share to Stelios, and I'm holding Maria's to go to her children.'

Yannis looked at his brother in admiration. 'There's more to you than I'd realised. A good many brothers would have taken the lot and considered it their due.'

'That would have been dishonest and unfair.'

'We would never have known. I'm glad you've told me. I was going to ask how you were placed financially and offer you help if you needed it. I've got five years pension saved up and nothing to spend it on.'

'I'll let you know if it ever comes to that. I appreciate the offer.' He poured another glass of brandy for each of them.

Yannis looked at the glass speculatively. 'This must be the last. I ought to see if Davros is down at the quay. He refused to bring me over, but he offered me a ride back.'

Yiorgo raised his glass. 'I'll see if Anna's finished.'

He pushed open the door of the living room. Anna was kneeling beside her mother's bed, saying a last prayer for her. Yiorgo waited until she stirred, then walked across.

'She looks beautiful, Anna.'

Yannis followed and looked down at the inert form. 'Thank you, Anna, for all your care. It can't have been easy for you all these years.'

Anna gave a tight-lipped smile. 'She was my Mamma. It was her due.'

Yannis took her hand. 'I'm going now. I'll ask Father Minos to say prayers for her. Come and see me when you can.'

He kissed her forehead and shook hands with Yiorgo, before bending over his mother and kissing her goodbye for the last time. 'Thank you for sending for me.'

He unlatched the door and limped and shuffled as fast as he was able to the shore, relieved to see Davros sitting in the stern of his boat. As soon as he had boarded Davros cast off. The sad, closed look on Yannis's face told him the news. 'Were you in time?'

Yannis nodded and they spoke no more until the tiny boat docked at the quay on Spinalonga. 'Thank you, Davros.'

'I'll bring you back any time you like,' his teeth flashed in a grin.

Yannis shook his head. 'I doubt I'll make the trip again.'

Yannis took the letter from Nikos to Father Minos and showed it to him in disgust. 'He says he'll be back over here in a couple of months or so. He has to clear his backlog of patients at the hospital, and then he'll come and take further tests as required by Athens. What do they think we are? Surely they must know from the tests they already have whether the drugs will help us?'

Father Minos frowned. 'Do you trust Nikos?'

Yannis considered. 'Yes,' he said finally. 'I do.'

'Then when he comes ask him for the truth. Did they lose the tests in transit, have you all suffered too long for the drugs to have any beneficial effect, is the delay political? You have a right to know, you all have that right.'

'Has Doctor Stavros spoken to you?' Yannis asked the question sharply.

'Not about the tests. Why?'

'There's something going on that I don't understand. I asked the doctor why there was so much delay and he said it was nothing to do with him and I'd have to ask Athens. I asked if he'd received the results through and he said that anything sent to him regarding our medical condition was confidential. I'm sure he knows something and won't tell us.'

'What he said is true, Yannis. He took an oath not to disclose medical confidentialities to anyone the same as I'm under oath not to reveal anything that's said to me in the confessional. I suggest you tackle Nikos.'

It was more than three months before Nikos arrived and was met with a cool reception. Puzzled by the hostility he sensed around him he sought out the priest.

'What have I done? I couldn't help being held up on the mainland. I had to treat my patients there.'

Father Minos looked at the doctor. 'You're losing the trust and respect of the people over here. Ever since Yannis first wrote there's been nothing but delay and excuses. These people want the truth, and then they want the drugs to which they're entitled.'

Nikos spread his hands in despair. 'I'm not sure if I know the truth. If I do repeat what has been told me from Athens I could cause more trouble.'

'Would it help if you came to confession? Whatever you said would be treated in confidence by me and maybe I could advise you on your course of action.'

Cautiously Nikos agreed. He felt very vulnerable on this island, despite his friendship with Yannis, and had no wish to antagonise the occupants. He followed Father Minos into the church and knelt beside the altar whilst Father Minos blessed him.

'I don't know where to start, Father. I don't understand what's happening.'

'Tell me as best you can.'

'It's not my doing, Father. I have to follow instructions.' Nikos moistened his lips. 'I've been careful and conscientious with the tests. The first ones they said were too long in transit and did not give true results. The second tests were sent by air. There was no delay and still Athens was not satisfied.'

'Do you know why? Are they too sick to benefit from the new treatment?'

'No.' The answer was a whisper.

'Are they too old? Is that the problem?'

'Then tell me, is it money? I'm sure there's money in a fund held by Father Andreas that could be used on their behalf.'

'No.'

Father Minos waited patiently. He could think of no other reason that could cause a problem.

'Athens says that most of them no longer have active leprosy cells.'

'What?'

Nikos turned anguished eyes to the priest.

'Explain to me. I don't know enough about medical matters to understand what you're saying.'

'The first tests that I sent to Athens showed no active leprosy in most of the people over here. Athens thought it was due to the delay in receiving the samples. The second tests showed the same result. That's why they've asked for more. If these tests show the same result there's no reason why anyone should stay on this island. They're burnt-out, no longer infectious. They don't even need treatment.'

Father Minos swallowed hard. 'So what will happen to them if these tests give the same results as previously?'

'I don't know.'

The priest laid his hands on the doctor's shoulders. 'The situation is not of your making. No blame can be attached to you.' His head was spinning and he could not think. 'I need to pray. Maybe a solution to the problem will be given to me.'

'Yes, Father.' Nikos rose, he felt relieved now he had shared his burden.

It was more than an hour before Father Minos left the church and went in search of the doctor. At first he had knelt at the altar and waited, hoping he would receive divine guidance, but none came. He turned the problem over and over in his mind, until he finally thought of a possible compromise. Nikos scanned the priest's face eagerly, but could read nothing. Father Minos sat beside him.

'I think it would be as well if you told part of the truth. They know Athens wasn't happy with the first results and now they want to confirm the second ones. You have to persuade them that it's for their own good and no fault of yours.'

'Suppose they ask what the results were?'

'They're hardly likely to. They all assume they're still contagious. Do you have individual results with you.'

'No, there was no need to bring them.'

'Then you can tell them honestly that you don't have them.' Father Minos smiled at the worried man. 'I'll ring the bell to announce a meeting. Compose yourself and speak convincingly. They have a great respect for you as a doctor.'

Nikos could not agree with the priest's opinion, but he saw no other way to carry out his instructions. Reluctantly he rose to his feet and brushed the dust from his suit. His mouth felt dry. 'Could you speak for me?' he asked.

'No. You're the doctor. I'll support you, but I'll not speak on your behalf.'

Gradually the people emerged from their houses, leaving their morning duties and gathering before the church. At a signal from the priest Nikos held up his hand.

'My friends,' he began, hearing his voice squeak with nervousness. 'I am pleased to be able to visit you yet again, but I wish it could have been under other circumstances. I have consulted with Father Minos and he and I feel you have a right to know why there have been the delays from Athens.'

An angry murmur ran through all of them.

'The first tests I took were sent to Athens by sea. There were the inevitable delays and the doctors were not happy with the samples. They were unable to find cultures of leprosy cells amongst most of them, and decided they were too old. I had to take new tests from all of you and this time they were flown to the city. I thought that would be the end of the matter, but then I was told Athens required a second set of samples to prove the results of the previous tests.'

'Don't they know what they're doing over there?'

'They want to be quite certain.'

'So when are we getting our treatment?'

An expectant silence settled on the gathering as they waited for Nikos's answer.

'I can't tell you that, but I'm sure it won't be very long now.'

'You ought to know. You're a doctor.'

Nikos looked pleadingly at Father Minos who held up his hand. 'The doctor has told you the truth. He cannot make promises on behalf of Athens. You have to be patient.'

'We've been patient long enough.'

'I agree with you. I know very little about medicine or drugs, but I do know that no doctor or hospital likes to make a mistake. That's why you have to bear with them a little longer, so they can study the results and decide on the best course of treatment for you all.'

'By the time they decide we'll all be dead.'

'How long is it going to take this time?'

'Just a few days.'

'So the first samples are going to be old when they reach Athens.'

'They've arranged to have them despatched directly from Aghios Nikolaos to Athens each day as soon as I return. They'll be completely fresh when they receive them,' Nikos tried to reassure them.

'How do we know that?'

'Trust the doctor,' interposed Father Minos. 'I will guarantee his integrity.'

'It doesn't matter to you.'

Yannis, annoyed and displeased with the news as he was, would not let the slight to the priest go by. 'If Father Minos says we can trust Nikos then I believe him. To prove that I have faith in him I'll give him my samples first.'

They grumbled, but if Yannis and Father Minos said they could trust the doctor half of them said it must be true, the others were undecided and rebellious.

'I'll be second,' shouted Spiro.

Yannis smiled gratefully at him for his support. 'Would it speed things up if we came up to the hospital?' he suggested.

Nikos nodded. His confidence was returning now and he felt annoyed that so much of the morning had been spent in gaining their co-operation and good will. Slowly the islanders made their way up to the hospital and stood waiting to be called. They were either sulky or garrulous and Nikos brought all his professional etiquette and natural charm into play whilst he explained again and again why Athens was asking for more tests.

Whilst with Doctor Stavros he once again read the notes the doctor had made on all the patients on the island, noting when the doctor considered that all outward signs of the disease had halted. He compared them with the list he had from Athens of those whose tests had returned a negative result and in all but two cases they agreed with Doctor Stavros's observations.

Yannis waited, growing more and more impatient as there was no word sent to him from either Nikos or Athens. He wrote again and again asking for the results of the tests, but received no reply. He wrote to Andreas, pleading with him to visit the government and investigate the delay, but Andreas was as evasive as Father Minos and Doctor Stavros had been of late. He began to brood on the problem, growing morose and sullen, until he formulated a plan.

He chose his time carefully. A stiff breeze rose during the afternoon, blowing towards the mainland, and when most of the islanders were busy with preparations for their evening meal he hauled a bathtub down to the quay and pushed himself off.

The journey was more dangerous than he had anticipated. The breeze had the effect of tipping him forwards in the unstable tub and although he travelled faster over the stretch of water than he had done previously he was exhausted by the time he reached the safety of the shore. He made no attempt to salvage the bathtub, but plodded slowly and cautiously up to the farmhouse.

No light showed from the windows and Yannis bit his lips. It was not yet fully dark so it was unlikely they would have retired for the night. He tried the door, which did not yield under his hand, then threw a stone up at Anna's bedroom window. The stone bounced back and Yannis threw it again without receiving any response. Hungry, tired and wet he made his way disconsolately over to the stable. He would at least get warm there, huddled up with the donkey. She objected to the intruder, grudgingly moving over a little on her straw to allow him room enough to lie beside her.

He dozed fitfully, the donkey disturbing him as she moved her position and it was only by a sixth sense that he rolled away from her hooves as she lumbered awkwardly to her feet. The stable door opened and a shaft of light dazzled him. Instinctively he held up his arm to shield his eyes and heard a quick intake of breath.

'Yannis! What the devil are you doing here?'

Yannis struggled to his feet. 'Yiorgo?'

Yiorgo lowered the lamp. 'Come inside.'

He followed his brother across the yard and into the kitchen. Anna looked up in surprise. 'Yannis! How lovely to see you. Why didn't you let us know you were coming?'

He sank into a chair and removed his shoes and socks, towelling his feet dry. 'I don't want anyone to know I'm here. I'm not staying. I'm going to Heraklion.'

'You're staying here tonight at least. You couldn't get anywhere at the moment. You look exhausted.'

Yannis smiled wanly. His determination for the journey was lessening as weariness crept over him.

'Warm milk,' announced Anna, 'then to bed. We can talk in the morning.'

Yiorgo opened his mouth, but Anna frowned at him. 'Anna's right,' he conceded. 'You can tell us what you're up to in the morning.'

Yannis slept late. When he awoke the sun was high in the sky and Yiorgo had long since departed for the fields. He dressed and crept timorously down the stairs. His sister emerged from the kitchen.

'Sit down and I'll get you some food and coffee.'

Yannis ate ravenously. 'Where were you when I arrived last night?' he asked. 'The place was deserted.'

'We'd gone to the taverna. It was Marisa's birthday.'

Yannis nodded. 'How old is she now?'

'Twenty one.'

'Twenty one,' mused Yannis. A cloud came across his face. 'I was that age when I went to Spinalonga.'

Anna laid a hand on his shoulder. 'She's turned into quite a beauty. What did you mean last night, Yannis, when you said you were going to Heraklion?'

'I need to see the government.'

Anna's eyes opened wide. 'The government? Whatever for?'

'To force them into telling me the results from Athens. We're still not getting any treatment. I keep writing to them. I either get no reply or they say they are waiting for Athens to send them the results. Well, I've waited long enough.'

'How are you going to get there? You can't walk. It's too far.'

'I need to talk to Yiorgo.'

'He's in the far field. Come into the kitchen and talk to me. I've plenty to do and there's no one around.'

Yannis shook his head. 'I'll go up to speak to him. I've wasted too much time already.'

Anna opened her mouth to reply, but Yannis was out of the back door and crossing the yard as fast as his misshapen feet would allow him. He reached Yiorgo and without pausing to greet him asked a question.

'Do you drive? A car, motorbike, a van; anything at all.'

Yiorgo shook his head. 'I've never even thought about it.'

'Then now is the time. You told me you were keeping some money for me. Do you still have it?'

'Of course.'

'Would there be enough for me to buy a small motorbike?' asked Yannis eagerly.

'You'd have to go to Aghios Nikolaos for that. There's nothing round here.'

'Then will you go, please, Yiorgo? Buy one and bring it back here.'

Yiorgo scratched his head. 'I doubt I'd get there before evening. Better to wait until tomorrow.'

Nothing Yannis could say would make his brother alter his plans and finally he had to admit that it would not be wise for him to try to ride to Heraklion in darkness.

Yannis was up before the sun rose, shaking Yiorgo into wakefulness.

'I'm coming with you and I can't walk as fast as you.'

Yiorgo looked at his brother doubtfully. 'Is that wise?'

'Of course, provided we leave early. It will save you having to come back here for me. I'll be able to go straight from Aghios Nikolaos.'

Yiorgo shrugged. He thought his brother's trip to Heraklion a crazy idea, but he had agreed to help and there was no turning back now. Unresisting he dressed whilst Yannis brewed coffee for them both.

'What about Anna? She'll wonder what's happened to us.'

'I'll tell her.' Yannis was almost at the top of the stairs as Anna came from her room. She took in the scene at a glance.

'You're going with Yiorgo?'

Yannis nodded. 'It will be quicker for me.'

Anna watched as Yannis stuffed packages of bread and cheese into his pockets. Her heart pounded as she kissed him goodbye and wished him luck. She watched, almost envious, as the brothers walked across the yard to make a slight detour over the hills before rejoining the road on the outskirts of the village. At first Yannis was able to keep pace with Yiorgo, but by the time they had climbed the low hills around Elounda he was limping badly.

'How about a rest?'

Yannis shook his head. 'I can manage.'

'If we went up a bit higher you could rest a short distance from the main road and I could go down to Aghios Nikolaos.'

Yannis thought about the proposal. 'It would be further for you to walk.'

'I might be able to pick up a lift, besides, you're tired. Even if I walk all the way I'll be faster without you.'

'How far is it to the main road from here?'

'A couple of kilometres.'

'And Aghios Nikolaos?'

'About ten.'

Yannis sighed. Yiorgo was making sense. 'Let's go up towards the road. I'll find somewhere to rest whilst you go down and buy a bike.'

Yiorgo smiled with relief. He would be able to make far better time without his brother. He left Yannis lying in a clump of gorse bushes a hundred yards from the road and began to hurry on alone. For half an hour he walked along the deserted road, until, with dust flying from its wheels, the bus from Heraklion nearly ran him down. He jumped onto the bank and waved vigorously as it passed by him. It slowed and he ran to board it gratefully.

YANNIS

He completed his journey and made his way to a taverna a short distance from the bus terminal. He felt in need of refreshment and also needed to ask where he could purchase a motorbike. The taverna owner advised Yiorgo to visit his brother-in-law; his son would show him the way when he had finished his meal.

The oily fingered mechanic looked up from the engine he was working on. He began to ask questions. What did Yiorgo want the bike for? Was it for work, over rough country, or just for pleasure, travelling on the roads? How big did he want the engine to be? Did he plan to use it every day or just occasionally? Would he use it for long or short journeys? How much did he want to spend?

Yiorgo was completely at a loss. 'I just want a bike that will be reliable for me to make the journey to Heraklion.' The man eyed his customer suspiciously, and Yiorgo decided it would be wise for him to enlarge a little. 'I've had a message from Father Andreas. You may remember him. He lived here, son of Yiorgo the fisherman. He needs me in Heraklion as soon as possible – an urgent family matter.'

'What's wrong with taking the bus?'

Yiorgo sighed in exasperation. 'All I want to do is buy a motorbike from you. Do you always question why people want them?'

'People aren't usually in such a rush. They like to look around, try one or two before they decide.'

'All I want is a reliable machine.'

The mechanic shrugged. 'Try that one.' The bike was cumbersome and heavy.

'How much?'

A crafty look came over the garage owner's face. He quoted an inflated price and Yiorgo peeled off the notes without demur. 'I want it filled with petrol.'

The owner cocked his head towards the boy who dutifully ran to get a can whilst Yiorgo began to look at the bike. 'How do I start it?'

'Haven't you ridden before?'

'Never.'

He pursed his lips. This man was mad. Never ridden before and planning to make a journey to Heraklion in a hurry. 'You'd be better by bus.'

Yiorgo's lips set in a firm line. 'Just show me what to do.'

He spent half an hour, listening intently and questioning the use of gears, finally nodding that he understood the principles. 'Have I enough petrol to get all the way?'

'Probably.'

'Then I'll take a spare can.' He handed over another note and waited for the change, which was not forthcoming. Gingerly he mounted the machine, kicking it to a start and nearly falling off as the engine roared into life.

'Take it slowly,' called the garage owner over the noise, doubting that his advice would be heeded, and he watched as Yiorgo departed in a wobbly line down the road.

It was not as difficult as Yiorgo had imagined. He crunched the gears as he changed them, skidded dangerously around the corners, but did not fall off as he had envisaged. He met few other vehicles on the road and as they approached him he used his horn vigorously, hoping they would give him a wide berth. By the time he reached the spot where he had left his brother he was beginning to gain in confidence and enjoy himself. He pulled the bike off the road onto the rough ground and called. Yannis emerged from the gorse clump and Yiorgo scanned him anxiously.

'It's very heavy, but not difficult to drive. The garage owner was a rogue. He took nearly five hundred drachmas off me, but I've got a spare can of petrol on the back.'

Yannis nodded. He was not interested in the cost. 'Show me what I have to do.'

Yiorgo ran through the intricacies of the gears, showed him the various gauges and their meaning, how to brake without shooting over the handlebars, and finally the kick-start.

'Thank you, Yiorgo. I couldn't have managed without you. I'll try to let you know what happens.'

'Where are you going in Heraklion?'

'To Andreas.' Yannis smiled with quiet confidence. 'He'll give me shelter.'

Yiorgo thrust the remainder of the notes into Yannis's hand. 'You may need this.'

Yannis placed the notes in his pocket and himself carefully astride the machine. He kicked the starter until the bike sprang into life and Yiorgo watched as he wobbled down the road to become a speck in the distance. The speed with which he was travelling meant nothing to Yannis, but he was surprised to come upon Neapolis so quickly and half an hour saw him in Malia. He was hungry and thirty, but he dared not stop, partly through fear of being accosted and partly because he was not sure if he would be able to start the bike again.

The outskirts of Heraklion were unfamiliar to him and he dared not try to take a short cut. He followed the main road until he reached Eleftherias Square and he knew exactly where he was. He swung inwards to the centre of the town, nearly losing control as he did so, and earning the wrath of a baker who had spilled his rolls as he moved rapidly from Yannis's path. Throwing all caution to the winds he continued on through the mean back streets until he reached the tiny church and adjoining house that Father Minos had occupied when he had lived in Heraklion. Slowing the bike to a halt and switching off the noisy engine he propped it against the wall and hammered on the door. A young girl answered his urgent banging and he pushed his way roughly past her before asking for Andreas.

'He's out.'

'I'll wait for him.'

'He could be gone a long while. You'd be best to come back tomorrow.'

'I'll wait. I know he'll see me.' Yannis made to go through to the living room.

'You can't go in there. It's private.'

Yannis dropped his head. 'Show me where you'd like me to wait,' he spoke wearily. 'And I'd be grateful for a glass of water.'

'You can sit there.' She pointed to an upright chair in the passage.

'A drink,' he reminded her as she disappeared towards the kitchen.

By the time Andreas returned home it was dark. On entering he spotted the figure slumped on the floor, his head resting on the hard chair and sighed. He was tired. It had been a long day. He walked over to the motionless figure.

'Can I help you, my son?'

Yannis raised bloodshot eyes to his cousin's face. 'Thank God you've come.'

'Yannis!' Andreas spoke incredulously. He took in the weariness of the slack body, the dirty and begrimed face. 'What's happened?'

'Nothing. That's why I've come.'

Uncomprehending Andreas helped him to rise. 'Come with me and make yourself respectable.'

He pushed his cousin through the door into the little sanctuary he had been forbidden to enter earlier and called to the girl. She arrived, excuses on her lips for having let the stranger stay until the priest returned, but Andreas waved them aside.

'You did right to let him stay. Bring a bowl of hot water and a towel. Get some soup heated, later we will want a proper meal. How long has he been waiting?'

'Some hours. I gave him some water when he arrived.'

Andreas nodded. He would have to talk to her about the reception of visitors whilst he was out. He turned his attention to Yannis, who was standing in the centre of the room, swaying slightly on his feet.

Aliki returned with a bowl of water and a rough towel, which she placed, on the table. 'I'll be back with the soup.'

'Have a wash, Yannis. You're covered in dust. When you've had some soup we'll talk and you can tell me what's brought you up here.'

Yannis dipped his hands into the warm water and rubbed them over his face. He looked in surprise at the dirt that ran off them. 'I hope I didn't frighten her. I must look terrible. Where's the old lady?'

'Pensioned off. It became too much for her. Aliki was orphaned in the war and I took her in hoping she'd be able to take old Marina's place, but she has a lot to learn.'

The soup arrived and Aliki hovered, hoping to find out the reason for the strange man's visit and the hospitality of the priest.

'You can take the bowl, Aliki. I'll let you know when we want to eat.'

As she lifted the bowl she looked at their visitor. What an ugly little man he was. He had a shock of hair, but no eyebrows, one side of his face was covered in lumps, and he had a tiny nose that seemed to have sunk into his face. She looked at his hand as he raised the mug to his mouth and almost shrieked as she saw the clawed fingers. Andreas saw her reaction and looked at her sternly.

'Yes, child, he's a leper. He'll do you no harm and he's in sanctuary here.'

Aliki's lips trembled and she crossed herself. She would remember which mug she had given him and never drink from it again herself. 'Yes, Father,' she answered hoarsely.

'And you don't tell people he's here. Sanctuary is confidential, remember.'

'Yes, Father,' she whispered again, longing to leave the room and dispose of the contaminated towel and bowl. Andreas shut the door and turned back to Yannis.

'I'm sorry about that. I doubt she's ever seen a sufferer before.'

Yannis shrugged. 'I've had enough people turn away from me. One more makes little difference.'

'You're very bitter.'

'Of course I'm bitter! You'd be bitter if your life had been ruined as mine has.'

'I will pray that the bitterness will leave you and you'll find peace and contentment with your lot.' Father Andreas crossed himself humbly.

'Pray! Pray! That's all you people ever do! It's action we need. Action and medicines. That's why I've come.'

Andreas looked at Yannis with troubled eyes. He had never heard him be derisive of the church or religion before and it came as a shock to him that his cousin's faith could be shaken. 'Tell me,' he said quietly. 'If I'm able to help I'll do so.'

'Do you know why Athens is delaying sending us our medicines?' asked Yannis directly.

'I'm not a doctor.' Andreas was evasive.

'Then who would know?'

'Nikos, if anyone.'

'Where can I find him?'

'I don't know where he lives. I see him occasionally at the hospital.'

Yannis switched his line of questioning. 'When does the government meet next?'

'Wednesday.'

'May I stay here until then?'

'I cannot refuse you sanctuary, but I'd like to know exactly why you've come here.'

Yannis's eyes gleamed. 'I intend to confront the government and ask why Athens hasn't sent the results of our tests or the medicines. I've written to them on numerous occasions and not had a satisfactory reply. I've written to you and you've been evasive, so I've come to ask you and them for the reason. I'll not be fobbed off with excuses. I want the truth.'

Andreas crossed himself fervently. He should have foreseen this long ago. 'Wouldn't it be better if you ate and rested thoroughly and I'll see what I can do about contacting Nikos through the hospital?'

Yannis rubbed his hand over his now throbbing head. 'Andreas, answer me, honestly, yes or no, do you know why there is this delay?'

Andreas stood dumbly. Had he the right to tell his cousin? The information had been given to him confidentially, but not under the sanctity of the confessional. What would Yannis's reaction be if he did tell him? He could be so impetuous.

'Yes or no, Andreas?'

'Yes.' Almost unbidden the answer came.

'Then don't you think I have a right to know, my own results at least?'

'I'm not competent. I haven't the medical knowledge.'

'I just want to know. I'm not asking for details.'

Andreas looked at Yannis with troubled eyes. 'Your results are negative.'

'Negative?' Yannis's voice had dropped to a hoarse whisper. 'Negative?'

Andreas nodded. He poured a glass of wine and handed it to Yannis, watching as he sipped slowly. The colour that had drained from his face gradually returned. He shook his head.

'I can't believe it. There must be some mistake.'

'That's what Athens thought also.'

'Am I the only one?'

Andreas shook his head. 'Nearly all of you.'

Yannis looked disbelieving. 'It can't be.'

Andreas leaned forward and clasped one of Yannis's trembling hands. 'I don't pretend to understand. All I know is that the first tests showed most of you to be negative. Athens thought the cells had died during transit and asked for more. They arrived at the laboratory more quickly, but still no cells showed up. They decided to wait awhile and then take more tests, getting them over even more quickly, and they still had the same results.'

'What about the medicine, the new drug?'

'If the results are true you don't need it.'

'But suppose the results are wrong, we're just wasting time.'

'Why should they be wrong, Yannis?'

'Because we're lepers.'

'Yannis, I told you, I don't pretend to understand the medical facts, but they've referred to you as "burnt-out". In other words the leprosy has run its course. You won't get any worse.'

Yannis sat back in his chair. He finished the last of his wine. 'I need to think about this.' He closed his eyes and Andreas thought he had fallen asleep. Suddenly Yannis sat bolt upright. 'What's going to happen to us?'

Andreas spread his hands. 'That's the problem Athens is up against. You have to understand, Yannis, they're frightened. If they declare that none of you are infectious and a danger to the populace they've no reason for keeping you on the island, but where will you go?'

'Go? I don't want to go anywhere.'

Andreas looked at his cousin. 'You don't seem to understand. They could probably close the island to you. Why should they keep you there and provide for you if there's nothing wrong with you?'

'They couldn't just abandon us.'

'Why not? You've said yourself that you've been an embarrassment and a nuisance to the government for years. They could say that as you're no longer sick, you're no longer their concern.'

Yannis moistened his lips. 'I don't believe it.'

'I'm not saying they will. I'm just mentioning it as a possibility. Put yourself in the position of the Athenian doctors and government. What are they to do? Continue to say you're diseased and send you medicines that could do you more harm than good?

Tell you that you may go and turn you off the island to return to the mainland and those families who would accept you back? Isn't it better to just leave things as they are?'

'The island is our home. They couldn't just turn us off.'

'They could. The island doesn't belong to any of you. It belongs to the government.'

Yannis looked at his cousin in horror. 'It would be inhuman.'

'They were inhuman when they sent you there, why should they be any different now?'

'What can I do?'

'You can't do anything.' Andreas frowned. He had expected Yannis to storm and rage indignantly.

'I must get back and tell them. We have to decide what to do.' Yannis rose from his seat, only to be pushed firmly back by Andreas.

'I thought you'd come up here to confront the government?'

'I'll do that later. First I must take the news back to Spinalonga.'

'You can't do that. Think what would happen if you told them. Some of them would rush off to try to find their families and would be arrested or stoned. You have to wait until the government in Athens has made its decision.'

'They have a right to know,' answered Yannis stubbornly.

'Of course they do, but in the right way at the right time. You mustn't encourage them to do anything foolish.'

Yannis challenged Andreas with his eyes. 'So what are you proposing to do?'

'Me? I can do nothing. It's a government decision.'

'As a man of the church you could influence them. Come with me to the next meeting, Andreas. If they know I have your support they'll listen.'

'I doubt it, but we have a couple of days to work something out. I'll have to ask you not to set foot outside whilst you're here. I can't give you protection against a mob.'

Yannis bowed his head. 'I'm grateful to you, Andreas.'

The two men walked down the road, Yannis keeping his head bent to hide his disfigured face. He slipped into a seat at the back of the council chamber, hoping Nikos would not notice him. The council members ignored him, along with a few other men who were sitting in the chairs at the end of the long room, waiting to present petitions or request a favour. At first he tried to follow their discussion, then gave up. They shouted across each other and at each other, with Dimitris continually calling for order and threatening to move on to the next item. An hour later there was a sudden silence, then hands were raised and Dimitris declared the motion carried. Yannis still had no idea what the motion had been.

The scene was repeated three more times before Yannis saw Andreas stand.

'I would like to ask a question.'

Heads swivelled and curious eyes stared at him. Nikos said something in an undertone to Dimitris and both men looked down at their papers.

'State your name and address.'

'I am Father Andreas, priest residing in Heraklion, with responsibility for Aghios Manathaeus.'

There was an uneasy silence. 'What is your question?'

'I would like to know what decision Athens has come to regarding the inhabitants of Spinalonga.'

'What is your concern in this matter?

'I am representing a man who has come to me for succour, protection and salvation. The way to salvation, gentlemen, is truth. I ask again, what decision has Athens come to regarding the inhabitants of Spinalonga?'

There was a sharp intake of breath, an uncomfortable shuffling, throat clearing and looking at watches. Andreas stood patiently and waited.

Eventually Dimitris cleared his throat. 'Do you mean by that statement that you are harbouring a diagnosed leper?'

'No. I am harbouring an ex-leper.'

'There is no such thing as an ex-leper. Leprosy is not a disease that can be cured.'

'I have with me a man who has spent the last twenty one years as an outcast on an island, designated as a leper colony. He was a leper, but the results of his tests show he no longer has active leprosy cells in his body. Therefore I call him an ex-leper.' Andreas spoke as he did from the pulpit, his voice resonant and clear.

Dimitris bent towards Nikos, who was playing nervously with a pencil and spoke quietly. Nikos shot Andreas a glance, shuffled his papers and rose to his feet. His voice was hardly audible across the chamber.

'Various tests have been carried out. They've been checked and double-checked. Athens still does not think the findings conclusive. They would not like to comment at present and raise the hopes of these unfortunate people.'

Before Andreas could say any more Yannis jumped to his feet. 'So what is Athens prepared to do about us? Forget us? If they leave us long enough we'll die of old age. We are human beings who deserve to live, to experience all that life has to offer us. We've had our share of sickness and suffering. If we're no longer contagious we deserve to have our freedom.'

Members of the council had shrunk back instinctively as Yannis moved forwards whilst he was speaking, until he stood directly in front of Dimitris. 'I beg you, Dimitris and Nikos,' he continued, 'For the sake of our friendship whilst we were students together, help us. Help us to become human beings again. Give us back our self-respect, our dignity, our lives.'

Nikos cleared his throat. 'Yannis, it's not our decision.'

'Then you must pressurize Athens. Insist that they either give us a clean bill of health or good reasons for staying as outcasts for ever more.'

'You have to be patient.'

'I've been patient long enough. We've all been patient long enough.' Yannis's gaze swept over the council members. He moved towards a young man at the end of the table who was taking notes of the proceedings. 'Would you like to join me on the island? Suppose I touch you, breath on you? If I'm still contagious you should be with us very soon. Are you frightened? You don't appear to fear me. Is that because you know I'm free of the disease?'

The clerk did not answer and Yannis swung towards the next man, extending his hand. 'How about you? Shall I shake your hand? Do you think I'm unclean?'

Nikos rose from his seat. 'Enough, Yannis. We are none of us frightened of you. We'll provide you with an escort back to the island and then I promise you we'll try and get a decision from Athens. You have to trust us.'

'Trust you? How can we trust you when for years you've denied us the medicines we've needed?'

'There were reasons. We could not defy Athens.'

Yannis thrust his face towards Nikos. 'You may not be able to defy them, but I can. If you send me back to the island I'll leave as soon as I can and make my way to Athens to petition the government there.'

Dimitris rose and faced Yannis across the table. 'Maybe it would be as well if we placed you in custody until we can arrange for you to be sent back.'

'No!' Andreas rushed forward. 'He is under my protection, the protection of the church. He won't go to Athens. I'll be responsible for him.'

Yannis glared at his cousin. 'Don't you see? If we don't keep on fighting we'll get nothing?'

'Calm yourself. Let me talk to them. Threats are no use. Go and sit down. Let me try my way.'

Yannis hesitated. If he were sent back to Spinalonga under

guard it was most unlikely he would ever be able to carry out his threat to petition the Athenian government.

'We want justice,' he muttered.

Andreas waited until Yannis had returned to his seat, then he looked at the gathering of ministers and directed his words to Dimitris and Nikos.

'You knew Yannis for a brief time during his stay at High School. Do you remember how he talked? How he wanted to attend University in Athens? Put yourself in his position. From being a happy student he is stricken with a disease that makes him an outcast from his fellows. He does not run away and hide; voluntarily he goes to the hospital, only to find the expected treatment does not exist.

From Heraklion he is sent to Athens, where again he finds no treatment. The hospital conditions are disgusting. He is kept a virtual prisoner, denied even the consolation of writing a letter to his family to let them know of his plight. Finally he could accept no more violence from the orderlies, no more mouldy food unfit for human consumption, no more degradation and neglect. All he and his friends asked of the hospital authorities was decent treatment and conditions. What did they get? They were sent to Spinalonga as criminals. How could sick people, who were merely asking for humane treatment, be branded as criminals? They were left on that island to fend for themselves. They had little shelter, no medicine, and were dependent upon the mainland to send them food and water.

It was to their credit and thanks to Yannis's spirit that they survived. You, Nikos, have seen the homes they made for themselves, built with their own deformed and crippled hands, how they have tried to be independent and how they suffered during the war years from starvation. Now, once again, they are an embarrassment to you and to Athens and you want to wash your hands of them like Pontius Pilot.

You may be able to send Yannis back to the island and detain him there for the rest of his life, but you cannot curtail my movements. If you will give no guarantee that Athens will give a decision within the next few weeks I shall visit Athens. I shall take his cause to the highest authority and not rest until I have satisfaction. He asks for very little. The medicine they need to help them recover from their disease, or the freedom to leave the island and go wherever they please if they are no longer contagious. You have no right to deny either course to them. It is not a criminal offence to become ill.'

Andreas dropped to his knees. 'I pray that you will exercise your judgement to do what you know in your hearts is right and just for these people.' He lifted his head. 'I will take responsibility for my cousin and his safe return to Spinalonga. I will guarantee that he will not attempt to leave the island again for two months. If, at the end of that time, there has been no decision from yourselves or from Athens, I take no responsibility for his actions as I shall be leaving Crete for Athens myself.'

Andreas rose and surveyed the gathering of ministers. They looked distinctly uncomfortable.

Nikos tapped his fingertips together and looked warily at Dimitris. 'What now?'

Dimitris's steady gaze was scornful. 'We wait for instructions from Athens.'

'You think he'll accept that?'

Dimitris shrugged. 'What else can he do? If he tries to live openly he'll very soon be picked up. Father Andreas can't shelter him indefinitely, so he'll have to return to the island and wait.'

'It's wicked. There's no good reason for them to stay there.'

'Wicked or not, the decision lies with Athens.'

'That could take years.'

'It could. Now, shall we break for lunch, gentlemen? Our morning has been badly disrupted. Maybe if we start promptly we can still complete our work this afternoon.'

YANNIS

Heads nodded, papers were shuffled together and chairs scraped across the wooden floor. The morning's outburst had been unusual and diverting. Each man wanted to discuss the event outside the sanctity of the government chamber.

For over an hour Nikos sat in a taverna. The pile of cigarette ends at his feet grew without him reaching a solution. Father Minos had been unable to help him and he doubted if Father Andreas would be any more help. Finally he ground out the last stub with his heel, the decision was made. He was already late for the afternoon session. He had nothing to lose by visiting the priest and Yannis. On reaching the small house he knocked timidly on the door, surprised when Andreas himself came to the door.

'Can I help you?'

'I would like to talk to Yannis.'

'What is it you want with him?'

Nikos shrugged. 'I want to help.'

'Help? How can you help? Whenever he asks for an answer he's told it's in the hands of the government in Athens.'

'I know, but maybe if I went to Athens, talked to the doctors there.'

'You would do that?'

'Yes.' Nikos made the promise rashly.

Andreas opened the door, which led to his private sanctum. 'Yannis, we have a visitor.'

Yannis did not bother to look up from the letter he was writing. 'I'm busy.'

'Nikos is willing to go to Athens on your behalf.'

This time Yannis raised his eyes. 'Why?'

'Because I want to help.'

Yannis snorted with derision. 'Help! What help were you when you took the tests on the island? The excuses you made. Why didn't you tell us we were clean? You must have known.'

'Please, Yannis, listen to me. Let me explain.'

Yannis's lip curled. 'Explain? There's nothing to explain. You don't want to be embarrassed by us.'

'Yannis, once we were friends, good friends. For the sake of that friendship, hear me out.' Nikos was pleading with tears in his eyes.

'Have the grace to hear him, Yannis,' interposed Andreas.

Yannis placed his pen on the table in front of him and leant his chin on his hands. 'Very well, but I doubt that you'll change my intentions.'

Nikos spread his hands. 'It was due to your letters that I first visited Spinalonga. The threats in your letters to the government forced Dimitris to do something. You have to understand that Dimitris has changed since our school days. He became a junior member of the government when Yiorgo Pavlakis was the leader. He resigned. It was a personal quarrel, I think, but he was tortured with guilt when the government were shot. He felt he should have been amongst them. He watched friends and relatives dying around him and he became disillusioned. He had watched an irresolute government become embroiled in a war that was nothing to do with them; then innocent people were subjected to wholesale slaughter, torture, imprisonment. We all lost people we loved,' Nikos shrugged, 'But we none of us felt that sense of guilt that Dimitris had. He felt it was his duty to form a strong government, a duty to those who had died.'

'That doesn't help me.' Yannis was impatient. 'I suppose he thought we'd all died and he could forget us.'

Nikos shook his head. 'He didn't forget you. We all thought that those of you who were left would be too old or sick to benefit from the treatment.'

'You didn't bother to come and find out.'

'Yannis, you have no idea of the way things were here after the war. We were short of everything, so was Athens. It was as much as the hospitals could do to keep going. Whatever we asked for we were told it was too expensive or they didn't have it.'

'So what's different now?'

'Now they don't know what to do. There's no point in sending you drugs you don't need. If you leave the island you could end up as beggars on the streets, harried from place to place, without a roof over your heads.'

'You don't understand. We've no wish to leave the island on a permanent basis. We want treatment if we need it, or freedom to do as we please if we're no longer infectious. All the time we're confined to the island we carry the stigma of a leper. We would none of us want to return to our families if we were going to cause problems for them. We'd just like to be able to visit. All we need is a piece of paper we can carry with us, a declaration, anything so we can live a normal life and not be prisoners.'

Nikos sighed. 'Do you really think a piece of paper will protect you from the outside world? Will people stop to read that before they throw a stone at you? Be realistic, Yannis.'

'Then what do you suggest?'

'I could go to Athens and say that in my opinion, as the examining doctor, you posed no threat to anyone and ask for a nationwide declaration to be made to that effect.'

'Would they listen to you?'

'I don't know. Even if they did, you'd have to be patient, Yannis. These things take time and you know how slowly the government can move. It could take months, even years.'

'We haven't got years. Some of us may only have weeks if we're to see our families again.'

'Suppose I managed to get a clearance that allowed you visits? Would that help?'

Yannis nodded. 'It would be a step in the right direction, but how long would that take?'

'It's possible that we could pass that locally, without reference to Athens,' Nikos spoke hopefully. 'It would still take time and you'd have to be patient until you heard from me again. I'd have to work on each member individually so I could be sure the motion would be passed. It's the best I can do.'

'Why this sudden change of heart towards us?'

'I feel guilty. We were supposed to be your friends, but once you'd gone we were all so involved in our own lives that we soon forgot you. I feel it's the least I can do to help you now.'

Yannis parked the motorbike in the yard and entered by the kitchen door. Anna was making pastry and looked up as he came in. 'I thought that must be you I could hear.'

'Aren't you pleased to see me?'

'Of course I am. Were you successful?'

'Partly. I have hopes, anyway.' Yannis proceeded to tell his sister about the council meeting and Nikos's promise. 'You don't seem very happy, though.'

Anna sighed. 'It's Marisa. She wants to get married.'

'There's nothing wrong in that. She's over twenty-one. It's high time she did think about it.'

'She wants to marry Victor.'

'Victor? Victor! You mean the Italian who was over here?'

'They've been writing to each other since the end of the war and he's coming over next week. She says if we won't let her get married she'll go back to Italy with him.'

Yannis raised the skin where his eyebrows should have been. 'She does sound determined. Maybe she'll change her mind when she sees him again. It's been almost five years.'

'Maybe,' Anna sounded dubious. 'Suppose she doesn't?'

Yannis frowned. 'What's he like, apart from an Italian and a soldier?'

'He's no longer in the army, he's an engineer. He was very kind to us when he was over here, more than kind.' A shadow of sadness passed over Anna's face. 'We certainly couldn't have kept the farm going without his help.'

'I'd like to meet him. Does he know about me?'

Anna nodded. 'He managed to get some supplies over to you occasionally.'

'How old is he?'

'Twenty four.'

'What have you got against him, Anna? The fact that he's Italian or that he was over here as part of the invading force?'

'It just doesn't seem right to marry a foreigner who held your life in his hands for years. How do we know that he's really suitable for her? We know nothing of his family.'

Yannis placed an arm round his sister's waist. 'Anna, she wants to marry Victor, not his family. You're the only one who knows him and you say he was kind to all of you. I can't say I approve, but it's not up to me. I think it would be better for her to marry with the family's blessing than run off with him and you spend the rest of your life wondering what's happened to her. I'll have a chat with her when she comes in.'

Yannis was up early the next morning, waiting by Davros's boat until the man appeared on the beach.

'Where've you been?'

'Heraklion. I had business with the government.'

Davros snorted in disbelief. 'Get in before you're seen.'

Yannis settled himself in the prow where the tiny cabin would hide him, watching as the island came closer. He felt relieved to be returning to the familiar place after the bustle of Heraklion. Flora greeted him with surprise and pleasure as he alighted and slipped her hand through his arm as he walked up the ramp.

'Where've you been? We didn't think you were coming back.'

'I visited my family, then went on to Heraklion and stayed with my cousin.'

'How did you do that?' Flora looked at him with wonder in her eyes.

'I bought a motorbike and rode up.'

'Where is it?' Flora looked behind them.

'I gave it to my brother. It wouldn't have been any good over here.'

'I'd have liked to see it. Did it go fast?'

'Fast enough. Where's Father Minos? I want to talk to him.'

'In the church. Tell me about Heraklion.'

'Later, there's not a lot to tell. How is everyone?'

'Fine, except Sevas. Spiro's taken her in and he doesn't think she'll last much longer.'

Yannis nodded. 'I'm not surprised. She was here ages before I came. I never thought she'd last this long. I'll see you later, Flora.'

He opened the door of the church and could see Father Minos on his knees. Yannis waited a good half hour before the priest rose and saw him. 'You should have interrupted me.'

'There was no urgency. I just wanted to let you know I was back and tell you what happened.'

'Come down to the taverna.'

'I got to Heraklion and I spoke to the government.'

'Tell me when we're inside. How were your family?'

'All well, but Marisa wants to marry one of the Italian soldiers who were billeted on them during the war.' Yannis spoke grimly.

Father Minos frowned. 'How does your sister feel about that?'

'Not very happy, but Marisa's of age. She can do as she pleases. He's coming over. It will be the first time she's seen him since the war ended so there's a chance the attraction will have died a natural death when they come face to face.'

'Of course; the man's a stranger to her after five years. What are you drinking?' Father Minos sat at the nearest table.

'At this time of the morning I'm still on coffee. Father, did you know that the results from our tests showed most of us to be negative, no longer infectious?'

The priest nodded.

'Why didn't you tell us?'

'I was told during a confessional.'

'So what happens now? I think we should tell everyone, they have a right to know, but Nikos is worried that some of them will return to the mainland and end up in trouble.'

'I think Nikos is probably right. Besides, not everyone is negative. It would be very unfair to tell someone they were no longer infectious, and then a doctor comes along and reverses the decision. Better for everyone to continue to live in ignorance.'

'Nikos is going to try to get the government to grant us visits from our family and friends. He reckons it could take a couple of months. He'll have to talk to the council members individually and convince them we're no risk to anyone. He's also going to Athens.' Yannis raised his cup. 'Let's drink to his success.'

The invitation to the villagers to visit the island was not taken up by any great number. Anna and Marisa arrived, along with Davros and Alkis. Anna led Marisa to Yannis's house, whilst the two men stood around, unsure what was expected of them now they had set foot on the island after so many years of delivering food. Father Minos took them to the taverna and bought them a bottle of wine.

'Feel free to go wherever you wish. We're all delighted to see you. We had hoped more of you might come over.'

Davros did not reply. He was staring suspiciously at the glass, wondering if it was safe to drink from it. Father Minos lifted his. 'Cheers.'

The two men raised their glasses, but Davros still hesitated to drink.

'It's quite safe,' the priest assured them.

Davros wiped the rim of the glass with a grubby finger; then placed it to his lips. 'What are we supposed to do over here?' he asked.

'That's up to you. You can wander around, sit and chat, have a game of chess or backgammon, ask to be shown the electricity. Do whatever you would normally do when you visit somewhere new. We're not really any different from you. Wander down the street and you could be in any village, walk down there this evening and it's a different story. Everywhere is as bright as day. That's worth seeing. I'm off now. I have my duties, you know, the same as anywhere else. I'll see you around, no doubt.'

The two men watched the priest leave. They refilled their glasses and looked at each other. 'Well, what do we do?'

'Wander around, I suppose. I must say you've got to admire their spirit.'

'We could find the one-armed girl who's always around.'

Davros drained his glass. 'Sooner we get on with it the sooner we can go fishing.'

They walked from the taverna up the path, taking their time and greeting those they met on the way until they found themselves at the end of the houses. Rounding the cliff they looked down onto the ramparts of the old Venetian fortress.

Alkis scratched his head. 'Makes you wonder how they built it. I'd like to know who they persuaded to work for them.'

'Slave labour, I expect. How did they get the materials here, that's more to the point. Half a dozen of those blocks in a boat and you'd be looking at the sea bed.'

The path narrowed and they looked down the sheer drop to the brilliant sea below before continuing on to where the tiny church stood. 'Shall we go in?' The door creaked as Davros opened it and he stood there waiting for his eyes to become accustomed to the gloom.

'Doesn't appear to be used.'

'Why should it be? They've got the other one and there's only one priest.'

The men crossed themselves before backing out through the door and closing it behind them. As they turned they met the steady gaze of a man on the other side of the path.

'Good morning. I'm Theodore. You must be visitors?'

The men nodded. 'Hope you don't mind us looking into the church.'

'Not at all. I'm glad to say it isn't used so often now. Care to join me?'

The two fishermen stood just over the threshold feeling embarrassed.

'Sit down.' Theodore placed glasses before them and drew the cork from a bottle of wine with his teeth.

'How long have you been here?' asked Davros.

'I don't know. I was in the second shipload from Athens. You tell me when that was and I'll tell you how long I've been here.' Theodore grinned, showing a number of blackened teeth, 'What was it like over there during the war?' He jerked his head towards the mainland. 'Tell me about the fighting. Were you involved?'

'Of course.' Both men answered in unison.

'Where were you?'

'Up near Heraklion at first, then Lassithi. I got shot there and that was the end of it for me, but I could tell you some stories.....'

Theodore leaned forward eagerly and Davros began an exaggerated account of his heroism that kept the elderly man enthralled for the rest of the morning, whilst Alkis poured himself more wine and smoked contentedly.

'Did you really build your house yourself, Uncle?'

'I only repaired and decorated it.'

Marisa looked at the sketches on the chimneybreast. 'Was that Phaedra?'

Yannis nodded. 'The other is Anna, the girl we adopted. She did both the sketches.'

'She was very talented. Have you any more of her work?'

Yannis smiled. 'Boxes and boxes; she hated lessons. When I tried to teach her she would always look as though she was writing hard and when I looked it would be a picture of me or someone else in the class.'

'I wish I'd been able to draw. Mamma could, and Yannis could if he bothered, but I'm hopeless.' Marisa twisted her fingers nervously.

'How is Victor?'

The direct question made her jump and blush. 'He's fine. We plan to get married in September,' she added, somewhat defiantly.

Anna rose from her chair. 'I'm going to find Father Minos. I have a message for him.'

Yannis looked at his sister in surprise. 'Shall I come with you?' he offered.

'No. The island's not big enough for me to get lost.'

Marisa watched her go, a smile playing on her lips. 'Aunty still doesn't really approve. I believe Victor when he says his family are willing to welcome me. You're not cross with me, are you, uncle Yannis?' Marisa asked anxiously.

Yannis smiled at her. 'Why should I be? Just be gentle with your aunt. She hates the thought of losing you.'

'We're going to have two weddings, one in Plaka and one in Turin. Will you be able to come?'

'I'm not able to, Marisa, you know that.'

Marisa pouted. 'There must be a way. I want you at my wedding.'

'We can think about it nearer the time,' Yannis promised. 'I'd certainly like to meet Victor.'

'I'll bring him over.'

'Come and find Anna.' Yannis put his arm around his niece. 'Just remember, Marisa, I'm here if you ever need me.'

For a fraction of a second Marisa hesitated, then she kissed her uncle's scarred and knobbly cheek. 'Thank you,' she said. 'I'll remember.'

Yannis was pleasantly surprised when Marisa arrived, glowing with happiness as she introduced the young man she intended to marry in a few days time. He sat comfortably in Yannis's house,

YANNIS

sipping wine and talking about his life in Italy. Yannis listened, asking a question to clarify a point that he had not quite understood and expressed his admiration of Victor's command of the Greek language.

'That is Marisa, she teach me in the war. I was very lucky to stay on your farm. When I hear the fates that befall many of my friends I would not like to think what would happen to me somewhere else.'

'What happened to your family during the war?'

'Many terrible things; I lose an uncle and a brother. Again, I was lucky. Many soldiers returned to their homes to find no one to give them a welcome. Our house need to be rebuilt, but,' Victor shrugged, 'that was no great problem, just a bit cold for a while, but you know all about that. I wish my uncle to visit you to see the work you have done. He is an architect and he would like to look at your buildings. I, too, would like to look later.'

'I'll take you round with pleasure. Marisa, suppose you try to find Manolis. I've some business I want him to see to for me.'

'Where will he be?'

'On the quay with Flora, I expect.'

Sulkily Marisa left. She knew it was an excuse to be rid of her for a while and she wanted to know what her uncle was going to say behind her back. Yannis leant towards Victor with a smile.

'What made you decide you wanted to marry my niece?'

Victor shrugged. 'Why you marry your wife? I love her. I think at first it is being away from home and war, but I could not forget her. Almost I dread meeting her again in case I am wrong.'

'Why didn't you ask her to marry you when the war finished?'

'I want to be sure. She was very young and in the war it is not the same. Besides your family would not be pleased.'

'I'm not sure they are now.'

'Are you against us?' Victor asked anxiously.

'No, I'm not against you two getting married. I just wish you were a local man for her aunt's sake.'

Victor twisted his fingers. 'I hope I make money. My family have money, but I want to make my own. I want enough for Marisa to come back when she want or aunt Anna to visit Italy. All of you are welcome.'

'Even me?' Yannis smiled thinly.

'Of course; I have told my family of you.'

'I'm sure they were very pleased to know they'll have a leper as a relation.'

Victor shrugged. 'Every country have. We treat ours a little gently. They are in hospital for treatments.'

'I hope your hospitals are a little more humane than ours then. Personally I would rather be over here.'

'Here is very good.'

'It is now. No doubt you've been told how it was when we first arrived and how we suffered during the war.'

Victor nodded. 'I have respect for you. I try to help in the war.'

'We were grateful to you.'

'I was very bad soldier,' Victor smiled as he spoke. 'Very pleased I was bad. I not shoot no-one. Marisa not marry man who shoot Greek people.' He leaned forward confidentially. 'I was student, told to join army for the glory of my country. No glory. All the time I frightened until I come here. I would like to run home. Never go into army again. Fight at home for my wife, my family, but not go in army. I do not like war, the starvation, the torture. I am sick when people scream.'

Marisa pushed open the door with Father Minos behind her. She turned to Victor with a smile. 'Father Minos has made a suggestion, Victor. I'm not sure if you'll agree. He has suggested that we have a third wedding. Over here, on the island, so uncle Yannis can come.'

'That is good idea.'

Marisa squeezed his arm. 'We'll be the most married couple in the whole of Italy. Three ceremonies. Wait until I tell aunt Anna; she'll be thrilled.'

YANNIS

'A problem. Where will the wedding party occur? On the farm or on the island?'

'Why not have two wedding parties?' suggested Yannis.

Marisa shook her head. 'I'd rather have just one. I want to get married over here on the same day as I do in Plaka and it would be difficult to get away if there was a party in full swing. I'll have it over here.' Her eyes sparkled. 'We can bring everything over in the boats and set it out in the square during the morning.'

The day dawned bright, promising greater heat to come as the day wore on. Yannis was up at dawn. He swept the tiny square clean of dust and sand, then struggled to bring out his table and four chairs before rousing his immediate neighbours to borrow theirs for the day. They grumbled. He was so early, they had not yet had breakfast; there was plenty of time. Yannis fretted and worried, would there be enough to drink, enough seats, enough food for all the guests as well as the islanders? Father Minos and Spiro did their best to calm him and all drew a breath of relief when a flotilla of small boats could be seen leaving Plaka. Yannis helped Marisa ashore and led her up the path to the church. She giggled.

'I wonder how many other people have been married twice in one day?' Marisa smiled up at him. 'I'm so happy. I only wish Victor's family could be here.'

'He will have his day when you go to Italy with him.'

'I shall wish you were there with me then.'

Yannis looked at her gravely. 'You're quite sure, Marisa? Even now you could say no.'

'Don't be silly. I'm already married. I'm looking forward to going to Turin.' She tilted her chin defiantly.

Yannis said no more.

At the door of the church he stood back for Yiorgo to lead her to the altar. Yiorgo shook his head. 'I did it last time. Your turn now.'

Proudly Yannis led his niece down to receive a blessing from Father Minos and stood to one side as Marisa and Victor renewed the vows they had made only an hour earlier.

Nikos read the letter through a second time. He had visited Athens and spoken at length to the doctors there, only to be told they were considering the situation and would let him know their decision in due course. Now their answer had come and he was not at all sure how the contents would be received by Yannis and his companions. He sighed. It would mean making the trip down to Spinalonga. It was not a meeting he could leave to others, much as he dreaded it. This was not what Yannis had asked for or wanted.

Throughout the journey he tried to marshal his thoughts and decide how to approach the subject. Yannis would know as soon as he saw him that he had news from Athens, he would not have made the effort to visit him otherwise.

He arrived in Aghios Nikolaos at mid-day and decided to seek out Doctor Stavros first. The doctor was out when he arrived and he hoped he had not gone over to the island. After a leisurely meal he returned to find the doctor eating a late lunch, a glass at his elbow.

'What brings you down here?' He placed another glass on the table and poured a generous measure of raki.

'I've had a letter from Athens. They want them back in hospital.' Nikos drew the letter from his pocket. 'Read it yourself. They say they can't give them a clean bill of health without a thorough examination carried out by their own specialists. To do that they have to return to Athens.'

'It's not necessary. You've examined them and taken all the samples they asked for. What more can they want?'

'I don't know. I was wondering if you'd come over with me to explain to them?'

Doctor Stavros shook his head. 'Impossible this week. If you can wait until my regular island day I'll go with you.'

'May I at least beg a bed for the night?'

'You know you're always welcome.'

Despite Doctor Stavros's insistence that he was far too busy to visit the island with Nikos he was able to spend the rest of the afternoon chatting and bringing his visitor up to date with the medical situation on the island before suggesting they adjourned to a nearby taverna for the evening.

'It made a tremendous difference to them when they were allowed visitors. Yannis's niece was married over there and that seemed to dispel the last of their fears. One or two have become such regulars that I've almost mistaken them for sufferers.' Doctor Stavros smiled. 'Most of them seem pretty content with their lot now. I see no point in uprooting them, even for a short time.'

'Athens makes no mention of how long they'll be undergoing tests and examinations, but I doubt if they'll be away for more than a month or two.'

'How are they to go?'

'Taken to Heraklion by bus and flown to the hospital.'

Doctor Stavros raised his eyebrows. 'That will be something of a harrowing experience for them. Couldn't they go by boat?'

'I'm only repeating what the letter says. They've also enclosed a list of names.'

'You mean, not everyone is to go at once?'

'I doubt if they could cope with them all at once. They're going to examine them in small batches.'

'Who do they want?'

Nikos read a list of names.

Doctor Stavros frowned. 'Two of those are dead. Do you have any instructions for substituting people?'

'No. I'll have to ask who they want.'

'Just add two and tell them when you arrive. I doubt that it will matter. Are you taking them back with you?'

'No. I've been told a doctor and nurse will arrive here next week to escort them and attend to their needs whilst travelling.'

'Then leave it to them to sort it out.' The doctor refilled his own glass and looked to see if Nikos's needed replenishing. 'Yannis should be pleased that things are moving.'

'I'm not so sure. He hasn't very happy memories of Athens.'

'I doubt it will be for long. Besides, once he's been officially declared clear he'll be able to have a holiday over there and see all the sights he missed before.'

Nikos nodded. He had not thought of that. Yannis should be very pleased at the way things were turning out.

One look at Yannis's face told Nikos he was wrong in his assumption that Yannis would be pleased.

'It's ridiculous. What tests can they possibly want to do that haven't been done already? If they don't believe the results why don't they come over here themselves? I'm not going. There's no need. The others can go if they want, but I'll stay here.'

'You can't, Yannis. Your name is first on the list.'

Yannis shrugged. 'Then cross it through.'

'Don't be silly. This is what you've been after for years. The only way you'll get a clean bill of health to move about freely is to go to Athens.'

'I've decided I'm not interested any longer. If they'd suggested this in the first place it would have been different. Now we can have visitors I'm quite content.'

'You may be, but what about the others? They'd like to see their friends and relatives again, no doubt, and until they have permission from Athens they haven't a hope. Some of them come from northern Greece and they'll never see their families again unless they have official clearance. If you refuse to go they'll have doubts. When you come back with your papers they'll be queuing up to go on the next flight. They trust you, Yannis. You started this and you're going to have to see it through. Besides, you'll be able to see Athens. You always dreamed of visiting there and seeing the museums. You could

YANNIS

spend a couple of months or even more and see everything.'

'I wish I'd never started to badger them. We've been left in peace for years and it could have stayed that way. I don't want to leave here, Nikos. This is my home. Phaedra and Anna are here.'

'Don't be ridiculous, Yannis. You'll only be away a short time. The way you talk you make it sound as though you'll never see the place again.'

Yannis sat morosely in the stern of the boat, gazing at the island as it receded into the distance. He felt a lump in his throat as the ramparts of the Venetian fort hid the houses from his view and finally began to dwindle into insignificant walls themselves. Aghios Nikolaos came closer and he wished they were going round to the beach where Yiorgo had always moored his boat, rather than the stone jetty that stretched out to make a sheltered harbour.

Along the waterfront he could see tables and chairs set out in front of tavernas and he realised how much the fishing village had changed since he had lived there. No one was there to greet the boat as it slid into the mooring space, but further down the quay were a group of spectators, anxious to see the lepers from the island as they landed, but afraid to come closer. They were shepherded aboard the waiting bus that bumped its way along the quay and onto the road leading to Heraklion, carrying its occupants who stared curiously from the windows and waved to passers-by who looked at them in surprise.

'When will we get there?' asked Flora anxiously.

'I don't know. About another hour, I expect.'

'What's it like to fly in an aeroplane?'

'I've no idea. We'll probably feel like birds, able to see everything down below. It will be exciting, Flora.'

Flora pursed her lips. Yannis might think the experience was going to be exciting, but she would have preferred to go by ship. At the sight of the aeroplane she shrank back. It looked so small and insignificant sitting on the runway and the burnt–out shells of three others did nothing to improve her confidence.

'What happened to those?' she asked Yannis in a whisper.

'That would have happened during the war,' Yannis assured her, hoping his surmise was correct.

They were escorted to one of the outbuildings where they sat at small tables and were plied with food and drink. The doctor and his assistant chatted easily to them, hoping to make their passengers relax and dispel the fears, which were obviously growing in their minds. 'We shall be in the air for about an hour. You'll find the view of Crete and also of Greece quite spectacular from the air. Have any of you flown before?'

Yannis gave the doctor a withering glance and shook his head.

'You may feel quite nervous. Very occasionally people become hysterical. If that should happen I have tranquillisers that I can administer. I can assure you there is no need for any of you to be fearful. Now, if you will excuse me, I'll see if everyone is ready to leave.'

Yannis did not enjoy the new experience of flying. He felt insecure so far from the ground. As they took off he felt his stomach churning and hoped he would not be the one to need a tranquilliser. He glanced at Flora and was amused to see she was gazing out of the window at the ground far below with a rapt expression on her face. 'Isn't it wonderful?'

Yannis smiled at her enthusiasm. 'I prefer to be on the ground.'

'You should look out of the window. Everything is so small. You can see for miles. I wish Manolis were here. He would love it.'

Yannis smiled again, but did not answer. His stomach was heaving uncomfortably. He shut his eyes and tried to relax, ignoring the doctor as he walked up and down the aisle asking his patients if there was anything they wanted and if they were comfortable. For him the flight could not end quickly enough. The landing found him gritting his teeth and straining his legs against the seat in front. To his disgust he found he was sweating with relief and his knees were shaking as he walked down the steps and on to the solid tarmac beneath his feet.

Once again they were placed inside a bus and he looked around with interest as they drove up the wide road from the airport. He craned his neck for a first sight of the Acropolis with the Parthenon on top and a strange thrill went through him. Maybe in a week or two he would be able to visit the famous site. As they dipped down into the centre of Athens he was no longer able to see the hill and he felt beads of perspiration breaking out on his forehead and top lip as remembered with clarity the hospital ward where he had spent the most miserable and uncomfortable years of his life.

The bus jerked to a halt, hooting violently to attract the attention of the gatekeeper, who stared curiously at the occupants of the bus. Yannis bowed his head, the almost forgotten feeling of shame welling up inside him. For the first time in years he felt he was contaminated and had no right to mix with his healthy fellows. He was last to alight from the bus and follow the group into the austere building, not looking to left or right. He heard his name called and muttered acknowledgement.

'Follow me, please.'

Yannis shuffled down the corridor after his guide until they stopped before a white painted door. 'Your room, sir.' The door was unlocked and the key handed to Yannis. 'I hope it will be to your liking. The bathroom is here,' another door was thrown open, 'and there is a communal dining room at the end of the corridor. Over here you will see a bell. Please use it if there is anything you need.'

Yannis lifted his eyes and looked around in disbelief. 'I'm not a doctor.'

'Mr Christoforakis, yes? This is the room that has been allotted to you. Number three.'

'Where are the others?'

The man looked at his list. 'Mr Chatzidakis is next door, number two, and Mr Psilakis is number four.'

'Do they have rooms like this?'

'Exactly, sir; they are all the same.'

Yannis sat down on the end of the bed. 'When I was here before we were all in one large ward together.'

'Things have changed, sir. We still have wards, of course, but they are a good deal smaller now. The patients don't stay so long in them. Is there anything else, sir? If not, I'll see to your luggage.'

Yannis shook his head. He was having trouble coming to terms with the speed with which things were happening. That morning he had been in his own little house on Spinalonga, now he was in Athens in a luxurious room. There was an air of unreality about the whole thing. He rose slowly and walked to the bathroom, stopping in awe at the doorway. He walked over to the basin and turned on the taps, watching, fascinated, as the water gushed from both of them. He pulled the chain hanging from the toilet cistern, stepping back as the water swirled before being sucked down the waste pipe and disgorged somewhere into a drain. The shower sprayed water at him and he pushed the handle the opposite way rapidly. This was unbelievable. A knock at the door made him turn to see the man returning with his two sacks of belongings and he fumbled in his pocket for a coin to tip him.

The man accepted the coin without a second glance, smiled at Yannis and shut the door behind him. Yannis wrenched it open, feeling beads of perspiration on his forehead and his whole body went limp with relief to find that it was not locked.

Mikalis leant out from his doorway and grinned. 'This is luxury.'

Yannis beckoned him in. 'Why do you think they've done this?'

'I've no idea. Maybe they thought we were used to rooms like this.'

Yannis snorted. 'They're not that stupid. They're up to something and I can't for the life of me make out what it is yet.'

Mikalis shrugged. 'Whilst I can live like this I don't mind. I'll unpack,' said Mikalis. 'Then I'm going to have a wash. I might even have a shower.'

Yannis nodded. There was something nagging at the back of his mind, which he could not put a name to, a feeling that was menacing him and making him feel very uneasy indeed

Yannis was annoyed and disappointed to find himself still there at the end of two months. Each day he asked when he would see a doctor and have tests and each time he was given an excuse. Finally he demanded to be taken to the doctor in charge, only to be told he was leaving the following day to attend a conference in Vienna and they would have to be patient. The International conference was of great importance, particularly to people who were in the same burnt-out condition as the people of Spinalonga. Yannis wrote a second letter to Nikos complaining of the delays, hoping the doctor in Heraklion would be true to his promise. Flora was pinched and miserable, Mikalis jubilant, he had received a visit from his wife for the first time in fourteen years, but the others were as despondent as Yannis.

'I just want to go home,' complained Sifis. 'My vegetable plot was flourishing. Now it will be over-run with weeds and I'll have lost a year's crop.'

'I'm worried about the hospital.' Spiro's face puckered into a frown. 'I'm not trying to boast, but I had it running pretty smoothly. How are they managing without me?'

'I just wish they'd get on with things. I'm worried that we're the ones who are not burnt-out and that's why they've brought us here,' said Tassos.

'Suppose, just suppose,' Yannis spoke tentatively, eyeing his companions, 'that there is no conference. It's just another excuse to keep us here. I know,' he held up his hand, 'it was always me who was discontented and made impossible demands on the government. I was the one that instigated the riot that saw us all shipped off to Spinalonga, I pressed for compensation, for medicine and treatment after the war, and then a clean bill of health. We have no guarantee they plan to give us that. We are as much prisoners over here as we were twenty-five years ago, and I think we've got to do something about it.'

Spiro grinned. 'I'm with you, Yannis. What are you planning to do? Another riot to get us all sent back?'

Yannis shook his head. 'The first thing is to find out how long this conference is supposed to last, then the address where it's being held.'

'What do you plan to do then? Go there?'

Yannis shook his head. 'My cousin's husband is bound to be there. I'll write to him and ask him to publicise our cause. The Greek government won't like it and they'll have to do something.'

Mikalis looked at Yannis in alarm. 'I don't want to go back. Whilst I'm here I can see my wife. She's promised to bring my son and daughter-in-law with her next week.'

'You stay.' Yannis shrugged. 'Anyone who's happy here can stay as far as I'm concerned. All I want is our rights. We were brought over here for tests and we've not had a single one. I want to go out and see Athens. I might just as well be back home on Spinalonga as here. Do you agree with me?'

All except Mikalis nodded.

'Then leave it with me.'

Yannis made his way down the maze of corridors from the annex of the hospital building and into the administration offices. He knocked on doors without receiving any answer until one yielded under his touch and he found himself looking into a room occupied by two men who were obviously not doctors.

'Can I help you? Have you lost your way?' The youngest rose, pushing his papers to one side with ink stained fingers.

'No, I'm not lost. I'd just like some information.'

The man frowned and looked at his colleague. 'What kind of information?'

'I'd like to know how long the International Conference in Vienna is scheduled to run.'

The young man opened a diary on the desk and flicked over the pages. 'According to this it will run for three weeks.'

'I see. I do need to send an urgent letter to a relative who'll be attending. Would it be possible for me to have the address?'

The clerk pursed his lips and looked to the other man for guidance again. There was a slight nod. With a sigh the clerk pulled a sheet of paper from a pile and wrote on it, handing it to Yannis who folded it and placed it in his pocket. 'Thank you, you've been very helpful.'

Jubilantly Yannis hurried back down the corridors to the lounge where he had left the others. 'I've got it! Now there's no time to lose. I'll write straight away and ask an orderly to post it tomorrow. It's worth a try, isn't it?'

Elias opened the letter in surprise, wondering whom he knew in Greece who would write to him. He had heard from his mother and uncle only the week before. He turned to the last page and read the signature "Yannis Christoforakis, your cousin." He sighed. There was no time now to wade through the half dozen pages. Any minute he was due to be speaking on the advances made for the treatment of leprosy in America and the way in which the leprosarium there was run. He pushed the letter into his pocket, gathered his notes, and strode into the lecture hall.

His hour-long address to the listening doctors was met with polite applause and he left the platform feeling he had accomplished nothing. When he had invited questions only one man had spoken, then there were a few minutes of embarrassed silence before he cleared his throat and vacated the platform to resume his seat. He spent the remainder of the morning listening to an Indian bewailing the plight of his nation in their unequal fight against not only the disease, but also the ignorance and poverty that the people suffered.

When he had finished Elias retired to the restaurant, choosing a table in the corner and whilst he ate his lunch he read the letter he had received. He would have to make some notes, then at least he would be able to ask relevant questions when the Greek representative spoke in two days time. He pushed his plate away and reached for his cigarette case.

He waited in eager anticipation for the day the Greek doctor was due to speak and settled back comfortably in his chair as the man took the platform. After the usual opening remarks he went on to say how deprived the country had been due to the occupation by the Germans during the war, how little money was available even now for treatment. He painted a glowing picture of the new hospital that had been built on the site of the old one, describing the facilities that long-term patients could expect, yet insisting that without international aid the treatment could not progress at the same rate as that enjoyed in the western world. Elias listened, amusement giving a small up-turn to his lips. This might be a medical conference, but it was turning into a begging campaign. Each country insisting they needed massive amounts of monetary aid to improve their medicine. Finally the Greek took his seat on the platform and waited for his words to be digested sufficiently before calling for questions.

Elias was on his feet. 'I should like to ask a question.' He waited for the nod of assent. 'What is going to happen to the lepers from Spinalonga?'

There was complete silence. The doctor looked desperately at the chairman, who nodded. There was nothing irregular about the question. The doctor took a mouthful of water.

'I do not fully understand the question.'

'Then I will repeat myself, sir, and also expound. The lepers from Spinalonga have undergone protracted tests that have proved most of them to be burnt-out. I understand some of them were taken to hospital in Athens to undergo further tests. When these further tests prove a negative infection, what do you plan to do with these unfortunate men and women?'

The doctor licked his lips. 'That's a very difficult question for me to answer. It's not entirely medical, but political also. I would not like to overstep the bounds of my ability.'

'Why should it be political? Why should these people not be allowed to leave and live wherever they please?'

'It's not quite as simple as that. Although many of them appear to be healthy we don't know enough about the disease to give them a completely clean bill of health. For all we know the disease could reappear at any time, striking them suddenly and fatally.'

'In my experience that has never happened with a burnt-out case.'

A chorus of voices agreed with Elias and the Greek doctor looked around desperately at the chairman, who kept his eyes glued to the floor.

'We do not feel we are in a position to be that positive.'

'So what are you going to do with them?' persisted Elias.

'It has not been decided yet. I have not had an opportunity to examine the patients.'

'Why not? I understand they arrived in Athens two months before you left for this conference.'

'We thought it better to give them a chance to rehabilitate themselves. We do not wish to overawe them by asking probing questions until they are relaxed and familiar with their surroundings.'

Elias snorted. 'These people are not primitive savages! A good many of them are well educated and had they not been stricken in their youth they could well be your politicians, lawyers, teachers or even doctors of today. I don't feel they would be overawed in any way simply by being moved to Athens.'

'We felt we should give them time. I intend to start my examination of their individual cases upon my return.'

'And should you find them negative what will your recommendation be?

'I would have to consult with my superiors.'

'What would you like to see happen if they are negative?'

The doctor stood, silent and helpless under the merciless attack.

Elias tried again. 'Would you like to see them kept in hospital if they have nothing wrong with them?'

'There would be no need.'

'So they could return to the island?'

'I suppose so, if they wanted.'

'Suppose they wished to live elsewhere?'

'That would be up to the government.'

'But you would be willing to see them leave the hospital and return to the island they consider to be their home?'

'It would seem the most practical solution.'

'I agree with you. For many it would probably be the only solution, but what of those who have families in other parts of Greece? Surely they should be allowed to return to them?'

The doctor shrugged. 'I can't answer that.' He turned to the chairman. 'Please, may I be released from this form of questioning? I do not feel it has any direct bearing on the conference.'

The chairman looked at Elias. 'How many people's lives are we discussing?'

'About seventy.'

'Then I think you should be satisfied with the answers given so far. The purpose of the conference is to discuss the suffering of some million or more, not to take up the cause of small groups, however worthy.'

'Thank you, sir. I trust my questions and the answers were recorded.' Elias resumed his seat. He knew he had discomfited the Greek doctor and he hoped it would have a beneficial effect. He would be visiting his family in Athens and could easily fit in a visit to the hospital, and if necessary, remind the doctor of the recorded conversation.

YANNIS

It was good to be home once more, to sit in the over-crowded, over-heated room and hear the sounds of Athens in the background. He wished he had been able to bring Annita with him, but she had become so Americanised he doubted that she would easily have been able to slip back into the role of the docile, Greek wife, even for a few weeks. She organised him, dictated to him and generally ruled his waking hours. He loved her dearly and admitted that without her continual management he would probably have become a recluse, dedicated to his research, and quite unfit to hold the important post that was his at the leprosarium.

It came almost as a shock to him when he realised he had already spent a week there and done no more than shopped for a present for Annita. He must visit the hospital and see Yannis. All the enthusiasm and fire he had experienced during the conference seemed to have dissipated from his body, leaving him weak and listless.

Without enthusiasm he propelled his steps in the direction of the hospital until he reached the gates. He traversed the grounds, pleased to see groups of patients sitting outside in the warm sunshine. At the information desk he asked for Yannis and was directed along the corridor to the unit of single rooms. There was no answer to his knock and he tried to find his way back, wandering as he did so into a small, secluded garden. The solitary occupant looked up and smiled.

'Can I help you? Have you lost your way?'

'I certainly have. I'm looking for Yannis Christoforakis. I went to his room, but there was no answer.'

'He's with the doctor. I don't expect he'll be much longer. You could wait here or go to the cafeteria. I can show you the way.'

'I'll wait here, if you don't mind. It's very pleasant.'

A look of sadness came over the girl's face. 'If only we could see the sea,' she spoke wistfully.

'You come from the coast?'

'From Spinalonga. You can see the sea wherever you are on there. I do miss it.'

Elias looked at her. 'Please, don't think me impertinent, but may I ask you some questions?'

She looked from Elias to the door leading back into the hospital. 'What do you wish to ask me?'

'I'd like you to tell me about Spinalonga.'

'There's not much to tell. It's just a small island, but at least you can walk where you please and do as you want.'

'Can't you do that here?'

Flora shook her head. 'We're not allowed to leave the grounds and they prefer us to stay round here rather than mix with the other patients.'

'Why is that?'

'I don't know. We're not infectious. It's almost as though they want to hide us. Yannis is getting very cross. He blames himself. If he hadn't continually pestered the government to say we could go wherever we wanted they wouldn't have brought us over here. We could have stayed on the island where we were happy.'

'Were you all happy there?'

Flora shrugged. 'Most of us were. I was. Yannis was. There's only Mikalis who likes being here and that's because his family can visit him.'

'A very good reason.'

'I agree, but let him stay and let us go home.'

'Wouldn't some of the others from the island like to come here? Maybe they'd be able to see their families again then?'

'Some of them would. That's why it seems so unfair to have brought us.'

Elias nodded sympathetically. 'What do you plan to do when you return to the island? Do you have a husband there?'

'No.' A guarded look came over Flora's face. 'Who are you anyway?'

YANNIS

'I'm a specialist in leprosy. You needn't be afraid of me.'

'I'll go and see if Yannis's returned.' Before Elias could say another word Flora had gone, rushing down the corridor, knocking on each door as she went. Grumbling the occupants came out, demanding to know what was wrong.

'There's a strange man in the garden. Says he wants Yannis, but he's asking an awful lot of questions.'

'Where is Yannis?'

'With the doctor.'

'I'll come.' Spiro reached for his jacket. 'You wait here until Yannis gets back.'

Spiro sauntered into the garden. 'I hear you've been asking for Yannis?'

Elias rose. 'Pleased to meet you at last.'

'I'm not Yannis. I'm a friend of his. What is it you want? Yannis is likely to be a little while yet, he's with the doctor.'

'Yes, the girl told me that. I don't know what I said. I seemed to frighten her. One minute we were chatting and the next she was running back inside the hospital. She is all right?'

'She said you were asking a lot of questions. Why did you want to see Yannis?'

'I'm his cousin's husband. He may have mentioned me to you. I was at the conference in Vienna and decided to take the opportunity to visit those of my family who still live in Athens. Yannis wrote to me and I thought it would be a good idea to visit him also whilst I'm here. We've never met, but we are related, and I thought my wife would appreciate news of him.'

A broad grin spread over Spiro's face. 'You must be Elias. You received his letter, then? He'll be glad to see you. Did they say anything about us at the conference?'

'I brought the subject up, which was what Yannis intended.'

'What did they say?'

'Let's wait for Yannis, then I can tell you and any of the others who may be interested.'

'They all will be. Wait here and I'll find them.'

Elias waited a good half hour before Spiro returned with a group of men and two women.

'We're still waiting for Yannis, but I've left a message pinned to his door asking him to come to the garden as soon as he returns. He can't be very much longer.'

'He's probably well into an argument with the doctor. He could be hours,' groaned Sifis.

'My son and daughter-in-law are visiting me this afternoon. I want to have had my lunch and a shave before they come,' grumbled Mikalis.

'There's plenty of time. You know your visitors are always late.'

'That's not their fault,' Mikalis defended them. 'They have to travel from Piraeus.'

Elias listened. They sounded no different from any other group of patients waiting impatiently for visiting hours. The door opened and a man entered. As if in deference to him the talking stopped and they moved back to allow him through. 'What's so important?'

Elias stepped forward. 'I can't be wrong again. You must be Yannis.'

'I am.'

'Elias. Elias from America.'

'Elias! What are you doing here?'

'You wrote to me in Vienna and I was coming to Athens so I thought I'd visit you.'

'You got my letter then?'

'I raised a question and forced an answer for you. It's not entirely satisfactory, but it was the best I could do before I was told to sit down.'

'What is it? Tell us?'

'I asked what would happen if you were declared negative and the doctor tried to hedge. He tried to avoid answering the question, so I changed it and asked if they planned to keep you here in hospital if you were negative and he said no. I then asked if you would be sent back to the island and he said it would be the most practical solution.'

Audible sighs of relief were heard.

'Suppose we don't want to go back?' asked Mikalis.

'That was when they made me sit down and keep quiet. It's all recorded and I've a copy at home that I can translate for you. They gave me mine in English, of course. If they try to keep you here against your wishes you can produce that and they won't have any grounds.'

'I can't thank you enough, Elias. We were beginning to think we were prisoners here.'

'They can't keep you here against your will. You came voluntarily for tests. If those tests show up negative they can't force you to stay in the hospital.'

'Suppose they try?'

'Then write to me immediately. I'll keep my copy of the conference minutes in a very safe place and if necessary I could take your case to the Court of Human Rights.'

'What good would that do?'

'I'm not sure. It would depend a good deal on how your case was presented. The Greek government could show that it was for your own well being that you were kept here, but at the same time it would high-light your predicament world wide. I don't think they'd like that kind of publicity. You could say it's a threat to hold over them if extreme measures were necessary.'

Yannis nodded. 'I feel that a great weight has been lifted from me. Can I ask you just one more favour?'

Elias grinned at him. 'I've done little enough, a favour won't come amiss.'

'Then send a copy of those minutes to Andreas. He's an independent person who would be able to look after them safely until we ever needed them. I just don't trust hospitals.'

'That's no problem. Now, would you like to see some pictures of Annita and the children?'

Yannis knocked on the director's door. He had waited two days for his appointment and was feeling very disgruntled. The genial smile and wave of a hand to a chair did nothing to dispel his annoyance.

'I want to know why I'm being kept here and how much longer you intend to do so?' Yannis glared at the man.

'Mr Christoforakis, no one is keeping you here. If you remember, when the first group of your friends dispersed we asked if you would be willing to stay for a few weeks, help the newcomers settle in, familiarise them with their new surroundings. This you agreed to do.'

'I then expected to leave.'

'We still need your valuable assistance. There are still a number of your friends to be brought over to the hospital. They've come to look to you for guidance over the years, they respect your judgement. When they have to make the important decision regarding returning to the island or to their previous homes they ask your advice.'

'That's rubbish,' snapped Yannis. 'They make their own decisions. Only five have returned to the island. The others took the chance to return to their families.'

'But they had you to discuss their decision with. Had they talked to me they might have thought I was trying to influence them one way or the other, but they know you have only their well being at heart.'

'So how much longer am I going to be asked to stay here?'

'A month, maybe two, then you'll be able to make your decision.'

'And what am I supposed to do with myself in the meantime? I'm bored. I've read all the books in the library; I've visited all the sites and museums until I could act as a guide to them.'

'Then maybe we could find a little job for you. Nothing too strenuous, of course, but to occupy you.'

'I don't need a job created just to fill my time. If there's a proper job that needs doing I'm willing, but nothing thought up just to keep me quiet.'

'I'm sure we'll find something satisfactory. I'll have a word and see where we're short staffed.'

'I'm not working on the wards,' Yannis warned him. 'I don't like sick people.'

'Maybe in the garden? You had a flourishing garden on the island, I hear.'

'I also built my own house. That doesn't make me an architect.'

'Of course, we will see. Leave the problem with me.'

Yannis left the office, doubting very much that anything at all would be done. He was bored. To have all his meals ready whenever he needed them, his room cleaned and his laundry done, left him with too much time on his hands. The novelty of such luxuries had worn off and he longed to occupy both his mind and body with something worthwhile.

He calculated the number of men and women still on Spinalonga and decided the director had been very optimistic when he had said two months, by his reckoning it would be more like five. With a sigh Yannis settled down to write his weekly letter to Anna.

He was interrupted by a knock at his door. 'Director wants to see you.' The door closed again.

The director leaned across the desk. 'I think the very thing has turned up for you, Mr Christoforakis. We need a controller in the hospital stores. We need a man who is reliable and trustworthy. The wards send down for medical supplies, the orderly presents a chit; you take the supplies from the shelf and make a note of the amount remaining. It is up to you to order more as they are needed and to ensure that we do not run short.'

'Who has been doing it?'

'Vassilis.'

'So why isn't he still doing it?'

'He's saved enough to have his veins done. That will take him off his feet for a few weeks.'

Yannis nodded. 'Is he there now?'

'He should be.'

'Then I'll have a word with him. He can show me how it's done.'

'You'll be paid, of course.'

'Paid?'

'Naturally. As a hospital employee you'll be paid a wage. It won't amount to very much as there will be deductions for your food and lodging as you're living at the hospital.'

Yannis rose. 'I'll find Vassilis.'

The director watched him go with relief. At least having something to do should stop him from causing trouble due to boredom.

Yannis was pleasantly surprised when he was handed his wage packet at the end of the week. It contained more than he had expected. He was beginning to enjoy the job. It was not arduous by any means, yet he had to concentrate when he worked out how much stock he had left. As yet he was nervous that he would run out of bandages or lint at a crucial time and placed two orders in quick succession, only to find when they were delivered that he had little storage space. He struggled with the cumbersome boxes, trying to fit them onto the shelves, cursing when they fell back on to him, when he heard a suppressed giggle behind him. He whipped round, ready with a cutting remark, only to see a middle-aged woman watching him with amusement. He placed the offending box on the ground.

'What can I do for you?'

She pushed a chit across to him. 'There's no rush. The nurses always panic when stocks dwindle.'

YANNIS

Yannis frowned at the piece of paper. 'Two dozen boxes of bandages. What size?'

The woman took the chit back from him. She sighed. 'I'll have to go back and ask. I'm bound to take the wrong ones otherwise.' She turned to go, limping across to the door.

'Which ward are you on?'

'Over the other side; Women's Surgical.'

'Wait a while. I'll phone up. How did you hurt your leg?'

'Oh, it's not hurt. I've had a limp for years.'

Yannis picked up the telephone and turned the handle. 'Women's Surgical, please.' He handed the mouthpiece to the woman. 'You can ask for what you want.'

Nervously she spoke into the mouthpiece and a look of wonder crossed her face as the instructions came back to her. 'Vassilis never did that for me. If I didn't know he always sent me back to ask.'

'Not necessary,' smiled Yannis. 'That's what it's been put here for.'

She gathered up the boxes of bandages. 'Do you have to go yet?' asked Yannis. 'It gets pretty lonely down here. Sometimes I don't see anyone for hours.'

'I mustn't be long.'

'I'm Yannis. What's your name?'

'Theodora, but people call me Dora.'

'I'm pleased to meet you, Dora.'

'I'm pleased to meet you, too, Yannis.'

They looked at each other in silence; then Dora giggled. 'What are we going to talk about?'

Yannis scratched his head. 'How long have you worked here?'

'About five years; since my husband died.'

'I'm sorry.'

'There's no need. It's over now. He was a good man, and what's done is done.'

'My wife died during the war, and my daughter.'

'The Germans?'

'Indirectly. They starved us.'

'Starved you? Where were you?'

'Spinalonga.'

'Spinalonga? I've heard of that place.' Dora shuddered. 'I managed to avoid being sent there.'

'You? But only lepers go to Spinalonga.'

'I know. That's why I limp.'

'Have you had treatment?' Yannis leant close to her. 'It's very important, Dora. What treatment have they given you?'

'After I came here I was given Dapsone. Until then I'd had nothing. I didn't want to be sent to that island.'

'What effect has the Dapsone had?'

'I don't know. They keep giving it to me and I don't seem any worse, so I expect it's doing me good.'

The telephone buzzed and Yannis answered it. 'Yes, she's just leaving. I'm new here and had trouble finding where the bandages were.' He grinned conspiratorially at Dora as she hurriedly limped to the door.

Yannis read the long letter from Father Minos and a wave of homesickness swept over him. He was still reading it when Dora arrived to collect supplies. She waited whilst Yannis drew his eyes reluctantly from the sheet of paper.

'What's wrong? Have you had bad news?'

Yannis forced a smile. 'No, just a letter from home.'

'And you're missing your friends?'

Yannis shrugged. 'There aren't many left to miss! Most of them have returned to their homes. Father Minos says there are twenty who haven't been over here yet, and five who have returned to their homes on the island. I wish I'd never asked for medical treatment.'

'Why? Because your friends have been able to return to their homes and families? I'd have thought you would have been pleased for them. Can you give me these?' Dora pushed the chit towards Yannis who did not even look at it.

'Of course I am, but what kind of a life is it going to be on the island? There'll be so few of us left.'

'You could stay here.'

Yannis shook his head. 'I've nothing to stay here for. My life has been spent on that island. My wife and child died there. My home is there.'

Dora did not know what to reply. 'I'd better get back,' she said finally.

Yannis glanced down at the chit. 'Is this urgent? Can't you stay a bit longer?'

'I'll be in trouble if I'm away too long.'

Yannis turned away to the shelf and took down the package of disinfectant, placing it on the counter with unnecessary violence. 'There you are.'

'I could come back later, when I'm off duty,' she offered.

Yannis shrugged. 'It's up to you.'

Dora limped away. She would not return when her duty was finished. Why should she try to cheer him up when he had spoken to her in such an off-hand way. All day the rebuff niggled at her until she felt so annoyed that she determined never to go down for supplies again. She could always make the excuse that her leg was paining her. She hung her overall behind the door and called goodnight to the nurse. She would go to her room, take off her shoes and have a cup of coffee. She had only tried to be friendly and he had been downright rude. Maybe Sevas would drop in on her when she had finished on her ward and she would be able to tell her how put out she was. Barefooted she went to the door to answer the gentle tap she heard.

'Come in.' The words died on her lips as Yannis stood there. She felt covered in confusion to be found without her shoes and she looked down at her feet in shame.

'May I come in?'

'Just a minute.' Dora pushed the door closed and shuffled her feet quickly back into her shoes. She took a quick glance around the room and poked a half darned stocking into her sewing box, then opened the door wide. 'Do come in.'

Yannis stepped inside. 'I came to apologise.'

Dora shrugged. 'What for?'

'I was rude to you. You offered to try to help and I was churlish enough to refuse. It's a bad habit of mine, I'm afraid.'

'Would you like a cup of coffee?'

'Are you making some?'

'I always have a cup when I finish.'

Yannis looked round the room. 'May I sit down?'

'Of course; I won't be a moment.' Dora busied herself over her tiny gas ring. 'I treated myself to this. I don't like to go down to the canteen all the time.'

They sat in silence, neither of them quite knowing what to say that would clear the air between them. 'When are you planning to return?' asked Dora finally.

'I don't know. The hospital has asked me to stay on. At first I didn't mind too much. I wanted to see Athens, but I've seen everywhere now. I think they've done it deliberately.'

'Done what?'

'Split us up. Brought us over here a few at a time. If we'd all come together we would probably have all returned together.'

'You mean you would have talked everyone into returning.' Dora looked up at Yannis from under her lashes. 'What about those who truly did not want to return? Think how happy they must be now.'

'They were happy on the island,' answered Yannis truculently. 'It's just causing problems. Spiro wanted to return to look after his hospital, now he hasn't any patients. Those cases have been hospitalised here.'

'Then why doesn't he come back here? He could be found something useful to do,' asked Dora reasonably.

'Then what would happen to anyone who was taken sick? There'd be no one to care for them.'

'Yannis, how many did you say were still on the island?'

'Twenty six.'

'Suppose those who still have to come here don't wish to return? How many will that leave?'

'Six, seven when I return.'

Dora looked at him in horror. 'You can't live like that, not just a few of you on the island. What happens when you're all too old to look after each other?'

'I suppose we'd have to come back here then.'

'But no one would know that you needed to.'

'Yes they would. The boatmen come over every day. They'd know if we were ill or needed help.'

'Are you sure they'd come every day if there were so few of you? They could bring enough supplies in one boat to last a week or more.'

Yannis felt a cold shiver run down his spine. 'We'd be all right.'

'Would you? Would you really want to be amongst so few people? You've lived in a large village for a number of years. Even here, although your friends have gone, you've made a number of acquaintances, friends that you can chat to, or play backgammon with during the evenings.'

'It's my home,' repeated Yannis stubbornly.

'It doesn't sound a very sensible idea to me. I wouldn't do it.'

'No one is asking you to,' replied Yannis tartly. 'I've lived there longer than anywhere else. My house is there, most of my belongings, my books.'

'You could have those sent over.'

'I can manage without them a little longer. Thank you for the coffee.' Yannis rose to go. 'I'll see you tomorrow.'

Dora watched as he let himself out and gently eased off her shoes once the door was shut. He was a strange man, an unhappy man, who did not seem to fit in anywhere.

1946-1957

Yannis brooded. A further ten islanders reached the hospital, two chose to return to Spinalonga, three remained at the hospital and the others dispersed to various parts of Greece to try to pick up the threads of their lives again with their families. Yannis received a letter from Anna, asking him to return to the farm and live with her and Yiorgo and he replied that the offer was tempting and he would consider it.

Father Minos wrote to him again and Yannis read the words in disbelief. He sought out Dora and handed her the letter. 'Read that,' he said bitterly. 'I thought that whatever they did to me they would never be able to punish me more than they had in the past.'

'Is it official?'

Yannis nodded. 'If Father Minos says so I'm sure it is. The island is to be officially closed once the last few come to the hospital. Those who returned earlier will come with them and be accommodated here.'

'What about the priest?'

'He's going to the monastery at Ierapetra.'

'What are you going to do?'

Yannis sank his head in his hands. 'I don't know. I wanted to go back. I could try petitioning the government, beg them to let us return.'

'Why, Yannis? What's the point? You have a home here, and it must be more comfortable than the island. This is a new start for you, to enable you to put all the bad years out of your mind.'

'I want my independence. I'm just a charity case over here. Looked after, fed, clothed, housed, nothing more than a parasite.'

'That's not true. You work in the stores and money is deducted for your living expenses.' Dora tried to reason with him.

'I've only got that for one more week. Vassilis is well enough to return.'

'Why don't you go and visit your sister for a while?'

'And be a parasite to her and Yiorgo?'

Dora sighed. Whatever she said appeared to be wrong. 'Maybe they could find you another job in the hospital.'

'Doing what?'

'I don't know. Maybe helping on a ward as I do.'

Yannis shook his head vehemently. 'I don't like sick people.'

Dora looked at him in disbelief, finally it dawned on her that he was completely serious and she could contain herself no longer, she began to laugh, her amusement growing until she was quite helpless, the tears rolling down her cheeks.

Yannis looked at her with annoyance. He saw nothing to laugh at. He waited for her mirth to subside, feeling it beginning to affect him, although he still had no idea why she was laughing. He began to smile and then to laugh with her.

'Oh, Yannis, you are funny.' She wiped her eyes with the back of her hand.

'What did I say?'

Dora began to giggle again. 'That you don't like sick people.'

'It's true.'

'But you've spent years with them.'

'That was different. We weren't ill; we were ...' Yannis's voice trailed away.

'Sick?' prompted Dora, and giggled more than ever. This time she controlled herself more quickly. 'I'm sorry. I shouldn't have laughed.'

'Laughing never hurt anyone, and that's the first time I've laughed since I've been here. Why have they done it to me, Dora?'

'I don't think it was meant personally. It isn't feasible to keep a tiny community supplied at great expense when they can have all they need here.'

'It's taking away our liberty. I'll appeal to the Court of Human Rights.' Yannis waved the letter in the air.

'Do you think you would be taken very seriously? Those who wanted to go back had nowhere else to go. Don't make any rash decisions until you've spoken to them again. If they want to return as much as you then it could be worth your while trying to get the decision reversed.'

'If only there were more of us. I see now why they brought us over a few at a time. They had this planned from the start.'

Yannis waited impatiently for the last of the islanders to arrive at the hospital. Spiro greeted him joyfully. 'I've brought all your belongings, Yannis. Packed them myself.' He looked round the tiny room. 'It's good to be back.'

'What?' Yannis was genuinely shocked. 'You wanted to come back?'

'We all did. Why? What's wrong?'

'I thought I could at least count on you.' Yannis turned away from his friend, bitterly disappointed.

'Now be reasonable, Yannis. No one but a fool or a raving mad man would go back and live on that island. Would you go back to a house that was cold and draughty? Having to walk to the top of the hill to get a bucket of water to wash your clothes, wait for a boat to come over before you could decide what you would have for lunch? Besides, it's so lonely. It's like living in a morgue. The shops and tavernas are closed down, there's nowhere to go, nothing to do, hardly anyone to talk to. Even Manolis is in a hurry to get away and has cut his trips to once a week. The island's dead, a cemetery. Leave it like that, in peace for those who never left. Here we can start again. Have a new life, forget what we suffered and the painful memories.'

Yannis shook his head. 'How can I forget Phaedra and Anna?'

'You won't, but at least you'll be able to accept it. There won't be the continual reminders. The geraniums that she and Flora planted, the curtains that she made, the rug.'

'Didn't you bring them?' Yannis looked at Spiro in horror.

'What was the point? You don't need them here. I brought all your books and papers. That took up four crates and I don't know where you think you'll put them.'

YANNIS

Yannis sighed. 'Then you won't back me in trying to get the decision to close the island reversed?'

Spiro looked at his friend levelly. 'Yannis, I've been with you in every one of your crazy schemes from the first time we met in hospital, but not this. Be thankful for the way things have turned out. I am. Everyone else is. Father Minos held a special service just before we left. We wished you'd been there. He thanked God for sending you to the island. Called you our saviour. Had it not been for you we would all have mouldered the rest of our lives away on that lump of rock. You made people remember we were there. You fought for us and for our rights, and now you're the one who wants to throw them away.'

Colour had suffused Yannis's cheeks. 'Am I really being so ungrateful and unreasonable?'

'You are. Now, let's forget all about it and go and enjoy ourselves.'

Together they strolled to Amonia Square and selected a table where they could watch the teeming life of the city passing before their eyes. Students, late for lectures hurried by, the flower seller on the corner, offering her rapidly wilting posies to all who passed her, the shoppers, strolling leisurely, the blind beggar, his stick tapping warily as he made slow progress, the scene shifted continually.

'This is what I missed most.' Spiro settled back comfortably in his chair. 'Life.'

Yannis did not reply. He was struggling to come to terms with the inevitable.

1958 - 1979

For three years Yannis stayed in his room at the hospital, gradually accepting the change. From a day-to-day existence he slowly made plans for the future. He would accept the charity offered him by the hospital, but only for so long as it suited him. He had written to Yiorgo and asked him to send his share of the money left by his father. His weekly pension was used up mostly on writing materials and stamps, keeping in touch with his cousin in Heraklion and Annita and Elias in America. He read the latest medical reports from the periodicals in the hospital library and often wrote replies or comments to the editor, until finally an abridged letter from him was published.

'Why don't you write an article and send it to them?' suggested Spiro.

'What could I write about?'

'Life on an island.'

'The government would love that!'

'Not if you slanted it the right way, saying how bad the old days were and how good everything is now.'

Yannis had laughed, but the idea had taken root in his mind. He began to jot down incidents as they occurred to him, making them tragic or humorous as the occasion demanded until he began to spend more and more time sitting at his table with a sheaf of papers before him, correcting and polishing each piece of writing until he was satisfied it could be no better. Finally he posted it, almost asking for its return as the stamps were stuck on and it was tossed into a sack.

The reply he was waiting for was disappointing. The editor had returned his pages saying they were unsuitable for publication in the medical periodical, but suggesting he sent them to one of the largest publishing houses in Athens, where he thought they might show some interest. Yannis pushed them aside. Postage was expensive. Spiro and Dora urged him to send them.

'You've nothing to lose, Yannis.'

'My postage,' he replied. 'I'm trying to save money.'

'What for?' Spiro was curious.

'I'm leaving the hospital.'

Dora's face blanched. 'Where are you going? To your sister's?'

'I've decided I've been here long enough in this tiny, cramped room. I'm for ever falling over books, so I'm going to buy an apartment.'

Spiro whistled. 'Yannis, that takes money.'

'I have money. My father left me a small amount and I invested it. Provided I'm fairly careful I should be able to afford a modest apartment.'

'All the more reason to send those articles away. Think of the money you could make if they're accepted and published.'

'And think of the money I'll waste by continually sending them and having them returned to me. No, they're just rubbish.' Yannis dropped the parcel into his bin. 'Come with me and buy a paper and I'll start looking for somewhere to live.'

Dora followed him to the door. Spiro hesitated; then scooped the parcel from the rubbish bin. 'I'll just get a pullover and I'll be with you.' He hurried down the passage to his own room, pushing the parcel out of sight under his bed.

The newspaper proved something of a disappointment. There were few apartments advertised and the prices being asked were ridiculously high. He could just about afford to buy one of them, but there was no way he could afford to live in it.

'I'll just have to wait a little longer. When I thought of this idea property was far more reasonable. Maybe it will go down in a few months.'

For the rest of the day and most of the night he turned the problem over in his mind, falling into a deep sleep in the early hours of the morning. When he awoke he found he had missed breakfast at the cafeteria and cursed again the fact that he had to live in the hospital and not be able to do exactly as he pleased. He began to shave carefully, studying the face that looked back at him. He was fifty-two, although he looked a good ten years older, his hair was so white. He had twenty, maybe thirty years ahead of him and he had to do something during that time. Maybe he should try to send his papers to another publisher as had been suggested. His face half lathered he returned to the bed-sitting room and reached into the rubbish bin. Empty. It could not be true. He had only put them in there late yesterday afternoon and the rubbish bin was never emptied until the next day. Surely he would have woken had they entered his room earlier. He towelled his face off hurriedly and rushed to Spiro, bursting in without a preliminary knock.

Spiro looked up in surprise. 'What's wrong? Why weren't you at breakfast?'

'My papers! Where are they?'

Spiro pulled the parcel from under his bed. 'I've got them. I thought you might have a change of heart.'

Yannis slumped down on a chair. 'You might have told me.'

'The mood you were in yesterday you would have thrown them into the incinerator. You're going to send them, then?'

Yannis nodded. 'I'll try. If I could sell them I could add money to the little I've already got. I'm determined to get out of here somehow.' Yannis cradled the package in his arms. 'Thank you, Spiro. I'll see you when I've been to the post office.'

Walking to the post office Yannis turned over the problem of his finances in his mind. So engrossed was he that he bumped into a priest hurrying in the opposite direction. The priest reminded him of Andreas. He stopped and returned hurriedly to the hospital, rushing into Spiro's room as unceremoniously as before.

'I've got it. I've got the answer.'

Spiro looked at Yannis patiently. 'What answer?'

'To the apartment. Andreas has the money.'

Spiro frowned. 'I know I'm not as quick as you, but what are you talking about?'

'Don't you remember? After the government were shot the doctor went to Andreas. Before he committed suicide he handed over all the money he'd kept back from the hospital patients. Andreas put it in the bank until it was decided how to share it out. It must still be there. There's so few of us left it could be a small fortune.'

'Yannis, I do believe you have something there.'

'I'll write to Andreas today.'

'How many of you are left to share it?'

'Three, but I think it would be fairer if we all had a share, if there's enough, of course. I'm going to write to Andreas then I'll go to the post office with the letter and the parcel.'

'You've still not had a coffee.'

'I'll have it later. This is more important.'

Yannis banged the door shut and Spiro smiled to himself. Yannis was getting better, gradually forgetting that his one desire had been to return to the island. It seemed he was only truly happy when tackling what appeared to be impossible.

The financial news from Andreas was good, better than Yannis had dared to hope. The whole transaction would have to be done through solicitors and a considerable time would have to elapse to allow any relatives to come forward and their claim be investigated. Yannis replied that he would leave the details to Andreas and trust him to place the whole affair in the hands of a reputable firm, asking only that an interim payment be made to him as soon as possible with the balance to follow when the solicitors were satisfied that all claimants had been recompensed.

He began to study advertisements for apartments with renewed interest, eventually whittling his choice down to a particular area of the city where he would be reasonably close to the hospital, yet away from the fumes and noise. The area had been developed tastefully after the war with small blocks of flats set in broad roads. He spoke to Spiro, asking him to visit with him, and waited for his reaction.

'Very nice; you should be quite comfortable here.'

'What about you? There's another going next door. I thought you might like to take that?'

Spiro shook his head. 'I'm content where I am. Why should I bother to buy an apartment and furnish it when I can live well enough at the hospital? Besides, I'd have to go back to doing my own cooking and cleaning and it just doesn't appeal to me any longer. You should think about it seriously, Yannis.'

'I have. I want my own home again.' He lowered his eyes. 'I'm going to ask Dora to share it with me.'

Spiro gasped. 'You sly old dog!'

'I've been thinking about it for quite a while, but I had nothing to offer her. A few inches in my room to call her own, but now she can have an apartment.'

'And you can have a housekeeper!'

'That's not why I'm asking her. I want a companion.'

Spiro nodded. 'You never did enjoy your own company for too long at a time.'

'Do you think she'll have me?'

Spiro shrugged. 'How do I know? I'd say she'd be a fool to refuse you. She'll never get a better offer.'

'I'll ask her to visit the apartment with me tomorrow and see what her reaction is then.'

'And if she says no?'

'I'll still take it. I need more space. Room to breathe and expand.'

Spiro nodded understandingly. 'I hope Dora feels the same way.'

'The solicitors have agreed to everyone having a share of the money. I think they thought it the easiest way out, rather than trying to trace any relatives. What will you do with yours?'

'You'll probably laugh at me, but I'm going to buy a car.'

'What ever for?'

'You may not have noticed, but I'm beginning to have a bit of trouble getting around these days. I think a little car to go wherever I wanted would be a good idea.'

'Where do you want to go?'

'Almost anywhere would do, just to have a look. If I liked where I ended up I could always stay a day or two at a taverna.'

Yannis smiled. 'We're not doing so badly considering that a few years ago we were outcasts.' His face clouded over. 'We're the lucky ones.'

'That's true, very true.'

Both men stood enshrouded in their own poignant memories.

The apartment enthralled Dora. She reminded Yannis of Phaedra as she had run from one room to the other in their tiny house and complimented Yannis on his cleverness in rebuilding.

'You can make it beautiful,' exclaimed Dora. 'You can put up shelves for your books and you could have a proper desk. Which room will you use as the living room?'

'I thought this one.'

Dora nodded. 'It's a little larger and the windows look out over the garden. You'll be able to make it look very pretty, Yannis. Are you going to leave the walls white or paint them a colour?'

'I thought I'd leave the choice to you.'

'To me? But I don't know what else you're planning to have in the room or what colour the curtains and rugs will be.'

'Maybe you could come with me to choose them?' Yannis

slipped his arm around her waist. 'I thought you might like to share it with me, as my wife.'

A deep red rose from Dora's neck, filling her cheeks. 'Do you mean that, Yannis?'

He nodded. 'I've thought about it for a long time, but I didn't see how it would be possible whilst I lived at the hospital.'

'I have nothing, Yannis. You know that.'

'I'm not asking you for anything.'

Dora pursed her lips. 'I'm not a young woman to marry again.'

'I know that too. You told me, you're forty-three next birthday, but age has nothing to do with it. Could you put up with having me around all the time, being bad-tempered and impatient when things don't go the way I want?'

'I've been able to put up with you whilst you lived at the hospital.'

'You could always get away from me there, or shut your door in my face. It won't be so easy here.'

'I can always visit my friends at the hospital if I find you difficult.' Dora smiled at him. 'Of course I'll marry you, Yannis. Did you think I'd say no?' She held her face up towards Yannis who frowned at her.

'I can be very difficult to live with. I'm terribly untidy. I like well cooked meals, clean clothes every day and coffee whenever I fancy.'

'And what will you be doing whilst I'm coping with all this washing and cooking you want done? Sitting and watching me?' asked Dora.

'I think I'll find enough to occupy my time. The publisher has accepted those little anecdotes and wants more.'

'Oh, Yannis, that's wonderful. You'll be famous.'

'I doubt that, but it should bring us in a little money to live on. Now, have you decided what colour you want the walls?'

Anna stepped from the aeroplane onto the hot tarmac. Her legs felt weak as she followed the other passengers to the passport control building. Yannis had promised he would be there and she hoped desperately that she would recognise him. The official gave her picture a quick glance and stamped the papers, slapping them onto the desk and holding out his hand for the next in line. Unsure what to do, Anna stood there.

'My case?' It was new, the first time she had ever owned a case, and it was packed with her possessions. It had been whisked away at the airport in Heraklion and she was now wondering if she would ever see it again. Feeling herself pushed from behind she repeated her question and the man she was hindering took pity on her.

'Come with me. You collect it through here.' He pointed through some swing doors, each time they opened a milling throng could be seen. 'First time you've flown?'

Anna nodded. 'My brother's meeting me. I can't see him.'

'He'll be waiting the other side. He's not allowed through here. What does your case look like?' He guided her skilfully through the people to the cases, which were going round on the conveyor belt.

'It's black. Maybe that one?'

Her benefactor held the label for her to read. 'Is this it?'

Anna recognised her rather childish printing and held out her hand to take it.

'I'll carry it through.'

'Thank you.' Dutifully Anna trotted along at his side, scanning the faces of the men and women who stood behind the barrier eagerly awaiting arrivals.

'How long is it since you last saw your brother?'

Anna thought, but gave up trying to calculate. 'A long time.'

'Then I suggest you sit there and wait. The crowd will thin and you'll be able to see each other.' He deposited her case on the ground beside her. 'I can't wait with you. I have an appointment. If you have any problem go to the desk over there. They'll help you.'

Before Anna could finish stammering her thanks he had gone, swallowed up amongst the moving mass that showed no signs of dispersing. Nervously she gazed around, the loud speaker making her start as it gave out a cracked message which she could not understand.

'Anna? It is Anna.'

She looked up to see her brother standing before her; the years had changed him very little.

'Yannis! You did come.'

'I said I'd meet you. You can't go running around Athens on your own.' He tried to pick up her case, his fingers too misshapen to slip through the handle.

'It's not heavy. I'll take it.'

Yannis nodded and held the door open for her. 'We'll take a taxi to the apartment. It's quite a distance from here.'

Swiftly the yellow cab found its way through the maze of one-way streets that they encountered once they left the main road from the airport. Yannis pointed out landmarks as they passed, whilst Anna gazed dumbfounded. Heraklion had been a nightmare of people and rushing traffic, but this was worse than she had imagined. She clutched alternately at Yannis and the seat in front as the driver applied his brakes at the last moment to enable them to skid around a corner. She took deep breaths as they finally came to a halt.

'We're here.' Yannis waited until the driver had opened the door for him, another small thing that he was no longer able to do for himself without great difficulty. 'Dora is looking forward to meeting you.'

He pushed open the front door and led Anna to a small door set in the wall at the foot of the stairs. She looked in surprise at the tiny box as Yannis ushered her in. He pushed a button on the

YANNIS

wall and she gasped as the box began to move upwards. With a slight shudder the lift came to a halt and Yannis opened the door.

'Much easier than walking up the stairs,' he smiled as he rang the bell set in the wall. The door opened and a small, dark haired woman appeared.

'Welcome. You must be Anna. Yannis has told me so much about you. Do come in. You must be tired after your journey.'

Anna followed her as she limped into a room that was beautiful beyond belief to Anna. The smooth, white walls, pale blue curtains and cover on the bed, a cupboard to hang her clothes and a chair to sit before a mirror to brush her hair.

'I'll show you the rest of the apartment later. I expect you'd like to wash and have a cup of coffee before you visit your brother. I'll show you the bathroom.'

Anna crossed the hall and gasped. The small room held a bath that filled from taps in the wall and also a basin. The toilet was the kind you could clean by pushing a lever and the walls were made of shiny tiles.

'It's so beautiful!' she exclaimed.

Dora smiled. 'It's very ordinary, but the tiles were replaced recently.'

Anna turned the taps over the basin on and off, marvelling as the water gushed out. She washed her hands and dried them on a soft towel before she emerged and looked timidly across the hallway. The first room was obviously her bedroom, but which was the living room?

Dora came from the end room, carrying a tray. 'In here, Anna.' She limped ahead of her, making Anna long to take the tray from her before the entire contents fell to the floor.

She nibbled the biscuit she had been offered and looked surreptitiously around the room. Brown velvet curtains hung to the floor, padded chairs were either side of the fireplace and in one corner stood Yannis's desk, a light above it. 'Is that where you sit and write?'

'Usually. I do very little now, apart from writing letters.'

She sipped her coffee. 'Your apartment is very grand.'

'You're in Athens, now, Anna. This is a poor place compared with many you could go to. We're comfortable, but it's not luxurious.'

'It is to me. I'm used to the farm at home.'

'Why didn't Yiorgo come with you, Anna?'

Anna lowered her eyes. 'He had to look after the farm.'

'Yannis is there. Surely he could have left it for a few days?'

'He didn't like to. He felt it was too much for Yannis.'

'He's a grown man, not a child!' Yannis snorted in disgust.

'Does it matter very much? You said yourself that when you went Stelios was unconscious and they wouldn't let you see him. It could be a wasted journey for Yiorgo.' Dora tried to smooth the matter over.

'Wasted journey or not he should have come,' grumbled Yannis.

Anna shifted uncomfortably in her seat. 'Do you know how he is today?'

'I telephoned this morning. They said he'd rallied. We'll take a taxi over when we've had lunch.'

Anna nodded. Her brother seemed very much in charge, both of her and his wife. Dora smiled. 'Take no notice of him. He doesn't like hospitals and sick people.'

'But you spent all those years with them!'

Dora wagged her finger. 'They weren't sick, were they, Yannis? You know, the first time he said that to me I laughed until I cried. I think that was what first drew us together.'

Yannis smiled at her. 'She made me laugh for the first time in years,' he explained. 'I decided there and then that I should see more of her.'

Anna studied her sister-in-law, taking in the dark, bird-like eyes and the ready smile. She obviously adored her husband and knew how to keep him happy.

YANNIS

It was with trepidation that Anna followed her brother along the corridor of the hospital. He had checked at the desk downstairs and had been directed to the fourth floor, now he scanned the numbers on the doors, before stopping at number seventeen. He laid a hand on Anna's arm. 'Ready?'

Anna nodded. She was completely over-awed by this large, white building. Her head was in a whirl with the new experiences she had crammed into the last twenty-four hours. First travelling to Heraklion and staying the night with Andreas, when she had never been further than Aghios Nikolaos or slept in a bed other than her own, then the airport and the flight in the early morning, and now this city which seemed so full of marvels that she did not know which way to look first.

As they entered three heads turned and looked at them with curiosity. The woman recovered herself first. 'You must be his relatives from Crete.'

Yannis nodded and watched Anna walk to the bed and take her brother's hand.

'It was good of you to come at such short notice. Maybe we could return to the apartment afterwards and get to know each other? Believe me, this situation is as difficult for me as it must be for you.'

Yannis stood motionless, looking at the shrunken form on the bed, remembering how Stelios had wanted to search for pottery with him; how he had brought his own little finds to him for approval, and then over the years all contact had been lost.

Anna returned to where her brother stood. 'He's conscious. Do you want to speak to him?'

Yannis stepped forward. 'Can you hear me, Stelios?' Stelios's lips parted and closed, no sound issuing from them. 'Thank you for making Mamma and Pappa proud of you when I failed.'

Stelios's eyes opened and he looked with shocked recognition at his brother. 'Yannis!' His lips framed the word. He struggled to move himself in the bed and his eyes closed again.

'We've probably tired him. The doctor said only a few minutes. Maybe we should go now.' Daphne bent and kissed her husband. 'We'll come again tomorrow,' she promised.

They tiptoed from the room and Daphne walked beside Anna along the corridor.

'You will come back to the apartment, won't you? I don't even know your names. Maybe we could get to know each other over a glass of wine?'

Anna nodded dumbly. In her confused brain she decided this must be Stelios's wife and the younger man and woman his children. 'I'm Anna, and this is my brother, Yannis.'

Daphne smiled and held out her hand. 'Daphne,' she said, 'And these are our children, Elena and Nicolas.'

Anna shook hands with them, a fixed smile on her face. They turned to Yannis and Nicolas held out his hand. 'I'm pleased to meet you.'

Yannis looked at the hand before him. Very slowly and deliberately he took his own from his pocket, giving Nicolas plenty of time to see the clawed fingers and shrunken thumb.

'You may prefer not to shake my hand.'

Nicolas stared. 'Good God – a leper!'

Yannis returned his hand to his pocket. 'I'm burnt-out. There's nothing to fear.'

'Can we get home, please?' Daphne suddenly felt very near to tears. So that was why her husband had not wished to acknowledge his family.

In silence they walked the length of the corridor and down the flights of stairs. Elena led the way to the car. 'Come on, it's big enough for all of us.'

Yannis hung back.

'And you – uncle Yannis.'

YANNIS

Obediently Yannis climbed inside, sitting between the door and his sister. Surprisingly Elena slid into the driving seat, switched on the engine and began to reverse the large car from the car park. She drove fast and skilfully, taking the road to Piraeus, before turning off into the most select suburb of Athens.

'Do you drive often?' Anna asked, her knuckles white from clutching at the seat in front of her.

'Every day,' she replied cheerfully. 'Don't worry, you're quite safe.' She swung the wheel violently to the right and brought the car to an abrupt halt. 'We're here.'

The apartment was larger and more opulent than Yannis's and seemed a wonder of modern conveniences to Anna as she followed Daphne into the kitchen.

'Is it all right for Yannis to be here?'

Daphne smiled. 'I'm thrilled to meet both of you. It was just a bit of a shock. When Stelios started talking in his delirium and saying he wanted to see you I didn't know what to do. I thought his only relative was a cousin. He had told me the rest of his family were dead.'

Anna's eyes filled with tears. How wicked to say Yannis was dead! She followed Daphne back into the lounge, carrying the bottle of wine that had been handed to her. Yannis was sitting self-consciously on the edge of the deep settee, whilst his niece and nephew were trying to think of something to say that would ease the tension. Daphne handed the bottle to Nicolas.

'Pour us all a glass of wine and then I think we should sit and talk. We've a good many years to catch up on. Where do you live on Crete? I only found out about you originally through reading a letter which Stelios had dropped.'

'Yannis, I think it's better if you do the talking.' Anna was beginning to feel very tired and she would have liked nothing better than to lean back in her chair and close her eyes.

'We heard nothing from Stelios once he went to Athens, and after the war we thought he must have died. Then Andreas wrote and said he was alive and well. We were obviously a great embarrassment to him as he refused to have anything to do with us.'

'Poor Pappa. He should have told us.'

'I think he really had convinced himself that his family were all dead.' Elena looked at Yannis with misty eyes. 'I asked him once to tell me about you and he spoke so sadly.'

'Then why did he suddenly want to see us?' asked Anna.

'I'm not sure. Maybe the doctor was confused. Stelios had been drifting in and out of delirium for some time. He kept repeating that he must see Yannis. The doctor asked me if I knew who this Yannis was and I eventually remembered the letter from years ago. I wrote to Father Andreas and asked him if he could help.'

"What other relatives do we have?" asked Nicolas.

'It might be better if I told you all about us. It could help you to understand.' Yannis looked at the attentive faces before him and began to recount the story of his life and the details of his family.

Nicolas drew in his breath. 'You lived on Spinalonga?'

'Yannis and his friends made it beautiful,' interrupted Anna.

'You went there?' Nicolas could hardly believe his ears.

'Of course I did, once I was allowed. My brother lived there. I made many friends over there.'

Nicolas shook his head in disbelief, whilst Elena gazed at her newly found uncle in astonishment. 'Are you really a leper?'

Yannis spread out his hands. 'I couldn't possibly deny it.'

'Is your brother Yiorgo still alive?'

'Yes.'

'Then why didn't he come over?'

'He had to look after the farm,' Anna defended him.

'And what about the children you brought up? What happened to them?'

'Marisa is married to an Italian; she has three children, all boys. Here, I've a photograph.' Anna delved into her bag and drew out a snapshot of her niece, the baby on her lap and her other sons on each side of her. 'Yannis is married, too, but he has no children yet.'

'And you?' Daphne turned to Yannis. 'I suppose not.'

Yannis smiled. 'You suppose wrongly. I've married twice. The first time was when I was on Spinalonga and then again when I returned to Athens. Lepers are human, you know.'

Daphne coloured slightly. 'I didn't mean....'

'I know what you meant. How could anyone find a leper attractive enough to marry? My present wife is also a leper. We accept each other's defects, although mine are a good deal more noticeable than hers.'

Daphne swallowed. She felt she had been extremely tactless. She leaned forward and refilled Yannis's glass. 'Will you visit Stelios again tomorrow?'

'I'll take Anna tomorrow, but I'll wait outside. He may not remember seeing me today and I don't want to upset him.'

'Suppose he asks for you?'

'I'll be there if he does.' Yannis looked at his watch. 'We should go. Dora will think something has happened to us.'

'Who's Dora?'

'My wife.'

'Can we meet her?'

'Of course; she'll be delighted.' Yannis rose to leave and held out his hand to help Anna from the deep armchair. 'If I could just call a taxi.'

'I'll take you home.' Elena picked up her car keys. 'Poor aunt Anna looks almost asleep.'

Dora looked at Yannis anxiously as he returned with his sister, his face drawn and his jaw set. 'Is Stelios dead?' she whispered.

Yannis shook his head. 'We've been chatting to his wife and children. They thought we'd both died long ago.'

Dora slipped her hand into his and squeezed it. 'How awful for you.'

Yannis slumped down in a chair. 'I suppose I was to all intents and purposes. Once a leper and sent to Spinalonga death was inevitable. You weren't expected to leave from there! It's Anna I feel sorry for. Why disown her? She'd done nothing.'

Dora could think of nothing to say that might comfort her husband. She placed a glass and bottle at his elbow. If he became drunk who could blame him? Anna had gone straight to her room and Dora knocked tentatively.

'Is there anything you want?'

'No, thank you.' Her voice sounded muffled.

'May I come in?' Without waiting for an answer Dora opened the door. As she had guessed Anna was crying. She pressed another handkerchief into her hand and sat beside her on the bed.

'Poor Yannis; fancy Stelios saying he was dead! Stelios used to adore him. Followed him everywhere.'

Dora placed an arm round her sister-in-law's shoulders. 'He was very young when Yannis was taken ill. Maybe he didn't fully understand.'

'We none of us understood. Pappa forbade us to tell anyone.'

'Maybe that's why Stelios thought it better to say he was dead.'

Anna shook her head. 'Why should it have happened to Yannis?'

'Why does it happen to any of us?'

'Oh! I'm sorry. I forgot.' Anna's hand flew to her mouth.

'That's all right. I'm not sensitive about it any more. I suppose I'm luckier than most. I've no outward signs that people can see when I'm dressed. When I first limped I said I'd had a car accident and everyone accepted it and was sympathetic. Had I told them the truth my own family would have driven me away.'

'We wouldn't have done that to Yannis.'

'You may not have, but your neighbours would. That was why your Pappa forbade you to tell anyone. It was probably easier for Stelios to say Yannis was dead; it saved him awkward questions and explanations. Now, how about helping me to lay the table for supper? You must be hungry. You've hardly eaten all day.'

Anna sniffed. 'I still think it was very wrong of him.'

To Dora's surprise Yannis had drunk very little, but she found his silence disconcerting. She tried to make up for it by chatting brightly to Anna, arranging how they would spend their morning in the city.

Yannis spent a sleepless night. He was more shocked and hurt than he realised. To have told people his family was dead! The words went round and round in his brain until he could see the sky begin to lighten. He seemed to have only just closed his eyes to try to stave off the coming of dawn when Dora was shaking him.

'The telephone, it's Daphne.'

Yannis rubbed his eyes. Stelios must have died in the night for her to be telephoning so early. He vaguely noticed that Dora was dressed and the sun was bright in the room.

'Hello? Daphne?'

'Yannis, I'm at the hospital. Stelios is asking for you.'

'For me? You must be mistaken. Is he delirious again?'

'No, truly. He seems quite coherent and is most insistent that he wants to speak to you.'

For the first time Yannis looked at his watch. It was ten fifteen. He could hardly believe it. Why had Dora left him so late? What must Anna think of him?

'Give me half an hour. I'll bring Anna with me.' Yannis replaced the receiver looking thoughtful. 'Why didn't you wake me?' he demanded of Dora.

1958-1979

'You spent all night tossing and turning, muttering away to yourself, so I thought it best to leave you when you began to sleep soundly.'

'But you and Anna were going into town.'

'That can wait until tomorrow. You get yourself dressed and I'll bring your coffee.'

It was a little more than the half an hour that Yannis had estimated by the time he and Anna reached the hospital. He was still unconvinced that Daphne had understood her husband and sent Anna into the room alone. He waited in the white, scrubbed corridor until Elena came out to him.

'Pappa wants to see you.'

Silently Yannis followed her into the room where his brother lay, small and wizened in the hospital bed. He stood where Stelios was able to see him. For what seemed like eternity to Yannis, Stelios looked him up and down.

'Not – too – bad,' he gasped finally.

Yannis moved a little closer. 'I'm burnt-out. I'm not infectious.'

'Doesn't – matter – now.' Speech was an effort.

'Why did you do it, Stelios? Me, yes, that was understandable, but why say everyone was dead?

'Education – career – Daphne. Might – have – found – out,' he panted. 'Better – all – dead.'

Yannis nodded. Tears were pricking at the back of his eyes. With a last supreme effort Stelios managed to raise his hand and touch Yannis's.

'Forgive – me – Yannis.'

Yannis took the fragile hand in his own disfigured claw. 'I understand. There's nothing to forgive.'

Yannis leant towards Daphne and whispered. 'Has he been confessed?'

'This morning.' She bent and kissed his thin cheek. 'You always made me very happy, Stelios.'

Stelios opened his eyes and smiled at her. He tried to raise his head, but it fell back limply on the pillow as his strength ebbed away. His breath rattled in his throat and his eyes began to glaze over.

Anna pushed Daphne away from the bed. 'Take them out, Yannis. There's nothing more to be done.'

Placing an arm round Daphne's heaving shoulders, Yannis led her from the room, followed by her two silent children. Anna closed her brother's eyes. She wondered if she should offer to wash and lay him out or if his family had made other arrangements. She decided she would ask them later.

Daphne, although white-faced, had regained her composure when Anna joined them and was busy apologising. 'It was just so sudden.'

'It always is,' Anna assured her. 'However prepared you are it still comes as a shock. How long had he been ill?'

'Almost a year. The doctors were surprised he fought for so long.'

'We'll go back to my apartment,' Yannis spoke authoritatively. He ushered his relations down the corridor and stairs, stopping at the front desk to inform the nurse on duty that his brother had died. She nodded, pressed a buzzer, murmured her usual sympathetic phrases to bereaved relatives and turned back to her work.

Elena drove across the city and was directed by Yannis to his apartment. The little party entered soberly, Dora guessing by their faces that the waiting was over. She fussed over Daphne, bringing freshly baked baklava and urging her to eat. Each did so automatically and in silence, occupied by their own thoughts until Anna finally spoke.

'Would you like me to wash Stelios and lay him out for you?'

Daphne looked at her in horror and shuddered. The action was not lost on Yannis.

'Anna is the local nurse back home,' he explained. 'She deals with everything as a matter of course. She just wondered if you'd prefer to have the essentials performed by a relative rather than a stranger.'

'No, I think maybe a stranger is better. Less,' she searched for the word. 'Less humiliating. It will be done by the hospital, won't it, Yannis?'

'Of course. All you need to arrange is the funeral, or I could do that for you.'

Daphne shook her head. 'No, I'm quite capable. I know what Stelios wanted. We discussed it when he first knew how ill he was. Would your brother Yiorgo want to come to the funeral?'

Anna shook her head. 'He can't leave the farm. There's little point in contacting Marisa or Yannis either. They hardly remember him and it's doubtful they'd be able to get here in time. I'll stay, Yannis, if I may.'

'I hope you'll stay a good bit longer. This is the first time you've ever had a holiday and I think you should make the most of it.'

'I did say I'd return as soon as possible,' Anna looked dubious.

'Yiorgo is quite capable of looking after himself for a week or two,' remarked Yannis dryly. 'It's time you had a rest and were looked after for a while.'

'Do stay. There's going to be a theatre show at the Acropolis next week and we could get tickets. You've never seen anything like it.'

'I've only been to the theatre once. That was on Spinalonga.'

'On Spinalonga?' Nicolas looked at his aunt in surprise.

She nodded. 'They were very talented. I didn't understand it all, but I did enjoy it.'

'It was "The Birds",' smiled Yannis. 'Very ambitious of us.'

'Did you really? You didn't tell us that yesterday,' Nicolas spoke accusingly.

'There's probably a good deal more I didn't tell you, and I expect I've forgotten more than I remember.'

'Were you happy there, Uncle?'

'Happy! Who can say?' Yannis shrugged. 'I had moments of great happiness and some of my saddest times. It was my home.'

'Weren't you glad to leave?' Elena looked at him in surprise.

'Of course not. We'd built Spinalonga into a community to be proud of. I only wanted to come to Athens to get a clean bill of health so I could travel wherever I wanted. I planned to return until the government placed a closure order on the island.'

'Haven't you thought of returning, just to see how it looks now?'

Yannis smiled sadly. 'Maybe. One day. When I have enough money.'

Daphne frowned. 'Surely you have enough money to take the ferry over?'

'Of course,' Yannis assured her. 'But I've always travelled at the government's expense. It's made me mean. Besides, I'd want to visit my friends, Andreas in Heraklion, Flora and Manolis in Aghios Nikolaos, Father Minos in Ierapetra. It would take a good deal of time and money.'

'I'd like to see the island,' mused Nicolas. 'I'd like to go there with you and see your house, the hospital, and where you held your theatre shows.'

'You'd be disappointed,' interrupted Anna. 'A good deal is in ruins now.'

'Is that why you don't want to go back?'

'No, I suppose I'm just getting old and it seems too much effort.'

'I'll take you. If you really want to go, that is.' Elena leant forward, her eyes glowing with enthusiasm. 'We'll load the car onto the ferry and I'll drive you to see all your friends, then to the island and back to Athens. Please say yes, Uncle. We could do it when aunt Anna has to go home and take her with us.'

Yannis looked at his sister. 'It's an idea, Anna.'

1958-1979

The car bumped down the gangplank from the ferry and Elena began to weave her way across the quay, avoiding the throng of people who were trying to board the ferry before the arrivals had finished coming ashore. Using her horn liberally she cleared a passage for herself between the people, luggage and animals.

'Where now, Uncle?'

Yannis peered out of the window. 'It's changed. I'm not sure if I know my way. Up the hill, I think. We should come to the Square. I'll know my way from there.' Following the line of traffic they rounded the corner and Yannis caught his breath. 'This is the same. Go to the left, down past the market.'

Yannis directed his niece, taking left turns all the way, until they stopped before the tiny church of Aghios Manathaeus. Leaving the car parked precariously on the narrow pavement they trooped into Andreas's little house, filling the room, whilst he sat there smiling proudly. He urged them to stay, but Yannis could sense that after four hours of reminiscing between himself and his cousin, Elena and Nicolas were bored.

'We'll visit you again on the way back, I promise,' vowed Yannis. 'We want to make Aghios Nikolaos tonight and stay with Flora and Manolis.'

Andreas crossed himself as Elena drew away. He had a deep mistrust of fast cars, particularly when they were driven by young women. He waved until they were out of sight; then returned to the peace of his sanctuary. The visit had been most enjoyable, but so many visitors at one time were tiring.

Manolis was still out fishing when they arrived, but Flora greeted Yannis rapturously. 'I never thought I'd see you again,' she exclaimed as she wiped away the tears of joy with the back of her hand.

'How are you keeping?'

YANNIS

'Fine. No signs at all. How about you?'

'Fitter than ever,' Yannis's eyes roved round the room. 'You still grow geraniums, I see.'

'Manolis wouldn't let me bring them back from the island. I had to start again with just a couple of pots. Let me show you our wedding photographs. I wish you'd been there. We had a tremendous party, just like Marisa, all the villagers came over.'

'What made you take Yiorgo's house?'

'Manolis had it all ready and waiting for me. He wrote to Andreas to ask if we could rent it and he replied it was his now Yiorgo had died and if he could afford to buy it he could do so. It was such a surprise. How long are you here for?' She chatted on, recalling for Yannis the years they had spent on the island, her indomitable spirit always coming to the fore.

Deftly she prepared a meal for them, refusing Anna and Elena's offers of help. 'I can manage,' she assured them. 'It took a while, but with practice I found I didn't even miss my arm, besides, it's much easier here than it was on the island. I think you're brave, going back, Yannis, even for a visit.'

'Why should he be brave?' asked Nicolas curiously.

Flora struggled for words. 'It's so "dead", somehow. It feels dead, dead and sad. I didn't realise how sad until I returned from the hospital and I couldn't leave fast enough then. Manolis still goes. He takes visitors over during the season, but I've never been back.'

'I'm surprised people can find anything to interest them over there. After all, it's only a deserted village.'

Flora shrugged. 'It pays well, and if they want to gawp at ruined houses let them.'

Manolis arrived, smelling of fish and tar. Yannis sniffed appreciatively. 'That takes me back to boyhood. Yiorgo always came in smelling like that.'

Flora wrinkled her nose. 'Now Yannis mentions it you do smell, Manolis. Go and wash and change your clothes or you'll drive our visitors away.'

Despite their protests Manolis did as Flora bade him, returning in his Sunday suit. Flora laughed at him. 'You didn't have to be that grand, Manolis.'

Gravely Manolis took his place at the head of the table. 'This is the first time I've entertained Yannis in my house. It's an occasion. I have dressed for the occasion. Had it not been for him you would still have been on the island and we would never have married. I have a good deal to thank him for.' Manolis raised his glass. 'To Yannis.'

To Yannis's embarrassment everyone followed suit and he felt his eyes growing moist. He wished Dora had been there with him, but he had bowed to her wishes that she stayed behind to keep Daphne company.

'It's only for a week, besides,' she had added, 'I don't belong to your island memories.'

Yannis rose the next morning with his head throbbing. He placed his head under the tap, hoping the cold water would help. Flora laughed at him.

'You are out of practice.'

'I'm just a little woolly between the ears,' Yannis assured her. 'I don't really want to meet Father Minos smelling strongly of drink. He might think I'd returned to my former habits.'

'Yannis,' Flora bit at her lip. 'It's just possible he may not know you.'

'Not know me? Of course he'll know me.'

'He's an old man now, well into his eighties. His memory's not what it was.'

'He'll know me,' Yannis spoke with assurance. 'We'll call in again on our way back, so be on the look out for us.'

'We will, and Yannis, thank you.'

'What for?'

YANNIS

'My life.'

Before he could answer she had shut the door swiftly and was waving to them from the window. Yannis settled back comfortably. He was enjoying himself.

They ran Father Minos to earth in a secluded garden at the monastery. The monk who escorted them to him warned Yannis gently.

'He has become very old of late, his sight has failed and his memory plays tricks. You must not expect too much of him.'

Anna touched Elena's arm. 'Let Yannis go first. We mustn't overwhelm him.'

Yannis approached softly over the grass and knelt stiffly before the elderly priest. 'May I have your blessing, Father?'

'Of course, my son.' He placed his hand on Yannis's head.

'Don't you remember me? I'm Yannis.'

'Yannis?'

'I was on Spinalonga.' Yannis felt a lump coming into his throat.

'Ah, Spinalonga. I was there a long time. With the lepers, you know. Sad cases, all of them, but they made a happy life for themselves, until the war, anyway. The Germans tried to starve them. They couldn't do it, though. We beat them in the end. Then they took them away. All my friends gone.' A tear slid gently down the priest's wrinkled face.

Yannis patted his hand, rose and walked away. 'He doesn't remember me. I left it too long.'

An anguished look on his face Yannis led the way back to the monastery. He did not see Father Minos rise to his feet, his hand outstretched before him, searching the air.

'Yannis? Is it you, Yannis?' He sank back on his seat. 'I could have sworn I heard Yannis's voice,' he mumbled.

Yiorgo eyed his visitors with something akin to suspicion. Stelios's children were not to be trusted if they were anything like their father. They would get nothing out of him except board and lodging. He would not deny them that for the sake of his sister who seemed so taken with them. He just saw their gesture as an excuse for a cheap holiday.

Anna took him to task in the privacy of the kitchen. 'Try to be more sociable, Yiorgo, they're your niece and nephew.'

'They're strangers to me.'

'They were to me at first, but I've got to know them and I like them.' Yiorgo snorted and Anna was reminded, not for the first time, of her father. 'They've been very good to us.'

'You've been good to them, you mean. Providing them with free meals from Yannis's friends and now staying with your relatives.'

'Don't be foolish, Yiorgo,' she retorted sharply. 'Who do you think paid our ferry passage and has put all the petrol in the car? They haven't allowed us to pay for anything. All I ask of you is to be sociable and make them feel welcome.'

'For you I'll try, Anna, but you know how I feel about Stelios. If he didn't want to know us for all those years why should we bother with his children?'

'Please, couldn't we just forget that? We don't want to start a family feud that goes on forever. Stelios asked Yannis's forgiveness just before he died. If they were prepared to be friends then we should do our bit as well.'

Grudgingly Yiorgo took the brandy from the cupboard in the kitchen. 'For your sake, Anna,' he reminded her, 'not theirs.'

The island shimmered like a mirage in the early morning sunshine as they boarded Davros's boat. Yannis watched, fascinated, as they drew closer. He had mixed emotions. Had he made a mistake to come back? He wished Dora were beside him to dispel his fears of the ghosts of the past that seemed to be beckoning him.

YANNIS

Davros skirted the customary landing place and tacked round to the shingle beach.

'What's wrong with landing at the jetty?' asked Yannis.

'Silted up, no one uses there any more.' Deftly he threw the rope over a tree stump and hauled the boat as close to the shore as he could. 'You'll have to jump for it.'

Nicolas spanned the gap easily and helped his sister and Yannis ashore. 'Where now?'

'What do you want? A conducted tour?'

They nodded and Elena slipped her hand through his arm. 'Please show us round, uncle. We want to see your house and where Flora lived, all the things you've told us about.'

Yannis led the way through the tunnel and stopped in the square. The houses on both sides were open to the elements, stinging nettles and weeds rising knee high from the doorways and across the rotten floors. He blinked. This was how it had been when they first arrived. He collected his thoughts and cleared his throat.

'It was almost as bad as this when we first came. Not the weeds, but most of the houses in ruins. Many of the lepers sheltered in the tunnel or the church during the bad weather before we really got things under way. That was my house.' He pointed to the arched doorway with arched windows to match, the remnants of a staircase showed inside and a cupboard hung limply on one hinge. A couple of geraniums struggled for their existence amongst the tangle of weeds that had once been his carefully tended garden.

Slowly they moved along the path, skirting a fall of masonry and ducking beneath the branches of a tree, through the next section of tunnel to the shops. Yannis ran his thumb lovingly over the carvings of ships on a wooden shutter.

'Anna did those. It was how she cut her finger.' He sighed deeply. 'That building there was where we kept our food and water when it was sent over from the mainland.'

Nicolas and Elena listened to him enthralled as he described the occupants or the use of the various buildings, not liking to interrupt him with questions. He smiled when he reached the house where Flora had lived; the geraniums had won their battle against the weeds and were a riot of colour, along with large headed daisies and bright pink roses.

'We must tell her that her garden is flourishing,' he smiled. 'She loved her garden. I think it was the first piece of colour she'd ever had in her life. They've left the church bell,' he exclaimed in surprise. 'Give it a pull, Nicolas.'

The mournful sound echoed round the island, bringing back memories for Yannis.

'The bell was a wonderful idea. Whenever we wanted to hold a meeting we tolled the bell. It wasn't just for services.'

They passed the washing troughs, and the patch of concrete where Kyriakos had sat for so many years, coming to the tower where Flora had once lived, now overshadowed by the gaunt, expressionless apartments that stared at them blindly. He led them round the rocky outcrop and they gazed at the remains of the Venetian fort spread out below their feet, now exclusively the home of sea birds, and down the gently sloping path where the sheer cliff fell down into the sea below. As they reached the other tiny church Yannis stopped and crossed himself.

'Phaedra is in the tower over there,' he said quietly and began to mount the steps opposite the church.

'Would you rather we waited for you?'

'No. You can come and pay your respects.' He looked across the graves to where the tower was half hidden by a low wall and long grass. 'We were too weak to dig a grave for her.'

They bowed their heads, the peace around them only disturbed by the bees searching for nectar amongst the profusion of yellow flowers.

'They say the lily is the flower of death, but here we only grow hamoleuka.'

YANNIS

'Was everyone buried here?' asked Elena, looking at the small number of graves and remembering how many occupants her uncle had described on the island compared with the few who had finally left.

'The others are in the tower, with Phaedra and Anna.' He pointed. 'You can see their bones at the bottom.'

Elena shuddered. 'I'll not bother. Can we go up in the fort?'

'You two can if you want a stiff climb. There's not a lot there, but you get a fine view across the bay. I'll wait for you here.'

Yannis settled himself comfortably on the ground, his back to the wall of the carpenter's house. He smiled. It was good to be back home. The flowers looked brighter here, the sun seemed warmer and the air was definitely cleaner.

'We won't be long, uncle.'

'Take your time. There's no rush. There never was over here. I was just impatient always. I wanted to get everything done at once. What a trial I must have been to live with!'

The bees buzzed more loudly. Yannis opened his eyes to see how far they had climbed. They must be behind the first of the walls that still remained for he could see no sign of them. He looked across the graveyard. There was Phaedra coming towards him, with Anna skipping along by her side.

As the pain in his chest squeezed him breathless, his fingers closed around the silver chain holding the charm his mother had given him so many years ago, breaking the slender links. Yannis rose easily and walked towards them.

The saga continues with the next title in the series - *Anna*.

See our website for up-to-date information:

www.beryldarbybooks.com